Praise for
VOYAGE OF THE SHADOWMOON
Book One of the Moonworlds Saga

"A brilliantly inventive, marvelously plotted sea-faring fantasy that surpasses genre expectations.... Australian author McMullen writes like Roger Zelazny at the peak of his powers: his dashing, flamboyant, cleverly resourceful characters trade off insults and reveal surprising abilities as they swagger bravely from one hair-raising scene to another. Exciting, suspenseful, vividly believable, and great, clever fun: a major fantasy-award contender."
—*Kirkus Reviews*

"McMullen has once again crafted a marvelously unpredictable and intricate story, full of swashbuckling intrigue and adventure on a grand scale."
—*Publishers Weekly*

"McMullen's *Voyage of the Shadowmoon* provides pleasures familiar from his earlier offerings: secret agents and ruthlessly ambitious adventurers in an epic-size story with a large cast and plenty of surprises in the who's-really-who department. It is a rambling and complicated tale, simultaneously busy and leisurely, woven through the several voyages of the spy vessel of the title.... We are treated to plots, crossplots, intrigues, betrayals, reconciliations, murders, massacres, genocide, secret identities, unmaskings, rescues, and paybacks—and also to displays of loyalty, courage, romance, and chivalry.

"The book's atmosphere and invention evoks both Jack Vance and L. Sprague de Camp: Vance in the elaborate intriguing of the characters; de Camp in the matter-of-fact treatment of what in Vance would be romantically exotic: sailing ships, ports, taverns, temples, aristocratic courts, and the practice of magic."

"A pleasure to read."
—*Locus*

"One of Australia's most inventive sf authors demonstrates his prodigious talent for fantasy in a standalone novel that belongs in most libraries. Highly recommended."
—*Library Journal*

"This novel represents world-building fantasy at its finest; complex characters and world-altering plots are interwoven to create a tapestry of great intricacy. McMullen is an expert craftsman whose stories will engage any fantasy lover, particularly those who enjoy such works are George R.R. Martin's *Game of Thrones* series. . . . This fantasy novel will be popular anywhere that epic fantasy is in demand, whether in high school or public libraries."

—*VOYA*

"With the Aussie-style rowdiness McMullen showed in his earlier Greatwinter trilogy, it's a fun read."

—*San Diego Union-Tribune*

VOYAGE of the
SHADOWMOON

VOYAGE of the SHADOWMOON

Sean McMullen

TOR®
fantasy

A TOM DOHERTY ASSOCIATES BOOK
NEW YORK

VOYAGE OF THE SHADOWMOON

Copyright © 2002 by Sean McMullen

Edited by Jack Dann

A Tor Book
Published by Tom Doherty Associates, LLC
175 Fifth Avenue
New York, NY 10010

www.tor.com

Tor® is a registered trademark of Tom Doherty Associates, LLC.

ISBN 0-765-34713-X

First edition: October 2002
First mass market edition: February 2004

Printed in the United States of America

0 9 8 7 6 5 4 3 2 1

To Trish,
my favorite reference librarian

Contents

Prologue

 Miral dominated the sky as the deepwater trader docked, an immense green, banded disk at the center of three scintillating green rings. The ship had scarcely bumped against the stone pier when there was a frantic scramble by the sailors and officers to get the gangplank over the side and secured. A thin, short figure wearing a calf-length cloak and carrying a small pack over one shoulder had been waiting beside the mainmast, and relief surged through the crew like a cool breeze on a summer evening as he stepped over the rail and walked from the ship.

"I've faced storms, wrecks, battles, a couple of sea monsters, and even a dinner party with all five sets of my parents-in-law, but I've *never* been so frightened as on this voyage," confessed the shipmaster to the steersman as they stood watching from the quarterdeck.

"So what now, sir?" responded the officer as he tied the steering bar.

"Unload the cargo, load another, and sail on the morning tide. We have seven hours. We can do it."

"After two months at sea, sir? The men will want to go ashore and carouse."

"Are you trying to tell me that any of them will want to be ashore in the same port as *that*?" snapped the shipmaster, pointing at the small, dark figure walking away along the stone pier.

"Ah, yes sir. Point taken."

"He casts no shadow in Miral's light, yet lamplight gives him a shadow," the shipmaster suddenly observed.

"I'm more concerned about why eight of our passengers vanished during the voyage. Now all the others want to go straight back to Acrema without setting foot ashore."

"Well, it saves us the trouble of advertising for passengers," said the shipmaster as he set off to supervise the unloading.

The night sky was clear, and three moonworlds were quite close to Miral: orange Dalsh, blue Belvia, and white Lupan. The color of Verral had been the subject of debate for millennia, but the weight of scholarly opinion favored green. To the people of Verral, Miral was the source of all magic, just as the sun was the source of all life. They knew plants died without sunlight, so the sun, obviously, was the source of life. Experiments to show that Miral was the source of magical ether were a little more difficult; in fact, only one experiment had ever produced results. Sorcerers had observed that the only vampyre on the whole of Verral slept as if dead when Miral was not in the sky. Unfortunately, this vampyre had escaped before further experiments could be performed, and generations of sorcerers had been pursuing him for centuries in order to do those experiments. Quite a few others had been pursuing him merely to try to end his undead life, but seven centuries on the run had honed his survival skills to be as sharp as his fangs. Now he had arrived in Torea.

"An entire continent, brimming with thieves, bullies, bandits, swindlers, slavers, and minstrels who sing long, boring epics out of tune," Laron whispered to himself as he stopped at the foot of the pier. "And they are mine! All mine!"

At an open-air tavern an elderly charmshaper had fashioned a small, scantily clad dancer out of pure ether for the amusement of the drinkers. Nearby, the vintner's pet dracel was blasting passing moths with puffs of flame, then snapping them up before they hit the ground. As Laron scanned the gathering, an ethersmith snapped his fingers over his pipe, and it began to smoke.

Plenty of ether here, thought Laron. *This venture will be far more pleasure than work.*

Ether was intertwined with life—it was magic that could be charmed out of the nothingness. Ethersmiths were the laborers of the magical arts; they were naturally strong in etheric energies, but lacked fine control. Charmshapers were the magical watchmakers, jewelers, and surgeons; they were artisans of life-force control. Initiates combined the talents of charmshapers and ethersmiths, and from level ten and above they were considered to have full sorcerer status. One had to be born with the right talents just to consider becoming a sorcerer, and even then it took long years of study to reach the tenth level.

As the last month of the year 3139 drew to a close, the people of Verral were unaware that the year to come would change their world more drastically than any other in the whole of history. A handful did know great danger and exceedingly interesting times were ahead, and one of those was Laron. For the present, however, he had more immediate problems. He sauntered over to the open-air tavern and stood at the serving-board.

"And what might your pleasure be?" asked the vintner.

"I would like one truly obnoxious and brutal bully," the vampyre replied in a somewhat archaic accent. He had not been to Torea for two hundred years.

"Plenty o' those in Fontarian," laughed the man, "and what's more, they're free."

"Wonderful," Laron breathed with genuine pleasure, as he placed a Diomedan silver coin on the board. "Kindly point one out, if you please."

"Er, might I ask why?" asked the now uneasy vintner as he accepted the coin.

"Because I follow the path of chivalry."

"Chivalry?" responded the vintner, who had a feeling he once might have heard the word mentioned somewhere, and now thought he should have listened more carefully.

"It means spreading happiness in one's wake," explained Laron.

"You mean like a rich drunk with a hole in his purse?"

"Yes, yes, a wonderful analogy," replied Laron, scanning the crowd of drinkers and rubbing his hands together.

Chapter One

VOYAGE TO ZANTRIAS

The walls of Larmentel had withstood the invading army of Emperor Warsovran for five months. Stone gargoyles poked tongues and bared buttocks at the besiegers beyond the outer walls, as its nobles sipped wine from glazed pottery goblets shaped in the likeness of the severed head of the invading emperor. Their confidence was justified. Larmentel had stood unconquered for the entire six hundred years since its foundation.

The city lay at the center of the continent of Torea. It was both beautiful and massive, with a high, crenellated outer wall circling the cisterns, market gardens, and storehouses that supplied its citizens. The citadel wall protected the inner city, where temples, palaces, and mansions built of white stone blocks rose in terraces to look out over the surrounding plain to distant mountains in the northeast. Larmentel was rich as well as powerful, and had been built to be pleasing to behold as well as strong. The warehouses were mighty domed cathedrals to honor prosperity, all built of white stone. They were clustered in the center of the city, as if they were palaces in themselves.

Einsel and Cypher watched the progress of the siege engines in the predawn light. They were standing just outside the range of a good crossbow in competent hands. Having lost a lot of men to direct assault, and several unwisely rude diplomats to direct negotiation, Warsovran's commander was resorting to machinery to take the walls. The three siege engines were towers of wooden beams, armored on three sides and crowned by a hinged bridge that would let the cream of Warsovran's storm climbers charge across and establish a bridgehead on the walls. The three towers were rolled forward together, approaching the wall like ponderous, powerful titans.

"When I see engines such as these, I sometimes doubt the

power of our leaders' brains," admitted Einsel, who was Emperor Warsovran's court sorcerer.

"When I see engines such as these, I *always* doubt the power of our leaders' brains," Cypher replied.

Both men were dressed in drab armor, with only the colored plumes fixed to the back of their helmets to distinguish them as nobility. After all, there was no sense in calling attention to oneself on a battlefield, where officers and nobles were prime targets for marksmen. Einsel's armor was ill-fitting, as he was somewhat shorter and thinner than most warriors. Indeed, he reminded many of a child dressed up in his father's war gear, but nobody said it aloud. This was actually his first time on a battlefield, which was a sign of how desperate the situation had become. On the other hand, Cypher was as concerned about his identity as his safety. Beneath his helmet his face was veiled with maroon cloth, leaving only his eyes visible.

The towers were almost close enough to drop their bridges onto Larmentel's walls when the thing appeared, a delicate-looking structure of beams and ropes, rather like the head and neck of a gigantic wading bird. It hoisted a huge beam of wood with stylized eagle talons on one end, and lowered it between the middle tower and the wall. Moments later two similar cranes stopped the two other towers in exactly the same way.

"The problem would seem to be that the honorable profession of applied engineering was invented in Larmentel's university," Cypher said.

"Ah, the University of Larmentel, I did my degree in etheric shaping there," sighed Einsel, whose mind had drifted away from the battle. "A truly lovely place."

Larmentel contained one of the five universities in Torea, but rather than being all dingy halls and overgrown, rambling colleges, the University of Larmentel was a cluster of slender, graceful towers joined at several levels by suspension walkways.

"I can see its towers from here," said Cypher. "Who would think that they are more deadly than all the spears of an army?"

"Did you know that the towers were meant to symbolically put learning above everyday life?" asked Einsel. "Some of the finest scholars in Torea's history were taught within them. The university shares the citadel with the royal palace—it's that great pile of domes, balconies, and towering archways. Part of the palace is set aside for citizens of Larmentel to visit, so anyone can walk the balconies of royal splendor and fancy themselves to be kings and queens for a few moments as they look out over the city to the plains beyond."

"Beautiful towers, but deadly," said Cypher.

"True. Even though they hide no weapons, and they are not even fortified."

"Indeed. The engineers trained therein are better than ours."

As if to confirm his words, an immense dragon's head on a long green neck appeared, dangling from another spindly crane. The mouth trailed smoke as it was swung over the wall, to reach out past the middle tower. The head swiveled, and a stream of smoky fire poured out of the dragon's mouth and into the open and undefended back of the tower. The two hundred storm climbers and archers within were set ablaze within seconds by the cascade of lamp oil, pitch, and sulfur. The tower was blazing and beyond recovery as the dragon head turned toward the next tower. The engineers controlling it need not have bothered, for those inside were already flinging their weapons away and leaping for their lives.

A torrent of flame poured into the back of the next tower, while those who had been pushing the third tower forward were now straining to pull it back away from the wall. Grapples had already been flung out over the wall, however, and the tower was immobilized. The dragon head slowly moved back toward the tower, which by now had been completely abandoned. Moments later it had become a pyre of bright flames, like its two companions.

"Only those storm climbers and archers who began fleeing when the first tower was burned have survived," Einsel pointed out.

"Cowards," sneered Cypher. "War is for heroes."

"War is the way that gods breed cowards," said Einsel.

"How so?"

"Cowards are less likely to die, so they survive to breed."

"They go home conquered."

"The cowards of both sides go home alive, which is what I hope to do. There they breed. Only the victorious heroes do that."

As they stood watching the rout of their own forces, a despatch rider came up at a canter and reined in.

"Most Learned Rax Einsel, your presence is required by Commander Ralzak," he called. "And sir, are you the one known as Cypher?"

"That is my name."

"Commander Ralzak requires your presence as well."

The young officer continued on as Einsel and Cypher returned to their horses.

"Ralzak must be growing desperate," said Einsel. "He despises his sorcerers even more than his engineers."

Agarif Ralzak was Warsovran's commander-in-chief. He had watched his siege engines and storm climbers thrown back from Larmentel's beautiful but solid outer walls in every attack so far, and those defeats had cost him dearly. The kingdoms of the southwest had been biding their time to see whether Larmentel would fall to the invaders' onslaught, but now they were beginning to lose their fear of Warsovran's forces, and to rally. Sitting on the thick Vidarian rug in his tent, Ralzak read the reports of his diplomats and spies while Silverdeath stood beside the open flap, gleaming with the sheen of quicksilver and somehow seeing through blank, reflective eyes. The walls, terraces, domes, towers, and spires of Larmentel were plainly visible in the distance, blushing red with the sunrise.

Ralzak looked from the city to Silverdeath. Silverdeath had the shape of a man, and was wearing Warsovran's band-plate armor and battle-ax over a black tunic. In the five months since he had become Silverdeath's master and assumed command over Warsovran's forces, Ralzak had been afraid to use his strange new warrior. For three years Warsovran had devoted fifty thousand slaves and ten thousand men-at-arms to digging it out from under a rockslide in the Seawall Mountains. Thus whatever it was, it had value and probably immense power, but Ralzak was just as unhappy fighting alongside the unfamiliar as against it.

When discovered, Silverdeath had had the form of a strange

metal tunic of circles, hooks, and mirror facets, but when
Ralzak had helped Warsovran to put it on, the fabric had melted
and flowed to become a skin of flexible metal that covered the
emperor completely. What remained of the emperor was his
shape alone. A hollow, ringing voice had declared that its name
was Silverdeath, and that it was ready to do Ralzak's bidding.

Ralzak was totally unprepared for this magical warrior. He
hurriedly announced that Warsovran was wearing a new type of
armor, and everyone but Ralzak thought Warsovran to be alive
and still in charge within his fantastic skin of living metal. His
famed judgment and acumen were gone, however, and the alliances that had been formed by the brilliant and charismatic
emperor were rapidly weakening. Warsovran was now only a
figurehead, and he gave no commands. For the past five weeks
Ralzak had been discovering that he, too, was not Warsovran's
equal.

"I never asked to become the supreme commander," Ralzak
confided to Silverdeath. "I'm just a soldier. I know my place
and my place is not here."

"Agreed," replied Silverdeath in a flat, metallic voice.

Is it mocking me? Ralzak wondered helplessly. "Defeating a
few of the homeland's neighbors, expanding our borders to advantage, that was my forte. Conquer a continent? I know neither why nor how. What would you do?"

"I cannot advise. I am only to be used."

Ralzak had heard those words before. He considered carefully, looking back to Larmentel. The city had to fall, but he did
not need its people or wealth. Nor did he want the luxury of its
mansions and towers for his own dwellings. In his own way he
was a simple man, fond of life in the field with his troops, and
politically unambitious.

"Can you destroy my enemies?" asked Ralzak, gazing over
at Larmentel again.

His voice was muted, as if he were just muttering his
thoughts aloud. Silverdeath regarded him with the blank,
metallic sheen of its face.

"The feat is at the limit of my powers," Silverdeath explained
in its flat yet ominous voice.

"So, you *can* do it," replied Ralzak.

"Yes."

Ralzak stood up and glared out through the tent flap at the distant walled city. "Larmentel is the strongest city in all Torea. With Larmentel gone, my other enemies are mere chaff to be swept up and burned. How quickly could you break Larmentel?"

"In tens of minutes."

Ralzak turned and blinked, his lips parted slightly. Silverdeath remained impassive. The metallic sheen that enclosed the head of what once had been Ralzak's master had the outline of human form, and Ralzak wondered if the man beneath was still aware of what was happening.

"So when can you, ah, strike?" Ralzak asked tentatively, when the silence began to lengthen.

"Now," replied Silverdeath, taking a step toward the tent flap.

"No, no," Ralzak said, with a hurried wave of his hands. "I want my troops positioned, ready to take whatever advantage you can give them."

"Not necessary," Silverdeath assured him.

"I still want to be prepared in my own way before you strike," Ralzak insisted.

"I am yours to command," replied Silverdeath.

Ralzak considered the incredible offer as he began pacing before the flap of his tent, favoring Larmentel with a scowl at every pass. What was there to lose? Silverdeath had said that conquering the city was at the limit of its abilities, so it would be exhausted and harmless when done, regardless of whether or not Larmentel had fallen. At last he beckoned to Silverdeath and they went outside together. Cypher was there, still wearing nondescript robes and armor, with his face obscured. Einsel stood beside him, looking fearful.

"Learned Einsel, I am about to give Silverdeath its first real test," Ralzak announced. "Do you have any advice?"

"Ah yes, esteemed lordship," replied Einsel, bowing and rubbing his hands together.

"And that is?"

"Don't."

"You have been giving that advice ever since Silverdeath was found. Can you not say anything new?"

"Ah, take it to the mountains, leave it at the bottom of a very deep ravine, and bury it with a very large rockslide."

"That is what the previous master of Silverdeath did."

"Very sensible of him," said the little sorcerer, bowing yet again to emphasize that his reply was not sarcasm—even though it was.

"Einsel, I want to hear you say something other than 'Don't'!" snapped the commander.

"Well, then, what about, 'Do not use it, esteemed lordship'?"

"I am rapidly losing patience! What operational advice do you have regarding Silverdeath?"

"Stand well back," said the sorcerer with a shrug.

"Cypher, do *you* have any suggestions?" Ralzak asked, turning away from the nervous and miserable little man.

"No, esteemed lordship," the masked man replied with studied deference.

"But you located it for us."

"I'm learning, too. From your mistakes."

Ralzak scowled. Cypher's expression was not visible beneath his mask and hood.

"Experience is an expensive school, yet fools are always clamoring to get in," Einsel cautioned.

"Are you mocking me?" demanded the commander, rounding on him.

"No, esteemed lordship, but I *am* trying to warn you," responded Einsel, staring the noble in the face this time.

Ralzak blinked. It was the first time he had known Einsel to stare anyone in the face for the entire fifteen years he had known him. "I cannot understand why you are so frightened," he said, folding his arms behind his back and turning away to scowl at Larmentel again.

"Commander, we barely understand the most basic features of this thing," cautioned Einsel. "All the ancient authorities do agree that it is immensely powerful, however."

"Rax, we don't understand why fire burns wood but not rock," said Ralzak dismissively, "yet we still use fire to cook, light our way at night, warm ourselves, and burn the towns of our enemies. The test will go ahead. Is there anything you would like to do?"

"I would greatly desire to stand well back."

"I meant, in the way of magical tests?"

"I should like to stand well back behind a very large rock, to test its ability to keep me safe."

Ralzak's preparations took two hours. Men on active, relief, and sleep shifts were all ordered to strap on armor and stand ready. The infantry were deployed at five strategic points to prevent the escape of anyone from the city, while elite lancers were stationed to ride for any breaches the enemy might make. Storm climbers with ladders and water-shields stood in closest of all. It was the eighth hour of morning before Ralzak was ready. Wearing his full skirmishing armor and standing with his battle-ax drawn, he faced Silverdeath before a small group of senior officers and nobles.

"Do your worst, destroy my enemies," he commanded, pointing with his battle-ax to the undefeated walls of Larmentel. "Today I will walk into the royal palace of Larmentel and spit at the feet of its king as the all-conquering victor."

Those close enough to hear began to cheer his words mechanically. Silverdeath's skin began to shimmer, then crawl, as if tiny silver ants were swarming over it. Its head slowly expanded, transforming into a shimmering silver globe. Those nearby began backing away, and Ralzak noticed that its hands had become white. Even as he watched, white skin was also exposed at the neck. Warsovran's jaw became visible, and by now the globe had expanded into a sphere the size of a small tent. Commander Ralzak stood his ground, watching as the mouth, nose, and eyes of Warsovran, the mighty emperor himself, were exposed. As Silverdeath detached itself from its host, Warsovran's body toppled to the ground and lay still.

Silverdeath floated free, a globe that shimmered and trembled like a soap bubble, and when it was the size of a house it began to drift upward and over toward the besieged city. Ralzak thought it was growing translucent, and soon it was so high and insubstantial that it was no longer visible at all. The sky was blue over Larmentel, and all seemed serene and calm. Ralzak began to wonder if Silverdeath might be playing some humiliating hoax on him. A half hour passed, then another quarter hour. All through the besieging army, the rank and file began to mutter.

"Can't wait to loot it," drawled Colcos as he stood ready with his spear, gazing wistfully at the distant towers.

"Its women are famed throughout Torea," added Manakar, licking his lips.

"They say its cellars hold enough wine to float a deepwater trader," sighed Lurquor.

"Their windows have glass in 'em," said Colcos. "You ever broken a glass window?"

"Can't say I have," conceded Manakar.

"Grand sound, so satisfying."

"You never broke one."

"Yes I did! I spent two years as a slave in a salt quarry to pay back its value."

"They say it could be today," interjected Lurquor.

"What could be today?" asked Colcos.

"The big attack, the big one that cracks 'em."

"It's already happened," Manakar pointed out. "Their armored engines burned our towers down to the wheels."

"Burned the wheels, too," said Colcos.

"Any city that can afford to pour boiling wine on us as we climb the siege ladders is a long way from being cracked," Manakar concluded with a sneer.

"They say Warsovran and Ralzak have a new weapon," Lurquor protested. "The thing that floated up from the command tent and over to the city."

" 'They,' 'they,' 'they'—who are *'they'*?" demanded Manakar.

"Folk who knows."

"Well, if it's that small, then it's not going to be any use against—" Colcos began.

With the abrupt, shocking swiftness of a bolt of lightning, a huge, circular rent burst open in the sky above Larmentel, spilling a curtain of brilliance that swept outward from a point above the palace. Abruptly it winked out. In its place was a towering column of yellow-and-crimson flames as a firestorm burst through roofs and poured through windows and archways. A blazing-hot wind flung heavy tiles about like leaves and turned great wooden beams to ash within the moments it took for the shattering thunderclap to reach Ralzak's army and shake each warrior like a blow from a mace. Most men flung themselves down in reflexive alarm, others stood petrified with fear. Breakers of flame cascaded outward, sweeping along the streets and out to the citadel walls where they burst like waves on the shore, then rose high into the sky. To the amazement of the besieging army, the circular wall of fire then curled back upon itself to focus above the very center of Larmentel. All that was left was smoke, which boiled up into the sky above the city like a mighty, malignant tree. The heat had been so intense that it scalded the faces of the nearest besiegers. Larmentel's heart was burned out. The circle of fire had spilled across a third of a mile at the center, its edges rolling upward, then backward. It was as if the flood of burning had been on a spring that had reached its limit.

The thunder's echoes took many moments to die away across the plain, then for a short time there was complete silence.

"Shit," said Colcos.

"Shit me," said Lurquor.

"Shit me senseless," said Manakar.

Someone nearby gave a strangled squawk that may have been a gasp for breath, but which those around him took to be a cheer. Their cheers quickly spread in both directions around the army encircling Larmentel as the troops realized this thing of hellfire was not to be feared, but was on a leash held by their commander. They cheered their invincibility under the command of Ralzak and Warsovran, they cheered the fall of Larmentel, and they cheered the end of a siege that would waste not one more of their lives.

"Brilliant!" shouted Ralzak. "The greatest of strongholds in all of Torea, annihilated!"

Riders were immediately despatched with a demand for surrender, but all gates were already open and the surviving defenders streaming out of the city. Larmentel had been stabbed through the heart, and its citizens were bleeding out through its walls.

Suddenly Ralzak realized that Warsovran was standing beside him, pale and thin yet somehow looking very healthy—even youthful. Ralzak dropped to his knees.

"You did well," the monarch who had brought down a dozen kings said hoarsely.

"Emperor Warsovran!" exclaimed Ralzak, now standing again to support his unsteady and swaying leader. "Sire! Are you all right? At'rik! Here, bring a medicar, now!"

"No medicar," whispered Warsovran, waving the man back. "Silverdeath was medicar enough. It is good to its host bodies, Ralzak."

"Your Majesty, how can I ever apologize enough for commanding you for all these months past?" moaned Ralzak, genuinely mortified.

"You commanded the machine, not me," replied Warsovran as he glanced across to the writhing nightmare of smoke and dust that was rising above Larmentel. "And no harm was done."

"Oh, indeed, Emperor, and many of your men have been saved by Silverdeath's magic. You can now enter Larmentel in triumph."

"No, I must return to my capital," said Warsovran as he beckoned for a horse. "You will remain here."

"But . . . But Larmentel has fallen. Sire, the triumph—"

"Is yours, Commander Ralzak. Stay here, do what you will with the city. Make an example of it for all others to know and fear. You are Silverdeath's commander, after all."

Ralzak glanced about for a figure with his face veiled with maroon cloth, but Cypher was nowhere to be seen.

"When Silverdeath first made you its host, Cypher was shouting at you to obey him," Ralzak confided to his commander.

"Was he indeed? And what did you do?"

"I had him thrown out of the tent for insolence."

"And Silverdeath accepted *you* as master? Curious. What did you do that Cypher did not? No spells, chants, castings, incantations . . . Curious, very curious."

For all his feigned puzzlement, Warsovran did know Silverdeath's secret. One did not wear Silverdeath to become its master, one provided it with a host, *then* commanded it. Ralzak had helped Warsovran to put on Silverdeath. *The person who puts it on the host becomes the weapon's master.* Warsovran said nothing. There was a great deal Ralzak did not need to know.

"Is Cypher nearby?" Warsovran asked.

"Yes," replied Einsel. "I was speaking with him only minutes ago."

"Have him killed, Ralzak. He knows enough to be dangerous."

"Consider it done, sire," declared Ralzak.

Cypher was in fact quite close, but hidden from view by those crowding around. Upon hearing his death sentence he slipped away, reversing his trail cloak to display military blue as he walked, and removing his helmet and masking of cloth. He had not concealed his face to hide his identity, but to be able to flee unknown when he removed the mask. He secured a new plume for his helmet and a fresh warhorse at the cost of two lives. Within a minute of hearing his death ordered, Cypher had become just another despatch rider. Many such officers were riding about with messages and orders, so nobody thought it odd that one more was riding away west. By this time Warsovran was pointing above the city.

"Silverdeath is still up there," he said to Ralzak.

"I do not understand, sire."

"I shall write out a series of incantations for you to make just before the eighth hour of morning on certain days over the months to come. They will invoke Silverdeath in ever more powerful and frequent fire-circles. You must invoke it again and again until its energies are exhausted, and then it will fall from the sky above the city in its original form. When that happens, find it and bring it to me. Einsel, you will ride with me now."

"But, Your Majesty, how do you know all this?" asked Ralzak.

"I wore Silverdeath for five months, Commander, and in that time I shared some of its thoughts."

The ink was still wet on his scroll of instructions as Warsovran set off with Einsel, accompanied by a strong escort from Ralzak's personal guard. Ralzak rode in triumph through the main gates of the city's outer wall at the head of a squad of heavy lancers. Larmentel now reminded him of a powerful and exquisitely beautiful queen in the grip of a deadly wasting disease. Except for the inner citadel, the place was intact and brimming with wealth and potential slaves, yet its spirit had been burned away. Well-dressed families hurried along with whatever they could carry down the straight, clean streets and across pretty, ivy-smothered plazas, all prey for the long-frustrated and unsympathetic troops of Warsovran. There were occasional piercing screams and cries of pain mingling with cheers and hearty laughter, and fires burned that were nothing to do with Silverdeath's stunning feat of martial magic.

Closer to the center, Ralzak looked toward the ruins of the citadel walls . . . the long, straight avenue was lined with the burning stumps of trees. The mighty ironbound gates of oak had been blown out and burned to ash, and beyond was a glowing ruin. The stubs of the university towers looked like burned-out candles, while the palace domes might have been a nest of huge, smashed eggs. Ralzak rode as close as he could urge his horse, noticing that the buildings touched by Silverdeath's fire were not just smashed, but partly melted as well, and heat radiated out from them as if from a baker's oven. Nearby houses had been set ablaze by the radiant heat, and the roadway was littered with the charred corpses of those who had been too close.

Finally Warsovran's commander dismounted and, wrapping his cloak about his head, strode toward the citadel's gates while a retinue of guards and aides begged him to come back. The hot air was barely breathable, yet oddly free of fumes. The soles of his warboots smoked as he trod the hot stones of Larmentel's devastated heart. Ralzak finally stopped just within the palace gates, spat, and turned back.

"I vowed I would spit in the royal palace as victor, and I have kept my vow!" he declared to the officers, guards, and aides around him as he swung back into the saddle. Parts of his clothing were singed where they had brushed hot stones, and the soles of his boots were charred and crumbling, yet standing in the palace and spitting on the royal sanctum was all the reward the dour, steady commander had wanted.

Upon leaving the city, Ralzak declared his eyes closed for three days, then gave his men the freedom of what was left of Larmentel.

✳ ✳ ✳

Nearly two months later, at the western port city of Gironal, Roval Gravalios stood waiting in the shadows of a dockside street, his tricorner hat pulled low over his face and the black lace collar of his cloak turned up. The air in the port was chilly, but there was something else nearby that was making him shiver. He was by now no stranger to the feeling. Miral was rising in the east, and its huge, ringed disk cast green light and inky shadows all along the street.

From one of the terrace cottages in the distance came screams and curses. Roval strained to hear the words as he waited. The gist of it involved hidden money, drinking, feeding the children, and someone wanting to go back to the tavern. Somewhere nearby a crier rang two hours before midnight and added that all was well.

The argument became screams and thumps, then the screams faded to silence. Presently a burly docker about a head taller than Roval came swaggering down the street, and he tipped the brim of his cap deferentially as he passed the ship's officer. Roval caught the scent of ale as the docker walked on.

Suddenly a dark shape detached itself from a balcony and dropped onto the big man. The attacker had planned the ambush well, as the place was within deep shadows, and further obscured by a row of parked wagons. The fight was a flurry of darkness against darkness, and curiously quiet. As Roval hurried over, he saw the docker pinned to the cobblestones and a dark shape bent over him. Traceries of etheric energy gleamed and writhed amid the shadows as the blood and vitality was drained from the big man. He struggled, grunted, wheezed, then lay still, but lights and sparkles still danced about his neck, and the face of his attacker, who was dressed the same as Roval.

"For pity's sake, Laron, what if somebody comes?" pleaded Roval.

The dark shape ignored him. After what seemed like an eternity Laron sat up, carefully wiped his lips, then fumbled for his victim's purse.

"Dammit, Laron, if you just wanted a couple of silver crowns you could have asked me for a loan!" snapped Roval as he knelt beside them. "That was the most disgusting thing I've seen since I walked in on my grandfather while he was treating his piles with leeches."

"Well then, next time do not watch," replied Laron softly.

"Our ship sails within the hour and— This man is dead!"

"I drank all his blood, that usually does the trick."

"But, but, but—"

"We are to be at sea for some time. Would you rather I fed on the crew?"

Laron stood up and moved out of the shadows. In Miral's light he began taking patches of hair from his face, licking their resincloth base and reapplying them to his cheeks.

"How does my beard look?" he asked as he finished.

"Ridiculous. Now, can we go to the ship?"

"Not yet," said Laron as he began walking away.

"What do you mean?" Roval demanded as he hurried after him. "The tide waits for neither live man nor dead."

Laron stopped before the door of a neat but shabby terrace cottage, then knocked smartly. Presently, a woman with a build not much different from that of the late docker, opened the door a fraction and warily peered out.

"I told ye, I don't 'ave any more m—"

She stopped when she saw the two cloaked officers, then opened the door to admit them. The bruises on her face were fresh and ugly in the light of the candle she held.

"Ma'yie Hulmork?" asked Laron.

"Aye, but me 'usband's not 'ere."

Laron held up the dead man's purse. "Your husband has just had a seizure of both hearts," he said solemnly.

"He's seized what?"

"He never knew what hit him," said Roval, somewhat more accurately.

"People's always 'itting 'im. Then 'e comes 'ome and 'its me."

"Please accept our condolences on his death," added Laron.

Suddenly catching on, the widow Hulmork swooned. Laron caught her and carried her to where a small fire of offcuts was burning in a stone grate. Five children in patched nightshirts sidled into the room as Laron held a vial of something sharp-scented beneath Ma'yie's nose. She revived with a jolt, then began rocking back and forth while moaning her dead husband's name over and over. Roval donated his kerchief to her.

"Your father is dead," Laron announced to the children when it became clear that Torea's most recent widow was not going to say anything coherent for now.

"Ooh . . . promise?" a boy of about five responded. A girl no more than fourteen smiled darkly for a moment, then put a hand to her face. "Can I 'ave 'is dinner?" asked a spindly child of about eleven. At that suggestion all five children turned and scrambled for the kitchen door.

"This is for the funeral of your much-lamented husband," Laron said as he dropped half a dozen silver crowns beside the purse on the table. After a sidelong glare Roval added two more. "And now we really must be going."

"Ye're true gentlemen," sniffled the widow. "Ye're too, *too* kind."

They swept off their tricorner hats, bowed, then left the household to cope with its loss.

"What was all that about?" demanded Roval as they hurried along.

"Hulmork drank his wages," Laron explained. "His wife's washing paid the rent and put food on the table. The family will eat better now, and live in peace."

"Obviously, but—"

"I always try to spread a little happiness when I select my prey."

"A chivalrous vampyre?"

"I was raised in the way of chivalry. In a sense, it is all I have left."

"Can't you prey on dogs, or maybe sheep?"

"The vitality of animals can sustain me, but the taste is foul. Imagine having to drink a jar of vinegar when a goblet of chilled Angelhair 3138 chardonnay is at hand."

The analogy struck a chord with Roval, who was five thousand miles from home and unimpressed by the local wine.

"I thought you can't have the food or drink of mortals."

"On the voyage from Scalticar there was a wine fancier aboard who could talk of nothing but wines, grapes, and famous vintages," Laron explained. "An intensely annoying man, but I learned a lot from him before I yielded to temptation. After I had drained him and flung his body to the sharks, I became unsteady on my feet, and the next day my head hurt. Something strange was in his blood and vitality."

"Can't you just drain off *a little* vitality?" asked Roval, who was not looking forward to traveling on the same ship as Laron. "Must you kill your victims?"

"Once I bite I am no longer in control. It is a type of frenzy."

Roval shivered, remembering the look on his face as he glanced up from Hulmork's neck. *Do not disturb while feeding,* he noted mentally.

"Now then, our bags have been put aboard the *Shadowmoon*, upon which you are to act as medicar and navigator," Roval said as they walked out along the breakwater.

"The *Shadowmoon*?" exclaimed the vampyre.

"Is that a problem?"

"The *Shadowmoon* is a tubby little schooner with a crew of six and the speed of a constipated jellyfish."

"Nevertheless, it is the most advanced vessel in Torean waters, and probably the world."

"And one of the smallest. What about my needs? I must have somewhere private and secure to sleep when Miral is below the horizon."

He gestured to the huge, ringed planet that loomed pale green in the eastern sky.

"A cabin has been added beneath the quarterdeck, although it is little bigger than a coffin," explained Roval.

"How appropriate. Are we liable to be at sea for more than a week? Longer than that, and my self-control begins to slip."

The word "slip" was like a dagger's blade being drawn clear of its scabbard. Roval shivered.

"After what I just saw, no way! I'll tell the boatmaster that you have special needs, like sleeping while Miral is down and going ashore weekly for fresh food."

"Weekly," sighed Laron. "I shall get ever so hungry."

As they walked Roval noticed that Laron cast no shadow in Miral's light, although in torchlight the vampyre's shadow was no different to his. The *Shadowmoon* was ready to cast off as they reached its berth. The schooner was short, broad, and squat, with two lateen-rigged masts, and a cargo gigboat clamped upside down to the maindeck. Instead of a steering oar there was a hinged pole projecting through the quarterdeck.

"*That* is the most advanced weapon the cold sciences can produce to counter Silverdeath?" asked Laron as they paused at the gangway.

"Yes."

"You are doomed."

"Then why are you here?"

"I was told to help."

Down on the middeck a couple was embracing in Miral's light while the crew made ready with the sweep oars and rigging.

"That is boatmaster Feran," explained Roval. "He has something of a way with the wenches."

"Given my circumstances, I shall not be competition."

"What do you mean?"

"I am liable to bite anyone that I come close enough to kiss, and being cold-blooded and dead is something of a social liability. I also have the body of a pimply, fourteen-year-old, pigeon-chested wanker, and after seven centuries I am getting mightily sick of it."

Roval noted the annoyance in Laron's tone. By now Feran was escorting his most recent lover up the gangplank. Laron and Roval swept their hats off and bowed to the girl, who giggled before embracing Feran one last time. They stood watching as she went mincing off along the breakwater.

"Is the special cargo aboard?" asked Roval.

"Carried on in a sack this afternoon," replied Feran. "Is this our new officer?"

"Boatmaster Feran Woodbar, may I introduce Laron Alisialar, accredited deepwater navigator with the Scalticar Marine Traders, and certified medicar with the Sargol Academy of Healers."

Feran looked him up and down. "Impressive credentials, but a little young to have been long at sea," he concluded in spite of Laron's carefully applied beard. "And I have been told that you are also sickly and have special needs. Do you have the strength to pitch in and be a useful member of my crew?"

The crew of the *Shadowmoon* paused to watch and listen.

Laron removed his glove and extended his hand. Feran grasped it firmly and squeezed hard. Almost immediately he gasped at the icy chill of Laron's skin. Laron squeezed back. Feran tried to pull away, then cried out and fell to his knees. Laron's lips began to curl back and his eyes bulged as Roval picked up an oar and struck at Laron's wrist. At the third blow Feran rolled free.

"Laron has the strength of five extremely strong men, and tends to become a little excited when challenged to such crude contests," Roval explained. "I trust you will take pains to spare him from any initiation roughhousing or . . . well, I cannot answer for the consequences."

Not a single man aboard the *Shadowmoon* required further convincing.

"Is—is there anything else?" asked Feran.

"Never stay at sea for more than a week, and never, never disturb Laron while he is asleep," said Roval.

The lateen-rigged schooner crept past the sleek, moored galleys of Warsovran's navy under full sail, keeping between the torch buoys. Feran stood at the steering pole, enduring jeers from idle marines and sailors aboard the galleys while his crew prepared to trim the sails once they passed the breakwater and reached clear winds. Feran was short, clean shaven, had curly brown hair, and looked younger than his age even though he was brawny. Some of the insults were about cabin-boy boatmasters. Most were far worse.

It was only when they were well out to sea that a passenger emerged from below and walked haltingly over the rolling deck to where Feran stood with Laron and Roval.

"You're safe for now," said Feran to his charge. "This is Roval, from the Special Warrior Service of Scalticar. He is here to protect you. Laron, here, is acting as the *Shadowmoon*'s medicar and navigator."

Laron's eyes gleamed green in Miral's light. The passenger scrambled backward and stepped behind Feran.

"He is also here to protect you from your enemies," Feran concluded.

"I never thought I'd feel sorry for my enemies," said the *Shadowmoon*'s only passenger, regarding the hawkish youth with suspicion and unease.

"Don't worry, he doesn't bite," said Feran.

"Much," added Roval.

"A Scalticaran name," the man said slowly.

"It is something to do with being Scalticaran," replied Laron, with good grammar but an old-fashioned accent.

"Part of his beard is peeling off."

"He can be trusted," Feran said dismissively. "How do you want to be known to my crew?"

"Lenticar is my real name," he replied as he gazed at the receding port's lights with relief. "I have had so many assumed names that I sometimes wonder who I might really be. Yes, let me be Lenticar for a while."

Lenticar was lean, tanned, and stooped from years of hard work in the open air and sun. He also had the fearful, furtive gaze of one who had been the slave of brutal masters for too long, and he wrung his hands and bowed involuntarily each time he spoke.

"How long before we reach Zantrias?" he asked, snatching at the wooden rail as a large wave rocked them.

"Fifty days would be a fair estimate," said Laron, examining his beard with his fingertips.

Feran nodded in agreement.

"Fifty days!" Lenticar exclaimed. "I could swim there faster."

"Then I suggest you dive overboard," said Laron. "We need to collect and discharge cargo to maintain the guise of a coastal trader."

Laron removed a strip of beard and licked the backing. Lenticar saw two long, gleaming fangs. The officer stuck the patch of beard back.

"But fifty days may be too late."

"Fifty days is all we can offer," agreed Feran.

"Is it about that fire-circle weapon Warsovran used to break Larmentel?" asked Laron.

"It may be."

"Did you know he used it again?"

Lenticar's eyes widened. "No. Which city was burned?"

"It was only a test over Larmentel's ruins, and apparently no lives were lost. It may have been to impress a prince from Zarlon who was in the area, but that's just rumor. In a circle of over a half mile across, there was not a scrap of wood, cloth, flesh, or food left."

"So it was bigger than the first time?"

"Oh yes, everything improves with practice," said Laron.

While they were speaking, Roval had breathed a tangle of etheric energies into his cupped hands, then spoken directive and formative words into it. Now Laron went to a wicker cage and took out a seagull. Roval spread the etheric energies over the bird like a tight-fitting net, and it ceased struggling. Laron put it on the warrior-sorcerer's arm.

"Messenger auton, listen carefully," said Roval. " 'Cargo loaded, sailed with the tide. Arriving in fifty from twenty-fifth of second.' Speak this to Elder, Metrologans, at Zantrias. Now go."

The englamored seagull took off at once, climbed into the darkening sky, then turned east under the messenger auton's control. It was soon lost to view. A steady wind filled the sails and drove them through the waves. The *Shadowmoon* was too small to be a warship, and sufficiently like a fishing trawler to move freely between the ports of all alliances. With so many of Warsovran's warships on the waters around Torea, the *Shadowmoon*'s company had little to fear from privateers. In a sense it was the emperor himself who gave them safe passage to Zantrias.

At that very moment Warsovran was in the port of Narmari, on the other side of the continent. The port was the base of his fleet, and contained the largest shipyards in the world. Admiral Forteron was a very junior member of Warsovran's Council of Advisors, but was a particularly brave and capable leader. He was from an old but respectable seafaring family; in fact, his ancestors had founded the port of Fontarian six hundred years ago. *These qualities are precisely what are needed just now,* Warsovran thought as they walked along a pier where a squadron of battle galleys was tied up. Behind them were the three sorcerers and three marines of the emperor's personal guard.

"I have been giving orders in the shipyards," the monarch said. "No new ships are to be commenced, and all hands are to work on ships currently under construction. Provisions for a campaign of four months are to be assembled, and fifty thousand elite marines are to be equipped and kept ready."

Forteron did not comment. Warsovran was the emperor, after all. They reached the flagship of the Damarian fleet, the *Thunderbolt*, and the deck crew stood to attention as they came aboard. The ship was an oceangoing battle galley, and could carry six hundred rowers, sailors, and marines. Warsovran did a tour of inspection, then climbed the stubby command tower at the rear of the big ship. For a moment the emperor gazed out over the vessels moored or at anchor on the placid waters of the bay, then he looked west to the horizon.

"Admiral, I want you to blockade Helion," he ordered.

"Helion?" Forteron exclaimed in surprise.

"Yes. The weather is mild at this time of year. The sailing should be easy."

"Emperor, do I have permission to speak my mind?"

"I would treasure true words, no matter what they be," replied Warsovran "One hears so few of them."

"With respect, Emperor, Helion is no prize. It is just a pair of volcanos, two miles long and a mile across."

"It is under the rule of my enemies."

"Emperor, half of the continent is under the rule of your enemies."

"Maybe so, but Helion is well placed between Acrema, Lamaria, and Torea. Whoever rules Helion will dominate trade in the Placidian Ocean."

That is certainly true, thought Forteron. *But why the sudden interest in controlling the ocean? Is he losing control of the Torean continent?*

"Your orders are mine to obey, Your Majesty," replied Forteron. "I shall take a squadron and secure the island. Do you want the prisoners brought here or sold as slaves in Lamaria?"

"Not a squadron. My entire fleet."

"The whole fleet?" Forteron exclaimed before he could stop himself. "Emperor Warsovran, it is scattered right around the Torean coast. It would take over two months to gather all ships together."

"You have one. Have the despatch vessels sailing within the hour."

"But, but . . . *Helion?* You could take the place with twenty ships and a thousand marines."

"Admiral, I said *blockade* Helion. Under no circumstances are you to attack the place. Any approaching deepwater traders are to be turned away. Any trying to leave are to be seized, but not one single sailor or marine is to set foot upon the island."

"Emperor, I do not understand," Forteron admitted.

"Splendid, that means that my enemies are unlikely to understand, either. I have already sent riders and carrier autons ordering some of my warships around Torea to assemble here, so it may not take even two months. On the twenty-fifth day of next month, and not one single day later, the fleet is to leave for Helion with every marine, sailor, weapon, sack of biscuit, and barrel of water that can be crammed aboard. Blockade the island as soon as you arrive. After another two weeks you shall receive further orders."

Warsovran paced the deck in silence for a time. Forteron paced respectfully beside him, but he was frowning. *Not the face of a man just granted a massive advantage over his peers,* thought Warsovran, with a glance to his admiral.

"You look troubled, Admiral Forteron," he observed.

"I am only ninth in rank among your admirals, Your Majesty. This appointment will breed ill will."

"Let me take care of that. Just get the fleet to Helion and have it battle-ready."

Forteron considered both his orders and position carefully. Warsovran liked his commanders to think as he did, and to act as he would if they ever found themselves cut off from the line of command.

"Would I be correct in assuming that Helion is not the real objective, Your Majesty?" he asked.

"If you were, I would not tell you."

That told Forteron all he needed to know. He bowed and set off to carry out his orders.

Within the hour the first swift, high-masted despatch clippers and dash galleys were sailing out of the harbor with Warsovran's orders. By then the *Thunderbolt* was being prepared to be beached, careened, and tarred, and Admiral Forteron was in his villa at the edge of the port, studying charts of the Placidian Ocean. *Diomeda,* he decided. Diomeda was a large port on the Acreman coast, and eight days due west of Helion. Diomeda was an important trade center; in fact, it was the hub of all commerce up and down the Acreman coast, but *why* Diomeda? There was still half of Torea's coast to conquer. Larmentel had fallen, monarchs everywhere were falling over themselves to negotiate treaties with the empire. *Still, a promotion is a promotion,* Forteron thought as he unrolled a scroll of common Diomedan phrases. Tomorrow he would visit the slave market, and the girl he selected as his companion for the voyage ahead would just happen to speak Diomedan, the common trade language of the Acreman east coast.

❊　❊　❊

Warsovran did not go to his palace until the gathering of his fleet had been ordered and set in motion. He was met at the inner gates by his son Darric, who had just turned fourteen. Unlike a certain seven-hundred-year-old teenager aboard a schooner on the other side of the continent, the prince was already tall, handsome, and well proportioned.

"Father?" Darric exclaimed, looking puzzled as he stood between the guards.

The squad captain nodded to Darric, and his shoulders gave the trace of a shrug.

"Yes, it really is me," Warsovran laughed, holding his arms out to embrace his son.

"But, Father, you are so, er, *young*."

"Hah, just the result of clean living, staying out of the sun, and bean-curd cheese."

"And some etheric sorceries."

"Oh yes, but only *natural* etheric sorceries."

They finally embraced.

"I'm sorry, I was away hunting when you returned to Narmari," said the prince. "Mother did not tell me; she tells me nothing."

"Then you must be growing up," replied Warsovran, looking the prince up and down. "Well, now, here's a laugh. I am nearly a youth, and you are nearly a man."

Darric laughed. He knew when it was expected of him.

"There have been reports coming back from the army," he said, again staring at his father's face. "You were said to be englamored, and could slay a dozen warriors with your bare hands."

"Oh, I can do that without being englamored," laughed Warsovran, who was in a very good mood by now.

"They said you can call lightning from the skies."

"Anyone can do that. Just carry a spear in a thunderstorm."

"They say you destroyed Larmentel."

"Walk with me," Warsovran said, gesturing down the corridor. He put an arm over his son's shoulders. "I made use of a device, Silverdeath, a machine of immense power. It destroyed the citadel area of Larmentel. By its nature Silverdeath is difficult to control, yet it did what I needed. It saved my army as many as a hundred thousand casualties. Larmentel would not have fallen easily."

"The reports said that it was an awesome sight."

"Oh yes. More awesome than your mother being served dinner on an unclean plate."

"I wish that I could have seen it."

"At the rate kingdoms are swearing fealty to me, I may never have to use it in anger again."

"Yet I hear that you did use it again."

"Oh yes, but just as a test, over Larmentel's ruins. As I said, the use of Silverdeath needs to be refined before it is turned toward any other city. It might just as easily have destroyed my own army, but this time luck was with me. Now, then, I have a new campaign planned, but this time you are going with me."

"Me?" Darric exclaimed. "I cannot believe it."

"You question your emperor's word?" chuckled Warsovran. "Arrest yourself for treason!"

Darric laughed, then drew his ax and swiped the air with it. Tiny whistles in the ornamented blade piped out chords in fourths and fifths.

"All these years I have pleaded for a chance to fight, yet you have kept me here, penned up and protected from everything but the lapdogs," Darric said with undisguised annoyance.

" 'All these years' began on your tenth birthday, and even now you are only fourteen. Consider yourself lucky."

"So am I really going to fight?"

"No."

"But I've killed two of my training partners."

"Both of them knew that your death would result not only in theirs, but those of everyone in their family, extended family, hometown, and province, along with anyone in Torea even sporting the same haircut. In battle, the enemy has no such inhibitions."

The prince put his ax back into his belt and stared at the path they were walking, shaking his head. "Then why send me anywhere?"

"You are going on campaign, rather than into battle," said Warsovran, patting his son on the back. "You will travel in one of my best galleys. I am planning an experiment."

"A new method of fighting?"

"A new method of *not* fighting. I have a theory that overwhelming displays of force can destroy any enemy's morale so completely that they surrender without a costly fight. To that end I am assembling the largest battle fleet in the history of Torea, seven hundred ships—"

Warsovran stopped as the empress stepped out in front of them. She had the bearing of one who had been brought up in the corridors of power, and could not display deference even if her life were to depend upon it. She did, however, cry out with surprise at the appearance of Warsovran. He looked scarcely five years older than his own son.

"My lady," said Warsovran, as he bowed to his wife.

"So, it *is* true," she said breathlessly.

"What your spies say about me? Quite probably."

Darric knew that relations between Warsovran and his empress had been less than cordial for a very long time. Darric also preferred simple situations, where the outcome could be settled with a choice of suitable weapons and a tourney marshal. This situation was very complicated. Rather than be part of a characteristically chilly reunion, he bowed to both of his parents, then turned to hurry away.

"Stay!" barked Warsovran, seizing him by the arm.

"Welcome home, my daring and devoted lord," said Empress Darielle, with all the warmth of a fish on a market slab.

"Returning to your side is always my greatest pleasure," Warsovran replied.

"Not so great as spending a half day in the shipyards and docks before rolling up to the palace, it seems."

"That was urgent business, where every minute saved was vital."

Darielle stared at his face, almost mesmerized. He seemed incredibly young. She wanted to touch his skin, to confirm that it was real, but they had not been in physical contact for fourteen years and Warsovran's orders to his bodyguards were very specific where his wife was concerned.

"Will you be sharing the secret of rejuvenation with your devoted family?" she asked pointedly.

"Once you are dead, certainly."

"Ah, so the secret will perish soon, and unspoken."

He folded his arms and looked down at the tilework of the floor for a moment. Dangerous thoughts entered his head. Darielle had been a princess when Warsovran was a minor noble with a small inheritance but large ambitions. He had turned the tide of an otherwise hopeless battle, and in return was granted the hand of the king's only daughter in marriage. The princess was a very accomplished sorceress, however, and just as ambitious as Warsovran. She also had been implicated in a string of assassinations, and soon after their wedding, the king had died in suspicious circumstances. Darielle became queen. By now she and her husband had developed a most intense dislike for each other, so she had sent him off on a campaign against several much larger kingdoms. She had hoped that he would soon be killed, or lose some important battle and thus become a candidate for execution. Instead he brought home a string of victories and declared himself emperor of an area several times bigger than Darielle's kingdom.

Darielle needed Warsovran's military genius to ensure new conquests, yet the heart of Warsovran's army was the Damarian nobility, who were loyal to Darielle. Being a good strategist, however, Warsovran had built up his personal control in the new territories and royal navy, so that Darielle was by now the lesser partner. Several very professional assassination attempts had been made on Warsovran over the past year, and he was in no doubt of who had been the sponsor. The dangerous thoughts in his head suddenly locked together into a vast and flawless plan, and he fought down an urge to smile that threatened to tear the muscles in his face.

"My loyal and dutiful empress, I suspect you are bored," he ventured.

"You suspect? You *suspect*? Do you also suspect that there is a hole in your—"

"Of course there isn't; emperors do not do that sort of thing."

"Very well, then. Get to the point."

"Darric and I shall be away with the fleet for two months. I think you should take my place, and administer the entire empire."

For once Darielle was speechless. On the only other occasion when she had been granted control beyond the borders of her own kingdom, a civil war had resulted.

"Mother, that's wonderful!" exclaimed Darric.

"Where are you sailing?" she asked, incapable of bringing herself to make a display of gratitude.

"There are several small islands around the Placidian Ocean where my—our—enemies are harboring privateer Vidarian fleets that attack our traders and steal our cargoes. They cost us dearly in trade, and I intend to annihilate them with a single, mighty blow."

Darielle frowned. "I cannot believe this! Only doomsday itself would force you to place your precious empire in my hands."

Warsovran put a hand to his ear and turned his head about. "I do not hear the heavens falling. Perhaps doomsday is not all that it is cracked up to be. Did you catch that one? Doomsday—*cracked*? Crack of doom . . . ? Oh, never mind."

The empress stood with her arms folded tightly, her lips a mathematically straight line between the edges of her mouth, and her foot tapping the ground.

"I cannot believe you would do anything that would not help me along that path which ends at a large wooden block, a big, hairy man wearing a black hood, and an exceedingly sharp ax."

"I swear I would never have any man strike off your head, my lady."

"Oh, so now you are pioneering the use of female executioners?"

"Think what you will—the offer stands. Without delegation I could never run the empire, could I? I shall be fascinated to see what you can do while I am away."

That night Empress Darielle lay awake, unable to stop thinking about what had been granted to her. Warsovran did not trust her—with good reason—yet he was about to hand absolute power to her. Warsovran was also taking their son with him on the fleet. The royal navy was her area of least influence, and it was not much better with his marines. Nothing made sense, but anyone could see that if she was being given a short term as supreme commander, then the position would be unimportant for that period.

What was really worrying the empress was what had not been discussed. Warsovran was forty, but now looked twenty. Darielle was forty-five and looked forty-five—a very healthy and well-groomed forty-five, but forty-five nevertheless. In days, weeks, months, or years he would become powerful enough to leave her for someone younger and more agreeable. One did not just *leave* an empress, however. One remarried after an empress died of some strange and inexplicably swift disease that generally manifested itself ten minutes after dinner.

Fontarian was the northernmost port in Torea, and at the center of the coastline under Warsovran's rule. Captain Mandalock leaned over the forward railing of the trireme galley *Kygar*, smiling with satisfaction as a fifth broken ship was painted in yellow on the bow. The oceangoing galley might not have been the biggest in the known world, but with two hundred rowers, a hundred and fifty marines, and thirty sailors and officers, it was a force to be reckoned with. The captains of enemy deepwater traders did not expect to encounter war galleys on the open ocean, and the *Kygar* had been invincible there. Five traders had been rammed and sunk, eleven burned, and fifteen captured.

All along the pier were jugglers, tumblers, and ether magicians, all paid for by Captain Mandalock for the entertainment of his men. Moored next to the *Kygar* but ignored by all, a tiny, squat schooner was taking on a load of lamp oil. Roval, the deckswain, and a crewman stood watching the show from the deck of the *Shadowmoon*, while discussing matters that would have had the *Shadowmoon* sunk instantly, had Captain Mandalock been able to hear.

"I shall be leaving you at Narmari," said Roval as he ticked off jars on a slate.

"And taking Laron with you?" Norrieav asked hopefully.

"I'm afraid he stays."

"Not half as afraid as the rest of us be," said Hazlok. "Every port where we've called there's been a terrible murder."

"But none aboard the *Shadowmoon*, you have to admit."

"It's only a matter of time."

"Laron knows how to behave. He has a strong sense of chivalry, and he attacks only bad or churlish people. Merely ensure that all the crew behave in a virtuous manner, and Laron will not take the slightest interest in you."

Fontarian was built on the edge of a vast plain, with no hills or mountains as far as the eye could see. The tallest building in the port was a four-hundred-foot lighthouse tower, at whose summit a pyre burned from dusk until dawn. It was built of sandstone blocks, and stood at the edge of the water. At its summit were loading beams for hauling fuel up for the pyre. It was at the base of this tower that a crier began bawling for attention.

"Attend if you will, brave and stout warriors of the *Kygar*, the Mighty Bendith!" the man shouted, and there was a scatter of applause and cheers.

The Mighty Bendith was tanned and muscular, and stripped to the waist. There was an ax at his belt and a crossbow strapped to his back.

"Today is a dark day for the fair princess of Fontarian, who has been captured and imprisoned in a mighty tower by an evil privateer," announced the crier.

The crier gestured to a girl with long blonde hair, waving from a window near the top of the tower, then to six figures dressed in black and waving axes, who were standing at the base. Those on the *Kygar* and the crowd on the wharf hissed and booed.

"What, O what can the Mighty Bendith do?" asked the crier.

"Climb the tower an' give 'er one!" shouted Hazlok from the deck of the *Shadowmoon*, and everyone except the performers laughed.

"See how the Mighty Bendith storms the very stronghold of the privateer chief himself."

With that, the Mighty Bendith sprang forward, engaging the privateer guards with much clanging of axes, and acrobatics. One by one the guards took mortal blows, pulled red cloths from their tunics to show they were now bleeding to death, and collapsed to the timbers of the wharf. At last only the privateer chief was left. He turned to run as the crowd booed and flung fruit peelings, then he stopped at the door in the base of the tower.

"Ha-ha, Mighty Bendith, you think you have thwarted me, but my tower has forty floors, and each one has a hundred brave privateers to stop you. You shall never rob me of the fair Princess of Fontarian."

He slammed the door shut, and a voice from the *Kygar* called, "Madame Nymphania's place is easier to enter!" There was more laughter, and the distant figure at the top of the tower screamed theatrically for help. The Mighty Bendith clipped his ax to his belt, unslung his crossbow, and with the aid of a crank bar drew back the heavy bowstring and loaded a barbed dart. He now began breathing a tangle of ether energies into his cupped hands while the crowd cheered. Finally he plunged his left hand into the ether and drew out a filament, which he attached to the crossbow's dart.

The crowd went silent as the Mighty Bendith lay down on his back, steadied the crossbow on the back of his left arm, and gripped the release with his right hand. He aimed straight up, paused for theatrical effect, then fired. There was no wind just then, and gravity merely slowed the dart rather than deflecting it. It struck a loading beam close to the window where the blonde girl was waiting, stringing a filament of ether all the way down to the Mighty Bendith. The audience cheered lustily. The Mighty Bendith handed the crossbow to the crier, did a casting to the filament, then began to be slowly drawn straight up.

"Hey, now, that's a mighty sorcerer," said Norrieav, nudging Roval and pointing to the ascending figure.

"*That* is an ethersmith of about level eight, with no more skills of sorcery than you have," Roval replied with a sneer.

"Esteemed sir, you have to admit that he has skill."

"Esteemed deckswain, a wharfer might be far stronger than a carpenter, but strength alone does not allow him to build boats."

"Look how high he is! Roval, you just *have* to be impressed."

"Two years ago I was at the Warrydale Plough Festival, where the farmers compete in an annual poo contest. They eat like pigs for days, without visiting a privy, then try to lay the heaviest turd in Warrydale. The winner's offering weighed in at just over ten pounds and I *was* impressed, just as I am impressed now. However, I had no urge to participate in Warrydale, and my feelings are unchanged today."

By this stage the Mighty Bendith had reached the level of the girl's window. He reached out his hand, taking the girl's in his. The girl pulled him toward the window.

"Bet 'e pops in fer five minutes to give 'er one!" said Hazlok to Laron.

"Could you do that?" Norrieav asked Roval.

"If I really had to," replied Roval.

Unfortunately for the Mighty Bendith, he was an extremely good shot. Far too good for his own welfare, in fact. His barb had struck in exactly the area where his seventeen earlier shots had impacted over the previous month. The area looked solid, but had been reduced largely to splinters. The barb pulled free, just as he was about to enter the window.

The girl's life was saved by the fact that she had sweaty hands. The Mighty Bendith fell, screaming the entire four hundred feet until he crashed down to the cobbles, narrowly missing the crier. For a few moments the crowd cheered wildly, then they realized that anything resembling the crumpled mess that was now the Mighty Bendith could not possibly be alive.

"There are, of course, good reasons for *not* attempting that sort of thing, except in extreme emergencies," added Roval in the moment of utter silence between the end of the cheering and the beginning of the collective gasp of horror.

With the entertainment over, the onlookers went about their business, most of which involved loafing in the sun. Roval and Laron climbed to the top of the *Shadowmoon*'s mainmast and began to tighten the braceline to the foremast, which had stretched in the heavy seas they had endured for the past week. At the base of the tower, the woman who had been playing the imprisoned maiden was staring down at the mortal remains of the Mighty Bendith with her hands pressed against her cheeks.

"Would that I was in some lady's service," said Laron, wistfully gazing across at her.

"Been awhile since I serviced—" Roval began.

"Not *that*, you boorish oaf!" snapped the vampyre. "I meant being in the *service* of a lady."

"Ah, as in *serving*. But you have been in Learned Wensomer's service."

"Learned Wensomer? She needs the service of a champion about as much as a battle galley jammed full of marines. She is a very senior and powerful sorceress, and would be the Consolidator of the Scalticarian High Circle if she did not spend so much time around cake shops, pastry markets, and gourmet wine vendors."

"Actually, I heard she has moved to Diomeda to lose weight by learning belly dancing, so there may be hope. But getting back to you, Laron, think more on your own achievements. You are in the elite Special Warrior Service, just as I am. You were the first dead person to be admitted."

"I am the *only* dead person to do practically *everything* that I do. What sort of existence do I have? Drinking nine pints of blood at every meal, always on the run."

"Anyone who drinks nine pints of anything would certainly be on the run."

"Very funny. Roval, I just want to be settled with a lady, to be her loving and devoted champion."

Roval laughed mirthlessly, then hauled in the stayline with all his strength. "Tie that fast, will you? Just a timber hitch, that's it. Laron, once upon a time *I* nearly married my beloved. Then I thought about what being settled would really be like. I realized that she had a voice that could shatter ax-blades, a temper that could set water on fire, and a social circle full of people who could talk very loudly for an entire week about nothing whatsoever. Why do you think I tried so hard to get into the Special Warrior Service? It was a stunningly good excuse to get out of my betrothal—I cannot even remember what the reason I actually gave was. Some vision from some god that I do not believe in anyway."

"How did she take the news?"

"Badly. Months later my head was still ringing from her tirade."

"It sounds like you made a good decision."

"My first tour of duty took me thousands of miles from her, and when I returned she was married to someone who . . . Well, let us just say that you could not have strangled him."

"Really thick neck?"

"No brain to starve of blood. Laron, Laron, even if a week seldom passes without having to fight for my life or endure great danger, it is still far more peaceful than living with her would have been. Now, you haul on the line and I'll do the final tie-down."

Laron hauled the stayline tighter than any mortal could, then Roval secured it to the top of the mast.

"Haul in the bracebar lines," Roval called to the men below, then he watched the knots for any slippage as the ropes of the rigging tightened.

"I want a lady who depends upon me, someone who adores me," said Laron, staring wistfully at the distant actress, who was now explaining something to a port constable and waving her hands a great deal. "Someone I may worship, someone I may love with the most pure and gallant of motives."

"Consummation is more pleasant—unless the lady concerned is Wensomer, of course. I have had the occasional dalliance, I must admit. The Special Warrior Service forbids members to make the first move, so the lady must always ask me first, and most ladies are depressingly coy about that sort of thing. Still, being tumbled infrequently is better than not at all."

"My motives are above such things."

"Your motives sound like a bit of a bore. Why cultivate a favored lady without some bounce and giggle as a prospect?"

"What a crass outlook. You do not understand purity in love."

"Laron, you have been fourteen years old—and dead—for seven centuries. You have no choice in matters involving women, so you are stuck with virtuous motives. Were you alive, you would be a dirty little boy with no more chivalric purity and self-discipline than—"

"You are wrong!" insisted Laron. "Were I alive, I would feel the same way."

"Were you alive you would be making up for seven hundred years of enforced celibacy, and every girl, woman, and sheep for a hundred miles around would be reaching for their chastity belts."

"This is pointless," said Laron. "I *know* my motives have the strength of steel and the purity of freshly fallen snow, yet nothing will convince you of that."

"True," said Roval, patting the now-taut stayline with satisfaction. "Let us descend."

"Nevertheless, I still desire a lady to serve."

"Laron, with your preference in food, not to mention some rather worrying table manners, you do not have a hope."

"I know, I know. I am doomed to be alone and misunderstood, yet I shall try to do good nonetheless. *That* also is the path of chivalry."

✦ ✦ ✦

Half an hour later the body of the Mighty Bendith had been loaded onto a cart and removed. Captain Mandalock was sitting in the sterncastle cabin of the *Kygar* with Dovaris, the commander of marines.

"I don't like entertainments that go wrong," Mandalock confided as he poured himself a drink.

"Oh, I don't know. The men say it was the best show you have ever put on."

"Carnival accidents are little hints from the gods about real life. I don't like them."

The officer of the watch rapped at the door and reported that a courier dash galley was entering the harbor and flying flags of the emperor's service. Mandalock went outside, and saw that the little galley was stripped of its weapons and shields. It was docked with the highest priority and Mandalock was waiting on the pier as the courier captain presented his credentials to the harbormaster.

"I am Captain Esar, and I require fresh rowers and supplies for departure within the hour." He turned to Mandalock. "You are the captain of the *Kygar*?" he asked Mandalock.

"Captain Mandalock, at the emperor's service," Mandalock replied smartly.

Esar called his clerk, who came running with a bag of scrolls. The captain selected one, broke the seal, and scanned what was written.

"Captain Mandalock, you are to assemble all fifteen galleys and dash galleys stationed in Fontarian into a squadron, requisition all deepwater traders in the harbor, and gather all available marines onto the traders. You will then escort them to the port of Narmari."

"Sir! I hear and obey."

Before the astonished harbormaster could protest, Esar turned back to him.

"Harbormaster, you will begin raising a town militia for the defense of Fontarian, and set the shipwrights building six dash galleys to patrol local waters. All expenses are to be charged against the treasury of the emperor, and you are hereby elevated to the rank of military governor."

The exchange had been conducted quite loudly, before a crowd of sailors, dockers, and wharfers. There had been no attempt at secrecy. Within earshot were Roval and Feran.

"I think that I should seek work aboard one of those deepwater traders," said Roval.

"For general advancement, or to get away from Laron?"

The one factor the *Shadowmoon* had in its favor was its lack of desirability in any sort of obvious military sense. It was too small to carry more than three or four marines and of no use in any harbor defense force, so it was ignored. By sunset Mandalock was the proud commander of thirty ships that were following the Torean coast southwest, his forebodings about the Mighty Bendith's death forgotten. Ignored by all was a tiny schooner, following in the wake of the fleet.

"With luck we can shadow them all the way to Narmari," said Feran with satisfaction. "No privateer will go anywhere near a force like that."

"But after that we may encounter convoys going the other way," said Laron.

"Then we will stand closer in to the coast, out of their way. I wonder why Warsovran has ordered this?"

"Doubtless Roval will find out. He is a spy of great skill and resource."

"Speaking of spies, have the boat's name painted over and changed to, er, *Arrowflight*."

"*Arrowflight*?" echoed Laron.

"Warsovran seems to be gathering ships together from the most remote of quarters, and someone from Gironal may wonder what brought a little trader like the *Shadowmoon* halfway around the continent so very quickly."

"*Arrowflight*?"

"Yes."

"*Arrow*? As in the small, pointy thing that moves really, really fast?"

"Yes."

"Are you not worried that such a name will seem suspicious when applied to the *Shadowmoon*?"

Feran stared at Laron for a moment, as if trying to decide whether he was worth a sneer.

"People are seldom suspicious of what is ludicrous," the boatmaster said patiently. "I want people laughing, and not asking questions."

✷ ✷ ✷

Exactly one hundred twenty days after the first fire-circle burst out of the sky above Larmentel, the *Shadowmoon* tied up at one of the long stone piers in the port of Zantrias. Its name was now the *Arrowflight*, and its rigging had been rearranged to present a new profile.

A large temple was visible in the distance, perched on a verdant hill three miles back from the coast. Feran escorted his passenger through the port to the safety of the temple complex, and at the hospitalier's portico they were received by the Elder's steward. Here Feran was told that his work had been well done, but that he was no longer needed. As he made his way back through the empty Gardens of Contemplation, someone hailed him. A blue-robed priestess with a pale face and tightly bound black hair was approaching, attended by a shorter student girl who wore the green robes of a deaconess, and whose dark brown, wavy hair was unbound.

"Worthy Terikel, how delightful to see you again," he said. "And Deaconess Velander, I see that you are still a deaconess."

"But you are now a boatmaster," Velander observed by the red shoulder-tassels of his deck jacket and his three-cornered hat. "Congratulations."

"Will you be in port for long?" Terikel asked.

"The *Shadowmoon* is temporarily the *Arrowflight*, and the *Arrowflight* is to be careened. There is also other work . . . maybe eight days."

"Velander and I need more practice with spoken Diomedan."

"Ah, so you are still studying that exotic tongue?"

"Oh yes. Are you available?"

"For Terikel and Velander, always. Why not walk back with me now, speaking Diomedan?"

Once through the gates and past the guards, Feran softly asked, "Have you any more news of Warsovran's weapon?"

"There have been two more tests," Velander replied. "One of

them was a week ago, and it burned a circle two and one-third miles in diameter. Some nobles from nearby kingdoms were invited to see it happen. The other was sixteen days earlier, and smaller."

"That's four tests. What have you learned?"

"The first fire-circle was a third of a mile in diameter. I learned that from a slave we carried on commission. As for the second test, we know almost nothing, just tavern talk by Warsovran's troops. Maybe he was not sure why it worked the first time, and did not want witnesses if it failed."

"All of this makes me wonder. The emperor is assembling a lot of warships at Narmari. He may be so confident that his weapon can smash any inland city, that he intends to claim the entire coastline."

"Can he do that?"

"He has the largest fleet in Torean history, but even that is not enough ships to beat the combined might of the southern sea-faring kingdoms. Besides, privateers will play merry hell with his unescorted trading ships while the warships are away. Those fire-circles are impressive against cities, but not all Warsovran's enemies are to be found inland."

All the way to the docks they discussed the statistics of the fire-circles, figures that encompassed destruction combining the swiftness of lightning with the power of a volcano. Velander talked earnestly about the fire-circles and smiled continually, yet within her hearts she was resentful. Feran was an intruder, introduced into her intensely monosexual society by her own mentor. The relationships and politics of the temple were balanced with exquisite care, and into this the boatmaster had intruded with all the delicacy of a stallion loose in a mustering yard full of mares. *Who are you, and why is my soulmate paying you so much attention?* she thought as they walked the neat, narrow streets down to the waterfront. His speech was deep and harsh to her ears; even his smell was sharp and nauseating. All she could do was stay with Terikel, weathering the barrage of strangeness, but angry and resentful.

"What can doing, ah, to fighting . . . fire-circle?" Velander asked, her Diomedan tortured and slow, yet almost aggressive in tone.

"Just what we are doing," Feran replied easily. "Study, record, and learn. My thought is that they don't work well over water."

"Perhaps Warsovran is going to put one mighty effort into smashing the coastal kingdoms, then use fire-circles on defiant cities inland," said Terikel.

"True, the fire-circles are invincible on land," said Feran. "No man can stand against them."

"But men are soft," said Terikel. "They boast of their prowess and power to impress mere women like us, do they not, Velander? We know their weaknesses."

"Yes. No match, for us," replied Velander, trying not to sound appalled at the thought of seducing men as a strategic tactic.

The narrow streets suddenly opened onto the wharf area, with cool but mellow sea air and a forest of masts. Velander felt herself relaxing as they approached the *Arrowflight* along the pier. The ordeal was almost over.

"*Arrowflight* here, being, is!" Velander declared in triumph, pointing to the name.

"Ah yes, and it's a special design," said Feran with a wink to Terikel. "Its masts can be lowered to pass under low bridges, for working in rivers."

"Just like, ah, old ship, *Shadowmoon*," Velander managed, trying to disguise her mood with an attempt at a joke.

"If you please, keep your voice down!" Feran hissed in genuine alarm.

Velander swelled with triumph at having discomfited the male invader, but she said no more. The little schooner was being unloaded, and the air was full of the curses of wharfers. Terikel searched for something flattering to say about the *Arrowflight*, failed, then Velander suggested that they should return to the temple.

"So soon?" said Feran, sounding disappointed.

"Velander has to prepare for ordination," Terikel said.

"Ah, how wonderful for you," Feran responded, still speaking Diomedan. "How many days more?"

"Eight, but five of, ah, being vigil," managed Velander, stubbornly refusing to revert to their native language. "Must fast, drinking, er, water of rain. Only. Endure, I must . . . ordeals alone."

"Ordeals?" asked Feran.

"Being interrogated by the Elder," explained Terikel, coming to Velander's aid.

"Hah, it's brave of you," laughed Feran. "Five days with only that old bat for company."

"Shall not alone, totally," Velander now added.

"One's soulmate customarily endures a fast nearby to give comfort," said Terikel.

"Worthy Terikel, fasting, nearby, will be," said Velander, as slowly and distinctly as she could.

"Yes, I shall be in the Chapel of Vigils while Velander fasts in the temple's outer sanctum."

"And then you become a priestess with twelve years of celibacy before you," Feran sighed. "Who could endure such a wait as that?"

"Not you, boatmaster?" asked Terikel.

"Not I, celibate and esteemed ladies."

Two of the crew paused to stare as the two women walked back down the pier.

"So which do you fancy of 'em?" asked the deckswain.

Laron put a hand on his chest and stroked it with the other.

"Me?" asked Feran innocently.

"You," chorused Norrieav and Laron.

"Velander's just a serious puppy—but Terikel! Ah, she's like a queen."

"They both have . . . allure," Laron said, his arms now folded and his head inclined as he stared at the shapely pair of departing figures. There was something about Velander that annoyed him, and he suddenly caught himself licking his lips. He hastily clenched his teeth.

"No chance. Ye look too small, pale, gaunt, and scruffy," said the deckswain, who was also looking at Terikel and Velander. "Besides, wash off that beard and ye'd look fourteen."

"I'm a qualified navigator and medicar!" Laron replied.

"Aye, and ye'd probably be stronger than the rest of the crew put together, but ye still look like a cabin boy."

"So does Feran," retorted Laron.

"But Feran has curly hair, blue eyes, and body. It gets 'em every time."

"Well, not quite every time," Feran demurred.

"Tread careful, boatmaster," warned Norrieav. "Ye can see that the little one adores the priestess, while the priestess is as protective as a mother cat. I'd not like to come between them."

"I would," admitted Feran. "Without a tom, there'd be no kittens."

The two women reached the end of the pier, passed between some stalls and vendors, then vanished into a lane.

"I've been asking around, as I always do," said Laron, turning away and stroking his beard to check that it was still all there. "There is far more to Velander than meets the eye. Just three years ago she was in deep trouble. She had killed several men, apparently agents of Warsovran."

"At seventeen?" exclaimed Feran.

"So it seems. She was also orphaned by agents of Warsovran. Terikel's sister Elasse got her into the temple academy. When Elasse died on a voyage to Acrema, Terikel made Velander into a sort of foster sister. She became her mentor, and even found sponsors for her years of study. As far as Velander is concerned, Terikel is her friend, sister, saint, and queen. She would die for Terikel, and probably kill for her, too."

"Kill?" said Feran. "As in, kill me?"

"You, in general, as opposed to you specifically," explained Laron.

With the unloading done, Laron went into the port and sought a merchant house not far from the water. The back room was nothing like an importer's office, however. Kordoban's Sacking and Cord was no more than a front for Kordoban the trafficker in machineries of doubtful ownership. Unlike sorcerers who studied the arcane arts for power or scholarship, Kordoban specialized in obtaining very powerful etheric machines for the use of others. Socially frowned upon, he was nevertheless much in demand, and fairly rich.

"This is a mock-up of your quarry," said Kordoban, holding a small, violet sphere up before Laron's face.

He dropped it into Laron's palm. Laron examined it for a moment, noting that it was very light, and probably hollow.

"I need an advance," Laron said. "The sanctum of the Metrologan's Elder will not be easy to breach."

"No advance, only results."

Unused to being denied anything, Laron growled and bared his fangs. Kordoban immediately drew two silver daggers and held them ready in the manner of a skilled fighter. Laron's growl subsided to a rumble as he backed away two paces.

"You are a fool, not helping me to help you," Laron warned.

"If I paid advances to everyone who claimed to be a master thief, I would soon be a master pauper. Now, then, this mock-up oracle sphere is nothing. You can get as many made as you want for five silvers each at Lapidor's. The internal structure and contents are another matter entirely."

"My price is three hundred gold circars," Laron said firmly.

"Produce, and I shall pay."

A quarter hour later Laron was standing before a stall in the market. "I am told you can make another of these for five silvers, Lapidor," he said as he held up the mock-up oracle sphere.

"That I can, squire, and I can provide discretion for another five."

"I shall take that option."

"Can you wait?"

"I certainly can."

✻ ✻ ✻

That same day the Councilium of the Metrologan Order met the agent Feran had delivered. The man was by now wearing the earth-brown robes of a lay scholar.

"This is Lenticar," said the priestess who was Councilium Elder. "He was captured early in Warsovran's wars of expansion, and worked in slavery for three years. Lenticar, tell the Councilium what you told me."

Lenticar bowed to the Elder, then to each Councilium member in turn, wringing his hands all the while. The six priests of the Brotherhood and six priestesses of the Sisterhood were all attentive and alert, which made Lenticar more anxious still.

"The, ah, essence is that I spent three years in an army of slaves, digging out a collapsed ravine in the Seawall Mountains. One day, late last year, there was a great commotion down at the base of the diggings. We had reached the rocks of the old riverbed, you see. The area was sealed off, and the six hundred slaves who had been working down there were put to the ax. Just like that! No reason, no mercy, just, just— But no matter. The other fifty thousand of us were marched off to build a fortress in Vidaria. I escaped as we traveled, because the guards were by then a lot less careful. I . . . cannot say why. Not precisely, but . . . something had been found. I just knew it. We all did. Sometimes we whispered it to each other."

"Did you see what had been discovered?" asked a priestess.

"No, but I heard rumors that even the guards of the slaves closest to whatever it was were killed. We heard the word 'cypher' whispered among the guards. Nobody knew what was meant by it."

"Worthy Lenticar, do you have anything else to report?" asked the Elder.

Lenticar squirmed restlessly. There was so much to tell, but it was not important here and now.

"I could report suffering, cruelty, death, and selfless kindness in the face of all those three, but those things have no place here. I have given all that I was able to harvest from three years of toil. Now it is up to you, most Learned and Worthy company, to grow what you can from it."

The Elder stood up again now, and gestured to a seat rather than the door. Lenticar sat down.

"Worthy Lenticar, you have as much right to what the rest of us know as anyone else. Perhaps you may even be able to make better sense of it than we who have not been digging for three years. Worthy company, we have learned that within a few days of the discovery in the ravine, Warsovran rode in with Commander Ralzak and a man named Cypher. Cypher is rumored to be one of the original thieves who stole Silverdeath from its shrine. Just over a month after digging ceased in that ravine, the fire-circle casting burned Larmentel's heart out. Now

Warsovran is testing it on what is left of the city, and is learning how to refresh it more quickly. Word arrived by messenger auton bird this morning that a fifth test scoured the life from an area four and two-thirds miles across. That is enough to destroy any army, and is probably adequate to conquer this whole continent."

There was a hurried, alarmed murmur among the members of the Councilium.

"Then why does he just detonate it over Larmentel, over and over?" the Examiner asked.

"Larmentel is a shell, and now worthless," said the Elder. "He wants the other cities intact, so he seeks to frighten his enemies with these obscene demonstrations of raw power over Larmentel's ruins. Worthy Sisters and Brothers, Warsovran has sworn to wipe out our Order, both priests and priestesses. Clearly we cannot fight this fire-thing, so it is now time for us to fade from sight, as we have often done in earlier times of tyranny. For a few of us, it is time to flee with the Order's records and treasures."

Laron sauntered through the twilight market alone, inspecting the stalls but making no attempt to haggle seriously. This was the market where goods of suspicious origins were offered by even more suspicious vendors, but Laron was in the market for nothing tangible. He stopped before a stall whose ragged banner declared, FARUGIL'S POISONS. The words were underscored with a line of little skulls, for the benefit of the illiterate.

"Dragon tears—would you have that?" Laron ventured softly.

"There is little call for it," replied the vendor.

"Could you get it for me?"

"I could show you where to get it, but the price is high."

"What is that price."

"Thirty-five gold circars."

"Thirty-five! For that, I could buy your soul."

"My soul is not for sale."

Their coded exchange over, Laron counted out the price and handed it to the vendor. He was given a vial of cloudy blue glass, which he inspected briefly. Something like a small scroll seemed to be within.

"Transcripts of the Metrologan Elder's guard autons," said the vendor.

"They had better be genuine," warned Laron. "You know what happens to those who cheat me."

"If you wish to complain, I am here every night."

The transaction complete, they bowed and Laron casually walked on. Moments later he was slipping through the crowds like an eel through long grass, and by the time he reached the docks he was running. Only the tip of Miral's outermost ring was above the western horizon as he scrambled into his cabin on the *Arrowflight* and slammed the shutter closed.

The next two days saw the *Arrowflight* dragged up onto a slipway at high tide, and scrubbed clean of barnacles and seaweed by laborers. After a wash with hot tar it was floated again, then rowed back out to the pier. Velander sat on a stone bollard and looked down at the deck of the moored *Arrowflight*, slowly combing and repinning her dark brown hair back from her face with little ornamental combs. Terikel was nearby, bartering for something at a pier stall.

Feran and Laron emerged through the deck hatch. Both were stripped to the waist, but Laron's skin was as white as fresh parchment, and his chest was painfully thin. He was also wearing black kid-leather dress gloves.

"Deaconess, should you not be keeping a vigil for your ordination?" Feran asked in Diomedan.

"As of noon, yes," Velander replied, choosing and phrasing her words slowly.

They strode up the gangplank and stood beside her, smelling of sweat, sacking, tar and resins.

"Have you had a good breakfast?" asked Laron, also in Diomedan. "There are five days of fasting ahead."

"Have hungered for longer," she replied enigmatically.

"In your travels?" asked Feran.

"Ah, yes. How is Diomedan sound? Could pass for, er, speaking native?"

"You sound more like a foreign scholar, but speak confidently," replied Feran. "Why do you ask?"

"Curious, only," she said, then her eyes narrowed. "Knowing about fifth fire-circle?"

"That's not common knowledge," Laron said slowly and uneasily, avoiding Velander's eyes.

"So, is true! I am hearing, four and two-thirds miles, across. How are you knowing?"

"I move among common folk," said Laron. "They have ways of finding out, just as priestesses, nobles, and kings do. They note odd things, Deaconess Velander, like the fact that you ask about your spoken Diomedan. Could it be that you might go to Diomedan soon?"

"Idea is, er, lacking, ah, lacking undergarments."

"I think you mean foundation," said the vampyre, smoothly switching to Velander's language for a moment. "The Diomedan for 'foundation garment,' as in 'corset,' and for 'foundation,' as in what a building is built on, are rather similar. Now, try it in Diomedan."

"Idea lacking the foundations."

"Close enough, for now. A few weeks in Diomeda will fix all that. Speaking of Diomeda, this morning I noticed crates from the temple being loaded onto a deepwater trader bound for Diomeda. The *Searose*, that big one with three masts."

"I know nothing," Velander replied, unconsciously squirming.

"Is it because of the fire-circles?" asked Feran.

"No!"

"Just no?"

"Worthy Terikel say speak Diomedan, I speak Diomedan. For her. Very well, am learning."

"But why would she say that?"

"She saying, ah, I am study too much of mathematics," Velander improvised. "Saying I am need balance of exotic language. No fire-circles then, when she say."

Feran conceded to her logic. "Well, it's meant your charming form and company whenever we dock here, so why should I complain?"

Nothing could destabilize Velander quite so readily as a man's opinion of her figure. Without any attempt at subtle wordplay, she instantly changed the subject—with a glance in Terikel's direction to see why she was taking so long.

"I cannot make sense, ah, of driving energies . . . that fire-circles having," she managed with considerable effort.

"I'm puzzled, too," said Feran. "Magical ether, one supposes."

"Magical castings are too limited in terms of sheer power," interjected Laron, "while hellbreath oil must be pumped out of a hose and does not burn hot enough to melt stone. A powerful and exact convergence of etheric and mundane energies is needed."

"What would you know of magic?" muttered Feran, surprised and a little annoyed that his strange navigator knew something of the cold sciences as well.

"I read a lot," replied Laron.

They were interrupted by Druskarl, a senior eunuch of the temple guard. He strode down the pier from where the deepwater trader was being loaded. Like the *Arrowflight*'s deckswain, he was a black-skinned Acreman, and was wearing the tunic of a pilgrim instead of his usual armor. His black, braided hair was covered by a sunhood.

"Deaconess, your vigil starting today," Druskarl said in sharp, heavily accented Damarian.

"I am under the escort of the Worthy Terikel," Velander replied, dropping back into Damarian, and with quite a good parody of Druskarl's hard, flat voice. She gestured to where Terikel was holding up a pilgrim's pack and arguing with the stallholder.

"Deaconess! Ordination vigil starting noon," Druskarl insisted.

"Nobody knows that better than me, Druskarl," she replied firmly.

By now Laron had noticed that Velander was under siege. Almost without realizing it, he found himself coming to her aid. "I note that the temple is shipping books to Acrema with you as escort," he said casually to Druskarl.

"No books," muttered Druskarl.

"I smelled the scent of old books as your crates were carried past to the *Searose*."

"What you know of books?"

"I am no stranger to libraries."

Velander nodded approvingly. Feran smiled and Druskarl frowned.

"Druskarl no stranger to ships, noting *Arrowflight*'s masts hinge between brackets," he countered. "Can lie flat."

"We need to pass beneath bridges when trading on rivers," said Feran.

"*Arrowflight* riding high in water."

"The *Arrowflight* is nearly empty, and our bilges are being bailed and scrubbed," Feran explained with a trace of condescension in his tone; when speaking with Druskarl, that was a mistake. "So, are the Metrologans moving to Acrema before Warsovran turns his fire-circle on Zantrias?"

"What are strange hatch-covers below load waterline?" Druskarl countered.

"They are for looking through," Laron answered smoothly.

Druskarl frowned, neither believing him nor seeing the joke. "Below waterline?"

"Yes, in an hour there will be cargo aboard, and they will definitely be below the waterline," said Feran.

"Druskarl say masts of *Arrowflight* easy for lowering. *Arrowflight* easy to sink, also. *Arrowflight* pretend sinking in shallow water when chased. Low tide coming, hatches closed by crew, crew bailing, then ship floating."

"But we are not fishes," said Feran. "We would drown."

"Gigboat bolted upside down to frame on deck."

"It would fill with rain otherwise."

"Gigboat holding air for breathing when *Arrowflight* sinking."

Feran's eyes narrowed. "Some people have minds so sharp, they could slice precious parts of themselves off," he said sullenly to the tall, powerfully built eunuch.

"They like to people having sharp noses, yes?" asked Druskarl.

"Well-parried," said Laron, standing back with his arms folded.

"Good sirs, we need to bid you both farewell," called Terikel, returning with the canvas pack. "Velander has to prepare for her ordination."

Terikel crossgrasped hands with all three men in turn, but only Feran felt a scrap of paper being slipped between his fingers.

"The guard knows our secret," Feran said softly to Laron when they were alone again. "The most advanced vessel on the waters of the world, and he knows what it really is."

"But he *told* us that he knows," replied Laron, who seemed calm about it. "Had he been an enemy, he would have said nothing. Besides, he does not know all the other secrets of the *Shadowmoon*."

"*Arrowflight*! Who is he?"

"Our next contact, perhaps. This could be his way of introducing himself."

Laron looked to the west, where the ringed disk of Miral was pale in the blue haze, just above the horizon.

"Miral is setting. I must go to my cabin."

"Perchance to sleep and dream?" asked Feran.

"I never dream, boatmaster. Neither do I sleep."

Laron walked down the gangplank, stepped down onto the middeck of the *Arrowflight*, then slid the hatch to his tiny cabin aside and crawled in. When he had slid the hatch shut again, Hazlok came up beside Feran.

"I allus feel easier when he sleeps," he declared.

"Apparently he does *not* sleep, matey."

"Then what's he do?"

"I have been assured that we are safer not knowing."

Hazlok folded his arms and shook his head. "I'se glad he be on our side."

The *Arrowflight*'s master cabin was about the size of a privy laid on its side, and the bunk, desk, chart locker, lamp, and weapons rack were designed to fold back against the wall. Feran sat on his watertight seachest, examining the scrap of paper Terikel had given to him. It was a scroll of tissue, the kind used on primitive messenger auton birds, the ones that could not speak. There was a preamble that was not easy to follow, but it eventually became clear the authors were two priests of the Metrologan's Brother Order. They had been disguised as peasants and were helping Warsovran's victorious army to strip everything of value from the ruins of Larmentel. They had also witnessed Warsovran's weapon being used. Included on the scroll were secondhand descriptions of the first four tests and quite accurate figures on the destruction's extent. Each test had been at the eighth hour of morning, and every time, a perfect circle had been blasted and scoured by the most intense fire imaginable. Many stones had partly melted or crumbled, and the fire had penetrated to the deepest cellars and tunnels. Not a scrap of wood, food, or even charred bone had survived, but they noted that the fish in a deep ornamental pond, while boiled, were at least whole and uncharred.

"It is our feeling that Warsovran's Commander Ralzak has a weapon of such potency that no city or army could stand against him," the report's minuscule writing concluded.

Total annihilation in a hopeless cause is far less constructive than surrender in the knowledge that Warsovran's day will pass. Our Order can continue to work in secret until more enlightened times return and—

There was a short pen-slash, as if the writer had had his arm jolted, then the fine writing commenced again.

We have just seen a fifth wall of fire over the city, one reaching right to the city's outer walls. It burst from the sky at the eighth hour in the form of a torus about a half mile above the center of Larmentel, spilling fire down the center to blast all before it, then rolling back into the sky and down its own center again. It covered a radius from the center to the outer walls in the time one needs to draw a deep breath, and made a sound like a continuous peal of thunder. The degree of annihilation was the same as before on the ground. Make what you will of this ghastly nightmare. We shall release an auton bird with this message and send more news as we are able.

    Worthy Deremi and Worthy Trolandic

Feran studied the figures and dates for the five detonations of Warsovran's weapon over the past one hundred twenty days.

He was intrigued by the fact the fish in the pond had remained uncharred. Appended in more elegant handwriting was the name of a dockside tavern, "Stormhaven," and the word "dusk."

He gazed through the cabin window's fretwork at the port. Were the fire-circle weapon to be used on Zantrias, the *Arrowflight* could be sunk with its crew, and with the air in the gigboat they could last as long as six hours. The only drawback was that the schooner needed several minutes to sink, while the weapon could raze the port in mere seconds.

"On the other hand . . ." Feran said to himself, then went out onto the deck.

"Norrieav, I want the, ah, *Arrowflight* taken through a practice dive drill tomorrow morning," he announced to the deckswain.

"Here, sir? In the harbor?"

"Just the drill, not a full dive. At dawn tomorrow, have the men secure and seal all goods that might spoil, and at, say, the eighth hour, have us standing over deep water with the masts down."

"There is a deep spot about a hundred yards straight out from the side of the pier. The big ships use it as a turning basin."

"That will do nicely. There we shall hold ready until I order a return to the pier. Nobody will know our secret unless we actually open the underwater sink hatches, and, of course, we shall not do that."

"Very good, sir. The worst time to practice is in a real emergency."

"Too true, Norrieav, too true."

Chapter Two

VOYAGE TO HELION

At noon that day Velander was presented with a summons to the outer sanctum, where she was to begin five days of fasting, and then endure the vigil that would see her emerge as a priestess. Although what lay ahead was sure to be taxing, she was comforted by the fact that at least it did not involve men—specifically, sailors, and more specifically, Feran.

"The *Arrowflight* will be gone by the time you are ordained," said Terikel as she brushed and braided Velander's hair.

"Good," Velander said tersely, resenting even the mention of the schooner.

"I do not understand why you are so hostile toward Feran."

"He is a man," Velander replied flatly. "Every suffering, every torment, every loss in my life, has been caused by men."

"Not all men do such deeds."

"But all such deeds are done by men!" retorted Velander, annoyed that Terikel was even being sympathetic to Feran's gender.

She was her soulmate, after all. Velander had tried to be a sister to Terikel after Elasse had been lost at sea. Now she was on the brink of an ordeal, however, and in need of Terikel's unreserved support.

Just before noon Laron was in one of the taverns not far from the temple grounds. This was the more salubrious part of Zantrias, high on the central hill, and with good views and cooling breezes. The vampyre pretended to sip from a pewter goblet, but he was doing no more than wetting his lips. Presently one of the temple guards entered and walked over to his table.

"May I sit?" asked the guard.

"No," Laron replied, glancing up and showing just a hint of fangs.

The man skipped back a pace, then seemed to gather back his composure. "Er, then, in the name of Druskarl, may I sit?"

"Garric, is it?"

"Aye."

"Then sit."

The guard dragged over a stool and called for ale. When they were alone again Laron jingled a purse that was hidden within his robes.

"Fifty circars," said Garric.

"Forty," Laron said firmly. "Druskarl has already given you ten."

"Fifty or nothing."

"Then nothing."

"I could denounce you," the guard warned confidently.

"Try," Laron responded smoothly.

"You're just a boy."

"I am a boy to whom a lot of very important people defer. I am also a boy in search of a somewhat less greedy associate." Laron stood up. "Now, you must excuse me—"

"Wait!" said the guard, standing also. "Look, I must be off Torea when Warsovran conquers this place."

"I know. This is not the first time you have betrayed a position of trust. That is why you were recommended, and that is why we approached you."

"Forty circars will barely cover the voyage to Acrema."

"Where you can get work in a mercenary army and start life anew with ten gold circars in your purse. The *White Wave* sails tonight, just after your shift ends. The shipmaster knows to expect you, and you can be gone before the outcry from my visit begins."

Garric's head sagged, and he put a hand to his face. "Very well, forty circars."

✳ ✳ ✳

Five days of drinking water and eating nothing had left Velander unsteady and weak but feeling strangely self-controlled.

At noon she was led into the inner sanctum of the temple by the Examiner, and they meditated together for two hours. The Councilium then entered and subjected her to an intense, aggressive barrage of questions about knowledge theory, verification, and her own personal loyalties. She was run ragged, but did not break. Presently she was left alone to meditate again while the Councilium discussed her candidature.

Velander could hear the bell at the end of the stone breakwater in the distant harbor, as it rang the change of tide. This was followed by coded rings for shipping movements. *Steady Prosper*, *White Wave*, and *Bright Leaper* had arrived, but there were no departures. *Arrowflight* was cleared to sail the following afternoon. So, Feran was still there. After the emotional flaying she had received from the Elder, even the *Arrowflight*'s boatmaster was beginning to seem like good company. Perhaps Terikel and she could go down to the docks and wave him off as priestess and priestess after one last hour of Diomedan language practice. She felt so weak, though, and three miles was a long, long way to walk. On the other hand, Terikel got along well with the young boatmaster, and Terikel was her soulmate. Grudgingly Velander decided she would go to the docks for the sake of Terikel.

Late in the afternoon Velander was led out to the plaza before the temple, where brushwood had been piled up in a open blackstone hearth shaped like a huge clawed hand. All priestesses and students in the complex had been assembled on the stone steps to watch Velander's last test begin. Everyone except Terikel, of course, who was in the little Chapel of Vigils farther down the hill. As the sun touched the horizon, trumpets sounded from the steps of the temple's outer sanctum. Velander lit a torch from the temple's eternal flame and plunged it into the brushwood. The blaze symbolized the light of knowledge being ignited against the onset of darkness. The brushwood fuel was a reminder that knowledge must be tended closely or it will quickly burn out. If she could endure through the night to stoke the flames until dawn, she would automatically become "Worthy Velander" when the sun cleared the horizon. The watchers filed down from the steps, leaving her alone to her task.

✳ ✳ ✳

As the afternoon began to fade into evening, Garric signed Laron in at the temple gate, then led him to the chapel in the Gardens of Contemplation.

"Careful, there's a priestess in there," hissed the guard. "She's keeping soulmate vigil."

Terikel, thought Laron without having to see her face. They kept to the back of the chapel, and the bowed head of the figure at the front did not turn.

"You know what to do now?" Laron whispered.

"Sign you out, then declare the grounds clear of visitors for the evening closure."

"Good. And after that?"

"Go to the *White Wave* just before midnight."

"They are expecting you, and they are also expecting forty circars. Now, farewell, and never mention this again."

"Look, about the Elder . . . I—I mean, you're not going to murder the old bat, are you?"

"I follow the path of chivalry," declared Laron.

"Er, what does that mean?" asked the guard, scratching nervously at his neck.

"It means that if all goes well, nobody will be hurt. Now, leave."

Once Laron was alone he checked that Terikel's back was still turned, then began climbing the stone wall of the chapel. Within moments he was amid the roof beams. A gong boomed in the distance. Laron cut the bindings on slats that prevented pigeons from entering, then squeezed through a ventilation gap and out into the lead guttering beyond. In daylight he could have been seen from the ground, but the deep shadows of evening covered his way. He climbed another sheer wall, his fingers clinging where mortals could get no grip.

The window to the Elder's chambers was protected by a guard auton, but it was just a primitive casting, designed only to stop any living intruder. Not being alive, Laron had no trouble slipping past it. Fortunately, the Elder was a neat and highly organized type of person. Books stood neatly on shelves, scrolls lurked in a carefully labeled lattice of cells, and behind a solidly built table was a high-backed chair, rather like a throne. Glittering machinery littered the table: pyramids of glass, a slab of slate with petrified ripples imprinted from some ancient sea, at least a dozen spheres of gemstone, crystal, and glass, un-gainly lumps of skystone, thin sheets of gold leaf, silver mount-ings and mechanisms, and cups cut from black glass and crystal.

What was on the table would have made him rich for several lifetimes, but faintly glowing filaments of alarm and accountant autons were threaded among them. To one side of the table was a heavy silver cover, bound to a silver platter by a separate au-ton. Laron put a hand down on the table. Immediately the au-tons there swarmed over his flesh, but soon concluded he was dead. He did not try to take anything. Confused, the autons re-mained enmeshed around his hand. Now he spoke the words of release, and the guard auton on the silver platter changed from a glowering red to an inoffensive green. With his free hand he lifted the cover.

Beneath the cover was a complex of mechanisms and autons, and at the top was an oracle sphere, a globe of violet crystal with an oddly metallic sheen. It was about twice the diameter of a fingernail, and rested on a spring balance and within tripod calipers. Both mechanisms were bound to glowing guard au-tons. This was something his informant had not warned him about.

Laron took an identical sphere from his tunic, then breathed a glowing tendril of nothingness at the mechanism. The guard autons blazed up at the threat, then began to pulse. There was the life force of something dead here, a contradiction in terms. The autons consulted with each other, verified the contradic-tion, then decided to recast themselves. In that heartbeat inter-val while the autons closed down to reset themselves, Laron deftly substituted his own oracle sphere for that of the Elder. His casting collapsed as the autons became active again, and Laron stood absolutely still as they checked the balance and calipers. Nothing was amiss, as far as they could tell. Laron put

the sphere away, replaced the silver cover, and unbound its
locking auton. Now he slowly raised his other hand from the
table. The autons there unbound themselves, continually checking whether anything had been moved or removed. Once his
hand was clear, they locked into the auton binding the silver
cover. It registered that one authorized access had been made.
The table's accountant autons disagreed. No living being had
touched the table or anything on it since the Elder had left. The
cover's guard auton was adamant that one authorized access
had been made. The accountant autons conferred, decided the
guard auton knew nothing about good accounting practice, and
left their records unaltered.

Relieved but still wary, Laron took the oracle sphere from his
tunic and examined it for a moment. Any gemsmith could
mimic the appearance, of course, but there were tests that
would distinguish empty fakes from those enchanted with . . .
whatever they were. On the Elder's desk he noticed a small, tapering cup cut from black glass. *Glass from the sky, no doubt,*
he thought to himself. Nearby there would be an eye, an eye of
greenstone. Looking around the room, he noticed an ornamental gargoyle supporting a ceiling beam. A single, green cyclops
eye stared sightlessly down at him.

There was no auton guarding the greenstone eye, and it came
out of its quill-and-resin mountings easily. It was about the size
of a peach. Again he put his hand on the table and again the autons swarmed to investigate it. Very carefully he placed the violet sphere in the concave bottom of the cup of black glass, then
breathed in fine tendrils of the life force from someone he had
fed upon the night before. He capped the cup with the large
greenstone eye.

A hazy face appeared in the greenstone, the face of a woman
with large, dark eyes and framed with greying hair.

"You can invoke me all you like, Elder," it declared. "The exchange must go *both* ways or I shall give you no more secrets."

The voice was faint but distinct, and the language was
vaguely familiar. *Latin,* he suddenly realized. Memories of a
world with a single moon and no lordworld flooded through his
mind.

"Elemental, can you hear me?" Laron asked in Latin, a language he had not used for seven centuries.

"Hear you? Yes," answered the voice. "I say, your Latin has improved a lot—no, you're new."

"Where did *you* learn Latin?"

"At school."

Ask a stupid question . . . Laron thought.

"Can you speak anything else?"

"Just a little Diomedan. Some witch called the Elder has been teaching me."

This made sense. Few in Zantrias could speak Diomedan, the trading language of the Acreman east coast. Thus the Elder had exclusive communication with the trapped elemental. *Is that why Terikel is learning Diomedan?* he wondered.

"Elemental, what is your name?"

"I call myself Penny. Who are you?"

"Laron," he responded, then added the name he had not used in centuries. "Laron de Belvaire. I was once like you, inside an oracle sphere. How were you trapped here?"

"Trapped? I'm n— Er, I don't know! Can you help me?"

"Perhaps. I hope so."

Laron found himself strangely moved. He had encountered elementals before, but they were nothing like this. Existence within the sphere was not pleasant. A thought came to him. "How many moons has your world?"

"Moons? There's only one."

"Who is the king of France?"

"There is no king in France! Remember 1789?"

Laron blinked. "No king? Are you sure?"

"France is a republic."

Republic. The ancient, ancient word stirred something within Laron's dead breast. France was now a republic. That seemed impossible, yet . . . yet it had been six or seven centuries. Anything might happen. Whatever the case, this elemental—no, this *woman* was from his world. Long, long ago his master had taught him to behave with honor and chivalry toward helpless women in peril, even at the risk of his own life. Well, he no longer had a life to risk, but there was a woman in need of defense here, so by Miral's rings he was going to behave with

honor and chivalry! A truly helpless woman of good breeding
and high degree, no doubt, because she knew Latin. Surely
some god was smiling upon him.

"Your image, it's breaking up and flickering—" Laron said.

She was gone, but that did not matter. Laron removed the
greenstone ball and allowed the remains of his life force to soak
back into his fingers. Placing the oracle sphere in a pouch
around his neck, he prepared to disentangle his other hand from
the table's autons—then noticed they had collapsed. Vanished.
Something had drained them completely, yet they had been
both powerful and deadly. Puzzled and wary, he replaced the
gargoyle's eye.

Laron did not bother to check that the room was as he had
found it. Were that not the case, the autons should have been
shrieking their alarms by now, and the place would be alive
with tendrils of fire that could slice any flesh, living or dead,
yet . . . they *all* seemed to be drained. The sun was below the
horizon as he squeezed through the window and past where the
last guard auton should have been. The Elder was going to get a
shock when she next returned.

Laron's client eyed the violet oracle sphere with satisfaction as he
held it between his fingers, but there was suspicion in his voice.

"This looks to be genuine," Kordoban conceded, "but so did
the sphere I gave you."

"They could well be the same," agreed Laron.

"I do have ways of detecting forgeries."

"Then use them. I have nothing to hide."

"Was this in plain view?"

"No, there were three gold covers protected by guard autons.
Being dead, I could bypass them, and naturally I took the
sphere from the cover with the strongest auton."

"You—you did?" he asked urgently. "Did you check the
others?"

"No. The auton that was strongest—"

"Damn you, that might have been part of the decoy!" cried
Kordoban. "Why didn't you check all three?"

"I had no way of knowing, and the cradles had weight-sensitive mountings keyed to the autons. You only gave me one decoy sphere, remember?"

Kordoban spoke to an auton guarding what appeared to be just another stone block in the wall. A stone plug began to unscrew, then it floated free of the wall and hung in midair. Kordoban drew out a padded iron box from the hidden chamber, and within this was a smaller version of the cup of black glass the Elder had been using. His greenstone globe was also smaller, and had several flaws and cracks.

"I shall check this oracle sphere. Wait."

Laron was kept only moments before Kordoban looked up from his etheric machine.

"A fake," he sighed, tossing the sphere to Laron. "The old fox. Are you sure that you disturbed nothing?"

"Yes."

"Then you must go back. I shall have two more of these made, and next time you will bring all three of the Elder's spheres to me."

"The temple guard—"

"—will be stopped at the docks, told to return to the temple as if nothing has happened, and offered another forty circars to let you in again. You will, of course, not be paid until you produce the correct oracle sphere."

"There is no fairness in this. I endured great danger."

"And brought me nothing."

Laron scowled and shook his head. "Miral is nearly down, I must get back to the *Arrowflight*."

"Whatever. Return tomorrow, I shall give you another two spheres."

"Why is the oracle sphere so important?" he asked, tossing the fake into the air and catching it.

"It is old, old sorcery, fashioned by a race older than the creation sagas of our world and commanding forces that we cannot even dream of. More than that, you do not need to know."

✳ ✳ ✳

Staying awake seemed such a simple thing until one had to do it after five practically sleepless nights and no food at all for as long. The supply of brushwood fuel was cunningly measured so that too much piled on at once would burn out before morning. One had to actually be awake, not to . . . *nod!* Velander caught herself falling forward. The fire was still burning: she had drifted away for only moments. She tossed a bundle onto the flames and sat back, again drowsy with the smoke and fatigue.

Someone to talk to was all she needed, but Terikel was keeping her own vigil after no more sleep or food than Velander had been allowed. Terikel was suffering, too, and her soulmate's ordeal could not be wasted. Velander cast about in her mind for a problem, and thought of Warsovran's fire-circles.

The tests had begun sixty-four days apart, halved to thirty-two, then sixteen, then eight. There should have been a test on the second morning of her fast, then one on the fourth, and one on the fifth. Convergence. Laron had mentioned convergence and Laron always knew more than he let on, she had noticed. Laron also liked forcing people to work things out for themselves. Somewhere in the temple complex a bell rang the eighth hour past noon. Another test would be happening at this very moment, then at two A.M. the next day, five A.M., six-thirty A.M., seven-fifteen A.M., seven forty-two A.M. . . . and soon after that the tests would converge on some time around the ninth minute past eight A.M. Larmentel time. That was it! Nine minutes past eight A.M. tomorrow Warsovran would become able to use the fire-circle *at will* . . . or perhaps it moved back to lengthening intervals after the convergence. Perhaps he had to make his conquests very quickly, or the interval would become sixty-four days again.

She thought to the years ahead. To be ordained in the Metrologan Order one had to do six years of study, then vow to follow ordination with six of travel, six of research, and six of teaching. It was not a totally celibate order, but marriage was not permitted until the teaching years began. She put another bundle of brushwood on the pyre, then circled it slowly to keep herself alert. Terikel had once endured this ordeal, after all, and now she was fasting again for Velander. *Don't fail Terikel,* Velander told herself as she forced her legs to walk.

✦ ✦ ✦

Velander was down to two bundles of brushwood when a brilliant bead of light appeared on the eastern horizon. Her fire was still burning brightly as the sun rose into the sky, and in tribute the temple bells began to peal out the good news. Priestesses and students streamed out of the darkness and Velander was swept away to warm broth, a bath, a suit of blue robes, and a lengthy audience with the Elder. All through the celebrations and ceremonies Velander thought of Terikel, who had endured the same privations yet received nothing more than the satisfaction of supporting her soulmate. A canvas pack with the symbolic contents of dried fruit, water, a writing kit, coins, and books was presented to Velander. The Elder signed her ordination scroll, blotted the ink, then rubbed it with beeswax to waterproof it.

"Twice the usual number of subjects in half the time," the venerable priestess said approvingly. "But what is your favorite?"

"Mathematics," Velander replied dreamily. "Oh, and languages! Languages, definitely."

She was taken back out to her room, where the seamstress was waiting to adjust the cut of her robes. After adding a few personal things to her pack, including some amberwood hairpins and a brass cylinder with the medicars' mark engraved on it, she stood still for her fitting. Sleep washed over her like waves over a sandbar, and she chattered to stay awake.

"What has been happening over the past five days?" Velander asked.

"In the temple, port, or world?" asked the seamstress.

"Start with the world and work back."

"The king of Zarlon has invited Warsovran to send an ambassador. That fire-circle thing of Warsovran's has him as frightened as our own monarch, you know. *I* think it's all a trick. Notice how it is always set off in the same place? I think it's just slaves spreading hellbreath oil. The eunuch guard Druskarl sailed on the evening of the first day of your vigil, and who do you think was waving and weeping on the pier? Why it was Worthy—"

"Has Warsovran's weapon been tested again?" Velander interrupted, shaking her head to clear it.

"Twice more, as I've heard."

"Twice more? In five days?" Velander asked slowly, pleased that her convergence theory—or perhaps it was Laron's—was holding true.

"I'm sure of it. I have my sources."

"Are they reliable?"

"Oh . . . yes and no. If a Councilium meeting is called within a quarter hour of an auton bird arriving, I know that another fire-circle has burned. Pah, the way that Warsovran has been squandering hellbreath oil! Just what is he trying to prove? He's just like a little boy playing with fire, and one day the fire will get out of control."

Suddenly a jumble of figures began to cascade into order in Velander's mind. The Elder's words returned, followed by those of the seamstress. . . . *twice the subjects in half the time . . . one day the fire will get out of control.*

Velander knew only four of the fire-circles' diameters, and even those were approximate, but a trend was there: a third of a mile, no figure, just over a mile, two and a third, four and two-thirds . . . And what of the latest tests? Six should have been nearly ten miles across; and seven, over eighteen.

A deep, cold chasm suddenly opened up within Velander. *Twice the diameter in half the time!* The fire-circle was doubling with each detonation, but after only half the previous interval. It was not being tested, it was out of control! Velander calculated frantically, oblivious of the seamstress chatting to her as she adjusted the pack's straps. Detonation eight, just under thirty-eight miles after one day. Detonation nine, seventy-five miles after half a day. The tenth would have been at two A.M. and a hundred fifty miles across, followed by one at five A.M. a staggering three hundred miles from rim to rim. It was nearly six A.M. now, so about half an hour ago a fire-circle must have seared the life from a circle six hundred miles wide. The next would stop a mere ten miles short of Zantrias in perhaps twenty minutes, and after that . . . Larmentel was an hour behind, on sidereal time!

Screaming the single word, "Run!" Velander tore away from the seamstresses and ran from her room. She fled down the stone corridor beyond, swaying and stumbling from five days of fasting. It was three miles to the beach, but Terikel had to be warned first. Velander ran across the plaza of the temple complex where her pyre was now ashes, and into the dormitory cells. Terikel's cell was empty, with the bed made up. *The refectory!* Velander ran down the stone steps and across a courtyard where stone dragons breathed water into a lampfish pool, then she burst into the refectory. The first shift of priestesses and novices was eating breakfast in silence while a novice stood at a lectern, reading aloud from an ancient text.

"Terikel!" Velander shouted. Silence and stares answered her. "Run for the beach, the fire is coming!" Velander added by way of explanation, then whirled and dashed out.

There was one last chance: that Terikel had fallen asleep in the Chapel of Vigils when the temple bells had rung out to announce Velander's ordination. The chapel was not far from the main gates to the temple complex, just beyond the Gardens of Contemplation. Velander screamed Terikel's name as she ran, shattering the serenity of those who were there to meditate, then stumbled up the steps to the chapel. The glowing stub of a coil of incense was tagged with Velander's name, but the benches beyond were empty. Velander hurried past each row, in case her soulmate was asleep on the floor. Outside, the thief-bell was ringing, and people were calling her name.

Soon they would catch her; they would think she was having a fit. Explanations would take time, perhaps hours, but only minutes remained. It was three miles to the docks. Druskarl had said the *Arrowflight* could be sunk, but still hold air to breathe. It would take long enough to convince Feran of the danger, let alone the Elder. Velander took the stub of incense and extinguished the glowing point in the skin of her left wrist.

"By this mark I'll carry your memory forever," sobbed Velander. "Forgive me for deserting you, soulmate, but I tried my best."

The gates of the temple complex were not yet locked as Velander neared them, but the two guards were alert with their glaves at the ready. Velander stopped and panted a tangle of life force between her hands, then flung it. One guard fell with glowing amber coils wrapped about his ankles, but the other tried to slam the gates shut. Already weak from the first casting, Velander breathed more etheric life force between her hands and flung it, binding the second guard to the heavy oak slats of one side of the gate. The effort of casting so much energy cost Velander greatly in strength. She shambled through the gate, barely able to hold herself upright. The pursuing priestesses would catch her in moments unless . . . The casting binding the first guard suddenly collapsed and streaked back to Velander, swirling around her head and quickly dissolving into her skin. As the second casting returned to her, she was able to break into a headlong, unsteady run again.

The Metrologan Order wore light sandals and loose trousers under a short outer robe, well suited to running. Velander dodged past a wood cart delivering fuel for a baker's oven then ran through the market square where stallkeepers bartered with customers. *So much life, but they will all be dead within an hour,* she thought. The sky was clear, and there was no wind. It was a perfect, flawless morning. Children were playing knucklebones on the cobbles, and two town constables were making a leisurely patrol with their spears held casually over their shoulders. *Should warn, must warn,* Velander told herself, but any delay was dangerous. She could snatch up one child and try to save it, but the constables would soon catch her and explanations would take hours. Pain lanced at Velander's side and her lungs burned, but still she ran. She cleared the square. Two miles to go, perhaps less.

She ran on more slowly, but still at her body's limit. *Down* was safe, *down* was to the sea. She looked up as the port watch-house loomed, then stumbled over a gutter and sprawled. Dragging herself up, she ran again. One mile to go now. Knives seemed to plunge into her bleeding left knee at every step. The wares of the streetside stalls became more nautical: netting, floats, cordage, sails, tar, ship's biscuit. Suddenly the buildings vanished, and Velander was facing clear sky and masts. The docks! Her legs betrayed her, she fell, crawled a few yards, then got up. She stumbled a few paces farther, fell again, then crawled for the pier.

"Worthy Sister, are you all right?" asked a docker in alarm.

"Leave me alone, pilgrimage," she wheezed.

With an ever-growing crowd behind her, Velander forced her aching legs to support her again and shuffled along the flagstones of the stone pier. Five ships along, unless they had sailed already. Five ships to—the *Arrowflight*! She literally fell down the gangplank and flopped to the deck, gasping for Feran.

Laron's pale face filled the blue sky that Velander lay staring into. There was a patch of beard hanging from his chin. He felt her pulse and put a hand to her forehead. His fingers were strangely cool.

"Exhausted," he concluded. "Deckswain, bring water."

"Boatmaster," Velander panted in a whisper.

"He is busy—" began Laron.

"Must see boatmaster. Fire-circles. Half the time, twice the distance."

"Fire-circles? I— Please, explain."

"Expanding, expanding as . . . convergence progression."

At the last two words Laron's eyes widened with alarm. "Cast off—now," he hissed to the deckswain. "Do it quickly."

"But sir, the boatmaster said to wait for his word before we cast off for our practice, er, drill, and it's still earlier than what he said."

"Cast off. Hurry!"

"But Laron, sir, we ought to ask the boatmaster—er, but like, after he's finished consultin' with his client—" said the deckswain.

"Damn the boatmaster!" snarled Laron, drawing him up off his feet then flinging him in the direction of the forward mooring rope. "I'm aware of the boatmaster's client. Cast off, *now!* The rest of you to the sweeps—hurry. Hazlok, not you! Take the steering pole, head for the deep turning area."

They were under way as Feran emerged. He was stripped to the waist, wearing only sailcloth trousers.

"Why are we under way—" he began, then he saw the girl on the deck. "Velander?"

"Release hatches," she panted, now louder. "Sink."

"Shush!" he hissed urgently, dropping to his knees and bending over her. "There are people on the docks."

"Soon—all dead. Fire-circle, coming."

"Velander, Warsovran's weapon is at Larmentel. Your fast has—"

"Out of control. Reach here, only minutes. Twice the distance, half the time."

Feran looked to the crowd gazing across from the stone pier, looked to the upturned gigboat bolted to its frame, then looked to Laron. "Well?" he asked. "What is she saying?"

"Twice the distance, half the time. I revised a few rough figures in my head, and they match what we know of the fire-circles better than my convergent regression theory. Its expansion parameters are called a progression, and it seems to be moving to a convergence."

"So what does that mean?" Feran demanded. "Will it kill us?"

"Yes," replied Laron, with the calm of one already dead.

The voyage from Gironal had taught them all to trust Laron's judgment, especially where mathematics was involved.

"How long?" Feran asked.

"A convergent progression would double the fire-circles' diameters as the intervals converge on zero, and there is a parallel progression expanding the circles to infinity. Considering the distance from here to Larmentel is a lot less than infinity—"

"How long?" Feran demanded, the veins of his temples standing out beneath his curly hair.

"Soon. Velander said minutes. I would have to check the figures more carefully, but her estimate looks depressingly sound."

"Damn," Feran said softly, striking his fist into the palm of his hand. He walked across to where the carpenter was rowing at a sweep oar.

"I'll row for you, D'Atro. Go below, and at my order release the sink hatches."

The man goggled at him, then gestured to the crowd on the pier. "But, sir, we're within sight of at least five hundred people. They'll know our secret."

"Soon it will not matter," Feran replied.

"But you're the boatmaster, sir. That Laron is getting too big for his—"

"Do as I say!" Feran shouted suddenly, his eyes blazing. "If Laron says jump, then jump! If Laron says croak, then croak! Now do—"

Directly to the north a curtain of light as intense as the sun's face streamed from a rent in the sky that spread up from the horizon to loom over the port city within three heartbeats. At the Blackstone Hills the dazzling light winked out, replaced by a wall of flames and smoke that towered over Zantrias. It was as if a god's guard dog had lunged for the port and reached the end of its chain. The flames and smoke boiled high into the air, and heat like the blast of an open oven seared the faces of everyone watching. Shatteringly loud thunder rolled over the port, reaching into the bodies of everyone there and shaking them to the very bones.

"Oh shit!" said the carpenter.

People began screaming even as the thunder was echoing away, and many on the wharves leaped into the water. Others rushed for the ships that were still tied up along the pier, and fights broke out with the crews as they tried to cast off, desperate to escape. Feran stared back at what Velander had spared them, then rushed to where Laron was helping her up.

"Navigator, how long have we got?" he cried.

"Worthy Velander?" asked Laron.

"Less than half an hour, more than twenty minutes," Velander replied, staring to the north where the sky was now a wall of brownish white, roiling smoke. "You *must* sink the *Arrowflight*. Now!"

"Soon, when we get to deeper water."

The *Arrowflight*'s masts were hinged, and a single bracing bar at the stern secured all the ropes holding the two masts vertical. As it was released, the masts came down together. Nevertheless, the masts and rigging took many precious minutes to secure. Several ships and boats had managed to get under way in the meantime, and one battle galley had actually cleared the harbor and was headed straight out to sea. With the hatch chocks knocked out, the *Arrowflight* began to sink. Feran ordered his crewmen under the gigboat, but Velander stayed at the starboard rail, gesturing intricately with her hands and muttering words of formation.

"Get back here, hurry!" shouted Feran.

"Another moment," she called back without turning. "I'm casting an ocular."

"We don't *have* a moment!" cried Laron. "Get back or die."

Water was already ankle-deep on the deck as Velander abandoned her incantation, splashed over to the gigboat and ducked under with the crewmen. The *Arrowflight* gave a loud gurgle, then sank on an even keel. Moments later it thumped softly onto the sand of the harbor's bed.

"How long till—" Hazlok began.

The water around them blazed with a whitish green light, brightening until they had to shut their eyes, then a deep, shuddering thunderclap resonated through the water and their bodies. There was a terrible hissing, with a rushing sound as if a huge gasp of pain was being drawn in by the world itself. Someone near Velander began to pray. Others joined in, not all in the same tongue. As suddenly as it began, the light faded. The rumbling merged into the declining hiss, but the water grew ominously warm around them.

"That wasn't so bad," came the deckswain's voice.

"Aye," agreed the carpenter. "Any number of folk might have survived by jumping off the pier and diving."

"Talk sense," panted Feran. "We're at least fifteen feet deep here, yet feel the heat. The air above will be as hot as from a smithy's forge for hours. How would they breathe?"

"But I've been in a smithy's shop, it's not so hot as to kill a man," replied the carpenter.

"He means inside the *forge*, not inside the shop," said Laron. "You'd burn from the lungs outward by breathing the air above."

Feran freed a sweep oar and managed to push it up vertically. The wood was charred at the end and crumbled in his fingers when he pulled it back down. Yielding at last to the torments her body had endured, Velander passed out.

✳ ✳ ✳

Hundreds of miles out to sea, Warsovran was cornered with his officers and Einsel on the quarterdeck of a caravel-type deep-water trader. The crew was in a state of blind terror after seeing an immense wall of fire, water, and steam surge out of the east to tower over them, then vanish. Another ship was standing by a few hundred yards away, and its master was already raising alarm flags.

"You can't make us sail into that!" shouted the bosun, pointing to the roiling mass of fog and ragged waves that now lay not a mile to the east. "What if that thing comes back?"

"Then we're dead anyway," Warsovran said in a clear, sharp voice that was firm with authority. "The fire-circle that follows is always twice as big." He lowered his battle-ax and let the edge rest on the deck. "What you have just seen is a god's weapon turned loose by a fool. Now it is spent, quenched by the sea, and I *must* return to Larmentel and get it back."

"Meaning no disrespect, Emperor Warsovran," said a midshipman, "but if you think we're goin' near what caused *that*, you can take a jump and swim."

"The lad's right," agreed the bosun. "We're six hundred miles out to sea and yet it was grand fearsome. What's Torea lookin' like after that's been over it? And what land are you plannin' to char next?"

"I am a ruler, I have no interest in annihilation. Until my idiot commander Ralzak unleashed that infernal weapon from the gods, I was uniting Torea's kingdoms under a single empire and bringing them order and discipline." He jabbed his finger to the east. "*That* was an accident. Now the weapon lies spent at the center of Larmentel for *any* scavenger to pick up. Would you rather it fall into the hands of yet another fool, or be safe in the hands of the only man in the world who can control it? You *must* help me! I *do not* need to use the fire-circle weapon, and I want to make sure that it is *never* used again."

They began to argue over his words, which did indeed make sense—provided one could trust him. Warsovran was adept at swaying crowds, especially when playing them for his life. He had got them wavering over a difficult dilemma, and now it was time to offer an irresistible reward.

"You need only take me to the port of Terrescol, where I shall take the horses and supplies we carry and ride on to Larmentel. While I am away searching for the weapon, you can amuse yourselves by digging for melted gold in the ruins of Terrescol's merchant halls, temples, and palace."

There was a highly excited mutter from the crewmen this time, and a great number of fingers pointed east amid the gesticulation.

"Wood burns, cloth burns, paper burns, and even people can be turned to ash, but gold merely melts," Warsovran continued. "If you get there first you may well dig out a half ton of gold before I return from Larmentel. We can sail to Acrema, buy a fleet of ships, then sail back and dig out more gold from all the other port cities. Imagine: a ton of gold for every man on this ship."

As he paused for breath the crew gave him three cheers and rushed to raise the sea anchors and unfurl the sails. Warsovran remained on the quarterdeck, glancing to the sun and fearfully estimating when the fire might return to sweep over them if he was wrong.

"Do we have a chance?" he asked Einsel, who was still staring at where the wall of fire and steam had stood.

"Cypher told me that a fire-circle will be quenched if either its entire circumference or more than half its area is over water," said Einsel, with the resignation of one who had accepted death so completely that he could not understand why he still had a pulse.

"According to the finest maps available to us, the latest fire-circle should have been the last."

"Mapmaking is by no means an exact science, Majesty," Einsel said glumly.

"That is not to be your concern," said Warsovran, taking a sheaf of sealed papers from his coat. "Take a gigboat across to the *Snowgull* and order the shipmaster to sail for Helion. At Helion you will present these to the admiral."

Einsel accepted the package gingerly, as if such a welcome

development was sure to have a dangerous or unpleasant catch. "So I am not to journey with you back to Torea?" he asked hopefully.

"Einsel, I trust only *myself* enough for that particular journey. Meantime, let us look to the positive results of the fire-circles."

"You mean *that* did *good*?"

"Oh yes. My supremely vindictive empress is now ash on the wind, my son is safely away with the fleet, and I have been restored to the age of about twenty. I consider all of that to be extremely good."

When Velander revived, Laron was holding her head above the water. Everyone under the boat was silent as they shared the wooden bubble of air. They waited in near-darkness. The water remained warm, but when a second oar was held above the surface it came down undamaged. Next a seaman swam clear of the upturned gigboat and held his hand just clear of the surface. He swam back to report it had been like plunging his fingers into boiling water.

The air under the gigboat became increasingly humid and foul. Another hour passed. They kept very still, not even praying now. The tide was on the way out, and when they could hear waves lapping more distinctly, another crewman swam up to the surface. He returned and said that the air was now hot but breathable.

"Laron, do we go up?" asked Feran.

"That would be sensible."

Feran gave the order to surface. Sailors swam out to release the four heavy anchor stones, and the schooner slowly rose through the warm water.

A blustery, hot wind was whipping the sea into a choppy confusion as Velander emerged from under the gigboat. Blinking in the murky daylight after hours of darkness, she waded through knee-deep water to the rail where Feran, Laron, and the deckswain stood. Behind them a sailor was setting up a valve-plunge pump while others dived to rechock the sink hatches. Parts of the port glowed like the embers of a campfire through a veil of steam and smoke.

"Is the whole of the world like that?" asked the deckswain.

"Hopefully not," Feran speculated.

"Over water the fire-circle may cool and disperse," said Laron, who was patting at his wet beard almost continually to stop it from falling off.

"But how do you know?" asked the deckswain.

"I do not."

Velander turned to Feran to ask a question, but noticed that another woman had come up beside him. She was wrapped in a blanket, with dripping, disheveled hair. Curly, black hair. A harlot from the docks, Velander assumed, then she did a double-take so abruptly that the bones of her neck clicked. Her mistake had been natural. She had never before seen Terikel without her blue priestly robes.

"Gods of the moonworlds, look at all that tangled rigging over there!" exclaimed Laron, and he hurried away with one hand pressed against his beard.

The deckswain glanced from Feran to the two priestesses, then hastened after the navigator. After another moment Feran ducked his head sheepishly and quickly waded off to help raise the masts. His back was a landscape of scratches, while his neck sported three lurid bite marks.

"Thank you for leaving the incense burning to keep soulmate vigil for me," Velander said icily, pushing her own hair back and feeling for her amberwood combs.

"Think nothing of it," muttered Terikel, shivering in her blanket in spite of the heat.

Terikel left the rail and walked to the aft deck hatch. Looking down, she saw that the pump had not yet removed enough water to let her enter and retrieve her clothes.

"I nearly *died* because I went searching for you!" Velander burst out, her fists raised and her eyes blazing. "You betrayed me!"

"I failed to be *Velander*'s Terikel," her mentor said as she turned from the edge of the hatch, "but that's not the end of the world, is it?" She stabbed a finger at the coast. "*That* is!"

Velander did not appreciate the comparison. "Ironic though it may seem, you are now the Elder of the Metrologan Sisterhood," the newly ordained priestess pointed out as she began to wring water from her blue robes. "Have you any pronouncements?"

"The celibacy rule is hereby annulled," Terikel replied sullenly.

Feran and Laron went as far as the stone pier in the corrak while the *Arrowflight* was being pumped out. The vista was not improved by being closer.

"I'm surprised that even fifteen feet of seawater saved us," said Feran. "The very stones and sand have melted."

"Well, don't get too close, the heat will still roast you."

"Are you sure you can go ashore safely?"

"Safely, no, but I *can* go ashore."

He was strapping on a pair of wooden work clogs, to which he had nailed iron cleats. Taking an iron barhook, he slipped from the corrak and waded up onto the beach. Even for one with Laron's powers, the heat was fearsome. His clothing smoked whenever it touched anything, and the iron-shod clogs on his feet were charring fast. Kordoban's house was in no better condition than any of the others, but one heavy stone block was still largely intact amid the ruins. The guard auton was, of course, disrupted and dispersed. Laron smashed the barhook down on the edge of the block. The glazed sandstone surface shattered and the rock beneath crumbled. After two more blows Laron lifted the iron casket out with the barhook. It was hot, but the thick stone had protected it from the worst of the heat. The point of the barhook broke the catch, and amid the charred and smoking padding within were the black glass cup and greenstone sphere. With a leather mooring glove, he took them out and put them in the folds of his tunic.

On the way back to the corrak Laron gathered some solidified splashes of gold and silver, and a chunk of vitrified sand. The gold and silver was from purses that had been dropped by people who had died and been blasted to windblown ash where they stood. A clump of his beard fell to the stones and began to smoke before he could snatch it up again. The clogs were charred almost all the way through by the time he returned to the corrak.

"Nothing could have lived through that," he reported, splashing water onto his feet as Feran began to paddle.

"So there is no food?"

"I checked, no food survived," said Laron, whose idea of food was rather different from Feran's.

"We can catch fish and drink rainwater," said Feran. "The *Arrowflight* is undamaged, so we might reach Acrema with luck. Could you guide us there?"

"Yes, but for now I must return to my cabin."

"You want to *sleep* at a time like *this*?" Feran exclaimed.

"I do not *want* to go to my cabin, boatmaster. I *must* go there. I have a disease, a magical disease. Unless Miral is in the sky, I must lock myself away."

Once they were back aboard the *Arrowflight* there was much speculation about whether the entire world or just the southern continent of Torea had been devastated by the fire-circles. Seasonal trade winds and favorable currents could take them the five thousand miles to the continent of Acrema, but was there any point to making the journey? Feran decided to take the chance, and they set sail in the early afternoon. Battling winds drawn in from the ocean to the hot land, the *Arrowflight* tacked away from the coast and by evening was on a northeastern heading.

At the third hour past midnight Velander stood at the stern, where the deckswain, Norrieav, was taking his turn at the steering pole. Laron emerged from his tiny cabin, stretched, then slid the hatch shut. He glanced about in the light of Miral, which was rising through the haze of Torea's demise. He nodded to Velander and Norrieav, then began taking sightings with his angulant from the few stars visible. Stepping up onto the quarterdeck, he gave Norrieav a fifteen-degree change in heading. For some moments he stood beside Velander, watching Miral's green, ringed disk hanging above the eastern horizon.

"I would like to thank you for saving us," Laron suddenly said to her in Diomedan.

"Was myself, ah, saving," she replied coldly in the same language.

He gestured down to the deck, below which was Feran's cabin. "Look, when it comes to choosing lovers, rules must be cut to the cloth," he said in Damarian.

"So I notice," replied Velander, stubbornly sticking to Diomedan.

"Don't blame Worthy Terikel loving the young boatmaster," said Norrieav. "She's spoken to me. She . . . she still wants to be your soulmate."

"Have new soulmate."

Norrieav scratched the tight curls of his hair, and Laron turned away to take another sighting from the stars. Velander looked up to the stars that were guiding them on their five-thousand-mile grasp at survival. The mathematics of progressions had saved her a bare half day earlier, and now the mathematics of navigation were taking her to safety. The Queen of Philosophies was ever faithful, and never let her followers down. Shivering, weak, tired, but in control, Velander imagined a cold yet comforting arm about her shoulders.

Has the world ended? Velander asked her new soulmate. *Was the fourteenth fire-circle the last?* the figures asked her in turn. She made some mental calculations. Eighteen fire-circles would have been needed to blanket the entire world in fire, according to current estimates of the world's size.

"After first fire-circle passed over us, ah, I am fainting," said Velander to the deckswain. "How many more, there are being?"

The deckswain gave a short, bitter laugh. "There was but one that passed over us, but that was enough to roast the world."

Velander allowed herself a smirk as a thrill of relief flooded through her. Only Torea, the Great Southland, had been destroyed. She thanked her new soulmate, the soulmate who had kept her awake to tend her pyre, and who had warned her to flee.

"I know the world's fate," she said softly. "Follow me through the shoals of reasoning and you can know it, too."

The deckswain shook his head, wondering if she was truly sane. Laron stood in silence, frowning with thought in Miral's light. Velander could hear Terikel just below, sobbing in terror of the world's end. She decided not to announce her latest discovery for five days and one night, by way of retribution for the vigil that her mentor and soulmate had not kept. Again she imagined a cold, firm arm about her shoulders. Lovers, kings, shipmasters, priestesses, and even sorcerers knelt before the throne of Mathematics, the Queen of Philosophies, and yet out of everyone in Torea she was soulmate to Velander alone.

"I've traced your reasoning, Worthy Sister," Laron said suddenly, breaking into her reverie.

"Uh— Yes?"

"Four more fire-circles would have been enough to cover the world, if Hirodoratian's solar-apex method of measuring its diameter is correct."

"With Hirodoratian, ah, I agree."

"Excellent. Well, there was only one fire-circle that passed over us. The seawater must have broken its regeneration cycle, so the thing was quenched at only two thousand four hundred miles across. The other continents have been spared!"

Velander looked up at him with her lips pressed together and her eyes bulging with fury. Then she paused to consider. This youth had consulted at the shrine of mathematics as well, and been given the same—verifiable—answer. Her expression softened.

"Very good," she declared with a shrug, then turned away.

She did not see Laron staring longingly at the back of her neck and licking his lips. Then he hurriedly reined himself back, and pressed his lips together as he gripped the angulant tightly in his trembling hands. By the time Velander turned back to him he was taking another sighting.

"If you know Hirodoratian's works then you should know the use of angulants," said Laron without looking away from a haze-shrouded star.

"Have used one. At temple."

"Navigation needs only mathematics, astronomy, and steady hands. I must rest whenever Miral is down, so there will be nights when I am not able to take sightings. I feel confident that you could learn deepwater navigation faster than anyone else on the ship."

"Crew, maybe not sharing your confidence," she replied, with the tone of one used to being patronized.

"You saved them once. I feel you have their trust."

✳ ✳ ✳

Once alone in his cabin Laron took out the violet sphere, then set up the mechanism of greenstone sphere and cup. He breathed in a very small tendril of life force. A face appeared in the greenstone.

"Greetings," said a small, faint voice.

"Penny?" asked Laron.

"Who are you?" the voice asked. "You are not the Elder."

Something was wrong, Laron realized that at once. This face was round, with short, brown hair. The image was clearly defined, but it lacked detail. It was almost like an ink sketch of a face. This was not the woman he had seen last time. This was almost like a child.

"No, I am not the Elder," said Laron. "Who are you?"

"Auton-9."

"Auton-9? So you are not— I mean, are you an auton?" asked Laron, perplexed.

"Auton, yes."

"But you sound almost human. Nobody has ever built an auton so complex and advanced."

"Auton construct, I am. The Metrologans made me. Concentricaren, second. 3139."

Laron was astounded more than disappointed. This was not who, or even what, he had rescued from the Metrologan Elder's study. This was an auton. A highly complex and advanced auton; in fact, the most advanced he had ever seen, but an auton nevertheless.

"Have you ever seen someone called Penny?" he asked.

"Penny, yes. She was very strong, with clever thoughts."

"That may be her."

"The Elder command me to learn Latin from her. A little, I have learned."

"Why does she not speak to me anymore?"

"The great fire came very close. Penny had the portal open. Things came in, to escape the great fire. Raptor things. They cut pieces from her. She fled. They chased her through the other portal, to her own world. I hid."

So, the fire-circle works in the ether dimensions as well, Laron realized. Penny had been holding the portal open—but from her world. His world. Earth. She had not been a prisoner, she had been looking in from another world. More to the point, she had been looking in when the several raptor elementals had come past, looking for refuge from the fire-circles. They must have made short work of her, then streamed through to ... Earth. *Well, they should liven the place up a bit,* he thought with resignation.

Meantime there was the matter of the auton in the oracle sphere. Her name was too strange; it branded her as an auton and might draw unwelcome attention were he ever to free her. But any new name would have to be interlocked with her old name, or it would not bind to her. Some slaves were known by a combination of a number and their master's name, and when freed they were still known by the number. The idea struck Laron as appropriate under the circumstances.

"Listen, you are Ninth. I name you Ninth."

"Ninth? Just Ninth?"

"Yes, names are strong. People and things can be traced and controlled using names; but now that your namer is dead, you can be renamed. I am a thief—that is, a thief sent to rescue you."

"Rescue? Truly?"

"Yes. Ninth is your worldname. Understand?"

"Yes."

"My worldname, it is Ninth."

"Ninth, do you have a truename?"

"Yes."

"Who knows it?"

"The Elder."

"The Elder is dead. Never tell it to anyone. Understand?"

"Yes."

"Now, try to understand this: We have to cross the ocean."

"What is the ocean?"

"Never mind, just trust me. It may be awhile before I can free you from this glass prison. I shall take you to Diomeda, or maybe Scalticar. There are people there who can help you. I— Ninth, your image is breaking up."

"The energy to keep the portal open is almost gone."

Out on deck the crew noticed a huge, glowing, insubstantial-looking jellyfish drifting in their wake. The creature appeared to be dead, and already a school of smaller fish were churning the surface as they began to scavenge from it.

"An etherfish," said Feran, scratching his head. "It seems to be dead."

"I've heard that they breed slowly, but are practically unkillable," replied Norrieav.

"Yes, they absorb ambient etheric energy, then use it for defense. Something seems to have drained that one completely, however."

As the seascape brightened with the dawn, Feran's crew petitioned that the vessel's name be changed back to *Shadowmoon*.

"Seems like bad luck came on us after the name change," Hazlok explained. "Fire-circles and all, like."

Feran stared incredulously at the man, pointing back along the boat's wake. "You're saying that the entire continent was blasted out of existence because we changed the name on this glorified beer barrel with sails?" he exclaimed.

"Er, well . . . Nothing like it happened while the name was *Shadowmoon*."

Feran shook his head, and let his arms drop to his side. "Why not?" he decided. "The people whose attention we were trying to avoid no longer exist."

The carpenter got to work at once. The again renamed *Shadowmoon* had not been provisioned for a voyage of several weeks, but at first this was not a problem. Dying fish were floating everywhere, along with charred timbers from ships caught in the waning heat from the last fire-circle. A brownish, opalescent pall glazed the sky, while the sunsets were as intensely colored as an orchid made from live coals.

Each of the seven crew and two passengers aboard the little vessel coped with the destruction of the continent in their own very different ways. Being an Acreman, the deckswain had not lost any family to the catastrophe. Velander had no surviving family anyway. Terikel was suddenly without her Order, rank, family, and friends, and with each day that passed she seemed to slip deeper into a chasm of loneliness. Her only relief was bouts of seasickness, which took her mind off practically everything. Feran mourned a great number of women, but managed to console himself by sleeping with Terikel. Hazlok seemed to cope with the deaths of his friends in dozens of Torean ports by talking about them to whomever was closest, as if by recalling them he could keep something of them alive. The carpenter began carving exquisite wooden busts of his dead wife and children, and was generally Hazlok's only audience. He used driftwood salvaged from burned ships, wood that had cheated the fire-circles, clawing back images of victims in the wood that had survived. The two remaining sailors, Heinder and Martak, played cards continuously when not on duty, eating, or sleeping. At stake were wood shavings produced by the carpenter.

Laron was the most calm of all those aboard, but even he sat staring in the direction of the murdered continent when off duty. At first he went about his work with unobtrusive efficiency, but after a week he grew increasingly restive. As always, when Miral set, he vanished into his cabin, where he was as quiet as one dead.

"I thinks he had a sweetheart in Torea," Hazlok speculated, looking down from where he and the carpenter were working in the rigging.

"Can't think who it might be—never seen 'im with any wench."

"Why does he glue on that beard? He's fooling nobody."

"Strange one, he is. Such a fine scholar and officer, yet he looks only fourteen."

"Wonder if he's a virgin?"

Laron was sitting at his usual place on the upturned gigboat one morning when Terikel emerged through the master cabin's hatch. She blinked in the sunlight, breathed deeply several times, then went over to the rail and retched for a minute or so. Presently she walked across the gently rolling deck and climbed onto the gigboat beside Laron.

"Lucky we have so little food," she said. "I have nothing to throw up."

"Every misfortune is attended by rewards," he responded, drawing his arms tighter around his knees.

"*I* feel like casting myself into the ocean," said Terikel.

"Death is no answer," answered Laron, "but it is so permanent."

"How do you know? Ever been dead?"

"Yes."

Terikel took the reply as a joke at her expense. She drew a deep breath. "We are alone on the Placidian Ocean with our homeland annihilated behind us, and the Acreman slave markets before us. My loved ones are dust on the face of the sun. I am sharing the bed of a youth who has the sex drive of a buck rabbit just released from a year in the stocks, being force-fed oysters and parsley. Every time I escape from his cabin I am watched by a sneer on two legs, who also happens to be one-third of my Metrologan Sisterhood. The boat has enough provisions aboard to provide a light breakfast for two, Helion is still about eight weeks away—if it still exists—and my only change of clothing is made of sailcloth."

"Still, you have to laugh," replied Laron.

Terikel took another deep breath. "Death is an escape. The dead are luckier than us."

"I am not so sure about that."

"Feran wants to do nothing but fornicate all night. I wonder if he ever sleeps! Navigator, I lost my family, my Order, my friends, my *everything* back on Torea. I want to grieve, I want to be left alone. Feran just says that it's his ship and besides, dalliance is his way of forgetting what happened to Torea."

Laron turned to look at her, leaving part of his beard attached to his knee, and his chin bare. "Would you like my cabin—"

"Navigator!"

"—when I am not using it?"

Terikel swallowed, then laughed out of embarrassment. "Ah, I see. I— Yes. Thank you. That's very gallant. I am touched."

Laron noticed the tuft of hair on his knee, licked the resin and cloth base and reattached it to his chin. Terikel twisted about to kiss Laron on the cheek, but he rocked back, then jackknifed forward onto his feet and stood up.

"I shall have a word with Feran," he said as he walked off.

A few minutes later Terikel was lying in Laron's cabin, which was about as large as two coffins stacked one above the other. The navigator knelt in the hatchway.

"When Miral is above the horizon, this is yours," he explained. "Otherwise, I must be here."

"You—you really meant it. I am so grateful. Ah, Laron, if only—"

"You had better get used to sleeping while I am awake," he interjected, then slid the hatch door shut.

He stared at the wooden panel, licking his lips—then he noticed Velander watching him. His mouth dropped open for a moment, but he hastily closed it again. She came over to him and gestured forward.

"Can we speak?" she asked in Damarian. "Privately?"

Privacy was not easy to come by on the *Shadowmoon*, but the tiny foredeck was as far away from the others as one might go. They stood together, holding on to the stay ropes.

"It took all of five minutes for Feran to propose that I take Terikel's place in his bunk," Velander reported.

"I see. Were you receptive to his, ah—"

"No, I was *not*!" she snapped. "Why did you give Terikel your cabin?"

"I felt sorry for her. Do you disapprove?"

His answer was not what Velander had been expecting. She thought carefully about her own answer.

"I disapprove of what Terikel did to me, not what you did for her."

"I am relieved. I had wondered if you would understand."

"I am very logical about things. You are also a very logical person."

"Thank you."

Velander licked salt spray from her lips, looking forward across the ocean as if seeing into the future. "I have plans for Terikel," she declared.

"What will you do?"

"Apply logic to her."

"That sounds very fair of you."

"Fair, yes. Pleasant, no. Shall I apply logic to you?"

Laron gave her a sidelong glance and checked his beard. He had always thought of Velander as a dangerous and predatory person trying hard to be sweet. It was obvious that she was now no longer trying.

"Feel free," he decided, although against his better judgment.

"In the days that the *Shadowmoon* was in Zantrias, the number of murders in the port rose to three times the norm."

"That is a rather esoteric fact."

"Hazlok told me that; he has a morbid interest in murders. He also told me there was a murder at each of the ports where the *Shadowmoon* called between Gironal and Zantrias. All the victims had wounds to the neck. Some were savage mutilations, others were just two punctures above the great artery. One of the Torean schools of martial arts identifies the area as a kill point, and several medicar and sorcery theorists have written that the life force that we use in castings concentrates in the neck."

"How very scholarly of them."

"You hide them well, but I have observed that you have two long, sharp fangs."

"They run in the family."

"I have never observed you to eat or drink."

"Boat food—can't stand it," Laron laughed. He was not comfortable with the direction of the conversation, but was anxious to know what Velander really knew of him. "What is it you wish to know, Worthy Velander?"

"You have gone a long time without food."

"For us sailors, food is like sex."

"How so?"

"One often has to do without for long periods."

"But *you* do not eat at all."

"All the more for you."

"Do you know what I think?"

"I have a fair idea."

"Day after day there are eight people named 'Dinner' walking the decks of the *Shadowmoon*, and within your reach."

"So what? Anyone aboard could make a meal of anyone else."

"But everyone else aboard can also eat other food. You cannot. Are we in danger?"

Laron thought frantically. "From me? No. From you, Worthy Velander? Well, I am glad to be skinny."

"I'm more likely to start on Terikel. Returning to you, Laron, I noticed that before the garlic ran out you shunned those who ate it."

"Doesn't everyone?"

"The travel pack that I was presented with for my ordination happened to include a clutch of garlic. Be pleased to bear in mind that I now wear it on a thong around my neck."

As Laron stared out to sea, his tongue kept caressing the points of his fangs. Hunger was driving him to the edge of his powers of restraint. Even a bird would have been enough to relieve the longing that was eating away what was left of his humanity, but they were in midocean and this was not the season when birds migrated back in Torea's direction.

"Navigator, do you know who I really am?" asked Velander one afternoon, again in Damarian.

"You have an unusual past, and have traveled widely," Laron replied. "You were caught up in several minor wars, too."

"I'm the daughter of Count Salvaras, who led the first attack against Warsovran ten years ago."

"Ah yes. That was the battle that touched off Warsovran's invasion of the rest of Torea."

Velander bristled. She was used to people showing somewhat more respect for her father's memory. "I like to think that my father woke up a sleeping people who were in dire peril."

"And gave Warsovran an excuse to attack."

"Indeed? So where were you ten years ago?"

"Biting people who antagonized me, and looking fourteen." There was brief silence. Velander's tactic was to cut down people who were standing on their dignity, but Laron was standing on something that was quite outside her experience. "Where were you?" he asked.

"I was a messenger in my father's army. Because I was ten years old and female, nobody bothered with me. I looked like a boy and I acted as a boy. I have carried messages and spied while disguised as the orphaned son of peasants, nobles, artisans, and merchants. Even at ten I could ride a horse, and use a dagger with some skill. I have killed several times."

"I hope they were horrible people."

"I— What?" Velander was starting to have the suspicion that he was making a fool of her, but could not pin down any specific insult or affront.

"Never mind, go on," said Laron.

"My point, navigator, is that I am not some silly, lowborn girl who has spent most of her life reading books. My father died in battle, then Warsovran's troops overran our province. When they came to our estate, I was ready. I disguised myself as a stable boy and fled into the darkness. Those in terror squads are fools. They come at night, thinking people are at their most vulnerable. Night is the friend of the victim. It is her cloak, her knife, her poison."

Laron clasped his hands beneath his chin. "Yes, you are quick of thought, I noticed that at Zantrias."

Already scanning every word of Laron's for any trace of affront, Velander suddenly decided that he had indeed gone too far.

"You dare say that I abandon my friends and loved ones when faced with danger?" she snarled.

Suddenly they were the focus of every other pair of eyes on the *Shadowmoon*. It was a very small vessel, and one did not have to raise a voice very far to attract attention.

"I do not," Laron said slowly, "but it is still clear to me that you are sensitive on the subject."

"I'll show you how I react to danger!" cried Velander, drawing her knife and slashing for Laron's face.

Velander had meant to merely give Laron an ugly scar, to teach him a lesson. In what everyone else saw as just a blur of arms, Laron checked her arm, seized her wrist, twisted her arm around behind her back, then bent her wrist until the pain gave her no choice but to release the knife. Laron pushed her away, then slammed the knife into the wooden railing, burying the blade right up to the hilt.

"Do not think of attacking me again, Worthy Velander," said Laron, although he glanced to the rest of the crew as well. "This moment's little act already has me on the edge of my very limited patience. Oh, and do not place too much faith in your garlic. I find it unpleasant, the same way that you would find a fresh, steaming turd unpleasant, but it will certainly not stop me."

Laron walked to the point of the foredeck, turning his back to Velander. She tried to pull the knife free, but without success. Feran tried next, then all the other crewmen. Finally the carpenter brought a crowbar, and extracted the knife after a lengthy and difficult struggle.

"There, see that splash?" exclaimed Laron, pointing ahead, and a little to port.

The group that had gathered around the extracted knife and damaged railing looked to him.

"This is the ocean," said Feran. "It's full of waves, they all splash."

"Boatmaster, I respectfully request a course bearing ten points to port," Laron called back. "An arcereon—see, the long neck?"

Feran came clambering over the cluttered decks to where Laron was standing. In the distance was something with a long, serpentine neck and a triangular head.

"Never seen one act like that," said Feran. "They seldom stay at the surface for long."

"I think that one was scalded by the last fire-circle. It could solve our provisioning problems at a single stroke."

"*Us*, attack *that*?"

"Yes."

"But it's twice as long as the *Shadowmoon*, and we don't even have proper harpoons aboard."

"We have shark harpoons and crossbows. The thing has been injured; that's several tons of fresh meat floundering about out there. What do you say?"

"I say no! It's huge!"

"It's seven weeks to Helion."

"And seven minutes to get killed, perhaps less."

"I have a bold and daring plan."

"That being?"

"I have special powers."

Laron did not elaborate, and Feran wondered if his stomach might be able to cope with whatever the vampyre considered to be "bold and daring." He thought for a moment, then turned to the quarterdeck.

"Deckswain, ten points to port."

The arcereon was shaped like a turtle but was as big as a medium-sized whale. It had no shell, and with its long, serpentine neck and tail it measured fifty feet in length. As the *Shadowmoon* closed with it, the creature paid no attention, and continued to fling its head high into the air, then smash it down on the surface. The carpenter had rigged up five spears with ropes and barbs, but the size and strength of the thing grew ever more impressive as they narrowed the gap.

"This may not be a good idea," Feran warned as he stood ready with his harpoon.

"Seven weeks to Helion, sir," Laron reminded him again.

Feran threw, but the harpoon did not even reach the arcereon's body. Velander and Terikel began to haul the harpoon rope in. The deckswain tried next, with no better result.

"Dare not get in closer, navigator," said Feran, staring intently at the floundering creature. "Some of those things can spout enchanted fire—"

"Burning oil, from a sac just behind the head," said Laron, then added "probably."

"Whatever! It's sticky and it burns. That's why they call them sea dragons."

He had not noticed Laron pick up the third harpoon. Laron flung it, and, being a vampyre, he had many times Feran's strength. The point buried itself at the base of the arcereon's neck, and it gave a bellow of surprise and pain. Laron picked up another harpoon.

"Stop! Don't attract its attention!" shouted Feran.

"Too late for that, sir."

The second harpoon struck low in the creature's throat.

"It's turning for us!" cried the deckswain.

There was a frantic scramble for the gigboat and hatchways as the arcereon bore down on them, then Laron jumped over the opposite railing as a blast of smoky flame sprayed the empty decks. The *Shadowmoon* shuddered as huge flippers smashed at its rigging and superstructure, and the spar of the mainmast smashed down across the gigboat. In their first act of agreement since boarding the *Shadowmoon*, Velander and Terikel screamed together.

Arcereons normally used their burning oil only to shoot large flying reptiles and birds out of the sky, preferring speed of escape as a defense against attackers. This one was in such a blind frenzy that it had no sense of discrimination. It clambered up across the schooner, spraying fire and thrashing wildly with its clawed flippers. After a few moments it discovered a new torment, however. The *Shadowmoon* was burning. While the arcereon's weapon was fire, its skin was never actually in contact with its own flames, and it was no more fireproof than the fire-breathing conjurers to be found in any market, in any city, on any continent.

Frantically the arcereon tried to scramble back into the water, but it was tangled in rigging and harpoon ropes. The *Shadowmoon* capsized, extinguishing the flames, but as it righted itself again the arcereon turned back upon it. This time, as it reared up onto the schooner, Laron was on its back, holding on to one of the harpoons as he chopped into the vertebrae of the reptile's neck with an ax. At the third blow the spinal cord was severed, and the arcereon went limp. Two more chops exposed an artery. Closing his eyes and steeling himself, Laron bit down and drank.

By the time the first of the crew ventured back on deck to see why the *Shadowmoon* was still largely intact and why they were still alive, Laron was chopping right through the neck of their attacker. He was drenched in blood, and they had no way of telling how much of it might be his.

"Free the body from the rigging and push it free," he ordered, and nobody was inclined to disobey.

Even though both masts had been smashed, the sails and much of the rigging burned, the bottom of the gigboat stove in, and everybody had cuts, bruises, and burns, still the circumstances of the *Shadowmoon*'s company had improved greatly. They had several tons of dead arcereon to harvest, floating beside the schooner at the end of two harpoon lines that were tied to the railing.

"My bold and daring plan succeeded, sir," said Laron, gesturing to the body with his ax.

"What was your plan?" asked Feran.

"Ah. You were under the gigboat, yes. You did not see."

"See what?"

"Er, my plan . . . sir."

Wide-eyed and speechless, Feran pointed first to the arcereon's severed neck, then to the floating body, then to the ax. "Navigator Laron, you provoked the arcereon into attacking."

"Yes."

"It got tangled in the rigging."

"Yes."

"It sprayed the boat with flames."

"Yes."

"Then capsized it."

"Yes."

"And by chance as pure as the wind-driven snow you happened to get close to the thing's neck in the confusion."

"Yes."

Feran raised his hands to the heavens before clasping them down on his soaking hair. "You witless bastard, you had no bloody plan at all, did you?" he screamed at the very limit of what his lungs and vocal cords could sustain.

"Er, no—sir."

"Next time you have a bold and daring plan I'm going to take the sharp and pointy end and stick it up your—"

The water beside the *Shadowmoon* exploded upward as two gigantic jaws surged out of the depths and closed across the headless body of the acrereon. They had the fleeting impression of a flipper the size of the schooner, then the vast head splashed back down with the dead reptile. The port railing tore away with the harpoon ropes, and the serrated back of whatever it was seemed to go on forever as the thing dived. A long, thick tail waved high in the air for a moment, then the *Shadowmoon* was alone again on the surface of the Placidian Ocean.

"You're welcome," Laron said softly, to the swirling confusion of water in the enormous predator's wake.

❊ ❊ ❊

The neck and head of the arcereon were twenty feet long, and turned out to have enough meat for several weeks of unstinted eating. The rigging and deck were a shambles. Both masts were down and the railings that remained were smashed. Great lengths of rope were badly singed and had to be cut out, but there had been another set of sails stored below.

Feran ordered all the smashed wood to be gathered, to roast or smoke the arcereon's flesh, then they rigged up the mainmast securely enough to take a small sail. They were soon under way again, and high among their priorities was lunch. The carpenter and Velander cut the meat from the neck as the cook struggled to light a fire.

"What we can't roast or smoke, we can cut into strips and dry in the sun," said the deckswain as he and Feran tied the head down on the deck.

"No scraps are to be thrown overboard," muttered Feran. "None! That thing was the size of a deepwater trader, and it had a definite taste for arcereon."

Laron lay resting in the sun, every so often feeling for the beard that had been washed from his face and lost. Terikel knelt beside him.

"Whatever Feran says, that was unthinkably brave of you," she said, smiling and clasping her hands.

"It smashed up the *Shadowmoon*."

"We cannot eat the *Shadowmoon*, and now we have food to last until Helion." She put a hand to his neck. "Navigator, you're as cold as death!" she exclaimed.

She put her arms around him and hugged the heady softness of her breasts against his skimpy chest. Laron squirmed, then pushed her away.

"Rest, need rest," he muttered. "I'll be in my cabin."

He got to his knees and crawled hurriedly away to the hatch.

"But don't you want your share of the meat?" she asked.

Laron had by now backed into his cabin. Looking out across to where Terikel was sitting, he could see the puzzled, hurt look on her face. Not far away, Velander was smirking.

"Miral disease, Worthy Terikel," he said, waving a hand in circles. "Best not to touch people. I appreciate your concern, though." He slid the hatch closed.

"And *he* is your *medicar?*" said Terikel, turning to Feran.

Lying out flat with the musky scent of Terikel in his blankets, Laron fought a feeling that would have been nausea, were he actually alive. The surfeit of raw, sour ether from the arcereon had almost overwhelmed him.

He breathed out gustily. Overcharged with the arcereon's blood and ether, his breath charred the planks above him. Whatever other problems lay ahead, feeding would be low on his agenda for three or four weeks. After that, he could fast for perhaps a fortnight more, and after that . . . If they were not at Helion by then, it depended on who aboard the little ship had been able to annoy him the most.

After a week of running repairs they had both masts more or less vertical and were able to fly full-sail. The arcereon's flesh lasted well, although most of the crew soon became weary of the oily taste. For Terikel it was a mixed blessing, for it meant that she now had something solid to throw up when she was seasick, which was most of the time. Feran did not allow any other scraps to be thrown overboard until he saw that a large shark was trailing along in the *Shadowmoon*'s wake.

Laron was sitting on the foredeck, sketching on the back of a parchment chart, when Terikel approached him again. It was a good charcoal likeness of the arcereon's head, split right down the middle.

"That is fine work," said Terikel as she sat beside him.

"Uh, thank you. Arcereons are difficult to hunt, and their bodies seldom wash ashore. Scholars in Scalticar have long wondered exactly how they produce their fire. Look here. This thing had a sac of oil here, behind its head, and a bladder here with muscles all around it. It blew oil through this little orifice here, at the back of its mouth, then ignited it with a white-hot casting suspended between its teeth."

"A mere beast that can do fire-castings? That could be seen as heresy by most of the main religions."

"Heresy or not, it seems true. The eleven fire-breathing animals that we know of, are all quite intelligent. Some can even mimic human words. Six are leatherwings, four are serpents, and the other is this one. I am the first to dissect and describe an arcereon. I might get a place in scholarly history books."

"I think that you already have a place in history books," said Terikel.

"How so?"

"As the only example of your kind."

Laron looked up from the sketch, his eyes narrowing. "Velander has been speaking to you."

"Oh yes. She was quite amused that I would try to embrace what she described as a cold, dead predator."

"But I *am* cold, dead, and a predator."

"Maybe so, but there is more warmth in your hearts than in Velander's. If ever I can come to your aid, Laron, just call."

"My thanks. And if ever Miral is down and you need a man you can trust, may I recommend my warrior friend Learned Royal Gravalios?"

"I suppose he is all terribly honorable," Terikel responded, sounding skeptical.

"He is actually honorable without being boring."

"That sounds like an oxymoron."

"Er . . . I don't think he's one of those. But he is alive."

"Honorable, warm-blooded, *and* fun to be with? No, not possible—too good to be true."

"You're right, he probably died like everyone else when—"

Laron caught himself, but knew he was far too late. Terikel squeezed his shoulder.

"No hurt done, little brother," she sighed. "And thank you for cheering me."

❄ ❄ ❄

Seven weeks after the battle with the arcereon, the ragged twin peaks of the island of Helion appeared on the horizon. There were weak but heartfelt cheers from the crew as the unburned pine trees on the slopes became visible in Laron's farsight. The two-mile speck of land was only a week's sailing from the coast of Acrema. It was an outpost of the seafaring Vidarian kingdom, a nation conquered by Warsovran only a year earlier. Not surprisingly, it was very hostile to the former Torean emperor, and had become a refuge for the remains of the Vidarian battle and trading fleets.

"I can see more trees, farther down the slopes," Laron called from the top of the mainmast. "I can also see . . . That's odd."

"Those are two words I dislike intensely when I hear them together," deckswain Norrieav muttered to Feran.

"Ships! Hundreds of ships!" cried Laron.

Everyone rushed to try to see for themselves. Even Terikel looked up from where she was being sick over the bracebar at the stern.

"Warsovran's fleet!" Feran exclaimed. "He must have known about the fire-circles. He sent everything that could float here, to safety."

The entire boat's company gathered on the middeck to confer. They had collected enough rainwater to survive a week, but their meat had almost run out. The Acreman coast was a lot farther away, and the *Shadowmoon* had required bailing several times a day since the arceron's attack.

"I say we surrender, sir," said Norrieav. "The alternative is death anyway."

"Why surrender?" asked Feran. "Nobody knows the *Shadowmoon* is a Vidarian spy vessel."

"And a Scalticarian spy vessel," added Hazlok.

"And a Metrologan spy vessel," added Velander.

"And a Sargolan spy vessel," added Laron.

"There are two Metrologan priestesses aboard," Terikel pointed out as she joined them. "Warsovran's feelings for Metrologans are less than sympathetic."

"If we dress you and Velander in sailcloth trews and tunic, then who would know?" suggested the deckswain.

"But what are we meant to be doing aboard your vessel, at sea, out of reach of the fire-circles?" Terikel asked.

"We'll say you were whores, working your passages to—"

"There's only one whore aboard this boat!" interjected Velander.

"The idea is nevertheless sound!" shouted Laron, waving his hands for order. "Terikel, Velander, you had best start changing."

"I'm a priestess; this is degrading," protested Velander.

"Then you can swim to Acrema. Make up your mind quickly. *We* are going to Helion."

"Why not just dress as sailors?" suggested Laron. "With a bit of rancid acereon oil rubbed on, nobody is going to come close enough to notice that you have breasts under your sailcloth tunics."

❋ ❋ ❋

On the flagship of Warsovran's fleet, the *Thunderbolt*, there was nothing that could have been of less interest to anyone in authority than the presence of one small and battered schooner sailing out of the east. A trader had just arrived with a despatch from the emperor. Its sailors and officers had also brought word of a gigantic wall of fire and steam that had reached to the sky and stretched from horizon to horizon. It had loomed over them, then collapsed into a boiling confusion of fog and wind. Warsovran had been on a nearby trader, and he had turned back to investigate.

In the small but luxurious state room of the *Thunderbolt*, the fleet council was gathered to hear what news and orders had been brought.

"In the meantime we have the emperor's original orders, sealed in this separate scroll," said Admiral Forteron.

His council of admirals and nobles watched, nervy and puzzled, as he broke the seal. Forteron was in a delicate position. While a duke himself, he was by no means the most senior of those present. Many were quite annoyed about that. He read, alternately raising his eyebrows, then frowning, then staring with surprise. At last he looked up to his audience.

"The invasion of Helion has been canceled," he announced. "We are to raise the blockade immediately and proceed straight to the coast of Acrema. There we are to attack, seize, and hold Diomeda."

This news was the cause of some consternation. Diomeda was a large port city. Diomeda was also sufficiently big, old, and central that the trading language, Diomedan, had spread all around the Placidian Ocean's rim.

"I shall post the official despatch in a moment," Forteron concluded, "but there is a little more. What I am about to tell you is for your own ears only. In his covering note the emperor has ventured fears that some terrible catastrophe may have taken place in Torea. If that is indeed the case, Diomeda may be our new home and capital."

"What?" laughed Duke Parthol. "The whole continent can't be gone."

"I hope you are right. Nevertheless, tell your men that Diomeda is not to be looted, vandalized, or its inhabitants molested in any way—other than to take and secure the city, of course. Above all, trade is to continue with the other kingdoms of Acrema."

While the others were reading the despatch for themselves, Forteron went on deck and gave orders for the blockade to be raised. All ships were to raise anchor, form into a convoy, and sail due west. Code flags began to be hoisted, and signal trumpets blared across the water. The dash galley that had been making for the *Shadowmoon* hastily broke off and returned to the fleet.

He knew, Forteron thought uneasily. Whatever had happened in Torea, Warsovran had known it was coming. As much of his military might that could be made to float had been sent to Helion and safety, while everything else—including the empress—had been left to perish. Was Warsovran to be trusted? In a way he had been quite logical. His enemies had been destroyed, and given no warning, or chance to escape.

Neither had anyone else, however, except for the cream of his fighting men and the ships that were now their only refuge.

There were few things Warsovran really loved—Forteron knew that was no secret: power, his son, his armies, and his fleet. The latter three he had preserved; yet if Torea had indeed been destroyed, then the emperor had been reduced from one of the most powerful monarchs in the known world to a mere refugee. A very dangerous refugee, in command of the largest battle fleet the world had ever seen, it was true, but a refugee nevertheless. No, Warsovran would not have destroyed his own empire. Some Larmentel sorcerer or engineer must have grown desperate during the siege of the city and unleashed hellfire itself. *Of course!* They had been destroyed by their own weapon, but then Warsovran had claimed credit. Any sensible tactician would do as much.

Duke Parthol, who was also Commander of Marines, emerged from a hatchway, looked around, then made for Forteron. "The men are going to be very disturbed by this," Parthol said doubtfully. "We will be fighting halfway across the world, with no chance of support. And for what?"

"Torea is definitely gone," replied Forteron.

"What?"

"Gone. Destroyed. Annihilated."

"But how can you be so sure? The despatch merely said that the emperor was turning back to investigate."

"I am not supposed to know anything, but I have ways of finding out. The emperor sought to have the final battle out here, far away from Torea. The fools of the southern kingdoms must have lost control of some weapon before they could bring it to bear."

"Our families, wives, mistresses, friends, estates—"

"All gone. Only hope remains, and that is hope of a new life in Acrema. With each day that passes, our stores diminish, and our ships have more need of servicing. So do our men, if it comes to that. We must make for Diomeda with the greatest possible haste, and win soil where our strength and numbers can grow again."

"But what of the emperor? Surely he should lead us."

"In this case speed is more important than the leader."

With that, Duke Parthol set off down the deck, calling for his scoreboat to be brought alongside. Forteron allowed himself a little grin. Warsovran *had* known; he was even more certain of it now. A fleet crammed with fighting men was a lot more effective than a fleet crammed with fighting men, their wives, and their children, however. Admiral Forteron was unmarried, an only child, and both of his parents were dead. The fleet was his homeland and family. Nearly everyone else would be somewhat less understanding if they thought the emperor had sacrificed their loved ones for the sake of optimizing the fleet's fighting strength. He looked to the west, toward which the fleet was now ponderously turning. When Warsovran eventually reached Diomeda they would have to have a long and discreet talk.

✳ ✳ ✳

Aboard the galley *Kygar*, the emperor's son had been briefed on the orders coming from the signal flags. The fleet was leaving for Diomeda, the fleet was going to attack Diomeda. All marines were to train and prepare for a battle in about ten days, depending on the winds. Siege engines were to be tuned and tested, ethersmiths were to practice their castings, and there were to be daily meetings of the fleet council to determine tactics. The youth had listened to everything that was said, then thanked the captain and retired to his cabin.

"Something wrong with that boy," Mandalock told his first officer as they watched the galley's mast being raised.

"I agree. He is far more quiet than I remember him. It could be seasickness, but the emperor has always said that he's a good sailor."

"Well, you know how rulers are about their children. Contradicting them is not a good idea, either."

"You don't think he may be lovesick over the whore he brought with him?"

"She looks twice his age."

"Maybe it's what she knows."

Down in the master cabin, Prince Darric's decoy was relating all he had heard to the empress.

"Something very strange has happened in Torea, and we have broken off the blockade of Helion. Our orders are to attack and seize Diomeda, on the Acreman coast."

"Diomeda? As in the large and prosperous city, and whose royal palace has never fallen to attack?"

"The very same."

"No wonder he gathered the entire fleet. But why attack another continent when half of Torea remains unconquered?"

"I was not told, Empress."

" 'Mother'! Always 'Mother'! Remember your role, and who you are meant to be. Go back on deck. Say little, but listen to everything that anyone within earshot says."

The empress looked out of the cabin window and saw that the *Kygar* was moving to flank the deepwater traders. At last she was slipping below the surface lies and deceits of Warsovran's schemes. She would claw back the power she had lost to him as he had expanded the empire, and she would be ruler of Diomeda by the time he arrived.

✳ ✳ ✳

By the time the *Shadowmoon* was nearing the outer edges of the huge fleet, Terikel and Velander were again dressed in sail-cloth, and standing among the sailors with their hair tied, braided, and slicked down with oil from the arcereon. The closer they got, the more activity was evident. Signal flags were being waved or hoisted on every ship, signal trumpets were sounding, and the crews were unfurling the sails and rowing galleys. By the time they had reached the harbor entrance, Warsovran's fleet was in motion and sailing west.

The *Shadowmoon* nosed into the harbor after being met by a pilot, and was soon berthed amid the galleys and armed traders of the exiled Vidarian navy. Helion was almost a double island, with two volcanic peaks joined by a narrow isthmus of sand and rock. The harbor was built into the waist of land, and Port Wayside clung to the side of the larger volcano. The smaller volcano was eroded into more of a gentle mound, and most of the island's farms were here.

"There must be ninety ships here," said Feran as they made for the quay, "and at least seventy are Vidarian traders and warships."

"Helion is a Vidarian outpost," Laron pointed out.

"True, but that fleet we saw departing could only have been Warsovran's," said the deckswain. "In ships they outnumbered the Helionese fleet by ten to one and they probably carried more marines than Helion's entire population. Helion should have been conquered in all of half an hour, yet those pennons flying from the masts and wharf towers are Vidarian, and the pilot said that they repulsed the blockade."

They tied up at a wharf of volcanic blackstone, and were met by the local governor, Banzalo. There had been a blockade, he explained. Seven hundred battle galleys and deepwater traders had blockaded the island for five days, then a single trader had appeared in the east. It had had Warsovran's arms on its mainsail, and made straight for the flagship of the mighty fleet. Almost as soon as it drew alongside, signal flags were hoisted and trumpets blared messages in intricate codes.

"As you saw, the ships began to get under way, hoisting sails and forming into convoy order," he concluded.

"I believe we can explain," said Feran.

In the meantime Terikel and Velander had changed back into their blue robes. They were quickly cleared to go ashore, and the governor's steward pointed out the Metrologan shrine, which was on the southern part of the island. The Metrologans managed the vinyards, and were Helion's biggest single landowner.

"But perhaps you ladies would like to clean up a little before you go to the shrine," suggested the steward. "Governor Banzalo is anxious to extend his hospitality to you, and his mansion is not far."

Terikel accepted the invitation, which offered her the chance to regain a little dignity before meeting with the rest of the surviving Metrologans.

"The mission here is ruled by Aspiring Serionese," Terikel explained as they set off for Banzalo's mansion. "She is eight years my senior as a priestess, but has had her title of 'Worthy' suspended."

"She must have done something serious to deserve that," Velander replied.

"Not really. She was in the Zantrias temple when I was a novice, but had a tendency to stab backs to gain power and influence. One day she stabbed the wrong back, so her title was suspended and she was sent here to minister to the harlots of Port Wayside, and to convert Acreman sailors and merchants to the Metrologan path of knowledge and love."

"Without a title she cannot act as a priestess," said Velander. "We need three priestesses to ordain any deaconess as a priestess."

"The Elder can restore her title, and I am the Elder. It will be my first act when I meet her."

✳ ✳ ✳

Predictably, the news brought by the *Shadowmoon* caused a sensation that was followed by an outpouring of grief across the little island. Except for a few Acreman sailors and merchants, nobody on the island had been spared the loss of relatives, loved ones, and friends when Torea had been obliterated. Services that had begun in the island's eleven shrines and chapels as thanksgiving celebrations for deliverance from Warsovran's fleet, quickly became the first remembrance services for the murdered continent. Banzalo was curiously unmoved, however. Feran and Laron were also invited to his mansion for a more extended briefing, and just two hours after coming ashore they were sipping the local wine on a stone balcony under the blue but strangely dusky sky. Laron was visibly restless, and his hands were trembling so much that there were standing waves on the surface of his wine.

"So, Laron, you were the first living man to set foot on the continent?" said Banzalo.

"In a manner of speaking, sir," replied the vampyre, who then feigned to sip at his wine.

"And what was it like? What survived?"

Laron took a misshapen splash of silver and handed it to the governor.

"This is all that is left of some merchant on the stone pier at Zantrias," he explained. "Apart from his copper belt buckle, of course, and I did not think to scrape that up."

"Fascinating. The people have been turned to ash, yet their wealth is untouched."

"Your pardon, Governor, but their wealth is a rather ugly mess," said Feran.

"But their wealth is still silver—and gold. The whole of Torea must be littered with gold and silver, just waiting to be picked up." The governor turned to Terikel. "You are now the Elder of the Metrologan Order," he said, again acknowledging her status. "In fact, you and your two priestesses are the only ordained Metrologans left in the world."

"That is right," Terikel agreed, putting her goblet down. "Our Brother Order had only two deacons in their mission in Diomeda."

"So your Brother Order may be considered dead?"

"As we speak, yes. However, three ordained priestesses can ordain a deacon. It has never been done, but I intend to begin the practice and create a single Metrologan Order under a single Elder."

"So, Torea's most powerful and respected scholarly Order is now based on Helion."

"Well, yes, and I shall be having the island's deaconesses ordained as a matter of urgency. The shrine already has an eternal flame, signifying that the light of knowledge and the warmth of love can never die, but we need to convert the shrine into a temple."

"A temple, yes, indeed," agreed Banzalo, rubbing his chin. "With the island's mason, three carpenters, and a dozen laborers, how long would it take to change your chapel into the most basic of temples?"

"Only as long as it takes to carve a vigil hearth in the shape of a clawed hand, set up some partitions, and erect a stone arch with 'MEASURE—CARE—TEACH—LOVE' chiseled in Oromac. The work of a week, no more."

"Splendid. It will be done." Banzalo turned to Feran again. "You say that a few feet of water was enough to shield you from the fire-circle's effect?"

"For us in the *Shadowmoon*, yes," Feran replied.

"That means silt survives in the river esturies. Rich, fertile silt. We can dredge it and grow crops. Shellfish, sea cabbage, lobsters—all of the ocean's bounty is still there for the taking, yet Warsovran and his armies are now dust on the face of the sun."

"Along with all other Toreans, sir," added Laron, whose hands were still trembling, and, who now had a nervous tic at the edge of his left eye.

"Well, yes, but we must look to the future. *All* Toreans are dead, you say?"

"Yes, Governor," said Feran. "With the exception of us on Helion, a handful of merchants and adventurers in foreign ports, and those in Warsovran's fleet."

"So, I am thus the most senior surviving Vidarian noble from our late and sadly lamented continent."

There was a long pause as Banzalo's guests began to assimilate his line of reasoning.

✳ ✳ ✳

Late in the afternoon the *Searose* appeared out of the east. Although the deepwater trader was faster than the *Shadowmoon* and had left Torea earlier, the shipmaster had turned back upon seeing the edge of the last fire-circle in the distance. They had reached the coast and sent boats ashore. All those aboard confirmed what Feran had reported. Terikel immediately ordered Druskarl to unload the precious archives that had been destined for safekeeping in Diomeda.

As soon as the governor had dismissed them, Laron went out and about in Port Wayside, which was the capital of Helion's three towns, five farms, and one vineyard. Of all those on the *Shadowmoon*, he had not yet eaten. The presence of so many potential meals going about their business had put him decidedly on edge. As the sun touched the horizon he made for one of the dockside taverns, ordered an ale, and sat down to watch the other patrons. Before long one of those patrons sauntered over with a mug in his hand.

"Assessing potential meals already?" he asked softly, sitting down opposite the vampyre.

"Roval—so, you escaped," Laron responded, moving no more than his eyes and lips.

"After a fashion. I was aboard one of Warsovran's ships, engaged in my usual trade."

"Spying."

"Correct. The captains decided to show some initiative and sent three scouts ashore here, dressed as Scalticarians. Because I speak Scalticarian like a native, I was chosen."

"Something to do with being born in Scalticar?"

"True. I posed as a Scalticarian merchant selling medicinal essences, borrowed from the ship's locker. I've made twenty-seven silvers in two days."

"And the others?"

"Caught, almost as soon as they entered a tavern called the Wayside Arms and tried to order two beers. One died of his wounds: he had put up quite a fight. The other was held for torture and questioning, but he managed to get a hand free and lick his fingernails. Their coating killed him within half a dozen breaths."

"I trust *you* have washed *your* hands?"

"Oh yes."

Roval took a sip of the island's wine, while Laron merely sat with his hands folded beside his untouched ale.

"It's also dangerous to be Acreman," said Roval. "Just now. On Helion."

"Why?"

"Silverdeath came from an Acreman shrine."

"But it was originally stolen by Damarian mercenaries from Torea. Besides, it was Warsovran who used it to turn loose those fires from hell."

"The Helionese are not particularly amenable to reason, logic, history, fact, or any other form of clear thinking just now. Nine Acremans have been murdered since you arrived. Even the Metrologans' big guard Druskarl has taken refuge in their shrine."

"Just who is Druskarl?" asked Laron, gazing through the window at the shrine on the crater hill, which was ruddy in the setting sun. "I notice things, and in Zantrias I noticed several very important people treating him with the deference worthy of a king."

Roval sipped at his drink. "Once he *was* a king, and his armies would have been a match for even Warsovran's. He was briefly captured by his enemies during some skirmish. Unfortunately for him, those few hours were sufficient for some, ah, creative modifications to be made to his genitalia. He decided to abdicate in favor of his son. Now he roams the world, seeking to restore his balls."

"An understandable but futile quest."

"Silverdeath can do it."

"Silverdeath? Silverdeath just reduced an entire continent to furnace tailings, yet he wants to use it to order a new pair of testicles?"

"According to some very ancient chronicles that I have read, Silverdeath needs a host to become active, and its host must have a whole and healthy body. When it is presented with any body that is less than whole, it conducts repairs. It can strip away decades of age, cure any disease, heal the most ghastly of wounds, restore the recently dead to life, and, of course, grow back severed testicles."

"While detonating a progression of fire-circles."

"Well, yes, the price was a little extreme this last time. Still, Warsovran emerged from Silverdeath's service two decades younger."

"How do you know that?"

"Druskarl told me. Kings know these things."

Laron was staring at a sailor who was particularly drunk and had just vomited over the table where he had been playing cards with three locals.

"He did that deliberately, he was sure to lose," said Laron. "I could see the hand he held from here."

"So, his name is Dinner?"

"Seaman Dinner, second class, if you don't mind. I look upon it as my contribution to the public good."

"Speaking of the public good, what about Silverdeath?"

"It is gone, and a good thing, too."

"Are you sure?"

"How could it survive the fire that burned out a continent?"

"Did you check?"

"Check? My clogs were charred by walking a few hundred yards on the surface of Torea. Larmentel was over a thousand miles farther away. I may be immortal, Roval, but I am not in-vulnerable and I *can* be destroyed. Burn me to ash, or starve me for enough months, and I shall lose my grip on this body and fade to nothingness."

"Nevertheless, now we need to either recover and destroy Silverdeath, or confirm its destruction. If we do not, our entire world will soon go the way of Torea."

Chapter Three

VOYAGE TO TOREA

It was to the small Metrologan mission and shrine Terikel and Velander went from the governor's mansion. The six deaconesses and one priestess were waiting for them, and had a hastily prepared but impressive dinner waiting. After the meal the resident priestess, Serionese, ushered her two refugee superiors into her small study. They sat down on seagrass and wicker chairs and related the story of Torea's death yet again.

"Your story is terrifying, but you still survived," Serionese said as she poured out freshly pressed grape juice. "Are you sure there are no other priestesses alive?"

"Very unlikely," Terikel replied, after she had drained her mug. "You were the only member of the Sisterhood stationed beyond the reach of the fire-circles. Only two Brother deacons may have survived in Diomeda."

"I shall, of course, put the Order as it exists here under your direct control, Worthy Elder Terikel," Serionese assured her guest.

"That will not be necessary," replied Terikel. "You can remain in charge of the shrine's running"

"That is generous of you, Worthy Elder, but what is left for you to do?"

"I must rebuild the Order. The shrine must be expanded into a temple so that we can perform ceremonies and ordain priestesses. I have convinced the governor to provide workers, stone, and timber. When the numbers increase I shall set up a teaching academy for Helion."

"But Worthy Elder, this is only a mission. We work among the harlots and poor, and preach to sailors from distant lands."

"What we have on Helion is all that remains of the Metrologan Sisterhood in the entire world. Helion *is* Torea now. The four principles of our Order are teaching, researching, love, and charity. We now have a monopoly on the sciences of Torea, so we shall be in demand. There is another important factor to remember, also. Governor Banzalo intends to claim and colonize Torea."

"Colonize? But . . . But there are only seventeen thousand people on Helion, and twelve thousand of those are refugees. Many are living on ships in the harbor."

"Banzalo is our monarch now, and that is his wish. He looks upon us with favor, Worthy Serionese."

Serionese clenched a fist to her mouth. " 'Worthy' is not my title, good Elder. In her wisdom the former Elder saw fit to demote me to 'Aspiring.' It was a matter of—"

Terikel waved her hand for silence, leaning back in the chair and closing her eyes.

"Bring me a writing kit and I'll restore you to 'Worthy' at once."

"But my case is not due for review for another two years, Worthy Elder."

"I am the Elder, and I can grant a review whenever I wish. I know your case, Aspiring Serionese. The politics behind it are as dead as the people who played them."

Terikel wrote out a proclamation elevating Serionese back to "Worthy," another appointing Velander and Serionese to her Councilium, and a third declaring the shrine now to be the headquarters of the Order. The six deaconesses were called to the shrine's sanctum, where they were told to prepare to be assessed for ordination in a very short time. The shrine's bronze gong was struck twenty-seven times to announce the Elder to be in residence, and chants were sung to Fortune in thanks for the Sisterhood being spared during the destruction of Torea.

"I now declare the first session of the Councilium on Helion to be open," Terikel declared, once the chanting was over. "Sessions will normally be only for members, but we need to apportion the work before us, resolve petitions, and bring any other local business to my attention. Are there any new or outstanding petitions?"

Velander stood up at once, drawing a scroll from her sleeve.

"I petition to declare just cause to impeach the Elder of our Order," she said in a cold, tense voice.

The eight other women and girls sat dumbfounded for a moment. Terikel said nothing, but turned as white as the plaster on the walls.

"Impeachment?" ventured Serionese, hardly believing her ears.

"During the voyage I felt it my duty to chronicle the circumstances of our escape from Warsovran's hellfire. This is part of the testament of Laron Alisialar, navigator and medicar on the *Shadowmoon*:

> " 'During the previous night the boatmaster had slipped aboard with a heavily robed woman at about the hour before midnight. He informed me that he had brought a female friend aboard, that they were to be sleeping together, and that they were not to be disturbed. Sometime after sunrise the boatmaster emerged and said that he and his companion had overslept, and that she could no longer leave because of it being daylight. Navigator Laron was instructed to cast about for a disguise for the boatmaster Feran's guest, so that she could leave without revealing her identity. Minutes later, Worthy Velander staggered aboard, completely exhausted, and warned us to cast off and sink if we wished to escape the fire that was soon to come.' "

Velander looked up, the trace of a grin on her lips.

"I shall skip forward a little now, but you are free to read what you will of this scroll, Worthy Sisters:

> " 'After the *Shadowmoon* had floated back to the surface, we observed that the port of Zantrias had been annihilated. The air was like that from the mouth of a smithy's furnace, and every trace of life had been seared away. I began helping to get the schooner ready to sail, and it was now that I noticed that boatmaster Feran's lover of the previous night had been the priestess Worthy Terikel. She was still only partly clothed—' "

"Enough!" Terikel barked. "You have made your point."

"I declare impeachment proceedings against Worthy Terikel

before this, the Councilium of the Metrologan Order," replied Velander. "The grounds are that she committed the act of fornication in flagrant violation of her vows."

"I pronounced the rule proscribing fornication to be annulled!" Terikel cried back. "You were the witness."

"And I confirm that you did so, Worthy Elder," Velander said smoothly, allowing herself a smile. "However, I can also confirm that your pronouncement was made only *after* the wall of fire had killed the previous Elder. You violated a properly constituted rule at the time you were bedded by boatmaster Feran of the *Shadowmoon*. It is now up to myself, yourself, and Worthy Serionese to vote on whether you are a fit and proper person to hold the office of Elder."

Within a quarter of a minute Terikel had been deposed as Elder, and Serionese had replaced her. Both acts could be done by a two-thirds majority of all the members of the Councilium, and Velander and Serionese made up just such a majority.

The sun was down by the time Serionese summoned Terikel and Velander to her study for the first of her official duties. She had taken the time to rearrange the furniture so the stone cube that was her strongbox separated her chair from the rest of the room. Over the chair she had draped a purple curtain. The deaconesses had removed the wooden guest chairs and replaced them with wicker stools, so visitors would be in no doubt of who was in charge. The shelves behind her contained over three-quarters of the books and scrolls on the entire island, and added further to her authority. On top of the stone cube were four cups and a beaker of grape juice.

A deaconess announced Velander. Serionese ordered her deputy to carry one of the wicker stools to the right of her chair, then called for Terikel. Terikel entered, glanced around, then stood before the stone strongbox and folded her arms.

"Worthy Sister, this is a disciplinary hearing," Serionese warned. "Your insolent bearing—"

"Worthy Elder, if you take the guard auton off your strongbox and give me all your money, I shall sign the ordination scrolls of your deaconesses. Otherwise, the Order dies when the last of us dies and you will *never* rule any more priestesses than the Worthy Velander."

"You threaten—"

"I certainly do. I also suspect that the governor will transfer his patronage to the Bluthorics, because their local patriach has the authority to ordain priests. Five priests can elect a new patriach, and, well, they do seem to have a future—which is more than I can say for the Metrologans if you do not conjure up an improved attitude."

Serionese was far better practiced at being forced to accept adverse rulings than handing them out. By now she had gone as white as sun-bleached bone, but her mind had raced along all the paths of logic and rule Terikel had already explored, with rather more leisure available.

"Worthy Velander, scribe out six ordination scrolls and sign each one," Serionese hissed with her teeth clamped together. "Blank sheets are on the lowest shelf, on my left."

Now she stood and came around the strongbox. She removed the tea service from it and placed her hand on the stone's surface with her fingers splayed. Red sparks and tendrils boiled up around it, then there was a dull clunk. The heavy stone lid hinged free on one corner, revealing two gold goblets, a ceremonial lamp, and a calico drawstring purse. Serionese breathed tendrils of force onto her hand, then reached into the cube. Tendrils of fire from the guard auton flared around her skin but recognized her. She drew out the bag.

"There are fifty-one gold circars in here," Serionese forced herself to say.

"I shall write a receipt for you."

"I'll have you expelled before the ink is dry!"

"Well, actually, you cannot. Expulsion of a priestess is a serious business. It requires a majority of Councilium—"

"I command such a majority!"

"—seniors of fifteen years standing. You can depose an Elder or demote a priestess to 'Aspiring,' but you cannot expel a priestess or even change the rules regarding expulsion without a majority of seniors. Oddly enough, the rules regarding sexual misconduct are within the ruling Elder's authority, so feel free to change my recent ruling on the subject at your discretion."

✳ ✳ ✳

In the privacy of his small room above the Midway Inn, Laron breathed his newly renewed etheric energies into the cup of black glass and capped it with the greenstone. Almost at once the stark little face appeared within the sphere's dusky green depths and looked out at him.

"Laron, you invoke me again," said the auton girl.

"And we have reached Helion! I have plenty to eat, and I have even been to the market. You will never guess what I have found."

"I cannot guess, that is true."

"It is something for you."

"For me? Great thanks to you."

The words were devoid of intonation, but who knew what feelings the auton might have? thought Laron. He opened the shutters of the window and carried the ether machine over.

"What do you see?" he asked.

"Only you. Fuzzy, with more distance."

"What about now?"

He placed a stubby tube against the greenstone sphere, and at once there was a tiny gasp from the imprisoned being.

"Ah! Yes! A picture. You are showing me . . . a picture."

Laron did not betray his disappointment. She knew about little beyond her oracle sphere.

"In the market I discovered the glass components of sundry farsights and other devices," Laron explained. "It took about an hour of fiddling with their arrangement until I achieved the opposite to the sphere's distortion. That is no picture, that is the real world."

"Ah! Beautiful, enchanting," the auton girl responded flatly.

"I cannot get you out of that oracle sphere yet, but at least I can open a window for your soul to gaze through. Soon you will be free, I promise that."

"What is 'free'?"

Laron turned the contraption of lenses to face himself, then sat down on the bunk and removed his tricorner hat. Slowly he unwound his headband, then he tapped something invisible at the right of his forehead. A silvery starburst materialized, with thin clasps of wire that vanished into his hairline. At the starburst's center, held by three claws, was a small, violet sphere with an oddly metallic sheen.

Laron raised his hand and tapped at his own oracle sphere.

"Fair Ninth, free is what I am, even though I am still in here," he said solemnly.

✴ ✴ ✴

The next morning Worthy Elder Serionese sat in her study, considering her position. The sale of all the current stocks of new wine had restored five gold circars to the treasury, and the governor's artisans were already converting the shrine to a temple. Thus, aside from some personal humiliation, Terikel's departure had not caused undue damage. Like Banzalo, Serionese also sensed personal opportunities presented by Torea's destruction.

"A small puddle, but my own," Serionese mused as she looked at her shelf of books and scrolls, then gazed out through the window.

The view was of vineyards carpeting the mountainside, giving way to sheep in the fields beyond, and it included the winding road that led to Port Wayside. The Metrologan Order owned the vineyard, and was thus an important part of Helion's economy. Serionese leaned forward. A man was visible, striding briskly up the steep slope. She picked up the shrine's farsight and focused on the visitor. He was dressed as an Acreman merchant, but carried no pack of samples. That could have meant he was very poor, yet his clothing was of fine-looking cloth, and well cut. A rich merchant, then, who was above mere samples. Serionese hurriedly finished arranging her study, selected a tome on the wordsmithing of etheric energies, and sat on a bench beside the window. Presently a deaconess announced that the merchant Roval had arrived and was seeking an audience.

The man who entered was in his thirties and had a closely shaven head, but with his travel cloak removed he had more the build of a warrior than the soft rotundity of a prosperous merchant. The two rings on his fingers were of plain and inscribed silver.

"Please be brief, I am rather busy," Serionese said in flawless Diomedan.

The man blinked, then smiled broadly. "All hail, young but Worthy Elder Serionese, and congratulations on your Diomedan. I am indeed impressed."

Roval had learned of the leadership coup from the deaconess who had shown him in, and had rethought his strategies with astonishing speed.

"You are not a merchant," Serionese observed.

Again Roval blinked. Serionese had intended the remark as a compliment, and she was about to say that he had the look of a warrior noble.

"Now I *am* impressed with your sources of information, Worthy Elder. On behalf of the High Circle of Scalticaran Initiates, I bid you additional greetings."

Serionese lowered her eyes to hide the surprise in them, and gestured to the other end of the bench. The High Circle was equaled only by the Metrologan Order in learning, but was more secretive in its teachings and activities.

"I fear that your brothers and sisters now have the advantage of us Metrologans in numbers," Serionese stated wistfully as Roval sat down. "I was contemplating a degree of cooperation with your Order in the future, but at this moment I have more pressing things on my mind."

"I see that you study etheric energies," he said, indicating the book on her lap with a circular flourish of his hand.

"Those energies destroyed Torea; in fact, my deputy Velander predicted what would happen—hence she is here, alive. My interest is now in what to do about them."

Roval sat forward, his hands clasped. "Have you heard of Silverdeath?" he asked.

"Everyone has," she replied cagily. "If Torea's death led to any good at all, it was the destruction of Silverdeath."

"Silverdeath was not destroyed. The High Circle believes that it lies in the ruins of Larmentel." Roval leaned farther forward, suddenly animated. "We *must* send a vessel back to Torea, find Silverdeath, and remove it from our world forever."

"Then do so."

"I cannot pay for a ship."

"Ah."

"You have money, Worthy Elder, and favor with the governor."

"Why not approach the governor yourself?"

"I cannot approach him directly."

"Why not?"

"If I may speak frankly, the governor is an ambitious ruler, and an ambitious ruler destroyed Torea with Silverdeath. Acreman and Scalticarian sorcerers have guarded Silverdeath for centuries. They have proved they can be trusted."

"Point taken," Serionese said warily. "What do you need?"

"A fully crewed and provisioned deepwater trader, with the shipmaster answerable to me. It would sail to Gironal's ruins, and from there a gigboat could be rowed up the rivers to within a few miles of Larmentel. The trader's crew could dig for gold and silver in the ruins in the meantime, so the trip would make a profit for you."

"I . . . have certain reserves that could be spared. All right, then, but only provided three of my own people make the voyage as well."

Roval thought quickly. His position was precarious, and speed was everything.

"I agree. We must trust each other, so—"

"Please, I have not finished: I have certain terms and conditions."

"Terms and conditions?" Roval echoed with foreboding.

"I may rule only two priestesses and a single shrine, but I am still Elder of the Metrologan Order and that gives me authority. If I hand over my gold, I want certain things in return."

"Like?"

"Like a seat on the High Circle, authority to send missionaries to your continent, and a priestess and two guards to oversee the recovery of Silverdeath."

Again Roval considered, frowning down at the rug on the floor.

"I cannot grant the first two conditions without consulting the High Circle, and time is against us. Someone else may stumble upon Silverdeath, someone who might set it off again."

"Well, then, you will have to find a quicker way to contact

the High Circle. Good afternoon to you, Roval the Not-quite-merchant."

Roval stood with his hands on his hips, his lips pressed together and his eyes wide. Serionese had shot blindly, but her arrow had struck the target. The Elder's eyes blazed with triumph as she watched Roval stride away down the mountainside. Suddenly she had something to offer, suddenly she no longer had to spend a lifetime building her Order up to a few dozen priestesses based on a speck of land in the middle of the Placidian Ocean. Whatever this scheme was, it could be of considerable worth to her.

She put the book of wordsmithery down on the bench, stood, stretched, then sauntered over and selected a book of Scalticarian grammar and vocabulary. She was pleased to see there was a common scholarly language above the jumble of regional tongues and dialects in that distant land. Walking back to the window she gazed after the departing speck that Roval had become.

"*Dulf weildera,* Roval," she said by way of farewell, then called for a deaconess. "I want you to take a message to Governor Banzalo," she said.

Laron heard the mob and saw their quarry before the pack of Helion's citizens surged into view. A burly, dark-skinned Acreman man hurtled around a corner, blundered over a pile of broken barrel slats, then ran on. Laron flattened himself against a wall as the panting Acreman ran past, smelling of sweat and fear. He dived for a pile of rubbish a moment before the first of the mob rounded the corner.

"Tha's 'im!"

"Slimy Acreman bastard!"

"Get 'im!"

"They killed Torea!"

In an instant Laron realized they were shouting at *him.* Acreman skin color varied from jet-black to golden brown, while—apart from the acne—Laron's skin was chalk-white. This important distinction appeared to be lost on the mob, however. Apart from the mob, Laron was alone in the narrow street.

"I am from Scalticar," Laron said in a cold, level voice.

Sweeping his hat off to show that his skin was pale and his hair not tightly curled, he also drew the ax from his belt. The mob was merely after a victim, so his origin meant little to them.

"E's chalked 'is face—get 'im!" a voice bawled, and the mob closed in.

Laron sliced and punch-chopped, using his ax to terrify rather than to kill. Most of those in the mob were used to brawls, but none were trained and experienced warriors. By the time a circle of bloodied, hesitant men, and women had drawn back from Laron, three bodies lay at his feet. Two of them were no longer moving.

"Acreman slime, ya killed Torea!" bawled a stonecutter with a broken nose.

"Look at me," Laron cried back. "I am not only Scalticarian, I am also an officer!"

They grew fearful at once, and began to disperse. Officers from any oceangoing vessel were considered minor nobility, and the penalty for assault on a noble of any nationality was death. Assaulting a titled noble brought death by torture. Had the real Acreman remained still beneath the rags and rotting vegetables, he might have escaped, but he chose this moment to make a break.

"Lookee there—the Acreman!" shrilled a voice.

The fugitive managed to run another ten yards before he was caught. The mob closed in, all anxious to be part of the kill. Now cornered and without hope, the Acreman fought back in spite of the blows flailing down on him. He lunged forward, seized the foremost man and head-butted him, then snatched the staff from the man's hands and straight-ended it into the face of another. Someone leaped onto his back, stabbing even as the Acreman seized his hair and ripped him away, then he went down.

Meantime Laron dragged his dazed assailant of moments past behind a handcart. By the time the vampyre emerged again, the cheering mob was sweeping away down the narrow street with the bloodied head of the Acreman raised on a pike.

Laron checked the bodies of the two other men he had dropped, but neither had a pulse. The decapitated Acreman was rather more obviously dead.

"Such a waste, such a criminal waste," said Laron, shaking his head sadly.

The new Elder decided that the crates of books, registers, archives, and records brought from Torea by Druskarl should be unloaded and taken to one of the caves they used to store wine. Velander was checking them against a list when Druskarl appeared on the gangplank of the deepwater trader with another case.

"Hard to believe," said the Acreman eunuch.

"But yes, Torea has indeed been burned to cinders," Velander replied absently.

"No, your denouncing Terikel."

Velander's attitude hardened in an instant. "She was properly and legally impeached and cast down by a majority of two against one. It was a tight case; it took but moments. The last Elder to be impeached was only unseated after five years of hearings."

"Still hard to believe," Druskarl insisted. "I spoke to Laron—he told me everything."

"What do *you* think of her behavior?" asked Velander.

"Unlucky. Got caught."

Velander laughed mirthlessly. "And that's all?"

"Yes."

"But she betrayed me!"

"You were unlucky, too."

Velander paced restlessly, her arms tightly folded. "You are a eunuch. How could you understand feelings?" she suddenly declared. *Feelings*, she thought as the word left her lips, and regretted what she had said at once.

Druskarl cleared his throat. "Not long ago—five years, in fact—there was a king who ruled the north coast of Acrema. The king was wise and just, very strong, and stunningly handsome. His queen had a liking for the captain of the royal guard, however, and they spent at least two years making secret assignations in the royal bedchamber. Eventually they must have grown careless with the logistics of seduction, for she became pregnant. As fate would have it, the king knew that he could not possibly have done the deed."

"So he had them killed," Velander said flatly.

"Oh, no. The king was wise and just, while the queen made an eloquent and passionate plea for mercy: 'Had I not been got with child, would you have ever known?' she pleaded. 'Had you never known, would you ever have cared?' The king agreed, and he forgave her."

"I do not believe it!" exclaimed Velander. "Nobody tolerates competition in that sort of business."

"True, true. That very night he had the captain brought to his inner chambers, where he was forced to write out a resignation, saying that he wished to go on a long pilgrimage. He then killed the captain, had the resignation posted, and appointed another captain. A day and a night later he dressed the captain's body in his own robes and gold codpiece, then dropped it into a garden pool full of small fish with sharp teeth. As the fishes rendered the body unrecognizable, the king left the palace dressed in the burlap robes and hood of a pilgrim. The young prince would have been crowned king on his fifteenth birthday."

Velander stood tapping her foot, with her head on one side. "Do not tell me that you are the king."

"It will still be true."

"And unprovable. The world is full of beggars claiming to be kings and princes, and generally anxious to sire a royal heir on any girl silly enough to believe them. I mean, why not just have the captain discreetly killed?"

"He had to silence the queen and remove all proof that the child was not his. A bloody war of succession between his brothers' children was avoided."

"You still make no sense."

"When the gold codpiece was removed from the body by the royal morticians, the royal dong and testicles were noted to have survived. This doubtless surprised the queen, but had she protested that the king was a eunuch, well, the body would obviously not be his. In that case, her son's legitimacy would be called into question. She had the good sense to remain silent. Her son died of a fever at the age of two, and to this day she reigns as regent and probably beds the best-hung of the palace guard."

By now Velander had gone pale and sat down on a crate. "When?" she finally asked; then added, "And how?"

"Eight years ago. I led my armies from in front, and was captured in a skirmish. The enemy warriors amused themselves by practicing some creative mutilation on me, which included gelding. The next day my own people annihilated them to a man and set me free. I treated my own wounds, and only my queen ever knew the truth."

Druskarl stood up and set off for the ship again. Velander went after him.

"Your words imply that had there been no fire-circles, I never would have known about Terikel and Feran."

"True."

"But I would be living a lie!"

"How many other lies are you living?"

"How should I know!" she exclaimed angrily. "Serionese may be vindictive and boring, but she has breached no rules. I *worship* mathematics, logic, and rules."

At that moment Terikel was sitting on a bollard not far away. She was contemplating the little schooner on which she had reigned as Metrologan Elder for nine weeks. She was still able to veto the appointment of any further priestesses, but such an act of spite would reduce her to the level of Serionese and Velander, and she found the thought distasteful.

"I am to return to Torea," declared an awkwardly pitched voice beside her.

She turned to see Laron. He was splattered with darkening blood and had bruises on his face.

"What happened to you?" she exclaimed.

"I need your help," he said, ignoring her question as he walked forward.

Terikel spread her hands wide. "*My* help? I'm no medicar. Who attacked you?"

"What influence do you still have in the Metrologans?" he asked, ignoring the latter two questions.

At the word "Metrologans" Terikel bristled visibly. "What is it to you?"

"This morning an associate of mine was arrested and imprisoned. Soon after that, the governor issued an order banning any ships from sailing until further notice. I have reason to believe that my associate was betrayed by the Worthy Serionese."

"Betrayal is the new fashion among Metrologans."

"So is gossip. Last night you charged over four dozen gold circars to sign the ordination scrolls of the deaconesses."

"True. Do you want a loan?"

"Actually, yes. I want to repair the *Shadowmoon* and take it back to Torea. Carpenters and shipwrights do not work for free, chandlers are not noted for their charity, and even the *Shadowmoon*'s crew would appreciate some pay."

"Why Torea? We just went through ten levels of hell to *escape* Torea."

"Torea is littered with melted gold and silver. There we can gather it amid the ruins, so we can return your investment a hundred times over. Then we would sail to Diomeda and live very well indeed."

Terikel did not need long to consider the proposition. Fifty-one circars could buy her a passage to Diomeda and leave enough to set up a small trading house. *Five thousand* circars could buy a very different lifestyle.

"So, this is why no ships may sail," she said. "Banzalo wants the melted wealth of Torea for himself."

"Yes."

"What is to stop me betraying you to Banzalo, just as the Worthy Elder did with your associate?"

For the first time Terikel could recall, Laron began to smile. Slowly his lips curled back—to reveal a pair of fangs three times the length of normal upper canines, and which tapered to needle points.

Terikel exclaimed softly, and slipped from the bollard to put it between her and Laron. He pressed his lips back together with obvious effort. He was not able to speak immediately, and seemed to be fighting for control.

"Please, come no closer," quavered Terikel, putting a hand to her throat.

"I have already fed this morning, do not be frightened."

"What are you?"

"Betray me, and your name will certainly be Breakfast, Lunch, or Dinner, depending when I eventually corner you. On the other hand, I can be a very powerful ally. . . . Well?"

"I'm with you, I'm with you."

Summoning her courage, Terikel came around the bollard. Laron pulled away a clump of his new beard and licked the base. Beneath it, his skin had the downy beginnings of a beard and a few acne pockmarks. He pressed the tuft back into place.

"How old are you, really?" she asked.

"Very, *very* old."

"You no longer age?"

"Being dead makes that a bit hard."

"So . . . And you have been like this for perhaps ten years."

"Longer. Thank you for agreeing to help, but Miral is nearly down so I must retire soon."

"Then return via my hostelry—I have some gold circars for you."

"I shall do that, and when I have your gold I may tell you about something else we hope to search for in Torea."

That night there was a massive explosion and flash of light from the vicinity of the shrine. Serionese later announced that lightning had struck and killed two of her deaconesses while they were meditating in the open plaza. She did not explain how lightning had managed to strike out of a clear sky.

Both Serionese and Banzalo felt that the people of Helion needed to see their rulers and betters at work if any sort of following was to be maintained. Thus the ordination ceremony was considered important as sheer spectacle, as much as for providing new priestesses. Every spare artisan on the island was called upon to help add the features of a temple to the shrine. A wooden partition was built to provide an inner sanctum. Outside, in the plaza that opened onto a view of the ocean, the air rang with the hammers and chisels of those fashioning the big clawed-hand fireplace of blackstone. Here each of the deaconesses in turn would keep vigil in a few days. Even now, islanders were arriving to donate precious driftwood and brush bundles for the fuel.

"The rules must be bent for our circumstances," Serionese explained to Velander as they inspected the work on the blackstone hearth. "The deaconesses will begin their vigils one day apart, so that the hearth will burn for four nights in succession."

To the west the sunset was luridly red with dust from their incinerated continent. It filled the survivors with more thoughts of blood than beauty. Every sunrise and sunset reminded Velander of the monstrous thing that had murdered her continent and put those colors into the sky. Still, life had to go on, and there were other matters that needed attention.

"What are we to do about the archive boxes?" Velander asked.

"Whatever is inside them must be of great importance. I have never heard of guard autons of such power being used to guard mere archives and books. Perhaps they are keyed to the touch of a priestess?"

"It is possible."

"Splendid. You shall examine the next crate."

Twelve days after leaving Helion, Warsovran's fleet sailed out of the dawn and descended upon the desert port of Diomeda. The Toreans had been the finest shipwrights and designers in the world, while their sailors and marines had years of battle experience, especially where invasion was involved.

The dash galleys were sent in first, and they had rammed, boarded, and set alight most of the defending vessels within two hours. By noon not a single vessel flying Diomedan pennants had not been sunk, burned, or captured, and ten thousand of Warsovran's marines were ashore and engaging the city's guards and militia. By evening the city had fallen to the invaders, but the highly disciplined marines did no more than impose a strict curfew.

The morning sun illuminated a harbor guarded by a massive battle fleet, but with deepwater and coastal traders arriving and departing unmolested. The Diomedans emerged to find practically nothing looted or damaged, and a lot of well-armed but courteous Torean marines doing a better job of keeping the peace than the former city officials had been able to manage. The markets opened and filled, and laborers were recruited to crew salvage barges and clear the wrecked vessels from the harbor.

The only people to notice any appreciable difference were in the impregnable island palace, Dawnlight, from which the king of Diomeda had ruled. It was blockaded by dash galleys, which were anchored just out of reach of the catapults on its high walls. In the distant past some monarch had reasoned that he could sit securely in such a place, even if his city were burned to the ground and his subjects slaughtered, to the last man, woman, and child. Now the city had indeed fallen to the biggest fleet the world had ever seen, but the only fires in the city were in the bakers' ovens, blacksmiths' forges, and pottery kilns.

Warsovran's young admiral proclaimed several new laws, lowered most levies, imposts, and taxes, and declared Warsovran to be emperor of Diomeda by right of conquest. A wealthy merchant was soon discovered to have committed treason, and dragged out of his mansion and executed by the Torean marines. His wives and children were marched straight off to the slave markets, and Admiral Forteron moved into the mansion. He declared it to be the new palace, and the other merchants of the city made haste to help supply, furnish, and decorate the place.

It was natural that no invasion could go quite as smoothly as that, however, and within hours of Diomeda falling, messenger autons were flying to the friends and allies of the blockaded king in neighboring states. Diplomats began to shuttle between cities on ship, horse, and camel, and more messenger autons flew about with despatches. Gradually the inclination would grow to assemble an army and drive the invaders out of Diomeda. The city had not really fallen, after all, not while King Rakera was safe in his island citadel in the harbor. Meantime, the invaders set about building barracks from tent cloth and the wood salvaged from the defenders' fleet, and began to strengthen the outer walls of the city. They also considered what to do about the person who was claiming credit for the victory.

Galleymaster Mandalock was actually older than Admiral Forteron, but he was very much in awe of the young duke and his strategic genius. The losses of the enemy warships in the battle to take Diomeda's harbor had been fifteen to one, and the city's fall had cost the lives of less than three hundred marines. They were in a fine position to defend what they had seized, and to expand their control, but first there was the matter of the woman who claimed to be empress.

Having paced the entire length of the *Kygar*'s deck in silence, they now stopped beside the forward catapult and looked back to the aft superstructure, where a middle-aged woman and an unhappy-looking youth were gazing across the water to Diomeda's towers, villas, and domes.

"What do you think—could it really be her?" asked Mandalock.

"I have met the empress twice," Forteron said, but he did not elaborate further.

"As soon as the fighting was over she came out on deck and demanded to see me. She gave me the pennon of the empress and ordered that I fly it in place of my own arms and colors, then she claimed victory in her own name—at least, in the name of the empress. There were still arrows flying about, so I ordered two marines to drag her back to the royal cabin and lock her in. She screamed and kicked, and threatened to have us all boiled alive in olive oil, then flung a casting at one of the marines and set his clothes afire. It took all three ship's ethersmiths to subdue her enough to be bound and gagged. Some hours later she was freed, but, while she has been behaving herself since then, she never ceases to tell us exactly what will happen once she is recognized as the true empress. I am very concerned."

"Justifiably so. There are important implications for us if she is speaking the truth."

"Oh yes, nobles like me are entitled to be boiled in hellfire oil, so the social disgrace of olive oil would be—"

"Yes, yes, nobody is going to use the wrong oil, galleymaster. You may not even be boiled alive at all. You were just doing your duty."

"Well, yes, but the decision concerning her is above my station. That is when I sent for you."

Forteron continued to stare at the couple who stood at the aft rail. Of all his attributes, Forteron's capacity for lateral thought was the one which served him best. He now brought it to bear with all the care and deliberation of a sniper aiming a crossbow.

"When did you first meet the crown prince?" Forteron asked.

"When he came aboard."

"No, I mean before this voyage."

"Never. I was really proud when the *Kygar* was chosen to carry the prince."

"And you've never seen the empress?"

"Only on coins."

Forteron began to gather in the diverse and multitudinous pieces of the puzzle. He had met the empress twice, and on one of those occasions she had been having a blazing row with her son. Crown Prince Darric was not known for submissiveness; in fact, he was well known for having the ambition and drive of both of his parents. To Forteron, the *Kygar*'s passengers seemed more like the empress and the crown prince's decoy. Were this the case, the real crown prince would be in Torea. Had he been in Torea when the continent burned, he would be dead.

"Arrange for them to be confined under heavy guard," said Forteron. "From now on, they are my responsibility."

✳ ✳ ✳

The early days of revelation and shock over Torea's demise were followed by a period of frantic reorganizing, planning, and maneuvering for power on Helion. The governor's mansion in Port Wayside was declared to be Banzalo's royal palace, and the blackstone fortress nearby was made the citadel, but the governor's ambitions ranged well beyond ruling a speck of land in the middle of the ocean. To him, the catastrophe that had destroyed his homeland was merely a divine act of purification, removing both Warsovran's contaminating invaders and those of his compatriots who were too lacking in courage and resolution to fight. The only true and worthy Vidarians were those who had fled to carry on the fight from exile. Return was their reward—in fact, it was also their duty.

Baeberan Banzalo despatched five deepwater traders to survey the Torean coast for sites to settle, and to mine for gold. His plan was clear and simple: Vidaria had been freed from Warsovran by fire from the gods, and now the surviving Toreans had to return and reclaim what was theirs. Even the total annihilation of life from the face of Torea could not keep the continent dead for long.

* * *

"*You* ordered this?" said Feran as Laron and he watched the *Shadowmoon* being beached amid a crowd of carpenters and shipwrights.

"Yes."

"Where did you get the money?"

"I have a way with ladies."

Of all possible answers that Laron might have given, this was the least convincing.

"The *Shadowmoon* is a very small vessel, and Torea is a long way beyond the horizon."

"We got here from Torea, and this time we shall be properly provisioned."

"Oh, yes, well, that makes *all* the difference. Do we have to do anything in particular, or do we just poke at the melted rocks and sand in the ruins and say, 'My, but that was a hot summer!' "

Laron glanced about, then drew closer to Feran.

"We are to find Silverdeath."

"Silverdeath? Silverdeath was destroyed, along with everything else in Torea. Everyone agrees about that. Regent Banzalo made a pronouncement; he said that it was destroyed like a fire arrow that is consumed by the house that it sets alight."

"Lies, guesswork, and wishful thinking. Silverdeath is no fire arrow, and if the weapon that destroyed Torea is still there, it can be taken by whoever would care to pick it up."

"What about stores?"

"I have secured stores," replied Laron, tossing a gold circar in the air and catching it.

"And papers?"

"We have papers to sail for Diomeda, once the embargo on sailing is lifted. That will be soon, or so I am told."

"So Banzalo is not to know that your destination is Torea?"

"Banzalo wants power. With Silverdeath in his hands he could hold the world to ransom. We are to sail up the Dioran River, then walk overland to Larmentel."

"But one of Banzalo's ships has already been sent to guard the harbor at Gironal, where the Dioran River reaches the sea."

"That is only to guard the river mouth, and the melted gold in Gironal. The *Shadowmoon* can slip past a single deepwater trader, remember? We have a very good chance of recovering Silverdeath if we leave within a few days. According to the old writings, it should have resumed its quiescent shape and fallen from the sky after the quenching of the last and greatest fire-circle."

"*If*—and I say *if*—the weapon fell from the sky as soon as the last fire-circle was exhausted, it would have fallen into a lake of molten glass and rock, and sunk to the bottom. By now it may be sealed beneath hundreds of feet of *solidified* glass and rock. Who would bother to try to recover it?"

"Warsovran bothered to have sixty thousand men digging for three years to find it. Besides, it may have drifted down slowly, landing only after the lake solidified."

"But now we know it can only be used to destroy continents. Who would dare to use it?"

"There are four living continents marked on maps of the known world. What is to stop the finder from demonstrating it on some rocky outcrop, just off the coast of Lemtas or Acrema? The sea would quench it at the first fire-circle, but it would still be very impressive. If you ruled an Acreman kingdom and saw that sort of power unleashed, would not you make haste to sign a surrender?"

Laron scribbled on a slate for some minutes, then began to make some estimates aloud. "If the island was only a few hundred yards across and far enough from the coast . . . perhaps the fire might not spread and regenerate. My studies of the figures and maps indicate that once the fire burned over an area where its circumference was all over water, it ceased to cycle. Yes, it could probably be demonstrated in safety, while easily visible from shore."

"That still does not tell me where we are going to find the horses for the overland journey, and how we are going to dig through a lake of solid glass."

"No horses are needed," said Laron as he began unrolling a map of Torea. "Larmentel lies at the edge of the Western Plains. The Bax River, a navigable tributary of the Dioran, passes fifteen miles to the south. The *Shadowmoon* could go at least half the distance with sweeps and prevailing winds, then we could take the gigboat when the current becomes stronger in the upper reaches."

"The gigboat could carry only a dozen men before the water came in over the edge. We would need hundreds to dig for the Silverdeath."

"I never said to dig for it. It may be on the surface. If not, we just need a sorcerer of sufficient skill to determine that it is sealed in there. I have arranged this, of course."

"And if it is?"

"Then Silverdeath's recovery becomes the problem of somebody else."

Feran raised his arms to the dusky sky, then let them flop to his sides.

"All right, then. Pah, I still don't see what anyone expects to find there. You were the first to land on Torea after the fire-circles had done with it. The stone bollards were so hot that the corrak's mooring-rope burned and I had to stay aboard and paddle to prevent it drifting. I actually saw smoke rising from your clogs with every step you took. Torea has been dipped in hell's furnace."

"Be that as it may, but it is what we may *not* find that chills me."

Feran walked off to supervise the work on the *Shadowmoon*. Laron stood watching the work on the vessel begin, then set off for the port. Terikel met him in the marketplace as he was buying provisions.

"So, repairs have commenced?" asked Terikel.

"Yes."

"And Feran is happy?"

"No."

"Well, I would be surprised if he had been. Are you sure you can survive the voyage? There will be none but those aboard the *Shadowmoon* to sustain you."

"I can survive on birds and fish."

"But you say that humans taste better."

"Unlike Feran, I know something of restraint."

The crates of archives had been stored in a cave near the shrine. The interior was illuminated by oil lamps, and there was no furniture other than a bench and table. Druskarl had volunteered to help, feeling sorry for the terrified Velander, and even Laron had offered to inspect the crates for vulnerabilities.

Laron picked up a crate by himself and carried it out of the cave in full view of the astonished priestesses and deaconesses. In order to spare the other crates from damage, or even set off a chain reaction of explosions, he had wanted the crate in an open space. He began to conduct his tests. Sure enough, the guard autons were like the thick iron bars in the windows of a dungeon. Primitive, but very, very strong. After an hour, even those watching from a distance lost interest, and left to go about their business.

Laron looked up into the night sky, where the stars were fuzzy balls of light and Miral was like a patch of green fog. *Glorious,* he thought. *Would Ninth like it?* He reached into his pack and drew out an assortment of tubes, lenses, spheres, crystals, and other etheric instruments. Almost reverently he took out the oracle sphere, mounted it in the cup, and set it on the crate. He spoke a casting and placed the greenstone sphere in the rim of the cup.

This time Ninth was there immediately.

Laron was astounded. Sometimes the thing worked, but only sometimes. The elemental looked out from her prison at the night sky as Laron moved the tube of lenses for her. Miral was near the zenith, and two other moonworlds gleamed intensely near the horizon. All but the brightest stars were swamped by Miral's light. Ninth's grasp of Diomedan was much better by now. Laron had even begun teaching her Scalticarian.

"The blue moonworld is Belvia, and the orange one is Dalsh," he explained as he moved the tube of lenses. "Lupan is not up just now, but it is white."

"What is this world?"

"Verral is the most common name. It is Diomedan for 'soil of home'."

"Strange, but wonderful," said Ninth. "What are the stars like when Miral is down?"

"I have never been conscious when Miral is down."

"Oh. Yes."

Definitely embarrassed, Laron thought.

"When you are restored, you will be as free to walk beneath a sky without Miral as anyone else on this world. That will be very soon, I suspect."

"What you mean?"

"I am trying to locate another oracle frame."

"When you find it, what then?"

"I will mount your oracle sphere within the claws. If a maid under the influence of a sleeping potion were to wear the frame, you would be able to walk, talk, see, and feel as if her body was your own."

"Until she awoke?"

"Yes."

"Laron, while you sleep does *your* body's owner return?"

"No. When I was summoned here, I was entrapped like you. My captors questioned me about the scholarship of my world, and in particular whether we knew about mounting the oracle spheres in the silver circlets. Presently I had an idea. Upon the soil of Earth I was one of the walking dead, so why not here, too? I told the priest who was questioning me to put my oracle sphere into a circlet, and mount it on the corpse of someone just recently dead. As I had hoped, I brought the corpse vitality, and enormous strength. I sprang from the table, snapped the priest's neck, and drank his blood. From his notes I discovered that very occasionally oracle spheres have been put on people who have lost their souls without dying, and these can become animate with any soul trapped within an oracle sphere."

"How can people lose their souls without dying?"

"Ah, now, *that* is for another time, and after you have learned a lot more words."

"Laron! Your image! Wobbling, flickering . . . I—"

The link to Ninth failed. Laron put everything into his pack and carried the crate back into the cave. He apologized to the Elder for being able to do nothing for her, then returned to Port Wayside. He had not noticed that the guard auton protecting the crate had become so severely drained that it had quietly collapsed.

Druskarl and Velander opened the second crate, but were astonished to find no guard auton. On the other hand, it contained nothing but a complete and definitive run of registers, official histories, and other useful but uninteresting reference works.

Velander watched Druskarl pull a board away from the third crate, noting the faintest trace of an orange sparkle that gleamed for a moment on the barhook's point.

"Put the barhook down and get back," said Velander as the nails squealed clear of the wood.

"But, Worthy Sister—"

"Put it down! Back away."

Druskarl did as he was told. Velander dropped to her knees before the crate. A board was now gone, and both books and bound records were visible within. There was a musty smell on the air, and dust motes danced in the lamplight. The gleam of something silver caught Druskarl's eye.

Velander picked up the loose board and prodded it through the gap. At once there was a crackling snap, and a flickering orange band snared the board and began to contract. The wood compressed, splintered, and was finally sliced through with a crisp *snick*. An orange sphere hung in the air for a moment, then vanished back into the crate. Wisps of smoke curled up, slowly dispersing.

"Guard auton," she whispered.

"It could have been my hand!" Druskarl exclaimed, visibly shaken as he held his hand before his face, rotating it as if to confirm that it was still attached.

Slowly Velander extended her hand toward the opening.

Terikel made her way down to the port and the Midway Inn. Miral was not yet above the horizon, so she sat down to wait. It was not a place where respectable women were normally seen, but she was a priestess, and her Order was known for its work among the harlots of the port. Two of them were among the deaconesses soon to be ordained. Most of the patrons of the Midway Inn were Acreman sailors and merchants. Druskarl was among them, showing a glass vinegar flask to the Acreman and Scalticarian drinkers for a few coppers a look. She suspected that his testicles were within.

After a time he noticed her and came over. He explained that Velander had been badly burned and lost two fingernails to the guard auton.

"Serves the little demon right," Terikel replied. "Still, she was luckier than those two deaconesses."

"Serionese is determined to have whatever is in the crates."

"Well, she can afford to lose three more of her followers before she has to ask me for help again. The woman's a fool; they were right to exile her here."

Just then Laron came down the steps, the new beard carefully stuck to his face. As he sat down with them, Druskarl pushed back his stool and stood up.

"No, stay," said Laron. "I hear that you want passage away from Helion."

"Yes."

"Where?"

"Anywhere. The locals are less than friendly to Acremans, even though they no longer murder them."

"There is room on the *Shadowmoon*, but I cannot pay you."

"I shall work for my berth."

"Will you? Then you have a place with us. We are bound for Diomeda."

Druskarl sat down again, and this time he was smiling.

"Druskarl was telling me that the archive crates and their guard autons are proving difficult," said Terikel. "The score is two dead and one injured—in favor of the crates."

"For what?" Laron asked. "Serionese doesn't even know what is within them."

"One was unguarded, it just contained archives," said Druskarl. "We pried a board off another. It was guarded by an auton, but contained much the same, as far as I could see."

"No treasure?"

"Only a silver tiara or circlet."

Laron blinked, then swallowed. "Describe it."

"Oh, just a starburst of silver with seven thin bands to secure it to the head. It's nicely wrought and inscribed, but the central jewel is missing. There were three claw mountings to hold it in place, and they were all bent back."

Laron rubbed at his head for a moment. "I see. Well, Druskarl, the Worthy Sister and I have much to discuss. Be so good as to pack, then report to the *Shadowmoon* tomorrow morning."

When Druskarl was gone, Laron's control weakened.

"I want that silver band!" he declared sharply, leaning over the table.

His eyes were bulging, and even his fangs were visible. Terikel flinched back.

"Your prospects are not good," she pointed out. "Those are very powerful autons."

"Do *you* know their keywords?"

Her eyes narrowed, and she drummed her fingers on the table. "What is it worth to you?"

"What is your price?"

"In spite of what Velander and Serionese have done to me, I

remain deeply committed to the Metrologan Order. I want to save it from the fools who have seized control, I want to prevent more deaths among its members. I want it to be *great* again. Can you restore me as Elder, Laron? Undisputed Elder?"

Laron pressed his lips together and closed his eyes. After a time he opened them again and stared at Terikel. It was an unsettling stare, but one of a predator warily facing off with another predator.

"I cannot make you Elder . . ." he said, smiling and folding his arms.

Terikel held his gaze. "But I have a feeling that you can help."

"Oh yes."

Terikel studied the crate in the lamplight as Velander looked on. After some moments she took a splinter of wood and prodded it at the opening. A glowing tendril wrapped around it at once, snapping it to leave a smoking stump in her fingers.

"I thought you spoke the correct keywords to these autons just now, while Serionese was still here," said Velander.

"I lied."

Nobody had been more surprised than Velander when Terikel had volunteered to unpack the crates. She said that she did not want to see any more Metrologans die because of Serionese's orders. That much was true. A crate had been carried into the ground level of an old tower, then Serionese had prudently left before they got down to the really serious work.

"What are you going to do?" asked Velander.

"Precious and sensitive records are obviously in here, hence the strength of the autons. I imagine there are other autons to destroy the crates if anyone gets past the warning traps."

"We bought that knowledge with two lives. Now what?"

Terikel breathed a streamer of ether into her cupped hands and whispered an incantation to it. The orange wisp enmeshed the seal ring on her finger. As she stretched her hand toward the opening, Velander gasped in alarm, but Terikel waved her away with her other hand. Her hand entered the space and a loop snapped into being around her wrist, all crackling orange fire and reeking ozone. It was hot and tingling against her skin, but it did not slice off her hand. Other tendrils of deep green danced about her ring, then dissipated.

"I seem to have passed a test," Terikel breathed, with considerable relief.

"I'm impressed," Velander admitted as she watched.

"A senior priestess loaned me her ring so that I could pass the gate auton to spend the night with Feran. She did not realize she had loaned me the ring, but that is all quite academic now, is it not?"

Very cautiously Terikel removed five almanacs and as many books of tables from the crate. A file with the Elder's crest stamped on it caused the glowing orange loop about her wrist to tighten painfully as she tried to remove it. She gasped with fright and dropped the sheaf of papers, which spilled within the space in the crate. Peering in, Terikel could make out part of a report on the Vidarian court sorcerer. Slowly, slowly, she reached down and removed it from the folder, keeping it within the crate. The guard auton did not give another warning squeeze.

"So, 'Reference Only,' " she concluded.

"Sorry?"

"Some items cannot be removed from the crate, but they can be handled and read *within* the crate."

"This does not make sense. Why take the thing out, if not to read?"

"The guard autons have been cast clumsily. They were probably fashioned in a hurry."

It took an hour for Terikel to go through the crate, removing what she could and glancing over what was left. It was carried out, and another brought in. The third and fourth crates contained nothing noteworthy, but the fifth contained a few artifacts. The silver circlet inscribed with archaic writing could not be removed from the crate.

"It feels . . . odd, powerful," said Terikel as she turned it over in her fingers. "It would suit me, do you not think so?"

"It belongs to the Order," Velander pointed out, sternly.

"Just as *I* belong to the Order," Terikel retorted. "Besides, it cannot be removed from the crate."

"What is it to you, anyway?"

"It looks like an immensely powerful and ancient machine, made by the same etheric sorcery as was Silverdeath."

Velander reacted predictably, and moments later Serionese was back in the tower.

"I must have it!" she exclaimed, peering into the crate at the circlet.

"Worthy Elder, were boatmaster Feran to tell me he intends to sneak into the governor's palace and roger his wife, I would point out that if caught he would probably be skinned alive before being suspended by his testicles and lowered into a pool full of ravenous crayfish. In the case of that silver circlet, I am pointing out to you that it is dangerous and powerful, and that you do not know what to do with it."

Tied to the circlet was an extract of the Annals of the Metrologan Order. Terikel reached in again, unrolled the scroll and began to read aloud, enunciating the words very slowly.

> "'Silverdeath: This artifact, also called Weapon, or the Demon-Cloth, is known to have belonged to a god in the very distant past. Halitos of Agrevan has written that it may be a way the god delegated powers to mortals, for he who puts Silverdeath onto another may then command Silverdeath to do mighty and terrifying martial feats. When inactive, it assumes the form of a shirt of finely wrought, interlocking metalwork and jewels, and while in this form it was stolen from its heavily guarded Acreman shrine in 3129. Once the thieves learned the true potential of Silverdeath, they were so terrified that they buried it under a massive rockslide. The Councilium of our Order has inspected the site and is satisfied that even ten thousand men could not dig it out in a decade. Thus Silverdeath may be considered to be lost forever, and so is no longer a threat to our world. Updated the tenth day of the eighth month, 3133.'"

"So many words, so little truth," said Terikel. "Warsovran stole it from the thieves, and it was in turn stolen from him by Velander's father, who buried it under the rockslide. Did you know that Warsovran seemed twenty years younger after Silverdeath released him at Larmentel?"

"Where did you hear that?" asked Velander.

"I knew a man who was in a position to know, and I got into a position to ask him."

Terikel lay on a sailcloth mattress stuffed with seagrass chaff, dressed in her priestly robes, with her arm in the crate and the circlet in her hand. The air was warm but bearable in the tower. Although Helion lay on the equator, its climate was mild, being moderated by cool ocean currents from the south. She breathed the incantation for a simple but concentrated auton to protect her tether. Orange shimmer drifted out of her skin like clinging smoke and settled on the smooth surface of the circlet—then slid off and collapsed to a point.

"Very, very strange," she muttered.

Her guard auton had not bound to the circlet. The auton that was protecting the inside of the crate was also protecting both the circlet and her while she used it, but her casting was within the auton. Why had it not bound? *Because it is not from my own world, perhaps,* she speculated. Terikel spoke the incantation for darkwalking detachment.

The lamplit interior faded, broke up into patches of darkness, then became all darkness. She had no weight; she was floating in a blackness where pinpoints of light gleamed and sparkled. Each was a concentration of enchantment. Most were clustered about the shrine, although some appeared to be beneath the ground. Her own tether had a distinct texture and density that she could sense clearly. In the etherworld she could see much that was not visible in her own plane of reality. Every few moments a gathering of shadows, a presence, or a cloud of glimmer would flit past to check her tether, then be gone again. She studied the tether intently, memorizing its feel and empathy before willing herself to drift farther away.

It was like stepping onto Helion after the long voyage aboard the *Shadowmoon.* She knew what to do, but she was still clumsy and awkward. One by one she examined the sparkles nearby. Most were simple medical and protective charms, several were tethers, but a few were quite potent concentrations that were unfamiliar to Terikel. Soon she recognized the autons guarding the crates on the floor of the cave. She began ranging farther afield.

The island was all points and sparkles of enchantment. None was particularly strong, but several had very large potential capacities. There were some fairly senior initiates on the island, but they were keeping their powers and identities to themselves. At least two other consciousnesses glided about near the guard autons of the crates while she was exploring the island's patch of Etherworld, but they quickly fled when she tried to approach them.

After what seemed to be a short time she returned to the tether. It was certainly different from everything else there. Not powerful or potent, but strange. It had no truename. She tried giving it a name of her own, but the name did not bind. That was odd; almost as if it did have a truename, but one that could not be felt.

She was about to return to herself when a light blazed up briefly beyond the island, a harsh, green light that made her look away by reflex in spite of its distance. When she turned her vision back in that direction the source had gone. Something powerful but well cloaked was in the vicinity. Returning to the immediate area of the anchor, she briefly cast about for another tether before settling back into her body.

The marked candle on the table had burned five hours! When darkwalking it was easy to stay away too long. Both time and distance were distorted. Terikel got up shakily and began to stretch the stiffness out of her limbs and body. She rapped at the door.

"I wish to speak with the Elder," she called when the guards did not unbar the door.

"Elder's orders are that you can't leave here until morning," a guard called back.

Terikel considered for a moment, contemplating what she had—and had not—seen while darkwalking.

"Bring the Elder here, then."

"She's asleep, it's nearly dawn."

"Then wake her. Tell her I have the silver circlet."

Serionese arrived with the deaconess Latelle before Terikel

had counted fifty breaths. She was hastily dressed and even more hastily groomed.

"Where is it?" she demanded.

Terikel was sitting on the edge of the crate. She did not stand up for Serionese. "Good morning, Worthy Elder, how liberal of your mother to let you stay up so late."

"Where is the circlet?"

"In the crate, protected by the auton."

"What? You lied!"

"I drew illuminations around the truth. I *can* remove it, but you will not wish me to."

"And why is that?"

"It will bind to whomever removes it from the protection of the auton. I cannot remove that auton, but I can remove the circlet."

"How?"

"With an iron case such as this."

Terikel lifted an iron case the size of a large book from the top of the crate and handed it to the Elder. Serionese hefted it.

"Put that case through the guard auton's fabric, drop the circlet into the case, and close the lid. The guard auton will no longer be able to see the circlet."

"Yes, yes, iron is proof against magical influences. Very clever and simple, just like all true solutions." Serionese sighed, suddenly satisfied that the problem had been solved. "All right, let us start."

Terikel stood up, then reeled at once and nearly fell. One of the guards caught her.

"Air, fresh air," she mumbled. "Think I'm going to be sick."

"Latelle, get her out of here," ordered Serionese.

"Don't do anything until I return," Terikel gasped as Latelle and a guard helped her out.

Taking a barhook, Serionese poked it into the translucent fabric of the guard auton within the case. The fabric colored angrily around the intrusion, but did not resist the steel tip. Next she put the open iron case on the flat of the barhook and pushed it through the auton. Sliding the case off the barhook, Serionese picked up the circlet on the barhook's tip and dropped it into the iron case.

"Now we shall see if she was telling the truth," the Elder said to the watching guard; then she flipped the lid of the case closed.

The auton registered that the circlet was gone, even though it was still within the crate. Following orders configured into it when it was created, it discharged all its energies in a single, intense flash of light and heat with a blast like a lightning strike. Serionese and the remaining guard died instantly, flung across the room and smashed against the stone wall. The wooden door was blown from its hinges, and flame belched out across the courtyard in front of the tower.

Terikel had expected something like that. Snatching up a discarded suncloak, she draped it over her head, took a deep breath, and dashed back into the tower. Burning paper and wood from the annihilated crate was everywhere, the air filled with smoke. Luck was on Terikel's side. The iron case lay within two yards of the door, and a tap on the release lever popped it open. The circlet was hot but undamaged as Terikel fished it out and hid it within her robes. She dragged Serionese's body outside just as Velander and the other deaconesses came running up.

It required only the briefest of examinations to establish that the Elder was dead. The surviving guard confirmed that Terikel had been outside when the guard auton had detonated.

"Your Elder has managed to kill herself," Terikel declared in hard, crisp words as she paced before them. "She disobeyed my order."

"You killed her!" Velander cried, genuinely shocked.

"Not so, Worthy Sister," said the surviving guard. "Worthy Terikel told her not to do anything until she returned."

"What did she promise you, to tell that lie?" Velander demanded.

"He speaks the truth," agreed Latelle.

"I am the Elder now!" Velander insisted. "I was Worthy Serionese's deputy and—"

"Actually, that does not make you the acting Elder," Terikel interjected. "The acting Elder's position automatically goes to the most senior surviving priestess—me."

"You were impeached and cast down while Elder!"

"I checked the law on that. I was only *acting* Elder, not having been voted into the position permanently. Only a permanent Elder can be impeached. What you and Serionese did was, well, merely to vote her to fill my position: that of acting Elder. I have committed no breach of the rules since Worthy Elder Serionese died, so unless you have new grounds to impeach me, I am indeed the acting Elder—again."

"You—"

Velander caught herself. Legally, Terikel was sure to be right. Velander knew the etheric and cold sciences well, but Terikel specialized in law and was sure to be on firm ground with whatever she said.

"When the ordeals are done and all four new priestesses can vote, we shall see who is Elder," she snapped.

"Why wait fifteen days?" asked Terikel. "Look, the sun is rising and it is the fifth day of Deaconess Justiva's ordeal. Shall we check the fire?"

Justiva had left her vigil fire at the sound of the explosion, and they had been talking for twenty minutes. With a cry of anguish the deaconess dashed back to the ceremonial hearth, followed by the others. The bundle of twigs should have lasted only a quarter hour, but somehow a distinct flame still danced amid a few last fragments of driftwood. Justiva looked about. One bundle remained. Had there been two when she ran to help? She was so tired . . . perhaps she had been seeing double.

"Congratulations, Worthy Justiva, your flame is still burning," said Terikel.

"But I abandoned it."

"Legally, you only have to keep it burning, not stand beside it. You are now a priestess. The Goddess of Measures saw fit to have you ordained to vote in our time of crisis. As acting Elder I hereby call for nominations for permanent Elder. I also nominate myself, and stand by my record of service, scholarship, and loyalty to the Order and its Sisters."

"*Your* record?" Velander exclaimed. "You fornicated, you defied the Elder, you betrayed my soulmate vigil."

"Do you wish to nominate?" asked Terikel.

"I nominate myself!" declared Velander.

"Do you wish to speak to your record?"

"*My* record? *Your* record is at issue. You have sinned, you can never be forgiven. A whore like you is not fit to herd a flock of geese, let alone the Metrologans."

"Is that all you wish to say?"

"Yes!"

There was silence for a moment. Suddenly Velander noticed a dangerous glint in Justiva's bloodshot, dark-rimmed eyes. With a qualm, Velander recalled that the local Metrologans ministered to the local harlots, and that two of the deaconesses had been recruited from among their number. Which two?

"Those supporting the appointment of Worthy Terikel to the position of Worthy Elder of the Metrologan Sisterhood . . . ?" Terikel was saying.

"No, wait!" cried Velander, but two hands were already rising, blood-red in the horizontal rays of the sun.

"A majority has been achieved—Worthy Terikel is declared Elder of the Metrologan Sisterhood," Terikel declared. "My first order is to put out the fires in the tower. Worthy Sisters, Aspiring Sisters, I also proclaim that makeup, tailored robes, and individual bedcells are permitted henceforth, and that celibacy is optional. Now, carry the bodies into the temple."

Except for Velander, the mood of the girls instantly lightened. Even as they carried the bodies away, they were discussing the relative merits of various cosmetics, fashions, and local youths.

After breakfast Terikel ordered Aspiring Latelle to continue her ordeal that day, then she set off for Port Wayside. The governor was informed of Serionese's accident and death, and of Terikel's appointment. Going on to the docks, she found Laron supervising work on the *Shadowmoon*, which was progressing well.

"I have the silver circlet," she announced as she took him aside.

"I had no doubt that you would succeed."

"Did *you* keep Justiva's fire alight?"

"That is between me and my conscience. Congratulations on your election."

"Thank you for telling me about Justiva's background, and for suggesting the trick with the iron case."

"It offended my chivalric principals," he mumbled between clenched teeth. "Still, you did appear to have pure motives. Well, now that I have fallen from chivalric grace and become a murderer, what next?"

"Serionese killed *herself*; you—and I—merely provided her with a very dangerous temptation. As to what is next, Banzalo sails on the next tide, and thereafter the ban on ships leaving Helion without his permission will be lifted."

"Splendid. The *Shadowmoon* will sail west with the following tide, then loop back to the east."

"Before you sail, I have a last request to make of you."

"Yes?"

"I must send Worthy Justiva to Torea with Banzalo. Aspiring Latelle is next in seniority, but I am not sure of her loyalties. Velander could cause trouble if she forced a vote over anything."

"Why not send Velander with Banzalo?"

"And let her have the governor's ear? Not likely. Can you take her away on the *Shadowmoon*?"

"As passenger or provisions?" Laron asked without emotion.

"As a passenger, unless she becomes really obnoxious. Just keep her away until I can get the others through their ordeals and build their loyalty to me."

Later that morning the nobility, military elite, and civilian leaders of the island met in the newly declared administrative palace. It was a villa of blackstone, three floors high, with a roof of imported terra-cotta tiles, and had been built around a courtyard. This featured a small fountain in which lampfish swam languidly, and a dozen marble nudes that had suddenly become the greatest collection of Torean sculpture in the world. One of the wings flanking the courtyard contained a dining hall, which was the largest single room on the island. It had been hurriedly fitted with a lectern, improvised throne, benches, and scribes' tables, while the musicians' gallery above the double doors had been furnished with seats for observers.

A Ruling Governance was announced for Helion, comprising Admiral Chanclar, the five landowner nobles, Banzalo, and one other, surprising member. As the Elder of Helion's Metrologans, Terikel was considered sufficiently important to be on the Governance. The Governance's first act was to pronounce Baeberan Banzalo to be emperor of Torea, as he was the highest-ranking Vidarian noble still alive. Terikel dutifully copied down the appointment's wording and terms, as none of the island's scribes were experienced in court protocol.

In his first address, Banzalo caused a considerable stir by reporting that Warsovran was still alive. One of his merchant shipmasters had just returned from the Ebaros Sea and had learned a great deal there.

"He will return here," said the master of the merchants' guild on Helion. "We must flee for Acrema."

"He has no interest in us," Banzalo replied. "We are causing no trouble for the rulers of Lemtas and Acrema, and much of his war fleet is made up of galleys that do not sail well in the rough waters of midocean. Remember, they only managed to maintain the blockade here for a few days."

"Then we are safe?" ventured the master merchant.

"As safe as anyone can be. He will hire his fleet out to some Acreman monarch and end his days as a mercenary. In the meantime, privateers and adventurers all around the Placidian Ocean are preparing to sail for Torea."

"That is hardly surprising," said Terikel. "There is a dead continent for the taking, and it is littered with melted gold and silver."

"Vidaria's gold and silver!" Banzalo insisted gruffly.

"Legally speaking, it belongs to whomever can salvage it," Terikel pointed out from the scribe's bench. "Morally speaking, whoever can prove prior ownership or can establish a defendable claim is the owner."

"Vidaria is now a settled kingdom," Banzalo declared. "As

the provisional regent of the restored empire of Greater Vidaria, I lay claim to all ruins and territory encompassed by Torea's coastline. I intend to establish five cities within the month."

"Using the Torean nationals on Helion, you have the followers to found a few hamlets, none of which will contain more than two hundred women," said Terikel. "There are eleven thousand marines and sailors in your fleet. This suggests a certain imbalance in the population."

"Those marines and sailors will use the gold from Torea to buy wives from the slave markets of Lemtas and Acrema. Five or six wives for every man! In a generation the population will be over a hundred thousand. With Torea's melted gold we can also buy ships, timber, tools, and weapons. The estuaries of the rivers can be dredged for silt, and crops planted on their banks. Sea cabbage and fish will be as plentiful as ever. Why, the folk of the Vidarian empire will eat better than we do here."

"Then why are you here?" asked the master merchant.

Banzalo shot him a glare. Everyone knew him too well here; the islanders barely knew the meaning of deference to rank. That had to change. What he knew he needed was an unfamiliar frontier, a place where people were insecure and frightened. Somewhere they would look to a leader who was all that stood between them and catastrophe.

"This very afternoon I intend to sail with the bulk of my fleet for the ruins of Port Kosamic in Vidaria. There I shall be crowned by the admiral of my fleet, and there I shall build a new city, Port Banzalo."

This resulted in a buzz of surprise and conjecture among the members of the Ruling Govenance. The map of Torea was pushed around the table.

"Are we to understand that you will leave Helion undefended?" asked Terikel.

"Helion needs no defense, but at this very moment looters from every port fringing the Placidian Ocean are sailing south to rob *my* gold in Torea. Torea needs defense. If anyone on Helion is worried about Warsovran coming here, they can come to Torea with the rest of us."

The ambassador from North Scalticar cleared his throat and gestured for attention.

"My homeland has a tenth the area of your new empire—"

"Restored empire."

"Whatever. My point is that North Scalticar has nine million souls to praise its gods, tend its crops, serve its king, build its ships, and defend its borders. You have a few thousand at most. How are you going to defend what you have?"

Banzalo reached out and drew the map across to himself. "The new settlement of Port Banzalo will blockade and defend the mouth of the Temellier River. Once I am crowned on my homeland's soil, my first act as emperor will be to also blockade the ruins of Gironal, where I shall build a fort and establish another Vidarian port. The tributary systems that feed the Dioran and Temellier Rivers are slow, wide, and easily navigable. They provide access to nearly the whole of inland Torea. Whoever controls them, controls the continent. There is no forage for those traveling by horse, and no game for those on foot, so invading looters must travel inland on the rivers or not at all. Besides, Gironal was the mightiest merchant port in all of Torea. Nearly a quarter of the gold on the continent was within its walls when the fire-circles burned it. By ruling Gironal, I rule Torea's wealth."

"Until you are robbed," Terikel pointed out.

Banzalo frowned as he turned on her. "For someone who hopes to head the principal religion in Greater Vidaria, you are showing precious little respect for your future monarch," he warned.

Terikel had been expecting such a retort, and was not deterred. "I was not questioning your motives, Regent Banzalo. I was pointing out that you will be hard-put to defend your claim to such a rich prize as Gironal, against the swarms of ships drawn to its wealth. Your deepwater traders will have heavy work ahead of them."

"Wealth can buy power and recruit friends. Other ships will be despatched to Lemtas to buy boatbuilding timber. Such materials will soon be precious beyond valuing on the seared, glassy coasts of Vidaria."

"What is left of Vidaria is a bleak and precarious place," said Terikel. "I have seen it. There are many places on other continents where Vidarians could live and prosper better."

"Vidarians have a just and sacred duty to rebuild the homeland. *You* are now Vidarian, Worthy Sister."

"But Vidaria is as dead as gnawed bones in a campfire's ashes."

"We are taking Vidaria back from the grasp of Death, just as we won it back from Warsovran!" Banzalo thundered. "I declare free passage for all Vidarians who would return to Torea's shores! Farmers and militiamen are especially welcome. Land will be granted in freehold. Come back and claim the homeland we rescued from Warsovran."

"You did *not* take it back from Warsovran," cried Terikel, slapping the armrest of her chair with exasperation. "His own enchanted weapon, Silverdeath, got out of control and destroyed the entire continent."

"Rhetoric, details, trivia! Our homeland is there for the taking, and so is the gold that will be used to rebuild it. The Imperial Vidarian fleet will sail for the capital of Port Banzalo at once. I have decided to leave the two galleys and six of the twin-masted war schooners to keep order here, at Helion. Further, I declare the whole of Torea as a protectorate of the Vidarian empire. As the only properly constituted kingdom on Torea it is Vidaria's duty to maintain order, and all ships and people of other kingdoms sailing for Torean waters must pay a levy for the upkeep of my navy. Will you return to Torean soil to establish the Metrologans, Worthy Elder?"

"I have already agreed to send one of my new priestesses to supervise the building of a shrine."

"So you will not return to your native soil."

"Soil? There is no Torean soil. There is only glass that was once sand and soil—oh, and lava—there is a lot of lava."

The thought crossed Banzalo's mind, that if he walked out now, the next gathering he would preside over would be his coronation, on the shores of Torea. There he would have respect, deference, and real authority. Without another word Banzalo stood up and strode out of the chamber, resplendent in his yellow-and-blue Vidarian half-jacket and red cloak with the new Vidarian imperial arms hurriedly embroidered on the back.

A retinue of brightly dressed officers, minor nobles, and atten-
dants streamed after him like a tail behind the brilliant head of
a comet.

That went rather well, thought Terikel as she sat alone in the
chamber. The young Elder had deliberately made a highly visible
stand against Banzalo. It was clearly stupid, because Banzalo
would regard both her and the Metrologans with disfavor. Terikel
could think strategically as well as tactically, however, and she
could also do that somewhat better than Banzalo.

The meeting broke up soon after Banzalo left. Word of the
deliberations spread quickly, and many of those on the island
felt it would be better to return to Torea. At least there would be
a proper military force to defend them.

Several dozen of the island's farm laborers gathered on the
docks with their worldly possessions soon after the regent's
court had ended. Free passage to Torea! Here was a chance to
become nobles, with more land than they had ever set eyes
upon, let alone dreamed of owning. Two brothers struggled
along the streets of Port Wayside with several sacks of tools,
seeds, and other supplies dangling from the pole between them.
Their wives and children trailed after them with their own
sacks.

"We'll have houses built of stone by the time ye come after
us," Prosus called back to the others as they approached the
docks.

"But why can't we come with ye now?" asked his wife.

"'Tis a matter of space an' needs. The regent wants farmers
and militiamen, an' in Crasfi and I, he gets both. Next ship as
has space, ye'll be sent on."

"But how to pay?" whined Crasfi's wife.

"There's nowt to pay, only what food as is like ter feed you
an' the brood," Crasfi explained, slowly and laboriously. "We's
explained it, wer'n yer ears open? Farmers is vally-ble in Torea,
like gold. They wants us, they needs us."

"Aye, we gets free passage when there's space. Crasfi an' I

will claim land grants near the port, where we can sell ter all who comes ashore. We's got ter be first ter do that, an' we're got ter claim berth on a ship early ter be first."

True enough, they found several deepwater traders admitting passengers for free passage to Torea. Prosus and Crasfi went aboard to claim hammock space while their children ran home for more sacks of food, and their wives stood guard over their tools on the wharf.

"So, Winte, d'ye fancy yourself as a lord's wife?" asked Prosus' wife, Heldey.

"Ah, 'tis a lot of servants ter be orderin' abaht," she grizzled in reply.

"But a great rise for a girl. Big house, servants, aye, and grand robes ter impress the other nobles."

Winte glanced furtively around before replying. "*Ye'll* be more like ter impress 'em with your clothes off, trollop," she sneered. "Like that merchant as brings ye Diomedan combs an' hairpins, an' that fisherman who gives ye fish for a little quick bargainin' behind stall. Prosus will find out, you mark my words."

"I'm a carpenter's daughter, I married below my station," Heldey said with a sniff. "I deserve finer things than a sodbreaker can give me."

"Well, just you mind yerself, as our men could just make themselves more than all your merchants and fishermen."

All the while, more and more people had been streaming down to the docks and seeking passage on the traders bound for Torea. For once it seemed that Prosus had been right, and that hard work and quick thinking might make them the founders of two great families with titles. It was what everyone on the wharf was dreaming.

Laron emerged from his locker-sized cabin to find Druskarl on the quarterdeck at the steering pole of the *Shadowmoon*. Miral was high in the sky, and the beacon pyre at the top of the island's new lighthouse was visible.

"You never seem to sleep while Miral is in the sky," Druskarl said casually, "yet tonight Miral has been up for hours and you have not."

"While Miral is in the sky I can be awake or sleep, as I choose. When Miral is down I can be neither."

"So what were you doing?" asked Druskarl.

"Being paranoid."

Druskarl waited for Laron to elaborate. Laron chose not to.

"Speaking of being paranoid, I hope you have eaten," Druskarl said as he rubbed his hands together in a parody of unease.

"Who told you about that?"

"The friend of a friend. Well, *have* you eaten, and were they meals that conformed with your chivalric principals?"

"Well, yes, and I do believe Port Wayside is a better place for it. Speaking of Port Wayside, I have been making inquiries there as well. You know: Who is humping who, who has plans to destroy the world for fun and profit, that sort of thing."

"And?"

"And I found out nothing about Feran."

"So?"

"So it continues a trend I have found in Scalticar, Acrema, and Torea as well. Before two years ago, Feran did not exist. He had no past. No parents, no home, no apprenticeship, not even a criminal record."

"He could have changed his name. Many do."

"I know how to trace the person even when the name dies and is reborn as something else. Nobody even *like* Feran ever existed before 3138, when he—"

At that moment Velander emerged from below, disheveled and scowling. She took one look at the rising sun and cried out in shock.

"We're sailing east!"

"That's the quickest way to Torea," said Laron.

"But the Elder ordered me to Diomeda."

"The Elder also ordered us *to* sail to Torea after sailing *for* Diomeda. You have to watch the prepositions very carefully.

Given your record of personal loyalty, you were not to be told until we were at sea."

The remark did nothing to improve Velander's mood.

"And why are we *really* going there?"

"To recover Silverdeath. We have reason to believe that it remains in Larmentel, intact. My associate Roval approached Serionese about financing an expedition earlier, but she went straight to Banzalo and revealed everything. Roval was made a guest of the governor in exceedingly well guarded lodgings, and then Banzalo dreamed up a fantastic scheme of repopulating Torea, then using Silverdeath to defend it."

Suddenly everything fell into place for Velander: Banzalo had known all along! That was the hidden agenda for blockading the Dioran River at Gironal: To make sure nobody else could reach Larmentel's ruins before he was ready to send an expedition to recover Silverdeath. Serionese had lied to her own priestesses and deaconesses.

"That slimy, evil, malicious betrayer—" Velander began, then she caught herself. "Did Terikel know?"

"Apparently not," said Laron, taking the silver circlet from his robes. "Do you recognize this?"

"Gods in their moonworlds!" exclaimed Velander. "The thing from the crate."

"It is very old, and even I did not realize that the Metrologans owned it. According to certain letters Terikel read for me from the crate, it was destined for Yvendel Si-Chella in Diomeda."

"What? She's a brilliant sorceress and an initiate *twelve*. She specializes in Etherworld studies and dimensional travel."

"She also has been associating with a group of, ah, concerned sorceric masters since Silverdeath was stolen. Apparently she may have found a way to neutralize Silverdeath."

Presently Feran came on deck and ordered the running lamps extinguished. Laron offered Velander the use of his cabin while Miral was up, and although Feran insisted that his own cabin was more comfortable and spacious, she declined the latter offer.

"It's true, his cabin does have more space and fittings," Laron said as he packed his few possessions aside to make room for Velander.

"Maybe so, but I know that he would like me in there as an additional fitting."

"How do you know that?"

"I am the only woman aboard."

"Terikel has decreed—"

"That sort of behavior is not to my taste, regardless of the new Elder's decree on celibacy. It is a bit like your chivalric principals, esteemed Laron. A silly notion, but one that I choose to follow."

Far to the east, on Helion, the constable banged on Roval's cell door and shouted, "Visitor." Roval got to his feet and straightened his clothing, then rubbed unhappily at the stubble on his scalp. The door opened, and Terikel was admitted.

"A quarter hour, Learned Elder," said the constable as he closed the door again.

"'Learned Elder'?" asked Roval, folding his arms and frowning. "As in, Elder of the Metrologans?"

"That is me. I am Learned Terikel."

"Indeed. But what about Learned Serionese? The Metrologan Elder whom I suspect had a hand in recommending me for complimentary accommodation in here."

"I deeply regret what happened to you, sir—please accept my word on it. As for Serionese, she met with an unfortunate accident. Unfortunate from her point of view, at any rate. My involvement in the accident is between myself and my conscience, and my conscience does what it is told."

Roval smiled, unfolded his arms, and gestured to the cell's stone bunk.

"But where are my manners?" he said genially. "Learned Terikel, we appear to be very much alike and have a great deal to discuss. Scrape up some straw, have a seat. Would you like some bread and water? It's reasonably fresh."

"Why thank you. Oh, and I brought this."

Terikel drew a slice of cake from her cleavage. Roval took a long breath while trying to think of how to respond.

"Sultana honeycake, my favorite. Thank you for keeping it warm, it's the only way to eat it."

"Really? I shall remember that for next time."

Terikel nibbled at Roval's bread crust while Roval consumed the honeycake in two bites, then licked his fingers.

"Our mutual friend Laron has told me much about you, and your dedication to our common interests," said Terikel, breaking the silence.

"Ah, Laron. Nice boy, but awful table manners. I trained with him in the Special Warrior Service. We have done five missions together. Actually, he did say a little about you after the *Shadowmoon* reached Port Wayside."

"Did he? He told me all about you, too."

Roval froze, with a look of alarm on his face. Terikel began to wonder whether she should have worn quite such a knowing expression for that last sentence.

"He—he what?" snapped Roval. "If it was about that revel in Palion where I was supposed to have laid on the floor with oysters in my nostrils while a belly dancer jumped on my stomach, it was not like that at all. And besides, he was not there. Miral was down at the time, so he was off in some bedchamber, being dead. You should have heard the scream when a young couple blundered in there looking for somewhere to— Are you all right?"

"Stop it! I put so much effort into being bitter and twisted, and you spoil it all by making me laugh."

"Anyway, they were olives, not oysters. . . . Why should you be bitter and twisted?"

"Roval . . . Seriously, life has not been kind to me lately. It is not just losing everyone and everything in Torea. The Elder before myself and Serionese had me do some things that I disliked with some people I despised, all to gather information for the Metrologan cause. When it became known, I had to play the part of a slut, again to protect the Order's reputation. Laron helped me when I was alone and at my lowest, and he did it with no hope or expectation of anything in return. Now I am Elder. The only company that I allow in my bed is an occasional book, even though I leave the recreational activities of my followers to their own consciences. I also pay my debts. Laron thinks highly of you, so as far as I am concerned, you can do no wrong."

"Oh really?" said the embarrassed Roval, rubbing his stubble.

"Roval, if Laron is your friend, then so am I. What can I do for you? If there is anything that I can do to make things more pleasant in here—within reason—just tell me."

Now Roval blushed. Terikel laughed.

"Ah, a daily visit from a barber to shave my head and face, and a weekly visit from you to keep me informed," Roval suggested.

"What about a daily visit from me, to give you a shave *and* keep you informed?"

"Oh, Elder, I could not—"

"Ah, but I have very steady hands, Learned Roval."

"Speaking seriously yet again, Elder, we might achieve some good by pooling our knowledge. When I am out of here we can even do some effective work together."

"And when you are out of here, I expect to be shown that trick with the olives, Learned Roval. Meantime, I really shall try to visit every day. Same time tomorrow?"

"I shall be here."

Chapter Four

VOYAGE TO LARMENTEL

 On the fortieth day out, Feran was standing by the handrail at sunset, drinking in the golds, crimsons, vermilions, and ochers that glowed from the clouds, reminding himself that the dust of uncounted millions of people was among those colors. To starboard was the dark, lifeless outline of the Torean coast. He climbed the five steps to the quarterdeck and peered down at the lodestone float, then took a bearing on the setting sun. Picking up an angulant, he took a sighting between Lupan and the horizon, then checked the drop-log figures on the watch's slate. Finally he relieved the steersman.

Feran had the meal watch that night, relieving for an hour until Laron took over. As he left his cabin he had seen flashes of orange light leaking past the sliding hatch that opened onto Laron's tiny quarters. Velander and all the others were below, at dinner.

Once alone on the quarterdeck, Feran lashed the steering pole and did a quick tour of inspection. All was normal—then suddenly he turned north, staring at a long line of faint lights on the horizon. *So, they're on the move early,* he thought, then he began to untie the steering pole. The running lamps of the fleet of distant ships were luminous specks gleaming yellow amid the dark waves. Feran thanked Fortune and Chance that he had been on watch alone when they had come into view, and that they were following the coast at a greater distance. Very gently he steered the *Shadowmoon* a few points farther southeast. The sails were not trimmed for quite this angle to the wind, but it would have to do. He prayed that nobody would notice the slight change and come on deck to investigate.

A quarter hour passed, then a half hour. The *Shadowmoon* was small and broad, but a fleet travels only as fast as its slowest ship, and—amazingly—that ship was apparently slower than the *Shadowmoon.* Slowly the lights winked out as they dipped below the horizon. Feran knew they were not visible, as the *Shadowmoon* now burned no running lamps. Being so small, it would be easy prey for virtually any fast privateer that chanced upon it, so Feran had even been using plain, olive-green sails and running a low profile on the lateen mainsail. He estimated there had been at least six dozen ships in the fleet that the *Shadowmoon* had skirted. He knew they would use the northwest tip of Torea to rendezvous, and while he had steered to miss that danger, he had not known *when* they would move. Another half hour passed, and more lights winked out.

A hatch scraped back on its runners and Feran looked down. "Boatmaster?"

Velander's voice. Her feet tapped on the steps as she climbed to the little quarterdeck. Feran shot a glance to the horizon where a few lights still twinkled.

"Look at all those ships!" Velander gasped as she joined Feran. "Sir, there must be six—no, eight, perhaps nine."

"Looters from the Ebaros Sea's ports," said Feran casually.

"So many at once?"

"They are drawn together for strength, though repelled by greed. Small boats like this one are easy prey for them."

"Is there a danger, sir?"

"The *Shadowmoon* is actually as streamlined as a fish below the waterline, and is surprisingly fast. All part of being a spy ship, really. That convoy travels as fast as the slowest ship, and that ship seems to be a washtub with a sail. We are definitely outrunning them."

Velander took a tube from a pouch at her belt, then pulled at either end until it had expanded to four times its initial length. Feran looked more carefully, and noticed that it was four concentric tubes of brass. She took metal caps from both ends, then held it to one eye and pointed it toward the distant ships' lights.

"Laron's farsight—he lent it to me," she explained.

"Laron? But I thought you and he, ah, had no time for each other."

"True. He adheres to some heresy that Miral's rings are dust, not solid. He said that with this you can see starlight through them, and lent it to me so that I should see for myself. Thus far, the dust and smoke high in the air have prevented me from getting a clear view, even with this device. It was invented as a toy a few years ago, but the leaders of Torea suppressed the use of it, allowing its use only for nobles and senior military. They didn't want the lower classes seeing too far, no doubt."

Velander continued to study the ships, but seemed to notice nothing that surprised her.

"The first I ever saw belonged to a Vidarian sealord, and was made from a single tube, as long as my arm," said Feran. "The image was reversed and inverted, but it brought out great detail in very distant objects."

"Laron disguised the version that he built, as container for medical powders—which is always empty. Now it doesn't matter, like a lot of old Torean laws. Those ships . . . They look to be long and low, like battle galleys."

"Oh, that's exactly what is intended," Feran quickly assured her. "The running lamps are attached low on the sides of deep-water traders so they look to be battle galleys. The ruse only works in the dark, but then that is half the day covered, is it not so?"

"Clever."

"Still, they are stronger than us, and that gives me concern. Anything bigger than a scoreboat gives me concern. The pickings are rich in Torea, and nobody likes rivals where gold is concerned. Strong rivals are met with threats, bluster, and displays of force. Rivals our size are sunk."

Velander turned away from the horizon, nodding in agreement. Finding the burned-out Silverdeath was only part of their agenda, Laron had told her. Gleaning melted gold from the ruins of the inland cities and towns was another. The river systems of Torea came close to most of the great inland cities, and Banzalo's miserable but sprawling empire was now the biggest gold mine in the world. If they were fast they would have first choice of the wealth, return to Helion rich, make the Metrologans rich, and remove Silverdeath from Banzalo's grasp, all with the one voyage. She noted that the distant ships were almost all out of sight now.

"It's as if a rich man's house has suddenly collapsed, killing him and leaving no heirs," said Feran. "All his wealth is there for the taking."

"In their haste to rummage through the ruins, nobody is stopping to ask what brought down the house in the first place," replied Velander. "Which of his neighbors' houses will be next?"

Feran did not wish to continue that line of thought, and he lapsed into silence. Velander turned back to the sea and watched the distant ships until the last light winked out.

Laron was still in his cabin when he heard a squeal of outrage, followed by a sharp slap. As he came out on deck to take the watch he was passed by Feran, who was hastening below. Velander was looking back along the *Shadowmoon*'s phosphorescent wake, to where the planet Caspelli was blazing brilliant just above the horizon. Laron took a bearing from the stars, using the angulant, then checked the rigging and the angle at which the steering pole had been lashed by Feran. Velander told him about the fleet.

"Could I take the angulant readings?" asked Velander as Laron lifted the instrument from its rack.

"Of course, Worthy Sister," Laron replied pleasantly, offering the angulant to her.

"Feran offered to teach me some of the finer points of navigation just now," she continued. "Very quickly his hands began navigating their way under my clothing."

"That should have been no surprise. Well, my cabin is now vacant."

"Your bed is never warm."

"Ah, but that is because I am cool in times of danger, and these are dangerous times. Have you finished with my farsight?"

"Yes, but I saw no stars through the rings," she said, returning it to him and being careful not to touch his skin.

"The truth is always there, should you wish to try again later. People can win arguments to the contrary, but truth is like me: unkillable."

The *Shadowmoon* landed on the north coast of Torea two days later, at the ruins of Fontarian. The shallow draft of the little schooner allowed it to go in quite close before the gigboat had to be launched. Fused sand crunched and splintered under the thick leather soles of their boots, but there were other footprints there already. There was also evidence of digging around some of the larger public buildings and mansions. Not a single plant grew, and there were no insects at all, yet the river that emptied into the harbor provided clear, clean water.

"Already the looters have been here," Feran concluded as he emerged from a roughly dug trench with a scrap of broken metal.

"Those who dug the trench, or us?" Velander asked.

"This is a piece of Cyronese ax-blade, probably from a makeshift hoe. You can tell by the shallow scalloping just back from the edge. The Cyronese did not have their homeland burned, however. The gold in these ruins is all that we have left; we have a right to it."

"Ah, so you are Torean-born, sir?" asked Laron.

"Just Torean," replied Feran.

Velander gave a slight sneer and tossed a stone into the trench. "Wherever you come from, you talk like Banzalo," she said.

Feran put the fragment of ax in a pouch and dusted his hands. "So, you side with the looters?"

"No, I merely point out that Torea is ruled by anarchy. We can keep what we find if we are able to defend it. All the seafaring kingdoms of Lemtas, Acrema, Scalticar, and Armaria will soon join the lucky merchant ship whose crew has been digging here. They will bring marines and battle galleys as well as slaves to dig, and there will be fighting. Nothing is as sure as that. Peace will only come to Torea when everything of value has been stripped."

They began walking back over the fused sand to the water's edge, where the gigboat was beached. Migratory seabirds were feasting on the body of something, fighting noisily over the putrid scraps. Other than that there was only silence and stillness.

"What is that thing?" asked Laron, oblivious to the smell.

"Dead," replied Velander.

"It has four flippers, and a neck longer than the *Shadowmoon*."

"Is it Silverdeath?" asked Feran.

"No, sir, but—"

"Then let's get back to the boat. There are looter ships only hours behind us."

"Another hour, that's all," Laron pleaded.

Laron took measurements of the thickness of melting in the sand, and the degree to which various metals had been affected. The other crewmen foraged for scraps of gold and silver spurned by the Cyronese looters, who had been after better pickings. Finally Feran gave Laron the choice of sailing on or being left behind. With curious and unexplained reluctance, Laron returned to the boat with them. More than a third of the voyage still lay ahead as they began skirting the coast of the dead continent.

"Expecting to meet someone?" asked Druskarl.

"Expecting a delivery of livestock, actually," admitted Laron.

"I wish you would not use that word."

"Why?"

"*Baa.*"

"Oh, very well, point taken."

"Are you sure you know what you are doing?" asked Druskarl as Laron measured out a few drops of potion into a mug of wine.

The sun was long down, and they were alone on the quarterdeck. Atmospheric dust from the fire-circles was scattering Miral's light to give the night sky the semblance of a vast, green dome.

"You will sleep for an hour, no more."

"But for what purpose?"

"For the advancement of knowledge, to enhance the study of natural philosophies, to push back the dark frontiers of ignorance—"

"To do something unspeakably stupid and dangerous."

"Not dangerous, just . . . difficult."

"Why not do it yourself?"

"The subject has to be alive."

"And is *this* subject liable to be alive at the end of an hour?" demanded Druskarl, tapping his own chest.

"You have my word upon it."

"That fails to inspire confidence."

"Druskarl, Druskarl, what I propose is a little exercise in the transference of souls. In time I might be able to do the same with your own soul."

"What do you mean?"

"I could very well transfer your soul into a body whose balls are still attached."

Druskarl thought about this for a moment, then held out his hand for the mug. He drained it with one swallow, settled back against the backboard, and quickly drifted into oblivion. Laron took out the oracle frame and placed it on the eunuch's shaven head. It sat loose as the vampyre pressed Ninth's sphere into the grasp of the three open claws. He spoke a casting, then clasped the double handful of luminous nothingness over frame and head. All at once the claws snapped shut, and the arms of the frame began to merge with Druskarl's skull. The eunuch stirred and opened his eyes.

Immediately the auton toppled sideways, then lashed out in panic. She had never controlled a real body, and the use of muscles was foreign to her. Laron tried to calm her.

"Don't try to move, Ninth. Don't move at all. Just lie there."

Ninth lay still, and gradually her breathing slowed. After some encouragement she was able to make a fist, then move an arm. After some intensive coaching she could sit up, but speech came only with difficulty. The effect of Ninth speaking with Druskarl's voice was more unsettling than amusing. More minutes passed. The auton girl's control of Druskarl's body improved.

"How . . . long?" she managed laboriously.

"Only a few minutes more. Your host is drugged, and when he wakes, you will be forced from his body."

"*Hisss* . . . body?" she exclaimed, with all the alarm that slow, slurred speech would allow.

"Well, more or less. He is a eunuch. It is the best I could do in the circumstances."

Ninth moved Druskarl's limbs experimentally, then looked slowly about. A light wind was driving them east, and the sea was choppy. The sky was clear but faintly green, and Miral loomed huge on the eastern horizon. Laron held out a dried fig, and Ninth accepted it.

"*Tassste* . . . good," she reported. "Chewy . . . but . . . *sssucculent.*"

"Like some of the people I have dined upon."

She stood up slowly, with Laron helping. She managed two steps, then had to sit down again.

"We can do this again, practice until you are confident."

"You . . . *ssso* . . . young."

"You mean you were expecting someone taller," laughed Laron. "Well, my body is but fourteen, and Druskarl is a head taller than most of us."

An awkward silence followed.

"What do you think of the *Shadowmoon*?" asked Laron.

"Neat, compact. . . . Feel faint. . . ."

"Druskarl is waking. Quickly! Sit down, lie back."

"Laron . . ."

Laron applied another casting, and the frame came free of Druskarl's scalp as he stirred. At a touch from Laron the claws released the violet sphere. Laron had everything packed away as Druskarl opened his eyes. The big eunuch immediately felt his throat.

"Such suspicion," said Laron, shaking his head. "I feel hurt."

"As long as *I* don't feel any hurt I am not concerned. Did your test work?"

"Yes, it did. In fact, the prospects for more advanced exercises along the same lines are very good."

Laron had a lot to think about after that. The auton could be taken for a girl with slow wits, but now what? She would need a large amount of coaching before she could be trusted to fend for herself.

The ruins of Gironal were utterly still as the *Shadowmoon* approached the entrance to its harbor. Scouts in the corrak reported that a two-masted Vidarian oared trader was already there, lying at anchor. It was heavily armed, with two ballistas mounted on the foredeck and maindeck, and boarding dropways drawn up beside the foremast. Feran gave the order to lower the *Shadowmoon*'s masts as they waited for evening.

"We must sink to just below the surface, then come in with the tide," said Feran as they sealed and secured everything that was not proofed against water. "We should be swept past the trader and near to the river mouth. After that we must rely on oars."

"Underwater?" asked Velander.

"It's hard and slow, but we have done it before," the deckswain assured her. "You twist them for a thin profile on the reach stroke, then twist them broad for the pull stroke. Of course, you only do a couple of strokes before returning to the gigboat for breath, so progress tends to be slow."

"When we reach the river mouth we shall be out of sight of the trader, so we can surface and bail," Feran concluded. "By morning we should be far enough inland that their scouting parties will not see us."

"There is an easier way," Laron suggested.

"That being?" asked Feran.

"I must retire to my cabin now, but be patient and lie at anchor for a couple of days. All of us shall profit."

The sailors of the morning watch on the *Oakheart* were not reluctant to go on duty. The ship was at anchor in a dead port, and there were some very special benefits to guard duty in this particular place. As they came on deck they were not surprised to find just a single man on the quarterdeck.

"All quiet, Hallas?" the officer called.

"Aye. The others of the night watch are ashore, guarding the city."

Those who had been ashore had found the usual splashes of silver and gold where purses had been dropped by Gironal's citizens, dead before they fell, while the gutters were choked with roofing lead that had flowed like rainwater then solidified. The heat had shattered, cracked, powdered, and melted the stonework, and every tiled roof in the city had fallen in after the timber beams had flashed into ashes. Across the water, the city moaned softly as the wind blew through the burned-out shells of the buildings. Some of the crewmen thought the sounds were those of ghosts, elementals, and demons warning them to stay away, but that did not stop anybody going ashore to literally pick up gold in the streets.

"Aren't they due back?" asked the officer.

"Aye, we want to guard the city as well," added one of his men.

They were interrupted by a trumpet's echoing notes from across the water. One long note, three shorter.

"That's for death!" gasped the officer.

When the boat finally reached the shore, the survivor was

found perched at the top of a broken column, with discarded bags of gold at the base. After being persuaded to come down, he guided them to where two others were lying dead. Their throats had been torn out and their eyes bulged with terror.

"Just found 'em like that," babbled the survivor. "I was only twenty yards away, behind that ruined wall, yet I heard nothing."

The officer examined both bodies.

"Both cold. They're long dead."

The following morning a pair on watch aboard the *Oakheart* were found dead, both lying at their posts. As before, their throats had been savaged.

"It's followed us out here," said the officer. "That spirit-thing from the ruins."

"Issue weapons from the locker, then search the ship," ordered the shipmaster.

The search was thorough, beginning at the bow and ending at the aft railing of the quarterdeck. Nothing was found, but one more man was found to be missing as the crew reported in. Another search found his body in the bilgewater.

"I'm beginning to worry about Laron," said Velander. "Two days, yet there's no sign of him."

"More to the point is the two days lost," said Feran. "We can't live off the land, and there's probably not even fish in the rivers."

He was interrupted by a signal from the lookout on the shore. He reported that the *Oakheart* was under way and sailing with the tide. They waited another hour, during which time the tide turned. Laron swam out and climbed aboard as they were raising the anchor.

"Just what did you do?" asked Feran.

"I had dinner with them."

"Dinner? You never even have dinner with us. What did you really do?"

"I shocked them with my table manners. Now, be quick and get moving."

By the next morning the *Shadowmoon* had ventured twenty miles up the broad Dioran River, with the aid of a strong easterly wind. The current was sluggish, so it was not hard to make headway at first. After another two days the wind died away, and the current strengthened as the river narrowed. Soon the *Shadowmoon* could no longer make good headway with sweeps. They tied up beside a stone bridge that had survived the fire-circles, although it was hung with icicles of melted stone. It linked the northern and southern ruins of a city that straddled the river. The gigboat was unclamped and launched. Feran, Velander, Druskarl, and Laron prepared to set off for Larmentel as Miral rose like a vast bow and arrow, about an hour before the dawn.

"What are your orders?" asked the deckswain as Feran prepared to cast off.

"Keep guard, forage for anything useful, and don't eat too much."

Five hundred miles north, at the mouth of the Temellier River, the town of Port Banzalo had swelled to two thousand souls by the time the regent had arrived to be crowned emperor. Masons had fashioned stone dwellings, and gardens of silt and seaweed compost had been planted with the first tomatoes, beans, and onions. Sea lettuce and veriden was being dried on racks, alongside fish caught offshore. Little had been done to mine the nearby ruins for gold, because there was no need for money yet.

Emperor Banzalo was crowned in the town plaza, which was smaller in area than the deck of his flagship. He then left for Gironal with his fleet. The tiny capital settled back into the routine of building, dredging silt, and planting crops. The chickens were flourishing on a diet of fish scraps and veriden, and newly hatched chicks were learning to scratch.

Prosus Hayport had become a landowner in return for serving in the town militia. He and his brother Crasfi took watches together to ensure that looters did not land to plunder the new emperor's gold, and to prevent the settlers from escalating petty squabbles into fights with axes.

"Cold night," said Prosus.

"Dawn soon," Crasfi replied.

"In ten years we could have quite a crowd, Crasfi," Prosus speculated.

"Got a crowd now," said his dour, terse brother.

"But in ten years we'll have a big town to feed, and a lot of scraps from the carters. I've ordered goats from Helion, two breedin' pairs. They'll change scraps into goat wool, milk, cheese, an' butter."

"Chickens," responded Crasfi. "Faster return."

"Can't wear feathers, brother, least I can't. Now—"

Prosus stopped in midsentence, staring hard out to sea and putting a hand on Crasfi's arm for silence.

"Thought I heard splashin'," he explained. "D'ye hear splashin'?"

"Hear a lot of that wi' oceans. Waves cause it."

"Could be a ship."

"Miral's up, we'd see a ship."

"Gigboats, then, from a raider," said Prosus, reaching for a brass handbell. "There! See the low shadows? Three gigboats, no, six—ten. No, no, maybe— Dragonshit! There's dozens!"

Prosus began ringing the handbell, still not believing what was before his eyes. All at once other raiders that had approached overland from a nearby cove charged. The two watchmen were wearing leather and band-plate, but their helmets were somewhere in the shadows and out of reach. Crasfi lunged at one charging shadow with his spear, skewering the man, but another engaged him as he tried to pull the spear free, chopping into his skull and dropping him where he stood. Prosus thrust out with his spear, catching a raider in the thigh, then he dropped his spear and drew his grandfather's campaign ax. He swung at shadows, hit armor and cut flesh. For an instant a head was silhouetted against the stars. Prosus chopped down and cut deep into the neck, then a mace smashed into his upper back, crushing his spine.

Other settlers burst from their new stone houses to find the enemy already swarming over the low drystone walls at the perimeter. The militiamen had been expecting to deal with undisciplined shiploads of looters, but this was a tactically well-planned attack by battle-hardened marines. Screams mingled with cries of pain as women and children tried to flee, only to be cut down without mercy. To their credit a few Vidarian settlers rallied and formed a line behind a drystone wall, but now screams and cries burst out behind them as the seaborne raiders struck from the beach at the enclave of stone houses. Some militiamen broke and ran for their families, others held firm at the wall.

"Helmets, they all wear helmets!" shouted a settler.

"Kill those with helmets—" another shouted before being cut down.

All the fighting was by the dim light of Lupan and Belvia, and the raiders were distinguished only by their plumed helmets and glimmering chain-mail. Their experience, discipline, and coordination overwhelmed the Vidarian defenders as much as their sheer numbers, and they showed neither mercy nor chivalry to the defeated and defenseless.

Prosus awoke, his legs paralyzed, his ax still in his hand. The sky was lightening with dawn. There were screams and entreaties all around him from women who had been kept alive for the amusement of the victors, and the *crunch, crunch, crunch* of boots walking nearby.

"This one's alive."

Thunk.

"Now 'e's not."

"Better get along, or there'll be no fluff alive for us."

Crunch, crunch, crunch, the boots came closer. Hands scrabbled for a hold on Prosus' leather and band armor.

"Hoy, nice ax—"

Prosus stabbed blindly for the figure towering over him, and the forepoint of his ax glided between chain-mail and trews, through a tunic, into an abdomen, sliced through a heart, and jammed into a shoulder joint. A mace thudded down, crushing his skull. The second, third, fourth, and fifth blows were quite unnecessary, but in view of what had happened to his companion in the darkness, the raider was taking no chances. Between them, Prosus and Crasfi had killed three raiders, a quarter of all the losses among Warsovran's marines.

∗ *∗* *∗*

Two days later the deepwater trader *Greenfoam* dropped anchor offshore and a gigboat was lowered to the water. From the window of the master cabin the shipmaster and Heldey watched the rowers pulling at their oars from the comfort of the bunk.

"We should get dressed," she suggested. "Prosus be as jealous as he be loyal."

"Ach, he can't get out to the ship without my say-so." He ran his hand along her leg, smiling into her face all the while. "I slowed our voyage to get a couple days more with you, but it was worth it. Heldey, you're too good for a shitraker like him."

"Ho, shitrakers like him will be great lords in ten years."

"And their wives will look like they've raked shit for ten years. Look at me. I'm clean, rich, and pleasing to be abed with—and my bed is comfortable."

"You have a wife in Palion."

"Aye, and another on Racital. So? You're shapely, even after two children, and look how fine your hair and skin have become after a few weeks of care on the *Greenfoam*. Stay."

"I love my children."

"Pah, their balls have dropped, they're practically men. Look, I used to spend much time ashore with my wives, but with all the trade and wealth that Torea's fall has spawned . . . I cannot afford not to be at sea, taking opportunities as they present. Heldey, you're beautiful, yet strong, a rare woman who can live happily on a ship yet be very pleasing to the eye. I am in my thirty-eighth year, Heldey, and I have maybe twenty years at sea ahead of me, the prime of my life. I want to live as a man for those years, not a monk."

Heldey turned away from him, looking wistfully to the shore.

"Such a ragged little ruin," she said. "Not even smoke."

"Pah, they have too little wood to burn, they light fires only to cook. Do you really fancy eating raw fish and onions with bread made from rough-ground corn?"

The shipmaster gave her an affectionate slap on the rump and rolled off the bunk to get dressed. The boat had reached the shore by now, but nobody had come out to meet them. This seemed odd to Heldey. The ship had fresh supplies, families, and . . . Where was Prosus? Prosus was very sentimental about his family; he doted on his sons. Those from the boat were walking to the township.

"Someone is waving flags!" exclaimed Heldey.

The half-dressed shipmaster stepped over to the bunk and looked out of the window with his arm around Heldey's neck and his hand on her left breast.

"This is standard code, it says, 'CATASTROPHE—ALL—DEAD.' O gods of the moonworlds!"

The shipmaster dashed out of his cabin in only his kilt and seaboots, shouting for the crew to make ready to sail in an instant. Word trickled back from the distant signalman. The town had been laid to waste, and every man, woman, and child was either dead or missing. The dead had been left to lie where they had fallen. The gardens had been stripped and trampled, the chickens were gone, the timber stores had been burned, and all the stone walls and buildings demolished.

"We counted eight hundred dead, all Vidarian men, women, and children," the oar sergeant reported to the *Greenfoam*'s shipmaster as they came aboard again. "I estimate there were about a thousand raiders wearing studnail boots of a common pattern, and their tracks showed good discipline and tactical work."

"But who were they, and why were they here?" demanded the shipmaster.

"They were from some army, and they were here to annihilate the place. Whatever could not be carried off was smashed or spoiled. Even the timber racks were burned. They were thorough and disciplined. Privateers are not like that."

"They even burned the timber? Timber is worth more than gold on Torea. It is useful to everyone, whether looters, settlers, or . . ."

"Warsovran's marines," said the oar sergeant, holding up an

ornate Darmarian knife that he had found embedded in one of the bodies.

There was a clamor from down on the maindeck, and after a few moments Heldey came clattering up the steps shouting colorful abuse at the sailors who had tried to restrain her. Her sons were behind her, and she came up to the shipmaster with an arm around each boy. The shipmaster spread his arms helplessly.

"Nobody ashore is alive," he said gently.

"But—"

"Warsovran's raiders. Had I not liked your company, and so chosen a slower current to dawdle on our journey here . . . we might have arrived a couple of days earlier. My thanks to you, Heldey. You saved us all."

They put to sea again, steering for the next settlement down the coast. Around sunset they met with a fishing boat that had been at sea when the invaders had struck. The crew reported seeing a large squadron of lateen-rigged galleys with the blue sunburst emblem of Warsovran on the mainsails. Miraculously, the much smaller craft had not been sighted. The fishermen had later landed at the settlement of Dramil and discovered two survivors: the Metrologan priestess sent by Terikel, and a young stonemason had been in nearby ruins on the evening that the invaders struck. They had watched the attack by Miral's light and stayed hidden until dawn, when the invaders began tearing down the buildings and hunting for survivors to abduct as slaves.

"You say you were surveying the site for a Metrologan chapel, Worthy Justiva," said the shipmaster.

"That is correct."

"At night?"

"I wanted to survey the effect of Miral's light on the chosen place. Light is very important to achieve a sense of serenity in our ceremonies."

"Miral was not up."

"I mean, er, the moonworlds Lupan and Belvia."

"And the stonemason?"

"He was advising me on technical matters."

"According to the fishing boat's master, your surveying equipment consisted of one bedroll and half a jar of claret—all the way from central Acrema."

The young priestess scowled. "Celibacy is now optional among the Metrologans," she muttered.

Oddly enough, this was the admission the shipmaster had been probing for.

"Ah yes, and the announcement was declared very recently. Too recently for a spy from Warsovran's fleet to have known. Very well, Worthy Sister, I accept your story. Your tumble with the mason has not only saved you from the Damarian marines, it has convinced me not to cut your throat."

Suddenly Justiva felt unreserved sympathy for Terikel, who also had been saved by being in the wrong bed at the right time.

Without further investigation the *Greenfoam*'s shipmaster turned from the coast and headed northwest with the fishing boat in tow. The shipmaster noted that on the twenty-eighth day of the seventh month of 3140, the towns of the new Vidarian empire had fallen to Darmarian marines from Warsovran's ships. It had been the largest empire in Torea's history, but had lasted barely a month from foundation to fall.

Velander noticed that the landscape of inland Torea was changing remarkably as they pushed deeper into the continent. The regions close to Larmentel had been repeatedly seared, so that instead of a crust of vitrified sand there was generally a layer of glass, lava, or rock slag. There were occasional choppy lakes of petrified red-glass waves near the river, breakers of glass frozen while bursting over hills, towns half drowned in glass that had flowed down hills and solidified, and cities that had melted into themselves. Most of the inland ruins were so severely melted and pulverized, that chipping the gold out of them probably would be far more trouble than it was worth.

Fifteen miles after leaving the *Shadowmoon*, the gigboat turned into the Bax River. The river water was quite clean and clear, as there was no silt and soil running off the land, only a little dust brought down by the raindrops. Wrecks of barges

were visible beneath the surface, and small fish fed on the remains of humans and animals who had escaped charring, only
to die when they surfaced and tried to breathe superheated air.
There were odd, sloping forests of glass spikes ornamented by
colored frills, and amid the nearby mountains they could see
glass and blackstone glaciers frozen solid, destined neither to
retreat nor advance ever again. The single sign of activity on
the landscape was the volcano, Mount Delchan, which was
sending a trickle of smoke into the sky, and occasionally rumbling.

It was six days after entering the Bax River that they reached
the little inland port of Tra'Vant, which once had serviced Larmentel. Very little that remained of it was recognizable, even as
a ruin. The vitrified surface crunched beneath the stubby spikes
of Velander's clogs as she walked ashore, but it was the sheer
silence that made the greatest impression on her. After weeks of
ceaselessly creaking ropes and timbers, then the rattle and
splash of oars, the hush over the inner continent was like losing
one's hearing.

The river port had endured eight of the fire-circles, and was
far worse affected than anything they had seen so far. The clay
in the bricks had shattered and crumbled, leaving only the mor-
tar outline in frail, fantastic lattices of fused glass in the vague
outline of walls. The thick crust of glass sometimes crunched
and splintered under their feet, slashing at the thick, spiked
hardwood clogs they had carved while at sea. Ruined stone
walls dripped with glass icicles in colors that had swirled,
blended, and flowed in the heat and now glowed and sparkled
as sunlight fell upon them and refracted through them. Frozen
cascades of lead, gold, silver, and copper filled the gutters beneath layers of semi-opaque glass. There was no stench of rotting offal or raw sewage; in fact, the glass which coated the
roadway was clean enough to eat from.

"This place has been burned many times over," Feran said as
he stood looking about.

"Eight," said Laron, a moment before Velander opened her
mouth to speak the same figure.

"Look there on the ground, the sand is not just a fused crust, it's thick, cloudy glass," said Druskarl. "The walls of brick have become red powder."

"Can you imagine death on this scale?" asked Velander. "Not a fly in the air, not an ant walking. I once passed through here, about four years ago. I remember the bustle, the street criers, even the stench of rotten fish-heads and dung carts. Now it is clean, pure and dead. They're all dead, every one of those who spoke with me or sold me bread and dried figs. Not a child, not a grandmother, nobody left alive. There was a boy named Massoff who sold me fresh apples. He was quite handsome and had a most charming manner. Who will remember Massoff, now that his family, friends, rulers, customers, lovers, and enemies are all dead? All their faces are ash upon the wind, coloring the sunsets as red as blood on a battlefield."

The others shivered, but did not reply. No words could possibly encompass death on such a scale.

Feran, Velander, Laron, and Druskarl set off in the early afternoon, leaving the gigboat sunk and weighted down with glass icicles in the river. After two hours of determined walking over the smooth, sterile ground, they passed over the boundary of the seventh fire-circle. A great ring of glass had been pushed up a yard high in an immense, circular, frozen wave that extended out over nine miles from the center of Larmentel. As they climbed over it, Velander noticed an ax-blade buried in the glass crest, the metal as perfect as when it left the master craftsman's shop where it had been forged. The wood, brass, and leather of the handle were gone.

A recent earth tremor had fractured a frozen ripple of glass, revealing nests of perfect crystals of green, orange, rose, and aqua. Velander carefully extracted a selection and put them in her pack.

"Are they worth something, Worthy Sister?" asked Druskarl.

"I cannot say. I just know that I must have a few."

From time to time they passed through little woodlands of spiral-shaped spikes of glass that freakish currents of air had teased up before they set. Some were the size of large trees, others were no longer than a dagger.

"These are like souls of the dead, held down and frozen on their way to the afterlife," said Laron as he caressed a lime-green spiral no taller than Velander. "The curves are so sensual, almost like breasts."

"And what are these tiny ones?" asked Velander, who was on her knees and peering at some little spirals of sky blue.

"Souls of mice?" said Druskarl.

"Well, then, nobody here will miss a few mice," she said as she reached for her pickhammer.

Rain had fallen since the fire-circles, and had collected in clear puddles that were quite fit to drink from. There was no dust but a thin smear washed out of the sky by the rain. Brought up in a world where dust is taken for granted, Velander had great trouble accepting the smooth, sterile lifelessness of the lands she was traveling through. For one mile the glass was cerulean-blue ripples, shot through with milky-white streaks, then it changed to speckled red. At five miles they reached another immense circle's rim, and after this there were jumbled mounds of white like ghosts caught in a pool of frozen milk.

"Four and two-thirds miles," Velander commented as they slithered and struggled over the glass.

Presently there were ruins, but these were just mounds of fused rock. Some were bubbled and jagged like scoria, other mounds were as smooth as the surface of polished jade inlay. Glass icicles hung here, too, but there were also long, flexible threads of glass that waved, tangled, and then untangled with every breeze. On some threads hung globes of glass, and the wind played tunes on the taut threads while the globes tinkled accompaniment.

"So beautiful," breathed Velander in wonder at a tiny cluster of glass chimes hanging from thin glass fibers. "Can this really be just an accident?"

"It's as if some god was trying to make up for all its devastation with these exquisite little gifts," Laron speculated.

"I once studied for a year at the University of Larmental," said Velander. "It was all towers and walkways, high in the air, and very serene and quiet. I hate to say it, and I know that the price of all this was millions of deaths, yet it is almost as beautiful in death as it was in life."

At dusk they stopped in a field of azure glass that was fringed by melted, skewed stumps of columns. Close by were the city walls, or more precisely, the breakwater of greenish grey glass that marked where the walls had stood. They decided to stop for the night and travel the last three miles in the morning. The surface was hard and cold, and not conducive to easy sleep. Velander took the first half of the watch, and Druskarl the second. Laron went some distance away to be dead in private.

The rising sun cast gleaming highlights and scintillations over the melted landscape as the travelers breakfasted. The last miles to the center were over a progressively more melted and uniform landscape of huge, circular, petrified ripples over which they had to clamber with the aid of handspikes and ropes. Between the ripples were shallow expanses of trapped rainwater. The sky was clear, and there was no wind. Neither were there any birds or leatherwings. Nothing but the four travelers moved or made a sound, yet they glanced about constantly, feeling very, very exposed. There was an irrational sense of being watched, as if everything nearby was lying still for fear that something huge and deadly would awake and pounce. They told each other that all was silent because everything was many months dead, but that did not seem to help. As they climbed over the last and highest of the frozen glass ripples, they beheld a circular lake, about a half mile across. Velander sat down and removed her clogs as the others entered the water. It proved to be only calf-deep and was absolutely clear, but as they waded out across the water their feet stirred up a thin layer of precipitated dust. They spread out as they reached the area of the center, where the water was knee-deep.

"Something ahead, something white," Feran called.

It was a skeleton. Decay progressed slowly in this sterile wasteland, yet the body had been reduced to bones and scraps

of clothing. Another body was found nearby. Velander was
shaken, wondering who might have reached this place before
them, and wondering, too, why they might have killed each
other.

"His coins and rings are untouched," said Velander, reluctantly examining the first body.

"Murdered for their silence," concluded Feran. "Marines in
Warsovran's navy wear standardized greaves like these."

"Found something," called Druskarl in Diomedan. "An imprint in the glass."

"You mean another body?" asked Feran.

"More like an area has been dug out. It's about a yard
square."

They converged on Druskarl, who held up a piece of broken,
greenish glass. Velander eagerly reached for it and held it close to
her face. There was a percussion point on one side, but imprinted
in the flat surface was a pattern of circles with triangular arms
and other decorations. Druskarl pointed to an area about the size
of an adult's torso, where the glass on the bottom had been dug
away. Somebody had smashed it out with a heavy pickhammer.

"The quiescent form of Silverdeath is a jacket of jewelry,"
said Velander. "The basic unit is made up of circles with three
arms. Each arm interlocks with an arm of three other circles."

She handed the glass it back to Druskarl.

"That's enough proof," concluded Druskarl. "Silverdeath *did*
survive the fire-circles that it generated, and it has already been
salvaged."

"Ow!" cried Velander, hopping about on one foot. "I found
another chunk of glass—or it found me."

"Keep it," said Laron. "If someone thought to remove the
other chunks, they might be worth something."

They spent the rest of the day examining the glass crater, but
found nothing else other than some more stray chunks of glass.
Eventually Velander and Druskarl left to set up camp for the
night.

"Well, there is not much more to do," said Laron to Feran as
they waded through the water, searching for anything that
might have been missed in earlier passes.

"So, navigator, what else should we do?" asked Feran. "It's a long way to come again if we have missed something."

Laron stopped, tossed a chunk of imprinted glass in the air and caught it again. "This glass came in contact with Silverdeath and was also at the center of every fire-circle. Its feel suggests quite a potent warp in the fabric between etherworlds."

"Ah, so that is why Warsovran chipped out all the other imprinted glass along with the mailshirt," Feran concluded.

"That is a logical premise, fit to be taken seriously. It is more likely, however, that some areas of the fabric were partly embedded in the solid glass and he wanted to remove them slowly, and at leisure. This piece probably just fell off and he ignored it. Look, here's another," he said as he reached down into the water.

They made their way to the camp, and sat down with Velander and Druskarl.

"Such an awesome place," said Druskarl, folding his arms tightly and shivering. "I can hardly imagine what happened here."

"The weapon assumed the form of an immense bubble when it was discharged," said Feran. "It floated high above Torea until it was lost to view, then the fire poured down. That's what the spies told us, anyway. As for the ending—who knows? I suspect the bubble reverted to a shirt of metal interlacings when the ocean's vastness quenched the fourteenth fire-circle, hundreds of miles away. With its cycle of doubled regeneration broken, it would have fallen from the sky into the molten glass and rock below. I expect it would have sunk deep and out of reach at once, but perhaps it floated down as slowly as a bubble, then reverted to its usual form only a few feet above the ground. That way the glass would have had a chance to harden somewhat."

"Whoever murdered the two marines arrived here just weeks after the catastrophe, and knew exactly where to go," said Druskarl.

Feran nodded. "The armor, the weapons, the coins—all are typical of Warsovran's marines."

"Warsovran must have known what would happen," said Laron. "He has the thing back, I know it."

"Then we have failed," said Feran. "Let us hope and pray that he has the sense not to use it again."

✦ ✦ ✦

The daylight was yielding to a brilliant tapestry of stars, Miral, and the moonworlds. A watch was not thought necessary, as by now they had accepted how very alone they were in this place. Feran was lying asleep, but Velander sat up in her bedding as Laron and Druskarl prepared to leave again.

"I am going to conduct some quick tests back at the central glass crater," Laron explained. "I only need Druskarl to help, but you are welcome to join us."

"And stand up to my knees in water again?" muttered Velander.

"Lacking a boat, yes."

"What are you going to do?"

"It seems to be a place of exceptional etheric power," replied Laron. "As Feran said, this is not an easy place to reach, so we should make the most of it. What do you say? Miral will not be up for much longer, so we need to get moving."

"You, not 'we.'"

"All right, all right," said Laron as they turned away. "What did I tell you, Druskarl? Cast pearls at swine and what do you get?"

"Muddy pearls?"

Once they were gone Velander crawled across to where Laron had dropped his bedding and shroud. If this was a place of exceptional power, then there were more ways to explore it than by merely standing in cold water and doing whatever he intended to do. She rummaged in his packroll. Sure enough, there was the iron case she had noticed him carrying. He had left it behind; he obviously did not wish to get it wet and rusty. Guard autons would not bind on pure iron, so it was probably a matter of merely releasing the catch to open it. As the hinges creaked open she saw the circlet gleaming in Miral's light.

Velander removed the circlet from the iron case and fingered it, contemplating its strangeness. It was plain but graceful to the untutored eye, yet very obviously from another world. The ma-

terial had a strangely silky feel. It was as smooth as glass, yet
not cold, almost like a leather strap. Perhaps an etherworld
tether of some sort? she wondered. She had never owned one
before.

Velander was aware that Silverdeath would stand out like a
beacon in the etherworld. Even if it was miles away she would
be able to see it. Nobody on the *Shadowmoon* had considered
the possibility that a boat from the *Oakheart* might have gone
up the river just ahead of them. Banzalo, not Warsovran, might
have taken Silverdeath. If that were the case, he might still be
nearby. After setting up camp, she had conducted several ether
resonance tests, and had found an exceedingly powerful presence close by. That could have been nothing else but Silverdeath, she was sure of it. It was just a matter of logic; the
Queen of Soulmates had come to her aid again. *She* had pointed
the way to Silverdeath after they had given up hope. Velander
put the circlet on her head, then smiled. She began to speak
castings. Just a few minutes, then she would raise the alarm and
give them Silverdeath's direction and approximate distance.

The gateway incantation was easy. It was like jumping into
a deep chasm: anyone could do it, but it was an exceedingly
bad idea unless one knew how to fly. Velander knew the me-
chanics of darkwalking, but had done it only twice, and under
close supervision.

A word of detachment allowed her senses to dissolve out of
her body into what she thought would be blackness shot
through with pinpoints of glow. Instead, lights blazed up
around her, causing her disembodied senses to reel and cower.
Starburst shapes drifted amid retinues of spinning violet rings,
while spiral-shaped comets spun showers of sparks that orbited
out to fall back again. Spheres of shimmering silver pulsated as
they hovered about an intense vertical line of orange light, and
Velander noticed that everything was slowly circling the orange
brilliance.

Velander hurriedly checked for her tether, the circlet. It was
close by, a band of firmness in the confused background of the
etherworld. Nearby, barely visible, were two thin lines of
light—the two larger chunks of glass from where Silverdeath

had fallen, Velander realized. They were a small part of the axis, and they retained its properties as tether points. No wonder the earlier visitor to this place had removed a bagful. She wondered what all the magical entities were doing here, at the center of a dead continent. A lazily rotating snowflake shape of silver and turquoise broke from its orbit and drifted in her direction. Velander retreated to the center of the tether's firmness. The snowflake drifted away again. She thought back to her years of study. Swarming here were probably the sorcerers, ethersmiths, charmshapers, and initiates whose souls were in the etherworld when the waves of fire lashed over their bodies. Across all of Torea, that had probably amounted to quite a large number. They circled the axis from which the burning tori had blazed out. Perhaps the fire-circles sucked them here or swept them up like an immense broom. They were consciousness, but unlike Velander, they had no anchor in her reality.

The young priestess drifted closer to the axis of orange light. There was nothing familiar there, but what she did find was a focus of attention. The deaths of all these initiates had originated here, and now their very awareness of it gave the place substance. Velander remembered her previous two darkwalkings. The forms had been somehow better defined then. Months had passed since the end of Torea, and all of these had been cut off from their living bodies. They were all dying, noticeably more transparent and faint than she remembered seeing in her previous experience. They moved sluggishly, yet some had sawtooth hooks and barbed tendrils. Even as she watched, a lurid snowflake sent a tendril floating lazily out after one of the glowing globes. The globe flinched away, but not quite fast enough. The tendril brushed the globe, caught, and drew taut. Slowly the snowflake began to draw itself over.

Raptor elementals, thought Velander, *predators of the etherworld.* The souls of living beings were too powerful for them to attack normally, but here they were all starving. Only the raptor elementals were equipped with weapons, and now the souls were losing their ability to evade them. The elemental closed with the globe and began to feed. Velander could watch no more, but as she moved away from the axis and back to her tether, something caught her attention. Something like light coming up from a well.

She moved across and looked into it. Her own world was laid out below her, lit by Miral's light. This was an ocular, she realized, an engine of pure etheric energy. Someone had left it to record the fire-circles, and it had survived. She was looking through the lens. The machine of ether was still chronicling images all these months after it had been set, but then, it was robust and simple. With no locks, and nothing to interpret the images it watched, it resolutely continued to function.

Suddenly the image jerked. A tracery of meshed fire had snared the filament binding the ocular to the ground. Velander watched, and presently Laron came into the field of view. The mesh extended from his hands, all the way across to—Druskarl. Their movements seemed strangely jerky and animated. That was due to the time-dilation effect in the etherworld, she realized. They had been trawling for oculars like this very one, and now she watched them attach it to a chunk of imprinted glass. They towed it back to the encampment and left it beside Laron's packroll. They did not notice that she was wearing the circlet before they left again.

"Miral is nearly down," said Druskarl as Laron selected a place to lie dead for the night.

"Less than a quarter hour," Laron estimated. "Still, time for a quick session of darkwalking."

"Is that wise? What if you delay your return until after Miral has set?"

"I have no idea, but this might be the time to find out."

"Sounds like I should stay and watch over you."

Velander gazed across at her own sleeping body. Her face was quite distinct in the light of Miral, and seemed utterly at peace. It was a body without the capability of consciousness. *Now,*

that is true innocence, Velander thought as she gazed at herself. With some amusement she recalled a story about a sorcerer who was watching himself through an ocular while darkwalking. He had not told his apprentice, though, and had watched as the youth spread a cloth on his chest, laid out a knife, bread, and cheese, then had lunch!

Suddenly Velander stared with disbelief. The body's eyes had opened. Velander's detached consciousness was paralyzed with shock for a moment. This was absolutely impossible. Very slowly, a hand came up, jerkily, as if it was being moved by invisible puppet strings. It touched the circlet. Her body now raised itself on an elbow, sat up, then pushed off the blankets. Its movements were now as smooth as those of a cat. It stood up and looked in the direction Laron and Druskarl had gone. Seemingly satisfied that they were out of sight, she minced over to where Feran was sleeping. She sat down beside him and shook him awake. They began to speak, and before long she took his hand and pressed it against her breasts.

Velander broke away from the ocular and made for her tether amid the sparkle-studded gloom of the etherworld. She poured herself back into her physical form—and spilled back out into the darkness. She tried again and again, each time with the same result. It was like trying to force water into a pail filled with sand.

By now terrified, she flashed back to the ocular. Something had possessed her body. *Impossible,* she thought, *only I know my truename.* Then the truth poured over her like a bucket of icy water. Her *body* did not have a truename! She had never thought to give it one, because she had never trained for solo darkwalking.

Velander dashed back to her tether and once more tried to flow back into herself. Again she was completely blocked. Something had probably noticed her and her tether, yet she had kept glancing back to her only link with her body . . . unless it had been an entity so faded that it was scarcely visible edge-on.

Desperate and terrified, she returned to the ocular. There, in the light of setting Miral, were she and Feran, naked on his bedding. She was kneeling, straddling him, and working up and down on his body. *I'm no longer a virgin,* Velander thought numbly. She began pounding with her control powers, trying to make them stop, shouting in a world with no sound.

Abruptly something jerked her back. She turned, saw a tendril embedded in her spherical form. She moved away with all her power, straining in the opposite direction. The barbs ripped out, trailing sparkles. Another barbed tentacle hit her, then another. Raptor elementals had surrounded her, lying edge-on in ambush. Wolf-pack tactics: Startle the prey into the middle of the pack. Raptor elementals were not known to hunt in packs, but then, they had never been studied at the center of a dead continent before. Something soundless that still had the effect of chittering and peeping boiled up around her as the elementals reeled themselves in. Sawtooth edges bit painlessly into her, yet she sensed the massive damage they were doing. Sparkles of light and color burst around her, sparkles of herself.

"Laaarronnn! Laaarronnn!"

There was no sound, yet she enunciated his name. Laron could help her, Laron had strange powers, Laron even knew mathematics.

✳ ✳ ✳

Laron abruptly returned to his body with a cry, then shook his head. He was still lying near the outer edge of the central crater. Druskarl was nearby, keeping watch.

"Was there a problem?" asked the eunuch. "What did you see in the etherworld?"

Laron drew breath slowly, searching for words.

"What a nightmare," he said at last. "So beautiful, yet . . . yet it was an island of despair in a rising flood of darkness."

"What do you mean?"

"I saw the souls of mortals who had been darkwalking at the time the firecircles killed their bodies. They were being stalked by starving raptor elementals."

"Mortals? How could they survive for so many months?"

"They were some of Torea's finest sorcerers when they died, so they had energy, speed, and skill. Now they are just slow bubbles of glimmer amid elementals that are little more than fangs and tendrils. While I was watching one mortal being stalked and killed, I heard it call my name. How could anything have recognized me in the etherworld, especially here? I was sickened and frightened." Laron sat shivering, hugging his knees.

"You? Laron, you have killed more people than I've eaten mutton pies."

"It was the feeling of despair, not the killing. It was hopelessness beyond words. Damn, Miral is nearly down. I am . . . unsettled. Will you watch over me tonight?"

"Of course. We freaks must guard each other's weaknesses, as well as benefit from our strengths."

"No, I mean if I get up before Miral rises again, cut me down and strike my head off."

"What?"

"Don't argue, just—"

Laron collapsed and lay limp. Miral was gone from the hazy murk at the horizon.

The sun rose a little before Miral the next morning. Druskarl had not slept at all, and had sat watching Laron for any sign of movement. The vampyre had remained as still as death, however, until the tip of Miral's rings was above the horizon.

"So, I notice that I did not move," he observed as he looked down at himself.

"And you owe me a night's sleep," grumbled Druskarl. "Shall we return to the camp?"

"Just one more matter," said Laron, taking a chisel from his pack. "I want a chunk of glass from where Silverdeath fell."

"Why? All the imprinted parts have been removed."

"Even the unimprinted glass remaining seems to have powerful etheric properties. Bring your ax, help me chip out a sample from the exact center of the chipped area."

"Why bother? I decided to do just that yesterday," Druskarl laughed as he tossed a greenish chunk to Laron.

They set off for the camp, which was not far away.

"Why were you so worried last night?" asked Druskarl.

"This place, it is swarming with powerful, clever things. Souls, elementals, raptors, things that probably have no name at all, and may never even have been studied by darkwalking initiates. I was afraid that something would know how to possess my body, in spite of the truename that guards it."

"Nothing can get past a truename, navigator."

"I am not so sure. If you had seen what I saw—"

Suddenly Druskarl made a sound like a gasp and a squeal forced into one. Laron's hand was already on his ax as he crouched and glanced about to see what was wrong. Then he gasped as well.

Velander was straddling Feran amid his bedding, their pale, naked bodies gleaming in the weak morning sunlight. There was no possible doubt of what activity they were engaged in. Velander was wearing the circlet.

"Don't mind us," Druskarl cried in Diomedan.

"No, don't mind us," agreed Laron in Scalticarian; then added, "That is, don't mind us," in Diomedan.

"I'm a eunuch."

"And I am—er, rather young."

"We are just bystanders," said Druskarl, now backing away.

"Yes, we are just, well, standing by."

Laron edged forward, snatched up his bedroll and iron casket, then stopped.

"Ah, my circlet?" he ventured. "Please?"

"I should like to borrow it, if that is not a problem," Velander asked. "I have no darkwalking tether, and—"

"Ah, no—no problem at all. One less thing to carry. I like to travel light. Just wear it and carry on—well, that is, as before. On Feran, I mean— No! I meant—"

"He means, don't mind us," Druskarl repeated. "We are just bystanders."

"Quite innocent, really."

"You might say we're innocent bystanders, in fact."

They suddenly ran out of words. The silence was absolute for a moment.

"Will you two go away?" said Velander's voice.

"Oh! Go away?" exclaimed Druskarl.

"Ah, yes," said Laron. "Go away. Quite an understandable request."

"Given the circumstances."

"Particularly *your* circumstances."

"We'll go behind those ruins over there until you are finished."

"Dressing, that is."

"Go away!" demanded Velander.

"Ah yes, we were just going," they said together.

They hurried away into the melted stumps of the nearby ruins.

"Why was she wearing my circlet? I wonder," said Laron as they sat down, still astounded.

"My former wife and queen liked to be seduced while wearing only her jewels," Druskarl replied.

"Whatever for?"

"Different things enhance the, ah, erotic mood for different people. Surely you have noticed."

"Oddly enough, eunuch, for all my strange and horrifying eating habits, and my peculiar sleeping arrangements, I am still something of a virgin."

Given what they had seen a quarter hour earlier, Druskarl and Laron were not at all surprised that Velander and Feran were sitting together and holding hands when they returned for breakfast. Most of the conversation pointedly involved the ocular that Laron and Druskarl had discovered. Druskarl even suggested they stay another day to see what else they could find. Velander advised against it.

"This is a disturbed place," she said as they prepared to return to the gigboat. "I can sense it."

"I know, the lives of many millions of people were obliterated from here, as well as those of countless more entities and animals," Druskarl agreed, gazing uneasily over the glass landscape. "Last night Laron spoke a word of detachment and looked upon this place from the etherworld. The sights he saw were disturbing. Many, many things are prowling here—wispy, frail, starving things that are slowly fading into true death."

"And they may try to follow us," Velander warned.

"So what should we do?" asked Feran.

"Put all our tether amulets in Laron's iron casket, along with the glass imprinted by Silverdeath, and the ocular tether. That way nothing can see us moving from the etherworld."

Druskarl nodded. "That does seem sensible."

"You will need to reset the circlet to be translucent to all but yourself," said Laron, speaking to the priestess without quite looking at her. "It currently can be seen from the etherworld as well as ours. You put it on, so only you can control it."

"Then you must tell me the settings," she replied.

She reset the circlet under his instructions, and the circlet and oracle stone winked out of view. *Clever girl,* thought Laron, as the priestess smiled in triumph.

Not much was left of Velander, only a faint collection of attitudes, motivations, memories, and values that once had formed the core of her spirit. That core could sense, and had limited movement, but hardly could be thought of as alive. She was now ignored by the raptor elementals as the ragged fragment of her being orbited the great axis. Out in the blackness was the starlike point of light that was the ocular, the lump of firmness that was her circlet, and the hair-thin beams of orange that were the chunks of glass from where Silverdeath had fallen.

She knew she was dead. Her body had been stolen, but nobody had noticed. Laron was the only other initiate in the group. *Laron.* He would eventually see something was wrong, but how long would that take?

The circlet's solidity suddenly vanished, along with one of the orange hairlines. Now only the star-point of the ocular and an orange axis to which it was tethered were out there. Velander suddenly realized that her party was preparing to leave, but first they were cutting off the anchor points that she might use to follow them. The elemental! She was doing it. Without even thinking, Velander drifted away from the great axis and toward the remaining hairline of orange light. It was moving as she reached it; she wrapped herself about it. It vanished, along with the ocular.

Now there was only the great axis in the distance, surrounded by circling sparkles of many colors. She was truly
dead, there was nothing to do but fade—yet there was something else nearby! The line of orange light was no more than
gossamer, like a strand of spiderweb that one could only see if
the light was favorable. Out here, away from the brightness of
the great axis, it was just visible. It moved. Velander followed.
The elemental must have advised Laron to put this, too, in his
iron box. Velander wrapped her tattered core about the line of
energy. It continued to move.

Velander clung to the orange line, savoring every moment of
awareness, savoring hope. Especially hope. Hope that she
would not suddenly find herself clinging to nothingness. Hope
of a future back in the world and dimensions she called home.
Hope for time. Time to remember being a tomboy who wanted
to punch, wrestle, and ax-fence better than any boy. Time to sa-
vor being a spy before she was a teenager, with blood on her
hands and the gratitude of kings. Time to recall the baffled fury
of being stared at and whispered about when she was an adolescent. *How dare they?* she raged in silence. She had followed
every rule, she had won, she had triumphed, yet youths her age
had called her a freak. The girls, too, if it came to that. Then
there had been Elasse Arimer. Elasse had convinced her there
was a place for the brilliant achiever among the Metrologans;
she had even found enough money to pay Velander's fees and
upkeep. But Elasse had been drowned. Terikel had lost a sister,
Velander had lost a saint. Of course, Terikel had done as much
as Elasse, and even more, Velander thought, but she was just
treating her as if she were her dead sister. It was all clear now,
with death so close. Death forced one to be honest, she realized.
Who would have thought the jaws of death could turn out to be
the lid of an iron case snapping shut? And after all her struggles, self-reliance, and independence, she called to a boy when
the raptors were closing in. *Not just death, but humiliation, too.
By now they think I am a slut, thanks to that elemental in my
body. At least nobody heard me call out to Laron for help. If he
had heard . . .*

If he had heard . . . ! Laron! The thread of orange was still there! She glanced to the great axis, but it was now some distance away. Laron was carrying this fragment outside the iron case, she realized suddenly. *He knows.* Laron somehow knew. He had left out the faintest of tethers for her to follow and cling to.

My chivalrous champion, thought Velander, suddenly overflowing with goodwill for the short, scrawny youth with cold blood and a pasted-on beard.

Laron had actually forgotten about the chunk of glass in his purse, and because he had no need for coins in the glass wilderness, there was nothing to jog his memory. They did not arrive at the river until nearly sunset. Without further delay they raised and bailed the gigboat, then rowed out into the current to return to the *Shadowmoon*. There was no living off the land, apart from the pools of drinking water.

They reached the *Shadowmoon* in a third of the time the voyage upstream had taken. The five men left with the schooner had discovered a large treasury barge that had sunk before it had totally burned away. They had raised more than their combined weight of gold, mostly as unmelted coins. The gold in the dead city where they were moored proved to be deep under melted rock and glass.

The trip back down the river to Gironal took only days. As Miral rose later in the morning, so, too, did Laron rise later. On the other hand, Feran and his new bedmate were hardly emerging at all, but the trip was uneventful so it did not matter. On their first day back aboard the *Shadowmoon*, Druskarl had the watch. Laron kept him company for a time.

"Velander and Feran seem anxious for each other's company," Laron observed. "What do they do for all that time? Sex only takes a dozen or so minutes, at most."

"Where did you learn that?" asked Druskarl as he raised his eyes to the sky.

"By watching sundry animals performing the act."

"You are still young," replied Druskarl, somewhat patronizingly. "When you are in love, nothing else exists except for your beloved."

"Young? In body I am fourteen, but in years I am seven centuries."

"Have you ever been in love?"

"Now that you mention it, no," Laron admitted sheepishly.

"As was required, has been proven. Are you jealous?"

"Of course not! I am dead. Are *you* jealous?"

"I have been gelded. Of course not."

"Then are you envious?"

"Now that you mention it, yes."

"So am I."

Not long after that, Laron went down to his cabin, crawled in, and bolted the hatch. He was a little earlier than Miral's setting, so he lay awake. The idea for another experiment to free Ninth had come to him, and he was thinking through the potential risks. Presently, there was a soft rattling and tapping at the inner side-hatch to his tiny personal space. "Laron, are you awake? Laron!" It was the soft, furtive call of someone who did not wish to wake others, and the voice was Velander's. After perhaps a minute it ceased. Laron lay still, counting to fifty. Then he eased the hatch open.

With his unique senses he could detect the heat leaking out of Feran's cabin, but there was only enough for one body. Down in the lower deck area were the enticing, succulent shapes of the other crewmen. Most were lying in their narrow cots, asleep—but one shape in the darkness was two bodies clinging together.

I may be a virgin, but I have a feeling I know what is going on here, thought the vampyre as he crawled back into his cabin and silently slid the hatch closed again. *If I had warm blood, I would be probably be blushing.* Within moments Miral was down and Laron was thinking nothing at all.

✴ ✴ ✴

The *Shadowmoon*'s last evening on the Dioran River saw a lot of activity, as Feran had the schooner prepared for its return to the open sea. Waiting for darkness, they stopped at the ruins of what once had been the winter palace of the Gironal monarch. The salvaged coins were hidden in the bilge, the decks scrubbed, and their rubbish was weighted down and sunk in the river. Only the supplies of wine had run really low, although rainwater collected from glass pools meant they still had plenty to drink.

Finally there was no more to do, and a few of them chose to go ashore and look for melted gold. Laron was among them, but he kept far from the others. This would be his last chance to wander on the Torean wasteland, and he wanted to soak in the experience alone, with his heightened senses extended to their limits. It was not long before he had the feeling of being watched. *What is here?* he wondered. The place had been a playground for very rich and generally stupid people, it was not a place for magic strong enough to survive the worst that Silverdeath could do. Then he realized what it was.

For Velander, it was a time of confusion. The ocular brightened as Laron approached, then there was the flare of the casting that he used to bind its anchor to the glass fragment from the great axis. Suddenly she could see the world again!

There was Laron, walking amid the ruins. Her view was from a perspective of a single eye about two or three feet above his head, but by moving around she could get almost any view except straight up. After a time Laron ceased his random ramblings, and walked purposefully until he reached the edge of the river. There was the *Shadowmoon*, and someone on the quarterdeck was beckoning him to come aboard.

The casting off of ropes and heaving on the sweeps to get the vessel into the center of the sluggish current was comforting and familiar to Velander. The elemental in her body was helping, although with little enthusiasm.

Laron went down into the now-deserted lower deck and did a casting over the glass that was the ocular's anchor. A rough but adequate viewing sphere materialized between his hands, then

remained floating as he withdrew them. He spoke other words
and did a few more minor castings.

A scene appeared in the flickering sphere, a scene containing a large, somewhat overweight, rather hairy and totally
naked man; three rather well fed and naked young women; a
few cushions; and a large, well-upholstered recliner. Laron
stared at what they were doing for some time. Velander stared,
too. There was no sound in her world, but presently she saw
Laron put his hands to his mouth and call out. Druskarl came
down the steps, froze for a moment, then hunkered down beside Laron. Feran arrived, hand in hand with the elemental.
Norrieav arrived, an open wine jar in his hand. Martak
climbed down next, closely followed by Hazlok, D'Atro, and
Heinder.

Velander watched in disbelief and outrage as the men
stamped their feet, pointed, made rude gestures, passed the jar
of wine around, and apparently even whistled at the antics of
the figures within the glowing sphere. Laron elbowed Druskarl
in the ribs, pointed at the sphere, and said something that
caused the eunuch to double over with laughter. *You dirty little
boy,* thought Velander, quite disgusted with the behavior of her
supposedly chivalrous champion. Hazlok suddenly dropped his
trews and bared his pale but hairy buttocks at the sphere. *Why?*
Velander wondered, but then she noticed the arms of the
Gironal royal house on the wall. *You filthy lecher,* said Velander
soundlessly to the dead king of Gironal. She had read that his
queen was a pious and holy Metrologan priestess who barely
knew the meaning of the word *vice.*

There was a massive lurch as the unguided *Shadowmoon*
struck a sandbank.

✳ ✳ ✳

Thanks to an hour stuck on the sandbank, they reached
Gironal's ruins somewhat later than sunset, but Miral was quite
bright enough for navigation. As they cautiously edged out of
the mouth of the Dioran River they were astounded to see a forest of masts rising out of the water. There were just masts and

rigging, with no ships. All were silhouetted against the ruddy sky. There were dozens, probably hundreds of masts: a fleet of rigging with no ships.

"Could it be an entire fleet sunk here without a fight?" Laron wondered aloud as he stared across the harbor from the bow.

Faced with the unknown, Feran wisely turned back at once. The *Shadowmoon* dropped anchor just inside the mouth of the river. Druskarl was ordered out to investigate.

"I should go out, too, sir," Laron said as Feran supervised the lowering of the masts in case they had to submerge in a hurry. "There may be sorcery and castings involved."

"You stay here," Feran said firmly, kneeling to tie down the rigging and ratlines on the deck. "I shall go with Druskarl in the corrak."

"But, sir, I am an initiate—" Laron began.

"Look around you, your place is here!" Feran snapped back. "The men are near shitting themselves with fright. With a strong initiate aboard they will not be so fearful, and with the deckswain to run the ship and you to navigate, they will be able to take the *Shadowmoon* back to Helion if I am lost. Stay here, keep order, and let nobody do anything stupid."

The corrak was launched, with Feran and Druskarl aboard, and they warily paddled out into the harbor. The nearest of the ghostly masts was no more than a hundred yards distant.

"Vidarian rigging, sir," Druskarl said as they reached the mast and spars standing sentinel above the calm water. "The cordage and timber is from everywhere, but the knots, wrapping style, and deadeye locks give them away."

"Most did not burn before sinking," added Feran, reaching up to touch the furled sail still on the main lateen spar.

"Nearly all sank on an even keel. The harbor is shallow and the sediment soft. On a rough count, this is most of Emperor Banzalo's fleet. There must have been quite a battle here."

"It's too dark to see the sunken wrecks properly, so we'll have to come back in the morning. The men will be restless and frightened."

"And so they should be. At least we shall have no trouble getting past Banzalo's blockade."

They spent the night on their guard, keeping a watch of two, and with everyone else sleeping clothed and near their weapons. Sunrise again revealed the ghastly forest of masts and rigging projecting above the calm, shallow waters of the harbor. Feran now launched the gigboat and dispatched it with Druskarl, Hazlok, and D'Arto. Druskarl dived to several wrecks, and confirmed that they were all Vidarian. Some had been rammed, a few had burned before sinking, but most had been scuttled. They finished their survey, scouted the nearby bays and coves, then returned to the *Shadowmoon* at midday. After hearing their report, Feran immediately ordered the schooner's masts to be raised.

"Make sure you use the plain green mainsail," he shouted as the crew scrambled into action. "Whoever did this may not be concerned with mere privateer looters."

"Boatmaster, someone on the shore," the lookout cried from the quarterdeck. "Five men, over there. They're waving to us."

"Waving what? Their fists? Battle-axes?"

"Just their arms, and they seem pleased to see us."

Feran sent Druskarl in the gigboat to investigate while the mainsail was being untied, and by the time he returned with the castaways, the rigging was nearly ready and the anchor was being hauled up. Banzalo was barely recognizable, and the five survivors of the Vidarian fleet were emaciated and wearing rags.

"Battle galleys, hundreds of them," Banzalo croaked as he was helped aboard. "Leave this place. Hurry!"

They towed the gigboat while the sail was being raised, then it was hoisted aboard as they passed between the masts of the lost fleet. It was not the best time to sail, and they had to struggle against the tide to get out into open water. Once clear of the harbor, the *Shadowmoon* headed north as the wind picked up, but there was no pursuit. Laron tended the survivors of the Vidarian fleet until the vessel was well clear of the coast.

"They came in out of the morning sun—there were battle galleys and dash galleys," Banzalo babbled as Velander and

Feran helped him below. "Out to sea there were support caravels and deepwater traders."

"But who? Who were they?" Feran asked.

"Warsovran's accursed fleet, his entire fleet! They caught us unawares. We're so far from anywhere, who could have suspected? They came in with firepots. Nearly all of our men were ashore. It was a calm morning with no wind to fill the sails of my ships, but the galleys could go where they would because they have oars. The battle raged for hours, but the galleys were crammed with marines and as soon as they grappled with our traders it was sheer slaughter. No prisoners were taken. I gave my flagman the general order to scuttle all ships. Even in defeat I denied Warsovran my fighting ships."

They laid Banzalo out on the mattress from Feran's cabin, and Velander brought some of their dwindling store of wine. He continued his story between gulps, red wine spilling from his lips and onto the pillow.

"I had ordered that no food was to be taken ashore, so that my men would not desert to live in the ruins and dig gold for themselves. After a week of starvation most of those ashore gave themselves up to Warsovran's fleet, but they were slaughtered where they stood and left to rot. The Damarian marines carried off our sacks of recovered gold, then burned everything that could not be carried away."

The telling of the story had filled Banzalo with emotion, and tears now streamed down his cheeks and mingled with the wine. The other four castaways had been brought below by now, and Laron examined each in turn. All had wounds, but none were in immediate danger from them. Those who had survived were obviously the toughest.

"They hunted us with tracker dogs, they herded us like sheep. I rallied a few dozen men and made a stand against the tens of thousands that came after us. We killed two for every one of us who fell, but more kept coming. Finally I gave the order to split up and flee, then I dived into the river and hid among the slabs of a collapsed stone bridge where the dogs could not catch my scent. Four others had the same idea, and they are with me still. For thirteen days we lived on raw fish and rainwater while Warsovran's sailors and marines hunted us; then they sailed away. I kept my men low, awaiting someone, anyone. Within hours of the last ship leaving the harbor, a few other survivors emerged, only to be trapped by a force of marines who had been left in hiding. Two days later a trader returned to pick up those Damarians who were left. We have been truly alone ever since."

"We should get farther from the coast," said Feran. "Warsovran may have caravels on patrol and the *Shadowmoon* is not as fast as them."

"But they may attack my new colonies!" Banzalo cried. "We must warn them to stand ready."

"I suspect they may already have done that, my lord," replied Feran. "If they could crush your fleet, then your settlements must be ash."

"We must go there at once, we have to warn them," croaked Banzalo, trying to sit up.

"The settlements will be gone by now," Feran pointed out, "and we are heading for Helion."

"No! You will steer for the colonies. I *order* it."

Feran had no choice. He steered back to the coast, trying to stay in water shallow enough to submerge safely. The boatmaster spent most of his time at the masthead or on the quarterdeck, scanning for Damarian ships. There were no other ships to be seen and no fires on the shore, but rather than seeming bleak and forbidding, this was the most welcome sight imaginable to everyone on the *Shadowmoon*.

The next day Velander was taking the air in the afternoon sun while Laron stood at the steering pole. For a time she sat on the gigboat, throwing him coquettish looks and smiles, but was rewarded with only nods. Finally she made the short journey to the small quarterdeck.

"Navigator, do you think the colonies will be all right?" she asked.

"No," he replied simply, looking away to the distant coast.

"Why not?"

"Warsovran's admiral knew just when and where to catch

Banzalo's fleet where they could not scatter once the battle was lost. If he had the power to locate and wipe out the Vidarian fleet, he would not have spared the colonies."

"I see," said the elemental, who had been planning to leave the *Shadowmoon* at the colonies. "What do you think has happened at the colonies?"

"Annihilated, probably. It is all very odd. According to the regent—"

"The emperor."

"Whatever."

Laron did not continue. The elemental waited. The silence lengthened.

"What is odd?" she finally asked.

"Banzalo said hundreds of galleys attacked, no prisoners were taken, and everything that might be of use to anyone was burned or smashed. Druskarl saw no evidence of mass slaughter ashore, however. Further, once Banzalo was safely drugged and asleep, I spoke with his four marines. There were no more than a dozen galleys in Warsovran's squadron, and two thousand marines. Banzalo had ordered all but a couple of watchmen ashore from every ship. He was too greedy for melted gold, that is why he posted so few guards.

"The Damarians rammed three ships before they realized they were unresisting. About thirty ships were captured merely by putting a few sailors and an officer aboard. After a while the individual Vidarian watchmen began burning or sinking their ships to deny them to the Damarians. Meantime, Banzalo had gathered his men on the old wharf to repel the invaders. These same invaders had meantime landed marines in another bay, probably before dawn. These marched overland, waited for the Vidarians to gather to watch the naval battle, then attacked them from behind."

"But Banzalo said that Warsovran's whole fleet attacked."

"What would *you* say? 'Er, sorry, I left the ships unguarded, and while I was watching them being captured without a fight, someone sneaked up behind us, pulled our collective kilts over our collective heads and tied a knot'? Warsovran has defeated the second-biggest fleet on the Placidian Ocean, gained thirty undamaged ships, and captured five thousand slaves at the cost of one dead marine—he was killed by a falling sack of gold, apparently."

The elemental licked her lips, which were pursed and engorged with blood. "Warsovran must be a military genius," she purred, gazing into Laron's eyes.

"He was well informed. Someone betrayed Banzalo, someone from his fleet or colonies. Warsovran followed in Banzalo's wake, most probably. First the colonies, then the fleet, and now the Damarians are proceeding south in search of other looters. There would have been only thirty ships in their original fleet, according to Banzalo's marines. Fast, deadly, but few."

"Faster than us?"

"The galleys? Oh yes, but then they have continued south while we have turned north. I think we are safe."

"If Banzalo has been defeated, why do we still obey him?"

"Banzalo still rules Helion. Just how long he will *continue* to rule is quite another matter, judging from his scorecard so far. He has the right to requisition any ship on Helion's tax register, and the *Shadowmoon* is certainly in that particular book. He also has four fighting men to back up his orders."

"So he can force us to go to Helion after we check the colonies."

Interesting—she does not know we were going to Helion anyway, Laron thought.

Interesting—he has no interest in women, thought the elemental.

"I noticed that you sleep with your cabin's hatch locked from the inside," she observed invitingly.

"Ah, yes," Laron replied flatly.

"Why?"

"My mother told me never to trust sailors."

As Feran and Laron had predicted, the settlements had been annihilated, and seabirds and seals were feeding on the bodies of the dead. Having convinced Banzalo the worst had happened, they began the long journey around the continent and back to Helion. There was still no sign of Warsovran's battle squadron, and the tropical skies were overcast and dull.

"The fleet would have come in from the north," Feran speculated to Banzalo, based on an earlier conversation with Laron. "If they razed the settlements first, then smashed your ships at Gironal, my guess is that they continued south, working their way around the coast and setting upon anyone they found scavenging in the ruins. When they have circled Torea, they will establish their own mining settlements in the richest of the melted cities, and keep other ships on patrol."

Banzalo looked down at the waves. "There is so much for everyone in Torea. Why did he have to do this?"

Laron thought back to when Banzalo had claimed the entire continent as his own, then thought better than to mention it. "This way he can control the amount of Torean gold that finds its way into Acrema and Lemtas," was what Laron actually said. "If he spends only a moderate amount at a time, it will not cheapen the value of gold elsewhere."

"Wise words from a little boy," Banzalo sneered.

"Your pardon, Regent, but you asked the question."

Frustration and anguish had been building in Banzalo for a long time, yet wise rulers know better than to vent such emotions on their subjects without discrimination. Though a noble, Banzalo was neither a wise nor an experienced ruler. He had led his subjects into the unknown, but he had never needed to rally goodwill in the face of defeat. He straightened, then backhanded Laron across the face. At least, he attempted to backhand Laron's face. The youth's hand snapped up and seized Banzalo's. He squeezed. Banzalo cried out, drowning the soft crackling sound of his hand being crushed.

Two of Banzalo's men clambered up the steps to his aid, but stopped at the sight of Laron's huge, gleaming eyes and bared fangs. Slowly, Laron fought down the hunger that had been given its head for a moment. Finally he released Banzalo, whose hand was by now only about as wide as his wrist.

"Nobody else aboard the *Shadowmoon* knows deepwater navigation, Regent," said Laron. "I suggest you show a little more respect for those who stand between you and a very unpleasant death."

Banzalo dropped to his knees, holding the wrist of his stricken hand.

"Medicar, get the medicar," Banzalo wheezed, barely able to breathe from the shock.

"Ah, that would be me," said Laron.

Warsovran stepped from the gangplank of the deepwater trader and onto Diomedan soil. In fact, it was actually the stones of a Diomedan pier, but the symbolism was no less potent, for that. The emperor had arrived, Torea had conquered a slice of Acrema. Warsovran had had plenty of time to be impressed by the grandeur of Diomeda and its island palace as his ship was being towed into the harbor, and now his gaze was steady on the representatives of his new subjects.

The most senior of the local nobles and merchants had been assembled at the base of the pier, and were under the scrutiny of several hundred Torean marines. Warsovran stopped before the assembly, arms folded.

"You have been told who I am," he said, in smooth but accented Diomedan. "You are my subjects."

"Kneel!" barked one of the marine captains.

Every Diomedan merchant and noble present knelt. Warsovran paced before them, alternately looking from the sky to the cobbles at his feet. It was more symbolism, for those caring to look for it.

"I am not a privateer. I am a conqueror. I have conquered Diomeda, and I have conquered you."

He continued pacing, but now in silence. His audience realized they were required to ponder his words. They pondered.

"I have no intention of plundering your wealth. I am very, very rich. I have no need of plunder."

Warsovran raised a hand into the air and snapped his fingers. Two dozen marines strode forward, half of them carrying baskets. The other marines reached into the baskets and began to pelt Warsovran's captive audience with pebbles of pure gold. The nobles and merchants cowered, then some sprawled, stunned by the rain of precious metal. Warsovran snapped his fingers again. The shower of gold ceased. Bloodied faces looked up to him.

"As long as you continue to produce more wealth, I shall leave you alone. Cross me or resist me, and I shall destroy you. I shall destroy you by having you flayed alive, then flung into a pool of hungry crayfish. Should you be loyal, however, you are safe. If anyone crosses you, tell me and I shall crush them. Now, go forth. Trade, prosper, and build my new empire's strength."

With that he turned his back on them and walked away. The guards dispersed as well, leaving the gold pebbles scattered on the ground.

After inspecting his makeshift royal palace, Warsovran unpacked Silverdeath. His court sorcerer, Rax Einsel, was standing before him as he ran Silverdeath's metal fabric through his fingers, pensively examining the shimmering circles and linkages with their multihued highlights. Einsel watched, nervous in the presence of a weapon that could sear all traces of life from an entire continent.

"The Vidarians should be out of the way by now, so I have the gold of Torea behind me and all Acrema before me," Warsovran said calmly. "I also have Silverdeath beside me. What do you think, Einsel?"

"It is a superb talisman, Warsovran. The craftsmanship—"

"Does not concern us. It is to be used, not admired."

These words alarmed Einsel. If it came to that, they would alarm anyone. "It reduced Torea to melted glass when Ralzak tried to use it to take a single city," Einsel pointed out deferentially.

"Ralzak knew none of Weapon's rules, powers, and limitations. I can use it without losing control. What do you think of my plan for Helion?"

"It is a gamble, master, you cannot know how Silverdeath will act," Einsel pleaded, emboldened by fear.

"I will be using it a long way out to sea, when at Helion. Nothing can go wrong."

"On Torea a great deal went wrong."

"On the contrary, Einsel. On Torea nothing went wrong at all."

The pop-eyed little sorcerer bowed his head in Warsovran's direction, trying to look at Silverdeath while averting his eyes. What little he could understand made him frightened.

"You have observed Silverdeath from the etherworld," Warsovran prompted. "What did you see of this fine machine from there?"

"Silverdeath sat as a heavy mass in the darkness of the etherworld," Einsel replied, studiously composing the neutral response as he spoke. "It is like nothing I have ever seen. Massive, powerful capabilities, able to drain energies in from other etherworlds, able to channel torrents of radiance and heat."

"Yes, Einsel. There is nothing so powerful as this engine, even though it has some limits. All the kingdoms of Acrema together could not stand against me now."

"Warsovran, surely you cannot be thinking to use Silverdeath on another continent. It is so far beyond our understanding. Why not build on your fleet?"

Warsovran continued to run the metal fabric through his fingers. "Build *what* on my fleet?"

"You have a powerful fleet. None on the Placidian Ocean can stand against you. You now also rule the biggest port on the east Acreman coast. Why use this doomsday thing on Helion? Surely the monarchs of Acrema will heed the lesson of Torea."

Warsovran shrugged. He was a trained initiate in his own right, but of indeterminate power and rating. He was also a scholar of great and deep learning, and had good tactical and strategic judgment. The combination of talents had given him half of Torea without Silverdeath's help.

"Why, Einsel? Because poison is leaking into our world. I have cut off the infected limb, and now I must cauterize the wound. Helion is that wound."

Einsel wrung his hands together, then finally sat down and uncorked a jar of fortified wine. He swallowed several mouthfuls.

"I have been to Helion," he said sadly. "It is a pretty, tranquil little island."

"The Metrologans have been pouring poison into our world for a thousand years. With the main temple in Larmentel gone, along with all the regional temples like that at Zantrias, there is only one surviving. It is on Helion. The Metrologans were destroying magic in the name of knowledge, Einsel. Somebody had to stop them, and I am doing just that."

Warsovran shook his head, as if trying to recall something amid a maelstrom of issues calling for his attention. The city had fallen, his fleet was at full strength, trade was continuing . . .

"My son," he said suddenly. "Where is Darric?"

"Ah, er, Admiral Forteron wishes to see you about that," said Einsel.

Forteron was expecting to be summoned, so he was already at the palace. He was sitting in the supplicants' room when Einsel had him fetched. As Forteron knelt before Warsovran, Einsel stood to one side. He was trying hard to seem inconspicuous.

"I wish to see my son," said Acrema's newest monarch.

"He is said to be aboard the flagship, Your Majesty," Forteron replied.

" 'Said'? Admiral Forteron?"

" 'Said,' Your Majesty."

"Do I have to start killing people before anyone will give me a straightforward answer?"

"No, Your Majesty. I am speaking as plainly as I can."

"Then speak until I comprehend."

Forteron wanted to pace, wave his arms, embroider the truth, and flatter his monarch, but he knew from experience that Warsovran liked cold, hard facts from cold, hard people.

"Just after Diomeda fell, I was approached by galleymaster Mandalock of the *Kygar*," Forteron began, his arms folded tightly behind his back. "He said that your son had been acting strangely for most of the voyage, and that his courtesan was now acting even more strangely."

"How so? Is he ill?"

"Not ill. His manner, voice, health, and appearance were all unchanged from when last you saw him, but he seemed somehow . . . empty."

" 'Empty'? Please explain."

"He was reluctant to talk on any but the most superficial of topics, and when he spoke at all he said very little. It was as if he were hiding a secret."

"That is odd. Darric is generally a little *too* open than is good for a future monarch. Perhaps he is trying to rein himself in, now that he has been trusted to go on campaign."

"Perhaps. In fact, I thought just that myself until Mandalock went on to tell me about his courtesan."

"What about her?"

"She is no younger than forty, and she claimed to be the empress, after we took Diomeda."

Admiral Forteron knew when to stop and let other people draw conclusions. Warsovran put a hand to his chin and frowned with thought for a moment, then his eyes stretched wide to protrude more alarmingly than those of Einsel. His breath became quick, snatched gasps and his jaw hung open, working soundlessly.

"Where?" he whispered at last.

"I had them locked in their cabins on the *Kygar*, and posted a strong guard. They have been held there ever since."

"Take me there," Warsovran demanded, his voice so contorted that the words were scarcely intelligible.

✳ ✳ ✳

Warsovran approached the *Kygar* aboard a harbor gigboat. They had to board from the port side, as a small dash galley was anchored hard to starboard as part of some sort of battle-damage inspection. A boarding ramp was lowered, and he went aboard with Einsel and Forteron. His bodyguards flanked the group. The fifty marines who lined the deck saluted, then Warsovran turned to galleymaster Mandalock.

"Bring both of the prisoners out on deck," he ordered, his voice soft but his words as cold as a polar gale.

Mandalock strode the length of the deck and spoke to the guards at the aft hatchways. Moments later two figures emerged. Darric looked quite normal, but his courtesan had been working hard at her face, hair, and clothing for the whole of her incarceration, and was now the very image of the empress.

"Darric, come here!" barked Warsovran.

The prince began the long walk along the one hundred twenty feet of the *Kygar*'s main deck. After what seemed like an eternity, he arrived before Warsovran.

"Well, Darric, did you enjoy your first campaign?" asked Warsovran, embracing the prince.

"Oh, Father, I would like many more."

"But did you enjoy it?"

"Why, yes."

"Well, I hope you are overcoming your fears. When do you think you will be ready to actually fight in a battle?"

"After seeing Diomeda fall, anytime you say. My fears are gone."

Warsovran's left hand reached into his right sleeve and drew out a dagger. Darric's decoy first became aware that he had not lived up to expectations as the blade plunged into his back and found his right heart. There was a loud shriek from the other end of the *Kygar*'s deck.

"Kill her!" barked Warsovran, but the empress had already spoken a casting, and a dazzling flash burst from her hand.

Forteron blindly tripped Warsovran and flung him down on the deck as Einsel burst a dazzle-casting toward what he hoped was the direction of the empress. The blinded Darielle had the sense to drop to the deck and crawl between the legs of the marines who were chopping at each other in search of her. She moved to the right, felt the starboard rail, slipped under it, and fell to the water between the two galleys.

Moments later people's vision began to clear aboard the *Kygar*. Two marines were dead and several more had wounded each other. Forteron had flung himself across Warsovran.

"Where is she?" demanded Warsovran.

The empress was nowhere to be seen. Marines flanked by ethersmiths made for the aft hatch as Einsel stood blinking with a fire-casting held high. When someone finally thought to look over the side, the dash galley's oars were already digging into the water.

Warsovran ran to the rail, in time to see the dripping-wet Darielle fling her own fire-casting. He dropped and twisted aside as it hit, leaving the rail charred, splintered, and smoking.

Einsel flung a casting at the deck of the dash galley, setting the galleymaster and several marines afire, but missing the empress. Marines on both ships began exchanging arrows as more ethersmiths came to the rail and flung castings. The gap between them widened.

"Chop through the anchor ropes—after them!" shouted Mandalock.

"Signal the patrol galleys. Have them rammed!" cried Forteron.

The *Kygar* was four times heavier than the dash galley, and although it was under way in less than thirty seconds, the gap between them continued to widen. The patrol galleys moved to blockade the harbor, but the dash galley was not headed their way. It was being steered straight for the island palace, and it had a truce pennant flying from its mast.

A few rocks from the palace, catapults splashed into the water around the dash galley before someone on the walls noticed the truce pennant and ordered it to be given safe passage. No such consideration was given to the *Kygar*. As the larger ship approached through a shower of rocks and fire arrows, the dash galley was beached and those aboard jumped into the shallows and ran for the opening gates. Galleymaster Mandalock ordered the *Kygar* brought about just as those on the walls found its range. A rock crashed through the deck, killing several rowers below, then its forward ballista landed a clay pot of hellfire oil on the dash galley. Arrows were falling so thickly that everyone but the steersman and ballista crew took cover. A second shot hit the oar ports of the dash galley, setting the interior awash with burning oil, but moments later a rock from the palace hit the ballista, smashing it to kindling and killing three of the crew. By the time the *Kygar* was out of range again there were five gaping holes in its deck, but it was still afloat. The dash galley was burning fiercely.

Subsequent interrogation of the wounded decoy prince revealed a thread of treason toward Warsovran—or loyalty to his empress, according to which side one was on. Burning slivers of bamboo were pushed under hundreds of aristocratic fingernails, their owners having been named by those who had already been broken. Several dozen noble and senior heads were then separated from their bodies.

Even though she had been confined to the *Kygar*, the empress had managed to convince some Damarian guards to take messages to trusted men in positions of power. One of those had been the dash-galley commander who had had his vessel drawn up beside the *Kygar*. When the emperor had seen that the decoy was not Darric, a contingency plan was activated.

The decoy revealed that Darric had been tricked into staying in the capital by a forged letter, and the prince had died when the final fire-circle obliterated the city. The empress had commissioned the forgery. Admiral Forteron was sure that Warsovran had intended Darric's fate for the empress, but he kept his opinion to himself. For the very first time he now saw Warsovran genuinely distraught with grief, and thus at his most dangerous.

"Some powerful sorceress took on the form of the empress and used Darric's decoy to get passage with the fleet," Warsovran declared to his council of shipmasters. "They hoped to get into my confidence, but the decoy was foolish enough to think that my son had been afraid of battle. When I stabbed him, the sorceress escaped to her true master, the former king of Diomeda."

The story was plausible, and most heads nodded. Forteron mentally noted which heads had not.

"Prince Darric was probably killed by traitors within the royal palace," Warsovran continued. "As we have seen, there were even traitors within this very battle fleet, but perhaps some of those were merely tricked into being loyal to whom they *thought* was their empress. Make no mistake, the empress is dead—only an impostor in the pay of a foreign king survives."

"But, Your Majesty, what was their intent?" asked Mandalock.

"I had a reason for coming to Diomeda," replied Warsovran. "I had made a pledge by the gods of the moonworlds, and because I sought to honor this pledge, we were all spared the fire that swept Torea away."

He paused, surveying their expectant faces.

"I expect that you want to know my secret reason."

Several hundred shipmasters nodded.

"It will become clear in time. For now, repair your ships and keep your men in fighting trim. This place is our only home and we must defend it."

The meeting broke up with a resolution of loyalty to the emperor. Warsovran and Forteron left the court hall together.

"I do believe that the empress has been completely discredited," Warsovran muttered quietly.

"I never knew that she was such a powerful initiate," admitted Forteron.

"She is a renegade Metrologan, and carries one of their very rare death orders. That is the reason she has compelled *me* to persecute the Order for so long."

"What did she do to bring that upon herself?"

"I do not know, it was before our marriage. Judging from what she has been trying to do to me, it must have been fairly serious. How ironic. In order to spy on me, she came here in disguise, allowing me to brand her as an impostor. She commanded loyalty among the Damarians, Forteron, but she was also an initiate of the twelfth level—even Einsel is only qualified to the eleventh. Those two things made her very hard to kill. When the fire-circles destroyed Torea, I thought the old bat was dead at last. Alas, she escaped, and that escape cost Darric his life. Still, at least I am free of her. That is some small compensation for losing my empire."

"And your son?"

"Nothing is compensation for that."

Forteron thought quickly. Warsovran would not admit to knowing in advance what the fire-circles would do unless some sort of test was being conducted.

"Sire, you know that I know," Forteron said warily.

"Yes. You saw through the empress, yet you were loyal to me. Why?"

"The fleet is my life; you are my emperor."

Warsovran stopped and turned to face Forteron, his hands on his hips. He looked him up and down, then closed his eyes and shook his head.

"Had Darric lived, I would have asked no more than he turn

out like you," the emperor said with rare sincerity, then strode off alone.

Forteron was left contemplating his future. The truth about his loyalty had actually been that Warsovran was a superb commander and Forteron enjoyed winning. Had the emperor been a bungling incompetent, Forteron would have taken his services elsewhere many years earlier. More than anything else, Forteron feared the prospect of inglorious death resulting from some idiot superior's stupid decision. Now he was the emperor's favorite and possible heir, all the while sure that Warsovran had deliberately left the families of every man on the fleet to the fire-circles. Perhaps the emperor was showing favor to buy silence and complicity? Forteron doubted it, but a good tactician always considered every possibility.

It was twelve days after leaving Gironal that the strains on board the *Shadowmoon* began to tell on the crew and passengers. The winds and currents were against them, and the small vessel was very cramped with five extra people aboard. The stores definitely would not last all the way to Helion no matter how Feran calculated the allocations. Worse for Feran, Velander had forsaken him for Banzalo, and they had appropriated his cabin.

By now Miral was rising well after sunset, and Druskarl was on the night watch. Feran joined him as the sunset splashed the sky with lurid colors.

"No fish on the lines, boatmaster," reported Druskarl.

"If you were a fish, would you go near Torea?" sighed Feran.

"Not being a fish, sir, I cannot venture an opinion."

There was a prolonged giggle from below their feet. It was from Feran's cabin. The two men glanced at each other.

"Your romance with Velander has, ah, foundered?" asked Druskarl.

"The wench has all the constancy of a weather vane shaped like a rabbit."

"Banzalo?"

"Who else did you think—Hazlok? Banzalo is no longer an emperor, but he is still a regent. A very minor regent, perhaps, but a regent nonetheless. Start with a boatmaster and work up, hah!"

"Sir, Laron did mention that her behavior was a little—"

"Laron! What would he know? Cold, bloodless little fish, he has no life in him. He must be the only man on the *Shadowmoon* that she has not flirted with."

"She obviously takes no interest in me," Druskarl protested.

"That's not the point! I am boatmaster but I must bunk with the men. How can I maintain my authority? I must have a cabin. Come to think of it, Laron has no right to a cabin of his own."

"Laron has special needs."

"Laron just goes limp when Miral is down, I saw it on the journey to Larmentel."

"Crossing Laron is not a good idea. Banzalo could tell you that. Besides, he knows deepwater navigation."

"I know some deepwater navigation, too. Laron challenges my authority—and the authority of our regent. He needs to be constrained; my mind is made up. I'm going to fetch the carpenter. Laron will be taken from his cabin while Miral is down, and he will be bound."

Feran studied Druskarl's face, but the eunuch gave no sign of caring. Leaving Druskarl at the steering pole, Feran went below. The sound of splintering wood soon came from beneath Druskarl's feet as the hatch to Laron's little cabin was smashed in. A cry of alarm followed.

"Dead!" shouted Feran. "The navigator's dead!"

✦ ✦ ✦

An hour later Laron's body lay on the middeck with the passengers and crew gathered around. It was meant to be a service, but had taken the form of an argument.

"He had to sleep undisturbed," Druskarl muttered as he prepared Laron's body to go over the side. "You killed him by smashing in that panel."

"He was long dead," Feran retorted. "He had no pulse and his body was cold. He must have died hours ago."

"When he slept, he slept close to death. Any shock would tear loose his grip on life. He explained his affliction to me when I first came aboard."

Banzalo spat on the deck. "What is one more death after all the death we have seen?" he sighed.

"This youth's death removes the only qualified deepwater navigator from the *Shadowmoon*, Regent," Druskarl replied. "How do you suggest we navigate across the Placidian Ocean to Helion without him?"

This problem had not crossed Banzalo's mind. He glared at Feran.

"I can do anything that Laron could have," retorted Feran.

He paced the tiny length of deck, annoyed and embarrassed, then seemed to make a decision. Laron's body was a symbol of bad judgment, so it had to be disposed of.

"Druskarl, prepare to drop him over the side."

Druskarl held Laron over the rail. The others bowed their heads. Druskarl slipped a noose around Laron's ankle, then intoned a few words of the burial service for seamen:

"Why should those, who have sailed upon the waters for so long, have fear of their dark and soothing depths? Sleep well, Laron, and rise again as a reflection of your life's worth."

He heaved the body over the rail, and it splashed into the water and sank immediately. Twenty minutes later Miral rose on the eastern horizon.

Laron awoke being dragged along by one leg through the dark water. Twisting his body around, he seized the rope that attached him to the *Shadowmoon*, then began to drag himself back to the little vessel. Druskarl had attached the other end to an outboard rigging pin, and before long Laron was clinging to the side of the *Shadowmoon* and listening for voices. There were none. He peered over the side. Two of Banzalo's guards had been stationed to watch for other ships, but they seemed to be asleep. Apart from these and Druskarl, all the others were below.

Laron slowly eased himself over the rail. Druskarl saw him, but the two marines were sitting dozing, their backs to Laron. Druskarl lashed the steering pole, then stepped forward and jammed the hatch shut with his knife.

Laron and Druskarl attacked together. Druskarl spun his marine and simply hit him squarely on the jaw. Laron seized his companion, twisted him to the deck with the skill of frequent practice, then bit. Druskarl watched Laron feeding with a mixture of curiosity and repulsion. Once the bodies had been dropped over the side, they sat on the quarterdeck, whispering.

"They must all be asleep below," said Druskarl. "I heard the giggles from Banzalo's cabin cease about half an hour ago. Velander sang for a while, and the marines on deck slumbered. The words of her song were from some very strange language."

"Her singing induced sleep, except in those whose ability to appreciate female charms is impaired."

"Such as us?"

"Well . . . you have been subjected to a few modifications, and I am dead."

"So what now?"

"Banzalo will be asleep, and she will be astride some man of lesser rank."

"I can hardly credit the change in Velander."

"It is not Velander. I have been studying her. She is as stealthy and cautious as a rat robbing a cat's food bowl, but I have caught her out several times. She did not know we were returning to Helion before Banzalo came aboard, and she thinks Terikel is her friend. Something possessed Velander in the ruins of Larmentel. A succubus, is my guess. It is in the oracle sphere held in the circlet."

"How can you know?"

"Velander changed from prude to temptress within mere hours while in Larmentel. Around the same time I saw a soul being torn to shreds by elementals while darkwalking. That was when I heard my name being called. I am now sure that I witnessed Velander's death without knowing it. Everyone aboard except us has been increasingly lethargic ever since Velander returned from Larmentel. I can recognize a fellow elemental, Druskarl. We both feed on the life force of others; I just do it more violently."

"So what now?"

"I am weary of the whims and orders of fools and idiots. I am going to do some serious eating, then I am going to take command."

Laron slipped quietly belowdecks and made for the boatmaster's cabin. Banzalo was asleep, and alone. Laron fed quietly, then moved on. Feran was asleep in the navigator's cabin, while the succubus was visible in the blackness, astride one of the marines. The other marine was behind them. Again Laron fed. Presently the elemental left the remaining marine in a deep sleep and slipped from his bunk. Laron seized her by the throat and pressed hard on the main artery. The elemental struggled soundlessly as he held her at arm's length. Presently she went limp. Laron bound and gagged her.

Back on deck, Laron held up a little chunk of glass from Larmentel. Now he whispered a truename to the fragment of glass and spoke a more complex casting. Faint violet fire skittered over its surface for some seconds, then expanded to surround it like a faint bubble. He put it on the lid of the iron casket.

"We are over the Arcosta Sandbanks," said Laron, leaning on the rail with his hands clasped. "The water is only about ten feet deep, but that should be more than sufficient. Furl the sails and drop anchor while I bring out the dead."

Soon there were three bodies on the deck. The elemental's eyes were open as Laron tied a small sack of gold to her feet.

"Druskarl, throw Banzalo and his two marines over the side," Laron said without looking up.

The elemental's eyes watched as the bodies were heaved over the side, one by one. Laron now lifted her, weighting and all. He bared his teeth at her, then spoke.

"A captured succubus is worth far more than the gold I am weighting you with," he said as he lifted her above the rail. "I know that Velander is dead, so what happens to her body is unimportant. *You* are alive, however, and I have prepared a tether amulet and entrapment-casting on deck. You may stay with this body and drown. You may also leave it and flee into the blackness of the ocean and be lost. Then again, you may consent to be captured. The other tethers are sealed in the iron casket. Think quickly."

The elemental's eyes glared, and her head shook emphatically from side to side. Laron released her without another word. Velander's body splashed noisily and vanished. Laron began to count, and sat down to watch the bubble of violet around the chunk of glass. The sound of men stirring came from below, but Druskarl had jammed the hatches again. Laron reached one hundred twenty-seven.

The elemental held on, hoping this was a trick. When her host body's lungs began to burn she tried to dissociate, but she could not speak the word. She breathed water, thrashing and struggling. Velander's body was dying. Serenity replaced terror, then the body's life force ebbed so low that the elemental was able to tear free. There in the etherworld was a well of light and a violet sphere, just as Laron had said, and beside it was an ocular. Laron was patiently watching the chunk of glass on the iron case. Druskarl sat nearby, cleaning his fingernails with the point of a knife. If they reeled in the ocular and closed the casket there would be total blackness. There was really no choice involved for the succubus, and in her despair she had not noticed another, gossamer-thin line of light with a vanishingly faint cloud of glow surrounding it.

Laron saw the surface of the glowing bubble shimmer, then change to red. Instantly he spoke a bright ball of yellow fire into his hand and leaped straight over the side.

Velander's bound body was just below the ship, and one tug at the slipknot freed it from the bag of coins on the shallow oceanbed. Moments later Druskarl was helping him to haul the body over the rail and onto the deck.

"Cut off the gag and bindings, quickly!" barked Laron. "Now turn her on her back, breathe into her mouth like I showed you."

Laron ripped open Velander's tunic, then spoke more tendrils of fire onto his hands. Spreading his fingers, he pressed down on her upper chest. The body heaved, and Druskarl pulled away.

"Keep breathing for her!" Laron cried, clamping his glowing hands down again.

Velander's body convulsed. This time it coughed, vomited water, then lay still, breathing raggedly. Laron sat back and absorbed the etheric fire into his hands.

"I thought you said Velander was dead," Druskarl asked.

"She is; she died at Larmentel. This is a body with no soul, no consciousness." He tapped the sphere held in the newly visible circlet that she wore. "The subsequent tenant has just been evicted."

Laron spoke a casting. Velander's body became wrapped in glowing threads that skittered over the surface without binding. He spoke another casting. Druskarl recognized some words from the experiments he had helped with.

"Luckily, I am the devious type," said Laron. "Back at Larmentel I gave her more than the settings to render the circlet opaque, I also had her reset it to release itself to this type of casting."

"What? You mean you knew back then?"

"No, I just wanted control of the circlet restored to me."

Druskarl whistled. "Your paranoia has no bounds."

"Who told you to say that?"

They both chuckled, then Laron twisted a ray on the circlet. Tendrils of fire danced along the metal, then soaked into her skin.

"Her hair!" exclaimed Druskarl. "It seems to be growing right through the metal."

"That is because the metal does not quite exist."

Laron shook the body by the shoulders.

"Ninth?"

Her eyes opened. She stirred. "Laron?"

"I am here."

"Laron, there was a thing in here with me. It was burning and greedy, and it was terribly strong. I was so frightened—"

"Ninth, Ninth, just calm yourself. It will never be back."

"Never?"

"Never."

"Am I to practice walking again?"

"No more practice. This body is yours."

The auton girl slowly sat up, again clumsily because of the new body.

"My clothes. They are wet."

"It must be wash day. Cover your breasts, we don't want the sailors getting the wrong idea."

Ninth pulled her torn tunic across her breasts and folded her arms. Laron put the chunk of glass with the imprisoned succubus into the iron case and closed the lid.

"I am never going back?" Ninth asked.

"You have not left your sphere," replied Laron. "You are reaching out from the sphere through the circlet and controlling a dead girl's body. If the circlet is ever removed you will be confined to the sphere again."

Velander watched everything from the etherworld. She was puzzled. The succubus elemental had been driven from her body, then a simple, almost formless elemental had replaced it. An auton, from what she could make out. What was Laron doing? Had he betrayed her? Then she realized what the problem was. Most of her was gone. She was like a tree with its roots and branches cut away. Life lingered, but she was weakening. The moorings that could attach her to a body had been torn off. Laron was doing nothing because there was nothing he could do. Nothing, except preserve her physical body, that is.

What was his plan, she wondered. Did he have a plan, or did he just hope in the face of hopelessness?

Whatever the case, she could not wait indefinitely. Velander had by now realized that the etheric energy in her chunk of axis glass was fading. Her needs were not great, but in order to maintain herself she was slowly draining it.

Perhaps he does not know I exist, she thought in despair.

After diving to retrieve the bag of gold that had weighted Velander's body, Laron allowed Feran and the rest of the crew up on deck. They huddled together in Miral's green light, looking up at Laron, who stood on the quarterdeck. Ninth and Druskarl were behind him. Slowly the vampyre smiled, baring his fangs.

"I would like to announce that I have just killed Banzalo and his four marines, drunk their blood, and dropped their bodies overboard."

There was very little that anyone could say to that. Nobody tried.

"As most if not all of you will appreciate by now, something happened to Velander in the ruins of Larmentel. I have finally discovered that she was killed by elementals while dark-walking, and her body was possessed by a succubus. The succubus concerned has been feeding on all of you for the fifteen days past, but only boatmaster Feran was awake during the, ah, proceedings. I have managed to drive it out of Velander's body and capture it."

"But if Velander is dead and the succubus is gone, who is that?" asked Feran, pointing to the girl beside Druskarl.

"That is Ninth, a child-creature, an auton built during Metrologan experiments before the fire-circles. The silver circlet around Ninth's head enables her to live through Velander's body."

Laron paused for emphasis. There were curious stares, but no questions. Ninth looked on with unsettling innocence.

"Now, a few words about me," Laron continued. "I am over seven hundred years old. Seven centuries ago, when the Metrologans captured me, they captured the mind and soul of a vampyre, an undead thing that feeds on both your blood and ether, and which cannot die. I was dragged in from another world, and I turned my host body into the only vampyre on your own world. I have many powers that mortals do not."

The crew of the *Shadowmoon* had suspected there was something very odd about Laron from the day that he first stepped aboard, but if they had further questions they did not ask them.

"When I was alive, I was the young squire of a good and chivalrous knight on another world. On that world, horses have hoofs instead of claws, and people have round ears and only one heart. Although I am now a monster, I try to cling to at least a scrap of chivalry, however. That is why I feed upon people who I consider to be bad, objectionable, annoying, or even unduly boring. I do try to make the world a better place."

Laron paused. After an awkward moment the crew began to applaud. Laron cleared his throat to continue.

"Although Ninth inhabits the body of a woman, she is just a child. If any of you so much as lays a finger on her, makes an unseemly suggestion, or even winks at her, his name will be Dinner. As an added bonus, before I begin to feed I shall do something so unimaginably hideous to you that you will curse the day your parents first set eyes upon each other. Ninth is not the one you have been coupling with for the weeks past. She is a little-girl auton who is lost and frightened, and I have sworn to be a very, very protective big brother to her. Do I make myself clear?"

He bared his fangs again. To a man, the crew of the *Shadowmoon* shrank back, all nodding.

"Boatmaster Feran, Ninth will have your cabin. You will sleep where the crew sleeps."

"Ah, yes! That is, yes," replied Feran.

Given the circumstances, there was no loss of face here.

"D'Atro, repair the door to my own cabin. I am *never, never* to be disturbed again when Miral is down."

Once more, everyone nodded.

"Boatmaster Feran, I am assuming command of the *Shadowmoon* until we have returned to Helion. Now, go about your duties."

In a strange fashion the general mood of the *Shadowmoon*'s crew improved considerably after Laron's act of mutiny. He was merely a ruthless, strict, but fair officer, and had not fed on any of them for all the time he had been aboard.

Laron locked himself in his cabin. The chunk of glass just fit into the black cup of obsidian. He breathed energies into it and capped it with the greenstone sphere. A jagged, malignant-looking red snowflake resolved itself within the sphere, but the voice that tinkled out was cool and silky:

"Laron, I was beginning to think that you dropped my prison over the side."

"Oh no, I want to give you a chance to misbehave before I do that," replied Laron. "I want your truename."

"You what? Vampyre, you're mad!"

"Oh yes, I certainly am. Now, we are a very, very long way out to sea, and if you go over the side you would fade to nothing over a few weeks, within the total blackness of midocean. Velander died quickly, but you would die with exquisite slowness. What is your truename?"

"Nobody knows my truename."

"I want it."

"You would make me a slave."

"Your truename, if you please. It's either the safety of slavery, or the security of oblivion."

"I'd rather go to oblivion!"

"As you will, good-bye," said Laron, reaching for the greenstone globe.

"Wait! Wait. I will make a deal—"

"No deals. Good-bye."

"Jorpay'thr-ak! Jorpay'thr-ak!"

"I am going to summon you into another tether and drop this chunk of glass over the side. Provided you have given me the right name, you will be quite safe and very, very secure."

"You *lied* to me! You said I would be safe."

"You lied, too. Now, if that truename is wrong, well, you will be in ever so much trouble."

"Jorpar'thr-ak, anus-breath," she replied sullenly.

Laron performed the summoning, but the second truename the elemental had given was valid. He transferred her back to the imprinted chunk of glass.

"Now, being your master, I would like a couple of things from you," Laron announced.

"I can be such an alluring, pleasuring slave."

"Actually, they're both information. What is your worldname?"

"Rasmey."

"Very pretty. Now, I was both prudent and skilled enough to revive Velander's drowning body and install my, ah, soulmate therein. What truename did you give the body?"

Rasmey's response was a howl of outrage that trailed into pain. "You tricked me!"

"Oh, yes, and I did an excellent job of it, too. How does it feel, resisting a truename summons? According to the texts I have read, you will burn from within, as if you have swallowed a white-hot poker. I used some very advanced medicar techniques to revive Velander's body and some even more advanced techniques to install another soul within it, but not having the truename is a real annoyance. Are you ready?"

Rasmey was not ready, and she never would be ready.

"Jorpar'thr-ak, I command you to speak the truename of the body of Velander."

There was a short pause, followed by a short, whining moan that quickly grew in intensity.

"Illi-einsielt!" Rasmey gasped resentfully.

Laron sat at the opposite end of the boatmaster's cabin to Ninth, his hands clasped tightly together.

"Now that we have changed your body's truename, you must guard it from all others," he explained. "Carelessness in such matters cost the previous owner her soul."

"I shall be careful."

"Whisper a new truename name for yourself into your cupped hands, using the same form of words that we just used for naming your new body."

Laron listened as Ninth named herself with a truename. It gave him power over her, but it also allowed him to heal her with his own strength.

"Very dangerous, letting someone else know your truename," Laron emphasized. "Even more dangerous to let someone else name you."

"This body, it has been mating," said Ninth bluntly.

Her frankness rattled Laron a little, but he held firm. "Ah, yes. Are you worried that you might be with child after so much dalliance between Feran and the succubus?"

"I just need to know, for the maintenance of the body."

"The previous, ah, tenant, was taking precautions against

that sort of thing. Precautions based on enchantment. If you want to know what is involved, I can show you."

"No," she replied, her voice devoid of emotion as only an auton's could be.

Leaving Ninth to have her first sleep as a living person, Laron went on deck to be alone. It had been quite a strain, yet he had won. The bag of gold was still on the deck, forgotten during the dramas and mutiny that had raged through the little craft this night. *Never hurts to keep some handy,* he thought, then he scooped up a handful and opened his purse. He noticed the chunk of glass to which he had bound the ocular. For some moments he considered his options, tossing it up into the air. Then he spoke a casting over the glass. It absorbed an unusual amount of energy, but the ocular did what he wanted.

In the etherworld, and unknown to Laron, the tattered, fading remains of Velander's spirit were totally focused on just one thing: clinging to the etheric beacon anchored to the chunk of glass at the bottom of the purse. The blaze of etheric energies flowed into her, giving definition to every facet of her remains.

It was some time before Velander noticed that the ocular was now registering and storing sound.

Chapter Five

VOYAGE TO ACREMA

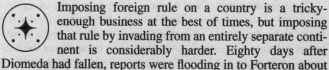

Imposing foreign rule on a country is a tricky-enough business at the best of times, but imposing that rule by invading from an entirely separate continent is considerably harder. Eighty days after Diomeda had fallen, reports were flooding in to Forteron about local preparations to attack the Torean invaders. In this case, "local" meant any other kingdom on Acrema. A dozen or so monarchs felt that their thrones were sufficiently secure, and their armies sufficiently idle, to justify getting together and getting involved. The matter of a reason posed a serious problem, however. The king of the Diomedan Protectorates was not liked, and had been disrupting trade with high taxes, levies, and customs charges. On the other hand, the Toreans were foreigners, even though they were far more reasonable about trade. It seemed a good idea to invade the place and set up a friendly, Acreman administration. On the other hand, each of the kingdoms wanted their own minion on the Diomedan throne and all the other kingdoms excluded.

In order to at least get some sort of response in motion, the northern kingdoms formed the Alliance, but immediately began to bicker about who was to be in charge. Several meetings and exchanges of messenger autons resulted in a declaration. Significantly, their declaration spoke of restoring the rightful monarch rather than putting the Diomedan king back on his throne. The eleven kingdoms in the Alliance harbored no less than fifteen of the pretenders to the Diomedan throne. Then there was the hidden agenda of desert trade routes. Any army traveling south would have to use them—and thus would gain control of them. All eleven kingdoms wanted this control, to the exclusion of the other ten.

All this, Forteron had expected. His intention had been to occupy the city, establish a firm but humane administration, lower the tariffs on everything, and keep his forces in a defensive posture. In time the Toreans would become part of the status quo, and eventually he and Warsovran would be getting invitations to royal weddings, tournaments, and orgies in the neighboring kingdoms. What really surprised Forteron was a threatened declaration of war that had arrived from the Sargolan empire on a deepwater trader.

The Sargolan empire was a union of five kingdoms of the fertile south of the continent. The Portcullis Mountains divided the desert from the forests, plains, and farms, and these were in Sargolan territory. The empire covered barely a twentieth of the continent's total area, but it was the greatest single military power. It was taking now taking a very unhealthy interest in the Toreans in

Diomeda. It was also sending messages to the northerners' Alliance, suggesting that they combine forces for an attack.

"The Sargolan emperor wants his daughter back," Forteron explained to the marshal of the Diomedan City Garrison.

"Who is holding her?" the marshal asked crisply.

"We are, apparently."

The marshal opened his mouth, closed it for lack of any immediate and sensible reply, then thought very hard.

"If we were, Admiral, I think I would know about it," he managed.

"And I would expect as much. So where is she?"

The marshal was one of those people who preferred to say nothing at all while he thought. Aware of this, and inclined to tolerate people's peculiarities as long as they got the job done, Forteron waited patiently.

"One can leave Diomeda by sea, the Leir River, or three main roads. We monitor the roads and port only to collect customs fees, and to make sure that armed infiltrators are not trying to sneak in. If the princess were here, she would have had no trouble leaving in disguise and under an assumed name. I would have been told if she had left openly."

" 'Openly,' " Forteron repeated. "Now, that is a good point. Suppose this princess, er . . ." Forteron picked up the Sargolan scroll and unrolled it. "Senterri, that is her name. Suppose Princess Senterri is in Diomeda covertly."

"But, Admiral, why?"

"*Why* does not concern me, Marshal. But if she *does* happen to be in Diomeda covertly, we shall ask her—once she is located. Sargol's fleet is no match for ours, but their army is quite formidable, and not above crossing five hundred miles of desert to teach us a lesson. The Alliance kingdoms might have all the unity of a room full of cats, but Sargol would be a politically neutral leader, as far as they are concerned. That combination would be very bad for us."

"I agree, that would be a force of half the continent's armies. Lucky that we have a larger navy."

"Wrong. The Sargolans are threatening to build a thousand ships and sail here. They are quite serious about teaching us not to throw Sargolan royalty in the slammer."

"Oh no, Admiral, I'm positive she is not in custody."

"Then, that's a start. The Sargolans have vast forests for ship-building, but we have only what wood is shipped down the Leir. By the gods of the moonworlds, who would have ever guessed that a girl's face could launch a thousand ships?"

"My wife's mother had a voice that could etch glass," volunteered the marshal.

Forteron pinched the bridge of his nose. "Find the princess, Marshal," he said wearily. "Find her quickly. Our lives may be at stake."

"If she is in the city, she will be with the local Sargolan community. There are a few dozen Sargolan merchants, students, and general wayfarers just south of the river docks."

"Good," Forteron concluded, rubbing his hands together. "Locate her, then tell me. *Do not* apprehend her like some common thief. The last thing I want is the girl to be shipped back to her father with a bad opinion of us."

The marshal bowed. "Your lordship is a wise and cunning diplomat," he observed.

"That is why I am still alive, Marshal. You would do well to follow my example."

✳ ✳ ✳

Fontarian's ruins were the last chance for the *Shadowmoon* to take on water before the long stretch across the Placidian Ocean to Helion. They arrived to find they had company. At anchor in the harbor was a triple-hulled Vindican trader. Feran's first thought was to put to sea again, but Laron pointed out that the Vindican craft could quickly detach a hull to send off in pursuit.

"It is the *Rashih-Harlif*," said Laron, peering through his far-sight. "We can approach in safety."

"Aye, and pigs may fly," Feran said fearfully.

"Then best to wear a hat; pigs have no sense of responsibility."

"How can you be so sure we are safe?"

"It is a merchant vessel."

"And that makes you trust it?"

"No."

"Then why?"

"Because I was expecting it to be here."

The gigboat was unclamped and launched, and Laron, Ninth, and Druskarl rowed across to the much-bigger vessel. They were helped aboard with deference, but Ninth and Druskarl had to wait on deck as Laron was shown into the seagrass-and-oilcloth cabin of shipmaster Suldervar. Suldervar bowed to Laron, who bowed in turn. The hospitaler brought wine, and they sat on cushions exchanging pleasantries for a while.

"Why were you not here weeks ago?" asked Laron, with just a suggestion of annoyance.

"My times and schedules are not my own. There is turmoil right across the Placidian Ocean. Warsovran has seized Diomeda. I am due back in Vindic in just two weeks because of it."

"Diomeda," said Laron contemplatively. "Large, rich, strong, yet on a desert coast and very isolated. If I had a fleet with nearly a quarter of a million fighting men, but no backup at all, why, Diomeda would be ideal. The armies of other kingdoms must travel a long way to attack."

Suldervar sat uneasily. Laron was young, highly educated, a spy, and very strange. The possibility that he might also be important had Suldervar puzzled. He was, after all, a youth of about fourteen, with acne, and a beard pasted onto his face.

"So, what of Silverdeath?" Suldervar inquired.

"We failed," Laron said tersely.

"But is there hope?" asked Suldervar.

"Perhaps. We reached Larmentel. The place where the fire-circles burned from is a powerful, disturbed artifact, but Silverdeath was not there."

"Our employers must pay it a visit someday. What else?"

"Warsovran has wiped out the new Vidarian colonies, along with Regent Banzalo's fleet. I saw the aftermath with my own eyes. Regent Banzalo is also dead."

"I have heard about the colonies. The deepwater trader *Greenfoam* crossed our path on the open sea after calling on them. Warsovran's squadron seems to be working its way south."

"A few Vidarians are left on Helion," Laron pointed out. "They should be warned. The surviving Metrologan priestesses are on Helion, too."

"I cannot take this ship all the way there. I have orders to return to our masters with either Silverdeath or your report of it."

"Where?"

"Our masters do not like to be noticed."

"Druskarl wishes to transfer to the *Rashih-Harlif*, is this permitted?" asked Laron. "We have discussed it, and he has my leave if you can take him."

"Why not? The ship is large, there is room."

"And Ninth. Can she go, too?"

"Ninth? The girl who is— How is it said? Like a cage with the canary missing?"

"She has been through a lot. It has made her somewhat withdrawn. I have patrons in Vindic; they can care for her, and place her in suitable work. It will be no trouble for you."

"No trouble, no trouble at all," replied Suldervar.

"Then, that is settled. I shall take the *Shadowmoon* to Helion and warn them."

They returned to the deck. Ninth stood listening with a serene and uncomprehending expression as Laron and Druskarl spoke.

"Will you not come to Vindic as well?" asked Druskarl. "The *Greenfoam* will warn Helion about Warsovran's attacks long before you get there."

"I gave my word to Terikel, I *must* return to Helion."

"But—"

"It is a matter of chivalry, it has nothing to do with logic. She is a woman in need, and I made her a promise. That is the end of it."

"The more I hear of this chivalry business, the less contact I want with it," said Druskarl, unsure of whether a smile or frown was more appropriate.

"When I will see you again?" asked Ninth.

"Druskarl will take you to Vindic, where an associate of mine will arrange for you to be looked after."

"That is no answer."

"Vindic is close to Helion; it is only twenty days away if the winds are fair."

"That is no answer, either."

"Ninth, I am a vampyre. I am dead, dangerous, and vicious, and my eating habits are revolting at best. I can only ever be a visitor in your life, girl, but visit I certainly shall."

This seemed to satisfy Ninth. "Nice," she responded.

"Yes, very nice. Vindic is a big, strong, prosperous kingdom, where you can live safe from Warsovran and his marines."

Ninth was below as the *Rashih-Harlif* got under way. It had twice the speed of the *Shadowmoon*, even with only a moderate amount of canvas in use. Before long, both the *Shadowmoon* and the Torean coastline were out of sight. Druskarl and Suldervar stood in silence beside the steersmen for a long time, as if nervous that Laron could hear them if they were still in sight.

"It is good to serve Your Highness again," Suldervar finally said, bowing deeply as he spoke.

"I appreciate the risk you took, my friend."

"I must counsel against a return to Vindic. The regent is not popular, and with the crown prince dead you would find yourself at the head of a restoration rebellion whether you wanted it or not. Your enemies know it as well as your allies, and—"

"Please, please, I accept your counsel. I never intended to go there anyway."

"Ah! Yet you wished the strange youth, Laron, to believe that?"

"I wish everyone to believe that."

"What about the girl?"

"I shall take her with me, to Diomeda."

"Diomeda? But, but Warsovran reigns there."

"And Warsovran has what *I* must have. You will change course and take us straight to Diomeda, then sail north to Bantak, on the Valestran border. Do you still have those two spies from my wife's faction aboard?"

"Yes."

"Look after them. Those two, Silverdeath, yourself, and one small, isolated island are vital to my plans."

Life in Diomeda had changed little since Warsovran's fleet had sailed out of the east and taken the port city in a single day. His fleet was the largest in the world, and he had been wise in deciding to use it to gain a new home while the fleet was still at full strength. Dawnlight, King Rakera's palace, was holding out, however. Built, manned, and provisioned to withstand a siege of up to a year, and being on an island in the middle of a bay, it had resisted two direct assaults using marines and scaling ladders, and another by the massed catapults and ballistae of the entire fleet. Warsovran's answer to this was to blockade Dawnlight while building five massive floating catapults that could fling quarter-ton rocks from beyond the range of the defenders' weapons. This was taking time, but Warsovran had time on his side.

Diomeda was in the middle of a wide desert, and Warsovran's fleet controlled the coast. Thus the allies of the besieged king had to assemble and equip an army to march overland, carrying all their water and supplies. Not only was this taking a lot of time, it would provide no tangible benefits. The invaders from Torea were not preventing the passage of trading ships, and had actually reduced Diomedan customs charges, levies, and taxes by fifty percent. This was very good for trade. By sending part of his fleet back to Torea to mine and defend its melted gold and silver, Warsovran had also gained control of more wealth than any single kingdom on Acrema. He could thus afford to be generous to his newly conquered subjects and his neighbors.

The emperor's mansion-turned-palace was on a hill near the shore, and had been carefully chosen by Admiral Forteron. The mansion's balconies and towers commanded an excellent view of the harbor, city, and surrounding desert. Were there to be a massive invasion from the desert, Warsovran could be on his flagship within minutes. Were his fleet to be destroyed, he could quickly flee into the desert with several squads of his newly formed mounted lancers.

What did appear out of the east one evening was not an enemy fleet, but a messenger auton in the form of an albatross enmeshed in a fine web of energies. Einsel was waiting on the highest of the mansion's towers as the auton approached. It banked, drooped its tail and raised its wings, then landed at the center of a circle of flickering orange the sorcerer had cast only moments earlier. The circle began to contract. The combination of bird and casting stood quite still. Einsel's casting merged with the feet of the bird, and slowly began to draw the auton away. After perhaps two minutes the exhausted bird shook its head and looked around in alarm. With a squark it lurched into motion, launching itself over the edge of the tower, then soaring away over the rooftops of Diomeda. Where it had been standing was a tiny figure of glowing energies.

Einsel reached out and cupped his hands beneath the figure's feet. It dwindled to a single ball of orange that hovered just above his hands. Einsel straightened and made for the tower's steps, and before long he was standing before Warsovran.

"From Admiral Narady, Your Majesty," said the little man.

"You have checked the transit name?"

"Yes. It is a match."

Warsovran nodded, and at this cue Einsel bent over and spread his cupped hands. The ball of etheric energies resolved itself back into a tiny figure.

" 'Most Esteemed and Supreme Emperor, please accept this despatch from your servant, Grand Admiral Harric Narady,' " it declared, with a bow toward Warsovran.

" 'It is my pleasure to report that the battle fleet of the Vidarian privateer chieftain Banzalo has been annihilated. Thirty-one of his ships have been captured, the rest have been sunk. The chieftain Banzalo is presumed to have died in the fighting. All Vidarian hamlets on the coast of your continent of Torea have been razed. In addition, fourteen illegal settlements of privateers from other kingdoms have been conquered, and twelve thousand prisoners of able body have been taken as slaves. About half are mixed privateers and the rest are Vidarians. These slaves have been set to work in the extraction of gold, silver, and other metals of worth from the ruined cities of Torea. One hundred and twenty privateer vessels have been captured either singly or in small squadrons so far, and your fleet has reached as far south as Wynsel's ruins. Losses have been confined to just five vessels, and these have been made up many times over by those which have been captured. It is my intention, subject to subsequent correction by your Esteemed and overwhelmingly wise Self, to divide the fleet, with one-third returning to Gironal in order to mine its riches by means of our slaves, while the rest of the warships circle Torea and sweep away all other privateers who would plunder the wealth that is rightfully yours. I am yours in service and soul, Grand Admiral Narady.' "

Einsel lowered his hands again, and this time the little figure dissolved into them and was gone. The sorcerer straightened, then bowed to Warsovran.

"The Grand Admiral is trying hard to win back my favor," Warsovran observed. "Glorious victories, untold plunder, a continent taken, and yet he is sensible enough to confess that Banzalo's fate has not yet been confirmed."

"Is there a problem, Your Majesty?" Einsel asked, safe in the knowledge that here was a political situation in which he had no stake at all.

"No problem. Narady uses the best of my ships and elite marines to great effect, and is as loyal as a hunting spaniel. Forteron is at his best against bad odds, but is inclined to go too far without a firm hand on his leash. That is why I sent him against Diomeda, but that is also why I keep him close to me. Narady can be trusted to do as I say, especially after I elevate him to prince regent of the Torean coast and award him one ounce of gold for every twenty recovered."

"That is generous of you," muttered Einsel, who had never been paid particularly well, for a courtier.

"It is sufficient: neither too much nor too little. Forteron has the illusion of being my favorite and hero, so he is no problem, either. That leaves the matter of what to do with Griffa? The man is a fearsome warrior, but limited if he has to command more than twenty ships. Some say the problem is that he cannot count beyond twenty."

"That is indeed the total of his toes and fingers," Einsel pointed out with a shrug.

"Nice joke, but this particular joke wants to become Supreme Admiral," sighed Warsovran.

"Such men often consider themselves better than their monarchs."

"True. They need to be beaten in a show of power, and I have just such a show planned, now that Banzalo has been plucked from the game's board. Admiral Griffa is to command a small squadron of my fastest ships and train a new millenary of marines. It will be called the Hellfire Squadron, and it shall be used to raid distant ports and harass the shipping of my enemies."

"Griffa will see that as a slight."

"Not if he is also the designated escort for Silverdeath whenever it is used."

Einsel gasped, and was unable to hide the dismay on his face.

"Your Majesty, you cannot be serious. The first use of Silverdeath annihilated a whole continent, and even now the climate here in Diomeda has become cooler from all the dust and smoke from Torea blocking the sun. You cannot—"

"I shall!" Warsovran said firmly. Einsel knew better than to protest further. "Griffa will escort me to Helion, where he shall see the power of Silverdeath for himself. Certain ambassadors and envoys to Diomeda from Acrema's other kingdoms will be aboard my ship as well, and I think everybody will be very impressed. Griffa will be flattered to be known as the escort of Silverdeath, yet he will be overawed, too."

"And after Helion, there will be no more use of Silverdeath?" Einsel asked hopefully.

"Lessons always need to be repeated, Einsel. Now, cast a messenger auton for me to speak into. Narady will be wondering how I reacted to his news."

Across the city, two women were lying on cushions on a balcony and fanning themselves in the evening heat. Sairet was a teacher in the Guild of Dancers, but although she was held in high regard, she had never prospered. For the year past she had been teaching the Diomedan version of windrel belly dancing to a rich client named Lady Wensomer. Wensomer was a Sargolan noble who had arrived on a coastal trader from Palion, bought a villa, hired servants, then enlisted Sairet's services to learn dancing. One rumor had it that she was an exiled princess. Another was that she was the daughter of a rich merchant, sent out of reach of some unsuitable suitor.

Every morning Sairet would arrive at dawn, drag her rich and slightly overweight client out of bed, endure a tirade of pleas, curses, and abuse as she forced Wensomer to wake up and get dressed, then spend the morning teaching her dancing technique, steps, and music. At noon the steward would pay Sairet, and she would return home to her other students. Wensomer paid well, and seemed to do little more than lie about eating and reading when not engaged in her dancing lessons. In the evening Wensomer had another personal lesson, so that after a year of such intense tutoring she had become quite an accomplished dancer.

"I like the darkness, it makes this drab city more exotic," said Wensomer, gazing at the rooftops between the marble supports of the balcony's railing.

"It does seem different at night," Sairet agreed. "Now it's all shadows, soft outlines, and flickering lights."

"Like people," said Wensomer. "The more you see of them, the more boring they become."

"Not like you," replied Sairet, shaking her head. "The more I see of you, the more I wonder. You are not really the daughter of a merchant."

"Why not?"

"You have no interest in the trivia that daughters of merchants find amusing and distracting."

"How should you know, dancemistress?"

"I have taught a great number of them. I have a real one on my register book at present. She has to be careful not to bump her head, else the hollow, booming sound is a source of embarrassment." Wensomer tapped at her own head.

"It sounds full. Am I failing a test?"

"Only one of many. I have watched you over the year past. You read at least three languages and speak another two."

"Very useful for a merchant's daughter."

"True, but still, I wonder."

Sairet stood, raised her arms into the air and began to sway her hips from side to side while her upper torso remained perfectly still.

"Why do you really want to learn how to dance?"

"Dancing is a talent. Rich, important suitors take more of an interest in girls who can do more than just look decorative."

"You are already rich," Sairet began, but Wensomer also

stood up, and peered out over the bay that was Diomeda's harbor.

A squadron of Warsovran's ships was under way, heading for the open sea. Miral was not up, but a bright display of etheric fire was lighting up the sky.

"Eighteen, nineteen, twenty ships. Six of them dash galleys, and fourteen battle galleys. Now, where might Warsovran be going?"

"How do you know Warsovran is with the squadron?"

"The really big galley is his flagship."

"You know ships well for a merchant's daughter."

"I know ships well *because* I am a merchant's daughter." She turned away from the harbor, leaning with her elbows on the balcony rail and trying to look relaxed. Sairet's experience allowed her to see the tension nevertheless. "This is a good time to end the lesson," Wensomer declared.

"Whatever you say," agreed Sairet. "You are beginning to tire, and will learn little more tonight."

They descended the stairs then sidled through the curtain of hanging beadwork and gauze drapery onto the long, locksquare-pattern floor of the passageway.

"What now, most excellent torturer?" asked Wensomer as they walked. "Do you go straight to bed once you are home, to build up your strength, all the better to torment me tomorrow?"

"Not at all, I have another pupil. Her name is Senterri."

"The brunette girl? The one with the two handmaids?"

"Yes. She is a rather spoiled young Sargolan."

"A Sargolan? That empire is half a thousand miles down the coast. Your fame has indeed spread."

"Not entirely. Her family has a trading house here, Aramadea Silks, Spices, and Fine Wines. Rather than sit about in idle splendor while her father arranges an advantageous marriage into another trading house, she learns dancing."

"And do you also torment her with such dedication?"

"I merely teach, whether my pupils choose to call it torment is their own business. Senterri is . . . lacking in focus. She seems to be learning dance because it is a daring thing for a merchant's daughter to do."

"But it is. I'm a merchant's daughter, I should know."

"*You* have the drive of a war galley. Senterri is just a silly girl. Still, she is a silly girl who pays for dancing lessons, so I am not going to complain."

The steward was waiting at the door, and with him was a eunuch carrying a purse on a velvet cushion. He began to count out Sairet's fee as the women bowed to each other.

"Have dancemistress Sairet escorted home," Wensomer said as the steward opened the door.

"Try to be in bed early, my lady," advised Sairet. "Rest is as important as practice."

The eunuch saw Sairet safely to her lodgings. There, Senterri was waiting, along with her two handmaids. All three of them had already done their stretching exercises. Dolvienne was the sensible handmaid, who made the other two practice rather than gossip. For Perime, her mistress could do no wrong, and she would do anything for her. This included arguing with Sairet when she tried to correct her mistress's mistakes. It had been a particularly long day for the dancemistress, as there had been no cancellations and all lessons had gone full-time.

"There are times during daylight hours that might suit you better," Sairet suggested as they began.

"Oh no, I am only able to slip away during the night," Senterri insisted, trying to seem conspiratorial and failing completely.

"Mistress Senterri is watched very closely," Perime added unconvincingly.

"Mistress Senterri might be recognized by other servants were she to come here in bright daylight," said Dolvienne. "They would betray her to her father."

"My father disapproves of dancing," said Senterri. "He says only harlots, windrels, and clowns dance, and that it is not a skill that any respectable girl should learn."

"But Mistress Senterri is none of those," Perime said hurriedly.

"The mistress thinks dance is important in courtship," said Dolvienne.

"Yes, why should harlots dance and be seductive while good girls just sit about and try to look winsome?" asked Senterri.

"But Mistress Senterri does not want to be a harlot—" began Perime.

"Enough!" snapped Sairet. "You are paying to learn dancing.

If you want to gossip you can do it for free elsewhere. Now, then, I want to see your hip rolls."

Sairet followed the city's gossip closely, and even had a web of informers among her associates. Senterri did live in a Sargolan trading house, but the merchant there never made the slightest attempt to restrict or constrain her. It was almost as if she were a tenant, yet there was better accommodation in Diomeda for a woman who could obviously afford two hand-maids and a lot of quite expensive clothing. Wensomer had her own mansion, after all, and was open about her wealth. Senterri was playing the role of a daring and rebellious girl, yet doing it with two personal servants to look after her. Neither of Sairet's two best-paying pupils were what they seemed, the dancemistress was sure of that.

After what seemed to Sairet like the longest lesson in her teaching career, Dolvienne paid, Perime packed up their costumes, and the three girls vanished into the darkened streets, accompanied by a guard from one of the escort guilds. Sairet retired for the night. As she lay on her small pallet bed she could not escape the feeling that her two most wealthy pupils had some agenda far larger than learning to dance to impress their friends, relatives, and suitors. In particular, Wensomer had allowed a carefully crafted mask of glittering bubbles to slip for a moment. Beneath her laziness and indulgence was a hint of hard, sharp acumen. The real question was why Wensomer was trying to hide it.

At that very moment someone else was puzzling over the behavior of Sairet's two most mysterious pupils. He was, however, a lot better informed than Sairet. Admiral Forteron read the scroll that he held while displaying no more emotion than a slight scowl. Presently he looked up and glared at his surveillance marshal.

"Now, let me repeat all this back to you in my own words," said the Torean admiral. "That way you can see what is actually in my mind, and hence can judge it to be true or false."

"Very good, Admiral."

"A dancemistress named Sairet lives in this city. She specializes in belly dancing, she is insane, and she is also the former queen of Diomeda—deposed when the king that *we* deposed led a palace rebellion and had her husband and children killed."

"Yes, Admiral."

"Why did he not kill her, too?"

"Diomedans consider it unlucky to kill mad people. Their gods—"

"Enough, question answered. Apparently this mad, former queen and teacher of belly dancing has many pupils. One is a quite lissome Sargolan princess named Senterri, who has been living in secret in Diomeda for some months, but whose presence was known to authorities from the minute she stepped off her ship."

"Yes, Admiral."

"Why was I not told about this two months ago?"

"Most of the former king's informers and spymasters joined the underground resistance against us. Yesterday one of those spymasters fell into our hands. After we tortured him briefly with a large bag of gold, and free passage to the port of his choice, he revealed the location of the Royal Surveillance Archives."

"Ah, I see. I wish to speak with him."

"He was assassinated this morning, Admiral."

"Understandable, I suppose, given the circumstances. Getting back to this report, the other . . . peculiar and worrying student of belly dancing is an extremely powerful but somewhat overweight sorceress from North Scalticar. Her name is Wensomer."

"Ah, by your leave, Admiral, Wensomer is not considered to be a problem—"

"I know, I know. The note on her file says, 'Harmless, except to a cake stall,' and goes on to say that her mother lives in Diomeda. The reason given for her visit is stated rather baldly in the Wayfarers' Register as, 'For her weight.'"

"Ah . . . yes."

"She has come to the pastry capital of the known world to lose weight?"

"Er, well, yes," replied the surveillance marshal, running his finger around the inside of his collar.

Forteron stood up, walked over to his subordinate, and sniffed the man's breath.

"You don't appear to have been drinking."

"No, lordship."

"Yet you wrote *this*?"

"Lordship, it is all true."

Forteron returned to his chair. He sat down and began massaging his temples.

"I am an admiral," he said presently. "I manage large numbers of warships, determine strategy and tactics, fight battles, and look after the welfare of my thousands of sailors and marines. Belly dancing is a little out of my experience. I mean, as entertainment during the occasional dinner it is all very pleasing. I am as fond of the sight of minimally clad dancing girls as the next man."

"Speaking as the next man, lordship, I most wholeheartedly agree."

"So I am rather badly in need of someone to explain what is going on here."

"As am I, lordship."

This was not the answer Forteron had been hoping for.

"Wars are fought on the whims of royalty as often as for pragmatic reasons," he explained with more of an edge to his voice. "If some princess has a whim to have dancing lessons, her father may have a whim to declare war if we don't clap loudly enough at her graduation performance."

"My feelings entirely, Admiral."

"I suppose it will not hurt to have a meeting with her."

"I advise caution, Admiral. If she is having the lessons in secret, you may spoil some surprise she is preparing for her father."

"Then we shall have a *secret* meeting. Arrange one."

"If you please, Admiral, for what day?"

"Today."

"But—but, Admiral, it is nearly midnight."

"Then you had better *run*, Marshal."

✷ ✷ ✷

Although Senterri had a love of adventure, she had never been in circumstances that could be even remotely described as perilous. She liked to do things in secret rather than really take risks, and that was the current appeal of being in Diomeda. There had been an invasion, and the city had been occupied, but the markets were open again the following day, and no restrictions had been placed on shipping. Confident that she could return home whenever she wanted to, Senterri had decided to stay in the city. Her letters home were, however, full of stories about danger, chaos, lawless streets, and fearsome, invincible invaders. She had gone on to describe how there was a warrant posted for her arrest, that she could not flee the city, that she had been bravely hiding in the house of the merchant Aramadea, and that she was helping distressed citizens to escape the Toreans and hide.

The problem was that her letters had been believed, and her father was an emperor.

Senterri arrived back at Aramadea Silks, Spices, and Fine Wines with her two handmaids and contract guard, weary from the night's dance lesson and anxious to collapse into bed as quickly as possible. She rapped at the door, but the steward did not answer. A group of men appeared at the end of the street. Just as her guard drew his ax, another group appeared, to block their retreat. Now the door was opened—to reveal a Torean noble flanked by two guards of his own.

"Your Highness, I am truly honored to meet you," he said smoothly as he bowed. "My name is Admiral Forteron, late of Damaria."

Senterri backed into her cowering handmaids, looked about, realized she had nowhere to flee, then turned back to Forteron.

"Wha— Wha— What are you going to do to me?" she stammered.

"Nothing at all, Your Highness," replied Forteron, spreading his hands wide as if to show that they were empty. "Your father has sent word that he is concerned for your welfare. I was not aware that you were here at all, but now that you have been located I am at a loss. Your father wants you home, but you seem to have no immediate plans to return home. Normally that would be no concern of mine, but your father's army is on its way here across the desert. He intends to lay siege to Diomeda until you are released. The only problem is that you are not being held in the first place. Now, according to my sources, you are visiting the city for dancing lessons. Belly dancing, to be specific."

"It is not what it seems," said Senterri, unused to being interrogated, and now thoroughly alarmed.

"Oh, I am sure of that. Well, Your Highness, far be it for me to be ordering royalty about, but I need to have you off the premises, so to speak. As soon as it can be arranged, you will be put on a warship and sent to a place of safety. Your father will be informed, and that will be the end of his siege. Have you a problem with that?"

"No, no, not at all," Senterri replied quietly.

"Excellent, would it be that all my problems were so easily solved. Well, then, I must be on my way. A true delight to meet you, Your Highness."

With that, Admiral Forteron and his two guards left. The other guards had already vanished. Senterri, her handmaids, and her contract guard found themselves in an empty street.

"Ah, I'se brought ye home," said the guard, hurriedly shifting his weight from foot to foot. "Best be on wi' it."

He hurried away. Now Senterri and the two girls were alone.

"Perime, Dolvienne, we must flee, now!" Senterri whispered to the handmaids. "The admiral is toying with us. Men love to toy with women."

"Your Highness, he said you will be kept safe," Dolvienne pointed out.

"Oh, yes. Safe in a dungeon, as a hostage to stay my father's hand against the Toreans. We must flee. This very night!"

"Your Highness, they will be watching—" began Dolvienne.

"No! We shall go before they think to stop us. All we need is a dozen guards, a wayfarer's wagon, and a driver. At dawn the city gates are opened, so we have the rest of the night to get ready."

✳ ✳ ✳

Thus it was that the following dawn saw six guards, a guide, two drivers, and a wagon with three young women arrive at the Great West Gate of Diomeda. The customs officers noted little in the way of trade goods on the wagon, although the passengers did declare thirty gold pagols. They were, they said, going to the inland city of Gladenfalle.

"Ah, it's not as if I want to seem awkward, excellent ladyship, but d'ye know it's five hundred miles to Gladenfalle?" the shift sergeant asked Senterri.

"Aye, it's not like a trip ter the markey," added another guard, leaning on his spear.

"Ah, we shall being shopping at Gladenfalle market," said Senterri.

"Buying costumes," added Perime.

"We are dancers, trained in Madame Sairet's academy for dancing," said Senterri, producing a scroll she had forged only an hour before, and which gave her handmaids honors and herself first-class honors. "We are going on a great dancing tour of Lioren Mountains, starting with Gladenfalle."

The guards let them pass. Senterri's plan had been to go west to the river port of Panyor, then turn south and begin the five-hundred-mile trek to the city of Lacer, in the Sargolan empire. By the time Forteron realized Senterri was missing, this plan had been modified rather considerably, however. The guards had waited until they were forty miles from the capital before turning on their charges, killing the guide and two drivers, stealing the thirty gold pagols, setting the wagon on fire, and abducting whom they believed were three dancers. Two days later Senterri and her two handmaids were sold—as dancers— for two pagols each; though the nomads who bought them were more aware than the guards of the value of white-skinned girls who knew windrel belly dancing. After a little more coaching they could be sold in Hadyal to a caravan going north, and ultimately they might fetch a hundred times more than the turncoat guards had been paid.

The voyage back to Helion took the *Shadowmoon* thirty-five days, through some unseasonably rough weather. Laron nevertheless kept the schooner trimmed to catch every breeze, and crowded on as much canvas as he dared whenever they came within sight of any other ship. They used the plain green mainsail, and did not light the running lanterns at all. At last they picked up the cold polar current that moderated Helion's climate, and a few days later Helion's two volcanic craters appeared on the horizon late one afternoon. There was a heavy overcast, and the crew was very relieved to see the navigation pyre on the higher of the two peaks.

News of the annihilation of Banzalo's settlements and fleet had reached the island already, and ships departing for Scalticar were already crammed with refugees. The sun was long down as the *Shadowmoon* berthed, and there was an ominously large number of spaces along the piers.

"Do I get my ship back now?" Feran asked sullenly as Laron stood beside the gangplank.

"No," the vampyre replied impatiently. "It is not your ship."

Laron breathed a thin, glowing streamer into his hands, then squeezed them closed. When he opened them again, the streamer lay coiled in the palm of his hand. He stood still for a moment, then flung the coil into the air. When he drew it in, there was a small bat snared at the end. He breathed a fine red mist over the little animal, enmeshing it.

"Fly to the temple, little brother," said the vampyre. "Tell Worthy Terikel that the *Shadowmoon* has returned, and that Laron awaits her instructions."

Driven by the auton, the bat launched itself from Laron's hands and disappeared into the night. On the deck of the *Shadowmoon*, the crew stood watching.

"Wait here," said Laron in a thin, distant voice, then he strode off down the pier.

"Suppose he's to do some eating," said Hazlok, but nobody else was inclined to comment.

Laron returned some time later, with patches of his beard missing and the rest caked in blood. He put his hand over one of the bollards to which the *Shadowmoon* was tied. A small, faintly glowing figure materialized, sitting hunched over with its hands clasped. It had large, soulful eyes.

"Did any of them leave the ship?" asked Laron.

"No, master," the figure peeped in reply.

"Did anyone visit the ship?"

"The crew called vendors over and bought bran cakes and wine."

"Good work. Come to me."

The figure floated up from the bollard and dissolved into Laron's hand before the astonished eyes of the crew.

"Prepare to sail on the next tide," said Laron in a flat but firm voice.

"What?" exclaimed Feran. "Why? You said I could have the *Shadowmoon* back at Helion."

Laron flipped him a coin. Feran caught and examined it.

"A Timagric coin," said Feran. "So?"

"I found it on someone named Dinner. Look at the date."

"The third month of 3140."

"A new coin from an inland Torean kingdom, minted just before the fire-circles. The crew of this vessel salvaged many such coins, but they had no other way to reach Helion."

"You're saying the *Rashih-Harlif* called here? Why not check with the harbormaster?"

"I did. It did not. However, the General Movements Register notes that a Sargolan deepwater trader met the *Rashih-Harlif* in midocean a few days ago and sold them supplies in return for gold. Druskarl's gold. It was sailing due west, straight for Diomeda. My figures say that it did not have time to call at any Vindic port to set Ninth and Druskarl ashore. She is being taken to a dangerous place, perhaps to be sold into slavery. I am very concerned, Feran, and very disappointed with Druskarl. When I become disappointed with someone, I also become ever so hungry."

At that moment Terikel appeared at the base of the pier, with two men dressed as deacons, but whom Laron remembered to be temple guards. Laron stood waiting as they approached.

"Worthy Elder," said Laron, sweeping off his tricorner hat and bowing.

"Laron, you—you all survived," she responded, casting her eyes over the scene.

"I am very hard to kill, Worthy Elder."

"We heard tales of terrible massacres on the shores of Torea."

"The massacres did take place, I am saddened to say. Ah, what is the status of these two gentlemen?" he asked, indicating the guards.

"I have decided to confirm deacons as well as deaconesses. These two are the first. They are former guards, and when not doing their own study they have been instructing all Metrologans on Helion in the use of weapons."

The two deacons bowed to Laron. He looked them over. They had the bearing and confidence of trained fighters, but there had been no shortage of trained fighters in the settlements.

"Regent Banzalo's fleet was wiped out, and Banzalo himself is dead," said Laron, trying to give an idea of the odds rather than comment on the futility of making a stand on Helion. "Warsovran is alive, and he reached Silverdeath before I did."

The news was as bad as it could possibly be. It was some time before Terikel was able to untangle her emotions sufficiently to reply.

"I do not see Worthy Velander or Druskarl on the deck," she ventured softly, fearing yet more bad news.

"Velander's soul was destroyed at Larmentel, but her body is currently occupied by a worthy tenant. I sent her away to a safe place, with Druskarl as escort." Laron did not feel inclined to mention that Druskarl had probably betrayed his trust. There was already more than enough gloom in his news.

"Again the Metrologan numbers shrink," Terikel sighed. "I have secretly sent the archives and most of our books to Scalticar with my four new priestesses. It is only a matter of time before Warsovran attacks Helion."

"Then why are you here?"

"Helion's temple and vineyards are all the Metrologans have left in the world, and after what the *Greenfoam*'s people said about the fate of the colonies, nobody has been willing to give me a fair price for them. Having heard your version of the story, however, I think I shall put my new followers aboard the first available ship and abandon whatever we can't carry to whoever wants it."

"Ah, there I can help," said Laron, bowing to her again. "Aboard the *Shadowmoon* is gold collected in Torea, and part of it is yours by agreement."

"Gold?" replied Terikel, who had long ago given up hope that this promise would ever mature. "How much is there?"

"In weight, six hundred pounds."

The astonished Terikel was led onto the *Shadowmoon* and down belowdecks, where the gold was stored. Laron remained on the quarterdeck, looking around the harbor. In spite of all the refugees who had streamed off the island, it was still a busy place. Opportunists, vagabonds, thieves, and tricksters were flooding over from other ports on the Placidian rim to take advantage of the breakdown of authority and the confusion. Terikel came back up from the hatchway, holding a handful of gold.

"At a single stroke you have saved us," she said in wonder, hardly daring to take her eyes off the coins.

"Then leave tomorrow morning," replied Laron.

"We shall leave as soon as we can pack—"

"Pack tonight, sail on the first tide tomorrow."

"And Roval is still locked up. We need to free him and take him with us."

"Learned Terikel, this is getting to be very complicated, and we have little time."

"Roval *must* come with us. I've been visiting him every day in the lockup, and— Look, he just comes with us, and there's an end to it."

"Then we need to free him tonight, and tonight's schedule is filling rapidly. This reminds me of Acre, just before the final siege."

"Acre? I do not know the place."

"If you did I would be very surprised. I sense impending doom hanging over this place—but no matter, and first things first. Is the division of the gold fair?"

"Laron, if you can be trusted to bring *any* gold back here you can be trusted to divide it fairly. You could have gone to any port on the Placidian Ocean's rim; you need never have returned here."

"I gave my word of honor, and honor is all that I truly value. Here I am."

Terikel removed a gold seal ring from her finger, put it into Laron's hand, and closed his cold fingers over it.

"This belonged to a Metrologan priest who died here years ago. It is probably the last in existence. I think that you should have it."

"Worthy Elder, I cannot accept this," he said, holding the ring out to her. "It belongs to your Order."

She took the ring but slipped it onto his finger before he could withdraw his hand. "Take it, Laron, because there will never be another Metrologan Brotherhood priest. Only my new, merged Order's priests, which are not the same—"

"Quiet!" barked Laron, suddenly alert.

He stared out into the darkness, holding his hands to his ears. Miral's light was blocked by the clouds, but there was little wind and the ocean was placid.

"Muffled oars," said Laron. "Many, many muffled oars. . . . Feran, Hazlok, cast off, now! Everyone else to the sweeps."

Before a minute was past, the *Shadowmoon* was clear of the pier and moving into deeper water. By now the approaching squadron was in sight, and alarm gongs and trumpets were sounding all across the island. Huge, sleek shapes with raised boarding ramps loomed before the *Shadowmoon*, and ballista shots flung up the water around it.

"We're smaller than they expect," said Feran as he and Laron heaved at the steering pole. "They're misjudging our range."

The *Shadowmoon* passed between two dash galleys five times its length and attracted a shower of arrows. A battle galley loomed ahead of them, but as they steered to avoid it a boarding ramp was swung out over the water. As it passed the *Shadowmoon* it smashed into the mainmast, and a dozen marines dropped onto the deck before the far-bigger ship had slid past on its way to the wharves. Several more marines missed, and sank at once with the weight of their armor.

Terikel's two deacons abandoned their sweeps and drew their axes, engaging the marines who were scattered along the length of the *Shadowmoon*'s decks. Laron cross-blocked the downward chop of an ax, seized the arm that held it, then grasped the man's belt and flung him over Feran's head and into the schooner's wake. The sailor Heinder traded several blows with a marine before an ax chopped into his side from behind. Staggering around, he took a chop to the shoulder before wrapping a brawny arm around the marine's neck and tumbling over the rail with him. Another marine tried to take the quarterdeck, but Laron cross-blocked again, twisting the ax out of his hands and thrusting the handle's butt into his face.

Norrieav and Hazlok fought back-to-back, doing little damage to the veteran marines but at least staying alive. D'Atro stood just inside the hatchway, defending it with a pair of facing hatchets. Just then another battle galley glided past, sending another shower of arrows into the *Shadowmoon*. A marine and both temple guards went down, crippled or dead. The Acreman sailor Martak stood on the foredeck, using the mast as a shield as a marine chopped at him. His own ax bounced off armor, but he had no armor against the knife that was flung from the maindeck and into his stomach. He collapsed across the spar, and an ax-blow to the neck ended his life.

Even though four had died on each side, the sailors were not professional warriors. Leaving two to engage Norrieav and Hazlok, the remaining six marines converged on Laron. In spite of being fast, strong, and immune to injuries that would kill most people, he was not proof against being hacked to pieces by six axes. With no sails up and nobody rowing, the schooner was moving only because of a current. Feran abandoned the steering pole and drew his ax, but as he stepped forward he noticed that the *Shadowmoon* was settling in the water. Someone had opened the ports below deck. *Terikel.* Turning immediately, he chopped through the two ropes holding the bracebar. The remains of the rigging hinged forward, crashing down.

The horrified marines also now realized that the schooner was sinking. They were, unlike the crew, fully armored. They began frantically stripping off their helmets and plate, but the crewmen had not stopped fighting. The *Shadowmoon* was designed to sink very quickly. The ruddy light of burning ships and buildings illuminated the *Shadowmoon*'s final moments on the surface, then it vanished, to the cheers of another passing battle galley.

The island was effectively in Warsovran's hands by midnight, but it was not until dawn that he came ashore to survey the damage. Barely two hundred Toreans had survived the fighting, and the rest of the island's population was drawn from the entire rim of the Placidian Ocean. Eleven ships had been sunk, and about a quarter of Port Wayside's buildings had been burned. As a prize of war, it left a lot to be desired.

"The elite stalkers who came ashore ahead of the galleys, killed all the lookouts at their posts," Admiral Griffa proudly explained to Warsovran. "The locals had no warning before we were actually in the harbor."

"This is all looking too easy," Warsovran commented doubtfully. "The ambassadors aboard the fleet were told that we triumphed against superior odds. Make sure they see the remains of a great battle."

"It will be done."

"Have you found their regent?"

"One of the prisoners said that Banzalo died off the coast of Torea, apparently from loss of blood. The acting regent was killed in the fighting for Port Wayside."

"What about the Metrologans?"

"According to your instructions, the temple was spared. Scouts report that two dozen militiamen in their pay have barricaded themselves in the place, and they have crossbows. One scout was killed; another brought back a bolt in his shoulder as well as his report."

"Pity. I was hoping to have just one leader for this morning's show."

"Oh, we have a priest, Your Majesty. Well, that is to say, we found a youth wearing a Metrologan priest's seal ring. Several of the islanders say that all the priests are dead and that he must have stolen it, but he insists that he is the only Metrologan left alive."

"Bring him to me."

Laron was brought to Warsovran in chains, still wearing the ring Terikel had given him. His beard had been washed off, and he had reset the circlet and oracle sphere that he wore for invisibility.

"You look very young for a priest," said Warsovran.

"Island life agrees with me," replied Laron.

"You say that you are the only Metrologan left on Helion."

"Yes."

"Where are the priestesses?"

"They were trying to escape on a schooner when your ships attacked. It was sunk in the harbor, with no survivors."

"The *Vodaren*'s master reported seeing a schooner sink, Your Majesty," Forteron added.

"Your Majesty, there is no need for more killing," said Laron. "Those in the temple are only servants and militiamen. I can convince them to surrender if you promise to spare their lives."

"But I am sworn to wipe out all Metrologans," Warsovran replied with a shallow smile.

"Then kill me after the temple surrenders and you will have succeeded."

"Well, Griffa, here we have someone who thinks ahead," responded Warsovran. "Very well, try to get this place looking like a battlefield, then bring the ambassadors ashore. I believe this young priest can save us a great deal of trouble."

Warsovran was the only person alive who knew that the Metrologans had been studying methods to destroy Silverdeath for the past thousand years. Warsovran did not know that all Metrologans who knew about that project had perished with Torea, so he continued to hunt the survivors. He liked the irony that an order dedicated to Silverdeath's destruction would instead fall victim to the fantastic machine.

The marines were set to work putting armor on the civilian dead and arranging the bodies to give the impression of heavy fighting. When the ambassadors finally came ashore, they saw burned-out, half-sunken ships in the harbor and bodies littering the piers and streets. The marines escorted them to where Warsovran waited with several guards and a single prisoner. The emperor was holding what looked like a mailshirt of strange and intricate jewelry.

"Most of you are from kingdoms that are even now raising armies to attack Diomeda, which is mine by right of conquest," Warsovran began. "Thus I have decided to give you a little demonstration of my powers, so that you may give your monarchs fair warning."

Warsovran drew his ax and held it high.

"This youth here, is the last of the Metrologan Order. He was captured in the fighting and now awaits my pleasure. *This* is my pleasure."

With that, he chopped Laron through the ribs with his ax. Laron gaped at the blade as it was withdrawn, then had the presence of mind to topple to the ground with his eyes closed. He felt his chains being removed.

"The Metrologan Order is now no more," continued Warsovran. "Correct?"

Several heads nodded.

"Of course, but I am master of both life and death. I can bring him back."

Laron was held up and Warsovran maneuvered Silverdeath onto him. As the ambassadors watched, the metal melted and flowed, dissolving beneath Laron's clothing and covering his skin with a sheen of silver. Laron became animate, and got to his feet.

"Serve me!" commanded Warsovran. "I am Melidian Warsovran."

Silverdeath bowed to him. "Your hands applied me. Command me, as I serve and protect."

"Are your powers at their greatest?"

"This host is damaged. I must repair it."

"How long will it take?"

"Moments."

Warsovran turned to his audience. "As you can see, I can

bring the dead back to life, but I am no mere hedgerow healer. Across there, is a small temple where a few militiamen have gathered for a last stand against my marines. I could order that they be attacked and the battle would be over in a half hour, but I do not like to waste my men. I could starve them out, but that would take weeks."

"The host has been optimized," Silverdeath reported.

"Instead I have decided upon a humane method to pacify those in the temple. First, however, I wish to provide another entertainment for your diversion. Ambassador Raichamur of Vindic, take this ax."

The ambassador hefted the weapon clumsily. The axes of his country were lighter, with more sharply curved blades, and they were balanced differently. Still, an ax was an ax.

"Now, strike me with that fine Torean weapon," said Warsovran.

The ambassador stared at him, but otherwise did not move. Warsovran waved the marines back.

"Come on, swing," laughed the emperor. "Surely your king would be delighted, were you to kill me."

The ambassador considered. There was some trick here, perhaps another demonstration of the magical weapon's powers. After all, Raichamur was the ambassador of Vindic, the most powerful Acreman kingdom on the Placidian Ocean, a man of importance. Warsovran would not allow him to be harmed. Raichamur swung the ax.

A flash of white light from Silverdeath's eyes sliced the ambassador's arm from his body, then slashed down through his rib cage. The ambassador's body fell apart, messily. Two more ambassadors who had been standing behind the Vindican noble also collapsed in bloody heaps. The building behind them tumbled down in ruins with a noisy rumble.

There was understandable consternation among the surviving ambassadors. Several closed their eyes, resigning themselves to what was hopefully to be a quick and merciful death. Others tried to hide behind each other, and two merely turned and fled. These were quickly caught and returned by the marines.

"Silverdeath does not like attempts upon my life," said

Warsovran. "Make sure that everybody knows." He turned back to Silverdeath, pointing to the temple. "Silverdeath, destroy my enemies. Use fire-circles."

"The feat is at the limit of my powers," warned Silverdeath.

"Do it."

Silverdeath began to withdraw from Laron. The surface of his silvered skin began to crawl like a swarm of ants, and a sphere of reflectivity began to expand where his head had been. Laron collapsed as the sphere detached from him and began to float away to the south, in the direction of the Metrologan temple. Warsovran beckoned the ambassadors over to where Laron lay on the cobblestones. Two marines heaved the youth to his feet and a third removed his tunic. There was no trace of a wound on his skimpy, hairless chest.

"You see, I *can* cure," Warsovran declared, "and look at his face. All the pimples are gone as well. Whether they stay gone is another matter. But in all seriousness, were an aging monarch to present himself to me, I could restore him to the prime of youth in return for, say, a border province, or a thousand stout trading ships. Remember, too, that I can and *will* restore myself."

The ambassadors might not have been entirely convinced, but they certainly were taken aback. Laron was confused by his brief encounter with Silverdeath. Being a vampyre, his body would have restored itself after a half day, and he had only collapsed when struck because it had been what Warsovran had expected.

Warsovran continued to harangue the ambassadors. Half an hour passed. People began to get restive, but nobody dared to cross Warsovran after what had just happened. On the western horizon Miral's disk was already low. The rings touched the horizon, then the disk. It was not long before only Miral's rings were still up. Laron knew that he was about to collapse again, with every appearance of being dead. Warsovran would be exceedingly embarrassed.

"Remember, I can both kill and cure!" Warsovran was declaring. "My powers are those of the gods in the moonworlds. Look to that temple if you would see—"

A fire-circle detonated, spilling a blinding column of light from the sky for a moment, and sending a roiling cascade of smoke, dust, debris, and hot air boiling out from the southern part of Helion. Heat blazed against their faces for a moment, then the blast of thunder hit them. The target of Warsovran's attack was quite invisible, and a rain of ash, dust, and pebbles began to fall.

"Name me an army, name me a fortress that could stand against such forces!" Warsovran shouted above the rumble.

Nobody was inclined to try, and Warsovran went on to explain exactly what he would do to any monarchs who stood against him, and in what order. By now Laron was being hurried away by two marines. They were taking him to the island's watch-house, the only prison on Helion.

"How does it feel to be the last Metrologan?" laughed a marine.

"Aye, next time the emperor kills you, Silverdeath won't be used to bring you back to life," said his companion.

By now the streets were sufficiently empty for Laron's purposes, as everyone had rushed off to view the fire-circle. The vampyre twisted in their grip, pushed the guard on the right against a brick wall, and lunged for the neck of the guard on the left.

Something was seriously wrong, however. The guard on the right was not stunned by his impact against the wall and the guard on the left merely cursed and pushed the youth away. Laron fell sprawling, and was struck smartly across the ear by the butt of a spear.

"Ach, the little bastard bit me!" cried the guard, who then struck Laron's head again.

Laron saw brilliant stars, and could not get up. It was no act this time. The other guard kicked him in the ribs. They hauled him to his feet again. Laron could not stand unaided.

Dazed and bleeding, Laron was dragged the rest of the way to the watch-house. He was dimly aware that Miral was well and truly down by now, but he was in too much pain to give the matter much thought. What was more, his strength had deserted him. The guards had wrenched him about like a child, yet he should have been able to toss them through the air with ease. Finally he was flung into a cell, and the door was slammed shut.

From within the etherworld, Velander had seen an orange axis suddenly blaze out in the darkness, transfixing a cold, white sphere. Another fire-circle, she realized. Where would it end this time?

Through the invisible ocular tethered to the glass in Laron's purse, she had seen and heard everything. Laron thought she was dead! He had never been trying to save her. Her survival had been due to Fortune alone. Now Laron appeared to be alive again, restored by Silverdeath. Even though there were other tethers nearby, Velander decided to stay with Laron. She had concluded that chivalrous behavior was worthwhile in a man, even if it was occasionally misdirected to benefit the likes of Terikel.

It was evening before the area near the temple had cooled sufficiently for anyone to approach. Wearing wooden clogs, the ambassadors were given a tour of the destruction. They were then put back aboard the flagship, where a feast was held to celebrate Warsovran's victory over the last of the Vidarians.

The following morning, surveyors were hard at work with instruments, string measures, and marker pegs. When they had finished, Terikel and the surviving islanders were given shovels and hoes, then set digging sand and rock out of the narrow isthmus that separated the southern part of Helion from the main peak of the island. It was to be an underwater refuge from the next fire-circle, according to one of the rumors. At the end of the first day's work Terikel was signed off in a register and given her rations.

"Where am I to stay?" she asked when the marines took no further interest in her. "The farm where I used to live has been melted and I had to sleep on the beach last night."

"There's the houses of a lot of dead Toreans on the island," said the marine with the register. "Choose whichever you want."

Terikel looked around as she walked to Port Wayside. Six dash galleys and twelve battle galleys had been left to hold Helion, along with about a thousand marines.

After selecting a clean, pleasant little cottage with a view of the harbor, Terikel settled down to eat her rations and contemplate escape. The marines had kept good order on the island, so the cottage had not been looted. The beds looked very inviting.

"Terikel?"

The voice was male, and Terikel was not armed. Taking a broom and holding it like a quarterstaff, she emerged from the bedchamber. Feran was waiting just inside the main door, looking back out through the window beside it.

"Where in all the hells have you been?" he rasped. "I've been looking for you. We need to raise the *Shadowmoon*."

These two sentences and his general attitude told Terikel a great deal. Feran had said nothing about sex, and he was quite agitated. He probably knew where the ship was lying, the marines were probably not aware that he was on the island, and he was obviously anxious to get off the island.

"Good evening, Feran, you're looking . . . alive."

"Norrieav, Hazlok, and D'Atro survived. We have been hiding in a loft near the docks. I saw you returning from the diggings, but I had to wait until it was darker. As soon as the sunset fades completely we can raise the ship and float out with the tide. By the time Miral rises we should be well clear of the island. We can bail it out, repair the masts, and flee to Sargol."

"Am I to assume that I am invited?" ventured Terikel.

Feran turned from the window, gave her an intense, appraising stare, then smiled and nodded.

"That you are."

"To keep *you* company on the voyage west?"

"It's only fair that you should work your passage."

"Then the answer is no. Find some other girl or sleep alone. Good-bye."

"What? If you stay you will be burned to ash by the later fire-circles."

"Maybe not. If we finish digging that refuge in time—"

"But I'm offering you a chance to escape."

"And I'm refusing it. Good-bye."

Feran made no move to go. He took one step toward her. Terikel smiled, opened her mouth, and took a deep breath. Feran stopped. A squad of marines marched past outside. Feran took a step back. "All right, all right, you can have Laron's cabin."

"Admirable idea, I know it well. Let me know when the ship is ready."

"I— That is, we need you to help with raising the *Shadowmoon*. Like, we thought of you first, even though there are others."

It was just as Terikel had thought. The sunken schooner was in a highly visible part of the harbor. People seen diving there while they ought to be digging the fire-circle shelter in the isthmus would be treated with suspicion. They would also be treated to leg irons and a shovel. That meant salvage at night.

"You need me, Feran; you need someone who can not only dive, but can also breathe a casting into her hand to light her way below the surface, at night. You have an additional problem because I have evacuated all initiates capable of doing that from this island. Even if there were any others, I also happen to know where the sink-weights are tied, and which ropes to cut to release them. Have I missed anything so far?"

"Need I point out that it was *you* who seduced *me*, that last night at Zantrias?"

"And need I point out that *you* just burst in *here* pretending to rescue me in return for supporting your weight on the way to Sargol, while you really needed my help all along?"

That had in fact been precisely Feran's intent. He hung his head, but in resignation rather than shame. "So you won't help?"

"Oh, I'll help, but at a price. Free passage for myself and . . . others. Oh, and remember, the use of Laron's cabin for the entire voyage."

Feran brightened, then frowned. "Ah, who might 'others' be?"

"They include Laron."

"Laron? Laron is currently the most heavily guarded person on Helion."

"Correction. Laron is the *only* person currently under guard on Helion. Besides, I could have him free within half an hour if there were anywhere for him to hide."

"I am not anxious to have Laron aboard."

"Ah, yes. Laron took control of the *Shadowmoon* and now you want to be boatmaster again. I can speak castings, Laron can speak castings, but *you* cannot, Feran."

"Yes, but—"

"But nothing. I owe a lot to Laron, and he has more loyalty and integrity than everyone on Helion put together. I shall not leave him behind."

"You are endangering your passage off Helion," Feran warned.

"Oh no, I am endangering *your* passage off Helion. Do we have an agreement?"

There was no doubt at all that Feran would have to agree. Whatever his feelings of resentment against Laron, there were no others on the island he could trust to help. Terikel wanted the terms and conditions of the voyage absolutely clear before they sailed, however, and that included Feran saying so in quite unambiguous language.

"All right, damn you all, yes," he muttered grudgingly.

"What was that? 'Tonight, fan you for less'? I can fan myself for free."

"I said yes! Yes! *Yes!* I agree. Get the *Shadowmoon* off the harbor bottom without the Damarians noticing, and you can have passage to Acrema with as many others as will fit aboard!"

Terikel approached the watch-house just as the newly appointed island's constable was relieving the two marines who had stood guard over Laron during the day. She waited in the shadows of a nearby laneway as they stood talking.

"We'll be back around dawn," a marine was saying.

"And he'd better still be here," said the other.

"Else you might end up a prisoner, too."

"Yeah, but in one of them farmhouses on the other side of the island."

"When the next fire-circle's due."

The two marines walked away in the direction of the main camp. Once they were out of sight Terikel hurried into the watch-house. The constable had been digging all day, and was washing the clay, sand, and grime from his hands and arms.

"Roval, it's me," Terikel said as she entered.

"Worthy Elder! Your company's welcome."

"Please, not too loud."

"Sorry. To tell the truth, I was half expecting you here. My new name is Peeler, by the way."

"How the hell did you get made constable?"

"The Toreans seemed to think that if Banzalo had locked me up for treason, then I was just the man to be put in charge now that Banzalo is gone. I was released and given a contract."

"Can I see Laron?"

"Aye, but he's to stay *there* if my head's to stay *here*," said Roval, pointing to the cell door, then to his neck.

"Actually, I was meaning to discuss precisely that with you before I see him."

Some minutes later Roval unbarred the door. Laron was lying on the moldy seagrass that covered the floor, dressed only in trousers. His eyes were closed, but he was breathing. He had not woken when Roval had unbarred the door, yet Miral was down. Could it be . . . ? She went down on one knee and shook the youth. He opened his eyes. Terikel sat back as Laron painfully pushed himself up into a sitting position. His face was bruised, and his eyes red-rimmed and unfocused as he sat blinking at her.

"Vampyre, you do not seem yourself today," said the priestess.

"Worthy Elder?"

"Myself, and nobody else. Thank you for taking my place. That was most gallant of you."

"My honor."

"I see that Warsovran has sensibly decided to test Silverdeath on something smaller than a continent this time."

Laron groaned as he tried to stand up. Terikel helped him to a bench, then he sat holding his head in his hands.

"What was it like, wearing Silverdeath?"

"When Silverdeath was put on me, everything went very

calm and cold. Odd voices and thoughts went through my mind, but although I could see everything that was going on around me, I had no control of myself at all. Finally Warsovran launched Silverdeath against the Metrologan temple, and I was released. I don't understand. It healed my ax wound, yet I am suddenly so weak! What happened? What did Silverdeath do to me?"

Terikel took Laron's wrist and felt his pulse, then put the back of her hand to his cheek. She went over to the cell's small window and looked out for a moment, then turned to face the youth.

"Pulse strong, temperature normal, and Miral is down," she said, tapping a finger for each point. "Laron, in order to make you a proper host, Silverdeath has restored you to life."

Laron swallowed. "Life?"

"Life."

Terikel had the distinct impression that he was disappointed.

"You're joking," he said hopefully.

"No, I am not."

"Tell me I'm not alive."

"You're not alive."

"But you're lying."

"Yes."

He fingered his cheeks. Acne pockmarks that had endured for over seven hundred years, and even had individual names, were now gone.

"Life," he sighed.

"Are you not pleased?"

"In a word, no."

"Laron, I can hardly believe what I am hearing. You are a perfectly healthy young man of fourteen—or maybe fifteen. Your pimples are gone, your blood is warm, your hearts are beating, and I even suspect that your fangs are not quite what they used to be."

Laron checked his teeth with his tongue. The etheric fangs were now just normal teeth. He felt for his pulse, and discovered that he had one.

"But why am I so weak?" he protested. "Those marines, I

mean they just pushed me around. I was as weak as a newly hatched chicken."

"You have the strength of a normal fourteen-year-old youth, not the supernatural strength of a vampyre. The average marine is considerably stronger than the average youth of fourteen, so here you are with a cut ear, split lip, a bootmark in your ribs, assorted bruises, and a lot of adjustment ahead of you."

"My stomach hurts."

"*That* is known to mortals as hunger. The constable will bring dinner in once he has cleaned himself up. Meantime, would you care to try the water?"

She took a ladle from the bucket that had been standing by the door all day. Laron eyed it suspiciously, then took a sip. He drained it.

"Strange. It has no taste, but it is so refreshing."

After another five ladles of water Laron was feeling marginally better, but he was by no means happy.

"Wish I was dead," he said sullenly.

"It's 'I wish I *were* dead,' the subjunctive—"

"Stop it!"

"But you have been restored to life! You should be pleased."

"Life? I'm in a position to make comparisons. I have no strength, yet I am in a world full of people anxious to discuss my past behavior and eating habits."

"Ah, speaking of people of that type, I have been discussing you with Feran. He is prepared to offer us passage to Sargol aboard the *Shadowmoon*."

"Feran? 'Us'? 'Us', meaning to include me with you? After what I did to him?"

"I never said he was happy about it. He will be sleeping alone, too."

"Then why?"

"I have him by his figurative balls. Only *I* can raise the *Shadowmoon*."

Laron's eyes narrowed. "Make sure you wash your figurative hands when we reach Sargol. But what is to stop Feran demanding new terms and conditions once we are under way?"

Terikel rapped at the cell door. Roval unbarred it and opened it wide, then stood there with his arms folded and an ax in his belt.

"Constable Peeler, also known as Learned Roval of the SWS, is very good at enforcing existing terms and conditions. Life may not have the same compensations as being undead, young man, but life is all that you have left to you. Should you get yourself killed you will not rise with Miral and prey upon the living, you will remain in your grave, become extremely smelly, and keep the worms company. The alternative is to get out of here and live the next six or seven decades as if they were your last—which they will be."

"Well, yes, but you have nothing to gain, I shall just be a burden—"

Terikel put a hand to Laron's cheek and pressed her lips against his. Presently she stood up and held out her hand to him.

"I owe you so much, Laron," she said, as he sat staring up at her in astonishment. "Do the chivalrous thing and let me assist you."

Laron hung his head, then reached out without looking up and let himself be raised to his feet. Roval returned his tunic and sandals, and handed him a light ax from the confiscations rack. Laron fingered the large gash in the tunic that Warsovran's weapon had made.

"Before we go, there is one condition that I do insist on. The *Shadowmoon* must leave me at Diomeda. I sent someone there I must—"

"Diomeda!" exclaimed Terikel. "Have you not heard? Warsovran conquered the place months ago. He's even made it his capital. If I so much as show my face on Diomeda's horizon I'll be frog-marched off to the headsman's block so fast the city magistrate will not even have time to sell tickets for the execution. The same applies to you, and the *Shadowmoon* is known to have been in Metrologan service."

"I know about Diomeda. *You* are known to be dead, the *Shadowmoon* is known to have sunk, and anyway it's been sailing with the name painted over since we left to return to Torea. *I* am the only person aboard with anything to worry about."

"Absolutely not," declared Terikel. "We are not going to Diomeda."

"This is a matter of honor!"

"No."

"A girl's honor!"

"The defense of honor is for those who have the strength to do it. Your chest measures less than my waist, and I pride myself on a good figure. As for your biceps . . . ! If someone were to auction you as a warrior in a slave market, there would be strong men rolling about on the ground, helpless with mirth."

Laron was not anxious to hear any of this, particularly since most of it was true.

"What about—" he began.

"No! The answer is no! If you want to leave Helion at all, it is on the condition that we go to Sargol. *Then* you can go north to Diomeda and get yourself killed. Understand?"

✳ ✳ ✳

Damarian warships were everywhere as the *Rashih-Harlif* entered Diomeda's harbor, and the pilot who came aboard wore Warsovran's crest on his hat. By the time they had docked, the master's unease had abated somewhat. According to the pilot, the refugee navy was behaving itself well, and life in the big trading port had changed little since before the former king had sealed himself in his own island castle.

"Mind, if you know where a Sargolan princess named Senterri might be, there's a reward of two thousand gold pagols," said the pilot as he stood with the master on the quarterdeck.

"Why, what has she done?"

"Nothing. She was in Diomeda until a month ago, then she decided to leave, dressed as a dancer. Seems that she was a mite too good at dancing, as her guards sold her to some slavers as soon as they were out of sight of the city."

"We come from the Placidian Ocean, yet you ask us about slavers in the desert?" asked the master.

"Well, there's two thousand gold pagols on offer, and questions are free. I ask everyone."

"It is very honorable of the Toreans to offer so much for the safety of a foreign princess."

"Not quite, excellent and esteemed master. The emperor of

Sargol thinks the Toreans are lying, and that they have her as a prisoner. He has threatened to declare war."

"Ah, now I see. Were I a Torean, I should be worried."

Druskarl and Ninth were not known to anyone in Diomeda. Both spoke the language, and the eunuch had even exchanged some of his Torean gold for Vindican gold and silver during the voyage. Both were now dressed in Vindican robes, and would be unlikely to attract any attention.

"Remember, sail north to Bantak and wait," Druskarl said to Suldervar as they docked.

"For how long, Your Highness?"

"Three months. Say that you are Vindic's contribution to Bantak's defense against privateers. Nobody will question an offer like that."

The Inspector of Travel registered Ninth and Druskarl as a servant girl and a eunuch returning from Vindic, and once they had cleared the docks they were as anonymous as anyone could be in a big city. Ninth was uneasy in the jostling crowds, having only ever seen Port Wayside, and even that was from within her oracle sphere. Diomeda was hundreds of times bigger. A wide river, the Leir, flowed to Diomeda across the desert from the lush, wine-growing mountains of the inland, and barges of jars and barrels floated down to be unloaded at Diomeda's wharves. The city was also midway on a desert coast, making it the only refuge for ships sailing between Acrema's northeast and southeast kingdoms.

"Where we staying?" Ninth asked nervously, overwhelmed by the crowds, the smell, and the noise.

"I know a kind lady named Sairet, who is on hard times. We go to her first."

Sairet was known to teach poor girls dancing in the market-place during the afternoons. This she did for free. They arrived just as she was finishing for the day, and Ninth had the impression of a thin, attractive woman in her mid-forties. Even though she was tired, she still somehow radiated command and charisma.

"Well met, Mad Queen," said Druskarl, going up to Sairet as she washed the dust from her legs, and giving a formal and elaborate bow.

"Druskarl! Most welcome, eunuch king," responded Sairet, with a different but no less formal bow and flourish.

Druskarl bought them date cakes at a stall, and they left the market with Druskarl and Sairet exchanging stories. A considerable number of Druskarl's stories were heavily edited.

"So, I find myself with this quite sweet but, ah, limited girl," he concluded, after recounting a quite untrue story of how Ninth had lost her memory after nearly drowning.

"Ah, so you want me to take her as an apprentice . . ." Sairet said, with a little genuine surprise.

"I can pay well."

"Even better."

"She means a lot to me. If she can be looked after for two years while she recovers her wits and learns a skill, Madame Sairet, I could not ask for more."

"Well, she is fit and attractive. What do you have to say for yourself, girl?"

"Ah, I was on a small ship, and I nearly drowned," said Ninth. She tapped at the scarf on her head. "My forehead has—"

"Enough, leave that scarf on your head if you have a scar. I dislike scars. So, you had an accident and lost your memory. Druskarl decided that you were worthy of rescue, so here you are. What can you do?"

"Do?"

"What can you do? Cook? Wash clothes? Clean out a grate? Buy and barter in the market without getting robbed?"

"She learns quickly," said Druskarl.

"I can learn mostly anything, if shown," said Ninth.

"I see," Sairet said slowly, frowning as she thought, then brightening. "Druskarl, what can you pay?"

"Torean gold," he said, reaching into his purse and drawing out some coins.

Sairet's eyes widened. "Ah, indeed. All fees in advance. Would that all of my clients were so considerate. Are you sure she is not a fugitive or runaway?"

"No more than any of us, my dear Mad Queen."

"As bad as that, King Eunuch?"

They reached the building where Sairet lived. Now it was clear that Druskarl was about to leave, and Ninth had become quite fearful.

"Are you going?" she asked. "Shall I never see you again? Like Laron?"

Druskarl laughed. "I am going to find somewhere to sleep. You are to sleep here, in your new home."

"Will you visit?"

"Yes, starting tomorrow. Meantime you must learn dancing, and other things that may bring you advantage."

"Yes, and in time I'll marry you off to a handsome merchant," added Sairet. "You will dance in the marketplace, wearing the robes that he wishes to sell. Druskarl, until tomorrow."

"My dear Sairet, the night will drag slowly."

"Good-bye."

Sairet lived a mile from Wensomer, on the roof of a grain warehouse. She rented the whole of the flat roof, which she had covered with frames and tenting, and used as a dance space. The dancemistress slept in one corner, with her chests of costumes and materials, cushions, mirrors, makeup, and ornaments. The autons, cats, and dogs that guarded the grain kept her space secure as well. Sairet worked a rope and lowered a hinged ladder. They climbed it to the roof.

"Well, there seems to be no language problem," Sairet chatted as she prepared a place for Ninth to sleep. "Is that little bag all that you have?"

"Yes," replied Ninth.

"Ah, poor waif. First we must get you sewing and dressed like a Diomedan. You can tell me about yourself as we work. Later we shall take you through some dance steps."

Warsovran's squadron soon returned from the conquest of Helion, bearing news of the fire-circle's use. Druskarl listened to the tales of the Torean sailors and marines in the taverns that evening, grimly noting every detail in his mind. From what he remembered, Helion was longer than it was broad, and would require four or five fire-circles to blanket it completely. That would mean Silverdeath might not fall to the ground until one hundred twenty days after the first detonation.

That was worth remembering, yet there was a mystery amid all the descriptions of the incredible blast of light, heat, and sound. Warsovran had apparently executed a Metrologan priest on the island, then brought him back to life with Silverdeath. Druskarl knew that to be within Silverdeath's abilities. The odd thing was that the priest's name had been Laron. Laron was a Scalticarian name, and Helion was a Torean outpost. Back in his hostelry, Druskarl chalked dates and sailing times on the stone floor. The *Shadowmoon* could have reached Helion no more than a day or two before Warsovran arrived. It seemed unlikely that Laron could have been ordained in such a short time, yet there was no doubt about the name. Whoever it was had been subsequently imprisoned on Helion, yet that person's identity remained tantalizingly out of reach.

Druskarl decided not to make any decisions until the matter had been clarified. He lay down on his narrow bunk and closed his eyes. There was still a chance for him. He knew where Silverdeath was to be found, and nobody suspected his true intentions.

"Are any of us truly not traitors, deep in our hearts?" he asked himself out loud.

Elsewhere in the city, several other men were not sleeping quite so comfortably. One of the guards who had sold Senterri to the nomad slavers had been unfortunate enough to return to the city, and had been recognized. Forteron paced around the hearth beneath the contract guardsman, who was tied spread-eagled to a wheel, and facing down at a bed of live coals. The hissing of his perspiration hitting the coals was almost continuous.

"At least part of your story can be verified," Forteron said, reading from a scroll. "We did find a burned-out wagon, dead horse, and three mutilated bodies about a day's journey west of the city. It was made to look like a nomad attack, but nomads would not have killed the horse, neither would they have left nomad arrows in the dead bodies. Nomads tend to be rather frugal with iron arrowheads and horses. Next, *you* return. You tell your friends that you have just spent a month escorting three dancers all the way to Lacer. Your friends turn you over to the authorities, for a five-hundred–gold pagol reward. My sources tell me that you spent half of your time away in Lacer, spending a lot of money."

By now the guard was uninterested in anything other than stopping the pain.

"We killed guide, drivers . . . sold girls," he wheezed.

The guard had repeated this sentence several hundred times over the previous four days. It was either true, or he was very, very brave in the face of torture.

"We gathered as much from the wreckage of the wagon," said Forteron. "Who did you sell them to?"

"Nomads."

"Palver Windstriker, I am a very powerful man. I am powerful because I pay that most excellent hooded fellow who is slowly lowering you face-first toward those coals. Now, as far as you are concerned, that makes me the most powerful man in Acrema, but that is not really so. The most powerful man in the Acrema is the man commanding the most powerful army in Acrema, and that man is the father of the girl that you abducted and sold into slavery, and probably raped."

"Not so. . . . Pale virgins worth . . . triple."

"Who were the nomads?"

"Leir Valley windrels."

"What names?"

"Didn't say names."

"Where were they going?"

"West, Zalmek markets."

"No white dancing girls were sold in the Zalmek markets over the month just past. I say you ravished the three girls, then buried them in the desert."

"No."

Forteron broke off his pacing and made for the door, saying,

"If he dies, you will take his place," to the torturer as he passed him.

The surveillance marshal was waiting outside.

"Still no confession, Admiral?" he asked.

"I suspect that what he is saying really is his confession. The girls were certainly sold to nomads, and their high value in the northern kingdoms is beyond question. The trouble is that we are at war with the northern kingdoms. That will tend to hamper inquiries."

"Besides, the northern kingdoms will be keen to add the Sargolan empire to their Alliance. That will make them even less cooperative."

Forteron rubbed his face in his hands for a moment, as if he wanted to shut out the world. There was a truth looming before him, and a quite unpalatable one.

"Senterri is either dead or out of our reach, Marshal. In either case, I have nothing to offer the Sargolan emperor except what is left of that wretch in there—and the names of his companions in betrayal. Summon the Sargolan ambassador, have him witness the guardsman run through his confession again, and have him list his companions. After that, the guardsman's head is to be struck off, pickled, and sent to the Sargolan capital, with the ambassador, aboard a dash galley. It may not be enough for the emperor, but he shall have it whether he wants it or not."

"I fear that the emperor wants his daughter or blood, Admiral."

"Well, drain the guard's blood and send that to him as well."

The *Shadowmoon* limped into the harbor of Diomeda under the pennant of a Sargolan coastal trader. It was riding low in the water, and the hasty repairs to the damage to the rigging were coming apart.

"I'm still unsure of how you convinced me to sail here first," Terikel muttered as she leaned over the rail to be sick one last time.

"The *Shadowmoon* is leaking almost as fast as we can pump the water out, and Diomeda is the closest port to Helion," replied Laron. "As arguments go, I've heard worse."

Terikel wiped her mouth, adjusted the shadeframes over her eyes, and pulled her shawl forward to cover more of her face. Of all the cities in the world, this was the most dangerous one she could have been compelled to visit. After helping the pilot on board, the deckswain bartered convincingly for a lower landing fee because of storm damage, but the full fee was still charged.

"Have you been here before?" the pilot asked as they navigated between the ranks of traders, galleys, coasters, and river barges.

"Our first trip," replied the deckswain as he took charge of the steering pole again.

"Ah, well, then, note that little island there, the one with the palace built on it. That is the former king's palace. It is still under siege, so keep your distance from it if you have no interest in being rammed by one of the dash galleys."

"What threat could a tiny trader like this be to the mighty Warsovran's fleet?" the deckswain protested. "We are but honest seamen."

"So keep your distance. Ah, yes, and do not be tempted to swim in the harbor, either. Agents have been caught swimming out to the island by Miral's light. Now scraps from the butchers and fishmongers of the city are thrown into the water several times daily to encourage the sharks, and the sharks are feeling very encouraged. By the by, would you have heard anything of a Sargolan princess named Senterri, who was abducted and sold into slavery last month? It was in the desert, to the west of Diomeda. The reward for her return is up to six thousand gold pagols."

"The desert? We arrive from the other side of the Placidian Ocean and you ask us about an abduction in the desert?"

"Ah, well, questions are free, and six thousand pagols is a lot of gold. Have a prosperous stay in Diomeda."

Feran joined the deckswain on the quarterdeck as the others dropped anchor and furled the sails. They were over a sandbar, which would support the *Shadowmoon* once the tide was out. The pilot went amidships to wait for his gigboat.

"Those leaks were bad; we were lucky even to reach Diomeda," said the deckswain.

"The repairs will cost plenty," grumbled Feran.

"So? We have plenty. Have you forgotten the Torean gold?"

Laron, Terikel, and Roval went ashore in the pilot's gigboat, leaving the others to have the *Shadowmoon* assessed for repairs.

"Sometimes I am tempted to tell the harbormaster just who they are," said Feran as the gigboat receded in the distance.

The deckswain shrugged. "They could in turn tell him some very entertaining stories about you."

"Which is why I have little interest in a trip to the harbormaster. Norrieav, as purser would you be so kind as to count out my share of the gold? It should not take long."

"Aye, whatever you like. Are you planning to impress the Diomedan wenches and raise hell?"

"No, I need money to buy a commission aboard a deepwater trader. I now know enough deepwater navigation to qualify as an officer, and as a former boatmaster and veteran of three voyages across the Placidian Ocean, I should be much in demand."

The deckswain rubbed his chin. "Ah, well, yes. I'll be sorry to see you go, as will the others."

The tide went out, leaving the vessel on the sandbar. The water was pumped out as hired carpenters repaired the rigging. Norrieav inspected the hull, but the leaks were not obvious. As the tide returned, the carpenters packed up and a dockswain waded over. He inspected the hull and gave Norrieav a price and date for careening the barnacles and weed from the hull. He had, however, been quite unable to find any leaks.

By the time the sun was low in the sky the surviving crewmen had gone ashore for a well-earned rest, and Norrieav was planning what else had to be done to get the *Shadowmoon* fit to reach a Sargolan port. The damage to the rigging had been trivial to repair, once new spars, ropes, carpenters, and the right tools had become available. Two days for careening and a coat of tar, one day for provisioning and loading the sacks, barrels, and jars of a cargo to maintain the guise of a trader, and then they could sail, Norrieav decided. The *Shadowmoon* could not carry as much as the deepwater traders, but it could fit under bridges and reach inland river ports that were denied to bigger ships. Once Terikel and Roval were gone, the crew technically could earn an honest living as genuine merchant sailors. Obviously, that did not seem likely with Laron as boatmaster, but perhaps Norrieav could buy out the former vampyre's commission, eventually.

Norrieav began to push at the bellows pump, so that the *Shadowmoon* would not accumulate too much water now that it was floating again. There was no water. Surprised, Norrieav went below. The leaks had stopped. Completely. He lit a lamp and began an inspection of the hull's interior. Sure enough, there were dozens of points where the caulking had apparently melted.

Sometime later there was a bump at the side of the vessel, and someone called out to come aboard. It was the voice of a woman. Norrieav crawled out of his small cabin and helped Terikel and Roval to haul the Elder's contingency sack of gold aboard.

"The Harbor Proclamation Board has Feran signed off," said the priestess, coming straight to the point.

"Aye, it's true. He's set upon becoming an officer on some bigger ship."

"There's another line on the board now. Laron has signed off as boatmaster, and named *you* to take over."

Norrieav was speechless for a moment. "Just like that? With no fee?"

"He says he has his share of the gold, and he wants nothing more."

"Boatmaster Norrieav," Norrieav whispered experimentally. "Boatmaster."

"And what will you be doing with the *Shadowmoon*?"

"Honest work, unless dishonest is on offer at a sufficiently tempting rate. I assume that you still want to go to Sargol."

"Will you take me to Scalticar instead?"

Norrieav whistled. "That is a long trip."

"I sent my priestesses there with the Metrologan library and archives, so I must join them. With my gold we can begin the Metrologan Order all over again in Scalticar, safely out of reach of Warsovran. Will you take us? I'll pay the value of a cargo plus another half."

"Aye, agreed," said Norrieav without hesitation, impressed by the offer.

"When will the repairs be done?"

"Except for the careening, they're finished."

"But what about the hull? All those leaks?"

"I've inspected the hull in greater detail than was possible at sea. My theory is that Laron caused those leaks with small, subtle castings, then resealed them just as we docked."

For some moments Terikel was inarticulate with rage. Pressure seemed to be building up behind her face. Finally the explosion came.

"The little bugger!" she cried. "I'll have his scrawny little balls on a silver platter!"

"I'll settle for pickled mutton and ship's biscuit," replied Norrieav.

"The ratty little worm! Damn him to every level of the hells within. Roval, fetch the two crewmen. We leave *now*. Boatmaster, what more do we need to sail?"

"We only need provisions."

"Damn provisions! Sargol is just days south and I bought a basket of bread, wine, and smoked sausage at the market. That will keep the five of us alive."

"But—"

"I insist! I am a Metrologan priestess in a city controlled by Warsovran, and I have enough gold in this sack to buy a deepwater trader outright. Thus I am feeling *exceedingly* vulnerable, Norrieav, and I wish to be away from here."

"Nobody knows about the gold."

"Feran knows."

"He would never tell a soul."

"Indulge my suspicions. Remember, you shall earn half again as much as an honest cargo to Scalticar. What do you say?"

Norrieav shrugged and spread his hands. "What else but, 'Welcome aboard.'"

Roval was gone for about a quarter hour before the sound of distant singing came floating across the water.

> " *'Drink ter the ship, lubbers,*
> *Drink ter the crew,*
> *Drink, drink drink.*
> *Drink up the sky,*
> *Drink the ocean so blue,*
> *Drink, drink, drink.'* "

"That sounds like my crew," said Norrieav. "Ah, they don't write songs like that anymore."

"Let me guess—it's about drinking," said Terikel.

"You're sharp as a blade, Worthy Elder."

"When will they be fit to sail?"

"Who knows, but we don't need them yet."

"Is that wise?"

"It's common practice. There's hardly a shipmaster on the Placidian as does not recruit sailors by getting them blind drunk and having them carried aboard."

"Very well, but Roval will want to return to Diomeda in the scoreboat. Unfinished business, apparently—oh, and this is your commission and deed of ownership."

She handed Norrieav two scrolls. Within a single hour they were at sea with the sails up and heading south. Hazlok and D'Atro were belowdecks and fast asleep, Norrieav was steering, and Terikel was counting the gold yet again.

Chapter Six

VOYAGE TO NORTH SCALTICAR

 An hour after Miral had set behind the hills that ringed the plain on which Diomeda was built, Feran walked to the Amberstone tavern. He sat by himself, savoring being alone as much as the smell and taste of the food after more than a week of soggy ship's biscuit and an occasional fish. The floor was steady beneath his feet, the timbers did not creak, and the only orders he had to give were for his meal. The seagrass mats that made two of the walls had been rolled up to admit the evening breeze, and lissome Vindican maids in plain but elegant orange sarelles glided among the tables with trays of food and drink. He bought a goblet of wine and drank it slowly.

He had a lot to think about. He had been to the heart of a dead continent, and discovered that the most hideous weapon imaginable was again in the hands of a clever maniac. He also had discovered that Laron was mortal again, and was thus weak in body.

Someone loomed over his table. "There sits a man whose mind is filled with dead cities of glass, and fleets of masts without ships."

Feran looked up to see Druskarl standing before him. "Actually, it wasn't, but sit down anyway," he replied, gesturing to a square wicker stool.

"So, you're alive."

"And you are not on Helion."

"Neither are you."

"Very astute."

"Is Ninth well?"

"Never better, safe and sound, and placed in honest work. Word is that Laron was executed as a Metrologan priest on Helion, then brought to life by Silverdeath."

"Indeed."

"How did it happen?"

"I saw it all, but at a distance. Silverdeath needs a healthy host in order to function. It cured Laron of death itself."

"Clever. It kills continents, then cures death. I don't suppose it could bring Torea back?"

"Doubt it."

"Why Laron? Did Warsovran know that he was a vampyre?"

"No. He was merely found wearing a Metrologan ring. Warsovran wanted someone for a public execution, and nobody else was to hand."

"So in the confusion nobody bothered to check his credentials?"

"Nothing like a war to cause confusion. Warsovran axed him,

not knowing the little wretch was already dead and that wounds mean nothing to him. Silverdeath was then put on him, and it accepted him as a host. After Warsovran launched Silverdeath to cast its fire-circles, Laron was left with no wound, and able to stand and speak. Nobody but me noticed that he was now awake although Miral had just set, however. Silverdeath had brought him back to life. He has warm blood, may be awake whenever he pleases, and, alas for him, has a tenth of his former strength."

Druskarl leaned back and folded his arms, thinking over the gaps Feran's story had just filled. Things were suddenly looking promising.

"How did you escape?" the eunuch asked.

"I am a good swimmer."

"And presumably you swam to where the *Shadowmoon* had been sunk just as soon as the sun was down and the tide was favorable. Who was with you?"

"Norrieav, Hazlok, and D'Atro survived. Heinder and Martok were killed when Warsovran's squadron attacked."

"And why are you now in Warsovran's very stronghold?"

"Silverdeath will eventually be brought here," replied Feran.

"Getting it out of Warsovran's hands will be as difficult as reattaching my balls."

"After all those years in a jar of vinegar, I'm not sure the prospect should attract you. Still, there is a way—to secure Silverdeath, that is. Had we been quicker we might have carried it off at Larmentel. The opportunity may present itself again."

"At Helion?"

"Here. A large army from several northern Acreman kingdoms is on the way, and should arrive late next month." Feran gestured across the harbor. "If Warsovran uses Silverdeath to destroy yonder island palace, the commanders and kings at the head of that army are liable to say, 'Sorry, big mistake,' and go home. That is when one might try to reach Silverdeath first."

"But Warsovran and his men would immediately fill you so full of arrows that one would be hard-put to tell your body from a large sea urchin."

"Not so. I had a chance to observe Silverdeath on Helion. It protects itself and its master; an entire army could not have killed Warsovran while it stood beside him. The fire-circles seem to take all of its strength, though, so it releases its host when commanded to make them. That is its weakness, and our opportunity. Are you interested in helping?"

"I might be," admitted Druskarl.

As he left the tavern sometime later, Druskarl looked out over the water to the east, where Helion lay. Again Silverdeath was moving within his reach.

The sky was overcast and devoid of Miral's light as Laron lay sprawled on the cobbles of the alleyway. He knew he did not have much time, but the pain that racked his body was all but blotting out his thoughts. Farther down the lane a figure was counting coins by the light of a distant street lantern. The alley was a dead end, there was no escape. He began to crawl. After about a yard he found his discarded, empty purse. Beside it was a chunk of glass, from the glassy ruins of Larmentel. Scooping up both, he crawled on.

Laron felt smooth, curved wood. Barrels littered the place, in various states of repair. Barrels. Frantically his fingers probed and groped, as he hoped against hope that the gods of the moonworlds would smile on him. He found it! A barrel with one end smashed in. He crawled inside, then heaved it vertical.

Footsteps approached. "Come now, are ye in pain? I can soon end all that."

The hunter probed and groped now. He thumped Laron's barrel, went on to another, then rummaged about in the smashed pieces.

"Come out, else it will go worse for ye," came the voice, but this time there was an edge of doubt to it.

Laron barely breathed. How long before he lost interest? An hour? Two? The entire night? He had the gold, after all, yet—

Suddenly there was a hollow knocking. His attacker had found a low door. Where there were barrels there was sure to be a cellar, and where there was a cellar there was sure to be a cellar door.

"How did ye get in there?" the voice demanded. "Some slackard bugger left it open, I'll wager." Laron heard the sound of kicking. "Open up, I say!" his enraged pursuer demanded. "Open up. I'll not warn ye again!"

A furious barrage of kicks and curses erupted and echoed along the dark alley, but within moments there were other voices calling out, and someone was ringing a gong. There was the sound of running feet, people shouting, the flicker of torchlight, then silence. Laron pushed the barrel over and crawled the length of the alley on his hands and knees, then hauled himself to his feet as he reached the street. He limped along for a few yards, leaning against the walls of the shops and houses. The owners of the cellar came running back, torches held high.

"Alms for the lame, in the name of the gods," croaked Laron, hoping that he looked even marginally as bad as he felt. "Alms for the lame, in the name of the gods."

Laron was ignored. By putting all of his concentration into heaving one leg ahead of the other he managed to reach the end of the street. The only public fountain on the entire rim of the Placidian Ocean bubbled and splashed there, and Laron plunged his head into the water for a moment, then drank greedily and wiped some of the blood away. Again he forced his legs to support him, and staggered away into the shadows, hoping that he was no longer being watched.

Sometime after midnight Laron finally found the Academy of Applied Castings. By the light of the rising disk of Miral the youth could see that it was a door made from salvaged bargewood set into an ancient wall of crumbling bricks, and flanked by a herbalist's store on one side and Madame Lorica's Services on the other. Burned into the door in unsteady pokerwork were the words YVENDEL and ACADEMY, but the nature of the academy was no better specified than were Madame Lorica's "services."

There was no handle, latch, or knocker. Laron knocked. There was no response. He knocked again. There was still no response. He pounded at the door continually for a full minute. There was not so much as a curse from within. Laron sat with his back to the door and thought through both his options and the facts to hand. Slowly and stiffly he got up and walked over to the herbalist's store and pounded at the door a dozen times.

"Geeroutafereyabastard!" floated across from a neighboring building.

Laron stood back and raised his fist in triumph. Sound did not carry more than a few feet from the academy's door. It was a muffler-casting. He wandered the length of the street, collecting scraps of wood and splinters, then piled them at the base of the door to the academy. With a small tinderbox he struck sparks into a handful of straw and applied it to his pile of kindling. It blazed up quickly. Laron stood back. Presently a thin scream sliced the air as the guard auton that had been muffling any knocking on the door began to lose its battle to protect the wood from the flames, and disintegrated. Moments later there was the rattling of a crossbar being removed and the door was wrenched open. An amorphous-looking figure shouted for water, then vanished back into the gloom beyond the door. Laron stepped past the flames.

Presently three figures came running with buckets of water and doused his fire. They then swept the charred and sodden scraps down the street, returned to the door, and pulled it shut. Just as they renewed the casting for a new guard auton, they were joined by someone carrying a pottery lamp. It was a woman dressed in a silk kaftan and with her hair combed out.

"Some idiot lit a fire against the door, Rector," explained one of those who had put out the fire.

"It disrupted the guard auton," added another.

"But the fire is out and a new casting is in place," concluded the third.

"All my own work, Rector Yvendel," announced Laron, stepping out of the shadows in a corner.

The three students whirled and gaped for a moment, then frantically spoke castings of tangled fire into their hands and held them ready to throw. The woman did not move.

"You are obviously not a thief, or you would be farther down the hall by now and in the grip of another guard auton," said Yvendel. "Who are you?"

"My name is Laron Alisialar. I am under the patronage of Lady Wensomer."

Laron noticed that Yvendel twitched at the mention of Wensomer's name.

"Have you a scroll of introduction?"

"Direct me to her villa tomorrow morning, and I shall return with one."

"This is all very well, Laron Alisialar, but why not wait until morning?"

Laron reached out with a scratched, bruised, filthy hand. The students flinched back, still holding their fireballs at the ready. Yvendel gave him her lamp and he held it up to his face. One of his eyes was blackened and nearly closed, his lip was split, and there were bruises on his cheeks and jaw.

"I was set upon and robbed. The thief thought me beaten senseless, for he emptied my purse and walked off. I dragged myself here because I know where Madame Yvendel is to be found, but not Lady Wensomer."

Yvendel took back her lamp.

"I can shelter you here until morning, but without your gold you cannot enroll."

"I merely said that my purse had been emptied," explained Laron. "I converted one gold coin to silver and used that to weight my purse. The rest of the gold is in my boots."

"I see," said Yvendel, tapping her foot on the stone floor. "Our tests for resourcefulness and cunning should not be necessary in your case, Laron Alisialar. Jarris, clean him up, put his gold under a casting, and assign him a bed in the dormitory. Breakfast is a half hour after dawn, Laron, and after breakfast you will be directed to the villa of Lady Wensomer. Return with her recommendation, and you can come to my chambers to discuss your strengths, weaknesses, and a course of study. The rest of you, back to bed."

✳ ✳ ✳

Laron ate breakfast with the other students. It was a mixed-sex academy, which was very unusual, if not unique in the known world. The dormitories of the girls and youths were separate, however. For the most part, Laron was ignored. He was quite short, and looked somewhat too young to be of interest to the girls. Besides, many students stayed there for a day or two while being assessed, then left for home and were never seen again. Madame Yvendel had high standards as well as high fees.

Laron became aware of shadows across his table. He looked up to see three Acremans and a Vindican standing over him.

"Who he?" asked the largest, surliest-looking Acreman.

"From Scalticar," said another.

"Know him, Starrakin?" the third Acreman asked the Vindican.

Starrakin reached down and poured Laron's mug of grape juice into his lap.

"Needs watering, make him grow," said the Vindican.

Laron watched them saunter away, his eyes lingering on Starrakin's neck as he felt with his tongue for his missing fangs. Adjustment to being alive was proving harder with each hour that passed.

The academy itself was rather like a maze of woodworm tunnels through a large and intricate piece of furniture: invisible from the outside, but very extensive and with few entrances. As far as Laron could tell by the faint sounds from the city beyond, it occupied buildings spread over several acres that were connected by tunnels, enclosed walkways, and corridors, and shared many buildings with the outside world.

He blinked in the sunlight as a neophyte student took him out into the street, then across the city to Wensomer's villa. By now he was uncertain whether he wanted her recommendation to the academy or something far more sinister.

Sairet was already out of bed as dawn was beginning to overwhelm the stars. Sargolan missionary priests were chanting syncopated organum prayers in a nearby temple. She woke

Ninth, and they washed, ate, prayed to Fortune, and shook out the bedding to air. Next she pulled on a pair of loose silk trousers and laced them at her ankles and waist, then laced herself into a blouse of raw silk that fitted tightly around her chest but had loose, flowing sleeves.

She began her stretching and limbering exercises, and Ninth followed her example. After Ninth's limbs had become supple and warm, Sairet began to teach her to move her arms and legs through some basic dance moves. Even though she had been living in Venander's body for some weeks, her movements were clumsy and abrupt. Ninth had only ever known the rolling decks of ships and the rigidity of dry land had come as a shock to her. Still, she had developed a pleasing grace about her walk, and she had definite promise.

Leaving Ninth to clean up and sew for the rest of the morning, Sairet climbed down the ladder and set off to work. As Diomeda awoke all around her, she walked briskly to Wensomer's villa. Neither Wensomer's servants nor Wensomer were stirring as she arrived. After rousing the steward to admit her, she went to Wensomer's bedchamber and dragged the curtains aside.

"Hail the morning, Esteemed Wensomer!" she declared brightly.

"Go away," Wensomer mumbled from beneath her pillow.

"As usual you are awake and supple already," said Sairet, dragging the covers from the bed.

"That I am," Wensomer moaned, her hands clasped over the pillow that covered her head.

"Would that all my other students had your dedication," Sairet said as she snatched the pillow away. "Ah, then, what magnificent, enchanting spectacles could be performed!"

Sairet poured part of a pitcher of water onto Wensomer, who shrieked and tumbled from the bed. Eventually they began stretches and exercises, and an hour later, when the trays of food and drink were brought in, Wensomer was actually alert and reconciled to being awake.

"How is your apprentice progressing?" asked Wensomer as they ate the light but expensive meal which featured sugar figs stuffed with candied honey ants.

"My, my, but word spreads fast in Diomeda. How did you know?"

"A strange man comes up to you in a crowded marketplace, introduces a girl to you, walks you back to your home, then counts out some coins and leaves the girl with you. You do not have to be a senior sorceress to work out what happened. So, how is she?"

"Her name is Ninth. She learns fast, but has had an accident and is strangely blank in the most basics. In two years she will be able to support herself, unless I have found a suitable young man for her in the meantime. There is one strangeness about her, though."

"Describe it."

"She talks in her sleep. Partly in Diomedan, and partly in a strange, sharp language that is nothing like I have ever heard. Last night she seemed to be dreaming that she was back aboard some ship. She said aloud that ships could move with great precision on the open ocean had they but accurate timekeeping machines."

Wensomer thought for a moment, then shook her head. "Preposterous."

"In the morning I asked her what she meant, but she could not say. She did say that she must have been Visitor."

"You mean *had* a visitor?"

"No, 'been Visitor.' The really strange thing is that when she was dreaming, her speech was very much more complex and confident."

"Curious," said Wensomer. "Perhaps a village somewhere is missing its idiot."

"She seems bright enough, just . . . empty."

They resumed the lesson. It was difficult to get the dance movements and gestures to work properly, even with well-toned muscles and a lean figure, but Wensomer had neither. It was all the more urgent because they did not have much time. Wensomer had some agenda, some reason to perfect certain aspects of windrel dancing by a certain, unspecified date.

"Now, legs straight and bend forward from the waist, arms above your head," Sairet said, demonstrating as she spoke.

Wensomer tried to follow her example, but could not bend as far. Sairet tried to be encouraging.

"Hold there, count one, two, three, four, five, now swing your right arm down and push it up and behind you. Right around, a full circle. Good, now the left, and straighten."

"But I did this an hour ago," groaned Wensomer unhappily.

"That's an hour in the past. Since then you have had a meal. Now, repeat the stretching exercise. Twenty times."

Wensomer did as she was told, and Sairet was pleased to see that she was steadily improving in her bending and stretching. A supple body could make up in part for the experience she was lacking.

"Contract the muscles of your stomach and bottom, while pushing your chin and chest forward—no, no, keep your head up. Push back and up with your arms, keeping them straight. Relax, then repeat it. Twenty times."

"Twenty times! I thought this was meant to be dance practice, but all we do is stretching. How can I improve my dancing without . . . well, dancing?"

Sairet was patient. Wensomer was not the first such student she had instructed, and their arguments and complaints were all the same. Nevertheless, she was different. Once out of bed and awake, Wensomer was driven, dedicated, and did what she was told in spite of all her complaints. Still, Sairet was being paid well for driving her hard, so she continued to drive.

"You already know the steps and sways, but you do them with the grace of a camel. If we can remove the stiffness from your body, even those basics would be enough to have Warsovran himself sit forward on his cushions and leer."

The exercises went on until the sun was high, then Sairet finally went on to dance steps. Wensomer grudgingly admitted to herself that her teacher had been right. Many of her problems in the previous day's lesson were gone, now that she had done a proper routine of stretches.

"Move your hips in a circle, and as your left hip rolls out, take a small step with your left foot—yes! Now roll your hip back and around to the right—"

"And take a little step with my right foot?"

"Yes, and so on for as many steps as you wish. Walking backwards is similar. Good, very good."

By now Wensomer was quite impressed by her own progress, and she had a increased respect for Sairet. The thin, wavy-haired Diomedan was a patient and perceptive teacher, always able to see what the problem was and how to solve it. She did not use ridicule to excess, but she did work her students very, very hard.

"That walk-step is vastly improved on yesterday's. I thought that I could never do it so fluidly. You are a fine teacher, Sairet."

Sairet folded her arms and shrugged, then looked away over the sunlit water to where part of Warsovran's massive fleet lay blockading the island palace of the king.

"The windrels of Diomeda are the finest dancers on the continent," she said without turning around, "but I am different from them, and in my own way I am better."

"Let me guess," said Wensomer. "Secret royal blood?"

Only Sairet's eyes moved, to give Wensomer a sidelong glance. "I merely remember what it is like to be at your level: awkward and ashamed. That makes me a sympathetic teacher."

At Wensomer's villa Laron presented a note to her steward. He was left seated in a parlor, and a servant brought wine and a tray of candied fruit. After a short time the steward returned and led him farther into the house. Wensomer was lying on a wicker couch in an upstairs room. The rugs about her were surrounded with scrolls and books, and half a dozen little green, blue, and red autons were darting about with mouse bodies, either hard at work or playing. Wensomer had fair skin, the beginnings of a weight problem in spite of her dancing, and sharp, darting eyes.

"Ah, welcome to my new villa, one and only vampyre," said Wensomer, looking up.

"Learned Wensomer, the mere sight of you is my pleasure," Laron responded mechanically.

"But you have bruises!" she exclaimed, suddenly sitting up and staring. "*You* can't get bruised."

"Pox take my bruises. I need your recommendation; I want to study."

"Study what? Better table manners?"

"The skills that living people need. I no longer have supernatural strength, my wounds take weeks rather than hours to heal, and I can be killed very easily. I also need normal food."

"So, you can eat?"

"It's good for my health."

"Anyone would think you were no longer dead."

"They would be right."

Wensomer stared at him for a moment, then got up and walked over. She felt his forehead, examined his teeth, then pulled away his beard.

"Warm blood, no fangs, no pimples," she said, circling him with her hands on her hips. "How?"

"A fortuitous accident."

"I've heard of people dying accidentally, but not being brought to life by accident—apart from accidental conception, of course. Quite a lot of *that* happens."

"True. The average haystack in spring probably sees more accidents of that type than I want to think about."

Laron suddenly threw himself down on the wicker couch and began to weep. "I want to die," he sobbed, inconsolable with misery.

"Uh—again?" Wensomer asked, stroking hair that had grown for the first time since she'd known him.

It took quite some time for Laron to finish the story of what had happened to him, and to sundry other relevant people.

"I thought I could trust him; of all people, I thought I could trust Druskarl," Laron concluded. "Now Ninth is somewhere in Diomeda, or maybe already sold as a slave. I have visions of her brutalized, violated, murdered. Lady Wensomer, she is so innocent, she is a baby in a woman's body, a totally trusting child."

"Ninth is a constructed soul, you say? An auton?"

"Yes. I think that the Metrologans were experimenting with drawing the experience and memories of demons into oracle spheres. When images of normal souls are used in the spheres, they often go insane with the contradictions. The Metrologans must have fashioned her with no memories of her own to get in the way."

Wensomer held up a slate, upon which she had been writing.

"I have a little list, Laron. May I check it with you?"

"I'm flattered that you were paying attention."

"Well, I am your friend—and I'll expect the favor returned."

"How altruistic of you."

"Firstly, you want to die. Why is that?"

"I preferred being a vampyre. Life was simple when I was undead. Now I get beaten up, I have to eat food, and I have no strength. I really miss my fangs. I feel like getting a false set made up. I am constantly bullied, humiliated, imposed upon, and laughed at. I wouldn't wish life on my worst enemy."

"Welcome to mortality. Second, you want a recommendation to Madame Yvendel's Academy of Applied Castings."

"I need a reason to be in Diomeda. Besides, I may need the skills and qualification to buy food and clothing as I try to live as a mortal."

"Thirdly, you want to find Ninth."

"If I ever get my hands on Druskarl, I'll—"

"Four, you want to kill Druskarl."

"Well, yes."

"Five, you want to recover Silverdeath."

"We all do, I suppose."

Wensomer picked up a piece of chalk.

"There *may* be a way to render you undead again."

"Hah! I would have to drink the blood of another vampyre first, and I am—was—the only vampyre in the world. How can—"

"I am the sorceress, I shall determine that. Second, you want a recommendation to Madame Yvendel. Splendid choice; I'll write one out before you go."

"Thank you."

"You also want to find Ninth. Druskarl apprenticed her to the finest dance teacher in all Diomeda—"

"What?"

"Roval will be past soon, he can take you to her."

"She—I—Roval, too?"

"Fourth, you want to kill Druskarl."

"Not anymore."

"Oh, good. Fifth, you want to recover Silverdeath. Well, if I could tell you how to do that, I would recover it myself."

Laron paced before Wensomer's couch several times, shaking his head as he silently read over the points on her slate.

"How do you do it?" he finally stopped and asked. "I walk in unannounced, after years away, and you know everything. It's like magic."

"Well, I *am* a sorceress."

"But *how*?"

"I know a lot of people, and I listen to what they tell me—not just what they *say* to me. You told me that Ninth's benefactor is Druskarl. My earlier informant did not. Now I know that he is in Diomeda, and that my informant is being discreet about the fact. They can hardly be having an affair, so I am left to wonder why."

At that moment the bell rang. Some seconds later, the steward entered.

"The Learned Roval awaits your convenience, ladyship."

"Splendid, show him in. Laron, I think that your colleague in espionage should give you some lessons in surviving life, at least while I do a little more research into the first problem on your list."

Roval entered, and Wensomer immediately arranged that he teach Laron a few elements of the fighting techniques used by the Special Warrior Service. Laron then left, and was shown to the door by a servant. He had taken three steps along the street when there was a piercing shriek from an upstairs room.

"He's *what*?" demanded Wensomer.

"Warsovran is recruiting dancers next month," came Roval's barely audible voice.

"*Next month?*" screamed Wensomer. "Just look at me!"

"All of what I can see is quite lovely," Roval said diplomatically.

"That's just the trouble!" cried Wensomer. "There's far too much of me. At least fifty pounds too much, and *this* is to blame!"

Pastries, sugar figs, candied fruits, and honey delights showered down around Laron, and a large jar of sweet frost wine shattered at his feet. Laron sidled out of range.

"*You* are going to make me *fit*," commanded Wensomer. "You know how to do that sort of thing, with all your SWS training."

"But that would take years."

"I didn't say I wanted to *join* the Special Warrior Service, Roval, I meant that I want you to put me through its fitness program for the next month!"

Could I but sell tickets for that, I'd need never work again, thought Laron as he hurried away.

Late in the afternoon, the former vampyre was escorted to Yvendel's chambers by one of the more senior students. The rector was reclining on featherdown cushions on a thick carpet in a room whose walls and ceiling dripped with hangings. The air was thick with incense, and scented smoke from aromatic candles. Yvendel wore a violet tunic over scarlet silk trousers with a sunburst across the midriff and embroidered silver stars all down the sleeves. Her hair was combed out but pinned by silver combs in the shape of skeletal dragons.

Laron bowed, presented his petition, and backed away several paces. Yvendel studied it.

"Recommended for admission by Learned Wensomer," she said slowly.

"Yes, Rector."

"You seem too normal to be in her favor."

"Er . . ."

Laron was not sure how to respond to this observation. The silence stretched. Eventually the rector stretched, yawned, and continued reading.

"You wish to be graded to the eighth level of initiation," she stated, as if to confirm what was on the parchment.

"Yes, Rector."

"But you currently have no grading at all."

"No, Rector."

"But nobody is without grading. Girls washing linen on the riverbank, beggars, and sweepers can manage two. The parrot chained to a perch at the Bargeman's Pole could probably manage level one. I once met a drunken harlot who graded as four. She's now the academy's nurse, as a matter of fact, and is even studying Etheric Physiology. Why are you without grading?"

"I've not been well."

Yvendel picked up a slate that lay beside her.

"Well, Wensomer would not have recommended you unless you were capable of grading at seven. Health and physique . . . normal. Unusually normal, according to the medicar autons that examined you this morning."

"Is this a problem?" asked Laron.

"Probably not—for me, at least. Have you been observing celibacy?"

"Yes, Learned Rector."

"Well, if you have not, we shall soon know. So, you survived the fire-circles while millions died. You do not look very charred for someone who has lived through the fire-circles."

"I had a nice, deep refuge."

"Why are you in Diomeda?"

"I wish to study with you. Am I acceptable?"

Yvendel had a dilemma. In a conventional sense Laron had no redeeming features at all, but then she was not particularly conventional where sorcery was concerned. Being interesting could make up for a lot, and if nothing else, Laron was certainly interesting. Still, there was no point in letting him know that, or he was liable to get ideas. Everyone knew how dangerous *they* were.

"If you were to enter this academy, then you might be able to reach a very high level of proficiency in a very short time. You may study with us for a year, after which your progress will be examined before you go on to further study."

"Thank you, Learned Rector."

"For this you will pay fees equal to a year of study."

Laron swallowed. It was a lot of money to part with at a single stroke. His confidence and self-esteem had been under severe strain over the previous two weeks. Nevertheless, here was an opportunity to recover some strength and independence.

"Learned Rector, I accept," Laron announced.

Yvendel allowed herself a smile.

"Splendid. See the accountant about the fees, then call in at the registrar's chambers to arrange a syllabus and tutors."

Sairet and Ninth looked up as the bell beside the ladder tinkled, then Ninth went to the edge of her rooftop tent and looked down. Sairet had a great many visitors, mainly students, but these were men. Or at least one of them was a man. The other was a youth dressed to make himself look broader in the shoulders and trying to stand as straight and tall as possible. He also had several lurid bruises on his face.

"Laron!"

A minute later they were sitting on cushions at the edge of the dance floor, exchanging the dozens of adventures they had lived through in less than a single of Miral's months. Roval and Sairet stood across the other side of the roof, arms folded and steadily regarding their respective charges.

"He has come from a . . . Perhaps you could describe it as a *sheltered* background," Roval explained. "His hearts are in the right place, he just lacks the body to back them up."

"Yet it was he who rescued Ninth from drowning?" asked Sairet, doubt plain in her voice.

"I have it on good authority, yes. As you can see, however, he has a build that attracts bullies and thieves. That is where you come in."

"Me? If I teach him belly dancing he is going to attract a lot more than bullies and thieves, and—"

"No, perhaps I expressed myself badly. Lady Wensomer says that you seldom use this dance space in the mornings."

"No, only Ninth is here, doing the sweeping and cleaning."

"It is large, open, yet totally private. I wish to hire it from you for a month, possibly longer."

"Really? This is a good week; everybody I meet wants to give me money. What do you propose to do here?"

"When I was a youth, my master lived for five years on the island of Zurlan, off the Scalticar coast."

"I have heard of it. They use a strange ax with a curved handle and long, thin blade. Their word for people who use shields means 'eunuch/coward/tax collector/man-who-does-unsavory-things-with-sheep-on-dark-nights.' "

"Yes, well, the Zurlanese have an extreme code of honor. They have never been invaded, you know."

"They also execute visitors to test their ax-blades. How did you and your master survive?"

"There is actually a small trade enclave on the north coast of Zurlan. The products of certain plants used in their medicine, cuisine, and sorcery do not grow in such a cold climate, so they are forced to have some contact with the outside world. When my master went there to learn their language and study with their sorcerers, he took me along. A local javat master took a liking to me, and decided that I needed to learn to defend myself. After five years, I was expelled after an incident involving a girl."

"It's always the way."

"You do not understand. I challenged someone in defense of the girl's honor, but Zurlanese girls are expected to defend their own honor, and . . . Well, I would rather not talk about it."

Sairet looked at Laron again, and the direction of the conversation suddenly became clear. "You are going to teach Laron javat, and you need the privacy of my dance space to do it."

"You have my intention to the very letter, dancemistress."

"Very well, I agree, as one teacher to another. Will you be starting tomorrow morning?"

"Yes, thank you. Oh, and one more little thing. Could you take the girl, Ninth, to Wensomer's lessons? Javat is not to be taught to anyone considered unworthy by the Keepers of Style. That essentially means anyone who does not live on Zurlan."

"Which Laron does not."

"Actually, Laron has been to Zurlan, and is well regarded there."

"What? He cannot be fourteen."

"Seventeen—at least that is his story. Regardless, he is known to be worthy, and so can be taught some elements. A lot of javat teaches you to dodge, deflect, trip, bend bits of an opponent's anatomy into excruciating positions, and generally put an opponent's strength to one's own advantage. It will be ideal for Laron."

Almost unconsciously Sairet rolled and swayed her hips as she thought, and Roval could not help but watch. Her sheer grace made her seem much younger than her years, and the sorcerer found himself attracted to, and even aroused by, the dancemistress.

"No, I think that Ninth can do no harm here," Sairet suddenly decided, breaking Roval's trance. "There is a good number of wits missing from her original quota, but if you tell her to look the other way or not listen, she will do precisely that."

"Are you sure?"

"I have been teaching her to dance for fourteen days. Believe me, Learned Roval, she learns fast, but only when *told* to learn."

Roval considered now, unconsciously beginning to sway in time with Sairet. Abruptly he caught himself, then clapped his hands together.

"Why not? Sometimes I need to stand back and watch while my student fends off an attacker with a knife or club."

"Knife, club?" Sairet exclaimed. "Ninth? I don't want her hurt or frightened."

"Oh no, I promise no harm will come to her. The weapons will be harmless mock-ups."

"She will not be a convincing fighter."

"All the better. Just look at some of the fools who are already wielding knives, clubs, and axes all across Diomeda."

Two hours into the next morning's lesson Laron was beginning to grasp the basics of Roval's mysterious solution to his less-than-impressive physique. Roval and Laron were both stripped to the waist, and Ninth watched as man and youth squared off against each other again.

"This time use my weight against me," said Roval as he advanced.

As Roval's hand grasped Laron's wrist, the youth pulled

away for an instant, then stepped forward and hooked a leg behind Roval's. His free hand snaked up to push against the big man's throat and Roval tumbled to the threadbare rug on the floor.

"That was better, but you don't have to put so much force against my throat, Laron. Throats are soft, if you push against them they yield very easily."

"Sorry, sorry," Laron panted. "I'm still trying to use strength to do everything."

"Well, don't. Pretend that you are weaker than you are—and speaking of strength, time for a break—"

"Praise the gods of the moonworlds."

"—to do thirty push-ups."

Presently Roval stopped for a genuine rest, and Laron drank greedily from a waterskin as he lay against the wall.

"That post over there is a thief and he wants your purse," said Roval.

Wearily Laron drew his dagger and flung it. The point thudded squarely into the post. While Laron had lost the strength of being undead, he had retained some of the weapons skills he had accumulated over seven hundred years. The trouble was that he had tended not to bother with weapons for most of that time.

"Now his two friends have jumped out with their axes drawn," Roval added.

Laron drew a second dagger from behind him and flung it at the same post, then breathed a thin etheric streamer onto his hand. He stood up and held the yard of glowing fire like an ax.

"Now what?" Roval asked.

"I advance on him, hoping he does not realize that the casting cannot stand against a steel ax-blade."

"For whatever reason, he does not run," said Roval.

Laron shut his eyes and clenched his fist. The casting-blade collapsed in a soundless but brilliant flash. Ninth had not quite raised her hand in time, and afterimages of a jagged starburst of brightness danced before her blinking eyes.

"I now step forward, cross-block his ax arm," Laron continued, "bending my right wrist up while hooking a leg behind his and pushing his wrist up and twisting to force him to drop his ax as he falls. I then bring my forearm down against the back of his elbow, breaking it, then snatch up his ax and chop him through."

"Actually, you run away as soon as he is dazzled," said Roval.

"What? But—"

"Only ever fight when there is no other way, Laron. He might flail about with his ax and slash you by blind chance—no pun intended."

Laron groaned. "I should hope not."

"Having been cut open, you are now in pain and losing blood every second, while the third thief is quickly recovering his eyesight. Can you see as yet, Ninth?"

"Seeing, yes. A little."

"Who has the advantage?" asked Roval.

"But if I was cornered—" Laron began.

"Ah, but you were not cornered this time. Repeat this to yourself every hour of every day, my friend: You are no longer supernaturally strong and your wounds do not heal overnight. Walk with confidence and take no nonsense from anyone, but never fight unless you have no choice."

Roval departed, to go about other business. Laron was left with Ninth, conducting a bland but cheerful conversation. Above them one of Diomeda's rare thunderstorms was developing, and the beginnings of a lightning bolt was building up. A massive static charge between Diomeda and the clouds increased as rain poured down. An immense amount of the etheric energy suddenly began to discharge through Ninth. She collapsed, arching around and writhing on the floor of the dance space. By the time Laron reached her side she had gone limp. Then she opened her eyes.

"What— Where the hell am I?" Ninth exclaimed.

"Ninth?" said Laron, although he already knew that whatever he was talking to was not Ninth.

"What is this?" demanded the creature that had possessed Ninth. "Who are you?"

"Er . . . Penny?" Laron ventured.

"What's going on? Why are you in fancy dress? What happened to my school? Where is my cell phone?"

"I do not understand your words," said Laron.

She put a hand to her chest, then shrieked and snatched it away. "I've got two hearts!"

"Hasn't everyone?"

"If I feel my ears, are they going to be pointed, just like yours?" said the elemental, suddenly looking very worried. "I have never, *never* had a dream like this. I remember going to the school fancy dress ball. Absolute bore, none of the boys would dance with me, they are all frightened of me for some reason. I got back to my room, I just lay on my bed without getting changed. . . . I must have gone to sleep."

"Penny? Is that you?"

"Penny—? Penny, as in my grandmother?"

"I do not understand," pleaded Laron. "Who are you?"

There was a pause.

"I might ask the same question."

"My worldname is Laron. Where is Penny?"

"Penny Gisbourne is dead."

"What? How?"

"That is a matter of some debate. The coroner said she just stopped living. Did you know her?"

"We met once," said Laron. "Sort of."

Suddenly Laron understood. Intense, immense quantities of etheric energy surrounded them. This creature was Penny's grandchild. Penny was dead, but her grandchild had now inherited the circlet and oracle stone on the other world. She must have worn it to the ball and not taken it off. It was a chance in a million.

"What is your name?" Laron asked.

"No sensible sorceress would tell her name to strangers."

A sorceress from another world, thought Laron. *Even better. A whole new scholarship of magic. She might even be of use against Silverdeath.*

"No sensible sorceress would be without a worldname," Laron explained.

There was another pause.

"You may call me Elltee."

"Elltee, a name with good definition. Listen carefully—this link between our worlds will not be open for long. We can be of great benefit to each other. Are you interested?"

"I am interested in anything strange," said the girl from some inconceivably distant world.

Feran looked carefully at the sign that hung above a doorway in the outfall level of the port. The sign bore the symbol of a charmshaper and healer. He took out a dagger and flung it at the door. The timbers oozed blue scintillations that swarmed over the dagger, burning away the wood, horn, and leather handle, but leaving the steel blade untouched.

"You might have knocked," declared a voice from behind the door.

"You might have ignored me," replied Feran.

A bolt rattled back. A man of early middle-age, dressed in robes of a priestly cut, opened the door. His hair and beard were very short, and his eyes were large and unblinking.

"That was a Torean dagger," he commented.

"What I have to offer comes from Torea," Feran replied in a tone that was more eager than confrontational.

He reached into his robes and took out a thorn of glass as long as his hand from which five spirals of milky glass hung suspended by thin, flexible glass strands.

"I am saving this in case I ever have to ransom a king, but I may be inclined to part with something else in return for a favor from you."

He held up a tiny spiral of clear green glass. It looked for all the world like the horn of a unicorn no bigger than a cat.

"What is it?" whispered the charmshaper.

"Apart from beautiful, I cannot say. The vitrified death throes of a mouse caught in the fire-circles, according to the rather poetic lad who collected it. Personally I think that any mice in the area would have been long dead, and that it is the manifestation of some tortured forces of enchantment. Can we talk?"

The Sargolan charmshaper motioned Feran through the door. It closed behind him, untouched. The Sargolan spoke a short, sharp word and blue tendrils leaped from his mouth to the door, penetrating the boards and binding into the door's frame.

They stepped through a sparkling, insubstantial curtain that tingled on Feran's skin. Something seized his wrists, and the Sargolan barked a casting that surged along his arms and down his body. The tingling stopped.

"The visitor carries an ocular, two knives, and what appear to be several powerful tether charms, Tilbaram," reported the curtain behind Feran. "He has initiate training to level two, but his skills are of a very basic nature and he can do no more than minor heal-castings."

Satisfied, Tilbaram led Feran to a stone room where they both spoke guard words before sitting down within a hemisphere of interlaced tendrils of light blue.

"I expected something more impressive to be hidden upon you," said Tilbaram.

"It's in my nature to disappoint, what with being a merchant," Feran replied.

"Apart from those toys, what could someone with such weak powers as yours have that I would want?"

"If it would profit me to impress you, I would indeed impress you," said Feran. "Tell me, what is your interest in Torea?"

"Torea? I have no interest in Torea."

"Why do you lie to me, Gasmer Tilbaram? The Placidian Rim kingdoms have been in turmoil for the past six months. There is no precedent for death on such a scale as happened in Torea, or swiftness. *You* pay real silver to question mere sailors who have walked the melted sand of Torea's shores, you even have a blackened knife blade found in the ruins of Gironal and several Helionese silver coins made from silver recovered from the melted cities. Oh yes, you have an interest in Torea, Gasmer Tilbaram. You and all the other initiates and charmshapers of Acrema want to know what unleashed the fire-circles."

"What do you know about it, merchant?"

"I am in a position to offer certain items for sale," Feran said casually. "Do you know what this is?"

"Probably the anchor for your ocular."

"Correct. Would you like to inspect what my ocular has imaged?"

The charmshaper spoke a casting at the anchor. A point of light appeared in midair, then drifted slowly across to a wall hung with cheap Sargolan tapestries depicting some of the more noteworthy frolics between their gods and goddesses. As the ocular touched the wall it spread out into a white, featureless disk. When the circumference was touching both the floor and the ceiling it ceased to grow and the charmshaper spoke a control-casting into the palm of his hand. He flicked it at the disk with his finger. The wall suddenly presented them with a view of a sunlit plain with a hamlet and a few trees in the foreground. People were visible going about the business of staying alive and earning a living. Quite without warning, and in less than a heartbeat, a wall of flame lashed up from the horizon. There was a moment in which pure, white light overwhelmed the ocular. Feran and Tilbaram blinked the afterimages out of their eyes, but now there were only swirls of thick dust and smoke over a blighted countryside.

"My ocular recorded a fire-circle," Feran explained.

The scene winked out, leaving the blank, glowing disk.

"I must see that again," the charmshaper said eagerly, standing up.

"You may see it as often as you like, once my price has been met."

"What is your price? I do not have the gold of the highborn amateurs farther up the hill, but I can teach you words, grant energies to you, even give you books of etherworld links."

"I want none of that. I wish only to have an introduction to the local representative of the Sargolan Governance of Initiates, with a view to affiliation."

"What?" Tilbaram hooted. "They even have apprentices with greater etheric powers than yours."

"Have your apprentices walked the shores of Torea and collected objects there? Have they been to Helion and spoken to the surviving Metrologan priestesses? I have done all of that. I have chunks of fused glass from the ruins of Larmentel. Would you like one?"

Strangely enough, there was more gold and silver from the

dead continent available in Diomeda than fused sand from the Torean beaches. The prospect of a gift also had a curiously powerful allure for the Diomedan charmshaper. Feran held up a long, tapering sliver of glass.

"I can speak words on your behalf, but why do you want to affiliate with our Governance?" he asked suspiciously. "Granted, we have a good name, but why us?"

"Certain initiates from Torea did survive the fire-circles," said Feran. "I am acting on their behalf, scouting out the cities ringing the Placidian Ocean."

"For what?"

"For support."

"And what is the nature of that support, and its end?"

"That is not for me to say; it is of a confidential nature. I have only goods to trade with, and instructions on what to look for. I also note that you are of a suspicious nature."

Feran had been watching Tilbaram, while allowing his eyes to scan the shadows at the edge of his vision. Tilbaram was standing quite still, with only his lips moving. That was marginally suspicious, as behavior went. The light from the blank viewing circle was casting his shadow on the opposite wall, however, and Feran had turned so that he could watch that shadow. Now there was another shadow moving behind his, that of an ax in midair.

Feran whirled and stabbed behind him with his shard of glass, thrusting into something like thick jelly. The ax that had been floating without apparent support dropped to the floor. Blood began to drip out of midair, then there was a hissing crackle as a casting collapsed. Tilbaram toppled forward on his chair, clutching his abdomen. Blood seeped between his fingers.

"Dangerous things, simulself-castings," said Feran. "They transmit damage just as effectively as they hold weapons."

Tilbaram writhed and gasped, too agonized and shocked even to cry out.

"I could get help, but do I really trust you anymore?" continued Feran. "I'll tell you what: Why not croak out the name of someone on the Sargolan Governance, and he can come to your aid after I have met with him?"

Tilbaram survived, until the next morning, at any rate. Four days later the Governance met, and Feran was presented to them. As it happened, what he had to say to them interested them considerably.

Across the desert, three hundred and fifty miles to the southwest, Princess Senterri was swaying to the music of a pair of windrel musicians while her owners haggled and bickered with prospective buyers in the Hadyal slave market. The town was barely two hundred miles from Sargolan territory, but that was over waterless desert. None of the locals spoke Sargolan, and even their grasp of the Diomedan trade language was limited.

"Five pagols each," declared the slaver D'Alik, folding his arms to show that his offer was final.

"But they dance, they are white," insisted the windrel man.

"They are suntanned, and their hands are filthy from having to milk your goats and tend your cooking fires. It will take a month in Madame Voldean's College of Domestic and Exotic Skills to get them cleaned up and suitably pale once more."

"Twenty pagols, all three. One is princess! Worth hundred."

"Then sell her to someone who wants a princess. I want dancers."

"Princess is dancer. Twenty."

"Eighteen, all three. Three at six. Madame Voldean is going to cost me gold as well."

"Twenty!"

"If you had kept them clean and shaded, yes, but they are tanned and filthy."

"Twenty!"

"Then keep your girls and find another buyer. If you change your mind, see my steward."

The windrel man went straight to D'Alik's steward almost as soon as the slaver went on to the next vendor. Face was saved as eighteen pagols were paid, and the scrolls for the girls were handed over.

"Robber, is D'Alik. Princess, is," muttered the windrel as he inspected each pagol in turn.

"And just which of them is the supposedly royal lady on hard times?" asked the steward.

"Name Senterri, hair long-fire."

"So, she's brunette? You would never know it with all that dust and grime on her. Ah well, a pleasure doing business with you, Malovot, as always."

The three girls were huddled together, and had a fairly good idea that money had just been exchanged in return for themselves. Only Dolvienne had any grasp of the desert languages, however, and she was translating for the others.

"The big, hairy one with the gold embroidery in his robes," she said, inclining her head without pointing, "I think he is the buyer."

"The one who looks like a middle-aged warrior with about ten years of good eating since his last fight?" asked Senterri.

"He surely intends to take us home and ravish us this very night," said Perime.

"We are worth more as virgins," said Dolvienne, not sounding at all worried. "Every time we are discussed, that matter is raised."

"I am so tired of intimate examinations by old windrel women," said Perime.

"Would you prefer it was old windrel men?" asked Dolvienne.

"After sixty days of windrel food, windrel clothes, windrel smells, and windrel punishment, I'll never allow a windrel dancer or musician in my palace again as long as I live," Senterri said firmly.

"That presumes you ever get back to your palace," said Dolvienne.

"Someone will recognize me," said Senterri. "It is only a matter of time."

"The windrels keep trying to tell people that you are a princess, but nobody believes them. I don't like your chances. We might have to look after ourselves."

"We tried that. We were betrayed and abducted almost as soon as we were out of sight of Diomeda's walls. I should have trusted that nice Admiral Forteron."

"He had such good manners," added Perime.

They stopped talking as a muscular but well-proportioned man in his thirties walked over and bowed to them. Unlike most of the other men in the market, his black beard and hair were neatly and even sharply trimmed.

"My name is Toragev, ladies, I am steward and chief of guards to D'Alik, Slavemaster by Appointment to three northern kingdoms," he said in flawless Diomedan as he unlocked their chains from the display rail. "Please accept my pardon for leading you away by your chains, but it is a matter of protocol. I have to be seen to be in possession of you, on my master's behalf."

"Polite," Perime whispered approvingly to Senterri.

"What is to become of us?" Senterri asked tentatively, her nerves badly shaken by nearly two months of windrel punishments, yet encouraged by the steward's polite manner.

"Oh, first you shall be given a very thorough bath. The windrels never learn to bathe their slaves, praise be to the gods in Miral. For the cost of water, oils, and soap worth a few coppers, a full gold pagol can be added to a girl's value. After you are clean again, there will be a month's or so lessons in manners, customs, and the arts of pleasing noblemen of high degree in the northern kingdoms. Then, I am afraid, you will have a very arduous and boring trip of a thousand miles to those very same northern kingdoms. Is it not remarkable? Here in the southern desert you are worth six pagols, but if we take you sufficiently far north, your value as slaves can increase twenty times over what has just been paid for you."

"Slaves?" echoed Senterri.

"Do not sound so dismayed. Do you realize how many girls *volunteer* to be sold into our trading house? You are to be the very finest of slaves, treasured and admired, the mistresses of the mighty and powerful. What girl of low birth could normally aspire to that?"

The question was carefully designed to provoke a response, and the response was quick to come.

"But, Toragev, I am not of low birth, I am the daughter of, er, a very wealthy Sargolan merchant," Senterri burst out.

"Oh, please, if I had a copper for every—"

"It is true! Read my scrolls."

Toragev stopped in the shade of a nut tree, took the scrolls from his bag, and read. The forged certificates from Madame Sairet's dancing school were in the Diomedan trade language, but there were others in Sargolan, which he did not speak. He pretended to read the scroll declaring Senterri to be the daughter of the merchant Aramadea, of Aramadea Silks, Spices, and Fine Wines in Diomeda. He feigned surprise.

"This changes everything," he said in a much softer voice. "The Sargolan border is two hundred miles to the south, but the road is difficult, and thick with bandits."

"So you will help?" asked Senterri, dropping to her knees in a mixture of relief and supplication.

"Please, excellent lady, none of this," said Toragev, offering his arm to help her back to her feet. "The only safe passage south is with the great caravans, and there are none going that way just now. For the present it will be safest for you to play the part of a slave dancer. You will be well looked after by Madame Voldean and D'Alik, but do not let anyone know that you are from a grand Sargolan merchant house. Leave the rest to me."

The girls showered their thanks on the steward—Toragev did not realize that what Senterri had told him was basically true, and Senterri and Perime did not realize that he was lying. Dolvienne distrusted any proposal that seemed too cheap or easy, but played the part of an unquestioningly grateful girl in dire peril because it was what the steward expected.

None of them realized that just two hundred miles away an army was being assembled to march north on Diomeda. Hundreds of thousands of warriors and sailors were preparing to fight for the freedom and honor of their emperor's daughter. Farther south, the keels of a thousand dash galleys were being laid. They were small and fast, and each could be built within two or three months. The larger, existing galleys were assigned to defend Sargolan ports, where the new ships were being built. All over the Sargolan empire men flocked to answer their emperor's call for a million warriors to defend Senterri's honor or to avenge her death. The trouble was, they were going after the wrong people.

Even though it was all being done to rescue Senterri, it came down to the same point Toragev had made earlier. Effectively, Senterri really was no more than a lowborn dancing girl in her current circumstances. She was in a hostile and alien place and culture, and totally cut off from all the power, wealth, and deference that made her a princess.

"There sits a man whose mind is full of glass cities."

Druskarl twisted slowly in his seat to see a man with a bristly beard, who was wearing a black kaftan and sun shawl weighted down by winged silver globes held in sea eagles' talons—the Racital symbols for souls in the grip of a slavemaster. The slaver's hands were folded invisibly into his voluminous sleeves.

"You again," Druskarl responded to the shadowed face. "But where are my manners? Sit down, have a drink. Ba'do, bring another cup for my Racital friend."

They sat together with their sandaled feet on the table and toasted the distant island in the harbor, which was encrusted with Dawnlight palace and surrounded by Warsovran's fleet.

"A nice chal'vik, thirteenth year of Magestril the Sixth, I'd say," Feran commented.

"Fifteenth, actually. They put oak slats in the jars to get that mellow bouquet."

"How inventive."

"So, what do you want?"

"To toast our escape from Torea."

"I'm touched. To escaping."

"To escaping."

"I forgot to ask last time, where is Laron now?"

"Here in Diomeda, lurking and hiding," said Feran with an unconcerned shrug. "Having mere human strength and being compelled to eat normal food has left him somewhat vulnerable. He will even die normally in a few decades—sooner, if some of his enemies catch up with him. Will Ninth ever come here?"

"A city filled with wenches and you yearn for Ninth?"

"No, I just . . . take an interest in women. Pah, you keep your balls in a jar of vinegar, you could never understand the love of women and hate of celibacy."

"To celibacy," said Druskarl.

"Long may other men practice it!" added Feran. "So, is she in Vindic?"

"She is with kind and caring patrons."

"Good, good. She was such a fearful, vulnerable creature. I am currently seeing a wench who works the taps at one of the taverns. Did you ever have a lover?"

"Yes. Ba'do, another jar of chal'vik."

"A special lover?"

"I had a wife in North Acrema, but we are obviously somewhat separated now. She is exploring new opportunities for advancement, and I am following the path of duty."

"To duty!" exclaimed Feran, draining his wine again. "Especially in the name of love."

They lapsed into silence for a while, watching Warsovran's fleet on the bay. A huge catapult barge shot a stone ball high into the air, and it crashed into the red tiled roof of Dawnlight's southwestern spire. Part of the roof collapsed, sending a shower of tiles cascading down onto the defenders. Moments later a scatter of firepots came over the wall. Most fell into the water, but one hit a dash galley and two struck the catapult barge. There was a flurry of activity to put out the fires and drag the stricken vessels to safety.

"King, two; Warsovran, one," said Feran.

"The palace has the advantage of height and strength. Presently the Alliance and Sargolan armies will arrive overland, and Warsovran will be forced to sail away with his fleet."

"And what about you?"

"I am in nobody's employ just now, but I have plenty of Torean gold. I have a mind to go north and consult certain Turiac medicars about my, ah, medical condition. What of you?"

"Actually, I have been consulting with certain sorcerers about a scheme, and refining and improving certain other plans. One item is currently missing from our plans, however."

"And what is that?"

"As I have said, Laron is no longer a vampyre, and no longer has quite the same strength that he is known for. You, on the other hand, remain as strong as ever and we need the services of one very strong man who has proved his trustworthiness. What are your feelings concerning Silverdeath?"

"I think that it would be best kept in more responsible hands."

Feran sipped at his wine, then pointedly examined his own hands. "And whose hands are they?"

"After what has happened in Torea and Helion, anyone's but Warsovran's."

"We have a scheme to capture Silverdeath."

Druskarl stared for a moment, the put his drink down. "And do what?"

"Our intentions are good."

"I'm sure they will be added to those that pave the road to the underworld."

"But will you be part of it?"

"First tell me more."

"Just now, I cannot. Give me a few days, however, and I shall show you."

Feran stood up, bowed in the Racital manner, then dropped a coin on the table and left. An Acreman serving girl bustled up as Druskarl sat thinking.

"Will you be having another drink, sir?" she asked as she scooped up Feran's mug and slid the coin into her cleavage.

"No, I must be about my business," he replied, then left, too.

Within a half hour the serving girl was in the Metrologan mission to Diomeda, speaking with Deacon Lisgar.

"I also heard the eunuch speak about consulting Turiac medicars about his medical condition, then Silverdeath was mentioned twice. I did not hear any more."

"And you did not see the slaver's face?" asked Lisgar as he scribbled down what she had said.

"No. Another shadow took over to follow Druskarl when he left."

"Excellent. Return to your work now, and remain alert."

"What does it all mean, deacon? I'm frightened of Sil-verdeath."

"So am I, but I have faith in those who I answer to."

Some days later Druskarl sat under the vine-smothered pergola of another tavern, sipping wine while an itinerant barber shaved his head and face.

"Mighty warriors, yessy?" said the Turiac barber with a flourish of his razor to the harbor below.

"You watch my head, I shall watch the ships," replied Druskarl.

"If I draw blood, worshipful sir, free shave you to have."

"I would prefer to pay and lose no blood." Druskarl wiped his head with a moist towel, paid the barber, ran a hand over his skull, and sat back to watch Warsovran's catapult barge being rowed back for another assault on the palace. Presently Feran found him, and pulled up a chair.

"Have you considered my scheme as yet?" he asked.

"You wish to capture Silverdeath. If I had a copper for every-one who wished to possess it, I would never have to work again. You said that you would show me something today."

"Yes. It is a matter of the greatest secrecy, but I feel sure that you will be convinced when you see it."

Together they set off for the shipwrights' yards near the docks. In a long, narrow shed used for storing and curing mast wood, a boat such as Druskarl had never before seen was taking shape. It was long, thin, and very light, and had extremely long oars. Most of it was enclosed, except for where the two rowers sat. It was constructed from hides over an ashwood frame.

"Those who built it think it's a messenger boat for travel in-land on the rivers," Feran said softly as they circled it. "It should easily outrun a dash galley on a light sea, and the seas generally are light around this time of year."

"It is a very handsome craft."

"Thank you. It cost a considerable amount of gold. The de-signer of the *Shadowmoon* once described the design to me; he called it a racing shell."

"I can see why. Just a bare shell of a boat, good for nothing else but going fast."

"Not quite, esteemed eunuch. Like you, it has certain luxuries missing, but in other ways it is vastly superior to its peers. Not only is this thing fast, but if inverted and tied down to rocks in the shallows it can hold enough air for four or five hours' breathing."

Druskarl suddenly made the connection between Silverdeath and the highly refined little craft. "I do believe that you have recruited me," he announced as he stood with his arms folded.

Outside, a harlot rejected yet another offer of employment as she waited, watching for Druskarl to come out again.

Roval had heard of Madame Yvendel's Academy, but had never entered it until now. It was not at all to his taste. In his experience, academies were meant to be cold, scrubbed, drafty places where youths wore sacking, drank rainwater, and ate brown rice flavored with olive oil. This place was dark, soft with carpets and hangings, and was reputed to train both girls and youths in etheric sciences and crafts. Learned Yvendel confirmed his worst fears by her comfortable and gaudy clothing. As they bowed to each other and exchanged ritualized flourishes and badge-castings, a short, pop-eyed man of about forty emerged from behind a curtain. He smiled ingratiatingly at Yvendel, while cringing with apprehension. He was not known to Roval.

"This is Einsel," announced Yvendel.

The name changed everything for Roval.

"Einsel, as in Warsovran's court sorcerer?" Roval asked the unlikely-looking little man, who had dark bags beneath his protuberant eyes.

"I suspected I might need no introduction, heh-heh."

"How many tracts on etheric fashioning have you written?"

Einsel blinked at the question. "Ah, thirty-one."

"And how many children have you sired?—and think carefully."

Einsel looked down at his feet. "One," he replied, then muttered, "Probably."

"You could be genuine," Roval conceded.

Yvendel cleared her throat. "As court sorcerer, Einsel raises no suspicion by visiting places such as this," she explained.

"Indeed, I am expected to make such visits, Learned Roval. I am something of an inspector for the emperor."

"Yet you are not inspecting at this moment."

"No, and I must be circumspect with what I say. Anyone might betray me, including you. My head is filled with facts of the most delicate character, and in return for presenting it to Warsovran on a platter you would be given gold sufficient to ransom a king. I am not willing to have myself exposed to people who could verify who I am by what intelligence I might pass on. For example, *you* might not be Roval."

"My sources are reliable," Yvendel assured him. "If you can trust me, you can trust this man."

"As court sorcerer to Warsovran," continued Einsel, "I had a great deal of information shared with me. Too much, perhaps. The emperor made me nervous. When nervous I am sometimes forced to take drastic action."

"He makes a lot more people than you nervous!" exclaimed Roval. "Did you see what he did to Torea?"

"Yes, and South Helion besides. Other than Warsovran, I have probably seen more fire-circles than any other living man."

"Why are you here?"

"That weapon, Silverdeath. I have seen it, touched it, even probed it as well as a mere initiate of grading eleven can manage. What I have seen and heard frightens me. Warsovran intends to use it, over and over again."

"He *what*?" said Roval incredulously. "Has he not seen what it can do?"

"He seeks to intimidate his enemies. The problem is that one accident, one miscalculation, and he could destroy this world. This is of rather great concern to me, because I have nowhere else to live."

"Why are you confiding in me?"

"Some of us are plotting to put a little distance between Warsovran and Silverdeath. When it is in our hands we shall need to keep it very secure. It cannot be destroyed, only removed from temptation's way."

"From what I know of Helion, and Silverdeath's 'double diameter in half-time' pattern of fire-circles, it will run out of land to burn in one hundred and twenty days."

"Not so," Yvendel interjected. "If more than half of a fire-circle's area is over water, it also will be quenched. Come over here."

She led them to a table where a map of Helion was laid out. It was an ugly, functional map, like those used by navigators, and was all exact lines and positions, with none of the illumination and embellishment more often seen on decorative maps in libraries.

"I risked my life copying this thing," explained Einsel. "See, the first fire-circle centered on the Metrologan temple was all over land. The second will all be over water, except for the isthmus to North Helion."

"Ah, and the third fire-circle will thus destroy part of Port Wayside," exclaimed Roval, "but otherwise be mostly over water. It will fall after ninety-six days."

"Correct, but wrong, heh-heh. As Admiral Griffa was sailing around Torea, purging Warsovran's rivals from the coast, his navigators did a survey that pushed the art of cartography to the very limits. The final fire-circle was definitely over more land than water, yet it was still quenched. The *entire circumference* was over water. This appears to be another quenching condition."

"*Appears* to be . . . but even Griffa's navigators and surveyors may be wrong."

"Perhaps, but as soon as Griffa's carrier auton landed, my emperor decided to conduct an experiment at Helion. Even now his marines and the islanders are digging out the isthmus between North and South Helion. The second fire-circle's circumference will be entirely over water, and Silverdeath may fall from the sky. Learned Roval, you must get there first, find Silverdeath when it falls, and flee with it."

"How? Visitors and sightseers will be discouraged with great enthusiasm until South Helion island is cool enough for Warsovran to walk upon, and even if I got past the guards— well! After a few hundred yards my body would be fit only for presentation with rosemary, chives, garlic, and a red-wine sauce."

"Made with a nice cabernet from the central Acreman highlands, I should think," said Yvendel, "but *you* could do it another way."

"The Learned Rector will not, however, tell me," said Einsel, a little resentfully.

"If you know nothing, you cannot crack under torture," explained Yvendel.

"Will you tell me?" asked Roval.

"Presently. After Learned Einsel is gone."

Once the little sorcerer had left the Academy, Yvendel explained what she had in mind. Roval thought it over as he studied the map Einsel had left.

"I could do it, but I would have to practice in complete secrecy," he concluded.

"That can be arranged."

"I would need the *Shadowmoon* to get me to Helion, and a very fast galley for when I am fleeing."

"That can be arranged as well."

"In that case, I agree."

Yvendel now flourished a leather-bound folder, which contained about two dozen pages.

"There is another plot to seize Silverdeath being planned in Diomeda," she announced. "It involves a former Vindican king by the name of Druskarl. Another conspirator is Feran Woodbar, the former boatmaster of the *Shadowmoon*, who appears to be building a fast, light boat of some description. Do you know anything about this?"

"Druskarl wants Silverdeath so that his castration can be reversed. Feran is just an agent, but he is sure to be working for dangerous people. My guess is the High Circle of Scalticar."

Yvendel's eyes narrowed. "But I also work for the High Circle of Scalticar."

"If you are surprised, then you have obviously not visited the grand palace of the High Circle of Scalticar. Two senior sorcerers with two separate budget allocations are perfectly capable of administering two separate projects with the same aim. Unless someone complains, let us continue with what we are doing, and regard Feran and Druskarl as a backup."

"But if Druskarl becomes master of Silverdeath—"

"Then he is sure to be an improvement on Warsovran."

The great port of Alberin was shrouded in drizzle and woodsmoke as the *Shadowmoon* tied up. This was nothing unusual, as most of North Scalticar seemed to be shrouded in drizzle most of the time. There were Acremans who said that North Scalticar got all the rain that should have fallen on the vast deserts of Acrema, but the Scalticarians replied that if the Acremans could find a cooperative weather god, then they were welcome to all the rain they could divert.

It was early in the tenth month as Terikel stepped ashore. The very first thing she did was embrace the nearest bollard. Next she swore that she would never set foot on another ship for as long as she lived. There was no welcome other than a customs official. A bribe was paid, so the official did not search the box the crewmen were bringing ashore for her. Terikel walked awkwardly, unused to solid ground beneath her feet after such a long time at sea. Norrieav, Hazlok, and several wharfers followed, carrying her box of gold in a sailcloth sling hanging from a pole.

Alberin was designed for rain, so awnings, walkways, and public shelters featured heavily throughout the city. A member of the city guard directed them to the rented house which the Metrologans now called their temple. In spite of the number of public coverings, they were soaked by the time they reached it. Terikel knocked on the door. Footsteps were heard approaching. An eyeslit slid open.

"Possible to help, yes, you are who?" asked a heavily accented and awkward voice in Scalticarian.

"I am your Elder, and you can start helping by letting me in from the rain," declared Terikel.

The door was flung open just as soon as the bolts could be thrown back. Soon the four Metrologan priestesses were helping Terikel out of her sodden clothes before a fire while Norrieav and Hazlok helped themselves to smoked fish fillets on toast in the kitchen. Justiva donated her spare blue robes to her Elder.

"There is great goodwill toward us here," Justiva explained as Terikel dressed, "and this is a very tolerant city. It is also a city where all pay their own way. The four of us are already serving in taverns to keep the roof over our heads and food in the pantry."

"Still, you are alive and safe," observed Terikel.

"And in need of *you*. We were all rammed through our last studies just to get us formally ordained and preserve the Order. We know nothing about organizing things."

"You seem to be doing superbly," replied Terikel, who had been expecting far worse. "A warm, dry house with no leaks, and everyone clothed, well fed, and healthy."

"That's just it! I can run a house with a few girls in it. Fortune knows, I used to run a rather different one in Port Wayside. What I can't do is be the deputy Elder for the entire Metrologan Order. I can't deal with senior sorcerers and nobles, discuss policy, loans, or even what we have to offer Alberin as priestesses."

"We have a couple of rooms out the back for street girls without shelter," said Latelle, "and I run a herbalist service once a week for those in poor health."

"From where?"

"Where you're standing."

"We have been managing without money, but we really need experience and leadership," said Justiva. "Otherwise we're just a house full of girls—we might as well be looking for husbands."

Terikel eyed her box full of gold, then looked over the faces of her four priestesses again. There was so much faith, and it was all directed at her. She could, of course, tell them about the gold, but that would just tell them wealth solves all problems. They had achieved miracles merely by getting here and surviving, and much of that probably had been under Justiva's direction and brilliant leadership. Now they needed to be shown that an Elder could work miracles, and that they were supposed to be training to do the same.

"Why has the Scalticarian High Circle not given us a temple, rooms, and staff?" Terikel asked Justiva.

"A *temple*? I—ah . . . I—"

"Did you ask for them?"

"I, ah—no."

"Did you tell them what we have to offer?"

"To offer?" asked the suddenly exasperated Justiva. "Us? Two reformed whores, a cook, and a nurse who can do windrel dancing? What can we offer the Alberin Branch of the High Circle of Scalticarian Sorcerers? A small orgy, with food, entertainment, and a complimentary checkup for the pox included?"

"You might have done those things once, but you are now Metrologan priestesses with between three and five years' study to your credit. We have a charter to teach, research, and do charitable works, and wherever we are, we are going to do just that. All of you, come with me—and bring my box in the sling bag, two at either end. Shipmaster, Hazlok, look after the house. Justiva, take me to the local tower of the High Circle."

Twenty minutes later, and again soaked, Terikel entered Alberin's tower of the High Circle. She brushed aside clerks, guards and lackeys until she was in the chambers of the tower master, then told her priestesses to wait outside. The tower master did not at first realize that Terikel was a new arrival.

"Just who do you think you are, bursting into my chambers!" he shouted, rising from his chair. "I said we were willing to allow sanctuary for your Order, but remember that you are just destitute refugees with—"

Terikel dropped a chunk of dark green glass onto his writing desk. The man had not become tower master without having a good eyes for powerful etheric talismans. There was the impression of what looked like elaborate chain-mail.

"*That* bears the imprint of Silverdeath itself, and was dug from the lake of glass at the center of Larmentel, where it fell," declared Terikel, in a voice as cold and level as a frozen river.

"It also has the last Torean succubus in existence bound to it."

"I, um . . . Succubus?"

"I know its name."

"Ah. Oh."

"And this is for us destitute refugees to pay our way!" shrieked Terikel, flinging a handful of gold across his desk.

A half hour later Terikel emerged with the tower master.

"Justiva, we have a temple, living quarters, and school. Freehold. The tower master will arrange for the local militia to clean and vacate it by tonight, when we shall move in. You will administer it. Latelle, you will be lecturing on Torean healing arts at the university every afternoon, then talking about the benefits of windrel dancing for the treatment of bad backs. Jeles, you will turn that rented house into a sanctuary for sick or injured harlots."

"But the owner said—"

"In one hour the owner will be me. Kelleni, present yourself here tomorrow morning. Some students of sorcery wish to speak to you about Torean cuisine and the enhancement of etheric energies through good cooking."

Terikel turned back to the tower master. "You! Find me dry robes. Find us all dry robes."

"Ah, yes, Elder. Certainly."

Terikel stalked after him as he hurried away.

Latelle finally remembered to close her mouth, then turned to Justiva. "Are we all meant to be able to do *that* when we grow up?"

"Apparently so," replied Justiva, who was still looking after Terikel, her eyes shining with admiration.

Six days later it was the Festival of the Etheric Lights. As if in deference to the great occasion, the clouds above Alberin broke up, then vanished to leave a flawlessly blue sky, which soon melted into a deep-red furnace as the sun set. Miral glowed brightly, attended by Dalsh, Lupan, and Belvia, while a stunning wash of stars covered the entire region around the south celestial pole.

The Sisters of the Metrologan Order filed into the ornate and soaring Etheric Cathedral of Alberin, with antiphonal choirs of boys and girls singing the carols of the season. The cathedral was packed with the nobility, academicians, sorcerers, and the wealthier merchants of Alberin, and carols and readings echoed into the darkness amid the rafters. Midway through the service Terikel was called upon to give the Metrologans' blessing to the season, and she spoke in carefully translated and memorized Scalticarian. Latelle sang one of the Order's hymns, "The Lamp in the Darkness," while holding up a Torean pottery oil-lamp that had come over on the *Shadowmoon*.

At the end of two hours the crown prince led the huge congregation in one final carol, then they streamed out into the city's main square, where all the soak torches had been extinguished. High above, a brilliant splash of etheric lights rippled and danced among the moonworlds, stars, and Miral. People laughed, cheered, and passed around jars of fortified wine and mead while initiates flung dazzle castings high to burst in the air.

Terikel embraced Justiva and Latelle, and decided that she was feeling truly happy for the first time since leaving Torea. She was the Elder, and the Order was secure in a strong and prosperous kingdom. They had patronage, money, and something to offer. The weather was admittedly abominable most of the time, and there was more work than the five of them could easily cope with, but that was better than being hunted or—even worse—ignored.

She felt a hand on her arm. The tower master. She was hurried away to his chambers.

"I have to leave *tonight*?" Terikel ranted in Diomedan as she paced before the tower master's chair.

"Er, yes," said the tower master. "There is very little time."

Outside, the festival was still in full cry, with the enthusiastic support of her four priestesses and four new Scalticarian deaconesses and deacons. Although she was not yet thirty, the young priestess suddenly felt old, tired, and very, very lonely.

"I can invoke the auton's message again," offered the tower master.

"No, thank you, I'm good at picking up bad news the first time. Why me? Surely in all of Alberin, the biggest port on the continent of Scalticar, you can find one bloody sailor extra for the *Shadowmoon*."

"Learned Yvendel insisted on you. Her message was quite explicit."

"But I've only been here *six days*! I love this place, I've just been to the most beautiful ceremony and festival of my life. My Sisters need me."

"Justiva is highly capable, merely less, ah, forthright than you. Elder, *nobody* wants you to go, but this involves Silverdeath. The Sargol Governance is backing a scheme to snatch it from Warsovran, and we must do it before them."

"Every monarch and sorceric organization in the world has delusions of possessing Silverdeath. It brings immortality and limitless power, after all. Why is the Sargol Governance worth worrying about in particular?"

"Their agents are Obanar Druskarl, former King of Vindic—"

"Damn his pickled testicles."

"—and Feran Woodbar, former boatmaster of the *Shadowmoon*."

"The little worm! Doesn't surprise me in the slightest."

"The Sargolans have made a dash galley available to Feran, and have reportedly built another submersible like the *Shadowmoon*. We have been trying to gather together the survivors of the *Shadowmoon*'s crew, those who know submersibles and know how these two men work and think."

"They are both bold, brave, and resourceful, whatever their faults," muttered Terikel.

"Roval will meet you on the Acreman coast, a day south of Diomeda. You will command the expedition until he joins up with the *Shadowmoon*. If he does not make the rendezvous, you will remain in command until Silverdeath is recovered."

"I can't believe the others were willing to go."

"They were not. Hazlok had to be dragged out of Madame Feather's Vale of Perfume by the city militia; D'Arto's wife chased my guards with a broom as they fetched him away; and boatmaster Norrieav was carried out of the Flash Frigate on a stretcher shouting, 'Pump, ye buggers, pump!' and singing something about hauling on the bowline."

"You're trying to tell me that the entire world is about to be placed upon my shoulders?"

"Well, yes. They are the only shoulders strong enough. I mean, very shapely shoulders they are, but just think: You are a proven commander, you are a priestess and initiate nine—"

"I want to take my tests to be graded to ten. I'm ready—"

"I'll arrange for that as you are walking to the docks. The examiners will sail on the galley with you and do the tests there."

"I'm not awake. This is a dream."

"I would not bother pinching myself, Elder. *You* must go. You know Helion, you know Roval, you know the *Shadowmoon* and its crew, and you are an experienced sailor. Above all, you can be trusted."

"The *Shadowmoon* needs a month in the dockyard before it will be ready for another voyage."

"The *Shadowmoon* is currently being hoisted onto the deck of the battle galley *Megazoid*, where it will be serviced, careened, and refitted on the voyage north. From now on you will even have new, watertight lockers to keep things dry when it submerges, and a depth measure to show how deep you have gone."

Terikel rubbed her face in her hands. Months of seasickness stretched before her, to be relieved only by brief periods of extreme fright.

"So the entire trip will not be on the *Shadowmoon*?"

"No, no, of course not. You will be commander of the whole expedition, the *Megazoid* as well as the *Shadowmoon*. You can have the *Megazoid*'s master cabin as your own; you can have whatever luxuries can be carried aboard in the next, er, three hours. You can even have the *Megazoid*'s galleymaster, if he's to your fancy."

"No thank you."

"Less than half of the voyage need be on the *Shadowmoon*."

Terikel flopped into a chair. Her shoulders slumped, and the tower master knew that he had won.

"*Commander* Terikel, I knew we could count on your sense of duty."

Chapter Seven

VOYAGE TO SICKLE BAY

Warsovran was careful to create the trappings of a royal court in his makeshift Diomedan palace. The nobles from his fleet were now dressed in rich robes, of a type more impressive to Acreman eyes, and gold featured heavily in the decorations and furnishings. He had already ordered work commenced on a new palace, which was to be sited on a hill commanding panoramic views of the harbor and city. The message was that he was rich, powerful, refined, and here to stay. On this particular day he was recruiting dancing girls for the entertainment of his new court.

A procession of eunuchs began serving as the girls sprawled on huge cushions, and serving maids discreetly moved about with pitchers of honeyed goat's milk, limewater, chilled caffin with marshmallow foam, and vanilla yogurt.

"Spiced partridge hearts on handwatered lavender rice under young lettuce leaves and cornflower petals," called the lead eunuch.

"Here," Grand Admiral Narady said without looking up.

The next eunuch in line stepped forward and cleared his throat. "Young marrows stuffed with candied wild locusts, and spiced, seedless cherry tomatoes in oiled vine leaves."

Sonmalin, the city governor, waved languidly but did not bother to call out.

"Leek fronds stuffed with curried sea urchin on maidenhair noodles."

"Mine," called Admiral Griffa, sitting up on his cushions.

The next eunuch had a look of undisguised distaste on his face. "Plain brown rice and raw celery, with *one* sardine in olive oil," he said, as if every word caused him pain.

"For me," called Admiral Forteron.

A servant poured out a goblet of limewater. Forteron sipped at it, then handed it to Warsovran.

"They will become soft," Forteron observed quietly to his emperor.

"I want them soft, that way they are easier to mold," replied Warsovran.

The band changed from background music to a dance tune, and identical-twin Locnarii dancers entered from the doorway at the back of the hall. Warsovran thought at first that he was seeing double as he stared at the approaching girls. Their languorous dance was perfectly coordinated, and even the loops of pearls on their midriffs and their pendant earrings swayed synchronously, and in time to the music. The technical precision of the dance held Warsovran's attention firmly, like a rat hypnotized by an approaching snake. Time seemed suspended as they danced . . . then they were bowing and backing away. The music changed tempo, slowing a little.

Standing just out of sight were Sairet, Wensomer, and a muscular eunuch.

"Are you sure you are strong enough to go through with this?" Sairet hissed anxiously. "I mean, a month of nothing but brown rice, raw celery, and rainwater—"

"Shut up and help me tie that veil," snapped Wensomer.

"Not to mention a daily regimen of three thousand sit-ups, a ten-mile run up and down the beach, a sauna—"

"I lost *sixty-one* pounds, that is all that matters."

"Everything is black or white for you, Wensomer, that is your trouble. There are no shadings or colors. I have been advising you on measured and sensible weight loss ever since you arrived in Diomeda and you just ignored me. Now you—"

"Gorien, bend down, please," said Wensomer to the eunuch.

"Sairet, I appreciate your concern, but for now please help me onto his shoulders."

The music changed yet again, and the muscular eunuch walked slowly in from one side of the throne room as the twins completed their exit. Wensomer was draped over his shoulders. Gorien was dressed as a windrel snake-charmer, and as he came to a stop in the center of the floor, Wensomer began to slide down and around his body to the flagstones. As the eunuch backed away, she rose to her feet, her head swaying all the while, her tongue flickering over her lips every few seconds. She began by rotating her hips in a tight circle. Gradually the circle grew wider and lower, and soon she was on her knees. Her waist-length hair, dyed a blazingly bright shade of red, streamed out as she gyrated again and again. Without taking a single step she then slithered into an undulating body roll, and worked her way through a series of floor glides and back bends that made her body seem as fluid as a suit of fine chain-mail. Her dance culminated in a shimmying back bend that had Warsovran and Forteron clapping wildly.

The eunuch walked slowly back to where Wensomer was doing another floor glide and stopped just beside her. As he stood there, legs apart and arms folded, Wensomer slithered around his legs, then up and around his torso until she was again draped around his shoulders like a snake. Slowly, steadily, he walked away, as if there was nothing heavier than a small velvet python curled around his neck. They vanished through a door.

"Now, *that* was something to remember," said Warsovran, rubbing his chin.

Forteron smiled and nodded. The governor just folded his arms and sat up, as if anticipating that even better was still to come.

Wensomer reappeared, her forearms held horizontally just below her eyes, fingertips touching. Dark blue veils now hung from her arms to the floor.

"She's swathed in veils, she will spend much of the dance disrobing," Forteron said knowingly as he winked.

Wensomer took several steps, swaying to the music, but at a sudden quickening in the tempo, swept her arms down to reveal only fringed, sequined breastcups and a tasseled bikini whose belt was covered in coins and silver bells. Her sash was worn low on her hips, and was of translucent blue silk. The month on the SWS training program had removed a third of her body weight and replaced it with a set of abdominal muscles few men in the room could have matched, but the overall effect was definitely lissome—if a little astonishing.

Forteron and Warsovran gasped together and sat back. Wensomer stood perfectly still for some moments, only her eyelids batting, then her torso slowly expanded as she breathed in. Her arms swept upward, drawing up the veils like blue wings. Rhythmically jingling the zills on her fingers, Wensomer began to rotate her hips slowly in a flat circle while holding her upper torso perfectly still. As she began the first of several figures she had been practicing, her movements were so light and serpentine as to make her limbs seem like wisps of smoke. Her balance was such as to make her seem to defy gravity. A glowing green stone was set in her navel, lit from behind with luminous paste extracted from moon-beetles, while makeup based on the same paste gave her face the suggestion of a glow from between her curtains of long hair.

Warsovran stared at Wensomer with his mouth hanging open, mesmerized, not even realizing that he had joined everyone else in the hall in clapping to the rhythm of the musicians' playing.

"Is she hired?" laughed Forteron.

Warsovran did not reply; he had not heard him. Wensomer's eyes were half shut as she began the second figure, suggesting effortless ease rather than exhaustion. Snake arm-rolls, head slides, back-bend shimmies, pivoted hip-swings—all of her movements flowed from one to another with ease yet intensity, and she never seemed to tire. This dance was not actually meant to be spellbinding, it was mere background now, a setting for talk between rulers. Warsovran beckoned for the city governor to join them.

"I would wager you Toreans never had such art as this," he said offhandedly.

"We Toreans are the greatest sailors in the world," replied

Warsovran, already aware of where the governor was trying to lead him. "We buy and sell artists."

"So, you have come here to buy the best art in the world?"

"Indeed. How much is that last dancer?"

"She is a citizen, for hire only."

"Then don't just sit there, hire her!"

All the while, Wensomer continued to dance, showing no signs of fatigue, but she had noted that the men had begun to talk again. She was once more part of the general entertainment, and had no special reason to seek their attention. She danced sinuous, easy moves, enduring rather than impressing. It was twenty minutes before the governor gestured for the remaining dancers to begin, and a troupe of windrel girls took over the entertainment. Wensomer was almost totally drained as she slipped behind the heavy curtains by the archways. The windrels were more overtly sensual in their dancing than Sairet's dancers had been, Wensomer noted as she watched through a narrow gap. Sairet came up beside her.

"The news is that you are hired," Sairet announced.

"Ah, wonderful," panted Wensomer. "And you?"

"I was not available. The time will come soon when the allied army comes marching over the horizon and anyone known to work for Warsovran's court will view the victory celebrations from the top of a twelve-foot pike while their bodies feature in a special underwater festival for loyal and patriotic Diomedan sharks."

"By then I shall have what I want, and be severely missing from Diomeda."

Sairet sighed. "Ah, the eternal question: What do women want?"

"Who said anything about women?" said Wensomer, turning away from the gap. "When this is all done, I swear I shall do nothing but eat for a year! I'll never complain about your training again, it was like a rest after the SWS program."

"So, first thing tomorrow morning at your villa?"

"Yes, yes—and this time I might even be awake."

✳ ✳ ✳

Laron's instinct told him that Roval was planning to leave soon. The Scalticarian had said nothing to that effect, but there was something in his manner that worried Laron. A slight distance in his conversation, a reluctance to talk about anything in the future, his readiness to give Laron extra lessons in javat whenever the dance space was available. In order to train, Laron had been missing lectures at the Academy and copying the notes of others, paying for the favor in real silver. Between study, etheric focus meditation, and javat training, he was lucky to get five hours of sleep in a good night. Every second evening he would visit Wensomer, and they would share dinner and a jug of rainwater together while complaining to each other about injuries, aches, and the fact there were not enough hours in the day. Wensomer also hated feeling hungry all the time, and the way her body seemed to put on half a pound if she so much as thought about a honey pastry. Laron specialized in complaints about the difficulty in adding muscle to his body, hair to his face, and the fact that even the smell of roast lamb raised pimples on his cheeks.

"Here I am, eating fish, rice, and plain rolled oats to keep my skin clear, and for what?" moaned Laron a few nights after Wensomer had been recruited as a palace dancer. "My skin is clear, but I do not have a girl to caress it. Why do I bother?"

"Hah, try my predicament," muttered Wensomer. "Desired by every man who sees me dance, yet too busy and tired to take any of them to my bed."

A gong downstairs announced Sairet's arrival.

"Well, my torturer is here," Wensomer said as she and Laron stood up.

"Luxury," replied Laron. "My torturer does not make house calls."

"He does when he trains *me*," retorted Wensomer.

"Well, then, same time, day after tomorrow?"

"See you then."

After a brief and rather limp embrace, Laron went on his way. The sun was down, but Laron could have cheerfully aimed at a bed, fallen, and not moved until dawn. He was bruised, aching, very tired, and desperate for a meal with a bit of flavor. As he passed the Bargeman's Pole, the scent of minced lamb patties with herbs wafted out and secured his attention. His foot froze in midstep. He thought about yielding to temptation, thought about Wensomer's need for moral support, thought about the risk of generating half a dozen pimples, then decided that chivalry had its limits and if he could risk death he could risk pimples as well.

A quarter of an hour later he belched contentedly as he pushed his plate away, then took a sip of grape juice. Being mortal again was quite a strain, but good food was certainly a compensation. The thought of Wensomer suffering through her dance lesson gave him a twinge of guilt, but the thought that she was unlikely to find out about the lamb and kidney pie eased the twinge.

Because he was nervous about being seen eating anything remotely enticing, he had seated himself in a shadowed corner of the room. Thus when Feran entered, followed by Druskarl, they did not notice him as they glanced around, looking a trifle furtive. Laron dropped his face into his hands and watched them through his fingers. If they stayed . . . But they did not stay. They bought a bag of dried figs and two skins of grape juice, then walked straight out again. Laron hesitated for a moment, then followed as they made their way to the shipwrights' yards on the bank of the Leir River.

The pair disappeared into a shed, where a guard was posted. Laron debated with himself about whether to try and get a look inside. He noticed that at least one large dog was just as concerned for the shed's security as the guard. Laron's dilemma was resolved with the rattle of a chain on the doors facing the river. Even at a distance he easily discerned four men carrying something long, thin, and obviously very light. They waded into the water, and two of them climbed into the lean, frail-looking craft.

"Panyor," and ". . . back before dawn," floated across to Laron as four oars the length of the *Shadowmoon*'s sweeps splashed into the water. The craft shot out into the river at a speed that nothing afloat should have been able to achieve, then turned inland. Laron followed for half a mile, but the exertions of the afternoon quickly caught up with him, along with the weight of the pie in his stomach. The thing was traveling up-stream at the speed of a horse doing a light canter! Panyor. That was an inland port, a place where the wine barges broke their journey from the inland mountains. The barges took from dawn until dusk to make the trip, yet Feran's voice had implied the strange boat could make the round trip in perhaps six hours. That was over four times the speed of a barge, assuming they would not stop to rest in Panyor.

All the way back to the Academy Laron thought about what he had seen and heard. If Feran's boat was to leave the inland mountains at dusk and travel perhaps six times faster than a barge going downstream, he could have wine prices and vol-umes to Diomeda in half a day, yet a relay of horsemen could do almost as well, and a carrier auton could do it quicker still. What advantage could a very fast boat confer? Then it hit him like the light of a dazzle-casting. They could bring the small sample jars of new vintages to Diomeda smoothly, without bruising the contents. That was something a rider could never achieve. Vintages could be presold to the masters of the deep-water traders who could taste them directly, rather than them having to pay tasting fees to inland merchants.

Laron keyed into the guard auton at the Academy's door and let himself in, then went to the library to study. Sitting in the golden light of the oil lamps he estimated that it would be only one season before all the other merchants commissioned versions of Feran's boat and recruited strong rowers, but one season with a monopoly on wine prices would be enough to establish Feran as a man of importance in Diomeda. The boatbuilders and mercan-tile spies had probably come to precisely the same conclusion however, and Laron suspected that there were over a dozen iden-tical racing shells being built in other sheds on the riverside.

Another spy, with quite different masters and interests, con-tinued the wait at the riverside long after Laron had left, how-ever. He looked and smelled like a homeless drunk, but the reports he returned were extremely coherent.

✳ ✳ ✳

The docks of Panyor were silent as Feran's racing shell glided out of the desert night. Leaving Druskarl to guard the craft, Feran slowly stretched, straightened, then hobbled off into the silent streets of the river port. He had never visited the house he sought, and was relying on memorized directions in streets lit only by Miral's light. At last he found a door with lamplight seeping out below it. He knocked.

"Aye?" asked a voice.

"Torean gold," replied Feran.

Feran was admitted, and the saddlemaker led him to the workshop. In one corner was something like a suit of armor for a hunchback. Iron-shod clogs stood beside it.

"It looks somewhat big for you," said the artisan.

"That is because it is not for me," Feran replied as he un-buckled a strap. "Good—plenty of felt padding and a second layer of leather beneath. That improves ventilation, you know. A man can fight under the hottest sun for hours wearing a suit like this. Now, show me how it packs away."

"Suppose you show me your gold first?" said the artisan.

Feran counted out the fee, and added a bonus. Even packed away, the suit was a large bundle. Feran hefted it.

"What inn are you staying at?" the artisan asked as Feran prepared to leave.

"There are not many to choose from in a town of this size. Why do you ask?"

"I did not see you arrive on any of today's barges. The gate-keeper said that no horses or camels passed in, either."

"Perhaps I arrived yesterday, and spent a day resting."

This had not occurred to the artisan. "The militia's captain is interested in your fine new type of armor. He wants to know whether it is for Warsovran, or loyalists in Diomeda."

Feran considered. The town was, in theory, within Diomeda's domain, but almost certainly was loyal to the besieged king, even though it was trading with Warsovran.

"Well, if he wants to discuss it, I can be found at Hergon's establishment," Feran replied, naming an inn he had passed on the way there.

Minutes later Feran crept out of the shadows beside the docks with the huge bundle on his back. Back in the center of the port a fire was taking hold and a gong was booming out amid cries of alarm and screams. Druskarl already had the aft covers of the racing shell open.

"Pack it in, hurry," Feran hissed as he handed the three main sections down to Druskarl. "The artisan betrayed us to the militia. The militia's captain is loyal to the king of Diomeda, and I am a Torean. I thought all the possibilities through in advance."

"Very logical of you, but then why come here at all?"

"It is beyond the reach of Warsovran. There, all secure."

Feran pushed the racing shell away from the pier and scrambled into his seat as Druskarl began to row.

"We have to row like demons of—" began Druskarl.

"No! Row slowly until we pass the edge of the town wall."

"The militia will have guards on the way there by now."

"Good."

"Good? Guards with bows? Bows that shoot arrows? Arrows that really hurt? While we row *slowly*?"

"This boat is a strange shape, O eunuch of little faith. On one of its trial runs Dorimithy the shipwright said that it looked more like a small, short boat closer to the shore than a large, long boat far away. By the time the guards get the range right we shall be gone."

"They will send lancers."

"Lancers who think we travel slowly. Once we are clear of the walls we shall indeed row like men possessed."

Nine arrows did strike the racing shell as they passed the river edge of the town wall, but as Feran anticipated, most shots went wild. Once out of sight they rowed with all their strength, sending the racing shell hurtling down the Leir faster than any other craft in its history, yet there were none to witness the feat. From Miral's movement Druskarl estimated that it was nearly an hour before riders with flaming torches appeared in the distance.

"We are dead now, there must be thirty of them," panted the eunuch.

"Just row, I'll decide when we are dead," Feran replied with confidence.

A few more minutes passed, and the torches of the riders grew more distinct. Suddenly Feran slowed the pace of his rowing.

"Long, deep, silent strokes from now on," he said softly.

"But that will slow us even more."

"We have just passed the place where we stopped on the way upstream, O eunuch of little faith and maximal fears. Remember that sack I took ashore?"

"Yes."

"It contained some handfuls of splinters, a small ax, half a bag of oats, a pair of strap-on hoofs and one Torean gold coin. Now, do as I say and row softly."

As Feran had hoped, the militia cavalrymen assumed that the fugitives had chopped up and sunk their boat before riding off into the sand dunes. When the lights of the torches were almost invisible again, the rowers resumed their former pace. Miral rose ever higher in the sky, and Druskarl noted its progress.

"At this rate we should be back in Diomeda at least an hour before dawn," Druskarl commented as they passed a marker cairn on the shore.

"Splendid, then we shall be clear of the harbor and well down the coast by first light," replied Feran.

"What? Just what is going on here?" Druskarl asked.

"By tomorrow evening we should be exhausted, sunburned, and approaching the little harbor of Saltberry."

"Saltberry? That's a hundred miles down the coast, to the south!"

"Yes, and on the northern border of a state which is not currently at war with Warsovran. A dash galley will be waiting for us there, and we shall be hauled aboard after nightfall. It will put to sea that very hour. Long, long ago I learned to move faster than those in pursuit of me, and to do what they least expect."

Druskarl shook his head. "I never thought I would say this, but it is a relief to be going with you," he admitted.

The sky had just begun to lighten was when the racing shell swept back down the Leir through Diomeda, riddled with arrows, yet even faster than before, thanks to the current. By now

Laron had returned to the riverbank, and he saw it flash past the boatsheds without even slowing. He immediately got up and gave chase, but after an hour under a bridge his legs were stiff and cramped. By the time he reached the mouth of the river the racing shell was lost on the harbor's dark water.

Something seldom appreciated by nondancers is the amount of training and stamina required by even a competent amateur doing a folk dance. An intensive bout of axwork requires no less exertion, and the risk of injury shadows both elite dancers and beginners alike. As Sairet's apprentice, the auton girl had already discovered this, but she had the foundation of a strong, fit body and her progress was rapid. Wensomer was in constant need of novelty for her entertainments at court, and had hit on the idea of fire-breathing. There was nothing especially novel about it, except that the exponents were all well-muscled and oiled windrel men. Were a girl to breathe fire at court, the Toreans would really be startled.

Ninth's first lesson in fire-breathing was in the marble courtyard of Wensomer's villa. Sairet was there to supervise, but she sat at a safe distance. Wensomer watched, impassive, as a windrel man took a swig of clear, pungent liquid, then squirted it in a thin spray from between his tongue and teeth. He swung a torch through the stream, and suddenly a great tongue of flame shot from his mouth. Ninth cried out in surprise, even though she knew what was going to happen. The windrel spat another streamer of flame, this time at the feet of the novice. She jumped into the air and scampered back several paces.

"Not to be frightened of fire, if to be breathing it," the windrel said sternly.

Ninth walked over to the water gourd and took a mouthful, then squirted it out in a heavy stream.

"Am I doing it properly?" she then asked.

"Too much at once. Had that not been water, *poof!* Half the courtyard ablaze, yourself including."

The auton girl took another swig. This time the stream was thinner, and traveled farther. She tried again, and again. By the tenth mouthful she could manage a messy but consistently thin stream of water.

"Better, better," commented the windrel.

Ninth held her hand out for the gourd that the windrel carried. This was moving faster than the man was willing to accept. He looked to Wensomer, who shrugged then nodded.

"Take the torch away first," Sairet called. "Let her practice by just squirting spirits. You will decide when it is safe to start igniting them."

The windrel bowed, and handed the gourd to Ninth. She took a swig—and immediately spat out the mouthful and dropped the gourd. She staggered about, spitting, spluttering, and rubbing her eyes. The windrel scooped up the gourd, grinning but not laughing aloud. Sairet put a hand to her mouth. Ninth washed her mouth out with water, then turned to face the windrel again. She held out her hand for the gourd.

By taking smaller swigs Ninth accustomed herself to the foul taste of the spirits, and began practicing at squirting the fluid between her teeth. After another quarter hour she had become fairly proficient at it, although her face had gone pale from the taste and fumes.

"Don't let the fluid trail away, or the flaming spirits will dribble down onto your clothing," the windrel called anxiously, aware that his strangely fearless pupil was determined to spit real fire, and to do it soon. "End the stream sharply. Purse your lips, like so! Make sure that not a single drop falls on you."

The torch was brought. Ninth held the gourd in one hand and the torch in the other. She took a small swig of spirits as the windrel led her to an area where there was no spilled fluid.

"Hold flame of the torch up, so. Spit as before, but through flame. Remember, blow sharply, close your lips fast when to stop."

Ninth sprayed the spirits from her mouth, and a long streamer blazed out beyond the torch. Suddenly she was out of breath, but not liquid. She pressed her lips shut for a moment, then lost her control and swallowed some of what was left in her mouth. She coughed out the remainder, and a large gout of orange flame erupted before her. The windrel jumped back even though he was well out of the way. Ninth stood panting, then tossed the torch to the windrel man, handle-first, and stood with her arms folded. Wensomer and Sairet applauded.

"That last fireball was very impressive," Sairet commented.

"A wonderful finale," agreed Wensomer.

The astonished windrel handed Ninth the gourd of water and she washed her mouth out. Unbidden, she picked up the gourd of spirits again.

The steward appeared, bowed to Wensomer, and whispered something to her. She excused herself from the lesson and went quickly to her parlor. Waiting for her was Laron.

"Hail the morning, former Prince of Vampyres," she said, giving him a bow and courtly flourish.

Laron smiled, revealing two long, pointed fangs. Wensomer gasped and skipped back. Laron reached up and removed the fangs, revealing two normal teeth beneath.

"I carved them from sea-dragon tusks," he explained. "They will discourage those in search of revenge for my past feedings."

"I have no doubt of it."

"Look what else I have." He took a locket from within his tunic, where it hung by a chain around his neck. He opened it to reveal a chunk of greenish glass held in silver claws.

"Glass, from the very place in Larmentel where Silverdeath detonated," Laron explained. "We collected other pieces, but Feran stole them when he left the *Shadowmoon*—along with an ocular showing a fire-circle."

"Damn, what a pity it was lost."

"On the other had, an ocular is attached to this piece of Larmentel glass as well. It shows the late king of Gironal indulging in amorous frolics with sundry wenches."

"Indeed?" exclaimed Wensomer, pressing her fingertips together. "I have heard of him. An overweight king with a taste for comfortably built courtesans, or so reports have it."

"Indeed. I have viewed it—but purely for historical research."

"Of course. What was it like?"

"Astonishing."

"I hate you."

"But you are no longer, ah, weighty."

"When I am finished with what I am doing in Diomeda, I have every intention of taking great pleasure in putting my lost sixty-one pounds straight back on. Having done that, I will be taking renewed interest in sex for sensibly upholstered people. What, er, price are you asking for that ocular?"

"I had intended it as a present for you."

"Really, Laron, how sweet of you," said Wensomer. "But why?"

"I, ah . . . violated the spirit of chivalry."

"What? How?"

"I consumed a lamb and kidney pie, when I should have been supporting you as a soulmate."

Wensomer opened her mouth, drew a breath while composing a look of astonished outrage on her face—then slowly exhaled.

The fire in her eyes has died down, Laron thought as he glanced up.

"I . . . may have stolen a cold pork cutlet in the market, smuggled it home in my cleavage, and consumed it," she admitted sheepishly. "Sorry."

"But—but you need not have told me," the relieved Laron babbled at once.

"You told me about the pie."

"I am male, I have chivalric obligations."

Wensomer batted her hand across his face several times. "Women have chivalric obligations, too," she said. "Thank you for telling me."

They circled the parlor, both with their arms folded behind their backs, and in silence.

"I suppose I don't really deserve that ocular now, do I?" sighed Wensomer.

"Don't be silly," muttered Laron.

"Was it interesting?"

"Well . . . more so than the fire-circles. You can have the Larmentel glass in . . . oh, a month. I need to finish some work on it. It has some etheric energy which is gradually fading for no apparent reason. I am going to probe it and write a thesis for the Academy, then it is yours."

"Laron! Thank you!" exclaimed Wensomer, skipping in front of him and throwing her arms around his neck. "When I have studied it, and have been eating properly for at least a month, I must invite you to join me for some experimental verification.

Fifteen years! You were my tourney champion before I had even met my first lover."

"You have had nine lovers since then. One of them was a king."

"What— Oh, him. I was a bit drunk."

There was another extended silence between them.

"Laron, were you jealous when I slept with those men?"

"I was dead; jealousy was out of the question. Why do you ask?"

"Well, you killed eight of my former lovers and ripped off their heads."

"They were not nice to you."

"Why did you spare Roval?"

"When he awoke, he made it plain that his intentions were honorable."

"What? Garbage! When he awoke he said, 'Gods of the moonworlds, what have I done?' Then he swore never to drink fermented potato-mash spirits again. The bastard. Now, getting back to us . . ."

"My exams require virginity."

"Pox take virginity."

"Well, in five minutes I might be dead," laughed Laron.

"Oh, again?"

"And so may you."

"Oh. Do vampyres do that sort of thing?"

"The females might. The males cannot get it up."

"Really?"

"I should know."

"But what about now?"

"None of your business— Wait a minute! Why did I come here?"

"Tell me."

"I mean, I remembered why I came here. Feran and Druskarl left for Panyor in a two-seat gigboat last night."

"Horrid place, right in the middle of the desert. I had to spend a night there last year."

"They returned before dawn."

"So they did not reach Panyor?"

"I saw their boat in action," said Laron urgently, greatly relieved that sex had vanished from the conversation. "It is very, very fast. Even the fastest dash galley would be hard put to overhaul it over a short distance, and it is far more agile."

"I'm impressed. What else?"

"Their boat was decorated with a lot of arrows that were not there the night before. They rowed straight out into the harbor."

"To where?"

"I did not see. It could have been to Dawnlight, to Warsovran's fleet, to some foreign trader, to some pier on the beachfront, north along the coast, south along the coast, or east to Helion."

"That does not really narrow the options, does it?"

"It excludes inland."

"Along with straight up. Still, I think that their scheme is now under way, whatever it is, and we shall not see them again until after Helion's next fire-circle."

Velander had watched and listened to the entire conversation from the etherworld. Part of her wanted to release the orange thread of light, drift away into the darkness, and fade into nothingness. Laron—how could he? Laron the chivalrous, embracing that—older woman! She had proposed a dalliance, a liaison founded upon pure lust. And he had refused her. Well, he had evaded the issue, at least. Very chivalrous. Yes, of course. Just like Laron. Remorse tugged at Velander's spirit. He would face death for a woman, but Velander had also seen him stop her from making a stupid mistake, then try to make sure that her feelings were not hurt.

Stupid mistake? Surely he deserves something after seven centuries. Is this really me thinking this? What is sex like? she wondered. She had seen her body doing it with Feran. It had seemed . . . embarrassing, unplanned, unplannable, messy, dirty, and not at all enticing. On the other hand, that was what she had actually seen. What about between Laron and Wensomer? Would that be any better? By now they probably knew each other too well to be anything more than friends, even though Laron was again alive. That had to be it.

Velander was not capable of feeling lust, but sadness was

sufficiently intellectual to register with her, being a disembodied spirit. *Very foolish, Laron, it might have been fun,* she decided on his behalf, then watched through the ocular as Laron returned to the Academy through the crowded streets of Diomeda.

The Sargolan dash galley was under sail with its oars shipped as Druskarl paced the deck in the suit of leather and felt armor. He was now six inches taller and covered with the thick, white, insulated butt-leather. A plate of polished quartz crystal was his eyepiece, and every breath he took was passed through a water cooler similar to those used by many patrons of Diomedan taverns.

"Three hours now," said Feran as Druskarl continued to pace. "How does it feel in there?"

"How? Smelly and very damp, but nothing beyond bearing," came the muffled reply. "How much longer will your tests last?"

"You have already lasted well over the time required. Just two more tests today."

Feran nailed a leather jacket to the deck. Druskarl approached it and seized it in one clawed glove while chopping clumsily at the nails with a hatchet. After a minute the jacket came free. The sailors removed the helmet from the eunuch; Feran poured water over his head.

"Many ships from many kingdoms will be gathering to watch the second fire-circle," said the shipmaster, looking at a slate. "We should not stand out among them."

"And Miral will be down for the second half of the night," said Feran. "We shall row to Helion in the shell, then invert and sink it just before dawn. When the fire-circle detonates, Druskarl will go ashore. He will make for the site of the Metrologan temple. There he shall find Silverdeath, or there he shall wait until Silverdeath floats down from the sky."

"And if I die?" asked Druskarl.

"Then I shall try again, myself, with an improved suit," said Feran. "One thing we can be sure of: While Silverdeath exists, it shall be used, again and again."

The inland city of Baalder existed for its location, and as locations went, they did not come much better. It was where the border of the Sargolan empire and the Alear Principalities met the largely uncontrolled nomad regions, but it was also where the desert abruptly gave way to the natural defensive wall known as the Portcullis Mountains. The Sargolans had little interest in defending the city, and nobody had a reason to attack it. Trade was the only reason that Baalder was on the maps.

Although slavery was outlawed in Sargol, a certain amount of that trade went on in Baalder. People in the border regions were always inclined to sell surplus children for the quite competitive prices that the slavers from the north paid, and D'Alik was a specialist in what he called "domestic merchandise." On this particular trip, however, there was no merchandise of that sort on offer. Baalder had been transformed as he had never seen it before. An army was streaming through.

"Been passing through for a week now," said his agent as he lounged beneath an awning. "Great for the suppliers of dried foods and such-like, but the slave market's not worth a fly spot. They're actually enforcing the laws that prohibit it."

"But—but . . . why, where are they going?" asked D'Alik, gesturing to a column of heavily laden footsoldiers who were tramping past. "There's just five hundred miles of rough pasture mixed with real desert until you reach the Leir River."

"And that's where they are bound. Word has come back that the river port of Panyor has fallen to the Sargolan vanguard, and that they are seizing every barge and boat from the Lioren Mountains. Diomeda is being blockaded, and soon it's to be attacked. When the emperor's forces join with the Alliance army, the Torean invaders will face the largest army Acrema has ever seen."

"I did not think the emperor thought so very highly of the Diomedan monarch that he would come to his aid."

"True, but the Toreans are said to be holding Princess Senterri, the emperor's daughter. Mind you, the Toreans swear that windrel nomads abducted her after she left Diomeda by road. . . ."

The agent's voice seemed to fade into the distance. Senterri. Sargolan princess. Abducted by nomads. The words amounted to an opportunity so vast in scope that D'Alik felt giddy just trying to fit it into his mind.

". . . Of course the girl is certainly dead. The Alearan princes are letting the army pass unchallenged because they are weak—"

"Enough!" barked D'Alik. "I want an audience with the Sargolan governor. Now."

"The governor!" exclaimed the agent, standing up and brushing at his robes. "Ah, yes, I can try, but—"

"Tell him I have information about Princess Senterri. Tell him that I bought her from windrel nomads. I also have her two handmaids. Their names are Perime and Dolvienne."

Senterri's name was widely known, but those of her handmaids were not. Because he had known those two names, D'Alik had his audience with the governor within the hour. He said that he had recognized the princess instantly, and had bought all three girls for five hundred gold pagols and placed them in Madame Voldean's academy for their own safety.

Governor Roilean was less excited than D'Alik had expected. There had been many sightings of Senterri, but all had turned out to be hoaxes or wishful thinking. On the other hand, the slaver had known that Senterri had two handmaids. That was significant. He even knew their names, which the governor did not.

"I am inclined to have you bring the girls here at your own expense," Roilean said as the slaver knelt before his audience throne.

"O esteemed and generous Excellency, but slavery is illegal here, on your most beautiful, rich, and fertile Sargolan soil. Whatever the truth behind the story of these girls, they will walk free, be they princess and handmaids, or be they three scullions named Senterri, Perime, and Dolvienne."

"Are you a gambling man?" asked the governor, who did not wish to dignify the slaver by speaking his name.

"Esteemed and just Excellency, all commerce is a game of chance and odds."

"And you are a man of commerce, so the answer must be yes. Take a gamble, it can be quite exhilarating. The palpitations of uncertainty, the sharp, cool pain of loss, the soaring, glorious triumph of winning. Bring the girls here. If they are as you say, you are a richer man by one hundred thousand gold pagols. If they are but clever scullions, you lose a trifling amount and they walk free. What do you say?"

D'Alik drew a breath that seemed to go on for longer than should have been anatomically possible while he made up his mind.

"Esteemed and perceptive Excellency, you are a most canny judge of character. I shall indeed play your game of chance and bring the girls here, with all haste possible and no expense spared."

✳ ✳ ✳

Ninth advanced on Laron with a knife, slashed the air before his face, then thrust for his throat. Laron moved one foot in a quarter circle while batting her arm aside with the back of his hand. Seizing her wrist, he twisted. She shrieked from surprise rather than pain, and dropped the knife.

Roval called for a break. In most martial-arts academies of the region, the favored topics of conversation during rests were muscular injuries, women, and Academy politics. With Ninth present, the second was out of the question, and the third did not apply, so they generally discussed aches, sprains, massage technique, oils, anatomy, and shared stretching exercises, and advice that medicars had given them over the years on all of the foregoing topics. Today, however, the mood was somber and there was little idle talk. Roval was leaving.

"In a single month, you have come a long way," said Roval, "but even the basics of these arts take one at least six months to achieve competence."

"Will you be away long?" asked Laron.

"Perhaps weeks, probably forever."

"But as you said, I have barely begun to learn your defensive fighting skills."

"I have given you the name of a good instructor."

"He lives in Scalticar!"

"Then go there."

"I have studies to do here, in Diomeda."

"Then find a Diomedan teacher, I'm sure that will not be hard. Laron, you now know enough to drop someone of even twice your weight. That should be enough to help you escape trouble."

"Have you forgotten how little I weigh?"

Further argument did not weaken Roval's resolve. His travel pack was ready in a corner.

"We finish with the armlock," said Roval at last. "Ninth, you are a two-hundred-pound drunken docker who has caught Laron in an armlock and intends to remove his purse."

Ninth walked forward with quite a convincing swagger, seized Laron's wrist, twisted it behind his back, and pushed a foot into the back of his knee. Laron snaked his free arm behind his back, slipped it under Ninth's wrist, twisted until the pain forced her to release him, then twisted her arm in turn until she doubled over and he could bring his other hand down in a fist. He stopped short of striking her.

"At this point the large and drunken docker has had his elbow snapped and is feeling very discouraged," said Laron.

"I *am* feeling very discouraged!" reported Ninth, who was in pain.

"Oh, I am sorry," said Laron as he eased off the pressure on her arm.

"At this point you should also be fleeing down the cobbles as fast as your legs can carry you," chided Roval.

"But he's down and disabled."

"He's down, but he might have friends nearby. Some people also feel pain less acutely than others, and he still has one good arm."

Laron let Ninth up. Roval bowed to him and declared the lesson over. As Ninth began to wind down the ladder he slung his pack over one shoulder.

"Can't you tell me anything about where you are going?" asked Laron. "If you don't trust me, who do you trust?"

"I trust those who need to know. You do not need to know. Do *not* try to follow me."

Roval's departure was as cold and unemotional as his bearing. He merely bowed to Ninth and Laron in turn, wished them good fortune, and climbed down the ladder. Laron counted to twenty, then hurried down the ladder as well. He immediately found himself bracketed by three men. They had a vaguely familiar style of clothing.

"I wouldn't try following the Learned Roval, young sir," one of them said casually.

"And I wouldn't try using his unarmed fighting arts on us," said the second.

"Because I'm his teacher, and these are my sons," said the third, who looked to be about fifty. "Why don't you just come to the Beer and Barnacle with us for an hour or two?"

Zurlan exiles! Now Laron remembered where he had last seen such clothing.

Precisely two hours later Laron emerged from the tavern, having been signed up as Magister Jialam's new javat pupil. What Magister Jialam did not realize, however, was that Laron had deliberately lost the battle to win the war. Laron walked straight for the docks area, but did not bother to go near the piers. Instead he went to a small, stone building whose door bore the sign, MISSIONARY CENTER FOR HARLOTS, beneath which someone had scrawled, *Bollocks, they both be men.* Laron knocked, and was admitted by a man wearing the brown robes of a Sargolan missionary priest. When Warsovran had arrived, the Metrologan deacons had hurriedly converted their facade and clothing, but Laron had ways of finding out about nearly anything or anyone.

"Laron, welcome," the deacon declared warmly.

"Horvey, such a pleasure to enter this sanctuary," Laron replied as he entered. "How do your studies progress?"

"Well enough. And yours?"

"Slowly but surely."

By now the door had been closed behind him.

"Worthy Laron, your presence honors this house," Horvey said softly, with a bow.

"Aspiring Deacon Horvey, it is this house that does *me* honor," Laron now replied.

Laron had met the deacons at the Academy, where they were fellow students. Having quickly worked out who they were, he had recruited them to his service. By assuming the guise of the only surviving Metrologan priest, Laron had gained their loyalty faster than might otherwise might have be the case. Having the ring that Terikel had given him had certainly helped in that respect. To account for his extreme youth, Laron had said that he had been ordained in haste, with some of his optional studies incomplete. This also accounted for his presence at the Academy as a student.

"As I suspected, Deacon Horvey, Learned Roval had me detained," said Laron.

"No matter, he was kept in sight by some of our clients. Pellien? Pellien!"

A woman appeared at the end of the corridor, wearing robes that featured a décolletage that reached down to the wide belt at her waist, and a skirt split from hemline to upper hip. Her breasts were unusually large and almost oblong.

"So nostalgic, wearing the old rig once more," she said in a husky, simpering voice.

Laron swallowed. The muscles behind both his knees began to twitch involuntarily. *What did I do when I was vampyre?* he asked himself. *When I was a vampyre my knees certainly did not go to jelly at the sight of so much female flesh,* he recalled.

"Well, I'd best let Pellien brief you alone," said Deacon Horvey, slapping Laron on the shoulder. "The less I know, the less that can be tortured out of me, what?"

Laron followed Pellien into the waiting room, on legs that had suddenly taken on the properties of warm baker's dough.

"And, Pellien, you behave!" called Deacon Horvey from the door. "Worthy Laron is meant to be observing celibacy."

"Oh, and whose celibacy is he observing?" she asked.

Laron sat down on the end of a bench, his hands clasped in his lap. Pellien sat down, too, draping her arm along the back rest of the bench—and put a leg across Laron's thighs.

"Now that we are more comfortable, I have quite a brief report for you," Pellien began, her fingers ruffling Laron's hair.

"The most handsome and impressive Learned Roval took a circuitous route from Mad Queen Sairet's establishment to the docks."

"Er, queen?"

"Former, of Diomeda."

"And mad? As, like, a couple of arrows short in the quiver?"

"Yes, but not dangerously so. Returning to Roval, he boarded a ferry scoreboat and was followed by Deacon Lisgar. The brave deacon already had with him a traveler's pack and was dressed as a pilgrim, so as not to call attention to himself. The scoreboat made the rounds of several traders, and Roval boarded a Sargolan coastal trader that was being readied for departure. Deacon Lisgar did, too. A galley boat towed the trader clear of the harbor, where it turned south. The deacon sent a brief note back to me with the master of the galleyboat. It said that although the trader was slated for the small port of Saltberry on the Lodgements Board, he had overheard Roval arranging with the shipmaster to call at a small bay on the desert coast."

"Do you, ah, have the note?" asked Laron, jerkily holding out one hand.

"Why, certainly."

Pellien took his hand and guided it under the silk covering her left breast. With one of his fingers Laron could feel her left heart beating. With the other he could feel a rather hard nipple. After several lingering moments he also realized that he could feel a piece of paper, and he clumsily withdrew Lisgar's note. *Sickle Bay,* he read. Roval had asked the shipmaster to call in at Sickle Bay. He slipped the note into his pouch.

Interesting. Laron hastily glanced about, wondering who was mocking him. There was nobody else in the room. He blinked and shook his head. A look of surprise was passing over Pellien's face.

"This, ah, is good—ah, excellent—ah, wonderful—ah, work. Tracking Roval, that is. I, ah, must reward you—er, well. Very well, that is."

"Oh no, I no longer accept money from men. I am studying dancing under the tuition of Mad Queen Sairet. She thinks that I may get into a position in the palace."

Laron was sure that she could probably get into a great number of positions in the palace, and one of them might even involve dancing.

Interesting. The word whispered itself so softly that Laron had more of an impression of remembering it being said, rather than having heard it. Pellien suddenly froze for a moment, then blinked.

"I, ah, need to go, ah, er, that is. Soon, that is. I have to go."

Pellien took her leg from his lap. Laron stood up. Pellien did not let his hand go; in fact, she drew him closer.

"Laron, you are so, so young for the study of boring, initiate books," she said, looking at the ring that he wore.

"I, ah, am older than I look."

"You must eat the right sorts of food."

"Ah, oddly enough, yes. Until recently, that is."

Deacon Horvey opened the door and peered in.

"So, was your transaction concluded successfully?" he asked, looking suspiciously at Pellien.

"One might say so, yes," Laron replied weakly.

"And is Laron in much the same state as when he entered?" he asked Pellien pointedly.

"His virginity is alive and well, if that's what you mean," she said, releasing Laron's hand and standing up. "Well, then, Worthy Laron, I am honored to have worked for you."

Pellien pulled at a couple of straps within her robes, and at once the two alarmingly revealing slashes in the fabric vanished. She picked up a suncloak that Laron had been too distracted to notice until now, and in an instant her red robes were hidden beneath a mud-brick–colored layer of cotton.

"Thank, you, ah, that is," stammered Laron, bowing to Pellien.

Pellien bowed slightly in turn, smiled, winked, then left without another word.

"Remarkable woman," said the deacon when she had gone. "She is proving to be a very talented dancer, according to Madame Sairet. Ah, but in ways of the flesh, well . . ."

"Yes?"

"She disliked harlotry, that was why she came to us, but she does enjoy seduction as such. Sometimes I get discouraged; I think that she just can't help herself."

Sometimes she probably does just that, Laron concluded to himself.

"Please remember us to the Elder when next you see her," the deacon was saying, "and if you could ask about the possibility of our ordination we should be extremely grateful. When Deacon Lisgar returns, I shall send word to our mutual contact."

"Ah, thank you. I appreciate the deacon's bravery. It really is for a good cause."

"Hah, I'm not such a provincial yokel as you think. I know that the Metrologans were fighting Silverdeath before Torea burned, and I suspect that us few survivors still are. Good fortune attend you, Worthy Laron. We are your loyal and dedicated servants."

Laron was noticing very little as he started out for the Academy, but once out of sight of the mission he noticed that a woman of about Pellien's height and wearing the same sort of dusky suncloak was walking just ahead of him. He slowed slightly as he made to pass her. She quickened her pace slightly. It could not possibly be Pellien, she did not know which way he was going—but she *might* assume that he would go straight back to the Academy. Out of the corner of his eye he glanced at her face. *Pellien!* They walked together for a while, without exchanging a word. Pellien began to slow. When she finally stopped at a street corner, so did he.

"The, ah, my place is away up that hill," he said, although looking down at his sandals.

"Ah, and this is my street," she responded. "I have a room just down there."

"My, ah, er, the Academy . . . is that way," was all that Laron could reply.

"Maybe so, but my street curves around and also leads to the Academy."

She turned away and began to walk slowly toward her rooming house. Laron looked at her receding back, tried to make a decision, discovered that his mind had been wiped clean, then hurried after her and fell in beside her again. They did not even stop to discuss whether or not he was going to climb the steps when they reached her place. Laron noted that it was not in a red-lantern area, and appeared to be inhabited by artisans and travelers.

Pellien shut the door to her room behind him and barred it. Laron stood anxiously rubbing his hands together, wondering what came next, but certain that when she unbarred the door to let him out in an hour's time he would no longer have the slightest chance of passing his Academy tests. Pellien batted her eyelashes at him as she unclasped her suncloak, then she fiddled with the straps of her robes again. Once more her neckline plunged to the wide, kid-leather belt she wore at her waist. Slits appeared at both of her hips this time. Laron swallowed.

Quite casually she reached out to a shelf of books made from mud-bricks and old decking planks, then selected *Definitions and Precedents in Comparative Anatomy*. The title caught Laron by surprise, almost distracting him from what was visible of her body—which was quite a lot.

"So, you are required to preserve your virginity until tested," she said as she flicked through the pages, her right hip turned jauntily toward Laron. She was swaying as if to the beat of an unheard tune, exposing a tantalizing line of flawless, smooth leg at each sway.

"Er, that is, yes."

"Is the status heavily monitored?"

"Er, well, not really, but . . ."

" 'But'?"

"There are tests for level-nine initiate status from Yvendel's academy that really do require one to be innocent of the pleasures of the flesh—in order to pass an ordeal, that is."

"Ah yes, to become a non-commissioned sorcerer."

"Yes, but I, ah, rather suspect that I am in the process of failing that particular ordeal, ah, right at this moment," Laron stammered. "With your permission, that is. I mean, I would not like to impose . . ."

"Well . . ." Pellien seemed to find the page she was looking for. "Before my merchant father was lost at sea and my stepfather sold me as a harlot, I was studying for a life in the etheric arts."

"Hence all these books?" asked Laron, wondering if they had

been on display when she was still entertaining paying clients. "I mean, were they your father's?"

"Well, no. I have managed to buy, steal, and scavenge a few books in the years since, but they all relate to the healing arts. If I cannot be a sorceress, I can at least become a courtesan, then find a patron, enter the Academy of Medicars, and graduate as a healer. Dancing may make me a courtesan, Laron. See? All very simple—ah-ha, here we are. 'Virginity . . . definition difficult to specify precisely . . . exchange of etheric energy . . . unions must be theoretically capable of producing offspring. Hence . . . man with female sheep, invalid . . . woman with—' My goodness! Invalid, at any rate. 'Either sex with any Dacostian . . . long a source of controversy, but resolved by Peppard the Ungainly in a paper presented to the Eighty-seventh Council of Sorric. Four experiments involving virgin slaves from Torea and Dacostia resulted in six out of the eight being able to subsequently pass certain etheric ordeals whose prerequisite is virginity—' "

Pellien snapped the book shut, then replaced it on the shelf.

"You must, of course, be familiar with the Eighty-seventh Council of Sorric, Laron. It is on the Metrologan syllabus, Deacon Lisgar once told me."

Laron had fed upon several people in Sorric a few centuries earlier, but his memories of the place were vague, and he had never attended a Council meeting.

"Yes, all of that is true," he bluffed.

Laron watched, mesmerized as Pellien hooked her thumbs into the fabric below her belt and pushed back. It retreated until all that he could see in the mirror behind her was a long tassel of red silk running down the cleft of her bottom. Now her thumbs moved forward, until a single, narrow strip of red hanging almost to the floor was all that was left between her thighs to cover her doomed modesty. Laron's hearts seemed to be not far from battering their way out of his rib cage and fleeing for some less intense sanctuary. Finally she reached to her waist and plunged both thumbs into her belt above her navel. She drew them apart, taking the red silk with them. Her breasts strained against the fabric, then popped out. Something was wrong . . . they were too low, and—another two breasts appeared!

Pellien stood smiling at Laron with her thumbs still in her

belt and her four quite shapely breasts proudly thrust out. *A Dacostian, from the double continent in the west,* thought Laron. *Four breasts.* The males had four testicles; he once had read that somewhere. By now she had advanced upon him, and was unlacing his tunic at the neck. She pulled it over his shoulders, and it fell to the floor. Summoning all his courage, Laron experimentally ran a finger from her throat down between her breasts, and onward to her belt buckle. He tugged at it, and it snapped open. The belt fell away, and her robe fell open. She began unlacing his trousers, then reached between his legs as they were exposed.

"Ah, only two. That puts my conscience at ease. According to Peppard the Ungainly you can no more lose your virginity to me than to a sheep."

This came as a great relief to Laron, who was by now in some degree of pain from his interest in verifying the results of Peppard the Ungainly's experiments. Pellien slipped her by-now redundant robe off and it fell to the floor. She slid her arms around Laron and he wrapped his arms around her back.

"Er, sorry," he whispered.

"About what?" she purred back.

"Being scrawny, like I'm fourteen while I'm really seven h— Ah, seventeen."

"Worthy Laron, you have not yet learned to let women be the judge of what they like."

She led him over to the bed and pulled him down with her. The entire world suddenly became focused between their respective pairs of legs.

"Gently, no hurry, all the time in the world," Pellien whispered as all manner of bodily and etheric stimuli cascaded through Laron. Blue sparks and streamers of ether crackled and danced between their loins, enhancing their sensations all the more.

*   *   *

Velander watched through the ocular, but there were various energies present from the encounter between Pellien and Laron, even in the etherworld. In spite of her ineffectual, tiny reserve of energy, she had been able to modulate some of the energy to enunciate the word *interesting* twice, when the two lovers had first met.

Now she watched with interest, and approval. *This encounter is quite beautiful,* she decided, then tried to work out why she had come to that decision. There was something between them—that was a possibility. What would Laron do for a lover that Feran would not? Now Velander decided that *Laron* was her soulmate, not mathematics. *His* seduction was *her* seduction. Through him, she had experienced sex as it should be. She would probably soon fade to nothing and become truly dead, but should she ever return to life, she swore to herself and to Fortune that she would be the most special person in Laron's life, and that she would exist for no other than him.

Two hours later Laron made a quick excursion to the Bargeman's Pole for two nutmince pies, a bag of oysters, and two jars of Arkendian claret, but it was an hour after dawn before he began to contemplate leaving for the Academy. He was pinned below Pellien, and had to wake her before he could move.

"Best be leaving," he said.

"Why?" she murmured.

"Must make the breakfast at my lodgings."

"You had fifteen oysters last night."

"Five of them didn't work."

"Poetry is written about my breakfasts."

"I'll have to make do with reading it, then. A roll is marked at Academy breakfasts. Priest I may be, but mere student I am, as well."

"Ah."

A Sargolan prayer gong was sounding as Laron finally kissed Pellien beside her now-unbarred door. Breakfast at the Academy always started just after the neighbors' gong was beaten.

"You know where I live," she whispered in his ear.

"But you may have company if I call unannounced. Company that may beat me up."

"There are no other lovers; I like to stay independent. A boy like you could never have thoughts of possessing me, of forcing me to wash your clothes or give up dance and study. Think of this as a convenient student romance."

As he set off for the Academy Laron realized that he had not had a single thought of guilt involving the auton Ninth from the first moment he had set eyes on Pellien. He had not had any thoughts for Ninth at all, if it came to that. *Well, at least my feelings for her are genuinely founded in pure chivalry,* he thought, *and not burned by passions of the flesh.*

"Good old Peppard the Ungainly," he said aloud, walking as lightly as if he were made of gossamer. "Must burn a coil of incense to your memory one day."

While Laron and Pellien had been energetically locked together, several hours past midnight, the Sargolan coastal trader had anchored in Sickle Bay on the desert coast. No ship was there to meet it; neither were there any tents or riders on the shore. Roval was set ashore and the trader sailed back out to sea. Roval sat on the sand watching Miral rise and ascend into the night sky, which was streaked with unseasonal clouds.

"How long to get the *Shadowmoon* back on the surface?" Roval asked the darkness without moving at all.

"With a crew of six, we should be sailing by midnight," a voice replied from somewhere behind him.

"Six. Three, plus me—that's two *new* men," said Roval. "Can they be trusted?"

"I may not be a man, but I'm an experienced sailor and very trustworthy," said Terikel. "As for the sixth, he's no sailor but he may be trustworthy."

By now Roval had stood and turned. By Miral's light he could see five figures. One of them was kneeling in the sand, and two had axes raised above him.

"Noticed him slip over the side of the trader when you came ashore," said Norrieav.

"Claims to be a Metrologan," said Hazlok.

Roval walked up and put his hands on his knees, scrutinizing the youth's face by Miral's green light. He did not recognize him.

"Learned master, I meant no harm," quavered the intruder.

"People who mean me no harm generally don't go to so much trouble to follow me, in my experience. Who are you, who is your master?"

"I am Aspiring Lisgar, deacon in the Metrologan mission to Diomeda. I am studying a special syllabus in the academy of Madame Yvendel in preparation for ordination. A priest asked me to follow you, but not to—"

"Lies! There are no Metrologan priests left!" exclaimed Hazlok.

"I saw his ring."

"Rings can be stolen."

"Please, not so hasty," cautioned Terikel. "I do have a deacon named Lisgar in Diomeda."

Lisgar gasped. "Elder?"

"What was this priest like, and what was his name?" asked Roval.

"Worthy Laron, and he was very fresh and young looking—"

"—in a scrawny sort of way," the exasperated Terikel finished for him. "Congratulations, Aspiring Lisgar, you have just left the service of the not-quite-Worthy Laron and joined the crew of the *Shadowmoon*."

"I noticed him being seasick all the way from Diomeda," Roval warned. "Still, we have more important things to worry about, like practicing the etherwing casting. Those cliffs yonder should be high enough, and do you have the mailshirt and stilts that I asked for?"

"All farther back on the beach," said Terikel.

"And Miral is being clouded over. Good, let's start while we have the right intensity of darkness."

❄ ❄ ❄

Governor Roilean's appointment originally had been seen as the poorest of Sargolan postings. It was a desert outpost that was more of a customs collection point and market town than a regional capital, and its population was made up more of foreigners than Sargolan citizens. With the impending war, all that had changed. Tens of thousands of troops were pouring through each week, and the local economy was booming as never could have been imagined. With the troops came nobles, commanders, and even the occasional prince and king. Roilean was getting introductions to the powerful and influential, and setting up associations that might help him into some more important and congenial posting.

On this particular night, Prince Stavez, the eldest of the emperor's sons, was spending a night in Baalder. He was staying in the governor's mansion, and Roilean had staged the most lavish feast the resources at his command could manage. On the other hand, the prince was a clean-living military campaigner, and not particularly hard to please. A dozen former slave dancers entertained the official guests, while a wholesome and healthy meal was presented to the prince and his five generals. The governor was torn between playing the part of a master of ceremonies and being waited upon in dignified splendor, and compromised by making hand signals to his staff behind his back.

"Everything has been working so smoothly," the prince declared approvingly. "Your servants act with military precision."

"Well, yes, I find that my own military background has so many practical applications in administration, that I have just continued to, well, run the province like a battalion."

"Ah, eminently sensible," agreed the prince.

"And the mansion. My servants are drilled and exercised in the courtyard each morning."

"Really? I would be interested to watch. My feeling is that the entire empire should be organized on military lines."

"Really?"

"Yes. Your household could well be the model for a Sargolan household military unit. Perhaps you could have your household scribe draw up the organization of your mansion's staff structure; I would be pleased to study it while on the campaign against the Toreans in Diomeda."

The governor's heart sank as he signaled for the next course to be brought out. He would either have to break whatever the existing record might be for raising a civilian militia, or he would have to manufacture a very plausible excuse for the household to be in total disorganization by dawn. Governor Roilean made a hurried hand signal for, *Call me away.* A servant dutifully came across and whispered, *"Excellency, I am whispering in your ear."*

"My apologies, Your Highness," the governor said softly. "A matter of extreme importance must be attended to."

The entire party turned and gave the governor stares that might have been glares of disapproval for leaving the side of a prince without being given leave, or could have been a coded exchange of facial configurations that only the most senior and powerful of nobles used among themselves. He scowled back, then suddenly remembered that one never, *never* takes one's own leave of royalty while at court, and this was indeed considered to be a provincial court. Roilean stood as awkwardly as a puppet whose strings were being fought over by people from three different schools of puppetry, then hurried away. What had he done? How could he have done such a stupid thing? One never dismissed oneself from the company of a prince. One dropped hints until they asked if one would like to leave, that was it! He went to his private audience chamber and padded around in a circle for several minutes. He had exited the company of a prince. He had broken protocol. He probably would be made the first ambassador to the melted continent of Torea as a result of this. It was so hard to remember protocols for the imperial court when one was stuck away with the camel drivers, spice merchants, dung carters, money changers, wholesale wine merchants, wholesale slave merchants pretending to be wholesale seed merchants—*slave merchants!*

Even as the two words blazed out in his mind, Governor Roilean had already broken out of his circle and was hurrying for the door. By the time he had returned to the crown prince of the Sargolan empire, he had his story, excuse, and disaster contingency plan all worked out.

"Your pardon, Your Highness—my most abject apologies for taking leave of your company on my own account, like some mere yokel, but a matter of the gravest importance has arisen."

Something akin to a glimmering fire flickered into life within the eyes of the crown prince.

"If it is of such great importance, then I should know of it as well," he replied. "Do we require, ah, discretion?"

The governor most certainly did not want discretion; he wanted everyone to know why he had made such a colossal blunder in court protocol.

"Your Highness, it may save time if all were to hear now. It is not as if I am a Torean sympathizer, but I have been plagued by doubts about your campaign."

"Doubts?" exclaimed the prince, a dangerous edge in his voice already.

"Your Highness, yes—doubts. I have been worried that if the Toreans are indeed right about windrels abducting Princess Senterri, then not enough effort is being put into searching for her inland, within the towns, villages, caravan camps, and slave markets of the deserts to the north. Thus I have had my own contacts hard at work, all paid for from my own limited treasury, of course. They are mere camel drivers, mercenaries, and even slavers, but true word of the princess would be no less welcome from the mouth of a beggar as from that of a duke—"

"You have been brought word of Senterri?" asked the prince, who by now had been brought word of Senterri many hundreds of times over.

"I have been brought word of a girl named Senterri, who was recently acquired in the slave market at Hadyal. She had flame-colored hair, and was sold in the company of two other girls."

The governor now had the undivided attention of the prince and all his generals. Senterri had two handmaids, and they had been abducted together, according to the Toreans. This was known only by the senior nobles and provincial governors.

"This information is indeed worthy of investigation by an armed patrol," replied the prince. "Have a dozen men sent to Hadyal to investigate. In particular, have inquiries made after the names of the two handmaids. There are millions who know the name Senterri, but the names of her handmaids are the filter through which impostors are discovered."

"My informant said they were Perime and Dolvienne."

The stare of the prince suddenly became so intense that Governor Roilean raised his hands to his face for a moment. The room was blanketed with absolute silence. Roilean stopped breathing.

"Governor Roilean, in a quarter hour I want you dressed for riding, along with a dozen guides to the roads and trails to Hadyal." The prince turned to his generals. "I want five thousand lancers riding behind me on the road north when I set off with the governor. Go!" He strode after them, then suddenly turned on his heel and looked back at the astonished Roilean. "Best get used to being called Duke Roilean," he called back. Then he was gone.

Laron made a show of yawning as he entered the refectory of Madame Yvendel's Academy. He was by no means the last to arrive and be marked on the roll, but as he sat down with his tray and began to eat, he became aware that he was redolent with the musky scent of Pellien. He glanced about his table. All were students, except for Lavenci but she was at the other end. *Well, if they are all genuine virgins they will not recognize the scent of what I've been doing,* he thought. Dacostians were almost unknown in Diomeda, after all. Laron yawned again, and this time it was not for show. In all he had wasted less than an hour of Pellien's delightful company by actually sleeping. Lectures and tutorials were going to be difficult to endure this morning.

"Been burning oil in the name of scholarship, Laron?" asked Lavenci.

She was an academician, but only a tutor. The fresh-faced but rather angular and tall albino girl always had her long, pale hair swept back in a tight ponytail.

"Yes— That is, yes, I learned a lot last night."

The students at his table began to pack their trays and leave. Laron gulped down his grape juice and munched a handful of raisins. The moment Laron was alone at the table, Starrakin sat down opposite him.

"Not expecting see *you* at Bargeman's Pole," declared the Vindican, coming straight to the point.

Laron stared back at him, but Starrakin would not be stared down. "I was studying last night," Laron declared.

"What? Studying bag of live oysters and two jars of claret with old whore?"

The word "old" was Starrakin's mistake. Laron had been aware only of Pellien being lovely, not of her age. Her age was, in fact, difficult to pin down. Somewhere between twenty and forty, perhaps. Suddenly honor was at stake. The honor of a woman. The honor of his lover. Laron attacked.

"If you spend so much time in the Bargeman's Pole, you must be living beyond your allowance," he said in an even, level voice.

"You have rich patron, plenty gold," replied Starrakin.

"Oh yes, very, very rich," said Laron. "And generous."

"Five gold pagols, make it difficult for me remembering you at Bargeman's Pole."

"I did nothing there worth five pagols of silence."

"With woman, you eat. Buy *two* pies, *two* jars."

"I was with a student friend, we ate while studying."

"Hah! Pull other leg, it play 'Gods of Moonworlds, Save Our Gracious King.' Virginity of yours, severely missing. Rich patron find out, five years' allowance of yours missing, too."

"My friend and I just study together—"

"Taverner say oysters and wine you buy—"

"He was lying!" Laron shouted, thereby securing the attention of all those still in the refectory, and fetching back most of those who had left.

"*You* lying!" Starrakin shouted back, determined to ruin Laron, having failed to blackmail him. "You cheat patron, never pass sorcerer test, jiggy-bump old whore—"

Laron flung his tray at Starrakin's face, then vaulted the table and came crashing down on top of him. They traded a few flailing blows then rolled apart, bounced to their feet, and squared off. Starrakin was over twice Laron's weight, and as he charged he swung a punch. Laron spun on his right heel, deflected the blow with his right arm, then brought up his left hand to seize Starrakin's wrist while he thrust his left hip into the Vindican's stomach and heaved his arm down.

Starrakin cartwheeled in midair, slamming down on the refectory table behind Laron. The table collapsed noisily. Laron sprang on top of him and managed three punches to his face before two of the younger male academicians seized him by the arms and held him back, lifting him from the ground. Starrakin lay dazed, bruised and winded. Laron shouted and cursed, challenging Starrakin to a duel with a choice of any weapons. By now someone had fetched the nurse. Pellien entered, carrying her medicar's bag, and began pushing through the crowd until she caught sight of Laron.

"They were fighting over some woman's honor," Lavenci whispered to her.

"Er, anyone I know?" Pellien managed.

"None of us knows her, but Laron still beat the Vindican senseless for saying she had bedded him."

Yvendel burst through the circle of onlookers at this moment. "Precisely *what* is going on here?" she demanded.

"He attack me!" cried Starrakin.

"He questioned the honor of a lady!" countered Laron.

"Who threw the first blow?" asked Yvendel.

"He did!" said Laron.

"Hah! First he throw breakfast tray, kick me in face!" Starrakin countered.

Starrakin was pulled from the wreckage of the table and hauled to his feet. Laron was lowered to the floor and released.

"What did you say to Laron?" asked Yvendel.

"Say he was, last night, ah, don't know polite word, ah, inseminating old whore."

"And what basis did you have for—"

Laron's etheric fireball exploded on the floor between Starrakin's boots, setting both floorboards and boots alight. Starrakin leaped into the air and shrieked. There were several more moments of confusion before the flames were smothered. Starrakin and Laron were forced to kneel before Yvendel. Pellien cowered in the background, her arms folded between her two sets of breasts and her eyes firmly fixed on a gold leaf in the top right-hand corner of a tapestry on the wall behind Yvendel.

"This is a scholarly academy, not the royal court," declared Yvendel firmly. "This sort of behavior is expressly prohibited."

"He challenged a lady's honor," Laron said again.

"Indeed, as myself, my academicians, my students, my cook, my cleaner, my laundress, my nurse, most of my neighbors, and quite a few passersby all heard, very plainly. Who is she?"

"I cannot say."

"Starrakin?"

"Not knowing. Guessing. Joking, I was."

"So this lady's identity was unknown to all but you, Laron, yet still you smashed a table, flung a casting in the dining hall, beat Starrakin to a pulp, then set him afire in defense of her honor? Just what does she mean to you?"

"She is a friend, no more. But if I do not defend her honor, who else will?"

Pellien shuddered, as a mixture of pride and guilt boiled through her.

"*You* attacked Starrakin, you began the fight," Yvendel concluded. "Thus you are in breach of my rules for Academy students. You must leave within three days."

Starrakin had the good sense not to grin. Laron gave this a moment's thought, then made a quick tactical decision.

"I can ask for examinations and a test of my etheric control at any time," he said firmly.

"For initiate level nine? You will fail the examinations as surely as the sun shines in the sky."

"The sky is quite cloudy just now, rector. Besides, the status of my virginity will be determined on the third day, when the etheric control test is done. *That* will vindicate the honor of my lady friend."

Yvendel ordered the registrar to make the arrangements at once. As Pellien treated Starrakin's injuries with her most sharply stinging ointments, her feelings of guilt, and of admiration for Laron, increased considerably.

In another part of the maze that was the Academy, Laron was standing before Yvendel.

"Laron, I agree, the Vindican is a turd, but my rules are my rules. You broke them in the most public manner possible. If you had fornicated with Lavenci on the breakfast table you would have had a better chance of staying."

"I'm not her type."

"Look, you already have almost enough background to attempt most examinations, and given a year I would be willing to let you try them, but a month?"

"Honor was involved."

" 'The more that he talked of his honor, the faster I packed up my glassware.' Well, I cannot be seen to favor you without provoking questions. Damn you, I could have made you a level ten, then an academician. You could have been lecturing here by this time next year."

"This time next year I might not be quite myself, Learned Yvendel."

There could not have been a greater contrast between the departure of Roval from Diomeda and that of Warsovran. The fifteen war galleys and ten dash galleys of Admiral Griffa's Hellfire Squadron escorted his flagship as it glided out of the harbor between rows of deepwater traders, with drum and trumpet bands massed on their decks. The city had been run on a mercantile rationalist philosophy for over a century, meaning that money was seldom spent on anything that did not contribute to the making of yet more money. While bridge and road maintenance, drainage, and civil and military defense qualified because they kept the city and its citizens efficient, dry, and unmolested, large public spectacles did not. The occasional brawl, fire, execution, or royal wedding was all that usually passed for free entertainment, and Warsovran's invasion was considered by most to be the greatest show since the great hurricane of 3097.

Thus all of Diomeda had turned out to watch and cheer as the Hellfire Squadron departed, and the forty foreign dignitaries of varied ranks and function who were coming along to see the power of Silverdeath demonstrated upon Helion were already impressed by the city's apparent enthusiasm for the Torean emperor. As always, Einsel stood beside Warsovran, nervously rubbing his hands together.

"This will serve to show all those in Dawnlight they have already been defeated, and that the palace is their dungeon," said Warsovran.

"They may soon surrender, and you can move into the palace yourself," Einsel suggested.

"I hope they do not. Dawnlight is a perfect size, shape, and position for a single fire-circle to destroy. That way I can mingle the ashes of that stupid, stubborn king and that vile, scheming bitch who killed my son, all in a single column of fire stretching up to the sky. I shall do it when the armies of the Alliance kingdoms arrive. I suspect that they will turn around and go back across the desert."

Einsel had long suspected such a use of Silverdeath was on Warsovran's agenda, but he had scrupulously avoided the subject. Now he lapsed into a depressed and fearful silence.

Unbeknownst to all of them, the besieged Diomedan king also had decided that public spectacle was a sure path to popularity. He had already ordered his men to build an extreme-range catapult out of spare parts, and when Griffa's squadron and the honor guard of ships had begun to form up, he decided that this was an ideal opportunity for a series of tests. The catapult fired its first shot, which was merely a rock of very precise weight. It flew well beyond the ring of encircling warships and even the honor guard, to splash harmlessly in open water. Few noticed, and nobody thought to have the two lines of ships break ranks. Six minutes later a second shot landed between the two lines, calling a lot more attention to itself and causing consternation among the commanders. Flags were run up, as signal trumpets were of no use above the bands.

Warsovran's flagship was now passing and within range, and high on the walls of the distant palace a hasty consultation took place between the king and his engineers. Was it worth chancing a precious barrel of spirits wrapped in tar-soaked cloth on only the third test shot? The king decreed that it would be so. The barrel was loaded, the sightings were taken, the elevation cross-beam was adjusted and locked down. The crew captain ordered the barrel to be lit as the rangemaster held up his hand.

"Steady three, steady two, steady one—release!"

The barrel traced out a thin arc of black smoke across the overcast sky, overshot Warsovran's flagship, but smashed squarely onto the deck of a deepwater trader in the guard of honor. Instantly the decks were ablaze, fire was pouring out of the scuppers, and sailors and bandsmen alike were leaping overboard with their hair and clothing on fire. The flagship passed the inferno without its oarsmen so much as missing a beat, but the wind blew the sooty smoke across the big galley.

A cheer went up from the palace, but the presence of several thousand elite marines among those ashore meant that any patriotic Diomedans there were somewhat more restrained in their reaction. The flagship was first in line, and Warsovran gave the order to raise the speed to battle pace. By the time the catapult on the palace tower was ready for a fourth shot, there were still five galleys within range, but Warsovran's vessel was well clear. The blazing barrel flew high and far, and this time struck the quarterdeck of one of the galleys. Three-quarters of the ship's officers had been assembled there in full armor and ceremonial finery for the procession, and were instantly drenched with flame. Knowing that four other galleys were in its wake, a junior officer on the maindeck rushed aft and into the flames. Seizing the abandoned steering bar, he sent the galley curving into one of the deepwater traders in the guard of honor. This cleared the channel for the remaining galleys, but left the galley and trader locked together, on fire and sinking.

The attack had caused considerable loss of face to Warsovran, but as far as the voyage to Helion was concerned, he had lost only one of his escort. The emperor was furious, but as for what his audience of foreign observers said or thought, he cared little.

"When we return, my very first act will be to burn that pile of degenerate, useless architecture to ash," he muttered to Einsel as he stood at the sternrail. "I shall put Silverdeath on you, Einsel, and restore you to youth again. Would you like that?"

"Your majesty is too kind," replied Einsel, who did not, in fact, appreciate the offer at all.

Back in the harbor, the honor guard was hastily breaking up and trying to get out of range of the new catapult. The besieging ships held steady, as they were clearly being ignored for the higher-profile targets. The king stood waving his ax atop one of the crenellations, while nobles and guardsmen alike raised their robes or chain-mail and bared their buttocks in the direction of the flagship.

A thousand yards out from the walls of the palace, a Sargolan mercenary sighted his crossbow through a farsight attached to the side. The farsight had been adjusted to allow for the drop over a thousand yards, and within the farsight a pair of stars had been marked by strands of silk glued down by resin. They were lined up on the triumphant king. The weapon had an ashwood stock that was a handspan across, and its bow was laminated battle-ax steel. The string was woven steel cable, which had taken a master armorer five months to make. In spite of its strength, however, the weapon had been made to very fine tolerances, and was mounted on a solid, heavy tripod. The water in the harbor was calm, apart from the waves raised from the distant galleys and traders. An apprentice watched for approaching waves; the mercenary tightened his finger on the release.

"Say when," called the mercenary.

"Looking steady—shoot when ye will."

The mercenary breathed out, then squeezed the release. The mercenary had been practicing for days, aiming just below the crenellations and hoping the guards would not notice. They had, in fact, noticed, but had assumed that someone was shooting with a weapon that did not have quite the range to reach them. The precisely-made steel bolt struck the king in the stomach. He doubled over, dropping his ax, then toppled from the wall and began the long fall to the water below.

Had the king fallen backward, or had the defenders had the

foresight to pretend that some mere minion had been killed, few would have believed that the Sargolan had killed the king. This was not meant to be. Five men jumped after the king at once, but all were killed by the long fall. Others began scrambling down the walls on ropes, but by now the dash galley captains had been alerted and were ordering their vessels into motion.

Two dash galleys were sunk and another five damaged in the frantic battle at the base of the palace walls, but the king's body was recovered by the Toreans. He had been imprudent enough to be wearing gold robes and no armor, so that he floated after hitting the water. A dash galley was sent to fetch the flagship back, and Warsovran displayed King Rakera's body to the overawed dignitaries that were his audience, explaining that the entire incident had been a ruse to lure the king into displaying himself in plain view.

Two hours later the squadron set off for Helion again. Ashore, the Sargolan mercenary sat on a large pair of scales as his weight in gold was measured out.

"Well, Einsel, it cost a good many lives and ships, but I successfully lured the king out into view for my marksman," Warsovran declared with satisfaction.

"A most cunning and finely balanced scheme," agreed Einsel, "but I am surprised that you did not share it with me in advance."

There was the slightest of pauses before Warsovran replied. The emperor never said "ah" or "um"; in fact he only paused when thinking—and he thought very fast. Einsel knew this well, from his many years as court sorcerer and confidant.

"Even you need to be shown that I am full of surprises," Warsovran now replied.

Einsel's heart sank. Every other time he had wanted to surprise Einsel, the emperor had said, "Wait and see, you should like this." Now Warsovran was improvising. This suggested that Warsovran did not always have his plans fully thought-out; in fact, he was probably a master at claiming credit for whatever accidents Fortune strewed in his path. This meant he was almost certainly liable to conduct dangerous experiments with Silverdeath again, even after Dawnlight was destroyed.

There were six examinations for Laron to complete: two verbal, two written, and two practical. Being seven hundred years old and something of a part-time scholar meant that he had gathered an immense background education, and now this all came to his aid. *Theory of Etheric Energies* was his best, for which he was awarded a credit. *Practical Applications of the Ether* was no problem, either, as Laron had been doing castings when Madame Yvendel's great-great-grandmother had been a laundress in North Scalticar. In the verbal examination for *Comparative Anatomy*, Laron had been failing until they reached the topic of Dacostian physiology. He began to improvise, once he realized the hooded academician knew less than he did. Wisely, the academician decided to recruit a second examiner. Unwisely, he chose the only Dacostian on the academy staff. Nurse Pellien was provided with a hood and shown in to the examination room. She proceeded to give Laron honors for a dissertation that was based partly on his one night with her, but mainly pure fiction. That was enough for the barest of passes to be awarded in the subject, but only a pass was required.

For the *Law and Ethics* paper, Laron constructed a system of government called "democracy," based on a fictitious people he called the Greeks. He was awarded a pass because this examiner, Yvendel herself, was taken by surprise at the sophistication of the scheme. The fact that the Greeks and their system of government had actually existed in some unimaginably distant place was not something Yvendel needed to know, not that she would have believed it anyway.

The final verbal test involved the historical use of etheric sorcery. Some of the examples Laron quoted were so obscure that the examiner did not even know they had taken place, yet Laron spoke with convincing authority. Not wishing to make a fool of himself, the examiner averaged out Laron's other results and awarded him a pass.

The sixth component of Madame Yvendel's grading process involved the use of ether in defense and attack. This was not to build up skills or subtle moves, so much as to test students' ability to channel raw power in ever-increasing quantities. Normally Laron would not have been given such a test until his second year.

He arrived at the lip of the arena, already stripped to the waist, and stood watching the Academy nurse examine his opponent, the Valestran, Arenkel. She signed him off as fit for combat, then turned. *Pellien,* Laron's mind shrieked. She held her face blank. He began to tremble all over. Her touch was cool and professional this time, although as she examined his eyes she whispered, *"Good fortune, virgin."* She signed him off, commenting only that he was inclined to be nervous when she spoke to Yvendel.

The arena was an ancient cistern with a sand floor. The arched vaults had been removed and seating installed around the rim, and the whole scene was lit by olive-oil lamps. There was no door. Laron and his opponent climbed down to the Sands of Challenge via a ladder, which was then withdrawn. By the rules of such contests, any participant who could not climb out unaided was declared the loser automatically. If both could climb out, the contest was decided on points awarded by a panel of judges.

Laron was wearing the red sash of a student under inquiry, while his Acreman opponent wore the white sash of the Academy. Arenkel was a student of two years' training, and looked about eighteen. He was also a friend of Starrakin's.

"We are gathered in judgment of the red challenger," said Yvendel, without getting up from her seat. "In judgment of his skills, power, and bearing."

Arenkel bowed to her. "In the name of the Academy of Applied Castings and as the Academy shall I fight."

By now it was clear to Laron that this was no test, so much as a trial. He would be subjected to considerable pain if he lost, and this would be in punishment for what he had done to Starrakin—who sat watching at Yvendel's right hand. Laron bowed to Yvendel, then glanced to where Pellien sat.

"Academicians, I dedicate this test to the honor of my friend, with whom I did nothing shameful. I pledge to uphold her honor as I fight."

There was complete silence. Pellien did not react at all.

"This is not a tournament, Laron," warned Yvendel.

"I trust not, Learned Rector," he replied.

It was, in fact, a tournament, it was just that nobody was supposed to say so. Yvendel stood up and tugged the scarf from her neck, then released it. The wisp of cloth floated slowly down. The Acreman watched, while breathing ether into his hands. Laron did likewise, except that he did not watch the scarf. He was watching his opponent.

The moment the scarf touched the sands Arenkel turned and lashed a filament at Laron's legs, but Laron jumped to let it whip harmlessly past. The Acreman reeled in the filament, formed it into a tangled ball, and flung it at Laron's head. Laron took the force on his own ball of ether, but spin-dodged to let the attack bounce from the circular brick wall and return. Arenkel snared it with a thin tendril of red, then formed it into a blade that extended a yard from his hand, and advanced on Laron.

Laron backed away, trailing his own ether weapon down his right arm in a blue shimmer. His opponent chopped down. Laron blocked. Arenkel stabbed. Laron deflected. Arenkel seized his own wrist and swung his projection blade. Laron ducked. Arenkel spun, Laron snared his leg with a thin cord of ether, and the Acreman fell, striking his head against the curved brick wall.

"I respectfully request my esteemed opponent to stand," said Laron.

Arenkel did not move.

"One fall to red," an examiner decreed.

By now Pellien and Lavenci were sitting forward on their seats, eyes wide. Starrakin had his fist over his mouth and was looking uneasy. Yvendel was stroking her chin and nodding.

A medicar descended to the sands, but it was a quarter hour before the Arenkel was declared fit to fight again. Laron won the next three bouts by forcing his groggy opponent to his knees, but slowly Arenkel recovered as Laron tired. Laron took five falls in a row, but won a sixth as the Acreman became overconfident.

The bouts became less elegant and more frantic. Laron faced

the white-belted Acreman student through a thundercloud of blue sparks and tendrils. Both were sweating and straining, trailing tendrils from their lips and fingers, while four examiners sat peering down and a fifth paced about the rim. A time-keeper looked down from a gallery in the wall. The sand about their feet was scuffed and chaotic from the struggle of the past hour and their trousers were soaked with sweat. Blood dribbled down Laron's chin from where he had bitten his lip. Arenkel broke past Laron's defense and grasped his hand in a mesh of force, but Laron twisted his whole body and raised his hand, forcing the Acreman around until he could bend his arm backward over his shoulder. Arenkel shrieked with pain, Laron prepared to force him down—then he released him and stepped away. He could smell that the Acreman had lost control of his bladder.

"I request a suspension," said Laron.

"Red requests a suspension," said the chief examiner. "Does white agree?"

"White agrees," panted the Acreman.

The ladder was lowered, and Arenkel climbed out with pee dripping from his trousers. Laron stood with his arms folded, unmoving. Presently the Acreman returned.

"Last bout, prepare to cast," warned the timekeeper.

Laron relaxed a trifle, bending his knees. His opponent's cloud surged forward eagerly, as if alive. Laron sidestepped, and the opposing castings slid across each other. As Arenkel stumbled forward to regain his balance Laron dropped to the sand and swept his leg out, and although his opponent's protective proximity-casting singed his boot, trouser leg, and skin, it was enough to make Arenkel stumble. Laron immediately grappled with his blue cloud of tendrils and hauled the Acreman in an arc with his own tangled casting. Propelled by his own momentum the youth could not stop, and although he flung himself to the sand in desperation it did not save him from sliding into the wall. Two examiners held up white flags.

"Break!" barked the timekeeper as the sands in the glass ran out.

The blue clouds of force-tendrils retreated back to the lips and fingertips of their initiates as the examiners gathered and conferred. The chief examiner called results to a scribe sitting in the gallery beside the timekeeper.

"Red has a tied contact over white. Red made a feint. Red sacrificed contact and used cold force to gain advantage. Red won within a single gradation of the nominated time. Red had superior cold balance. White had superior word power. Red had superior word control."

Yvendel stood up and gestured to the ladder. "The bouts are over, lower the ladder."

Both contestants were able to climb out of the arena, and they walked into a nearby auditorium behind the judges and academicians, but at the head of the other students. The judges called for Laron's opponent first.

"White, your petition?" asked the chief examiner.

"Fight with pure word power, did I. Forced red to knees, ah, eleven times. Collected forfeit. Declared ascendant, white should be."

Now all eyes were upon Laron.

"Red, your petition?"

"I assessed my opponent, giving ground to learn his weaknesses. I forced him to the ground five times, forced one touch, and won the first bout by a drop. I also proved my endurance by winning the last bout. I assessed that his word control grew careless and his attitude overconfident as he collected falls. I used that to advantage in the face of otherwise certain defeat. I should be declared ascendant."

Four of the examiners returned to their seats and the chief looked up to the gallery to address the record.

"The score is eleven falls and one forfeit to white; with five falls, one touch, and an outright drop to red. As casting vote, I assess that white was overeager to score, and in real life would have died in the first bout. Red studied a superior opponent, then used his observations to advantage. I declare for red. Scribe, declare the score."

"White: eleven falls and one forfeit, and thus fourteen. Red: five falls, one contact, and a drop, and thus fifteen."

"I declare red to be the winner," concluded the chief examiner.

There was no cheering or clapping. All five judges and the Acreman initiate bowed to Laron, who then bowed in turn. The judges began to file out of the auditorium while the black Acreman thumped a hand on Laron's sweat-soaked back.

"Good fight, sir," he said.

"Ah, thank you."

"For forfeit, especial thanks."

"Think nothing of it."

"Very embarrassing."

"Do you know what happens next?"

"Sir, not I. You passing four examinations, ah, that most students take five years to passing, prepare for. Some passing not after ten. You defending yourself, can. Very important. Now final stage. Not test, not exam. Ordeal. Ah, learning, just, it is, ah, but virgin only can learning."

Arenkel bowed hastily, then hurried out. The rector led Laron out to a small chamber, which was furnished with nothing more than a large and comfortable-looking chair, and a padded bench featuring a dozen stout-looking leather straps. A crystal goblet of something murky and blue was brought in by Lavenci.

"Drink," Yvendel ordered.

Laron drank. The liquid was alcoholic, bitter and cloying, but had a suggestion of peaches about it. Lavenci left with the goblet and tray. The door clicked behind her and was bolted from the outside.

"Strip," said Yvendel.

Laron pulled the drawstring of his sweat-soaked cotton trousers, then removed them. The rector looked his scrawny, naked body up and down, as if it were a piece of secondhand furniture that did not quite meet her expectations.

"Lie there," said Yvendel, pointing to the bench.

Laron lay down, and she began to strap him to the bench. He began to imagine lurid erotic rituals, where the rector stripped off her robes and mounted his unresisting body. Nothing of the kind took place. She just walked over to the chair and sat down, her chin resting against the tips of her fingers.

"Fly," Yvendel said cryptically.

The room began to spin unsteadily, but by now Laron had lost touch with his body and could not call out. His mind blanked, except for a single word. *Fly*. He could feel something, as if he were rushing through warm air, with a blue dome of sky above and a vast circle of sparkling ocean below. The sun was near the zenith. Laron had arms, but his legs were just an ability to twist his body. He glanced to his arms, which were outstretched. Fins. Huge, long fins. He was a finwing. Experimentally he gave a few flaps, dipped, banked, and climbed. He was clumsy, but could manage to stay in the air.

For what seemed like a half hour he flew on. He began to feel unpleasantly warm. Did he need to stay moist? Fly, not swim, yet finwings needed to splash into the water occasionally to keep wet and cool. On the other hand, he was not a finwing. What was he? He flapped higher, leveled out. Laron now noticed that his lung sac was uncomfortable; in fact, it was beginning to feel as if it were burning hot. What was he to do? Fly until he died? He told himself that this was all allegory. The water was some sort of vaginal refuge, while apart from his fins he probably was a phallic sort of shape.

What seemed like an another half hour passed. By now the joints at the base of his fins ached, and he was so hot and dry that even twisting his body was an effort. He dropped closer to the waves. Droplets of spray struck him. He dropped lower, bouncing on the wavetops. This was still flying, he told himself, but his lung sac was still a molten slug of lead within his ribs and his back was as dry as desert sand. Was crashing *through* the waves still flying? Laron flapped to gain speed, dived, and plunged through the crest of a wave—just as a vast shadow sailed over, clawing at the spray that he had just raised.

In a panic Laron gained height as the giant leatherwing banked and came around. *Fly.* Being eaten by a giant winged lizard would soon put a stop to that. He stared at it for a moment, mesmerized. There was something alluring, hypnotic about it, yet his fears pushed all this aside. As the leatherwing dived after him he folded his wings back and plunged for the water, then leveled out at the last moment and flew along the trough between two waves. A huge head full of teeth on a serpentine neck shot up at him, closed over him for a moment—then he was flung clear and high into the air as the leatherwing smashed into the sea dragon's neck.

Battered, bleeding, and with one wing badly torn and buckled, Laron circled the fighting giants as they thrashed spray high into the air. The droplets were cool on his skin, but all too soon the leatherwing vanished beneath the surface. He had to fly on. *This is like something in my recent past, a long journey over the sea,* he told himself as the sun dried out his battered body again. He could remember few specifics, just burning thirst, agonized longing without end, weakness, no end in sight . . .

Laron opened his eyes to find Yvendel unfastening the straps. When he tried to sit up, he nearly fell from the bench, and Yvendel had to hold him steady as he eased his weight onto his feet.

"How do you feel?" she asked as he took a few experimental steps.

"Like I've never owned a pair of legs in my life, Learned Rector. What was all that about?"

"You were learning a few basics of control. They are techniques specific to my academy, they must be learned unaided, they can not be taught."

"So, did I learn them?" he asked, casting his mind back to a recent tutorial in seduction with Pellien, as well as earlier, monosexual experiments with his newly living body.

"Only just," Yvendel said sternly.

"What do you mean?"

"The marginal status of your virginity was clearly visible. Describe what you saw and experienced."

Laron did so. Yvendel listened impassively until he had finished.

"Well, you were right, the sea was a parallel of sex. The other things were dangers and distractions that virgins ought to be able to avoid. Virgins recognize the allegory with the true path; in this case the leatherwing."

"What?"

"You heard me. You should have had no fear of celibacy—in the form of the leatherwing—because you had no experience of being devoured. Non-virgins dive straight for the ocean and show no fear of being devoured by the sea dragon. This directly contradicts the order to fly."

"I—I don't follow. I was *meant* to be eaten?"

"You were meant to be eaten by the *right* predator, which was the leatherwing. You would nourish the leatherwing's body, just as when you become a member of a religious or magical order you contribute to the strength of the whole. The greater body keeps your own body flying, whereas if you flew on alone you would be knocked out of the sky by misery and fatigue. You must have come closer to losing your virginity than ingenuity and scholarship has ever been able to devise, yet somehow kept it. The sexually experienced soon plunge into the water to refresh themselves, saying that it is all in the interests of staying fit enough to fly. However, the command is to *fly*, not to stay capable of flying. Your splashing through the wavetops was flirting with the ocean without really plunging into it. Nobody has ever flown without being eaten until now, but you flew, so you pass. What you will be able to do when next you try to use that skill will be truly interesting, but that is your business—just like whatever you did with whoever you did it with."

"I see," said Laron, feeling very uneasy. "So where does that leave me?"

"It leaves you as a non-commissioned sorcerer of the ninth grading level of initiation. Now that you have learned these controls, you can use them for the rest of your life. They cannot be lost."

"And if I'd not been a virgin?" asked Laron.

"I would have noticed. It is exceedingly obvious."

"Oh."

Laron considered this. He had been measured against some unimaginable standard and found satisfactory. He felt a trace of smugness, akin to the time he had set fire to the Academy's door. Suddenly doubts assailed him again.

"Learned Rector, have you heard of Peppard the Ungainly?"

"Yes, he conducted certain experiments that defined the boundaries of virginity."

"With Dacostians."

"Yes. He proved that virginity can be lost to a Dacostian as easily as to one of our own race."

Laron blinked. The bottom fell out of his stomach.

"Ah, what about those who *believe* they have kept it, even though they remember performing the very act itself?"

"You mean like silly girls and boys who think they can keep it by fornicating while standing up? That is for some future experiment to determine."

Not anymore, it isn't, thought Laron, feeling not a little betrayed. The only reason he had endured the final ordeal was that he believed he was technically still a virgin, and that he would have something new to experience when abed with a girl of his own species.

Yvendel suddenly stopped, her mouth slightly open. Laron stopped as well.

"Would you by chance have been recently conducting experiments involving etheric energies, your own virginity, and a Dacostian lady?" she asked.

"I, I, I— What makes you think that?"

"Your questions on the subject."

"Oh! Ah, well, I have actually been doing a lot of study on Dacostian anatomy lately. Hence my, ah, good showing in the examination, ah, of that subject."

"Ah, yes, of course. Besides, there is only one Dacostian woman in all Diomeda, and she is the Academy nurse. Had you been conducting applied anatomy experiments with her while doing your shopping at the Bargeman's Pole, then beating up other students in defense of that Dacostian lady's honor, well, her identity would very soon become obvious, would it not?"

"I never said she was Dacostian," Laron stammered.

"Neither did I."

They entered another room, lit only by a single oil lamp. A tiled pool was sunk into the floor.

"Is this another water allegory ritual?" asked Laron.

Yvendel gave him a push, and he splashed heavily into the clear, cold water then rose gasping with shock.

"This is a bath. You smell like a rower's cushion in a battle galley. Soap, a towel, and clean robes are on that ledge in the corner. Use them."

Laron emerged a quarter hour later, exhausted, bruised, disorientated, and confused, but nevertheless clean. Pellien entered and beckoned for him to follow.

"Never had anyone fight for my good name before," the nurse admitted. "Something to do with not having a good name, I suppose."

"It was the path of honor," Laron replied mechanically, then added, "Peppard the Ungainly indeed!"

"Ah, sorry," she admitted. "I, er, never realized that your status was going to be tested so soon—etherically, that is, I mean."

"But you knew that it would, eventually."

"Well . . . er, yes."

"But I believed that I could not lose it to you, so that saved me."

"Well, yes. Just."

"I am unimpressed."

"You could have said no at any time!"

"Just like a moth could abandon a lamp's flame. They never do, though."

"I'm sorry."

Laron did not try to hide the scowl on his face. He considered himself to have been wronged, after all. They walked the corridors in silence for two dozen steps.

"Laron, three days ago, while I was treating a man of twice your weight and strength for some quite impressive cuts and bruises, I had to keep reminding myself that the fight had been in my name. Nobody has ever been my champion before, Laron, and I . . . I can only hope that the experience of sleeping with me was as sweet as the way I felt then. While I was swabbing Starrakin's cuts and grazes with my most potently sharp and acidic ointments and oils, for one brief, sparkling, and glorious moment, I loved you. See? You made me do something I never thought I would do."

They stopped before a door. *This is all too unlikely for words,* thought Laron, *even though it is so intensely romantic. What does she really want?*

"Someday, sometime, please try to forgive me for deceiving you," asked Pellien.

Laron frowned and pressed his lips together. "Someday," he said slowly and reluctantly. "Sometime."

"Thank you. And I shall thank Fortune for repairing the damage."

She put a hand to Laron's neck and kissed him very softly on the lips, then whispered, *"My brave and valorous champion."*

As she drew back she snapped her fingers, as if breaking a casting spell. *She meant it, she really meant it,* Laron thought, as guilt for doubting her struggled to break through his relief that he had managed to keep his doubts to himself.

"Learned Laron, through this door is a revel in your honor," Pellien declared with a broad smile. "Get in there and revel, sorcerer!"

No tricks, no demands, no requests, no pleas, no knives, not even a casting. Perhaps she really meant it.

She opened the door. On the other side was the dining hall, which had been rearranged and decked out for a feast. All of the other students and academicians were there, as was Yvendel. They began clapping as Laron entered.

The Academy scribe cleared his throat for attention.

"Laron of Scalticar, also known as Laron d'Tyrll-ny, you have been graded to level nine of initiation, that is, non-commissioned sorcerer, having passed certain examinations, demonstrated knowledge and requisite skills, and provided proof of virginity. As has been agreed, from your deposit in trust you will forfeit five silver pagols to your esteemed opponent, ten pagols each to the examiners, fifteen pagols to the chief examiner, one pagol to the venue, and twenty pagols to the Diomedan Governance of Initiates. Are you agreeable?"

"I am agreeable," called Laron, rubbing at a bruise on his chin.

"Answer yes or no."

"Yes."

"The registrar has your scroll of articles, ring, and seal ready. Uh, registrar?"

"Here."

"One scroll, made out in your name. One seal cylinder carved from a sea-dragon tooth, on a leather thong."

"Be careful what you endorse with that," said the registrar, suspicious of Laron's apparent youth and lack of maturity.

"Finally, one ring of electrum."

"It marks you as a non-commissioned sorcerer," added the registrar.

"And now, eat and drink. This is all in your honor."

Laron sipped his red wine with his scroll safely in his pouch, his seal cylinder on the thong around his neck, and the new ring on his finger.

"Of course, the nicest thing about becoming a non-commissioned sorcerer is that virginity no longer confers any advantage for higher levels," the chief examiner was saying suavely. "Many don't bother to keep it, and still think they can drink the blue wine of pathways with impunity."

"Amazing," Laron said with a little shrug.

"Yes, and they spend years studying, thinking nobody will notice, then *snap!* The women, well . . . I'm not, ah, qualified to know. The men drink the wine and dive straight down into the, ah, ocean. Not every time, though. I always remember a young lady who was rendered blind drunk by a classmate and seduced, oh, a mere week before her test. Sheer stupidity, if you ask me. Anyway, she remembered nothing of the, ah, exercise at all, and surrendered to celibacy."

"Astounding," replied Laron, aware that his own story was far stranger.

"*He* didn't qualify, of course. Cost his parents a packet! They tried to sue, but then the girl's parents sued on account of his malicious intent to cost them five years of study."

"Inconsiderate of him."

"Quite so. Well, if you are inclined to exercise your new freedom, do so with care. There is an outbreak of red pox in Diomeda. All those sailors and marines from Torea, if you ask me. Are you, in fact, er, about to . . ."

"Celibacy can be more of an escape than a burden."

"Ah, well put."

Lavenci materialized out of the crowd. The tall, angular albino's wide lips were painted crimson. She had always reminded him of something predatory, and she had a strangely appraising look about her. She had taken him through the basics of casting words and protocols, and had assessed him as latently having a high degree of etheric control.

"Laron, I do admit I'd not expected you to pass today," she said in a strong but not intimidating voice. "You could collect your assessment charts and projections from my office if you wish to leave here."

"But, ah, I *have* to leave," said Laron, almost beyond decisions by now. "I was expelled."

"Oh, no. You can now stay as a tutor academician; you were only expelled as a student. You were very marginal in some areas, however, so you really should study them in greater depth."

This technicality came as a surprise to Laron. "Oh. Well, I'm still not sure."

"Come and get your charts anyway. You can always return them if you decide to stay."

She led Laron out through a small door that led to a walkway among the roofs of the Academy. Presently they came to a door leading into the side of a tiled roof. Lavenci rattled the latch, but it was bolted from the other side.

"Ah, damn, shortcuts always turn out to be the longest way," she sighed. "Sorry to drag you across here, I know how weary you must be."

She sat down on a flat, moss-covered brick divide. Laron, who had been standing for the hour since his bath, was grateful to do the same. Lavenci lay back and looked up at the sky, which was heavily overcast.

"They say the smoke from Torea's burning has changed the weather," said Lavenci.

Laron looked up, too. "Rector Yvendel says that the dust and smoke blocks out the sun, and that the world is growing cooler," he said.

"Did you ever notice how the pyre, beacon, and street-corner torches of a big city like Diomeda are reflected as a glow in the clouds?" asked Lavenci.

Laron had noticed. There was a faint light about the roof, just enough to see outlines. He lay back, looking up at the sky. A moment later a vast, dark shadow filled his field of view, and what seemed to be an unnaturally large mouth pressed itself down on his lips and nose as Lavenci rolled on top of him. For quite some time Laron could barely breathe, and while he was fighting for air he became aware that the drawstring of his trousers was being untied by quite expert fingers. Lavenci embraced Laron and heaved him along the moss-covered brickwork. His trousers stayed where they were, and she had already taken the trouble to gather up her own skirts. *Probably*

a graduation ritual, it's probably expected of me, thought
Laron as he began to take an interest in the proceedings.
Lavenci responded by settling down on him and locking his
legs between hers.

Wensomer arrived late at the reception, secured a goblet of
wine and a marinated chicken leg, then sought out Yvendel.

"I heard that my protégé graduated," she said brightly.

"Yes, and he was even a virgin," said Yvendel. "Rather surprising, for a protégé of yours."

"Well, it just shows you should not believe all those scur-
rilous rumors about me," laughed Wensomer. "Where is he
now? I can't see him."

Yvendel gestured to the small door leading onto the roof, and
Wensomer strode off at once, the goblet of wine still in her
hand.

Moments later there was a piercing shriek from outside, followed by the clang of a goblet being dropped. Wensomer
scrambled back inside, slammed the door shut, and stood with
her arms spread out against it. The expression of bloodless
shock on her face quickly crimsoned into anger.

"*Really*, Mother, this is *too much!*" she rasped, looking
straight at Yvendel.

"What, fair daughter?" asked Yvendel.

"I was but an hour late into this revel, and, and, and . . ."

"The pastries were all eaten?"

Wensomer strode across to where Yvendel was standing. "He
was *my* protégé!"

"Yet he remained a virgin. I was stunned when he drank the
blue elixir, yet—"

There was a clack from the door. The entire assembly turned
to watch Laron and Lavenci attempt to enter inconspicuously.
Everyone began to applaud.

"One bloody hour," growled Wensomer. "It must be a
record."

"Ah, no," said the registrar. "The record is held by Rector
Yvendel."

"Who was not then rector," said the scribe.

" 'Twas in the bath chamber."

"Took advantage of a new initiate."

"Gave him one."

"Thirty-one ten, it was."

"No, 3112, the year before the birth of . . ."

The voice trailed away. Wensomer's eyes narrowed. Thirty-one thirteen was the year of *her* birth. "Those who do not take a cheap lesson in history must pay for an expensive course in experience," said Yvendel.

"A plague upon the lot of you!" Wensomer snapped.

"Just because some of us do not flout our passions from the chimneytops, fair daughter, do not ever assume they do not burn. Why does a blacksmith pick up everything with tongs? Hot iron or cold, iron looks the same."

"I think enough hot iron has already been picked up tonight. We have business to deal with, Laron. Attend my villa tomorrow." With that, Wensomer swept out of the hall, slamming the heavy door behind her. It took some time for the level of conversation to progress from tentative whispers to loudly declaimed opinions again.

Chapter Eight

VOYAGE TO DETENTION

 Laron was full of apprehension as he was shown into Wensomer's parlor. His patroness had been clearly outraged by his behavior on the Academy roof. She had probably showed up at his graduation revel to invite him home to consummate their long and strange relationship, he now suspected. On the other hand, Lavenci somehow seemed a far preferable choice for that sort of activity.

He sat quietly, contemplating his future. On the one hand there was Silverdeath and the question of just which homicidal maniac would make the safest master for the infernal device. On the other hand there was Wensomer, and just what she might have in mind for the next hour or so for Acrema's newest sorcerer. If it involved raising anything more substantial than his eyebrows, he was probably about to make a fool of himself. Over the four days past he had experienced one fight, one duel, one initiation ordeal, four examinations, a night with Nurse Pellien, and then half an hour with Academician Lavenci, followed by the rest of the night with the very same academician. What he currently wanted more than anything else was at least twelve hours of undisturbed sleep.

The steward returned, bowed, and bade him follow. Laron was taken up one of the villa's two towers and shown into a sparsely furnished, whitewashed room where Wensomer stood waiting. The steward withdrew, closing the doors behind him as he left.

"Hail the, ah, rather late morning, Learned Wensomer," Laron mumbled.

By way of reply the sorceress walked over to one of two benches and flung back a sheet. Strapped to it was the very obviously dead body of a man of perhaps thirty. There were stab wounds over both of his hearts, and he had taken a severe blow to the side of his head. Otherwise it was a nicely proportioned body with a full beard, broad, hairy chest, and impressive biceps.

"This is about to become yours," Wensomer declared.

Laron looked up. "Well, er, admittedly, I don't have one of these, but—"

"I mean I can recast your oracle sphere onto it. My theory is that within your oracle sphere you still have the soul of a vampyre. Silverdeath only restored your body to life. You are about to become a vampyre once more."

Laron looked down at the corpse again. He reached out and touched its arm. The skin was cool.

"It is no more than three hours dead. Gr'Atos Arak's Necrotic Merchandise charged me eleven gold pagols. In another three hours it will be worth barely one."

Laron peered down at the corpse's genitalia.

"Not very well hung, was he? I mean, even mine are bigger."

"You didn't use yours for seven centuries, and you will certainly not be able to use these, so what do you care? You will have fantastic strength, immortality, and the ability to address every bully, thug, and varlet by his place on the menu. You will also be fully grown, broad in the chest, and ruggedly handsome. Remove your clothes and lie down on the other bench, if you please."

"Strip?"

"Yes, and reset your circlet to the 'share' option."

"Strip naked?"

"That is the most common meaning assigned the word 'strip,' in popular usage, at least."

"Why?"

"Why should you care?"

"You may, er, interfere with me."

"If I choose to, it will no longer be you, and should not concern you at all. Are you going through with this or not?"

Laron stripped and lay down. He closed his eyes. Wensomer spoke words of casting and then there was a soft crackle as she shaped the etheric energies. There was a tingling, glowing sensation as she applied the casting to his head, then all his senses winked out and he was suspended within metallic-violet nothingness.

Wensomer put the ether-enclosed circlet and oracle sphere down beside the corpse, and peeled back his eyelid. Satisfied, she felt for Laron's breath with the back of her hand and checked his pulse. Everything was normal. She picked up his penis between her thumb and forefinger, shook her head, and said, "What a waste." Next she hoisted up her robes, swung up onto the bench, straddled Laron, and breathed a fine-tendriled, sparkling casting into her hands. She put a hand either side of his head, and pressed her forehead against his. Slowly her mind merged with Laron's.

"Greetings—anyone home?" she inquired wordlessly.

There were only echoes of her own words in reply. Probing further, she met with resistance. The body was named; she could be no more than a visitor. Experimentally she opened the eyes and saw her inert face directly above, meshed with her casting's energies.

"My . . . my . . . you . . . are . . . pretty," she managed with the unfamiliar lips and tongue that had belonged to Laron.

Now she was taken by surprise by an even more unfamiliar stirring between the legs. *Ah, so this is what you men feel when you fancy us,* she thought. *The things I do to myself in the name of the cold sciences.*

Wensomer shook her own head as she detached her mind from the other body. There was no ancient soul there, smothered by Laron for seven hundred years. That soul had departed before the oracle sphere had been attached to the corpse. She got down from the bench, reached into a locker by it, and took out two sets of manacles. The new corpse was safely secured by cold iron before she picked up the circlet, spoke another casting, and attached it to the head. She stood back. Before her eyes, the wounds to the chest and head healed over with a flickering of etheric lines of force. Any moment now, Miral would begin rising. She saw an eyelid flutter.

Laron tried to bound up with something like a slurred howl. Wood splintered beneath chain links, but the chains held against the vampyre's struggles. Finally he lay still.

"As always, success," said Wensomer. "You will remain chained here until Miral sets, then someone from Gr'Atos Arak's Necrotic Merchandise will take your body inland on the river and dump it. In a day or two the army of allied kingdoms should be calling past, and you should have plenty of livestock to feed upon. Warsovran may even give you a medal—who knows?"

The vampyre Laron turned its head and looked across to where the teenaged body lay. It took a quite unnecessary breath.

"Wwwenssmerr," Laron slurred through lips he had never used before. "G-go. Ba-ba-back."

"What do you mean? I live here. The villa cost me twenty seven thousand gold pagols. I had to buy at the wrong time of the year—or so Honest Jerrik assured me."

The vampyre's jaw worked again. Long fangs gleamed in the noonday light streaming in through the tower's windows.

"M-mm-me. Go . . . b-b-back. A-live."

"To that body? After I spent eleven gold pagols on this body? You want to grow old and die, like the rest of us? Do you realize that you still have the soul of a vampyre, and when you do die, you will again revert to being undead? If you die of old age you could be a very unattractive vampyre. I suppose someone could do a purge-casting on your oracle sphere to really release your soul to its proper destiny, but—"

"Go . . . b-back!" insisted Laron, already in better command of his new tongue.

Wensomer removed the circlet with an appropriate casting, then replaced it on Laron's head and stood clear. He opened his eyes, shook his head, and sat up on the bench, swaying slightly.

"How do you feel?" asked Wensomer.

"Better." He hurriedly satisfied himself that he had teeth instead of fangs. "Better, but odd. Odd in some places more than others. One might almost say glowing."

He looked at the beams of sunlight and the shadows they cast through the windows of the tower. "I was aware of only minutes passing, yet I estimate that your procedures have taken over an hour. Just what did you do with me?"

"For that hour, the body was no longer yours, Laron the Chivalrous and Reasonably Well Endowed. I merged with the body's head, checking whether the soul of the previous occupant was not still there, suspended against time."

This possibility had not occurred to Laron. He swung his legs down and hastily climbed into his trousers.

"Well, was he?" Laron asked.

"Believe me, if he had been there, my own sense of ethics would not have allowed me to let you back into this weedy young body that nevertheless has plenty of potential. You are lucky indeed. You were very nearly stuck with that."

She gestured to the corpse, whose wounds had opened again now that the etheric forces of the vampyre soul had departed.

Laron shuddered. "Ethics. Hah! I have a feeling that your ethics nevertheless extended to taking control of this body and giving yourself one!"

"That, young man, is between me and my own conscience."

Laron pulled on his tunic and buckled on his ax. "Look, thank you for doing this for me," he finally said in grudging acknowledgment. "I'll pay for the depreciation on the corpse. Ten pagols, you said?" he asked, reaching for his purse.

"I think you will find that they are already missing."

Laron frowned and released the purse. "In that case, I should probably leave you to write up the results of this unique and edifying experiment."

"Just one matter. *Why* did you choose to return to mortality and life after you had been restored to your old state? Was it longing to again experience of the musky delights of Nurse Pellien or Academician Lavenci that changed your mind?"

Laron grinned pleasantly, then hefted his recently lightened purse. "What is it worth to you?"

Wensomer's mouth dropped open. "Worth? To me? After all that I did for you?"

"And *to* me. You learned a lot, and for free. You have payment on the corpse's depreciation, so I estimate that you are already ahead by, say, six pagols."

"Six pagols!"

"Not to mention use of my body for, er, whatever the term for male harlotry is."

"The body that you had abandoned at the time."

"Ah-ha! So you *did*!"

"I conducted tests, nothing more."

"'Tests'! I've heard it called 'humping,' 'jiggy-jump,' 'intimate entertainment,' and 'procreative recreational activity,' but never '*tests*.'"

"One pagol."

"One pagol! Thanks to me, you have just become the first woman in history to experience sex from a male perspective—for free. And now you want *my* fascinating, priceless and pioneering experiences, also for free?"

"I'm not interested in what you did with Pellien and Lavenci, I want to know why you gave up a chance to be undead again. Two pagols."

"Five."

"Three!"

"Four or nothing!"

"Four, if you throw in that glass thing from Larmentel which plays a pentatonic scale."

"Feran stole it. What about that ocular of the king of Gironal?"

"Done!"

Laron went to a window, leaned on his elbows and looked out over the city. Clouds were beginning to obscure the sun, and rain was threatening. Diomeda was somehow meant to be viewed in sunlight, and seeing it under clouds made it seem ill and diseased. Wensomer came up and looked out, too, leaning against him in the narrow space.

"Well?" she asked, nudging him with her hip.

"Uncertainty."

"Uncertainty? Just uncertainty?"

"Yes."

"Why?"

"Being undead was very certain. I knew precisely what I could do and could not. I never changed, and I knew that my intentions toward women were honorable because I could offer them nothing else but honorable intentions. Oh, that body behind us was superb, but I know that it will be precisely as it is in a century, and that becomes boring. Immortality is not living forever, immortality is total and absolute certainty."

"But being asleep and helpless when Miral is down must have been uncertain. Were your oracle sphere to be removed from your body and a purge-casting applied, you would become truly dead."

"No, that was *totally* certain. As a vampyre I was driven to survive. I did not say that I enjoyed it. Uncertainty is life. Certainty is worse than death. I had some problems adjusting to being alive again, but . . . Wensomer, after I had returned to actually being a vampyre, I realized that I could never again stand with someone who takes me in her arms and presses her lips against mine with the tingling softness of the most finely wrought massage-casting, then tells me that I am her brave and valorous champion. People could feel compassion and gratitude for me when I was undead, but never tenderness."

Wensomer attempted to stifle a sob. Laron turned to see that tears were running down cheeks.

"Dammit, Laron, *I'm* alive and *I've* never had a chance to call any man 'my brave and valorous champion.' "

Cautiously Laron draped an arm over her shoulders. "Well, ah, perchance you are spending time in the wrong taverns?"

She gave him another nudge with her hip, then put an arm around him. "You don't meet that sort of man in those sorts of taverns, Laron. Don't ask how I know."

Laron held up the little chunk of glass from the center of Larmentel, then smiled knowingly at Wensomer.

"Filthy pictures?" she said.

"Well, yes. Would you like them now?"

"I need a laugh. Why not?"

"Then do you have an anchor amulet that I can use to bind the ocular? I have not finished my investigations on the etheric leakage into the glass as yet."

Wensomer detached a garnetlike stone in a silver claw-clip from her navel and dropped it into Laron's hand. "It once belonged to a powerful sorcerer who was killed and eaten by a rather more powerful etheric leatherwing—the stone, that is, not the mounting."

"I should hope not," responded Laron.

"It stayed lodged in the creature's gut for ninety years, until the creature grew old and nearly blind. It became what one might call a creature of habit, then someone built a castle on a mountain peak where it was inclined to roost every summer. The following summer it flew straight into a tower, jamming its head into a bedchamber window and breaking its neck. When the beast was being chopped up for disposal the stone was found. It has an intense and dark solidity in the etherworld."

"Oh. So how did you obtain the stone?"

Wensomer frowned, then her eyes darted back and forth. Finally she hunched her shoulders slightly and stared at the railing. "I was sleeping in the bedchamber at the time, and Roval—"

"That's enough! I do not wish to know any more."

Laron made a fine etheric mesh and trailed it over the fragment of glass from Larmental. The ocular's base was now manifested as a pinpoint of bluish light, but this sank into Wensomer's red stone as he placed the mesh in the palm of his hand. Finally he made a fist over the stone, and when he opened his fingers again, the mesh was gone.

✳ ✳ ✳

Velander watched the operation with increasing horror. The etheric mesh that detached the ocular's base was too coarse to pick up such a weak and diffuse presence as her. She was left in the darkness of the etherworld, clinging to the filament of orange light.

When death comes, I shall not notice, she told herself. *Just a brief sensation of dozing that becomes nothingness. Perhaps I deserved it. A continent had been murdered, yet my only thoughts were for revenge on Terikel. What is evil, then? True evil? Terikel never ceased to fight Warsovran and his firecircles; she even paid for the* Shadowmoon's *voyage to Torea. Serionese just played games and gathered scraps of power about her like an ebonian bird collecting scraps of bright cloth and colored glass for its nest.*

Velander wondered if she would go mad before she faded completely. *Never liked Feran*, she decided. *Perhaps if I had surprised Terikel with someone nicer? Laron, perhaps? Poor Laron, but at least he has stumbled out of the briars onto the path to happiness. He fought for the good name of Pellien. Nobody else would have done that. Would he fight for me, if he knew that I still lingered? And Terikel—she was a spy for the Metrologans. Had the Elder ordered her into Feran's bed? Did Feran revolt her as much as he revolted me? It must have been so. We were soulmates, she must have felt precisely as I did. She must have hated Feran, too; it must have been duty alone. Poor Terikel. First defiled by Feran, then shunned by everyone. Except Laron. At the end, when all others have gone their various ways, Laron is always there. When I fade to nothingness and die, the glass that anchors my axis line will be resting against Laron's chest. He will be with me, I shall not die alone.*

So have I gone mad? Rejoicing each time Laron is seduced? Aching for Terikel's forgiveness, ready to beg to be her soul-mate again? Or have I become sane for the first time in a great many years? Probably I am sane. Suddenly everything is so clear and certain. Laron, I am not worthy to love you, but I do worship you. Were it in my power, I would be you. Should any means to serve alongside you cross the dark and narrowing path I tread, I shall take it without so much as a second thought.

Hadyal was such a small place that everyone knew when the camel caravan had arrived. Through the serving girls and eunuchs of Madame Voldean's school, Dolvienne also learned that it was heading south, to Baalder. That was a Sargolan city, even though it was hot, dry, dangerous, and filled with more desert people and nomads than Sargolans. It had a Sargolan governor and was the northernmost outpost of the empire. It certainly meant safety if she and her companions could reach the place.

Dolvienne watched and listened continually. She knew the rhythms of Madame Voldean's school, she knew the footsteps of most of the guards, and she knew who came and went from day to day. Dusk had almost faded as the rider arrived. At once, Dolvienne was at one of her many spyholes and saw Toragev arrive by the light of the guards' torch. He tied his horse to a rail, told a guard to fetch it a nosebag. *Toragev has authority,* she reminded herself. She hurried back to her room, fetched a thumb-lamp and frantically scratched sparks from the tinder-box until she had a flame. By the time Toragev strode up the stairs she was in the corridor, sweeping one of the rugs. She bowed low as she caught sight of him.

"Ah, well met, fair and devoted Dolvienne," he said, sweeping his cloak open with a flourish.

"Master Toragev, well met," she replied politely.

"Step into your room, I have something to discuss," he said without further ceremony.

He was furtive and cautious as he entered her room, as if he had no business there. He took Dolvienne's arm and led her to the window.

"The smoke and glow across there is from the fires of a caravan camp," he said, pointing through the fretwork and bars. "It has just arrived from Zalmek, and is heading south to Baalder."

"Baalder, in the Sargolan empire?" said Dolvienne, with a very good imitation of hope and innocence.

"Yes. Baalder is two hundred miles away, across open desert. In less than a week the caravan will be on your homeland's soil."

"It would be sweet beyond telling to be traveling with them tomorrow."

"If you could pack tonight, you could leave tomorrow."

"Tomorrow?" gasped Dolvienne. "Leave?"

"Yes."

"I—I have nothing to pack," she said excitedly. "All I need is a change of clothing, a disguise."

"Well, yes, that has been arranged. See here."

He took a bundle from beneath his cloak and shook it out. It was a man's roughweave tunic and suncape.

"But how may I escape this place?" asked Dolvienne. "There are armed eunuchs at the entrance."

"There is no need to escape. I do have your deed of custody, after all. We can just walk out."

"As easily as that?" she exclaimed.

"My dear Dolvienne, it is never as easy as that. Only one of you three may leave. If what your so-called mistress says is true, when the, ah, escapee reaches Baalder, the other two of you will be ransomed. You see, in order to verify your story, you have to be given into the custody of the Sargolan governor in Baalder."

"I don't understand."

"Officially, Sargolans do not keep slaves, even though there is some unofficial trading in that regard. That means that my master loses a slave if you are not what you say you are, and my master will take the price out of my wages and back, have no fear of that."

"You have our scrolls, you know who we are."

"I also know that scrolls can be forged."

Dolvienne certainly knew that scrolls could be forged. Her certificate in dancing from Sairet was in Senterri's handwriting, after all, but then, nobody had required Senterri to write anything since she had been abducted, so no comparison had ever betrayed her.

"What could convince you of our sincerity?" asked Dolvienne, now pleading very convincingly. "We have nothing of our own to give as surety."

"There is one thing," said Toragev, leaning against the edge of the window. "The three of you are virgins, and that rather fragile commodity is highly prized in the kingdoms of the far north. On the other hand, the girl who goes to Baalder will certainly cease to be the property of my esteemed employer, so the state of her innocence will cease to have relevance. Whichever of you three is to go must first spend an hour entertaining me in her bed."

Dolvienne gasped and stepped back. For some moments neither of them spoke or moved.

"Well?" asked Toragev. "Are *you* willing to pay?"

"I—I do not fancy the idea," she said slowly. "But there are three of us. What do the others say?"

"Clown, I have only just arrived!" laughed Toragev. "I intend to speak with them, then let you gather together and discuss the matter."

He left, and Dolvienne heard the bolt slide over to lock her door from the outside. She hurried about her room, pulling parts of selected furnishings out and piling them together. With the skill of practice she made a dummy for her bed, then dressed herself. Within only minutes she was six inches taller, dressed in a dark, hooded cloak made from a dyed bedsheet, and holding a light ax whose shaft was a cane curtain-rod and whose head was parchment and paste. She drank from a vial of something sharp-scented, then spat it out almost at once. Gasping and wheezing, she gradually got her breath back under control.

The handmaid tugged at her door. There was a soft snap as the resin holding the bolt gave way. Dolvienne stood in the doorway for a moment. Somewhere nearby people were talking.

"Who is he with?" whispered Dolvienne to herself, her voice

deeper and more ragged from the corrosive polishing fluid. "Is it you, Your Royal Highness, or is it Perime?"

At the far end of the corridor, at the head of the stairs, two eunuch guards sat playing dice by the light of a single lamp.

"Perime would die for you, my princess, she would even do more if she could. When you call, she is there, when you speak she agrees, but she is as dangerous as a pleasure barge on a river with the rapids rumbling in the distance. And what will you do? You have a good heart, but it is not yet wise with the lessons of the world. If you are to be free, there is no other way. This is not betrayal, I swear it."

Aware that her resolution could easily teeter either way, Dolvienne strode out into the corridor on her cloth, paste, and parchment boots. The eunuchs saw a cloaked and hooded figure of Toragev's height approaching in the gloom. Both hurriedly touched their foreheads to the floorboards as Toragev passed.

"Well met, master," they chorused.

"Well met," came the hoarse whisper of a man not anxious to be noticed leaving.

Once the figure had reached the floor below and was striding for the door to the courtyard, the eunuchs turned to each other, smiled, then giggled. The elderly servant dozing at the courtyard door stiffly got to his feet, pulled back the latch and pushed the door open. He scowled at the back of Dolvienne's cloak when she passed without tossing him a copper, and resolved to drop an accidental hint to D'Alik about this visit. The two eunuchs at the other gate saw Toragev's figure unstrap his horse's nosebag smoothly and toss it over the hitching rail, then slip the reins free and spring lightly into the saddle.

"Seems like he's lightened his load a trifle," snickered one of them, then they heaved the bar up and pushed one side of the gate open.

Dolvienne rode Toragev's horse through the gate, then turned for the caravan's campside as the guards closed the gate behind her. The desire to urge the horse into a gallop was close to being a physical ache, but she rode as Toragev might be expected to do through the darkened town. At first she made for the field where the caravan was camped, then she skirted it. The road south was marked by the remains of an arch, and beyond it was an earth rampart that passed for the town wall. Dolvienne rode for the gap the road passed through. The guards languidly got to their feet as she approached, but she tossed them a pair of coppers cut from the coinbelt of her dancing rig and rode past without allowing the horse to break stride.

Now clear of the town, Dolvienne now rode at a canter by the light of Miral. All the while she cringed in dread of some gong or trumpet announcing her escape, but there was nothing but silence in her wake. An hour from the town she saw another group of riders approaching, but they paid her no attention as she skirted them. *Two hundred miles,* she thought again and again as she rode. One hundred and fifty to the Zavi well. She might just be able to reach it without killing the horse. If the keeper accepted the remaining coppers she had cut from the coinbelt Madame Voldean had given her, she could buy water and feed, and perhaps reach Baalder in one more desperate dash. Toragev's horse was strong, and she weighed a lot less than the steward.

✳ ✳ ✳

Senterri swallowed as Toragev finished putting his terms to her. Since leaving Diomeda, all three of the girls had been threatened with violation more times than they could remember, but they had never suffered any worse abuse than being stripped, inspected, and fondled by prospective buyers.

"So, who will make the journey?" he asked in conclusion. "One of you, or none of you? I have a disguise, ah, in my pack. We can leave this very hour."

"If there is anything, *anything* that would convince you of my sincerity, I would do it," said Senterri.

"There is one proof of sincerity that you can offer," said Toragev, spreading his arms wide in the local gesture of harmless intention. "All three of you girls are virgins, certified by Madame Voldean herself. That is greatly valued by the nobles and royalty of the far north kingdoms. Whichever of you goes to Baalder will cease to be the property of the most esteemed slavemaster D'Alik, so the matter of whether she is a virgin or not will have no relevance."

By the look on Senterri's face, it was clear she had realized what Toragev was proposing.

"Yes, my lady," concluded the steward. "The girl that you choose to go to Baalder must first take me to her bed."

Senterri shank away from the steward, but he did not go after her. Folding his arms, he began walking slowly to the door.

"Wait!" she said sharply. "What— No, no, I mean, how did my handmaids— Did they . . ."

"They were both aghast," laughed Toragev. "I must indeed seem ugly. But nonetheless, both of them were willing to make the sacrifice that I have quite respectfully requested. They are so exceedingly dedicated to your service and protection that I am almost tempted to believe you might really be a rich Sargolan lady, and that they are your handmaids."

Senterri walked over and stood in front of the door. She folded her arms.

"Perime and Dolvienne *are* my handmaids," she said, as steadily as she could. "Perime and I were brought up together. Dolvienne has been in my service since she was seventeen. We are very close. Like sisters. The sisters I never had. I have four brothers and no sisters. Do you understand what it is like to be so close?"

"I have indeed dealt with slave families many times, I know how strong such bonds can be. I have also pursued a lot of escapees. None have ever eluded me, so you see I have a reputation to maintain."

"I am willing to pay you for our freedom!" insisted Senterri, her fists clenched. "I am willing to pay generously."

"And I am taking a gamble. D'Alik's wrath can be quite terrible. I must hasten to add that for me this will not merely be an act of intense but brief delight. It will be an act of faith. Now, I must gather you three to discuss this matter. The decision must be yours. Please stand aside—"

"No more!" exclaimed Senterri. "Enough. Leave Perime and Dolvienne out of this."

"What? There is no need—"

"The handmaids are my—my responsibility."

She reached up to release the strap at her shoulder. The robe fell to the floor, revealing a pair of full, firm breasts. Senterri fumbled at the knot of her cotton trousers.

"Excellent lady, are you entirely sure?" asked Toragev, rubbing his hands together nervously.

Senterri's cotton trousers fell to the floor.

"My bed awaits your pleasure," she said unsteadily. "I lack the benefit of your experience in such activities, my lord steward, but if I am what you want, here I am."

The two guards at the head of the stairs glanced out of the window at Miral, then down to a shadow cast by the fretwork on the floor. It had touched the foot of an ornamental table.

"That's the time," announced the Racital eunuch.

"Time?" the Vindician eunuch asked as he yawned.

"The shadow from the filigree point has touched the table leg. Time to do the rounds."

They closed and locked the barred door at the head of the stairs, then set off down the corridor. More than a few feet from their thumb-lamp, it was as black as the inside of a barrel of pitch. All oil in the town had to be carried in by the camel caravans, so it was burned sparingly and in very small lamps. For the first two-thirds of the corridor, all was well.

They stopped at Dolvienne's door and reached for the bolt. It was hanging loose, held up only by the socket in the frame. They rushed inside, the lamp held high. It did not take long to establish that the shape in the bed was just a dummy.

"She was here at dusk, and only D'Alik's steward has come and gone since then," said the Vindician.

"She will be with one of her friends," said the other eunuch, "comparing notes on Toragev's performance."

The bolt on Perime's door was secure. They threw it back and entered.

"Master, I took the liberty of changing into the disguise—" she began; then she gasped loudly and was silent.

The eunuchs at first had the impression of a small, cloaked

man standing beside the bed, but the voice was that of the slave girl. The bed was rumpled.

"Bring her, keep hold of her!" barked the Vindic eunuch. "There is more to this than a little girl-talk."

Now thoroughly alarmed, they flung open Senterri's door and burst into her room. For an instant they had an image of the scene, as if frozen in time by a painter. Toragev half-dressed. Senterri sitting naked on her bed, hugging her knees and looking frightened. Clothing strewn on the floor.

Senterri tried to cover herself. Perime suddenly realized that she had saved her mistress from nothing by taking the steward to her bed and trying so very hard to delight him. It was all a monstrous trick. Slowly Senterri realized that it was Perime, wearing a disguise. The truth suddenly blazed out before her as well. What she had been about to give Toragev would bring nothing at all in return.

Toragev laughed as he looked from Perime to Senterri.

"If only you could see your own faces—" he began.

The eunuch's grip on Perime's arm had gone slack as he stood there, astonished. Perime broke free and drew the eunuch's ax from his belt in one motion, then screamed with rage as she charged Toragev. The steward cross-blocked the descending ax on the shaft, then step-dodged as he tore the weapon from her grip. As the girl sprawled over Senterri's bed, Toragev's years of experience with armed and angry slaves took hold of his reflexes. He brought the ax down on her back, severing her spine and the reciprocant arteries between her hearts.

D'Alik had been nervous about riding through the night, even with three of his hired guardsmen to escort him. The stakes were high, however, so it seemed worth the chance. When the lone rider had passed his group going south at a canter, the slavemaster was surprised.

"He's either fleeing a crime or bent on being a victim," he called to the guardsman riding beside him.

"I give him five miles," the man called back, and they both laughed in spite of their fatigue.

By now they were so close to the town that D'Alik was not willing to camp until morning. They urged their exhausted horses onward, and reached the desert town nearly three hours after sunset. An unusual number of lights were gleaming in Madame Voldean's building, yet D'Alik had to ring at the outer gate's bell for some time before anyone admitted him.

D'Alik refused Madame Voldean's invitation to sit as he entered her audience chamber. Two eunuchs flanked the cushion on which she sat. She was in her sixties, but looked a lot younger for having stayed out of the sun for most of her life.

"I want an explanation," the slaver said quietly. "One of my stock is dead."

"Your steward did the killing," replied the mistress of the slave school, but she did not elaborate lest it be taken as a sign of weakness.

"What were the circumstances?" D'Alik now asked.

"A caravan arrived from the north this morning. It brought word that all trails north had been closed due to the Diomeda business. As I was having my evening meal your steward arrived, and I invited him to join me for wine and grapes after my meal. He showed me a note of commission from yourself, saying that in the event of market circumstances for the girls changing, they were to be retrained for whatever opportunities were available. Toragev's opinion was that attractive and sophisticated harlots would be much in demand by the officers of the army of the Alliance."

"I suppose he announced that he wished to commence tutorials himself?"

"Well, yes. You have sanctioned the practice in the past."

"Go on."

"It seems that he followed his usual ploy of pretending to offer them a chance to escape in return for some willing and intimate entertainment. Perime agreed. Next he went to the room of Senterri. Meantime the guards began an inspection and found Perime dressed to resemble an artisan wayfarer. They seized her and dashed into Senterri's room, where they found her keeping quite intimate company with Toragev. It was an intensely emotional moment."

"And you. Madame Voldean, have a gift for understatement. Pray continue."

"Perime snatched a guard's ax and attacked your steward. He disarmed her and buried the ax in her back, killing her instantly. Because he was not the slave's owner I had him bound and confined at once, because my charter from the Guild of Slavers states—"

"Enough! Where is Senterri?"

"In a spare room, asleep. At first she clung to Perime's body, begging her to come back to life. Eventually we managed to pour some sleeping draft down her throat and wash Perime's blood from her. She—"

"Well, feed her a stimulant. I want both her and Dolvienne ready to leave within the half hour."

"Ah, we think Dolvienne has escaped."

There was a pause that had all of the tension of a fully drawn bow.

"You *think* she has escaped," D'Alik said, very slowly.

"She may be still in the compound. We think she worked the nails out of her bolt's frame and stuck it back with resin. The guards allowed what they thought was Toragev to leave. Ah, and his horse is missing."

D'Alik squeezed his eyes shut for a moment. "Unless you think the horse is also hiding within the confines of the compound, might I suggest that she took my steward's horse and fled into the . . . desert."

The slaver had suddenly recalled quite a large horse with quite a small rider, heading south. It must have been Dolvienne. He turned, strode to the door, and flung it open. The chief of his escort was waiting outside.

"Take three men and fresh horses, ride with all speed down the south road," he barked. "If you overtake a lone rider, a girl wearing a slave collar, then kill her. Her skin is white, her hair is black and quite curly. She will be riding for Baalder, and will be on Toragev's horse. If you bring back her head, there are ten gold pagols waiting for each of you."

"At once, master. A mere inexperienced girl will not get far."

"If you fail, do not bother to return."

D'Alik returned to confront Madame Voldean.

"I wish to have some words with Toragev, in private," he announced.

"He has been bound to a stool in Perime's former room. Her body is still—"

"Take me there. Now."

A quarter hour later D'Alik emerged from Perime's room and bolted the door behind him. He advanced on the eunuchs at the head of the stairs.

"I am leaving now," he said. "Where is the slave girl Senterri?"

"Madame Voldean has her downstairs, and is trying to revive her."

"Have the girl taken to my horse. She leaves with me, now! Even if she has to be strapped behind the saddle."

Senterri was coherent enough to sit behind D'Alik and hold on when he rode through the gates and vanished into the darkness beyond. By then the sky had been obscured by clouds. Occasional large, heavy drops of rain thudded into the dust. By morning there was thunder rumbling in the sky, and intensely bright bolts of lightning blazed out. An elderly initiate said it was a portent of disaster. He was, in fact, the doorkeeper at Madame Voldean's, and before she had sat down to breakfast he had given his notice, packed a small bag, and hurried west as fast as he could hobble.

It was raining steadily by noon. Madame Voldean had returned to bed after breakfast, being quite tired after the traumas of the previous night. She was roused by a trainee slave, who was dripping with rain.

"What do you mean, dripping water over my best Racital carpet?" Madame Voldean demanded.

"Mistress, please—men to see you," babbled the girl.

"What men—?"

The door was smashed open, and five cavalrymen entered. They seized Madame Voldean and dragged her out into the corridor. There three eunuch guards lay dead, and over them stood at least another dozen cavalrymen. Madame Voldean was taken out into the compound, where four bodies lay in the red mud and rain before several mounted Sargolan nobles. Beside them was a girl, disheveled and drenched. With a qualm so sharp that it nearly stopped her hearts, Madame Voldean realized that it was Dolvienne.

"She is a runaway slave!" exclaimed Madame Voldean, more by reflex than common sense.

The response of her captors was to force her to her knees. A Sargolan cavalry captain emerged from the open door, and more Sargolans began to file out behind him. Two of them were carrying Perime's body. Dolvienne shrieked once, then was again still and silent. Toragev's body was carried out next.

"Lady Perime is dead," announced the captain. "We cannot find the princess, but we found that man's body."

"Who is he?" asked Prince Stavez, who was beside Dolvienne.

"Your Highness, the man is Toragev, a slaver's steward," said Dolvienne. "He visited us yesterday with a scheme to escape. The price for his scheme involved sex."

Her words, and the look on the face of the prince, helped Madame Voldean's grasp of the situation catch up with reality. The town was in Sargolan hands. For the town militia to have surrendered without a fight, which they obviously had done, the Sargolans probably were there in overwhelming numbers. The Sargolan empire's Princess Senterri herself had been imprisoned in her College of Domestic and Exotic Skills, made to learn menial tasks, been given several mild beatings, then had been seduced by Toragev. It looked very bad indeed. The mistress of the College of Domestic and Exotic Skills decided to add whatever embroidery she could.

"Toragev the steward ravished Perime when she would not agree to his scheme," babbled Madame Voldean. "Then he killed Perime when she tried to defend Senterri. He—"

Madame Voldean was seized by the neck and her face was forced down into the red mud. After the longest moment of her life, she was drawn upright again.

"The term is *'Her Highness,'*" Dolvienne said sharply. "Continue."

Madame Voldean spat out a mixture of red mud and horse droppings. "The steward ravished Her Highness—ah, that is, we think he did—before my guards could come to her aid—"

"What?" bellowed Prince Stavez, drawing his ax and holding it high, aching to find someone to kill to avenge his sister's dishonor.

"But we stopped him from killing her, too, we rescued her, yes we did. I ordered the steward bound, and the guards, they bound him, and, and . . ." She looked down at Toragev's body. D'Alik obviously had killed him before he had left, but who was to know? "And I ordered him executed."

With a shriek of impotent rage the prince leaped from his horse and began to hack at Toragev's body.

"Where is Her Highness?" asked Dolvienne as they looked on.

"The slavemaster, D'Alik, arrived here from the south, ah, just an hour after all this had happened. He demanded that Her Highness be given over to him, and, er, not knowing that Her Highness was, ah, Her Highness, all that I could do was agree. He must have taken her—Her Highness—to his own house."

"He is not there," someone reported from behind the line of nobles. "His groom said that he arrived back around midnight, emptied his gold and some supplies into a pack, then left again. Nobody saw which way he went."

Dolvienne appeared to have a rather strong influence over whomever was in charge, from what Madame Voldean could see. The girl sat thinking for a time, while the rain poured down on them. Clearly, inviting them inside for tea would do little good. Besides, inviting an ex-slave/ noblewoman inside for tea made by slaves would be less than diplomatic. Madame Voldean had not made tea herself in decades, and was a little unsure of just what was involved.

By this stage the prince had finished hacking at the body of Toragev. The largest of the pieces could have easily fitted into a reasonably small saddlebag.

"Take the remains of this—this thing back inside the slaver college," he ordered. "Soak the place in lamp oil and set it afire.

Not a trace of the flesh that violated my sister must exist when we leave this place."

"Your Highness!" Madame Voldean began to protest—

The prince spun about, lashing out with his ax and striking her head from her shoulders.

"Dolvienne, you will separate the slavers from the slaves," he ordered as he wiped the blade in the mud. "The slaves will be taken to Baalder, given five pagols each, and set free. All others will be put to death."

"My lord, Your Highness—" began Dolvienne.

"I am insane with grief and outrage!" he shouted. "I *want* death, and I shall *have* death. The Second, Fifth, and Ninth Pursuit Brigades will follow the three other roads and trails out of this place. Now!"

The commanders concerned rode off through the rain and mud. Dolvienne went into the college, and returned with some clothing and combs that had belonged to Senterri. Prince Stavez snatched them from her, pressed them to his chest, then fell to his knees in the rain and mud and began weeping hysterically. The College of Domestic and Exotic Skills began to burn. Dolvienne identified the genuine slaves from the college. The lancers executed all the others. Presently the prince stood up and got back on his horse.

"The Toreans clearly had nothing to do with the original abduction of Her Highness," he told Dolvienne. "As a matter of honor we must stop the war. Now. I shall ride east, and order our forces back from Diomeda. Will you consent to come, too, Lady Dolvienne?"

"Her Highness would want me to," she replied.

"Governor Roilean!" he shouted, and the governor urged his horse forward. "You will remain in charge here, with all the remaining men. Obliterate this village. Every stone is to be pounded to dust. The scene of the indignity and dishonor done to my sister must cease to exist!"

✳ ✳ ✳

The Sargolans had reacted as fast as mortals could have been expected to, but it had not been fast enough. The rains had already converted the desert ravines into torrents, and D'Alik had begun traveling just ahead of the flooding. Most of his wealth had been invested in property and slaves, and neither of those was particularly portable, given his circumstances. He had seventy gold pagols in his saddlebags, some jewelry, a horse, and Senterri. Senterri was worth a lot more than the average slave; in fact, D'Alik knew she could fetch a hundred pagols to the right buyer. After that, he could vanish into the mountains, where he had a different name and persona as a wine merchant.

"Where are we going?" asked Senterri as they sheltered beneath a rocky overhang for the night.

"Urok, on the Leir River. I have a buyer for you there."

"A buyer? How much will he pay?"

"A hundred gold pagols."

"But—but my father will pay a thousand times as much for my return."

"Your Highness, the story is already abroad in Hadyal that my steward ravished you. *My* steward. That story will soon reach Sargol. That means that the entire Sargolan empire will be falling over itself to place my head on a spear. A princess has been ravished. That princess is you."

"But why would anyone blame you?"

"I authorized Toragev to begin training my slaves for harlotry under certain circumstances. Those circumstances arose while I was away, so I am guilty. Besides, he is dead, and I am alive—and therefore eligible to be tortured."

"Your steward—dead?"

"Yes. I killed him for robbing me of a hundred thousand pagols by mounting you. My temper is not to be taken lightly. Rob me of the hundred pagols that you can bring me now, and the consequences do not bear consideration."

Senterri did not need much thought to decide that her life hung by a thread held by D'Alik. He only had to leave her behind and she would soon die.

"Who is to buy me?"

"A rich windrel caravancer. He wishes to found a royal dynasty of desert princes, and has promised me a hundred gold pagols for any woman of royal blood who is also of childbear-

ing age. You will be well treated, if you behave. You will be
treated like royalty, in fact."

※　※　※

The Sargolan dash galley *Waverider* was well within sight of
Helion's beacon pyre, riding at anchor, with three hundred feet
of anchor rope holding it against the current. One of
Warsovran's galleys languidly cruised past, checking that all
the observer vessels ringing Helion were outside the ten-mile
limit. No secret had been made of the fact that a second fire-
circle would detonate precisely sixty-four days after the first; in
fact, the event had been publicized by Warsovran's agents and
traders. As far as the emperor was concerned, the more who
were terrified of his powers, the better. As the Torean ship receded into the darkness, Miral's rings touched the horizon.
Feran's racing shell was uncovered by the crew.

"Easy, easy!" barked Feran as they worked. "The sides have
little more strength than parchment."

Frail it might have been, but it was also exceedingly light and
had the streamlining of a spearhead. Druskarl's padded suit was
packed aboard, then the craft was gently lowered to the placid
sea. Miral's disk dropped below the horizon, leaving only a
glowing arc of ring. Feran and Druskarl climbed into their seats
with the care of someone stepping over a sleeping crocodile,
then their oars were handed to them.

"We should be back two hours after the fire-circle detonates," called Feran as the current took the shell clear of the
dash galley. "With luck there will be no pursuers."

"Are you sure Silverdeath will fall from the sky with this second fire-circle?" called the Sargolan captain.

"Yes; this is not just a demonstration," Feran replied.
"Warsovran is refining his control of the thing."

Feran and Druskarl began to row, and within a few strokes
they were clear of the galley and pointed directly at Helion's
navigation beacon.

"We should be there well within an hour," Feran panted as
they rowed.

"You are placing much weight on Silverdeath falling after this particular fire-circle," Druskarl commented.

"If it does not, we shall just hide all day and return to the ship after dark. There will be another chance."

"You have never said why you think Silverdeath will fall."

Feran did not reply.

"Feran! It's not as if I can tell anyone now."

"It was the diggings," Feran conceded reluctantly.

"The diggings? The underwater shelters the islanders were forced to build?"

"No, not so. From my hiding place I watched Warsovran's surveyors marking out a great arc across the isthmus between Helion's two peaks. Its center is seven-tenths of a mile from the Metrologan temple and it is one hundred yards wide. Some very basic arithmetic will show that the islanders and marines could excavate this area to a depth of ten feet within sixty-four days, so that the circumference of the second fire-circle will be completely over water. The detonation will be at midmorning, which is also high tide."

"So, that is why Helion is barred to all outward shipping and messenger autons," said Druskarl, genuinely impressed at Feran's reasoning. "This is a vulnerable time for Warsovran."

As soon as the beacon pyre was eclipsed by Helion's lesser peak, they slowed to long, deep, and quiet strokes. There was a small bay beside the vineyards of the former temple, and it was here they stopped. Standing waist-deep in the shallows, they strapped the oars to the sides of the shell and unpacked Druskarl's heavy suit. While Druskarl waded to shallower water to clamber into it, Feran selected several large, heavy rocks and tied cords to them. With Druskarl wearing all but the helmet, they carried six of the rocks into deeper water, inverted the shell, and while Druskarl held the largest rock, Feran tied it to the shell's midspar. The weight of one rock was not enough to sink the shell, but by the fifth rock it was almost beneath the surface. The sixth rock was enough to anchor it securely to the bottom. By now the sky behind the lesser peak was beginning to glow with dawn.

A patrol galley glided past with its running torches burning brightly, but the two intruders were no more visible than drift-wood among the rocks and shadows.

"We should dive for the boat," said Druskarl. "That will not be their last patrol."

"No, we should gather some seaweed and hold it about our heads on the surface until the sun marks off the eighth hour. The air in the boat may have to last us all day."

"So, you doubt your calculations?" asked Druskarl, still watching the distant galley.

"No, but if the excavations are not adequate, we may not have Silverdeath in our hands."

"We could flee in daylight."

"Aye, and Warsovran would know that someone has a sub-mersible that can speed away faster than a dash galley. You can be sure that he will have his entire bloody fleet ready and ring-ing Helion for the final fire-circle, and remember, the lightest dash galley is actually faster than our shell over moderate dis-tances in choppy water."

Just after the sun had cleared the lesser peak, the next patrol galley came past. All that was visible in the bay were two clumps of kelp floating amid the wavelets. The galley moved on. It circled the lesser peak, which was now a separate island from Helion. The islanders and marines had completed their task, and Warsovran's surveyors and engineers had been true in their work. As incentive, they had been promised an intimately close view of the last fire-circle if the channel had not been completed in time.

❊ ❊ ❊

On the western slope of Helion's main peak, six observers sat to-gether on a large rock with a jar of wine and half a round of cheese. Like some of the other islanders who had been digging the channel, their faces and hands were smeared with a mixture of olive oil and white clay, as protection against the sun. This also served as a convenient disguise. Their view of what was now the island of Helion South included a vantage over Warsovran and his official party, who were two hundred yards closer to the newly dug channel. As they watched, a battle galley entered the narrow channel, passed through carefully, then headed out to sea.

"It would have to be over ten feet deep for that one to clear it so easily," said Roval.

"How deep you think it be?" asked Norrieav.

"As deep as the Helionese were able to manage," replied Terikel.

"Thought I'd never live to see another o' those fire-circles," murmured Hazlok.

"Thought I'd never live through the first," added D'Atro.

"Will it stop a fire-circle?" asked the deacon.

"We'd be safer back on the *Shadowmoon*, a mile out to sea and ten feet down on the sandbar," said D'Atro.

"There's not air for the lot of us to be breathing all day," explained Norrieav.

Roval stood up, stretched, and stood with his hands on his hips as he glanced to the sun.

"Nearly the ninth hour from midnight," he commented, then looked down to where Warsovran stood with his audience and squad of guards. "Time that I was moving closer."

"Closer?" exclaimed Norrieav. "Your view of something the size of a fire-circle will not improve for a few yards less."

"I want to hear what is said."

"It's liable to be little more than, 'Shit, look at that!' "

"Be that as it may, I'm going. Remember, when you see Warsovran's people crouch behind that wall, get behind this rock and close your eyes."

Roval strode off down the grassy slope. He was close enough to Warsovran to make out his face when a pair of marines challenged him.

"Hie there, islander, back the way ye came!" ordered one of them, pointing back up the slope.

"But I don't want to miss the fire-circle," protested Roval.

"You'd have to be in Diomeda to miss it."

"Oi, have I seen you before?" asked the second marine.

"Can't say," replied Roval calmly.

"Don't remember you."

"Perhaps the oil clay on my face makes me look unfamiliar."

"Don't remember anyone with a shaved head diggin' the canal."

"I shaved it this morning, to celebrate the canal being finished."

"You been diggin' the canal, then?"

"Aye, like everyone else on Helion."

"Then yer hands ought to be callused. Show me."

Roval's hands did have a few blisters from a week of helping with the *Shadowmoon*'s rigging, but not the sorts of calluses that sixty-four days of digging would have developed.

The fire-circle saved him.

"Oi, the nobles are ducking behind their wall," cried the other marine.

Everyone on the island had a pile of stones, earth, or rock to shelter behind, and the marines were no exception. They flung themselves into a shallow trench, dropped their spears and lay flat. Roval joined them.

"Get out, this is ours!" shouted the marine Roval was lying over.

"Thought you wanted to see my hands."

"Pox take your hands—"

Brilliant, soundless light blotted out everything. The next sensation Roval became aware of was the scent of burning grass. A thunderclap and groundwave lifted them into the air with a confusion of rocks and dust, then a blast of air lifted them again. Roval smothered the smoldering patches on his tunic as he blinked the dazzle out of his eyes. A pillar of smoke, steam, and flame seemed to reach right up to the vault of the sky itself, and a continuous, rolling thunder was all around him. As he rose to his knees a hand seized his shoulder and spun him around. It was Warsovran.

"Get down there and help—the wall's fallen on the ambassadors!" shouted the emperor, who then kicked at the two marines who were still lying with their hands over their helmets.

❉ ❉ ❉

Beneath the steaming surface, a few yards off Helion South, the water was beginning to heat up.

"Much more of this, and we're stew," warned Druskarl.

"It's tiny compared to the fire-circles that killed Torea," Feran reassured him. "The hot air will disperse quickly over the smaller area. Time to go up."

"This is too soon," Druskarl warned, even as he fumbled for his helmet in the cramped darkness. "The surface water will be scalding hot."

"Everything is too soon or too late in this life," replied Feran. "Better to be too soon. Besides, you have the suit and cooling machine. Only one man in the entire world could walk on Helion's south island just now, and that man is you."

Druskarl stepped out from under the shell and began to walk. The suit contained enough air for two or three minutes' breathing. After that he would have to open the pipes to the water cooler on his back. His head broke the surface, into thick steam and buffeting wind, and he rammed a short spear down in the shallows.

"Three thousand six hundred feet of this," he said as he lumbered out onto the shore.

Feeling his way through the hurricane of smoke and steam with an iron staff, Druskarl set out across the inferno. After perhaps three hundred feet he unstoppered his air pipes, and began to gasp air through the jars of cooling water on his back. It was still blazing hot and seemed like pure steam, but after a few more steps he had not collapsed so he guessed that Feran's device was working.

After a thousand feet the turbulent air began to clear a little, and he shambled out onto a level strip. This was the road to the temple, the road that led between the vineyards. To the right was to the former isthmus, and left was to the temple. He jammed his iron staff between two rocks as a marker, then turned left. Now his progress was faster, but the heat was winning. The outer layer of leather in his suit's joints was already crumbling char, and the heat was penetrating the steel, leather, and felt that separated him from a quick but excruciating death. The slab of crystal in his visor steamed up continually, and he pumped the lever on the side of the helmet that worked an internal wiper blade.

A pile of stones and tumbled columns loomed out of the swirl of dust and smoke ahead. If Silverdeath had fallen onto a building, he had virtually no chance of finding it, especially with his strength and breath failing in the heat. The center of the little temple complex was an open plaza, as he recalled, but would *Silverdeath* have considered it to be the center? The road led between two pillars that had fallen parallel.

The place was littered with ash, heat-shattered stones, and pools of things that had melted in the heat. Silverdeath would not be easy to find . . . but then suddenly Silverdeath was before him.

There was a definite form in the murk and swirling clouds before him, a vast sphere. Druskarl stared, and almost immediately noticed that it was shrinking rapidly and descending. The eunuch shambled in its direction, wondering how long it would be before it became a shirt of interlocking links and plates again, and if he could survive whatever the wait might be. *Of course, this was why it had not sunk into the lake of glass at the center of Larmentel's ruins*, Druskarl realized. *It had floated down slowly, reaching the surface only when it had begun to harden. Perhaps it had been cast that way, so that it would not be nearly impossible to recover.* The sphere was about ten feet across and still shrinking as it touched the baked cobblestones.

There was a bright flash, and as Druskarl blinked the dazzles out of his vision, he saw that Silverdeath had collapsed into a gleaming tunic of metal. It now seemed quite inert. Druskarl took a butcher's meathook from his belt, reached down as far as the stiff suit would allow, and snared the fabulous but dangerous prize.

Scarcely glancing at Silverdeath, Druskarl now turned to go back—but where was the road? He fought down a wave of panic, worked the internal wiper of his visor again, then began to circle the outer edge of the plaza. There were several tempting breaks in the ruins of the buildings, but he persisted until he found the parallel pillars again. Once back on the road, he walked more slowly than before, breathing what seemed like fire through the rapidly heating water on his back. Again and again he cleared the visor, but as the gusty wind lessened in strength, the smoke and steam seemed to become thicker. He missed actually seeing the thin iron staff in the murk, but struck it with his right arm as he passed, and heard the clang as it fell.

Druskarl turned right, tramping over broken ground again, hoping and praying that he was walking in a straight line. He seemed to be going downhill, and downhill was to the water. The leather joints at his knees were crumbling away fast; he could feel his flesh burning in the hot air. As he reached up to work the wiper lever, the entire right elbow-joint crumbled away. He smelled burning meat mixed into the steam that he was breathing. He could no longer feel his right arm, and could not work the wiper lever. Blinded, he kept walking, forcing the legs that he could barely feel to move. The light beyond his fogged visor began to brighten, then he fell with a splash.

Druskarl was barely aware that Feran was beside him, wearing a smaller breathing jar and a water-soaked leather coverall.

"You've done it!" came Feran's muffled voice. "You got Silverdeath."

Feran began to cut away Druskarl's charred, ruined insulation and plates as they lay in the shallows together.

"Take it, leave me," gasped Druskarl as the helmet came away, pushing Feran away with his left arm.

"Never!" Feran laughed in triumph, standing to straddle the eunuch. "You're part of the plan."

He stabbed Druskarl just below the ribs, jerked upward, then sliced across to cut open both of his hearts. Druskarl went limp as his blood poured out into the water. Feran hauled him up into a sitting position, then began to pull the metal fabric of Silverdeath over his head. With Druskarl alive and fighting back Feran could never have succeeded, but after no more than a minute the eunuch's burned, blackened right arm was in the second sleeve and the fabric was beginning to shimmer and melt into a silver skin.

Feran flopped down into the hot, shallow water, watching. Soon a gleaming, silver figure stood up, still wearing the charred and crumbling leggings of the insulating armor.

"Serve me!" Feran commanded in a firm voice. "I am Feran Woodbar."

Silverdeath bowed.

"Your hands applied me," declared the familiar, hollow-sounding voice. "Command me, as I serve and protect."

"Your host is damaged. How long will it take to make your repairs and reach your full potential?"

"Moments."

Feran ducked under the water and released the weights holding down the racing shell. It surfaced, and he began to unpack the oars.

"The host has been optimized," Silverdeath reported.

Roval had helped the squad of marines dig several ambassadors out from under the collapsed wall. Some had broken bones but none had been killed. All were exceedingly impressed, and several said they would recommend treaties with Warsovran just as soon as they could get letters to their respective monarchs. Slowly the smoke began to disperse over Helion South, while marines and servants bustled about with stretchers, ointments, and bandages.

The entire surface of Helion South was burned down to the rock, and a deepwater trader that had been anchored just offshore had vanished. Nothing north of the channel was melted, but several grass fires had been started, and a fruit vendor's cart and several sand wagons were burning from the intense radiant heat of the wall of fire that had stopped halfway across the canal.

Suddenly someone called out and pointed. A long, narrow boat was slicing through the water, skirting the tortured coast of Helion South. Warsovran gasped, then muttered a lurid curse.

"All of you, stay here!" he shouted, thinking quickly. "Not you!" he barked at Roval, dragging him aside. "You, clay-face. Do you speak Diomedan?"

Roval shrugged, raising his hands. "Glorious Emperor, I'm a poor fisherman, I only speak Vidarian," Roval replied.

"No Diomedan—then you're my man," said Warsovran in Vidarian. "Come with me."

Roval held the bow of the shell steady as Feran and Silverdeath got out in the shallows, then he dragged it onto the sand.

"Clay-face," Warsovran said in Vidarian. "Take my ax. If anyone comes within earshot, kill them."

"Yes, Emperor, Glorious Emperor," replied Roval.

Roval walked to about thirty feet away, then stood with his

back to them, holding up the ax and waving it every so often.

"Can you speak Diomedan?" asked Warsovran, jerking a thumb back over his shoulder. "That yokel doesn't."

"I not only speak it like a native, I *am* a native," Feran replied.

"Then we can talk freely. I am Emperor Warsovran."

"You look young for an emperor."

"I once wore Silverdeath. It reduces the age of one's body to about two decades."

"And one does not resume aging for another decade," added Feran.

"I— Does it? I mean, how . . . Who *are* you?"

"I am known to many as Feran Woodbar. When you ordered my death you knew me as Cypher."

Warsovran squeezed his eyes shut for a moment. In his experience, people with something like that in their backgrounds tended to be a little vindictive.

"So? You were trying to cheat me, just as I tried to cheat you," Warsovran countered, his reply being rather more honest than most.

"Quite so. Returning to my identity, I was once known to many as Nare'f As-bar."

Neither Feran nor Warsovran saw Roval's jaw drop, because his back was still turned to them.

"So, Silverdeath sponged away *your* years and scars as well?"

"Oh yes, but a little *too* well. When I was born, Fortune favored me with weak, puny etheric powers. I lived fifteen years as a nobody. I was a common stablehand, when one day a horse kicked me, cracking my skull. After a month I had healed enough to wake, but I awoke with an initiate potential that eventually gave me the twelfth grading of initiation. A glorious career as a sorcerer was mine, but after Silverdeath had finished healing me I was again at the first level of grading, or even less. I had nothing but restored youth after a lifetime of power. Is it any wonder that I have worked so hard to become the master of Silverdeath by way of compensation?"

The Diomedan sorcerer should have been in his nineties by now, thought Roval, but the facts added up. It was a fact that nobody had seen him for years. The man had had a misshapen skull, that was a very well known fact. Feran's voluntary control of etheric powers were almost nil; that was a fact Roval had sensed for himself.

"You wore Silverdeath?" Warsovran was asking.

"Briefly, after we liberated it from its shrine and guards. I made the mistake of allowing my, ah, professional associate to put it on me. We had no idea of how it worked until then. My companion used it to destroy a castle built upon a small island on an inland lake. He did not realize the owner of the castle was not home, but was in the process of returning. He also had quite a large squad of lancers with him. They struck from behind, killing my associate as he waited for the island to cool. Praise be to Fortune, but Silverdeath had stripped sixty years from me while I was its host. I pretended to be my associate's dimwitted young servant. I was merely driven off after a beating. I watched in the distance as my enemies rowed out to the island once it had cooled sufficiently; I saw them return with Silverdeath. Ah, I had lost Silverdeath, but I had learned that it can bestow immortality as well as invincibility."

"And now *you* are its master."

"Oh yes."

"Yet you must wear it again to become rejuvenated."

"That, former emperor Warsovran, is five or six decades away. In the meantime I require servants, and good servants are so hard to come by. You will help me build a new empire in Acrema."

Warsovran considered for a moment. "And in return?"

"You will be my supreme servant—aside from Silverdeath, of course. You will also be allowed to live."

Warsovran took the duration of one inward breath to make up his mind.

"Your terms are eminently attractive, Emperor Feran Woodbar."

"Splendid. Firstly, you are to do my bidding on a few small matters. A certain youth named Laron, currently at Madame Yvendel's Academy of Applied Castings, is to be delivered into my custody. A young woman named either Velander or Ninth is to be captured and brought to me from Vindic, as is a certain Metrologan priestess named Terikel to be fetched from Scalticar."

"A Metrologan survived?"

"Oh yes. In addition, I want certain devices fetched, buildings raised, and sorcerers collected. This racing shell is to be taken back to Diomeda, with me, on your flagship, and I am to be tended by three different girls, every night, all the way back to Diomeda. You will speed ahead in a dash galley, and prepare a fitting welcome for me from the entire city. Is all of that clear?"

"It is."

"One more thing. You are to refer to me as 'master' at all times. Spread the word that you have always been working in my name, and that I have finally chosen to reveal myself."

Thirty feet away, Roval heard the hiss of Warsovran's breath. Warsovran thought and assessed quickly, however, and it was clear that he had no option but to capitulate—for now.

"I agree—master."

"Have your personal barge brought here, and take me out to your flagship—with my racing shell in tow. I wish to be aboard as it rams the Sargolan galley *Waverider*. Make sure there are no survivors."

"I shall see to it personally, master."

"After that, I am to be provided with silk robes and your best food and drink. I am to be waited on by women only. No men or eunuchs. Anything without tits that approaches me with a tray or a goblet will be flung to the sharks."

"Yes, master."

Leaving Feran standing on the beach with Silverdeath, Warsovran strode up to where Roval was still standing with his back to them, now and then waving the ax at the distant onlookers.

"You, clay-face. Give back my ax."

Roval turned, and in the very instant before handing the ax back realized that the emperor had spoken in Diomedan. Roval thought very, very quickly.

"I do not understand," he said respectfully.

"Ax! Give it here!" Warsovran demanded, now in Vidarian.

Roval bowed and presented the ax to Warsovran on the palms of both hands, handle first. Warsovran pointed to Port Wayside.

"Now go."

Roval bowed again, then backed away to one side as
Warsovran brushed past him, shouting orders to his people in
Diomedan. When Warsovran reached the governor of the island
he did not shout, however.

"Nobody is to leave the island, except on my order," he said
softly and quickly. "I shall also send my galleys out to secure
all the ships that are within sight as well, and they are not to be
released until my order. Every islander and marine is to be interrogated about what they saw between noon yesterday and
this present moment. Everyone from every ship, from the shipmasters down to the cabin boys, are to be questioned also.
There will be an absolute blockade of the island. No ships or
autons may leave until after I give a release. All ships that arrive
are to be impounded. At first light tomorrow, I want the marines
to go over every square foot of Helion South for any clue of
how that clown reached Silverdeath while the island was still so
hot. Do you understand all that?"

"Yes, Your Majesty."

"Uh-uh—just 'Commander' for now, if you enjoy being
whole and alive."

As soon as he was sure that he was being totally ignored,
Roval began trudging slowly up the slope to where the rest of
the *Shadowmoon*'s company was waiting beside their vantage
rock.

"We have a problem that will challenge your capacity for be-
lief," he announced as he reached them.

Einsel had arranged a series of experiments to study the fire-
circle from the beach of North Helion. Some were etheric, involving recording oculars and trigger autons, others were from
the cold sciences. These were tissues and cloths of varying colors and thicknesses, open vials of liquids, spring-mounted wind
vanes, and such-like. Two marines stood guard nearby. The sorcerer glanced about and noticed an islander sitting on a rock
and drinking from a jar of wine as he looked across at the deso-
lation that was Helion South. The rock that was his seat had
been selected with great care, and many weeks earlier.

"Guards, I need help!" called Einsel. "Fetch that layabout over there, the one on the rock."

The guards brought the islander over. His face was coated with clay and oil. They then retreated to their former position, lest they be told to help with Einsel's work as well.

"I have some alarming news, Learned Roval," Einsel began.

"I already know it all," replied Roval. "I was the one with the ax who stood by while Warsovran and Feran spoke."

"My, but you find your way around with great facility, heh-heh. What went wrong? Our best estimate was that nobody could have walked on Helion South until at least twelve hours had passed."

"I know, but there are always lateral schemes. I had prepared a means to snatch Silverdeath just after sunset, the method was Learned Wensomer's—but none of that matters anymore. Will you be going ahead to Diomeda with Warsovran?"

"Yes, right after he returns from sinking the Sargolan galley that Feran arrived on."

"He is leading the attack in person?"

"Yes."

"I see. Learned Einsel, I suspect that your master will return with Feran's secret. If you also learn how he did it, make sure that Learned Wensomer hears of the method as soon as you return to Diomeda."

✦ ✦ ✦

The *Kygar* smashed deep into the *Waverider*'s side amid a barrage of arrows and fire-pots from the ballistas. The boarding ramp swung down and its spikes bit deep into the *Waverider*'s deck, locking the two ships together. Warsovran was among the first to storm onto the Sargolan galley, flanked by three of his personal guard. They fought their way aft, to the doors beneath the quarterdeck.

"Arthen, Tionel, guard the door!" said Warsovran as he kicked through the paneling. "Gratz, come with me."

They killed two sailors before bursting into the master cabin, where the navigator was burning the charts and scrolls. He backed toward the shuttered window through the smoke, keeping the flames between Warsovran and himself.

"You! Did you see Feran Woodbar's secret device?" Warsovran demanded in Diomedan.

"I— Yes," replied the terrified and desperate navigator. "What is this?"

"Do you want to live?"

"I am loyal to Duke Fujillios of Sargol," the navigator said firmly.

"I don't give a damn about your duke!" snarled Warsovran. "Will you describe the device to me in return for your life?"

Hope suddenly relaxed the man's features.

"Only if I do not betray my duke and emperor."

He stopped as Warsovran whirled and buried his ax in the throat of his own marine.

"Get into his armor and helmet, then dump the body through the window and come with me," said Warsovran, glancing back out through the door and along the narrow corridor. "Once we're on deck, keep your mouth shut and stay beside me."

As long as nobody tried to leave Helion, the locals had complete freedom of the north island, and nobody was particularly interested in visiting the south island. The *Shadowmoon*'s company spent the rest of the day scavenging driftwood on the beaches, and even traded their gleanings for two jars of wine and half a dozen smoked fish. They watched as the flagship and its escort squadron sailed west, and two hours later the sun set. Miral was high in the sky, and still climbing.

"It will be a long wait until Miral is down and we can swim out," said Terikel.

"No, it's not worth the wait," said Norrieav. "Miral down is only two hours before dawn. We would still be bailing at first light."

"And the *Shadowmoon* could be caught by a bathtub rowed by snails," said Hazlok.

"Drunk snails," added D'Atro.

"Is this leading anywhere?" asked Terikel.

"There will not be any sharks within a hundred miles of here after what happened this morning," said Roval. "In half an hour we can swim out past the patrol galleys to the *Shadowmoon* using breathing tubes."

"The *Shadowmoon* will be visible by Miral's light once it is on the surface," warned D'Atro.

"Perhaps we should take the chance," said Terikel.

Off to one side, at the marines' garrison, something flashed brightly and a speck of orange light rose into the darkening sky on flickering wings meshed in ether. As they watched, it curved upward, banked, then plunged at a steep angle. Suddenly there was a starburst of sparks and burning fragments.

"Raptor auton," commented Roval. "Someone tried to send a messenger auton west, and Warsovran's sorcerers were ready."

"Who?" asked Norrieav.

"There are other observers on Helion beside us," admitted Terikel.

"Who?" asked Roval.

"None of your business. All right, then, we shall definitely not wait. We swim out now, while they are watching the skies and searching the island."

By triangulating Miral against the beacon pyre, they reached the area where the *Shadowmoon* had been sunk. Tied to the schooner was buoyed netting, and a grapple towed by Roval soon snared it. All six swimmers dived for the vessel, and they presently had the weights released. The *Shadowmoon* rose to the surface.

"The current will take us west; leave the masts down," said Roval as they began to pump and bail.

"What? Are you mad?" Terikel demanded. "There's a fair wind."

"Just keep bailing," cried Roval.

"Worthy Elder!" called her deacon from the quarterdeck. "There's a galley turning for us."

Roval cursed, then began to bail all the harder.

"We must sink again!" said Norrieav.

"No! Drop the anchor stones."

"What? We're dead unless we sink. The galley will—"

"No. Keep bailing and pumping, and have everyone drink as much wine as possible. Terikel."

"Wine?" shouted Norrieav. "Why add a breach of the Navigation Act to espionage? We're already facing the death penalty."

"Terikel, open the sealed locker and put dry bedding in the master cabin," ordered Roval. "Then strip."

"Strip?" echoed Terikel, as did everyone else within hearing.

"Strip. You and I are about to simulate an exceedingly hasty affair."

When the galley *Seafire* reached the *Shadowmoon*, the schooner was anchored and with its masts tied down. As they approached, the galley's crew could hear the sound of singing. The galley drew alongside. Three crewmen lay sprawled on the maindeck, while another was throwing up over the side. A man who seemed to be a dark-skinned Acreman stirred, got to his feet, and waved a jar at the galleymaster.

"So where's this bloody fire-circle, then?" bawled the Acreman.

The galleymaster and his captain of marines stared at each other for a moment, then raised their eyes to the stars.

A boarding walkway was lowered to the *Shadowmoon*'s deck and a dozen marines hurried aboard. Moments later Roval and Terikel were dragged out of the master cabin. They were naked, and no more sober than the four crewmen. Presently the officer in charge of the boarding party returned to the galley and reported to the galleymaster.

"The schooner is the *Arrowflight*, sir. It has a cargo of lamp oil and olive oil, but was diverted by a merchant named Garretten to convey himself and a lady of, well, no particular virtue, to Helion to see the fire-circle. It cost him seven hundred and fifty Scalticarian . . . I couldn't quite catch the name of the currency, but anyway, he spent them to hire that pile of firewood and its crew—and I use the word loosely—to sail here."

"Have you told them that the fire-circle detonated this morning?"

"Yes sir. They refuse to believe it."

The galleymaster closed his eyes and took a deep breath.

"Take them in tow. They are to be kept at Port Wayside until word comes from Diomeda that all captive vessels are to be freed."

Aboard the renamed *Shadowmoon*, Roval was doing a casting while Terikel wrestled with a medium-sized fish. It had two extremely long fins.

"Are you sure this will work?" Terikel muttered with revulsion.

"No, but unless you can provide a fully grown hunting hawk for my carrier auton's host, then we have no choice. Now, hold it up."

The fish featured wide wing-fins and a lung sac that enabled it to fly for hours at a stretch. It needed to return to the water more often than that, to moisten its skin, but it could still match the speed of a seagull. Roval set the auton to swim west for three hours, then take to the air. He spread his hands, stretching the lattice of blue tendrils, then cast it over the fish. The tendrils covered its body and spread a faint glow over its wings. It ceased to struggle. Terikel dropped it into the water through the stern window of the master cabin.

"It should be out of sight by the time it is in the air," said Roval.

"What a relief," said Terikel, wiping her hands. "Now what?"

"Now you must cast another lure, we need to catch one more finwing."

✳ ✳ ✳

Warsovran's sorcerers were casting their hunter autons in a huge arc around his squadron, and one was lucky enough to sense Roval's first carrier as it flew unerringly for Diomeda. It dove. The finwing's auton sensed its approach, swerved, and escaped with a gash from the hunter's talons. The raptor auton pulled out of its dive and beat its wings as it climbed again. On its second approach the englamored hawk came in slower, its talons spread, but this time the finwing went into a steep dive. The hawk followed. The finwing pressed its wings against its body and dropped like a stone. The hawk dropped, too.

The autons that sorcerers cast to control animals were often amazingly complex, but they were quite deficient in both common sense and instinct. The hawk's auton assumed that anything in the air was either a bird or leatherwing. The idea that a fish might be able to fly as well was quite beyond it. The finwing hit the dark waves and vanished. The raptor auton pulled the hawk out of its dive and began to circle, confident that its prey could stay submerged for no longer than a few moments. The longer the carrier took to surface, the harder the hawk looked for a floating bird, cowering amid the waves. After ten minutes of swimming west, the finwing launched itself into the air again and flew off, this time staying low, near the wavetops. So intent was the auton hawk on its vigil, that it missed a second finwing passing high overhead, also flying west.

Warsovran had sent his own auton west, and it arrived in Diomeda a little ahead of Roval's. It also arrived half a day after the Alliance army had appeared on the desert horizon, to the east of the city. A detachment of cavalry had immediately left the main force and attacked the outskirts of Diomeda, causing every marine and militiaman who could hold a spear or fire an arrow to be rushed to the earthwork ramparts that passed for the city's walls. A short, savage battle had seen the intruders repelled, but there was still the matter of the main army. The commander of marines had every available fighter stationed on the ramparts to impress the enemy nobles, and the tactic had the desired effect. They stopped, made camp, and began planning the next attack with somewhat more care.

Admiral Forteron ordered four hunter autons into the air, to stop any messengers—friendly or otherwise—from entering the city. He then had a flying squad of dash galleys put out to patrol the approaches to the harbor and enforce a total blockade. All other warships were emptied, and their crews were rushed to the walls.

Aboard the dash galley *Watersprite*, the captured Sargolan navigator was in the only cabin, sketching the suit of leather he had seen Druskarl wearing during Feran's tests. In particular he was trying to recall details of the air-cooling jar that had been strapped to the suit's back. Warsovran and Einsel were on deck at the bow, away from the crew and rowers, and talking quietly about their new master.

"Feran Woodbar is as unstable as my former wife," muttered Warsovran, tapping his own head with a large scroll.

"Legally speaking, my lord, she is still your current wife," Einsel reminded him.

"Your are right, Einsel. Should I divorce her before I kill her? Now, that is an issue to ponder. For the present, however, Feran Woodbar is my problem. He is unstable, impulsive, and that is good. Goaded sufficiently, he could do something stupid."

"Then we had best treat him carefully."

"Oh no, we should make his life hell until he snaps."

"And sets off a fire-circle?" asked Einsel glumly.

"Yes, precisely, and after that . . . The Sargolan navigator has betrayed Woodbar's secret. He used a heavily insulated suit of armor with some sort of device to cool the air. Why, I could have the leather armor run up within a day of returning to Diomeda."

"But how to breathe? The cooling machine's secret is still just that."

"Hah! A large jar strapped to the back may hold just enough cool air for the trip."

"*May*. Large pottery jars are very heavy."

"And I am quite strong. We shall ply this Feran Woodbar with insults said to be from those in Dawnlight palace. Before long he shall turn Silverdeath loose upon the place. Then we shall kill him, and I shall be first to Silverdeath this time."

"My lord, he used a submersible boat. Suppose that he just slips away in that boat one night with Silverdeath, annihilates Dawnlight before we realize that he has even launched it, then gets it back again. Besides, there is an army on the way, to besiege Diomeda and return it to . . . Well, the former king is dead, but there is an heir. Suppose Woodbar decides that all Acrema hates him as much as those on Dawnlight, and he casts Silverdeath on land?"

"So? We can have a channel dug around it and filled with water in sixty four days."

"No, this is madness! Suppose the ground is rocky, or on a hillside? All Acrema, Vindic, Racital, North Scalticar, and even part of Torea would burn before the thing is stopped—and that is on the assumption the maps are accurate and the ice and snow in Scalticar and Lemtas are the same as water for stopping fire-circles."

"It is worth the gamble—"

"What? No!" Einsel protested.

"Keep your voice down and have faith in my calculations. We certainly shall be trying to provoke the little turd into casting Silverdeath. Where he does it, I don't care. Torea meant more to me than Acrema ever could. Besides, getting Silverdeath back is the key to immortality as well as infinite power. Einsel, Einsel, I know what a fearful man you are, but remember that you will be by my side, and safe. If Silverdeath gets out of control on the plains behind Diomeda, I shall build an underwater shelter in the harbor and endure the last of the fire-circles in there. Inverted and submerged ships' hulls will do it. Two thousand men, fifty Diomedan women for each of them, provisions and tools . . . Yes, I could build a new world. Perhaps it would even be the most sensible course."

When Warsovran went aft to check on the progress of the Sargolan's drawings, Einsel stayed at the bow, looking west. The sky was overcast and rain was threatening, but all he could see was fire.

High in the air and some miles out to sea from Diomeda, the finwing that was Roval's carrier auton was beginning to descend. One of the patrolling raptors sensed it, assessed its speed and direction, then went into a long, curving dive. Roval's finwing was carrying gashes from the earlier attack, and was dying in the air as it approached Diomeda. It folded its wings and dived. The hawk followed. A second hunter broke off its patrol to fly cover. The finwing plunged into the sea, but this time it was daylight and the hawk could see the outline of the fish still making for Diomeda. Slowing almost to a stall, it followed. With a speed of over ninety miles per hour the second finwing smashed into the hawk, annihilating them both in a brilliant flash and a cloud of sparks and charred feathers.

The second hunter auton descended, aware the other had been killed, but not that whatever it had been hunting was a fish, capable of staying submerged for a long time and swimming long distances. It began to circle the charred remains of its dead companion, waiting for what it thought was the first carrier bird to surface again.

The first finwing surfaced in Diomeda's harbor, so far into the patrol boundary that the hunter autons were not aware of it. It was weak now, barely able to leap above the rainswept waves, and it was not until its third attempt that it was flying again. Trailing intestines, the auton beat its wings and struggled to gain height. It passed over the battle fleet, barely clearing the masts, flew over the muddy streets, took its bearings on several of the large villas, then registered its target in the distance. The effort to gain that last three dozen feet of altitude killed the finwing, but the auton held the wings rigid in a glide, selected an upper level tower window as a target, and banked slightly.

It smashed through thin cedarwood shutters and a rushweave curtain, landing on the bed where the naked Wensomer was enjoying a morning free of dance practice. Her shriek roused her entire household, and a good part of the neighborhood besides.

". . . and I would strongly advise you to make sure that Laron is packed onto the first neutral trader going south. Do it this very hour. Feran may decide to send his own autons ahead of the squadron. Good fortune be with you, my lady."

The speaker was a small, translucent orange image of Roval, standing between Wensomer's outstretched hands.

"Would you like to see it again?" Wensomer asked Yvendel.

"I heard it the first time," replied the rector Yvendel.

Wensomer brought her hands together, and the auton's energies dissolved into her skin.

"There is a lot to think about," she said.

"Starting with Laron. We must get him aboard a ship."

"A ship? The harbor has been blockaded."

"Oh. Yes. Well, if any ship tries to leave and gets sunk, we can have a forgery done to list Laron on the passenger board."

"And meantime, where will Laron really be, most devious Mother?"

"I hate to say it, but probably in your villa, and replacing that dead fish as your bedmate, most peculiar daughter."

Unfortunately, no ship's master was sufficiently obliging as to try to run the blockade. Laron and Wensomer had a late breakfast in the upper sunroom of her villa, except that the sun was hidden behind unseasonal cloud, and rain was again threatening. The matter of getting to a foreign state was discussed at length. Although the nearest border was a day's sailing down the coast, there was quite a large foreign presence camped about three miles west of the city ramparts, and that made travel difficult. On the other hand, there was a fortified palace technically under foreign control on an island in Diomeda's harbor.

"All you would have to do would be pay five gold pagols to Jarrem the Bald at the Tin Flute," suggested Wensomer.

"And then?"

"He will send you to Chok-Tas, the shipwright, in the riverside yards."

"And then?"

"You will buy a small, fast rowing corrak for thirty gold pagols."

"Thirty!"

"You will then climb aboard this corrak with a knife and a packroll containing your weight in stones."

"Stones?"

"You will then wait under the Royal Esplanade Bridge until Miral sets."

"And then row out to the island palace and deliver the stones to the crown prince with your compliments?"

"No, you will slice a small hole in the leather that covers the corrak's frame, slip overboard, and let the current carry it into the harbor. As it leaves the river mouth, the guards stationed there will fire arrows at it while it is within the range of torchlight. By the time they launch a pursuit gigboat, the corrak will have sunk."

"Leaving me cold, wet, up to my armpits in water, and thirty-five gold pagols poorer."

"Precisely. You will then cover yourself with mud, climb out of the river, and complain to the guards at the river mouth that you have been beaten, robbed, and thrown into the Leir. They will say, 'Piss off, horrid, smelly little boy,' or words to that effect. You will do just that, and return here. You will then be bathed and hidden within this villa, and when Feran arrives in Diomeda and Chok-Tas the shipwright is eventually betrayed by Jarrem the Bald, he will confess that he hired a corrak to you for five silvers, that you rowed away with an exceedingly heavy pack sometime after midnight, and that you never returned the corrak."

"Feran will conclude that I have taken refuge in the island palace."

"Yes."

"Feran will reduce the palace and its eight hundred defenders to ash with a single fire-circle."

"No."

"The palace is a quarter mile across and surrounded by water—it would be an easy and tempting target."

"Feran would lose all Silverdeath's protection the instant that he gave the order. Warsovran would then have Feran diced into pieces no larger than an apricot, and recover Silverdeath at his leisure. Feran is unlikely to relish that prospect, so I imagine that he will use Silverdeath to intimidate the besieging army into leaving, then order Warsovran to take the palace by direct assault. Warsovran will take about ten weeks to build the requisite number of floating catapults, and after that—"

"They crack the place open, discover I'm not there, and post a reward so large on the public boards, that even *you* will be tempted to convert me into a pile of gold pagols."

"Laron, Laron, much of life is merely surviving for a day or two longer in the face of starvation, disease, war, or boring relatives dropping in unannounced for lunch. Trust that something will turn up. Trust me, Laron: Something *will* turn up."

"In the meantime, the auton girl is also walking about in the body of the late Velander, and Feran has some less-than-wholesome designs on that body, regardless of who is at the reins. Ninth *must* be brought here and kept hidden."

"Ninth? The auton girl? *Here?* Not likely!"

"Why not?"

"As soon as the sun is down and Miral is up, you will take her straight out onto the roof and give her one. I saw you at the Academy with that, that . . . woman!"

"Lavenci."

"Ninth can stay at Madame Sairet's."

"Madame Sairet takes her out to the markets, where she can be seen. If we asked that she be hidden, Sairet would become suspicious."

"Laron, you just want to get her in here and do what you ought to be doing with me."

"Not so."

"I have everything she has. It's just lower, wider, and weighs more."

Laron took the scarf from his head and tapped something invisible. The circlet and violet sphere materialized on his head.

"Do you have one of these?"

The Toreans had been the masters of oracle-sphere sorcery, but most of the mechanisms, texts, and people essential to its understanding had perished with the continent. Wensomer was seriously tempted. The device that Ninth wore was of incalculable worth, in terms of both gold and scholarship.

"I believe we can arrange that Ninth never returns from her next trip to the market. Freelance slavers, you know. One never knows where they will strike next."

"Admiral Forteron banned slavery—"

"*Illegal* freelance slavers, one never knows where they will strike next. Sairet will be upset, but I'll console her."

"Why not spread a rumor that she has fled with me to the island palace? That will give Feran even less incentive to have Diomeda searched."

Wensomer stroked her chin for a moment. "I'll do it, but only if you promise to sleep in separate rooms and not to—"

"Wensomer! Velander's body may be twenty years old, but Ninth's soul has existed for only a few months! She's an auton, she has no interest in sex—and as far as I am concerned, she is my baby sister."

Wensomer nodded to herself, then reached her decision. She

stood up and began to pace, her arms folded behind her back. Laron watched, his chin on his clasped hands.

"Laron, against my better judgment, I agree. By tonight Ninth will be locked in one of the villa's towers, safely tucked into a *single* bed. Meantime, you will be standing in the mud beneath the Royal Esplanade Bridge."

What Laron had not told Wensomer was that he had been conducting brief conversations with a very, very different part of the auton girl whenever he could find a strong guard auton or etheric field to drain, or when a thunderstorm was in progress. *Should I tell her, or let her find out for herself?* he wondered. It would be very, very satisfying to demonstrate superior scholarship in front of Wensomer.

It was not the season for either storms or rain, but then, neither of Diomeda's seasons featured much rain. The warm season saw no rain at all, and the hot season brought a hurricane every so often, but otherwise all of the port city's fresh water came from the Leir. Or *by* the river. Citizens who felt nervous about what was being dumped, dropped, poured, or peed into the Leir River by the kingdoms upstream were inclined to import barrels of meltwater from the snows of the inland mountains. The market gardens, date palm and fig orchards, vineyards, and horse troughs were all supplied by riverwater, however, and even the silt that was used to grow vegetables and make mudbricks came from the river.

The river was rising. Normally it rose five feet every year when heavy rains fell on the inland mountains, and the flood plain around Diomeda was underwater for a few weeks. Now the river was already two feet above the normal level, and most people suspected the clouds that were raining on Diomeda were also dumping a large amount of unseasonal rain in the mountains. The citizens shivered in the tepid air of what should have been the hot season, and they made daily trips to inspect the depth markers in the river. Apart from the more exclusive villas, mansions, and palaces—which were built on hills—the entire city was on ground that was precisely one foot above the high-water mark of the annual floods.

Wensomer looked out over the river from the larger of her villa's two towers. Ninth sat behind her. The river not only was rising, it was changing color to a rich, muddy red. Wensomer turned back to Ninth, who sat with her hands in her lap. Unless ordered to do anything, she did nothing.

"Take off your scarf, if you please," ordered Wensomer.

Ninth obeyed. Laron had left the circlet configured to be visible. On her forehead was a violet sphere held in a silvery metal circlet, whose edges blended somehow into the skin of her forehead, and which vanished back into her hair.

Laron was on the roof, in the rain, assembling a complex mechanism of crystals, metallic spirals, sea-dragon ivory, carved greenstone, and pure copper bars. Bats enmeshed by autons trailed wires high into the sky. Presently he entered, dripping wet.

"I seem to be tapping etheric energy down out of the clouds without inducing a lightning strike," he announced.

"I'm relieved to hear it," replied Wensomer.

"That cushion is now right at the focus of the etheric crystal inducers on the roof. Ninth, sit down upon it, if you please?"

Ninth stood, walked to the cushion, and sat down. She wriggled uneasily, as if an ant had found its way under her robes.

"You know that I am your new patroness, don't you?" asked Wensomer.

"Yes, ladyship."

"I have decided to make you my personal servant."

"Yes, ladyship."

"Would you like that?"

"Yes, ladyship."

"Have you ever been to bed with a man?"

"No, ladyship."

Interesting, thought Wensomer. *No memories of when the succubus controlled the body. Not so much a clean slate, as nobody to hold the chalk.*

"What are you, Ninth?"

"An auton, ladyship."

Wensomer continued to wait. Ninth remained Ninth. Laron ran about frantically, making adjustments. Wensomer sat back in a chair and began drumming her fingers on the armrest.

Velander cowered as the thing loomed over her. It had elements of cold, sharp hunger about it, and was quite powerful. *Almost a raptor elemental,* she thought, *but not quite.* It focused on her.

"You are very faint, but quite complex," it observed, without showing any hostility.

"I was once alive," said Velander.

"Are you saying you are a ghost?"

"I am dying, very slowly."

The thing circled the almost vanishingly faint axis, examining Velander.

"Can I help?" it asked presently.

The offer took Velander by surprise. *Help.* In a curious way the thing was already helping. Speaking with it was helping to focus what was left of her. It was like a huge, clumsy puppy, radiating etheric energy everywhere. Velander basked in the glow, like a cat lying in a sun-drenched garden.

"Just talk, be near," she said. "Your life force . . . reviving me."

The thing moved closer. An experienced darkwalker would not squander energies like this; most were so controlled that they were difficult to see.

"I am lost," the thing admitted. "My worldname is Elltee. I am a . . . scholar."

"I am Velander. I was once a priestess. Where are you from, what are you trying to find?"

"A sorcerer has been speaking with me. He tells me secrets, in return for secrets of the cold sciences from my world. I—I am afraid that I was experimenting with a new setting on my circlet when he called this time. Instead of focusing on the oracle sphere and body where I was being summoned, I found myself here."

"Elltee, please, stay with me. I shall tell you skills and secrets without asking for any in return. I have been alone for so long."

"Velander, I have no control of how long I can stay in this place, but tell me how to help while I am with you. I shall do all that I can."

✷ ✷ ✷

Wensomer had eaten two small pastries, drunk half a jar of wine, read part of a book on seduction castings, then fallen asleep before Laron finally cried out in triumph and dashed back into the room.

"The little wretch must have been fiddling with her circlet's settings!" he announced as Wensomer shook her head and sat up. "I have had contact all along, it was just the focus that was missing."

He made an adjustment to Ninth's circlet. Abruptly she writhed in the grip of a spasm, falling back with her spine arched. Laron held Wensomer back, and moments later Ninth sat up. She looked around slowly, as if seeing the room for the first time.

"Elltee?" asked Laron.

"Laron! Sometimes I just can't believe this."

Wensomer instantly knew this was not Ninth. The thing radiated energy and self-confidence.

"Where were you?"

"In a dark place, full of sparkles and shadowy shapes. I was talking to a sort of fuzzy bubble on a glowing, orange string. She said she was a ghost."

"What? You were darkwalking?"

"Yes, that's what she said it was."

"Elltee, you should never talk to strange elementals. They can trick you, even kill you. It might have been a succubus, not a ghost."

"Oh no, she seemed much too nice for that. Bit of a <dork>, to be honest."

" 'Dork'?" said Laron, echoing the inconvertible word.

"*Dork*. I thought I was supposed to think and speak in the language of my host."

"Not if the word does not exist."

"A dork is an overfocused scholar or natural philosopher with limited social skills. They tend to take themselves a bit seriously—"

"Not now!" snapped Laron. "I need to ask you some important questions."

"Whatever you like."

"*Dork*," said Wensomer, savoring the work like a pleasant sweet. "That describes a disturbingly large number of sorcerers."

"Who is your lady friend?" asked Elltee, turning from Laron.

" 'Lady friend' is putting it a bit strongly, but her name is Wensomer. It's actually she who wants to ask the questions."

He looked to Wensomer and shrugged.

"Where were you born?" Wensomer asked.

"The Royal <Memorial Hospital> in <November 1988>."

Several words were inconvertible, obviously from a culture, language, place, time, and world that had little in common with hers.

"How old are you?" Wensomer asked.

"Eleven," she replied, then added, "years."

"What are the most advanced etheric machines where you were born?"

"There are no ether machines there. We use a type of ether called <electricity>, though."

Wensomer shook her head, fighting to conceal her astonishment. On the other hand, she was learning nothing that a clever trickster could not have devised.

"Then what are some of your advanced machines?"

"<Space> shuttles, <robots>, <supercomputers>, the <Internet>, <lasers>, <nuclear bombs>, <comms satellites>, <cell phones>, <auto->tellers—"

"All right, that's enough!" Wensomer called.

Hardly a word had been intelligible. *A* something *shuttle. Did that mean they had very advanced weaving?* Wensomer wondered. And a *something* teller. *That might be a machine to tell stories to children while parents were out gathering the harvest. Teller.* Perhaps it was a machine to speak castings—and possibly to store ether. *Now, that would indeed be an advanced machine. But she said they had no ether machines there. There* were too many words that made no sense. The elemental could be of immense value, yet she was like a book of advanced castings in a dead language—with no pictures or diagrams. Long and careful study of her was clearly needed.

Wensomer came to a decision. "What are your last memories of the world you were born into?" she asked.

"I was doing my <homework> on my <laptop> using the <Internet>."

"And how long ago was that?"

"Just now, before I found myself in the etherworld with the ghost."

Wensomer's jaw dropped. She quickly closed her mouth, swallowed, and blinked. This had no precedent in the world's history. The oracle spheres could enclose the essence and memories of a soul from the moment of imaging, but never thereafter. This girl was not just an image, she was an image linked to a live creature. A thought came to Wensomer.

"Elltee, how many moonworlds circle the lordworld of your world?"

"None."

"What?"

"None."

"Ah, how many suns circle your world?"

"None."

Wensomer put a hand to her forehead. This was either the greatest hoax in history, or she was so far out of her depth that—

"How many moonworlds in your world's sky?"

"One."

Wensomer's shoulders sagged with relief.

"And does it provide all light and heat?"

"No, the sun does that."

"But you said there was no sun."

"I said no sun circles my world. My world circles a sun."

A world with a huge sun at an immense distance. Wensomer now wondered if Laron was playing some monstrous hoax on her. If not . . . Wensomer suddenly went over to a writing desk and began to scribble on reedpaper.

"Fantastic," she said to herself. "Instead of a sun circling Miral, the girl's world circles a sun."

Laron forced down the smile of triumph that was trying to curl his lips upward.

"No, Miral circles a sun, too."

Wensomer opened her mouth to say *Heresy*, but caught herself.

"How do you know that, if your world's skies are so different?"

"There are four of what you call lordworlds in our skies. <Jupiter>, <Saturn>, <Uranus>, and <Neptune>. <Jupiter> has four large moonworlds and a lot of smaller ones. <Saturn> has rings like Miral's. All those lordworlds circle our sun at a great distance and are very cold. Our world circles closer in, like Miral, and is warm enough for life."

Barely comprehending, Wensomer wrote it all down. This day, the universe had changed. Outside, there were people worrying about a rising river and a besieging army, yet in this tower the very order of the skies was being juggled. She was talking to something with the knowledge of a god. What did one ask a god?

"What is ether, what is the source of our magic?"

"Miral is known to our sciences as a <gas giant planet> with huge <magnetic fields> and <radiation belts> but it circles within the sun's <habitation zone>, allowing your world to ability to support a <greenhouse effect>. Your world circles Miral within its <radiation belts> and the tremendous energies stored there, so life on your <planet> has come to depend on them. If my real body were sent to your world, I would probably die within minutes from <radiation> poisoning."

"Would I die on your world?" asked Wensomer, gleaning a fragment of meaning from the last sentence.

"I think so. You probably need ether as much as food, water, and air. There is not much on my world."

All the important words were unintelligible to Wensomer. She sighed and laid down her quill. Suddenly Elltee cried out.

"<Laron, everything is starting to flicker and break up>," she began, then she collapsed again but this time she went totally limp.

From the roof came a loud crackling, followed by a sharp blast. Laron hurried away to investigate, and the acrid smell of something burning wafted down to Wensomer. Ninth shook her head and sat up.

"Ladyship? Should I wait upon you?"

"I—I feel a little faint; I must rest now," said Wensomer. "Go and find my steward, have him put you in the lower tower."

She left. Wensomer contemplated her notes, scribbled a few figures on a slate, consulted several texts, did some calculations on an abacus frame, then stared in disbelief and rubbed her eyes when she saw the result. Presently Laron came down again, carrying his sodden, blackened apparatus.

"The amberstone etheric insulators burned out and shattered," he reported. "That disrupted all my castings and the autons collapsed, letting the bats escape. Luckily, nothing I borrowed from the Academy was damaged too badly, except for the amber."

"Does Mother know you borrowed all that from her Academy?"

"Er, no, and getting it back is going to be hard."

"Oh no, let me do it. It's *my* turn to see *her* furious. Laron, do you have any idea how much etheric energy is needed to keep a link open to another moonworld's creature?"

"By the tone of your voice, quite a lot," the youth replied.

"The figure is truly immense. The Toreans also used to drain power down out of thunderstorms to achieve it; in fact, that is why their Concentricaren Arena was sited in an area notorious for thunderstorms. *This* is different, however. Ninth is linked to something that is not from the moonworlds." Wensomer pointed through the window and up into the night sky, out of which the rain was still pouring. "I say she is linked to the stars."

"So, you now believe me? Elltee and I are from the same world."

"Laron, I don't believe *that*! She is from some glittering paradise of scholarship and power. *You* were from a society on a level barely above the hairy-arsed, illiterate pig molesters of Bantriok Island."

"Now, just a moment—"

"Unless, of course, your world changed fantastically over the past seven centuries. I know systematic knowledge when I hear it, even if I cannot grasp all the concepts. So, there is a link between Ninth's oracle sphere and one in another world, a world so distant that we do not even have names for the immense figures needed to describe the number of miles involved. One thing I do know is that if Silverdeath were to be put onto her, her oracle sphere would soak up etheric energy on a scale not seen since Torea burned. Remember what those who witnessed the fire-circle castings reported? Silverdeath said, 'This is at the limit of my powers,' or words to that effect. Put it onto Ninth, and I would bet my seat on the High Circle that it will fade and vanish."

"'Fade and vanish'?" Laron scoffed. "The thing survived heat that melted a continent and you say that *Ninth*, an auton girl, can destroy it?"

"Not destroy it, jam it. Silverdeath does not quite exist, Laron. It is just energy and organization, fashioned by ancient etheric sorcerers who obviously went to a far better academy than I did. Jamming Silverdeath would be like scratching a channel at the top if an immense earthwork dam. Water would begin to trickle out, washing away a little earth in the process, and widening the channel. Come back in a day or two and you would find no lake and no dam."

"This sounds too easy, too convenient," said Laron, who was suspicious of any solution to anything that did not involve a lot of suffering.

"I think not. Warsovran had a vendetta against the Metrologans. The story put about was that they were plotting something involving the empress, but . . . well, after hearing what your elemental just said, I think it was because they were experimenting with a way to destroy Silverdeath with the very sphere Ninth is wearing. Silverdeath killed Torea, Laron. We must help the ghosts of Torea's finest sorcerers reach out from the grave and strike it down in turn."

Chapter Nine

VOYAGE
TO THE ABYSS

 Warsovran's dash galley reached Diomeda two days
before his flagship was due to arrive with Feran. He
made only a brief announcement, to the effect that
Silverdeath had a new master, and that none could
stand against it, but that Silverdeath was still their ally.

"By the use of cunning devices he got to Silverdeath before
the ground had cooled to below lead's melting point,"
Warsovran told Admiral Forteron. "These are the devices."

Forteron studied the drawings of the heat armor and racing
shell. The boat had no real secrets, it was just the idea that had
been refined to extremes. The heat armor was a different matter.
A medium-sized pottery jar was strapped on like a wayfarer's
backpack, with a tube leading to the face mask. Its purpose was
obviously to cool the air before it was breathed, but there were
no details at all of the internal workings.

"It is hard to believe that a mere youth could be so skilled in
the cold sciences," Forteron concluded.

"He is not a youth. He once wore Silverdeath, and before that
he was a sorcerer over eight decades old. Nare'f As-bar was his
name. Nare of the Academy of As-bar, which is Scalticarian—
although he claims to be Diomedan, so who knows?"

"What is he like as a master?"

"About as flaky as a bowl of wheat bran. Watch your actions
and tongue when near him. Give him the deference you would
afford me."

"Do you have a plan, my lord?"

"Oh yes. He is clever and resourceful, but ill tempered and
excitable, too. I can use that, and I can win back Silverdeath.

Meantime, round up a couple dozen skilled artisans and have them build these."

"The breathing jar is lacking in detail."

"Tell the artisans that a pit floored with glowing coals is being prepared. Tell them that each of them will be forced to walk in circles around the aforesaid pit until one of them is still alive at the end of a half hour. The first test will be in two days. Einsel will be in charge of matters technical; he is currently outside with the Sargolan navigator. Give him whatever he needs."

Rain continued to fall as Forteron and Einsel set about gathering the craftsmen together. It was persistent rain. It rendered the city muggy and uncomfortable, and the humidity made people's clothing stick to their skin. By noon a warehouse had been cleared and put under guard, and the first felt and leather was being cut. As the overcast afternoon began to fade into overcast evening, an artisan of Warsovran's height and build was walking about in a basic prototype suit of felt and leather while his colleagues labored over a helmet. At midnight he was able to stand beneath a scaffolding while marines emptied vats of boiling oil over him for a full minute, then he walked across a bed of glowing coals. Having accomplished all this, he collapsed.

The following morning Forteron called in to check on progress. Einsel had not slept at all, neither had any of the artisans.

"The iron-shod clogs work, as does the insulation of felt and leather," Einsel reported. "A plate of quartz crystal provides vision and is kept clear of moisture on the inside by two leather levers wired to lead weights. Sway from side to side and they wipe the plate clean. The hands work two pairs of blacksmith's tongs with felt wrapped around the handles. They serve as walking sticks as well as allowing Silverdeath to be picked up."

"Very, very impressive," said Forteron as he watched a marine striding back and forth on the bed of coals.

"There is only one problem," said Einsel. "The wearer has

only what air is sealed inside the helmet with him. After three minutes . . ."

The marine testing the suit collapsed, falling face-first into the coals. He was dragged clear with long barhooks.

"But you have written here that the suit has withstood a full quarter hour of walking on coals while flamethrowers roasted it with burning lamp oil."

"Yes, but all the while, cool air was being pumped down a long copper pipe using a blacksmith's bellows."

"Hardly practical for the aftermath of a fire-circle."

"True, but in two days we shall at least have a suit that can withstand the heat for a half hour."

"That will be of little comfort to the artisan balloted to try it out in the burning pit for that half hour."

"Well, I have had an idea for that, a brilliantly simple idea. Look at this."

The drawing Einsel placed before Forteron seemed better suited to a grotesquely deformed hunchback with an immense beer belly.

"Ah, I don't know this man."

"No, no, those are just cavities, nothing more than air enclosed by leather, tin, and felt. I have had one marine's head enclosed in a sailcloth sack of the same volume, and I was able to walk him around the floor for over three-quarters of an hour, according to the sandglass. In a pinch, we can use this for the half-hour test tomorrow; I am having the lads of the current shift make one up."

"I have a message from Warsovran about that. The test will be tomorrow morning, an hour before dawn."

Einsel's features sagged with dismay. "So soon?"

"Emperor Feran is expected to arrive not long after sunrise, according to the latest carrier auton from the flagship. Warsovran's movements may not be as free from surveillance as he would like after that. I think this will work. Have three suits made according to this design. One for your tests, one for tomorrow morning, and one to be hidden in the palace for Warsovran's use."

Einsel sat back with the sketch in his hand and sighed. "Heh-

heh, it is superlatively ugly," he said. "The mighty Warsovran, a beer-guzzling hunchback."

"On the contrary, Einsel, it is a most superlatively elegant design, far better than Woodbar's complex air-cooling device. As an engineer, you are the peer of the best ever to come out of Larmentel."

"Larmentel?" exclaimed Einsel, glowing with pride at the unexpected compliment. "Admiral, do you really mean that?"

"I may not be an engineer, Learned Einsel, but I have hired, dismissed, bought and sold thousands of them. I know quality."

"I wanted to become an engineer when I was a youth, but when my etheric potentials were discovered I was sent straight off to a master of applied castings."

"Perhaps 'engineer' will be carved on your gravestone. That is the one place where it really matters."

Forteron stood up to go, but Einsel hurriedly seized his arm before he could walk away. The sorcerer glanced around hurriedly, checking once again that nobody else was within earshot.

"Admiral, there are things I must tell you, things that could get my height reduced by exactly this amount," he said, tapping at his head.

Forteron regarded him steadily, his hands on his hips. "As your friend, Learned Einsel, I must warn you that I am also loyal to my monarch. Given the situation with our current head of state, however, I promise to listen and be discreet."

"It is not Woodbar, it is Warsovran himself. His plan is to goad Emperor Feran into annihilating Dawnlight, then seize Silverdeath, using the suit of heat armor that we are supposed to develop."

"So? A committee of village idiots chaired by Admiral Griffa could have told us that."

"But Warsovran intends to use it again, on the army currently outside Diomeda's walls and ramparts."

"Never! It would grow to melt Acrema within ten dozen days, and possibly the world. Warsovran is no fool. Besides, when the army sees Dawnlight roasted, they will pack up and leave within a week."

"He may not be a fool, but he certainly is a brilliant madman! He wants to detonate another fire-circle on the army as it camps on the flood plain, then divert water from the Leir to inundate the place before the second fire-circle happens, sixty-four days later."

"Apparently the plain only floods to a yard or so's depth. Will that be enough?"

"We don't know!" Einsel shouted, with his fists clenched, then he sheepishly looked around and waved the staring marines and artisans back to their work. "Look, Warsovran must be removed—I mean separated—from Silverdeath."

"You really mean killed."

"Neutralized."

"Killed."

"Rendered ineffectual."

"Killed."

" 'Killed' is such an extreme word," sighed Einsel.

"His inner guard of initiates, ethersmiths, and marines is almost as good a protection as Silverdeath itself, Einsel. Besides, I'm not sure that I want to be a party to all this. Even if I did agree, Admiral Griffa is in charge of his security. The man may be a blockhead, but he's a thorough and meticulous blockhead."

"You could have your own guards turn on Warsovran's, leaving him exposed."

"No, I could not. My guards are as loyal as I am, but it is loyalty to the monarch. I have no idea what their personal loyalty to me would be, because my own loyalty has never been in question. I could easily be helping the palace headsman provide some more free public entertainment to the citizens of Diomeda within a single hour of trying to recruit my own men as assassins."

"Then you will not help?" asked Einsel, rubbing his hands anxiously.

"*Can*not."

Forteron wanted to be out of the place and away from all of its moral dilemmas, but a sense of duty kept him there. Not duty to Warsovran, or even to Feran, but to the people under his command. Both the other men saw the marines and sailors as mere rough tools, just a means to power, but to Forteron they were as precious as a set of sharp and finely wrought chisels. The admiral wanted them to be used to carve and maintain something as beautiful, useful, and enduring as a fully armed deepwater trader. Would Warsovran ruin them just to cut up firewood?

"If the fire-circles did get out of control, how would Warsovran survive?" Forteron asked.

"Oh, he intends to have a few ships' hulls inverted and weighted down within the harbor. Food, drinking water, sheep, chickens, seed grain, and tools would be aboard, along with a couple of thousand men."

"Two thousand? If converted thus, the fleet could hold all the Toreans under my command."

"Warsovran intends that fifty women also be included for every man, heh-heh. He intends to rebuild a sizable empire under the cold, ash-laden skies of our ruined world."

Warsovran had always taught his commanders to think as he would, and now that worked against him. Forteron could easily imagine Warsovran following exactly such a plan, and burning alive nine out of every ten surviving Torean marines in the process.

"Einsel, I cannot help you," the admiral concluded nevertheless.

Einsel closed his eyes and swayed, his face contorted with real pain.

"Will you at least not repeat—"

"I have not finished. What I *shall* promise is to recover Silverdeath, should you somehow manage to persuade Emperor Feran to cast it as a fire-circle. In that, I certainly shall go against Warsovran—and I promise never to use Silverdeath."

Einsel beamed with relief and gratitude, and he bowed repeatedly to Forteron while rubbing his hands together. "My good and valiant Admiral, you may not have to endure the temptation for long. Certain sorcereric associates of mine may have a method of jamming Silverdeath's internal mechanisms until its energy is totally drained and it fails completely. It may result in a small explosion, but nothing catastrophic."

"How small is 'small'?"

"Watch it from no closer than a mile."

"You call that small?"

"Should you have the fortune to acquire Silverdeath, you will be contacted. One more thing, however."

"Yes?"

"Seize power. Become king of Diomeda. We need a wise ruler after these two fools."

"Easier said than done. Nobody is loyal to Woodbar, so he will be doomed from the moment he casts his next fire-circle. Warsovran is a different matter. Most of the fleet worships him."

"They don't know what we know."

"Precisely. If you can arrange for his life to be ended, however, I shall seize power and you will be appointed court engineer from the moment of his death."

The two days' notice for Feran's arrival had imposed a tight schedule on the officials of Diomeda, but on the other hand, large, cheering crowds, an honor guard of ships, massed ranks of marines and militiamen, a couple of dozen dancing girls, and a really impressive feast were all that were really required. Most of the aforementioned merely required the right people to be in the right place in the right clothing at the right time, so by the time the flagship was sighted through the early-morning rain, everybody was more or less in place.

Einsel stopped at Hass Harber Ballistics on the way to the docks, and went straight to a rack of crossbows. Nodding to the proprietor, he selected one of the smaller specimens on offer and took it down with a quite unsteady hand.

"Business prospering, heh-heh?" Einsel asked in a voice even less steady than his hands, as he fished a bolt from his robes.

"Oh, never better. It's the war, ye know."

Einsel laid the bolt on the groove. It was an adequate fit.

"I shall have this one, if you please," he said to Harber.

"I'se never seen nobody buy a crossbow fer a bolt."

"It's a family heirloom. It is all that I managed to bring with me from Torea."

"It's a heavy head for such a small shaft. Kill anyone special?"

"My grandfather—that is, it missed him in, ah, an assassination—attempt, that is."

"Ah-ha, yeah, so it's lucky fer you, because it missed."

"Yes—ah, yes. It brings good luck. Just now I am in need of good luck. The entire world is, if it comes to that."

"So why d'yer want to shoot it?"

"So I can miss. How much?"

"Well, it cost me three pagols, but I've done a lot of improvements—"

"Ten pagols, and would you draw back the string, please?"

"Draw back the string? How long yer keepin' it like that?"

"An hour, perhaps two."

"What? It'll be ruined!"

"Well, then, you had better sell me a second string, heh-heh."

Einsel counted out the gold coins, then pressed a small bead of resin into the groove and stuck the bolt down lightly. Concealing it under his raincloak, he then swept the cloak aside and raised the crossbow for a fast shot.

"Oi, I'd use me other hand ter steady it, I were you," said the proprietor.

"Ah, er, thank you."

Einsel tried again, and then a third time. They agreed that with both hands the little crossbow had a far better feel.

"So, yer gonna shoot at close range? Maybe ten feet?"

"How can you tell?"

"Yer aimin' flat."

"Ah, yes. Yes."

"I notice these things." Harber's eyes narrowed. "Yer not gonna do somethin' stupid with that thing, are ye?"

"No, no. Of course not. In fact, I'm going to do the most sensible thing of my entire life, heh-heh."

"Ah, well, that's all right, then."

There very few things quite so dangerous as a very timid person who is also seriously fearful. Einsel was just such a person, yet he was also very strong willed in his own way. He was determined that Warsovran had to die. Einsel was high in etheric rating, but Warsovran had initiates with even higher ratings than the court sorcerer, and these were guarding him, along with his other personal guards. A casting, an ax, a crossbow bolt—all of these could be stopped. A shot from a battle galley's ballista could well get past Warsovran's guards, but ballistas were fifteen feet long, ten feet across, had a crew of four, and were bolted to the decks of battle galleys. As the weapon of choice for a lone assassin, they did not even get onto the list. There was, however, one far more dangerous weapon available to the little sorcerer. Fear for the world, fear for the future, fear that his thirty-one tracts on etheric fashioning and biographical entry in *Notable Sorcerers of the Placidian Rim* would never be read by anyone ever again, and finally, fear for the future of an illegitimate child whose upbringing he had paid for even though he had always strenuously denied that it was his.

A gigboat met the flagship as it entered the harbor, and those watching from the shore saw several bundles being hoisted aboard. The galley then proceeded to the pier and tied up. Everyone waited, in the rain. The new emperor did not appear. A herald appeared with a decree. The rain was to be ignored. All rain capes were to be removed from sight. Another quarter hour passed. Everyone had by now grown sodden.

Finally Feran strode down the gangway with Silverdeath behind him. Whatever the powers of the mighty etheric machine, it could not or would not stop the rain. Feran was wearing exceedingly impressive silk robes, a jewel-encrusted belt, an exquisitely ornamented Diomedan battle-ax, and black riding boots made from the skin of a giant leatherwing. Everyone bowed as they stood in the rain, and water cascaded to the pier from where it had been pooling in the folds of the robes of the many thousands of those who stood waiting.

"I do not see the vampyre Laron," declared Feran, his hands on his hips. "I ordered you to have him here, waiting for me as I left the ship."

"I regret to inform Your Majesty that the vampyre fled to the island palace a week ago," Warsovran replied without looking up.

"I want the vampyre, not excuses!" Feran shouted back.

Far across the harbor a new floating catapult had been loaded with a barrel, and was being prepared for a test shot. It was behind Dawnlight castle, and the rain shrouded it from the view of those ashore. The engineers aboard had very precise measurements of the harbor, however, and the barrel in its sling was a tenth of the weight of the standard rock that it was designed to fire. An enclosed galley was towing the catapult's barge, and it was well within the range of Dawnlight's own catapults. The defenders held off with their firepots, waiting for the best possible shot. The barge closed, then fired.

The barrel flew between two of Dawnlight's towers, arced through the air above one of the patrol galleys enforcing the blockade, then descended. Its target was the pier beside the flagship. Silverdeath detected the approaching missile, turned and sliced it open in midair with a bolt of etheric fire. After a millisecond-fast spectrographic analysis of its contents, Silverdeath concluded it was of no threat to its master, and turned back to the pier. Seconds later Feran and all the waiting dignitaries were splattered with a carefully homogenized mix of piss and turds.

Feran screamed with outrage.

"Silverdeath, who did that?" he shrieked as soon as he was capable of coherent speech.

"It originated at or near the island palace known as Dawnlight," came the flat, hollow reply.

"The swine, the filthy maggots! Silverdeath, de—" With a quite remarkable act of self-control, Feran reined back his temper. "Silverdeath, desist from any retaliation," he added, slowly and clearly.

Warsovran stepped forward, reining in his equally strong sense of disappointment.

"Your Exalted Majesty, a message was flagged from the former Diomedan prince and heir-pretender when your galley was entering the harbor," he announced. "It said, 'Shit on you and

your exceedingly small and deformed penis, from the anuses of
the Prince of All Diomeda and the Elder of All Metrologans.' "

The words, composed by Warsovran, were meant to be generally insulting. He had not realized the current Elder of All
Metrologans had once been in a position to assess the size and
quality of Feran's penis. Contorted by blind rage, Feran turned
to see what appeared to be two warships ablaze near the rain-
softened outline of Dawnlight. Other ships nearby were now
exchanging shots with the defenders, and burning oil dribbled
harmlessly down its high stone walls.

Feran had been pushed too far, and nobody knew that better
than Einsel. Within another moment Silverdeath would be
launched. Soon after that, the biggest remaining pieces of Feran
would fit comfortably into a medium-sized beer mug, and
Warsovran would be climbing into a set of heat-armor of Einsel's own engineering to retake Silverdeath.

The crossbow under Einsel's cloak was a small, hunting
type, the sort used to stun birds with padded bolts. He had
coated his own standard-issue, armor-piercing bolt with poison,
just to be sure. Although Einsel had used such crossbows at social hunts in the past, he was not a good shot.

Warsovran was standing flanked by Griffa and Forteron, although each admiral was about a yard apart from their commander. Einsel was standing behind Forteron as he offered up
the first prayer to pass his lips in two decades—it was to Fortune—took a deep breath, lost his nerve, squeezed his eyes
shut, deliberately blanked his mind, then made his move before
his resolve cracked again. Sweeping his rain cloak aside, he
raised the crossbow as he lunged across the gap between
Forteron and Warsovran and fired at Feran. A moment before
he fired, three of Warsovran's guards had landed crossbow bolts
in Einsel's back, spoiling his already doubtful aim even further.
He missed Silverdeath's master, but after traveling another two
hundred yards the bolt managed to strike a seagull dead in mid-
flight. However, his aim and intention had been more than
enough to draw the attention of Silverdeath.

There was a bright flash of pure whiteness from Silverdeath's eyes, and two beams of star-hot energy sought Einsel. In the process they also sliced diagonally through several

innocent bystanders. Warsovran, six marine guards standing behind him, and Admiral Griffa fell in a tangle of steaming limbs, blood, and internal organs. Einsel saw Warsovran's head burst as the beams cleaved through it and the superheated brains blew the skull apart. In the instant between Warsovran's death and Einsel's own demise, the little sorcerer thought not of his child, nor of saving the world. His years as Warsovran's principal sorcerer were forgotten, and thoughts of his thirty-one tracts on etheric fashioning and biographical entry in *Notable Sorcerers of the Placidian Region* did not even flash through his mind. As Silverdeath's beams sliced Einsel apart, the image before his dying eyes was of a statue in some Diomedan plaza with the words *Rax Einsel, First Engineer of the Diomedan Court.*

Silverdeath's beams winked off. The ship behind the pile of body parts on the pier snapped in two, and its rigging came crashing to the deck. It began to sink. For a full quarter minute, nobody who was still alive dared to move. Very few dared even to breathe.

"Take me to my palace," ordered Feran, wiping a gobbet of foul sludge from his face and favoring Dawnlight with a glare. "I shall deal with *them* presently."

Forteron began to give orders, and a dozen porters came running with a two-seater sedan chair. Feran and Silverdeath got in, and the procession to the temporary palace began.

"I can barely believe that the sorcerer was foolish enough to threaten the demon's master," muttered the Commander of Marines to Forteron as they stood watching the entourage move off. "The marines behind him, Silverdeath before him—what chance did he have?"

"Call him 'Emperor Feran' if you value your life," cautioned Forteron. "Silverdeath is his servant, and Silverdeath is invincible."

"So, he is our new lord? I do not like the look of him."

"Very astute of you. There is hope, however. His servant's repertoire of tricks is very limited."

"Ah. So what can we do?"

"Get a look inside that," replied Forteron, gesturing behind them, to where the racing shell was being carried by a dozen more marines.

Fortern looked across to where Einsel lay, sliced into three pieces. The little bird-hunting crossbow was still clutched in both hands. *Died fighting,* thought the admiral while holding the trace of a frown on his face. Then Einsel's words of the previous day returned to him: "Should you have the fortune to acquire Silverdeath, you will be contacted." *You,* not *we,* Einsel had known that he would have to die, and intended to die provoking Silverdeath while catching Warsovran in the crossfire. Forteron found himself moved at the thought of how very lonely and desperate the sorcerer must have felt.

Forteron went down on one knee and picked up Einsel's severed head. The red eyes were open and protruding, but the expression on his face was oddly serene.

"Alas, poor Einsel, we hardly knew you," said Forteron.

"Your pardon, Admiral?" said the Commander of Marines.

"Sort these remains out with care," replied Forteron. "When they are buried I want no confusion about what bits of whom are buried where." He stood up and handed Einsel's head to the commander. "Have profile and contour sketches of the white-haired man done within the hour, then bring them to me."

The patrol autons were called in as soon as the flagship docked. Within a half hour Wensomer launched an auton pigeon into the rain. It flew unmolested out to sea, heading due east for Helion.

Feran's demonstration of power did not go unnoticed by the Alliance spies in the crowd. By midafternoon an envoy and his retinue had arrived under a flag of truce, seeking an audience. Feran declared that he had come to take direct control of the military campaign that had been so badly bungled by his commander, Warsovran. The envoy returned to the Alliance army and reported the change in leadership. He also reported that Emperor Feran intended to hold a royal court that very night. The envoy was ordered to return, and to report on any decrees that might be issued.

The fact of an invasion from Torea was at the heart of the matter, even though the Sargolans also wanted their princess returned, but the fact the invaders had a weapon the size of a man that could slice ships in two was clearly a factor to take into account. Then there were the fire-circles that the other envoys and ambassadors kept talking about. They were deadly indeed, although several sorceric advisors insisted that Feran dared not use them on the mainland. The leaders of the Alliance conferred. The general feeling was that experimental verification of the theory of their sorceric advisors might come at a very, very high price. They decided to take the course most favored by all sensible military commanders: let someone else do the fighting.

All the while the Leir continued to rise. By evening it was four feet above the seasonal average, and the rain still fell steadily. Out in the harbor, on the palace island, someone with a whistle sent out a coded series of peeps. Moments later the crown prince's guards were out on the short stone jetty, escorting a swimmer who had two inflated piglet skins strapped to his upper arms, and who reeked of pungent shark repellent. Crown Prince Selva was waiting at the siege gate as they escorted the swimmer inside.

"What news, and from where?" asked the prince.

"You must carry out the Sea Dragon plan tonight, by order of the Alliance," announced the swimmer.

"Sea Dragon? Tonight? But a night attack is unheard of. Predawn, yes, but night?"

"The Leir is rising fast, and has overflowed its banks. The defenders in Diomeda think the city now has a moat several miles wide, but that very water will be their nemesis. You must attack tonight, and use every man in the palace."

The plan had been worked out in secret over many weeks, and was one of several. All had imaginative names, and all names gave a clue to the nature of their plans. For Sea Dragon, the defenders in the palace were to swim to the moored warships and set them alight with skins of oil. When the Torean marines rushed back from the city ramparts to deal with them, the Alliance army would attack the ramparts.

"Without dawn's light, and under those clouds, it is going to be hard to coordinate the attack," warned Selva.

"Oh, there will be a signal that you will not be able to miss. It will light up the entire city," the swimmer replied.

Prince Selva was doubtful, but with only eight hundred men he had no alternative but to cooperate if he was going to regain control of his city. "What about that weapon thing? The one that split the ship in half this morning?"

"A trick. It was done with wires and a ship that had already been sawn right through," the swimmer insisted.

It was a lame explanation, but the prince wanted to believe it.

"Very well, I shall give the order."

✷ ✷ ✷

Ashore in Diomeda, the real Alliance messenger was lying in a cell as Forteron and Sairet observed him through the door's eyeslit. He bore the marks of torture.

"He revealed that the attack will be tomorrow morning," said Forteron. "After those in the palace slip out and set afire the moored ships of the battle fleet, the Alliance commanders intend to attack across the flood plain in barges."

"Their plans are no matter," replied Sairet. "You have been warned, and their plan was desperate at best."

"And how did you learn of this spy?"

"I am a dancer, and a dancer with access to the court. Someone thought that I might be so loyal as to spy for the Alliance and the Royal House of Diomeda. As you can see, I came straight to you instead."

"Who was that someone?"

"A recent arrival, one who did not know that fifteen years ago I was cast into the street by the assassin of my husband, who was then king."

"So, the late king had been fifteen years on the throne?"

"Yes, and it gave him great pleasure to see me reduced to the status of a windrel, dancing for coppers in the marketplace and teaching the women of the idle rich to sway before their jaded menfolk."

Forteron bowed, then kissed her hand. "I am not the supreme commander of the Toreans, my lady, but I shall show you what gratitude I can. This very night I shall commend you to Emperor Feran at his first court."

"No! No, please, do nothing to draw attention to me. Yet. Win your victory first. It will be my victory, too, and it will be reward enough. What orders did you pass on to Dawnlight with your substitute courier?"

"Those of the original," said Forteron with a sly smile.

"What?"

"Why not?"

Sairet pondered his question. "Indeed, why not? So, you will set a few traders afire before dawn, having already moved the battle fleet into the river or up the coast."

"Yes. The army on the flood plain will wade across to attack, thinking our defenders have been rushed to the docks. They will get quite an enthusiastic reception, I should think."

The exhausted auton pigeon flopped onto the deck of the *Shadowmoon*, hardly able to move. The patrol autons had not been cast to stop autons arriving at Helion, for how else could messages from Warsovran—or whoever was giving the orders—be received? The crewmen were playing dice by lamplight, while Terikel was making fish jump at images of ether insects. Roval was on watch on the quarterdeck, and he was first to the bird. He unlocked the casting and handed the pigeon to Terikel.

"Tonight there will be a fire-circle, I cannot tell what time it will detonate," said an image of Wensomer's face floating above Roval's hands. "It will be upon the marines' garrison, at Helion. Try to get to Silverdeath first. Use the *Shadowmoon* as it is best used. If no fire-circle happens before the second hour past midnight, I am either dead or there has been a change of plan. I may even command Silverdeath."

"The garrison," said Terikel, frowning. "That's near the geographical center of Helion, on the main island, so . . . four fire-circles will detonate before the things burn out. Sixty-four, thirty-two, sixteen, eight . . . that's one hundred twenty days in total."

"Wensomer as mistress of Silverdeath!" breathed Roval. "What a prospect."

"Ten dozen days, this makes no sense. Either Feran or Warsovran will be here with the entire Diomedan fleet in a mere eight days. The garrison is on what remains of the isthmus, so if a fire-circle happened over it, how much of its area would also be over water?"

"More than half," replied Roval. "Perhaps there will be only one fire-circle. Perhaps we shall indeed have a second chance."

Feran spent the entire morning in a series of baths. Baths of milk, baths of wine, baths of rosewater, and baths of scented oils. At noon he sent for one of the lower-ranking marine commanders, a man named Takeram. He promoted him five grades in seniority, and put him in charge of forming and commanding the emperor's Secret Militia. He also gave him a series of tasks to be carried out by sunset. Feran had chosen carefully, after talking to a great many senior officers. Takeram was known to be ambitious, and to think himself overlooked by superiors of less talent than himself. He was perfect for Feran's needs.

Takeram's militiamen visited the boatsheds of the riverside shipwrights in midafternoon. Here they found the shipwright who had constructed Feran's original racing shell, and who was now not only building more of them, but conducting tutorials for other shipwrights. Takeram chopped him through with an ax. The other shipwrights were gathered in the boatshed, the boatshed was sealed and set on fire.

Feran spent the entire afternoon in the company of a succession of girls in his palace chambers, and by sunset he was, predictably, exhausted and fast asleep. Even Takeram was not inclined to wake him with his report, instead ordering one of Feran's courtesans to leave the scroll on a cushion at his bedside.

Elsewhere in the improvised palace, the preparations for Feran's first court were both frantic and lavish. Apart from Forteron, a few nobles, and the envoys, Feran would tolerate no others into the court but girls and women, although eunuchs were allowed to carry the heavier platters. Thus the houses of

the rich were scoured for girls, women, and eunuchs with experience in court life and protocols, while cooks, bakers, and tai-
lors were brought in with ax-blades pressing between their
shoulders. Musicians and dancers were not in short supply in
Diomeda, and as the newly appointed royal dancemistress,
Sairet had no trouble in assembling a troupe of the finest on the
Placidian Rim.

Sunset took place behind heavy clouds and pattering rain.
There was very little of Diomeda that was not built of mud-brick,
and in a city that had known less than five days of rain per year
until now, the continual deluge was becoming a serious problem.
Roofs of mud and thatch began to erode, then leak. Torrents of
water washing down the streets weakened walls, and throughout
the city there was scarcely a fire to be found. The boatsheds on
the riverbank were largely immune to the downpour from the
skies and the rising level of the river. They had been built on
stone or wooden piles to withstand the annual floods, and there
were plenty of sails to rig over the roofs. Out on the city ramparts, Forteron's marines were camped in well maintained tents
between properly dug drainage channels. Much of their cam-
paigning in Torea had been in the rain, and in a much colder climate than this. One mile away, the army of the Alliance was also
sheltering under tents, but on rather less well drained ground.

The villas of the rich tended to be made of stone, and there
were plenty of servants to plug the leaks as they manifested
themselves. In the temporary palace, the throne room was
hastily prepared for its new monarch. The richest carpets and
hangings available had been appropriated from all the other villas, and a throne of perfumed cedarwood had been built to
Feran's dimensions and specifications. All others were to stand
or to lie on cushions. The new emperor would tolerate nobody
to be sitting, except himself.

Feran finally woke at eleven. He read Takeram's report with
approval. Takeram had discovered a very strange suit of leather
armor in a covert, unannounced search of the palace, along with
sketches of the sorcerer Einsel, the failed assassin with the
crossbow. They were all in Admiral Forteron's quarters. *This
could be the basis of some quite lively entertainment at court,*
thought Feran with satisfaction. He had himself bathed again,

then dressed. He was inclined to keep his new courtiers waiting, yet he was anxious to reign over them as well. The emperor called for a navigator's map of Diomeda's harbor, and noted with satisfaction that there was shallow water and a sandbar to the southeast of the island palace. That would be very useful for him later.

Those in the court had been called the moment the emperor had woken, but everyone had been anticipating a lengthy wait. The rehearsing of the music, fire-eating, windrel dancers, and jugglers provided a welcome distraction, and was watched by Forteron, the Commander of Marines, several Torean nobles, and the envoys. Duke Terracict, from one of the northern kingdoms of the Alliance, had volunteered to risk becoming a hostage in order to assess the enemies and their newly arrived leader.

A complex and subtle system of coughs, claps, and gestures signaled that Feran was coming. A trumpet fanfare by Torean marines behind a screen announced his entry, and he sauntered up the center of the hall, climbed the sandstone-and-marble steps, and sat on the throne. Silverdeath followed, and stood on his right. Feran was wearing a gold crown that had been improvised from the tiaras of four Diomedan noblewomen by a quick-witted and skilled goldsmith, but nobody dared to laugh.

Forteron stood at the left of the throne with a scroll, and at a nod from Feran he began to read.

"'Matters to be brought before His Royal Majesty Emperor Feran Woodbar are a follows: demands from the Alliance for the immediate surrender of Diomeda to its rightful monarch; appeals for relief from the misery brought about by the unseasonal rain to the citizens of Diomeda; a call for increased taxes to cover the housing, feeding, and equipping of the Torean marines engaged in Diomeda's defense; a petition from certain merchants for protection from privateers operating in the northwest of the Racital Sea—'"

"Enough," said Feran, languidly raising his hand for silence. "I decree my pleasure to be no, no, no, and no. Now, bring on girls to dance, and so to charm away the gloom of this night's weather."

Everyone there had been expecting something a little more substantial from the new emperor, but all had wisely concealed their disappointment. A tray with a goblet of wine was brought, and Feran accepted it after Silverdeath had checked it for poisons. The area before the throne was cleared. The dancers had been allowed a light meal in the midafternoon, and thereafter the servants had been preparing them. A troupe of girls was first, to be followed by Wensomer. The girls danced. Feran leered, then selected three to lie at the foot of his throne.

One of the serving girls approached Wensomer with a tray of pastries and whispered as she selected one. "The emperor is ready, what will be your tune?"

" 'Ocean's Dream,' " replied Wensomer.

The girl left immediately, even though other dancers were beckoning her over. Wensomer set the pastry down uneaten. A gong sounded behind Feran's dais and the music began.

Wensomer rose up from the floor with the first bars of "Ocean's Dream," just as if she were a wave gaining height as it approached the shore. She used the slow introduction to send undulations along her outstretched arms as if they were ripples on a placid sea, while her hips swayed back and forth, causing a very unsettling and difficult double direction effect that took the attention of all, the dancers in particular. Even Sairet stared in amazement.

The first tempo change cut in, and now Wensomer moved in a circle, bending down then swooping up, this time dancing as larger waves, again with the double motion and undulating wavelets along her arms. The tempo picked up further, and she spun the top of her body from the waist, swirling hair, pearl strings, and gauze veils around like spray bursting across rocks.

Another tempo cut in, very much slower. Now it was as if Wensomer were underwater, for she drew her veils through the air slowly, yet undulated them as if they were floating. Her body rocked with rhythms counterworked against other rhythms, like a frond of kelp suspended between rocks and surface.

There was absolute silence and stillness in the court, apart from the dancer and the musicians. Behind their curtain, the musicians had no idea how the performance was progressing, however. Feran, Forteron, the nobles, and the others followed Wensomer's every move, while Silverdeath appeared not to be taking any notice.

This was more than a dancer's dance, or an alluring and seductive display; this was spectacle, this was a dance that tuned itself to everyone in the room. Wensomer spoke a language common to all of them, and Wensomer spoke to them of the sheer beauty of movement for its own sake: of dance that allured lecherous monarchs, whirled through marketplace revels, and swayed in the privacy of marital bedchambers. Everyone read Wensomer's movements as if they were exquisitely crafted verse—they swayed in sympathy, they became the water on which she was the wave, just as if she were an elemental within a mortal body. Together their movements communicated what Wensomer's body was saying—without knowing that it was an ancient Scalticaran body-verse!

The music ended with a fading patter on a pottery drum as Wensomer rolled on the floor, drawing her sash and veils after her like a wave retreating back to the ocean after breaking on a beach. Wensomer lay before Feran and his court, the center of attention. The music had stopped, so she rose up and began a low, sinuous bow from left to right. As she moved Feran began to applaud, and everyone else joined in. Everyone who had been watching was now under Wensomer's influence. She was not controlling anyone, but all were compulsively anxious to please her. They clapped continually, rhythmically. Silverdeath remained impassive. Wensomer had trod the fine line between influence and control. Any attempt to control Feran would have brought instant death from his guardian, but the fact she was still alive meant that she had been successful.

Wensomer minced across to stand before Feran's throne, her hips still swaying. Feran stood, then walked down from the dais to her. All the while the applause continued.

"I like you," she purred. "Who are you?"

"I am Emperor, I am master of Silverdeath," replied Feran mechanically.

Wensomer looked up to where Silverdeath stood. She turned her head on one side and frowned.

"What can it do?" she asked.

"He can annihilate this continent," said Feran, sounding a little proud.

"But I like this continent."

"He can destroy my enemies, I am his master," he explained, now sounding anxious.

"His master? Make him do something for me."

"I can make him kill anyone who displeases me."

"Hah! What is so special about that? Many men have killed each other over *me*, and *I* am just a dancer. I think you are Silverdeath's servant. I cannot be impressed by a servant."

"I command Silverdeath!" exclaimed Feran, his intonation suddenly colored bright by strong anxiety.

Wensomer began to undulate her arms again, and rolled her hips in time to the rhythm of the continued clapping of the court. "Then make him dance, and I may be impressed."

"Silverdeath, do it, dance for us."

"Excluded function," entoned Silverdeath.

"Command him to stop the rain."

"Silverdeath, stop the rain," cried Feran, with a hint of pleading.

"Excluded function."

"At least make him take me in his arms and fly me above the clouds to see the stars."

"Do as she says, Silverdeath," again Feran cried, the hint of pleading now a streak of despair.

"Excluded function."

Wensomer continued to sway, but was now giggling. With one undulating arm she gestured east, to where Helion lay. "You're not a Torean, are you?" asked Wensomer.

"No, I am from here."

"I hate Toreans; they burned their continent and caused this horrid weather."

"I hate them as well," Feran insisted, desperate to please her.

"Yet you cannot destroy the Toreans in Diomeda."

"No, to do that would destroy Acrema, too."

"Well, there is a Torean garrison on the island of Helion. Can Silverdeath destroy our enemies there?"

The casting woven from the language of dance and body was

powerful, but Wensomer did not realize quite *how* powerful. Desire to please her was tearing Feran apart. He opened his mouth to cast Silverdeath to Helion, but Wensomer's casting had twisted his control and judgment too much. This was the first time she had used the dance-spell, after all. Feran was being wrenched by desperation to win her approval, yet how could a fire-circle eight days' sailing to the east impress her?

He caught sight of Dawnlight, in whose windows lamps had been left burning to create the illusion of occupation while the defenders set off to attack the Torean fleet. Those in Dawnlight were definitely his enemies, and a fire-circle over Dawnlight would be a spectacular show indeed.

"Silverdeath, destroy my enemies in Dawnlight!" shouted Feran, pointing at the island palace.

Wensomer's jaw dropped a fraction and her tongue began to form *No!* but she had already thought through the many alternative ways Feran might react, and so had contingency plans for all of them. This was regrettable, but the eight hundred in Dawnlight were less than the garrison at Port Wayside. This was war, after all—it was eight hundred lives or the entire world. She continued to undulate her body to the rhythm of the clapping, although she had stopped breathing.

"The feat is at the limit of my powers," warned Silverdeath.

"Do it!"

"Let us go out to watch," Wensomer purred.

Feran led the way out onto the nearest balcony. The entire court continued to clap. Feran shook his head, as if he had dozed for a moment. He was out on a balcony, standing in the rain. He was soaked. How long had he been there? He whirled and dashed back inside. Everyone was still entranced and clapping. Both Druskarl and Silverdeath were nowhere to be seen. The dancer was gone, too.

Betrayed! The word screamed in Feran's mind. *A spell, a casting.* Everyone in the court had been affected. *Forteron, damn him . . .* But Forteron was still clapping, his face smiling and vacant. Silverdeath should have protected Feran from all spells. *How had the woman done it?* Then he realized it. She had not attacked him; she had used the language of dance to allure him. She had no intent of harm whatsoever. That was how she had subverted the mighty Silverdeath itself.

Whatever the nature of the spell, it was certainly fragile. Any sudden noise or movement would rupture it. Feran began to sidle for the nearest door, stepping in a slow march, in time with the clapping. Taking Takeram by the arm, he passed through the door. The clapping continued. Feran backhanded Takeram, across the face, shattering the hold of Wensomer's casting.

"Fetch that fire-walking suit you found in Forteron's quarters," Feran cried as he and Takeram clattered down a flight of stairs. "Get twenty marines, fetch my racing shell from the palace courtyard, get everything to the Bridge of the Esplanade! Hurry! Surround the palace. Nobody may leave. Then send a squad to the home of that last dancer. Have her killed!"

Druskarl found himself lying on the floor beside the throne. He reached down and checked his scrotum. There were testicles within it. He was aware of everything that had happened since Feran had stabbed him and put Silverdeath onto his body. Wensomer's dance had meant nothing to him, but he was by now beginning to suspect that Feran had been tricked. The entire court was clapping slowly, in time. They were obviously under the influence of some casting, one so subtle yet powerful that it had slipped past Silverdeath.

Slowly, slowly, Druskarl edged away into the shadows behind the throne. Two swift, silent blows dropped an Acreman servant senseless to the floor, and mere seconds saw Druskarl wearing his robes and carrying his tray. In another minute the former eunuch was outside and fleeing into the rainswept darkness. In yet another minute, the palace gates were sealed behind him.

By the time Feran and his marines had cleared the palace, Wensomer's casting had weakened, and the people of the court had come to their senses in mild confusion. Feran and Silverdeath were gone. The dancer was gone, too.

"A superlative dance," remarked Forteron to Sairet. "Obviously the little devil could not wait to audition her for quite another type of performance."

Just then one of Forteron's aides rushed in, bowed, and hurried up to the admiral.

"My lord, there is something you should know," he hissed as he went down on one knee.

. *.* *.*

Wensomer stood on a balcony of the highest tower in the villa palace. She had been thinking very quickly, and making some decisions she might have condemned as morally odious only minutes earlier. The rain beat down on her skin through the wispy gauze of her costume as she breathed energies into her hands in glowing tendrils that wove themselves into two tall, thin spikes standing on the palm of each hand. This was a difficult and draining casting, and the fact that she had done it before made it no less exhausting. The spikes were each a hundred feet long when she finally began to speak shaping-words. The base of the spikes formed into a harness, with straps and handholds. The spikes began to broaden and fade, and even before they were fully formed into wings, Wensomer struggled into the faintly glowing machine of pure energies and plasmas. As she brought her arms down she felt the weight of rain on the huge area of her two-hundred-foot wingspan.

Wensomer leaped. For a moment she lost height quickly as she gained speed, then she leveled into a long glide over the darkened city. Diomeda had only a few public street-corner torches at the best of times, and with the rain falling, these had not been alight for many days. She hurtled through stinging raindrops, taking sightings on lamps in the windows of a few towers, and the light of the city's hilltop navigation pyre, which was under a stone canopy. It was difficult to maintain height, as there were few air currents to give Wensomer lift. Flapping the enormous wings was out of the question.

The murky shadows of domes, towers, treetops, and spires passed below, and she flew through a few plumes of smoke mixed with the smell of cooking oil, burning fat, and baking bread. There was a thin, piercing shriek from someone who happened to be looking up at the exact moment Wensomer passed overhead. A small dark flying thing dodged Wensomer with a loud squeak before vanishing into the saturated darkness. She realized that things no longer looked familiar, she had lost her bearings. She caught sight of the hilltop navigation pyre again, found the vast dark of the ocean, then saw the illuminated windows of Dawnlight and the faint running lamps of the three patrol galleys on the harbor. Not long now, but at a speed of over fifty miles per hour the windchill and continual sting of raindrops were rapidly wearing her down. At last she saw the bright beacon lamp that she had left in the higher of her own villa's twin towers.

The roof of the tower rushed up. Wensomer raised her wings and dropped her legs, descending in a near-stall until her bare feet slapped down on the wet flagstones of her villa's square-topped tower. Laron dashed out into the rain to her side.

"Silverdeath's been cast," she began.

"Good, good, the *Shadowmoon* is already there, so we just have to get Ninth to—"

"Not Helion, Dawnlight!" cried Wensomer. "Get Ninth, hurry, and bring that little crossbow from my sunroom—and mead! Bring a jar of my strongest mead!"

Wensomer stood waiting in the rain, still wearing her belly-dancing rig, but in a gratifyingly short time Laron returned with Ninth, the mead, and the crossbow.

"Put the jar to my mouth," said Wensomer between chattering teeth. "My hands are otherwise occupied."

"Are you sure you should be drinking and flying?" Laron ventured as he removed the cork.

"Damn you, Laron, it's not as if anyone will be able to arrest me! Ninth, get onto my back."

Ninth needed to be told nothing twice. Laron slung the crossbow's strap over her shoulder as she walked around behind Wensomer, then Ninth took hold of Wensomer and locked her legs around the waist of the sorceress. Laron held the jar to Wensomer's lips and she drank frantically between coughs and splutters.

"No, don't put your arms around my neck, hold those glowing things at my shoulders," Wensomer called to Ninth. "Are you ready?"

"Ready for what, mistress?"

"Laron, expect trouble. Try to escape if—"

There was a sudden shouting and commotion from out in the street. Wensomer jumped.

She had expected Ninth to shriek, but the auton girl merely held on tightly, precisely as ordered. Wensomer's villa was not as high as the temporary palace, but the etheric wings were adequate to the task. Rain stung her skin as she searched for traces of thermals and tried to gain height. All that she could achieve was a shallow glide, however, and that would not be good enough with Ninth's extra weight.

Back at Wensomer's villa Laron hastily chewed and swallowed a clove of garlic then opened the rapidly splintering door to the men of Feran's new Secret Militia. A bedsmock was over his clothing.

"Night greetings, liberators!" he said with what was meant to be a Sargolan accent but sounded more like he had a heavy cold and severe constipation. "I am speak very good Diamedan. House new steward am being—"

"Out of my way, frogeater!" bellowed the captain of the squad, seizing Laron and flinging him out into the rain before leading his men inside. Laron hastened away, discarding the bedsmock as he ran.

Wensomer was gliding over the beaches at the southern edge of Diomeda and only a hundred feet from the ground when a dazzling flash of light and an immense column of steam, smoke, and dust erupted. It reached from the sea to the clouds, and lit up the city and the entire surrounding countryside. It was centered on Dawnlight, or, at least, what had once been the island palace. Moments later a shock wave swept over Wensomer, buckling her wings and heaving her sideways and upward. Wings of ether cannot be broken, however, and she quickly had them re-formed. Suddenly the air around her was roiling with thermals from the heat of the fire-circle. Wensomer soared high, fighting for control, then banked to begin circling the ghastly column of steam, fire, and ash.

"That's the hot air from the remains of the island," called Wensomer to Ninth. "We need to circle it and use its thermals to maintain height."

Ninth did not answer, as she had not been asked a question. Wensomer continued to spiral upward, keeping her left wingtip toward the darkening column of hot air. All the while she counted, estimating times for passably fit men to run from the palace to the docks carrying a bulky leather suit, then to row from the docks to Dawnlight. By the time she reached her set number, they were flying through warm, roiling fog, and she was having trouble getting her bearings. The rain was still flaying her shoulders, head, ears, and arms, but at least the wind-chill had been swamped by the fire-circle's air. She began to spiral downward.

Within the etherworld, Velander saw the fire-circle blaze out as a bright line of orange. This time she knew they were in a very large city; she could see the teeming etheric castings, mechanisms, and autons. This time the world would end. She felt her sanity slipping, just as the energy of the crumb of axis glass was also slipping toward nothingness. *Not long now,* she thought, and it would be a relief.

As Feran reached the waterside he was wheezing from fatigue but driven on by despair. Takeram helped him into the ungainly heat-armor that had been tailored for a somewhat bigger man. Several marines lifted him into the racing shell.

Silverdeath detonated, out across the water. The marines looked about fearfully.

"Now, stand clear, all of you!" Feran shouted through his open faceplate above the echoing thunder that was spilling across them. "No, not you, Takeram. Come closer, listen, I have more orders."

"Your Majesty?"

"Jam your torch into the framework."

"Done, Your Majesty."

Feran smashed the long blacksmith's tongs protruding from the suit's arm across Takeram's head. Stunned, the marine commander fell across the racing shell. A second blow ended his life. Feran grasped the oars as well as he could with the tongs, then began rowing. The others saw only a confusion of thrashing limbs before the shell began moving. Behind him, Feran could see other figures rushing up. Then angry shouting and the clang of axes echoed out across the harbor.

Things splashed into the water nearby or whizzed overhead. *Arrows,* Feran thought as more missiles flew all about him. Forteron was showing his true colors, and had apparently swept Takeram's militiamen aside in a depressingly short time. *Should have killed him while he was entranced,* Feran thought glumly as an arrow struck the rear of his boat. Even with only one rower, and a body trailing arms and legs in the water, the racing shell was still very fast, however—though the torch gave the archers a point to aim at. Feran cleared the river mouth in two minutes. The battle fleet seemed to be burning fiercely on the southern side of the harbor. Ahead of him, the light from the fire-circle was fading, but even though the island was hidden in clouds of steam and the rainsoaked gloom, it was wide enough to find by dead reckoning.

* * *

Three hundred feet above, Wensomer noticed the gleam of a torch moving straight for Dawnlight.

"Only one person in all Diomeda would be visiting on a night like this," she called back to Ninth.

* * *

A sandbar trailed out into the water beside Dawnlight's island. It had built up to the southeast of the island, and this was where Feran was aiming. The shell grounded in the darkness, and Feran heaved himself out and drove a spike anchor into the sandbar. Taking his pitch torch, Feran waded ashore. The water was uncomfortably warm as it leaked slowly into his suit, but already the currents were mixing cool water from farther afield with the scalding layer that had ringed the island.

Wensomer's wingtip collided with the racing shell as she skimmed just above the water. Had she been higher up, she might have recovered, but at no more than a foot or so above the surface, she had no option other than to cartwheel messily into the sea. She and Ninth stood up, knee-deep in warm water.

"My lady, the crossbow is gone," Ninth reported.

"What? Where?"

"When crashing, the strap broke. I search—"

"No! You could take hours in this murk. Come with me."

Wensomer set about absorbing her wings as they waded. Soon they had found the shell, along with the body of Takeram.

"I believe we have found something suspicious," panted Wensomer as they examined the shell and its dead passenger.

"The man is armed," said Ninth, drawing the marine's knife.

"An eating-knife," Wensomer pointed out, tapping the man's belt. "Note that his ax is missing. Think about who might have it."

"Feran?"

"Your powers of deductive logic may one day rival mine, auton girl. Cut a hole in this boat's side and push it out to sea. After that, we wait."

Dawnlight palace had actually been a square, fortified wall with towers and halls built into it. In the middle were gardens and storehouses adequate for any siege. These either had been flat to begin with, or rendered flat by Silverdeath. The main walls had collapsed outward. Thus Feran had a straightforward and relatively easy walk to the place where Silverdeath had fallen. He spent precious moments searching in the murk, but presently found it on the flagstones. He scooped up his prize and started back. The suit was beginning to char and smolder, but the walk was only half as long as for Druskarl at Helion, and Feran had been able to get up to a slow jog on the flat surface. Thus he was back at the water's edge less than five minutes after setting foot ashore.

There was no shell. Feran removed his helmet and held his torch high. No boat, no body. He stuck the base of the torch in the sandbar and began to strip off the other pieces of heat armor. In a pinch he could float Silverdeath over to Diomeda on the empty, hunchbacked heat-suit and find a new host, but where was the shell?

A movement caught his eye, figures wading out of the darkness. Two women. One dressed in a servant's tie-blouse and trousers . . . Velander! The other was the dancer from his court!

"We gave him a nice burial at sea," said Wensomer. "It seemed the right thing to do, his being dead and all that."

Feran draped Silverdeath over his neck, then shook his arms into the sleeves.

"Ah, Velander, and my cunning dancer," he replied.

Wensomer breathed a casting into her hands.

"Interesting fact: Silverdeath cannot claim anyone as host who has put it onto *himself*, and it makes quite a good mailshirt," Feran declared with something approaching amusement. "In order to regain Silverdeath as my active servant, all I need is another body. Would you like to provide one?"

He drew his ax.

"My mother told me never to give my body to any man without checking his penis first," replied Wensomer.

The insult of the previous morning stung Feran like nothing else could have. His face went blank, and he began to wade purposefully toward the two women.

Wensomer flung the ball of glowing scarlet tendrils she had fashioned. The energies should have burst over Feran's head and wrapped around his neck, strangling him. Instead the ball was pulled down to vanish into Silverdeath's mass of jingling metal. Feran laughed. Wensomer stepped back, breathing more ether into her hands and this time fashioning a long, glowing whip, which she lashed at his knees. The tip snaked upward, to bury itself in Silverdeath, which then drew the rest of the whip into itself. Wensomer was pulled off her feet before she could let go, ether streaming out of her and vanishing into Silverdeath. Frantically she gasped a casting word that snapped the etheric whip, but she was now severely drained. As Feran came striding over, she detonated another casting in a brilliant flash, then scrambled to one side as he stumbled past, dazzled and chopping blindly at the water.

"Nice, but how many more of those can you do?" Feran laughed as he blinked the dancing afterimages away.

Wensomer responded with another flash, but this time Feran had closed one eye before it detonated. Wensomer turned to run. He followed her until she stumbled and fell. He raised the ax above his head—and a dagger flew through the air and thudded into the back of his hand. During the month past, Ninth had learned a little of javat defense skills, and by assisting with Laron's lessons she had certainly learned how to attack.

Feran cursed and dropped the ax. Wensomer lashed out with her foot, connecting with his testicles more out of luck than design. Feran staggered back; then, pulling the knife from his hand, he started after her as she made for deeper water. Suddenly he remembered he had dropped the ax. He tried to retrace his steps, but in the dark water and steam, and by the light of a single torch, it was hopeless.

Feran was far from beaten. All that he had to do was float Silverdeath across to Diomeda and there would be no shortage of hosts. He started back to where he had left the leather suit, but Ninth was standing in front of it, now empty-handed. No longer in a mood to be distracted, Feran waded straight for her, knife held underhand.

"Flee or die, it's all the same."

Feran stabbed, left-handed, but Ninth twisted where she stood and with one hand batted his hand aside while backhanding him in the nose with her other. Feran saw a brilliant blue star, at least as bright as Wensomer's castings, felt his leg snared by Ninth's, and went down with his wrist in her hands. Ninth spun her whole body around with her hands above her head, twisting her much-stronger opponent's arm behind his back as he fell. Feran breathed water, tried to raise himself on his other arm, then collapsed as Ninth's knee rammed into his back. He dropped the knife, gasped water, tried to rise again, then collapsed under Ninth's weight.

In a sense Ninth was puzzled. Feran was not fighting back in any of the ways Roval had taught Laron. Feran ceased to struggle and went limp. Roval had said to count to two hundred when suffocating anyone, and beware of tricks. Ninth tightened her grip on Feran's arm, and he started thrashing again. This time his movements were weaker.

From farther out into the darkness there was a splashing and swirling of water followed by, "Ninth! Don't let him catch you, I've found his ax!"

Ninth considered, like the well-designed auton that she was. The order was to not be caught, rather than to stay away from Feran. *She* had caught *him*, so logically she should remain there, pinning him down.

"Yes, mistress."

"Where is he?"

"Near the torch, mistress."

Wensomer came out of the darkness, holding the ax in a surprisingly professional manner. She glanced about wildly.

"Ninth! Where is he?"

"Underneath me."

"What! Get clear! Get back!"

Ninth did just as she was told, pulling away in a great splash of water. With the last of his strength, Feran reared up. Wensomer chopped at where his head seemed to be. The blade of the ax cut through the vertebrae of his neck, severed muscles, sinews, veins, and arteries before stopping halfway through his windpipe

Wensomer stood over Feran in the dark, bloody water, the ax in her right hand, still wearing her dancing coinbelt and the remains of her silk costume, but looking nothing like a court dancer.

"What— how . . ." she panted.

"I was drowning him, mistress."

Wensomer dropped to her knees and began laughing, and tears quickly mixed with the seawater on her face.

"Mistress? Have I made a joke?"

Wensomer shook her head, sending a spray of water onto the dark wavelets. "No, I am the only joke hereabouts. Hurry, get Silverdeath off his body."

"Yes, mistress."

"How did you pin him down?"

"A technique learned from Roval."

"What? The bastard taught *me* none of his javat fighting, in spite of all our years together."

Given the condition of Feran's body, and his lack of cooperation, getting Silverdeath off was considerably easier said than done. At last they stood together by the light of the guttering torch as Wensomer held Silverdeath high.

"I have only to put it back on Feran," said Wensomer. "Because it would be put on by my hand, I would become mistress of Silverdeath and he would be restored to life as its host."

There was no question, so Ninth said nothing.

"But no," Wensomer continued. "I cannot be trusted with command over Silverdeath. Nobody can be trusted with power like that. Besides, the turd deserved to die. He must have been over a hundred years old, and that's life enough for anyone. Silverdeath must be destroyed, and I think I know the only way. *You* must wear Silverdeath, my little auton girl."

"Yes, mistress," replied Ninth, holding her hands out for the metal fabric.

"Are you not curious about why?"

"No, mistress."

"It may kill you. Are you not worried?"

"No, mistress."

Wensomer could hear the splash of approaching oars. Without another question she helped Ninth into the metal shirt.

"Someday you must show me how you managed to pin the little rat," muttered Wensomer as Ninth shook her arms into the sleeves.

"It is simple, mistress—"

Her voice was cut off. Silverdeath had begun to assimilate her as a host.

"But not in this lifetime. I'm sorry, Ninth, I want to hope otherwise, but I doubt that I shall ever speak to you again."

As it had done with others before, Silverdeath flowed into a continuous skin beneath the girl's clothing, but instead of offering its services to Wensomer it went rigid and began to glow slightly. Purple shimmers flayed over its surface, and Ninth's clothing began to smoke and char. Rain falling onto her hissed and spat as if she were made of hot coals, and at her feet the water began to bubble. Wensomer backed away, then ducked down into the dark water as she heard shouts from the approaching boat.

"There, that glowing thing," someone called in an upper-class Diomedan accent.

Half a dozen long, low gigboats nosed into view through the rain and drifting steam. They were built to have a very low profile in the water, with the rowers lying almost flat on their backs. Wensomer quickly realized that these were loyalist nobles, absent from Dawnlight palace when the fire-circle burst.

"It's gone, it really is gone," the speaker continued. "The palace blasted from existence in an eyeblink."

"That, there!" exclaimed someone else. "The glow, it's not from a torch."

"It's what they called Silverdeath, Your Highness," said someone else.

"So, it's true. This accursed device can lay waste a palace . . . or a continent."

"Silverdeath not looking right," said a woman with a strident voice and a heavy Damarian accent.

Those on the lead boat got out and gathered around Silverdeath.

"Can anyone hear me?" shouted the nobleman. "Who is Silverdeath's master?"

Wensomer stayed crouched in the water.

"Highness, lookee here!" shouted one of the rowers. "A body."

. . . *Highness?* thought Wensomer. *Prince Selva.* They hoisted Feran's body up to a sitting position and held up his almost severed head.

"The emperor fella, I seen him on the pier. He commanded Silverdeath."

"But not anymore, quite obviously. I wonder if Silverdeath is here for the taking?"

Wensomer saw a figure take an oar and prod at Silverdeath. Oar and oarsman detonated in a shower of bloody fragments and splinters.

"Stay back," the former empress shouted, somewhat redundantly.

"What happened?" asked Selva.

"Said to be vulnerable, times, when using Silverdeath," said Warsovran's former wife, empress and sorceress, wading over from one of the other boats.

"This fella were its master, I recognize him from this mornin' on the pier," said the rower.

"Then what do you think happened, Learned Paditan?"

Paditan, thought Wensomer as another figure came wading over. *The court sorcerer of Diomeda.* The lanky, angular figure waded around the glowing form once, his arms folded behind his back.

"Someone killed this Feran buffoon just as he was putting Silverdeath onto this girl!" he concluded. "Zaltus, was it not on a man before?"

"Aye, and this be no man," said Zaltus, looking carefully at Ninth.

"Your Highness, Silverdeath now has a host but no master."

"Silverdeath, I am your new master!" barked Prince Selva at once. "Obey me!"

Silverdeath did not react at all. Wensomer nodded to herself.

"It must be jammed, as surely as a watermill with a broken axle," said Paditan. "Nobody can touch it, nobody can be its master."

"And the Torean battle fleet's gone, leaving only those decoys. Lucky we did a scoutin' run first—"

An arrow in the back cut Zaltus short. He staggered a few paces and fell—straight onto Silverdeath. There was another bloody explosion, but by now two squadrons of small boats were exchanging bowshots.

"Highness, make a break!" shouted someone through the confusion. "We'll hold them."

Forteron's men were in conventional, slower gigboats, but there were five times more of them, and they had a lot more archers. In no more than two minutes, those of the Diomedan squadron that had not fled, had been wiped out. Forteron waded over alone and stood before Silverdeath. Wensomer saw him pull an arrow from a body and toss it at the luridly glowing figure. The shaft flashed into ash and splinters. He knelt in the water and held up Feran's head by the hair, then an officer came wading over to report.

"The Diomedan prince is not among the dead, Commander, and one of their stealth boats got clear. Five of ours have set after it, but those stealth boats are very fast."

"So, I suspect that you may now call *me* prince of Diomeda," Forteron responded. "Look here."

"Feran Woodbar, dead! But how? Silverdeath could chop ships in half to protect him."

Forteron let go of Feran's hair and stood up.

"The Diomedan prince must have been making a treaty with Feran when we attacked. I managed to kill Feran just as he was putting Silverdeath on this girl, a heartbeat before Silverdeath became active. Now the thing has a dead master. Do you not agree?"

There were, of course, anomalies in this version of events. How had Silverdeath been glowing before they attacked if Feran had only tried to put it onto the girl afterward, for example? More to the point, Forteron had been armed with a boarding-spear, while Feran obviously had been killed by an ax blow. Forteron was the man's commander, however, and the marine officer was one of the elite royal guard. He went down on one knee and bowed to Forteron.

"It was precisely like that, Your *Highness*."

Forteron smiled, then they both looked at Silverdeath.

"So it cannot be commanded?" the marine asked.

"Watch. Silverdeath, I am your new master. Obey me! Silverdeath! Who is your master?"

There was no reaction at all.

"How long will it stay like that?" asked the officer.

"Until its energies run down, then it will shatter. Einsel had a theory that it could explode when that happens."

"Like another fire-circle?"

"No, but it would be wise to move well clear." Forteron pointed to Feran's body. "It would also be wise to evacuate the waterside areas of Diomeda. Alert the militia, say another explosion may be about to happen. Make sure the whole city knows, say that I will keep them safe. Now, call a boat over and load the late emperor's body aboard as well. I want it paraded through the city, then taken to the ramparts for all the marines to see. I want them to know that *I* rule Diomeda."

Once they were gone, Wensomer crept back to the glowing statue that Silverdeath and Ninth had become. The energies crawling over the surface had a very unhealthy look about them. Ninth was still linked to something on some other world, and immense etheric energies were draining away through the mechanism. The strain was sure to snap something soon, even in a being as powerful as Silverdeath.

"And when you snap, what then?" Wensomer asked the glowing thing before her. "Will you take me with you? Well, if the auton girl can face death, I can, too."

The rain was getting colder, and so was the water. What was more, Wensomer had been in the water for a long time. Silverdeath was looking more and more unsteady, flickering and changing its colors. What would happen when it finally lost its cohesion? It would probably collapse, freeing whatever etheric energy remained to it. *How much would that be?* Wensomer wondered. *Knowing Silverdeath, probably lots and lots and lots.*

Wensomer knew she had to get away, although there was no hope of that—but suddenly something was moving on the water, just at the edge of the light cast by Silverdeath. Another boat, a corrak, with a single rower. Wensomer stood up, giddy with exhaustion and drained of ether, clothed only in scraps of costume but with Feran's ax still in her hand. She only had to kill the rower and steal the corrak. *Only!* After that, she had to row back across a harbor alive with boats and ships, while blinded by the fog, then find her way through a city under martial law while practically naked, to—Where? A villa that was probably still swarming with marines?

"Wensomer?" called a familiar voice with an adolescent quaver.

"Laron!" screamed Wensomer, almost collapsing with relief.

She rushed through the shallows to where he had jumped from the corrak, and she was still holding the ax as she flung her arms around him, smothering his face between her breasts.

"We were right, Silverdeath is jammed and degrading," she managed between gasping sobs as she released Laron. "We killed Feran, me and Ninth. I chopped his neck through . . . almost."

"Ninth? You?"

"I put Silverdeath onto her. Now it's degrading, unstable. Your corrak, we can escape."

Wensomer pulled back, drawing breath and trying to remember the exact words her rescuer had spoken to her only a few days earlier. Now, finally, it was her turn. Small, scrawny, pimply, and pigeon-chested he might be, but he *was* her rescuer. The magically romantic words welled up and sat ready on her tongue—then suddenly the youth went down on one knee in the shallows and took her by the hand.

"Well, I hate to admit it, but *you* are *my* brave and valorous champion," he declared.

Wensomer snatched her hand out of his and backed away.

"Hey, I'm supposed to kiss that!" protested Laron, standing up again.

"What is this?" demanded Wensomer in a dangerously low voice as she unconsciously shifted her grip on the ax.

"You killed Feran and defeated Silverdeath."

In the desperate scramble to incapacitate the quite monstrous weapon, Wensomer had not paused to think of herself as a hero. Laron was right, but his disappointingly unromantic way of announcing it had plunged the exhausted, filthy, shivering, and practically naked sorceress into a particularly ugly mood. Laron now realized he had probably caught her at a somewhat vulnerable moment, and in hindsight should have chosen his words with a little more care. Hoping to make amends, he hastily removed his tunic and held it out to her. Wensomer snatched it from his hand.

"Someday, someplace, you had damn well better rescue me from something," she muttered as she put the tunic on. "Sarcastic little wretch. . . . Laron? Laron, what is it?"

Laron did not hear, he was staring at Silverdeath. Ninth's head was free of the pulsing, flickering skin of metallic orange liquid! It was slowly falling away from her like quicksilver honey.

"Get that body out of his tunic," said Wensomer, pointing to a shape in the water as they waded over. "Then prepare to paddle very, very fast."

Ninth was beginning to slump forward by the time Silverdeath was down to her waist and glowing green, and Laron carefully steadied her without touching the rapidly failing device. Soon it was down to her thighs, and as it reached her calves and turned deep blue, Laron and Wensomer began pulling carefully. Her feet came free. For a moment Laron stood with Ninth in his arms, staring at the violet mass that was bubbling and glowing just below the surface.

"Into the corrak, and paddle!" Wensomer cried urgently. "When Silverdeath finally turns black, this will probably be a bad place to be standing."

"Precisely what will happen?"

"Silverdeath does not quite exist, like the stuff of the circlet that holds your oracle sphere. When it collapses, all the etheric energy left to it will burst out at once, and that may be quite a bit."

Laron paddled, and within moments they were lost in the thick fog caused by the fire-circle. Rain continued to pour down. Wensomer wrestled the unconscious Ninth into the charred, bloodstained tunic, then leaned over the side and paddled frantically with her hands.

"How far to the docks?" she panted.

"What do you mean?"

"That thing will be destroyed by an explosion, not a firecircle. There will be a huge wave, we need to climb the beacon hill."

"But we could be headed out to sea, for all I know."

"What? Call yourself a navigator?"

"Well, clear the fog and give me something to navigate by!"

"How did you find Dawnlight in the fog?"

"By the glow from Silverdeath."

Wensomer waved her hands in the air. "Then that's the end, we'll die!" she exclaimed. "And to think I wanted to live to a hundred, and die in bed—in company."

"At least I charmed my way into the beds of a couple of ladies after seven centuries of longing," said Laron, still paddling.

" 'Charmed' them? Garbage! Lavenci was probably ordered to spy on you by Mother, who was working for the High Circle. Pellien is no ex-harlot, she's the first-ever Dacostian member of the High Circle, and she's in Diomeda to spy on Mother—and anyone else who looks suspicious."

"You're lying!" exclaimed Laron, his paddle frozen in midair.

"Why else would they take an interest in a scrawny little privy brush like you? And while we're telling the truth and getting ready to die, Mother had *no* scheme to neutralize Silverdeath. She just thought *she* would be a better custodian than the rest of us."

"You're just paying me back for what I said back at the island."

"Yes, but I'm paying you back with the truth! You were taken in—figuratively—by Mother, and literally by Lavenci and Pellien. *I'm* the only honest player in Diomeda. The rest of you are rogues, fools, and bungling incompetents."

"Why, you— What in all the moonworlds is that?"

Looming up behind them was something huge. It was also moving very fast. Oars dug into the water to the beat of an unseen drum, and an initiate at the bow was shining a brilliance-casting over the waters ahead.

"A dash galley," said Laron. "Over the side—swim with Ninth! I'll stay in the corrak, give them a target."

"I'll stay, you take her."

"This is no time for heroics—"

"Laron, I can't swim!"

"You can fly but you can't swim?"

"What do you think I am, a duck?"

"Too late!"

They sat dazzled as the brilliance-casting's beam caught the corrak.

"There, ten degrees to starboard!" called the initiate aboard the dash galley. "Another of the prince's boats. Archers, at my word . . ."

Again Fortune favored Laron. Silverdeath lost its cohesion at that very moment, and the energy remaining within it was released in a micro-millisecond. The dash galley shadowed the corrak from the moment of pure, searing radiance, and it burst into flame then shattered into a mass of burning timber and bodies as a pressure wave slammed into it a heartbeat later. The thunderclap preceded a ragged wall of water that they could not escape, however. It lifted them high into the air as they clung to each other, then it was spilling in over the corrak's sides as it flung them along.

The militia sergeant and his squad were amazed that the wave from the second explosion had not swept the entire city away, but in fact the harbor had been comparatively shallow and simply did not contain enough water to do more than swamp the docklands and a band of houses about twenty deep. Many people had been killed, but many more survived. Forteron had warned them. Everyone was saying the new ruler looked after his people, and that Forteron would be a good prince.

"Pollos, three more over there!" he called, pointing through the rain.

A woman in a tunic was leading a youth carrying a girl over his shoulders. Yes, the girl was hurt but not badly, they explained. Yes, they had been asleep when the wave hit. No, the man of the house was across the city, defending the ramparts. Yes, they did have friends they could stay with. In a moment of compassion for the thin but valiant youth, bravely staggering along under the weight of his unconscious older sister, the sergeant draped his cloak over them before setting off in search of more survivors. The moment the sergeant was out of sight Wensomer gave Laron a stinging slap across the face.

"*That's* for saying I was your mother!" she snapped.

"It was the first thing that came into my mind."

"And I'm a virgin. Well, do you *really* have friends who will not cash us in for whatever reward is on offer?"

"This way."

Pellien was awoken by a heavy, insistent knocking barely a quarter of an hour after she had managed to get to sleep. She rolled from her bed, struck a flame onto the lamp's wick, and padded to the door.

"Who is it?"

"Laron."

"What? Why are you here?"

"Please, open up. I need help."

"Men!" Pellien sighed, and rattled the bolt across. "Laron, this is not a good time—" she began, pulling the door open, but the soaked, scratched, bruised Laron fell straight through the doorway and into her arms.

"That's all right, I've been having a bad time, too," he mumbled.

"If it comes to that, all three of us have," said Wensomer, dragging Ninth in from the hallway.

As it happened, Wensomer was no longer being sought by anyone. Pellien, who had only been home for half an hour, reported that Feran's Secret Militia, the shortest-lived body of secret guardsmen in the history of the moonworlds, had already been disbanded, and its surviving members sent to the foremost defense lines on the ramparts. A pony cart was fetched for Wensomer, who returned to her villa. She was standing with her hands on her hips, surveying the remains of her front door, when Forteron arrived.

Over hot, spiced mead Wensomer explained that Feran had been so captivated by her dance that he had dragged her outside and cast Silverdeath at Dawnlight to impress her. She had become frightened when he then turned on her, so she had leaped from the balcony into the bushes below. The branches had broken her fall, but she had been badly bruised and scratched. She had seen a huge, birdlike thing leap from a tower and vanish into the night. She assumed it was the sorcerer Feran.

This was not quite the story that had been reported to Forteron by some particularly repentant marines, but he was aware that men standing before a very angry commander who is brandishing an ax at them tend to say whatever they think he wants to hear, rather than the truth.

"Did you know he flew here in search of you?" asked Forteron. "A street watchman said that a huge and ugly bat with etheric wings leaped from your tower just before the first fire-circle."

"No, Your Highness. I remained hiding in a garden bower all night while the fire-circles exploded, then I gathered the courage to go home. My servants said that a squad of marines had arrived to arrest me. Apparently a second squad arrived, smashed in what was left of the front door, and arrested the first squad."

Just as dawn was breaking, Diomeda's self-declared prince gave Wensomer his thanks and left. Wensomer was helped upstairs by her steward, and fell face-first onto her bed and into a deep, pitch-black sleep.

Pellien dressed, chewing a few leaves of the caffin bush that she had earlier stolen from the palace kitchen, then set off for the ramparts through the rain with her nurse's pack. She was a nurse, after all, and she suspected nurses would soon be needed there. The students of Madame Yvendel's Academy would have to tend their own cuts, scratches, headaches, and casting burns for a while. Back in Pellien's room, Laron heaved Ninth's body into Pellien's bed, lay out on the floor beside it, and fell asleep almost instantly.

Dawn was just a bleak lightening of the heavy clouds. Forteron stood at a window in his highest tower, looking west across the flooded farmland to the camp of the Alliance army. Sairet approached with two servants, one of whom was holding a tray. After a moment's thought Sairet took the tray and dismissed both servants.

"My lord prince, you should eat," she began.

"Again I am in control, but of what?" he said without turning.

"I have brought refreshments, Your Highness," insisted Sairet.

Now Forteron turned. "A sharp but alluring scent," he said, looking at the pottery bowl. "What is it?"

"Beans of the caffin bush, roasted and ground, then boiled and strained. I have mixed honey and goat's milk into it, to take the edge off the taste."

"And why is this better for breaking the night's fast than honey and sundried dates on flatbread?"

"Because it renders you alert as well."

Sairet took the bowl and drank a mouthful. Forteron accepted the bowl from her hand and sipped at it himself. He winced at the taste.

"Gah, this is like something a medicar would give the diseased."

"It is prescribed for some ailments, but being worth its weight in silver does constrain its use."

Forteron drank more, then gestured across to the Alliance army.

"The thick mud that has protected my ramparts is about to turn traitor," he said. "My enemies have been gathering wine barges by the dozen at their island camps, awaiting a good depth of water on the floodplain. Silverdeath is gone. Most of my fighting ships have been scattered and dispersed as a result of last night. There are only a dozen dash galleys in the river, and the deepwater traders that survived last night's huge wave. Most of my galleys will not be back until tomorrow, so I suspect our friends out on the floodplain will pay us a visit today."

"They have my curse, Your Highness."

"And you have my thanks, but fifty thousand warriors would be more useful. You were married to a Diomedan king once, I have been told."

"He was put to death, with all of our children. I feigned madness. I danced in my dungeon cell, I danced as I was paraded through the streets in humiliation, I danced at my trial, and I danced as I was led to the headsman's block. This cracked the nerve of the usurper, who was of a superstitious nature. I was led back to the dungeons, where I taught my jailors to dance. I was cast into the streets in rags, but watched for any sign of sedition. I danced with the windrels in the markets, and coins were showered upon me. I was given shelter by the stallholders, and in time I began to take pupils. Years passed, and the watchers grew bored with me. I even taught a few spies how to dance. By the time you invaded, I was under the patronage of the foreign merchant's daughter, Lady Wensomer. It has been pleasant to throw off the guise of madness under Torean rule."

"I am gratified that I have been able to discomfort the murderers of your family," Forteron said with mechanical courtesy. "But you should have delayed your move. Your usurper's son is about to take back Diomeda, and rumors of your sanity are sure to reach his ears."

Forteron drained the last of caffin from the bowl, then replaced it on the tray that Sairet still held.

"Have you ever wondered why Diomeda has been so passive under your rule?" asked Sairet.

Forteron had indeed wondered about the fact but had never asked the question. He had assumed that his strategy of restraining his marines and allowing the Diomedans to go about the business of making money was partly responsible.

"Yes, I have," he ventured cautiously.

"I still have influence, and I know a vast number of people. Whenever a cell of loyalists got together to hatch a plot, my own followers would hunt them down and kill them. When spies were sent over from the island palace, my people would catch them. When assassins sought shelter in loyalist safe houses, well you can bet your very life that at least one of my people would be there to discreetly betray them to your people or strike them down. It was difficult, dangerous work. Few people have survived long in my service."

Forteron stared at her for a moment, very surprised and genuinely impressed. He was not to know that in reality there had been no such resistance, led by Sairet or anyone else. The truth was that business had been so good under Forteron that the merchants, nobles, and freemen of Diomeda had turned most loyalist agents over to the new authorities on their own initiative. Who was to know that, however? Certainly not Forteron.

Forteron bowed low to Sairet.

"My lady and protector," he said with grace, and no hint of sarcasm.

Sairet set the bowl down on the marble railing of the balcony, then held her hand out to Forteron. Puzzled, he nevertheless took her hand in his. Her skin was refreshingly warm and dry in the cool, dank air that now enshrouded Diomeda.

"I *can* also provide you with fifty thousand warriors," Sairet said in a silky contralto.

* * *

The criers were on the streets within ten minutes, warning that
an attack was imminent, and that the crown prince was alive.
The criers also announced the crown prince had added the last
of his men to the Alliance army, and had vowed to slaughter
every man, woman, and child in Diomeda for not showing any
sign of resistance during Forteron's occupation. The fact
Forteron had already admitted that the prince was alive gave the
lie instant credibility. The criers concluded with the news that
Forteron had offered to cram as many women and children onto
his surviving ships as would fit. They were to stand out in the
harbor, and if Prince Selva and his allies breached the walls,
they would flee to Scalticar.

An hour later came another announcement, one that had an
impact hardly less dramatic than the fire-circle that had destroyed the island palace. Sairet, the former queen, was to
marry Forteron. Forteron was to restore her as queen. Sairet had
not been mad after all. Together, Forteron and Sairet would defend Diomeda. The wedding would take place on the balcony
above the main doors of the temporary palace.

Rumors began to spread. Warsovran had destroyed Torea.
That was not a difficult line to sell. The really stunning news
was that Forteron had mutinied and stolen Warsovran's war
fleet and marines to depose the Diomedan usurper and restore
Sairet to the throne. Forteron had rebelled against Warsovran to
come to her aid. Warsovran had only escaped the fire-circles
because he had been on the way to capture and execute
Forteron, and take back his fleet. With Torea destroyed, however, Warsovran had been forced to forgive Forteron and pretend the whole exercise had been his own idea. Forteron had
done it all for the love of Sairet. Right across Diomeda, people
forgot about fire-circles, giant waves, invaders, war, floods, and
torrential rain. A passionate, heroic, and epic royal romance
had been exposed. The gods of the moonworlds had smiled
upon Forteron's act of chivalry, and so allowed him to escape
the fire-circles. Now Warsovran was dead and Forteron had
killed the madman Feran. He had also smashed Silverdeath.

Forteron was a prince, and a strong, protective prince.

Another rumor was that Sairet had been forced to stay apart from Forteron while she bravely led the resistance against the loyalist agents. Within about forty minutes, Sairet's network of two dozen stall holders, harlots, spies, and informers had grown to ten thousand citizens and slaves, all claiming to be members of her underground. By the ninth hour of the morning there were thousands of citizens gathered before the villa that had been Warsovran's palace. Forteron and Sairet were to be married immediately. It was the ultimate free public spectacle—a royal wedding! Surely Diomeda was again in Fortune's favor.

While a priest of the Diomedan harvest god officiated, Forteron and Sairet exchanged vows in the pouring rain, then gongs rang out all around the city. The royal couple flung handfuls of silver coins to the thousands of spectators who were standing knee-deep in muddy water and cheering themselves hoarse. Wensomer then led a troupe of dancers in a space cleared by an arc of marines on the plaza below, while musicians played beneath umbrellas. As Forteron and Sairet stood waving, one of those chance happenings took place, something that meant little but could be construed to be quite a lot more. The rain trailed off, then stopped. This was instantly taken as a sign of divine blessing of the wedding. The crowd went wild.

"The Alliance will attack within the hour," Forteron warned his bride.

"Tens of thousands of newly recruited Diomedan militiamen are said to be flocking to the ramparts," Sairet replied.

"And no rain means that my marine archers will be able to keep their bowstrings dry," added Forteron.

The Diomedan crown prince had by now skirted Diomeda and reached the command tents of the besieging army. He swore that Silverdeath had been destroyed, and was no longer a danger. Word had already been brought to the Alliance nobles and kings that a large part of the Torean fleet had sailed away, and that Forteron's remaining ships were being loaded with people. The invaders were preparing to flee. Clearly this was a very unsatisfactory state of affairs. They were on the eve of a great and glorious victory, but now they were not going to have the satisfaction of crushing the enemy. Any pillage of Diomeda could not be allowed to be too excessive, for the crown prince did not relish the thought of having a ruined capital—especially since his entire kingdom was Diomeda, the Leir River, a few towns, and a very, very large expanse of desert.

When the rain suddenly stopped, it seemed to be a sign from the gods of the moonworlds. It was their way of asking the Alliance what they were waiting for.

The attack began with the wine barges crammed with warriors being rowed with the current from the islands of the Alliance camp toward the embankments. Away from the river the current was sluggish, although the water was now over six feet deep in most places. The ramparts loomed, topped by what looked like irregulars.

Without warning it began to rain arrows. The barges were not roofed, and the men aboard were very tightly packed. Worse, they were a mixture of pikemen, archers, and warriors armed with axes and shields. The rowers in the lead barges tried to turn back, but the crush of barges from behind prevented this. Pikemen desperately tried to shelter under shields and dead bodies. The archers fired back, but their opponents on the ramparts were more thinly dispersed, and each had a shieldman from the city to shelter him. The first of the barges landed, and Diomedan militiamen fell upon the survivors. Even so, there was a great number of Alliance warriors uninjured, and they were seasoned campaigners.

The rain began to fall again. The Alliance nobles tended to be in gigboats at the rear, rather than the barges. This was so they could get a better view of the overall battle, and so they would be safe from stray arrows. After all, they reasoned, a noble was worth ten or more commoners, yet arrows made no distinctions in matters of class. Thus they were the first to see Forteron's five dash galleys emerging from the river channel and turning into the flooded farmlands of the inner delta. The row up from the main channel had been slow and exhausting, but now Forteron's ships were like wolves among chickens. Two of them cut across to harass the rear line of the barges, while the other three made for the islands of the camp. These dash galleys were crammed with marines. The islands were thought to be well out of reach of the Diomedans, and defended by cooks, grooms, packmen, camp followers, and some of the more timid nobles.

With nowhere to go but Diomeda, those on the barges renewed their attack on the ramparts all the more. In several places they actually broke through and swarmed into the city. The city was flooded, however, and the high ground—the houses—was occupied by Diomedan militiamen and irregulars. Everything was soaked, so no attempt to set any building alight was successful. Back at the ramparts the dash galleys rammed the rearmost of the barges, while Forteron's own gigboats rounded up the nobility as they tried to row to safety. The warriors remaining on the barges swarmed back to attack the two dash galleys, and soon they were covered in desperately fighting men—robbing the Alliance of extra men to storm the outskirts of Diomeda.

Diomedans on the roofs pelted their supposed liberators with bricks and beams of timber. With their bowstrings soaked in the rain, the Alliance archers could not shoot back. Alliance warriors chopped holes in the two dash galleys, but they only sank only a few feet before they grounded in mud, leaving the decks above water. Having secured the Alliance camps, leaders, horses, camels, supplies, and servants, the three remaining dash galleys bore down on the ramparts, manned only by the rowers. Even the sight of the approaching warships was too much for the Alliance warriors. Some surrendered, some took to the water and swam, some flung down their weapons and pretended to be Diomedans, and others managed to push their barges clear and rowed into the main channel of the river. At the mouth of the river were two dozen becalmed deepwater traders crowded with women and children and crewed only by a few Toreans—but they were armed with catapults and heavy ballistas. Five barges were sunk before the others surrendered.

By the time the light began to fade from the sky, Forteron

was the undisputed victor, and at the price of surprisingly few Diomedan lives. Early in the evening the rain stopped again and the cloud cover began to break up. Miral was visible in the east, rising huge and luridly bright in the rain-washed air.

There had been no fire-circle at Helion. Roval was very agitated as he paced the decks. Finally, when the designated hour had passed and the garrison had not been obliterated, he ordered the crewmen to raise and lock the masts.

"The patrol gig will notice next time they come past," warned Norrieav.

"Boatmaster, the patrol gig has one inspector, and two marines to row. Besides, by the time they notice, we shall be under way, with a stiff wind."

"But Miral's up and the sky is clear. The patrol galley *Kygar* will be on to us faster than Hazlok with a willing whore."

"The galley is on the other side of Helion, we'll have a good start."

"You want to race the *Shadowmoon* against the *Kygar*? Learned Roval, I've crawled out of taverns faster than this thing can sail."

"We shall escape, Boatmaster. I have what Laron would call a bold, daring, and devastatingly stupid plan."

"So, as stupid as that?"

"There is no more to do here, and Wensomer may be awaiting execution. I must try to reach Diomeda and help her. Besides, there may be another chance to snatch Silverdeath. What else is there to do?"

Norrieav sighed. "What do we have to do?"

"Firstly, get at least five miles from Helion before the *Kygar* catches us."

"There is an easterly wind—yes, we can do it. And after that?"

"We put on a very credible act."

Boatmaster Norrieav struck the little gong by the steering pole with the back of his hand, and the four others of the ship's company quickly gathered.

"Listen carefully," Roval began. "We are going to make a break from Helion, and sail for Diomeda. Now. It will be dangerous, but we have a chance."

"As expedition leader I now give full command to Boatmaster Norrieav," sighed Terikel.

Roval stood back, and Norrieav scanned the harbor and nearby waters before turning to speak to them.

"I declare battle conditions until further notice," said Norrieav quietly but firmly. "Terikel, take the steering pole, notch it to fifth octen and stand by. Hazlok, D'Arto, and Lisgar, raise the mainsail then stand by to man the sweeps. Roval, you can tell me about the rest of your plan as we raise the anchors."

The *Shadowmoon* was under full sail and sweeps before the harbor inspector noticed the schooner was leaving the harbor. Within two minutes he was ashore and waving two torches to signal the lookout at the lip of Mount Helion's crater. Moments later another signaler was sending the message to the patrol galley. Immediately the galleymaster changed course, cutting close to the island to set after the tiny schooner. He also gave the order to ram. That was up to his discretion, but patrolling Helion had become boring, and this was an excuse to paint another broken ship on the galley's bow.

Aboard the *Shadowmoon*, Roval was at the masthead, and was first to catch sight of the distant galley's running torches. He came scrambling down to the deck.

"The *Kygar* is under way, sir," he reported. "Like us, sail and oars."

"Secure sweeps!" Norrieav shouted. "Terikel, strap the steering pole at zero octen, the rest of you drop and tie the sails. Hazlok, not you. Empty that jar of olive oil over the quarterdeck while I light a torch."

"Light a torch, sir? Wi' all that oil about to catch afire?"

"Well, I'll not wait till it dries. Hurry!"

❄ ❄ ❄

Galleymaster Mandalock saw the distant schooner suddenly blaze up, as if soaked in lamp oil. As his officers cried out in surprise, the fire began to diminish as the schooner sank, then the ocean was dark and clear again.

"It caught fire, then sank," said the Commander of Marines.

"Never seen the like," said the galleymaster. "Never so quick, anyway."

"We should slow—there may be survivors in the waves."

"Damn survivors, I want a ninth ramming to paint on my bow! Nine is my lucky number."

"But it sank."

"The hull may be just below the surface. Have the initiates do brilliance-castings. Search for it."

Not far below, the *Shadowmoon*, was sinking rapidly. Normally that did not matter, for the boatmaster chose to submerge in shallow water. This, however, was a long way out from shore. The five crew of the *Shadowmoon* were huddled under the gigboat on their knees, with dark water swirling around their waists and the timbers squealing under the increasing pressure.

"Light—someone do a casting!" ordered Norrieav.

Terikel spoke a casting into her hand and held it up. Norrieav took her wrist and held it near a glass tube with evenly spaced marks and figures painted on it. The level of water was just above thirty.

"Thirty feet," Hazlok read.

"But we're still going down," cried Roval as he watched the meniscus moving in the pressure glass.

"Well, it was your idea to sink in deep water," retorted Terikel.

"We had to look to be on fire, then sink," said Roval.

"Fifty feet," read Hazlok.

"Well, we're certainly sinking!"

"I'm open to constructive suggestions."

"Sixty feet," read Hazlok.

"Unclamp the gigboat," cried Terikel.

"No, the gigboat will right itself and spill all the air as soon as the clamps are—"

"Silence!" shouted Norrieav. "I am boatmaster, and you are all to remember it. Nobody is to speak except as part of their duties."

There was silence, except for the creaking of wood and an ominous gurgling.

"Seventy feet, descent slowing," said Hazlok.

"In tethered tests before we left the *Megazoid*, this craft reached ninety feet before its buoyancy stopped it. Is that not so, D'Arto?"

"Yes, sir."

"Seventy-five feet, still slowing," reported Hazlok.

"We should stop at eighty; the new airtight lockers and empty lamp-oil jars in the ballast will help the gigboat balance us."

"Eighty feet, still slowing," said Hazlok. "Eighty-two, eighty-three . . . balancing . . . stopped."

Terikel breathed out gustily and Roval slumped deeper into the water. An echoing boom shook the *Shadowmoon*.

"A locker collapsed, sir!" shouted D'Arto amid the cries from the others.

Another boom shuddered through them.

"Eighty-five feet," read Hazlok.

"We need to cut away two anchor stones," said Norrieav. "Roval, speak casting bands onto your wrists for light. D'Arto, feel around for the gig's tow rope and tie it around his waist."

As his tether was secured, Roval fashioned glowing bracelets of ether with bright points beneath his wrists. He took three deep breaths.

"Whatever you see, note it," said Norrieav. "I want good status reports."

"Yes, sir."

Roval ducked beneath the water and climbed out just behind the foremast. It took only seconds to find the port deadweight and another half minute to hack through its rope. Turning to starboard, he began cutting through the rope of the starboard deadweight as the slipstream of dark water flowed past him. His lungs were in some discomfort by the time the second rope gave way, but as he tried to return to the gigboat he found his tether was tangled in the foremast's mounting. More precious seconds were needed to cut himself free, but as he scrambled for the gigboat again, something large and pale glided past nearby.

Roval's head burst into the tiny refuge of air, and he gasped desperately for some moments.

"One hundred and twenty feet, slowing, but still descending," said Hazlok.

The timbers of the gigboat squealed and creaked almost continuously.

"Both forward deadweights gone, sir," panted Roval. "Decks cluttered, had to cut my tether. Saw things. Alive. Big, pale."

"Sharks?" exclaimed Norrieav. "There have been none since the fire-circle."

"One hundred and twenty-five," said Hazlok. "The scale ends there."

"Not sharks, but plenty of teeth. My lights, they drew attention."

"Things that don't go near the surface, but know that a sinking ship has tasty bodies to eat."

"You must write a paper when we get home," said Terikel.

"We're still sinking, but slower," said Hazlok.

"Should I go out again, sir?" asked Roval, already tying another tether to himself.

"At this rate, balance depth is five hundred feet, by my estimate," said Norrieav. "That's another way of saying we're all dead. The midships deadweights will have to be dropped also. Roval, come back for a breath between them, understand?"

"Still sinking."

Roval's shaven head vanished beneath the water again, and moments later there was a slight pop and lurch as the starboard deadweight dropped away. Roval returned.

"Dentards, they are. Three, four dentards. Fast, curious. Swam down after the deadweight."

"Rate of sink slowing."

Again he took a breath and ducked under. For some moments there was just the creaking of the timbers, then a thump and scraping sound, followed by another thump. Norrieav took an ax and ducked under while D'Arto hauled Roval's rope in. It

was almost a full minute before Norrieav and D'Arto dragged
Roval back inside. The sorcerer's left arm was gashed below
the elbow.

"Dentard had him," gasped Norrieav. "Whole school of them
out there."

"Port deadweight dropped, sir," Roval managed between
clenched teeth.

"Balance point," reported Hazlok.

Something bumped and scraped at the hull of the gigboat.

"They smell blood," said Terikel.

"Lisgar, hold him up. D'Arto, bind his arm, stop the bleeding."

"Ascending," said Hazlok.

"How deep are we?"

"Hard to say. We've been off the scale for some time."

There was a dull but powerful boom as something collapsed.

"That was an empty jar, I would guess, sir," said D'Arto.

"Descending again," Hazlok said unhappily.

"Sir, permission to drop the aft deadweights?" asked Terikel.

Norrieav looked at her, then rubbed his eyes for a moment.
"Go ahead," he said reluctantly. "But return between weights,
and wear the tether."

Her head vanished under the water. Norrieav took Roval, and
Lisgar spoke a pale filament that wrapped around his hand.

"Still sinking," said Hazlok.

They waited. D'Arto finished bandaging Roval's arm. There
was a muted pop as the rope holding the distant deadweight
parted, then a series of echoing bumps and scuffles. The tether
was pulled tight for a moment, then went slack.

"Pull her in!" shouted Norrieav. "D'Arto, Roval, help me."

"Too easy, no weight on the end!" cried D'Arto.

The end of the tether was roughly severed. For a moment
there was only the creaking and gurgling of the sinking
schooner.

"Terikel," whispered Roval.

"Slowed, but still descending," said Hazlok, his voice suddenly rising in pitch. "Not enough, boatmaster! That was not
enough—"

"Hazlok, quiet!" said Norrieav.

"—and the indicator float is jammed, and the air in here's

squeezin' with the pressure, soon there won't be room for our heads—"

"Hazlok!" shouted Norrieav.

Hazlok froze. Lisgar leaned over to the tube.

"Indicator float jammed," the deacon read.

"Terikel is dead," whispered Roval.

Hazlok released his breath in a cough, then took several great gasps.

"My . . . my station," he managed, seizing Lisgar's wrist and holding the light closer to the tube.

There was a distant pop. They stared at each other in the dim light.

"Terikel!" exclaimed Roval. "She must have almost severed the last deadweight before the dentards got her."

They cheered the dead priestess as one, but almost at once something was bumping and scuffling nearby. Something scraped at the gigboat.

"Dentard!" said Norrieav. "What's it doing?"

"Maybe it eats ships, sir?" said D'Arto.

"Maybe some crewmen live on in trapped pockets of air when ships sink," said Roval. "It might be common."

"So common that dentards have learned to unwrap the packaging on their food," said Norrieav.

Large jaws worried at the gigboat's hull. There were deep, ululating cries from outside.

"Roval, I'm taking an ax and going out," said Norrieav. "If I don't return, take command."

"Wait, sir," panted Roval. "I shall go. Less to lose than you."

He spoke a casting into his right hand, then fed it yet more etheric energy in a series of breathlessly chanted words.

"Indicator float still jammed," reported Hazlok.

Roval ducked under the surface, and a moment later a brilliant flash of light lit up the water around them. The dentards around the *Shadowmoon* bellowed and ululated, but the sounds quickly faded. Roval returned.

"They are creatures of the depths, sir," Roval explained. "It will be some time before they regain their sight and their nerve."

"Float still jammed."

"We still have the anchors," said Norrieav. "Roval, we both go out, but you just provide light, understand? Maybe we can work faster than one alone. D'Arto, Hazlok, help with the tethers."

Roval spoke another casting, then they went out together.

"Estimate, sort of really deep," said Hazlok.

There was a deep scraping, followed by a pop.

"Anchor gone," said D'Arto.

"Estimate, really deep and either going up or down."

Norrieav and Roval did not return. The scraping started again.

There was another pop, followed by a softer scraping sound amid the creaks and gurgles.

"Estimate, sir, er, hopefully not so deep."

Norrieav reappeared, then hauled Roval's head into the air. The sorcerer coughed water.

"Estimate, ah, um, deeper than is probably safe."

"Didn't we die a few hundred feet ago?" gasped Roval.

"Call the reading," prompted Lisgar.

"The reading is . . . one really tightly jammed gauge. Estimate, er, really, seriously deep."

"We're ascending," said Lisgar.

"What?" Hazlok laughed, with a slightly hysterical edge to his voice. "D'ye have your own gauge?"

"Actually, yes. That was at water level a minute or so ago. Now it is just clear."

He pointed to a small eating knife that he had pressed into the timber beside him. This time there was no cheer to draw the dentards back, but there was a definite improvement in the mood of the ship's company.

"I'll go out again, dump anything loose and heavy," said Roval.

"That would be helpful, but we are already ascending," said Norrieav.

"It is my way of saying good-bye."

"To Terikel?"

"Ah, yes."

"Look . . . just out of curiosity, did you ever, like . . ."

"Give her one?" suggested Hazlok.

"Open your heart to her!" shouted Norrieav, although he was now glaring at Hazlok.

"Never," said Roval. "It is not my place to make such suggestions."

"But why?"

"The Special Warrior Service turns men into something more than just exceptional fighters. We are trained to be stronger and faster than most, we are masters of all fighting arts, and on top of that we are tenth-level sorcerers, experienced darkwalkers, and have a university education. There is a temptation that goes with all that, a temptation to think of oneself as a god. To counter this, there are rules, and one rule is that we may only respond to the advances of a woman, we must never make such advances ourselves."

"Shit, glad I never joined the SWS," said Hazlok.

"So, all that business with you and Terikel in the master cabin—"

"I do not know!" confessed the warrior-sorcerer. "I think it was honorable. I certainly took no liberties with her."

"I'se definitely never joinin' the SWS," Hazlok said firmly.

Roval made a series of quick forays outside, and dumped some metal fittings over the side. D'Arto's anvil also went into the depths.

"Pleased to report, the gauge is working again," said Hazlok. "One twenty-five and ascending."

"Hear that?" said Norrieav.

There was a distant *boom—creak, boom—creak*. It did not sound at all like any animal.

"Shit!" exclaimed D'Arto. "The *Kygar*."

"What? After all we went through?" cried Hazlok. "Is the galleymaster blind? He saw us sink—we were on fire to prove it."

"Perhaps he knows the *Shadowmoon*'s secret," mused Norrieav. "Have you any more bold, daring, and devastatingly stupid plans, Roval?"

"My last one cost Terikel her life, sir," replied the sorcerer. "I am having trouble thinking of anything else just now."

"We can't sink again, not without the weights," said Norrieav.

"I adored her."

"If we tried to fight they would probably just laugh."

"Perhaps if I had just smiled at her more often. . . ."

"We could abandon ship and swim for Helion."

"Or maybe I should have paid her a few compliments."

"I don't believe I am hearing this, Learned Roval. We are a hundred feet below the surface, up to our nipples in water, ascending into the view of a fully armed battle galley, and armed with just half a dozen axes and one cheap crossbow, yet you sit there lamenting you never made a move with Terikel!"

"Seventy feet," said Hazlok.

"In fact, surrender is looking like a quite viable option, sir," Lisgar suggested.

"The rest of you should abandon ship and swim back to Helion, sir," said Roval. "I shall stay with the *Shadowmoon* and fight to the death to cover your escape."

"No!" Norrieav said emphatically.

"She died here. I would wish that my blood mixes with hers in these dark waters."

"Snap out of it!" cried Norrieav. "The *Shadowmoon* has more secrets than any blockhead on the *Kygar* could know. We will fight."

"Fifty feet, the mast top will be at the surface," said Hazlok.

"Fight?" Roval exclaimed numbly.

"With respect, sir, with what?" asked D'Arto. "We have a crossbow and a few axes. That thing above us is a battle galley."

"We got a couple of harpoons somewhere," said Hazlok.

"Stand by to surface," said Norrieav. "Hazlok, D'Arto, dive out and close the sink hatches. Roval, dive for the jars of lamp oil down below."

The decks of the *Shadowmoon* broke the surface, and they scrambled out from under the gigboat into Miral's light and the deliciously cool, fresh wind. The galley was nearby, turning in a wide circle.

"Hazlok, Lisgar, D'Arto, begin pumping," ordered Norrieav. "Roval, dive for the lamp oil while I unclamp the gigboat."

"Sir, why bother to pump if we're abandoning ship?" asked D'Arto.

"Because we're not abandoning ship, I—"

He was interrupted by a shriek from Lisgar. Roval raised his

ax and waded toward the aft cabin hatches, where something
was scrabbling out.

"Gets back, one of those dentards must have been trapped in
there," shouted Roval.

Terikel crawled out into Miral's light. Roval dropped his ax
and hauled her to her feet, wrapping his arms around her as the
other began working the pump. Almost as rapidly, he pulled
away.

"You—ah, seem uninjured, my lady," he said hastily.

"How?" asked Norrieav.

"Air from the burst lockers, trapped by the cabin's roof,"
croaked the priestess, falling to her knees in the shallow water.

"Why didn't you come back?" asked Roval. "I thought I'd—
that you were dead."

"Thought . . . more air for you under the gigboat. Also, too
frightened . . . to move."

※　※　※

Having found the fugitive vessel, galleymaster Mandalock ordered the *Kygar* back to get a really good speed established.
Initiates with brilliance-castings swept the darkness as the top
of the ram threw up twin waves. They closed.

"It must have capsized, then righted, who would have known
it?" cried the galleymaster. "Come around farther, get a good
run and bring us to maximum speed."

※　※　※

Aboard the *Shadowmoon* there were traces of order amid
murky chaos in the dark water under Miral's cold, green light.
The middeck was just above the water by now.

"Hazlok, unclamp the gigboat!" shouted Norrieav. "Roval,
unseal those jars of lamp oil."

"Lamp oil? Sir, we need oars!" shouted Roval.

"Lamp oil, damn you! *I'm* boatmaster! Pour it into the gigboat."

"But, sir, we're supposed to escape in that!" Roval pointed out.

"Shut up and do it! Terikel, can you cast one of those dazzle autons?"

"Yes, boatmaster."

"Do so, and bind it just inside the front of the gigboat."

"What? Sir, those things are highly unstable, they practically go off by themselves. A heavy-enough thump—"

"—will be ideal. Lisgar, D'Arto, keep pumping."

Norrieav rigged a canvas cover for the gigboat while the oil was being poured into it. By now the galley was head-on, but at a distance. As Roval poured out the last jar of oil, Norrieav began cranking back the crossbow.

"A tendril-casting with contraction, if you please," the boatmaster said to Roval. "Link the gigboat to this quarrel."

"I can't sink a galley with a casting!"

"No, but *I* can. Everyone, to the sweep oars and stand by—Not you Terikel. Stand at the steering pole and notch it to fifth octen."

It was a difficult shot, at night, at sea, and in only Miral's light, with a wet bowstring, but the galley was a huge target. Norrieav fired. A thin sliver of light flickered through the darkness and struck the bow of the galley.

"Now row!" shouted Norrieav.

The tendril began to contract, drawing the gigboat away from the *Shadowmoon*. The *Shadowmoon* moved sluggishly, being still largely full of water, but move it did. The *Kygar* had lined up to approach broadside, but the *Shadowmoon* was turning. The faint tendril was lost to sight. The galley began to turn as someone realized the alignment with the target was changing.

"Get ready to duck under," cried Norrieav. "If my device works, there's to be flame everywhere."

"Sir, under what?" asked the exasperated Roval. "That's our bloody refuge you've just thrown at them."

The gigboat struck the galley's bow. Terikel's dazzle-casting was disrupted. It detonated with a tiny core of intense heat amid a mixture of lamp oil and air. The mixture exploded. The sides of the gigboat had been designed and built to be exceedingly strong so they would withstand the pressures of being submerged. A plume of burning lamp oil was shot high into the air with a thunderclap blast, and it splashed down the entire length of the galley. Burning from bow to stern, the galley slid past the mostly submerged *Shadowmoon* and its astonished crew, oars clattering and splintering against its side and railings. The *Kygar* continued on, slowly losing momentum, then came to rest, trailing flames into the wind.

"Hazlok, Lisgar, return to the pump," called Norrieav. "Terikel, to the steering pole and lock into the third octen. Roval and D'Arto get into the rigging and unfurl the mainsail."

Norrieav tied down the sweeps as they worked, and the wind began to nudge the half-submerged *Shadowmoon* away from the burning galley. Presently he joined Terikel on the quarter-deck, working the pump while Lisgar and Hazlok went forward to unfurl the foresail. Terikel locked the steering pole and joined the boatmaster.

"We need to make headway," said Norrieav as they worked the pump handles. "They'll not be distracted for long."

"On the contrary, sir, I think they will be distracted for quite some time to come," said Terikel, staring back over the *Shadowmoon*'s wake at the blazing galley as it trailed flames and smoke into the easterly wind.

Those aboard the galley were very much under the impression they had been struck by a fire-circle, and quite a large number of rowers, marines, and officers had leaped overboard on their own initiative. The blaze touched off by the gigboat had not, in fact, been so very serious, but with most of those who should have been fighting the flames leaping overboard, the fire was free to take hold with a vengeance. Those watching from Helion thought the galley had caught the fugitive and set it ablaze. The fact this was the second fire to be visible was confusing, but the watchers assumed that the correct explanation would soon be brought home with the victorious galley. It was an hour before another ship was sent out to investigate. Fortunately, the dentards were sufficiently intimidated by the fire that they did not investigate those struggling in the water around the blazing wreck, so there were few casualties among the crewmen.

✳ ✳ ✳

By the time the *Shadowmoon* had been pumped empty and trimmed to sail due west, the *Kygar* was an orange point of light on the horizon. The sky had clouded over by then, and light rain was falling. Norrieav stood at the steering pole while Roval stared back along their wake for pursuers. Terikel sat hugging her legs beside the rail.

"I shall never, never set foot on another ship again once I return to Scalticar," said the priestess.

"I have lost count of the number of times you have said that," said Roval without turning. "Can we not change the subject?"

"My intent had been to spill burning oil ahead of the galley," Norrieav declared, breaking his silence of the hour past. "The fountain of fire was a timely accident."

Norrieav beat at the gong until the crew had gathered before him.

"I declare the vessel stood down from battle stations," said Norrieav. "Learned Elder, I am your servant."

The others returned below. Terikel cleared her throat.

"If you have any more creative innovations like that, sir, please keep them to yourself," she said, looking straight at Norrieav. "Ships are dangerous enough as it is. Submersible warfare is more than this world could take."

"You take the benefit of the device, yet you condemn it?" laughed Norrieav, shaking his head.

"You asked a dragon for help, boatmaster, and it amused the dragon to oblige us," said Roval. "Next time it may not be so charitable."

"And next time *we* may be on the galley," Terikel pointed out. "By the gods of the moonworlds, I hate the sea. After tonight it's going to be hard for me to cross a bridge or even step into a bathtub."

Norrieav went below, leaving Terikel and Roval to the quarterdeck and the rain. Presently Terikel stood up and put an arm around Roval.

"When—when the *Shadowmoon* surfaced . . ." she began, then let the words hang there.

"Sorry," he mumbled. ". . . should not have shown familiarity that way."

"I— What? Why not?"

"SWS training and protocols are very strict regarding unsolicited familiarity with women."

"Roval, this is ludicrous! We stripped off our clothes and got into bed together when the *Shadowmoon* was boarded."

"That was a military action, that was espionage. We were warriors."

"But— Well, why did you embrace me, then, when the *Shadowmoon* surfaced?"

"I was worried, I wanted to be sure that you were not injured."

Terikel shook her head. Roval folded his arms very tightly and squirmed.

"So, about Learned Wensomer," said Terikel casually. "If she lives still, are you—"

Roval made a sound like someone being strangled while attempting to throw up.

"Never!" he gasped as he recovered his voice. "The only occasions on which I have carried her to bed and removed her clothes have been when she managed to get blind drunk and vomit over herself. Actually, there have been quite a few of those, but— Look, she is my friend, I care for her, and I have risked my life for her many times, but bed? Well, once, but the very memory induces a sharp, intense pain just behind my left eye."

"So you—and she—that is, . . . ?"

"Hardly ever. The woman is as unstable as a brilliance-casting, however clever she may be. Give me credit for at least some good taste."

Terikel glowed warm in the cold, soaking rain and flying spray, but then remembered there was a second matter to clarify with Roval.

"Have you ever talked to Laron about his chivalry nonsense?" she now asked.

"I admire Laron for his strong principles—"

"Well, Hazlok has talked to *me* about what you said during the dive."

Roval opened his mouth, took a deep breath, worked his jaw soundlessly several times, glanced over the rail, seriously contemplating diving overboard, then decided to put all of his self-control and SWS discipline into stopping his knees from turning to jelly.

"Roval . . . my last bedmate was Feran Woodbar, in the master cabin that is directly below us. Torea was behind us, all glowing slag, and my family, friends, and Order were all smoke and ash on the winds, yet he just rutted all night until, well, until Laron stood up to him. I swore that I would never bed another man after that."

"Quite so, my lady, I had deduced that this was precisely the case," Roval babbled, with the most extreme of relief, "and of course I have the highest respect for your feelings, so—"

"Roval, please shut up and let me finish."

"Sorry."

"In the time since then a thought has kept nagging at the back of my mind. Why should Feran be my last memory of a man's arms and company? He was all lust and no compassion or tenderness, he was— Oh, I can't speak about it without anger flaring. Then there was you. Funny, charming, gracious, educated, and so handsome when your head is freshly shaven. Look, you seemed too good to be true, but you never showed the slightest interest in me—even when naked and sharing the same bed. I assumed you had a true love somewhere distant, or perhaps somewhat less conventional tastes. How was I to know about the Special Warrior Service and its rules about making border incursions with women?"

"I could not tell you about the SWS rules; you would have known I fancied you," Roval protested.

Terikel pressed her splayed fingers against her face. "Roval, I am not asking for anything lasting, but will you sleep with me for a night or two?"

"My lady, I could never ask—"

"I know, that's why *I'm* bloody well asking *you!*" Terikel cried, banging both fists against the deck. "Still, why should I complain?" she continued more softly as she got to her feet. She put her hands on Roval's shoulders. "It means that you are now before me, unencumbered with attachments to some other."

Terikel drew his face close to hers, then kissed him softly. Roval ceased to be aware of time, then Terikel's tongue was flickering teasingly over his lips and she was laughing into his face.

"Your arms are around me," she giggled softly.

"I—I'm sorry, I thought it permissible, my lady."

"Of course it is, but how are you steering the *Shadowmoon*?"

"Oh shit!"

With the steering pole locked, they again stood with their arms around each other on the quarterdeck. A head appeared in a hatchway, then vanished. Presently the sounds of laughter and the clink of coins could just be heard above the splash of the waves and creaking timbers and ropes.

"I believe we have just caused sundry wagers to be won and lost," said Roval.

"You care for me—you are charming and gracious," said Terikel.

"You are my princess, my true love, my goddess of beauty, and my angel of wisdom. And you have the wit to understand my jokes. Most women do not."

Terikel squeezed him as tightly as she could. "This is just wonderful. Now I shall take sweet memories of you as my last bedmate into the future, rather than those of Feran. You have lifted my curse, you have slain my demon. There is nobody in all the world that I would rather dwell upon than you."

"The thought of you and Feran, I—I . . . It makes me feel so ill, it squeezes my hearts like a pair of cold, taloned hands. I did not show it, because it is not my place."

"Do you think I have felt any happier about it?" Terikel sighed. "It was spy work. Dirty work. Filthy work. I am haunted by the thought of it."

They kissed again, for a moment that lingered like a polar sunset. In spite of the rolling waves, heaving deck, flying spray, and rainswept darkness, Terikel was not aware of any trace of her seasickness.

"Think you can beg someone to take your shift?" asked Terikel.

"I have favors that I can call in."

"Then I shall meet you in the master cabin."

Roval went below to where the others were playing at dice, beckoned to Hazlok, and led him to the middeck.

"I gather you made quite a tidy profit by your not entirely discreet words to Worthy Terikel," he said quietly.

"Learned sir, I meant no harm," whispered the grizzled sailor. "I'll make it up ter ye, just tell me how—"

"Oh, good, you can take over my watch. Now."

"I— What? Er, yeah, that I'll do. A pleasure. Gracious and mighty sir, my thanks and apologies. Are you sure that's all?"

Roval's hand snaked out to seize Hazlok's thin but wiry arm.

"Had money not been involved . . ." Roval began.

"Ah . . . I'd have told her just the same," admitted Hazlok.

Roval released him, leaned against the foremast, closed his eyes, and began laughing softly. Then he straightened and bowed to the sailor.

"There must be hope for the world if even you harbor a trace of romance, Hazlok. If ever you are trying to impress some tavern marm and want a few words spoken about your bold and brave deeds, just let me know."

"Ah— Oh. Kind of ye, sir. That I might."

About an hour later Hazlok was alone on the quarterdeck when Norrieav emerged and joined him. Below their feet, a lot of giggling and scuffling was coming from the master cabin.

"Sir, one thing worries me," confessed Hazlok.

"I may not have an answer, but ask anyway," said the boatmaster.

"Roval, like, has big muscles, is handsome as a prince, can probably fight better than any warrior in the world, brave as a sea dragon, right?"

"Well, aye."

"Terikel's got a figure that a goddess would kill for, she's more beautiful than any woman I've ever set eyes on, and by the sound of what's going on down there she bangs like a privy door in a really bad storm."

"Repeat that in front of Roval and you would probably find yourself overboard with a broken neck, but go on."

"Well, remember how like when we sat hidin', listenin' to them talk, they said they loved each other because they had nice manners, made each other laugh, that sort of thing?"

"Aye."

"But they said nothin' about either bein' strong, brave, beautiful, handsome, powerful, or any such-like."

"True."

"But—but . . . Were I chattin' with the likes of her, the first thing I'd say is, 'Hie there, ladyship, fine set o' norgs ye have there.'"

Norrieav put a hand to his forehead and massaged the skin while he thought about how he might bridge the chasm between the outlook of Hazlok, and the likes of Terikel and Roval. Presently he put a hand on the sailor's shoulder and gestured to the sea ahead of them.

"Hazlok, I may be your boatmaster, but I'm also your mate."

"Aye."

"When we get to Diomeda—if it's not been blown off the charts—trust me, and do as I am about to say."

"Er, aye?"

"Do not say 'shit,' 'bang,' or 'norgs.'"

"What? Why?"

"Trust me. Pour a bucket of seawater over yourself, shave, wear clean gear, and run a cloth over your teeth and a brush over your hair—and not the decking brush! When you meet with a woman, ask her about herself. Then listen. When she asks about you, don't go on for too long. Try to make her laugh. Scabby tar though you be, you will seem very like Roval in charm and manners, and look at where it got him." Norrieav pointed downward.

"That's all?"

"Aye."

"Well, shit me—I mean, I'll be buggered—I mean, I'll be f— I mean, er, ah . . . Goodness me?"

"Very good."

Two days later the *Megazoid* was sighted, and Lisgar, Terikel, and Roval transferred to the far bigger and more stable ship. All trace of Terikel's seasickness had vanished. The *Shadowmoon* followed behind the warship as it set a course for the Acreman coast.

Chapter Ten

VOYAGE TO DIOMEDA

A fanfare echoed out across the sodden city of Diomeda, announcing that the court of Queen Sairet and Prince Forteron was being held and receiving guests. A short time later three captured monarchs swore fealty to the royal house of Diomeda, as they knelt before its rulers. Wealth and ships would be bought by the ransom of the other captured princes and nobles, and soon Diomeda would control three times its former population. By the time Sairet discovered she was pregnant, she would be queen of half of the Acreman east coast, and in alliance with the newly restored King Druskarl of Vindic and the emperor of Sargol. All of that was still in the future, however, as Laron, Druskarl, and Wensomer watched the torchlight procession of Alliance prisoners, wading past on their way to newly built shelters above the floodwaters. They were at a window of her lower tower, and each held a goblet of mulled wine.

"I shall say this for Forteron—the man be as objectionable as a cow pat on a feasting table, but he is still a brilliant tactician," Laron remarked.

"I was dragged out of a hot bath to be a bridesmaid," said Wensomer, her throat inflamed and her skin flushed with fever. "Then I had to stand in the rain for a half hour while they were married—oh, and waved, and flung coins to the rabble."

"I secured a small stealth boat and hid it near the river," said Druskarl. "If you could spare me provisions for a few days and a handful of silver I really should flee north."

"So, you have what you wanted, yet the price was reasonable?" Laron said with a frown.

"You are hardly in a position to preach about ethics," retorted Druskarl.

"Were it not for Feran, you would currently be master of Silverdeath."

"I only ever sought it to be healed and restored."

"Yes, and at the cost of lives. Silverdeath only releases people to do fire-circles, and fire-circles are only done to kill people."

"So? All I would have needed was a small island and half a dozen condemned criminals chained to a palm tree."

"That is monstrous! You would buy your balls at the cost of lives?"

"Why is that any different from you when you were a vampyre? Whenever your stomach rumbled, well, whatever bully-boy, pimp, or wifebeater was to hand would be straight into the gutter with his throat torn out and his blood drained."

"I had ethical motives, it was a form of philanthropic work—"

"Just as vaporizing half a dozen murderers on an isolated island would have been."

"Just to restore your balls."

"Would you have killed so many miscreants had you not needed to drink their blood and vitality? What do you do these days, now that you're alive again? 'Whoops, I've not done anything to improve society this week, think I'll pop out and knife some slaver to make the world a better place'?"

"Gentlefolk, if you please," croaked Wensomer.

"He can say what he likes," declared Druskarl. "I am going back to Vindic, to reclaim my throne and sire an heir."

"Thanks to Silverdeath," jeered Laron.

"Thanks to Silverdeath you are no longer undead, and have been proving it with every woman foolish enough to—"

"Fine talk coming from a reconstructed eunuch who—"

"Gentlefolk!" Wensomer cried, in a badly damaged voice. "We are *all* monsters, but those who do not feel guilty about it are the only ones who are damned. Druskarl, here are three gold pagols and some silver. Take what you will from the kitchen but leave the cook, and Fortune attend your plans."

Druskarl left to pack, then returned to thank Wensomer. Standing in the doorway, he bowed to Wensomer and Laron for a last time.

"Gracious and learned lady, you have only my thanks for now. Should you ever be in need in years to come, do remember that I am in your debt, and that I always pay my debts. Laron, one day, somehow, you may find yourself very dead, and very, very hungry. When that day comes, and you are sinking your fangs into some plump and succulent throat, remember me, and what I said to you here, in this room."

With Druskarl gone, Laron and Wensomer returned to the window and watched the prisoners still shuffling past below in the rain.

"Speaking for myself, if I am going to be rained on I would prefer it to be in Scalticar," Wensomer announced.

"So, the rain is better there?" asked Laron.

"No, but in Scalticar I have my home, friends, colleagues, tenure in an academy, and two thousand miles to separate me from my mother. What of you?"

"I have been looking after Ninth, in the Academy. Perhaps I shall continue to do just that as I study for the next level of initiation."

"How is she?"

"Gone."

"As I suspected, but not as I hoped."

"What do you think happened?"

"Ninth was an etheric machine. Silverdeath could not repair a body that did not have a real spirit, yet it kept trying because the auton had the semblance of life. Perhaps it destroyed Ninth to try to release itself, but the link to the very distant world drained it."

Laron said nothing.

"Again, I can only beg forgiveness," Wensomer added.

"What is there to forgive?—you had no choice," said Laron, sounding almost surprised. "Ninth was a mechanism, just a small bundle of memories and motivations that could learn simple tricks."

"For the love of all moonworlds, Laron, *I* am just a *large* bundle of memories that can learn *clever* tricks," she shouted, raising her hands to her head. "We all are. You, me, Druskarl. You attack Druskarl, yet you defend me for doing the same thing."

"All right, all right, perhaps that was indelicately phrased. He was saving his balls, but you were saving the world."

Wensomer sneezed, then sniffled. The line of prisoners finally came to an end.

"Ninth had the mind of a baby, she was not a warrior," said Wensomer.

Laron clasped his hands, leaned on the edge of the window, and stared out into the rain and darkness. After a time he had another thought.

"Wensomer, I was once a dark and evil creature, I feasted on people for centuries, yet I tried to do good. Often I succeeded. Ninth may have been an auton, but she was very sophisticated and she *volunteered* to shatter Silverdeath as she did."

"Ninth had no will, she was built to serve."

"The Metrologan Order built the auton that was Ninth. How can you be so sure that she was not so well crafted that she really did have her own will?"

"Laron, that makes her death worse."

"Indeed, and it also makes her a brave and loyal warrior who happened to be under your command."

Wensomer considered this. The logic was built on untestable premises, but it was good logic. Was it correct, then? She would never know, yet she had related to Ninth as if she were a sentient and very intelligent being. Quite probably she was just that.

"Damn you, vampyre," she finally concluded.

"Ex-vampyre."

"Still, my hearts considered her as a baby."

"Then your head was right, and your hearts must go to the slateboard and write 'WE WERE WRONG' a thousand times before they can have dinner."

"Thank you," Wensomer said warmly. She sniffled, then blew her nose. "Laron, in the corrak, when I was angry: I said cruel things about Pellien, Lavenci, and you."

"Yes?" Laron said hopefully.

"I'm afraid it was all true."

Laron left Wensomer's mansion and waded back to Yvendel's Academy. When he arrived, the body of Ninth was lying quietly in a bed, while one of the younger initiates read from a book of simple castings.

"Any change, Dorios?" he asked as he sat down.

"No reaction at all, but she still breathes."

"Then I shall take over. While there is still breath, there is hope."

Dorios left. Laron bolted the door behind him, then returned to the bedside. Ninth was dead; before him was just a body that functioned. Form without spirit, life without sentience. Still, even this form was a gateway. The being from another world. Elltee. She was a floodgate, and when opened she would pour a torrent of scholarship into Verral. It would be Ninth's monument. There were a few communication problems to solve, like that of untranslatable words, and things in Verral totally outside Elltee's experience, but all that was trivial. Her accidental experience of darkwalking must have been beyond comprehension, and the gods alone knew what she had been told by the elemental pretending to be a—ghost!

Laron sat perfectly still for a moment, hardly breathing, stunned by the sudden realization. *"Dork,"* Elltee had said. *"An overfocused scholar or natural philosopher with limited social skills . . . take themselves a bit seriously . . ."*

Velander.

But Velander was dead, thought Laron. He had seen her die.

Laron tried to recall that day in the ruins of Larmentel. Something had been torn to shreds in the etherworld as he had been darkwalking. Something that had called his name. Velander? The succubus had stolen her body, leaving her defenseless against the raptor elementals . . . yet what was a spirit? Memories, experiences, personality, etheric energies, and reserves that allowed it to reside within a body. The raptors would have slashed away nearly all the etheric life and fabric of Velander—leaving what? Life without life force.

A sort of fuzzy bubble on a glowing, orange string. Laron took out the locket that he wore around his neck and opened it. He stroked the mounting of the flake of greenish glass. This had an orange axis line, when viewed from the etherworld. He had never looked at it closely. He had been so busy, he had been putting it off until he was ready to begin his thesis. It had never been in the iron casket. Velander might have clung to it with whatever scraps remained after the raptor elementals had finished with her. Was she still there?

Laron removed the girl's scarf and examined the circlet and oracle sphere he had put on her so many months ago. The settings were unchanged, but, then, that was no surprise. Only he and Ninth could change them, and he had ordered Ninth to leave them alone.

Laron hesitated. In a way he was almost reluctant to learn the truth. What if he was wrong? Worse—what if Velander had survived, but had faded to nothing by now? Stretching out on the floor, he spoke the words of power to detach and go darkwalking. He detached, and left the pain of his badly bruised body behind. In the odd reality of the etherworld he could see the shapes and lights of dozens of etheric devices and autons nearby. That was hardly a surprise; he was in Yvendel's Academy, after all. He knew what to look for. It would be nearby: a straight, orange line, no more than a hint of gossamer. Laron probed amid the sparkles and tendrils, as if walking through a rainshower of bright, glowing gems. It took some time to locate the axis, for it had faded considerably. The pale hint of shimmer was even more faint.

"Velander," he called into the blackness.

He strained for any reply. There was the faintest of mewls, like the cry of a kitten. Laron was not entirely sure that it might have been wishful thinking on his part.

"Velander, this is Laron."

"Laron." The word was softer than a whisper, but quite distinct.

"Velander! Do not speak again, or try to move. Save your life force—I can help you, it's not too late."

Laron's words were based on hope rather than fact, however. Nearly all the etheric filaments that had linked her spirit to its body were torn off, and her reserves had been stripped away, too. This was like the legend of the princess whose father discovered she had a secret lover. He swore the boy would never know another kiss from the girl, but she disguised herself as a page and stole into the execution chamber. After the headsman had struck her beloved's head from his shoulders, she darted forward and picked it up. The eyes blinked, and the lips moved for a moment as he recognized her, then she placed a kiss on his lips while his life lingered. In sheer outrage the king had then ordered her executed on the spot, but neither the bards nor their audiences cared about messy little details like that when heroic romance was involved.

In Laron's case there was, in fact, no romance involved; this *was* Velander, after all. On the other hand, that made it all the more . . . More what? Velander? She had nobody. She had been vicious, vindictive, opinionated, self-righteous, spiteful, scheming, and totally without real friends. Now she was helpless, and very definitely alone and in distress. Alone. That was the worst of all. The core of Velander's spirit had lasted a lot longer, but her position was little different from that of the princess's decapitated lover. Death was not inevitable, because it had already taken place. The echoes of life were merely reverberating, but for how much longer?

Laron wove filaments around the fading essence of the girl, and there was barely a tug as she came away from the orange axis line. The oracle sphere worn by Velander's body floated in the sparkle-studded darkness, solid with the inertia of the flesh merged with it. Countless thousands of etheric attachments beckoned, but less than a dozen were left to Velander's spirit. Velander. He had very nearly bitten her and flung her body overboard when they were on the *Shadowmoon*. She had betrayed Terikel, she had stupidly fooled about with his circlet and oracle sphere. He could never love her; even respecting her would be quite a strain, and anyway, she was not even alive.

But I am all she has, thought Laron.

With the sheer, bloody-minded persistence in the face of annihilation the legendary princess had once shown, Laron attached the eleven filaments remaining to Velander.

"You are back in your own body, Velander," he announced.

"Laron . . . only you . . . never doubted . . ."

She believed in him. Why? All he had done was put her spirit back into her body so they could die together. Still, Laron was nothing if not incurably romantic. Even though in life Velander was the sort of girl he would have crossed the street to avoid, she was now helpless, and Death's cold hand was descending toward her shoulder. Laron extended tendrils of his own life force, bridging attachment points with the echo of Velander's life.

"Hungry, cold . . ." murmured Velander.

"That is good, discomfort is life!" Laron said eagerly.

It was a lie. Discomfort was actually life under stress. Enough discomfort could kill. *Does having one's head struck off involve much discomfort?* he wondered. He knew his extra attachments would not last; they would have to be renewed. Eventually the strain would kill him. This was like old times, when he had been the pale shimmer of a life that had already been lost, yet was sustained by borrowed life force.

Borrowed life force, thought Laron. He returned to his body, which was lying on the floor. His limbs felt heavy from the loss of the vitality that he had spared to Velander. He stood up slowly, then looked down at the candlelit body of the priestess. The oracle sphere was sustaining her body, and given proper care it could live on for decades. On the other hand, once Velander was truly gone, the young alien sorceress Elltee could possess the body in further visits, pouring knowledge of the cold sciences into Verral from her own world. Once Velander was *truly* gone. Only then. People would be impatient for that to happen. Who would have the task of snuffing her out?

Laron leaned over Velander, gazing down at her pale face. A tear fell from his cheek and splashed on her lips.

"So many others deserve death more than you," he said sadly, then added, "even though you are a self-righteous, insufferable little dork."

Laron sighed, squeezed his eyes shut, then lay down again and spoke the words of darkwalking.

"Velander, can you hear me?" he asked the remains of her spirit. "This is Laron again."

"Laron . . ."

"Velander, you are going to have to trust me. I must know your truename. I shall be truthful with you: There is little hope. Only one path remains open to us, and it is a path that has never been taken before. Succeed or fail, I shall be hated and hunted throughout all of Acrema and Scalticar, but I am willing to try."

"Laron . . . wish I could say . . . I love you . . . but it would be a lie."

"That is a relief. Now, will you tell me your truename? Can you trust me?"

"I already trust you . . . Without you, what am I?"

With Velander's truename echoing through his mind, Laron again returned to his body. With the furtive haste and controlled terror of a thief slipping out of the royal bedchamber with the sleeping monarch's crown in his hand, he got to work. His legs trembled and his knees felt like springs as he held Velander's hands to the circlet, spoke her truename, then pushed. The circlet came free. Laron reapplied it with his own hands.

"Now there is no going back," he said as he drew his knife.

Laron decided to stay a week more in Diomeda, waiting for the freebooters and bandit deserters from the defeated army to be run down by the Diomedan militia's lancers, and allowing the roads to dry out. He was, of course, in hiding and wearing a disguise. With seven centuries of experience behind him, he was quite good at disguises. He had bought a horse and cart, and spent the days collecting bodies and weapons from the muddy fields to the west of Diomeda. The bodies he took to a barge, to be stripped of their armor, weighted, and sunk at sea. The armor and weapons went to the city marshal's storehouse, to be cleaned and repaired by his artisans.

There was no announcement that the body of Ninth had gone missing. A senior initiate had found the body dead in the morning, with the throat cut and Laron gone. Yvendel ordered that the circlet be removed, but it remained somehow locked onto the head of the dead body. The rector was intrigued. Circlets always became detached when the host body died. She ordered a detailed study to be made of the phenomenon. It was to take place the next day, after the body had been given the appropriate rites the following dawn. Early that evening, Velander's body vanished.

Quite a substantial reward was offered for Laron, by word of mouth. The circlet was worth enough to cancel the national debt of many kingdoms, and anyone who found it would not be foolish enough to trade it for any reward that the academy could offer, but Laron—alive—could be questioned about its location. Several dozen weedy teenage boys with acne were hauled into the Academy by hopeful bounty hunters, but the reward remained unclaimed.

Miral was above the eastern horizon but the sun had not yet set in the west as Laron unloaded the last of the rotting bodies from his cart and heaved them onto the barge. He wore a rag over his mouth and nose, and everyone avoided him because of the stench. As disguises went, it was perfect.

I had my life back, he thought as he paused to rest, gazing at the little schooner. *I had said farewell to being a wolf among sheep, I had been welcomed back to the fold.* Baaa. *I had said farewell to sleeping while Miral is down, and had offered greetings to dark skies full of glittering splashes of stars, unchallenged by Miral's light. I had tasted rabbit roasted on a spit, and the sour pleasure of ale. Best of all, I felt the warmth of a seductive embrace by soft warm arms. Now nobody will dare to try to seduce me. Did I really give all that up for Velander?*

The bargemaster walked up to the wagon, jingling coppers in his hand. He was one of the few people in the city who smelled as foul as Laron, and so did not shun his company.

"Many more out there?" he asked as he counted out the fee for the day's bodies.

"Still some dozens, but they'll be buried as where they be lyin'," explained Laron. "Graveworms been munchin' 'em, they're too far gone."

"So, big bath for us all?" the bargemaster laughed.

"Nay, I'm back ter haulin' nightsoil," said Laron, shaking his head. He pointed down along the pier. "What's the big battle galley down there, tying up?"

"She's Scalticarian, the *Megazoid*. Goodwill visit, probably, eh? Well, I'd best be on my way with this load."

Laron barely heard him. He was watching Lisgar, who had hurried down the gangplank, fallen to his knees, and begun kissing the timbers of the pier. They were followed by Roval and Terikel, who were holding hands. Now a second, far smaller vessel, approached the pier. The *Shadowmoon*. Laron noticed that quite a large number of people were glancing at it, then pretending to do something else. Yvendel had alerted the bounty hunters of the city that Laron would probably try to board the *Shadowmoon* or contact its crew. On the decks were Norrieav, Hazlok, and D'Arto.

Laron felt a tear leak from his eye and soak into his mask. They had been through so much together, and now he did not dare approach any of them. He wanted to exchange stories with the crew, to buy drinks for everyone, to stay up all night with Roval discussing castings and javat, and most of all to bow before Terikel and petition to begin studies as a Metrologan neophyte. They might as well have been docking on the shores of another continent.

"Intent and cargo, sir?" called an official as Norrieav jumped onto the pier to tie up.

"Just taking supplies and commissioning repairs," responded the boatmaster. "We were damaged in a storm, but the *Megazoid* found us and escorted us here after a few running repairs."

Terikel and Roval walked along the pier and stopped before Norrieav.

"How was the *Megazoid*, Worthy Elder?" the boatmaster asked.

"Compared to what happened to us during the—the storm, it was paradise," said Terikel. "I shall have my toenails extracted through my nose before I ever set foot on the *Shadowmoon* again."

"So you will return to Scalticar on the battle galley?"

"Yes. I imagine that Learned Wensomer will require the comforts of the *Megazoid* as well. What about you?"

"Oh, once the repairs are done and a new gigboat has been built, I will bring the schooner south at my leisure."

Laron caught himself unconsciously rubbing at a fang under his mask. He hastily lowered his hand.

"I thought Laron would be here to meet us," said Terikel, looking about with her hands on her hips.

That was too much for Laron. He climbed back onto the wagon, flicked the reins and set off along the pier. The crowd parted hastily as he approached, and he gave not a hint of recognition to his old friends. He passed the small, chunky *Shadowmoon*, then the immense and streamlined *Megazoid*. They reminded Laron of a swan's dumpy chick beside its large and graceful mother.

The darkening city was crowded as Laron drove his cart toward the west gate. In one of the plazas the masons were packing up for the day. A statue of the former king had been removed some days before, and a new inscription stone had been mortared into place. It read, *In Memory of Rax Einsel, Royal Engineer to Queen Sairet and Prince Forteron*. The city gates were about to be closed for the night as Laron arrived.

"Oi, bungo, off to harvest more bodies from the fields?" called a guard as he approached the wagon.

"Ter ye they be bodies, but they're my bread and butter," Laron called back.

"Ach, rancid swine! You'll put me off dinner. Isn't it a bit late to be gathering the dead?"

"Aye, that's true. But I'se been evicted from me room on account of me smell. Got a tent and roll in the back ter sleep in the fields."

"Dangerous in the fields, beyond the walls."

"Dangerous?" laughed Laron as the guard glanced over the tailboard of the wagon. "With all them 'orrible murders in the city? Two strappin' bully-boys wi' their throats torn out, and that furrin' student, er, um—"

"Master Starrakin."

"Yeah, like wi' 'is head torn off—and them's the only ones we knows about. Reckon it's a demon, I does."

"So you prefer bandits and desert wolves?"

"Ach, I'll just lie still. One sniff and they'll think I'm dead."

"Pah, on your way," laughed the guard, "and good luck for the night."

Laron drove the cart out across the muddy battlefield, then reined in on the low hill where the invading army's command tents had once stood. Amid the rubbish and wreckage were the waterskins, provisions, money, and fresh clothing he had cached there earlier, and he quickly had everything loaded onto the wagon.

Climbing back onto the driver's bench, he looked east to Diomeda. He knew the buildings would obscure the docks, but he still had a pang of disappointment that he could not see them. Taking a small plate from his robes, he stroked it with his thumb. It was his badge of rank as an officer on the *Shadowmoon*.

"Farewell, *Shadowmoon*, and thank you for everything," he whispered, then flicked the reins and set off along the road that ran west beside the Leir River.

The slaver D'Alik had been lucky in his flight from the pursuing Sargolan lancers. The rain had begun, and while it made his journey over the desert difficult and uncomfortable, it also washed away the tracks of his horse. His merchant house in the river port of Urok was quite modest, but it was safe and discreet. Over the weeks following his arrival, he gradually wound up his affairs while he waited for a caravan to arrive from the north. He sold his slaver license to his local steward after hearing that Diomeda had defeated the Alliance army, and that the Sargolans had actually signed a treaty with the Torean invaders.

At last the rain stopped. Barges were more common on the Leir River, now that the Sargolan blockade had been lifted. At last a particular caravan arrived, both camels and their drivers caked in mud. He sent a message to the caravan master, then had his nine remaining slaves escorted to the docks.

Barge traffic was mostly one-way on the Leir. The barges themselves were crudely constructed, designed to float down on the current with cargoes of wine, timber, and other such things that were in short supply in the coastal city. At the end of the journey the barges were broken up, because the wood used in their construction was worth several times more in Diomeda than the cost of hauling them all the way back to the mountains. There was often some room left over to pick up additional cargo on the way down, especially if it was light.

"Dunno about this," said Cenzel, the bargemaster of a convoy of timber barges that had stopped at Urok to pay customs fees. "Diomeda is not the place it was for slave tradin'. It's Queen Sairet—she's met too many folk who was slaves, like when she was pretendin' to be a mad dancer. She's killed the trade, like, ye know?"

D'Alik had been in the trade for three decades, and was not easily discouraged.

"But these nine girls all have pedigrees and certifications," he insisted, opening a cloth bag full of scrolls. "Every one comes from a good merchant family in the Sargolan states, and all can pay ransoms. There is no excise on ransoms in Diomeda."

"Diomeda is not Sargol."

"Aye, but Diomeda is a seaport. You can discreetly sell them to a shipmaster bound for Sargol, then have no more to do with them. Besides, you have eight barges, each with two crewmen. A girl each to keep them amused for a week would be a bonus that would cost you no money, take them off my hands, make you a profit, and restore the girls to their families. Everyone will be happy—you cannot lose."

"Nine girls," the bargemaster sighed.

"And eight barges," laughed D'Alik, elbowing him in the ribs. "Cenzel, I'm afraid you will just have to take two girls in the flag-barge."

"No, you said nine girls, yet I count ten."

"Ah, but one of them is not for sale."

D'Alik's deals were difficult to resist, and indeed, most were happy with the arrangement. The girls even had a good prospect of getting home, and seemed willing enough to supply whatever services were involved to pay for the trip. Cenzel took the seal from around his neck and concluded the deal. D'Alik

paid off the guards, saw the girls aboard the barges, then returned to where Senterri was chained to a railing. She was gazing west, to the Lioren Mountains. That was the territory of the
Gladenfalle principality. Slavery was banned there. It was only
thirty miles or so to the frontier. Nearly ten times closer to freedom than she had been at Hadyal, yet in a way just as far. What
else was there to do, though, except what she was told?

"Now, little Senterri, there is just you to dispose of," he declared.

"Master, I would fetch a better ransom price than any of
them," she said as he unlocked her.

"And get my head on the end of a very long pole if I tried to
claim it. Still, the market for slaves of noble origin is more
steady than that for common whores, especially in the kingdoms to the north. I have a very discerning buyer ready to make
an assessment, so come along."

Senterri looked longingly to the mountains in the west. They
were in a different kingdom, they seemed so close. There she
would be free . . . but they might as well have been on the other
side of the world. A few guards and some loyalty were all that
separated royalty from slavery; she now knew that only too
well. The sheer helplessness of her situation offended her like a
foul stench, but there was no escaping it.

D'Alik stopped before a tavern, checked a note, then led Senterri inside. A caravan master met them at one of the tables. He
beamed at the sight of Senterri, then circled her several times.

"At first sight, she is a rare prize," he declared, taking her
chain from D'Alik.

"There is more to her than just the sight," said D'Alik. "I
have her papers and certifications."

"Indeed? I shall be glad to inspect them, but I must insist on
inspecting the, ah—how shall I put it delicately? The entire
proposition?"

D'Alik's eyes narrowed. "I suspect that you wish to inspect
the proposition while staring down into her most beautiful
green eyes within a most comfortable bed. Such-like would de-
value her worth."

"Ah, but if you already have your fee, is her worth any business of yours? A princess, you say? I have seen a few from afar. Why do they always seem so much more fair than the common run of women?"

"Because kings demand—and get—the fairest of bedmates."

The caravan master stroked Senterri's breasts, then hefted one and nodded. Senterri shivered miserably, but had learned not to pull away.

"I have a room prepared in the town's finest inn," announced the caravan master.

"The Red Star?" asked D'Alik.

"The same. The bed has been scented with rosewater, incense is burning."

"So, you intend to set about bulling her all night? What sort of price will she fetch if her belly is bigger than yours by the time you parade her in the markets of the north?"

"Price, price, price—you think only of price, D'Alik. I think of destiny. I intend to set about bulling her until she brings forth sons, a line of princes to make my house great, to succeed me."

"And if you sire daughters with her?"

"Hah! They will still be princesses, and so will she."

They sat down at a table to examine Senterri's scrolls in greater detail, and presently the men were deep in serious bargaining. Senterri stood beside them, as unheeded as if she were a pony. *Not once has either of them spoken to me in this exchange,* she thought. She looked about the dimly lit taproom, aching for release. Every dream, every reverie was a prayer for escape, yet her master had decades of experience with the handling of slaves, and knew of more tricks and schemes to escape than she could ever dream of.

A young wayfarer with a soft-featured, almost girlish face was gazing at her. There was a disturbing intensity in his eyes, something that hinted at a hungry fire and lashing etheric energies within him. At first Senterri could not quite believe he was paying her any attention. He had to know what she was: a slave. She wore the padded yellow collar, it was there for the world to see. *Perhaps he is a young prince in search of adventure,* thought Senterri, savoring the dream rather than holding any real hope. *He might even be a warrior prince, wandering the world, having lost his kingdom.* He would rescue her with a

band of loyal followers, they would flee across the desert to
Sargol. Her father would welcome him, shower him with
wealth and honors. They would be married.

No! The word blasted through Senterri's mind. *No dreams,
no more futile dreams. What would Dolvienne do? Fight, of
course, there was no question of that. But how? Perhaps by
gathering allies. Perhaps the youth was a master thief, or a
desert brigand, who might start a fight, flee the tavern with her,
and take her to the sanctuary of his desert hideaway.* He was
still staring at her, a cold, bright, unblinking stare. He raised his
eyebrows. The gesture seemed to say, *Well?*

Locking stares with the youth, Senterri mouthed the word,
Please, with what was the most imploring expression she could
manage. The youth straightened the fingers of his right hand,
put them to his lips, then one by one curled them into a fist. The
gesture for words into deeds, thought Senterri with a shock.
Was he serious? There were two impressive and expensive
bodyguards flanking the table where the slaver and the caravan
master sat with her. Slavery was legal in Urok. Any attempt to
rescue her would be regarded as theft; the town militia would
be after them within the hour.

Beside her, a deal had been concluded. Papers were being
stamped, signed, and sealed on the table. As the two men stood
up to go, it was the caravan master who was holding the silver
chain attached to Senterri's collar. She cast one last glance at
the youth with the intense eyes. He put a fist to each heart, then
bowed his head slightly. *"My hearts are in your service,"*
thought Senterri. *But does he mean it?*

Miral was rising in the east above the low buildings of Urok
as they set off through the darkened streets. Urok did not have
much nightlife beyond the five taverns near the river docks, so
they saw nobody as they walked. Thoughts of the youth in the
tavern faded quickly from Senterri's mind. Perhaps he had had
good intentions, perhaps he had even thought seriously about
helping, but he would soon see that it was no use. Even half a
dozen men would be hard-put to defeat the four who were with
her. *So this is how I am introduced to womanhood,* she thought.
No sweetheart, no romance, no love, no coy glances and shy,
hesitant kisses, just a command to disrobe and a bed that gaped

like the mouth of a dragon to feast upon her innocence. However revolted she might be by the caravan master, though, Senterri knew she would have to try her very best to please and delight him. Were he to lose interest in her, she would be quickly turned over to his drivers or sold as a harlot slave.

"My purser is waiting at the Red Star with funds that will cover your most ruinous price," the caravan master was saying.

"Pah, for just a few grubby gold coins, you will transform the fruit of your loins into royalty—"

Something black dropped from a balcony and smashed down onto D'Alik and the caravan master. They both collapsed, shadows swirled. A tangle of glowing threads wrapped itself around the neck of the caravan master's bodyguard, then there was a sharp snap. Senterri had the impression of D'Alik flying through the air, to thud against a wall. He lay still. A shadow struggled silently on the dusty ground with the caravan master. Senterri backed away until stopped by the wall. Now she saw that another figure had engaged D'Alik's bodyguard, and they were trading ax blows. The smaller man ducked under a swing, closed, hooked the bodyguard's leg with his own. The bodyguard stumbled, recovered, there was a flailing of arms, then the bodyguard was bent over in an armlock. A knee smashed into his face. The bodyguard collapsed and lay still.

So far everything had taken place in near–total silence. To Senterri's amazement the smaller man began binding the bodyguard. He dragged him over to a horse and cart she had not noticed until now, heaved him into the tray, then hurried back to D'Alik. Senterri watched as her unconscious master was also gagged and bound. Next the youth lifted the other bodyguard into the tray—and tossed a severed head after it. Suddenly he looked up, appearing to notice Senterri for the first time. It was not the youth from the tavern. This one had a scruffy beard and wavy hair.

"Who the hell are you?" he demanded in an urgent whisper, speaking Diomedan.

"A slave," replied Senterri, tapping her collar, then pointing to D'Alik. "He is my master."

"Not anymore. Hurry! Help me drag him to the cart."

D'Alik was heavy, and it was a struggle to get him into the tray of the cart, and concealed. Senterri followed the youth back to an untidy black pile of shadows on the ground.

"Velander, for goodness' sake!" he hissed, dropping to his knees. "What if someone comes?"

By Miral's light Senterri could see that the one called Velander had her teeth buried in the caravan master's neck, and was sucking and swallowing rather messily. Tendrils and sparkles of etheric fire played about her lips in the gloom. *Her* face! The youth from the tavern, Senterri realized. A girl? A girl who had the strength of half a dozen men, and who drank blood?

"Velander, *please!* We have to go."

Velander's head shook without detaching her teeth from the caravan master's neck. The youth hurriedly searched the man's body.

"Purse, scrolls, seal, notes of credit and debit, rings, knife, another knife, sheepgut contraceptive . . . that seems to be all," he muttered. "Velander, will you hurry up!"

Velander raised her head and snarled sharply, then returned to her feeding.

"No use, it's been three days since her last meal. You know how it is with those thin desert outlaws. Give her one, and before you know it, she feels like another."

"I, I, I— What is it—er, she?" asked Senterri.

"The technical term is 'vampyre.' She is the only one, but she's quite a handful. Velander! Snap out of it! It's no good; you will have to help me, young lady. I'll bring the wagon over to them, then you lift Velander while I try to get her dinner in."

"Me? Touch *that*?" gasped Senterri, catching sight of the claws on Velander's fingertips as the horse plodded over with the cart.

"She's quite clean, it's just that her eating habits are a bit messy. Now, lift her at the waist and I'll get his shoulders onto the tray. Just be careful, her thinking is not too clear when she is feeding. Ready? Heave!"

Senterri put her arms around the supernaturally strong bundle of shadows, claws, and fangs, and was not really surprised to discover that she had no body heat at all. They heaved.

"No! Mine! Mine! Mine!" mumbled Velander, her teeth still buried in the caravan master's neck.

With a frantic flurry of pushes and shoves, Senterri and the youth managed to get the vampyre and her victim onto the tray of the wagon and raise the tailgate. Senterri's rescuer draped a ragged tent over them, then sagged against the wheel and paused to catch his breath.

Senterri glanced about her. The street now looked quite normal, almost innocent. The horse seemed quite unperturbed, and obviously had seen a lot of this sort of thing. The youth had worked with efficiency that could only have come from extensive practice. He snapped his fingers, and a pinpoint of light appeared above the palm of his left hand. With his right hand he reached under the seat of the wagon.

"Now, what do we have here? Which scroll? Are you Senterri/Sargolan/Five?"

"Senterri is my name, and—"

"Good. This scroll must be yours, I'll just stamp it. There, you are free. Take the scroll, and his purse."

He thrust them into Senterri's hands.

"What?" she whispered.

"Go. You're free."

"Free?" Senterri gasped. "What do you mean? You can't just set me free."

"I just have."

"But you can't!"

"Why not?"

"Because I am a slave."

"Not anymore, I stamped your scroll. Just here, see—"

"No, no. I mean if I was found wandering the streets with my master's purse and my master missing, I would be tried for his murder, sentenced to death, and executed so fast the town crier would be able to announce the lot in one breath," Senterri hurriedly explained, stamping her foot with exasperation.

At that moment Velander's head appeared over the edge of the wagon's tray, her chin dark with blood.

"Girl is right, Laron," she hissed in soft, heavily accented Diomedan. "With us, comes."

"What? No!" snapped Laron. "Next time your stomach rumbled you would be onto her faster than a sailor with a—"

"No, safety, I pledge, for her. From tavern, young lady. Remembering, one I said about? With evil slaver? With filthy ravisher?"

"I— Yes, yours was a brave and valourous deed, quite beyond—" Senterri began.

"Succulent ravisher," Velander said wistfully.

She bared her fangs and flicked her tongue over them, then her head vanished again. Laron glanced up and down the street, but it was still empty. He unpinned his cloak and draped it over Senterri's shoulders.

"Here, hide your collar and chain under this."

The guards at Urok's desertside gate were more interested in keeping raiders out than preventing anyone from leaving, whatever the hour of the day or night. However, at night they charged double the bribe for an unrecorded opening with no questions asked. Laron paid with one of D'Alik's coins, borrowed from Senterri.

"If they knew what they were letting out of Urok, they would have let us pass for free," said Senterri, glancing back at the covered tray of the wagon, and shuddering.

"Thinks with her stomach," Laron muttered without turning. He urged the horse to a brisk but sustainable pace.

"My lord, I am truly grateful to you for your valorous rescue," said Senterri, once the town's lights were no longer visible behind them.

"Think nothing of it."

"Oh, but—"

"Look, this was Velander's idea, not mine. I did not even know you were being rescued until the fight started—but don't feel hurt or anything. If I had known about you—ah, I suppose I would have suggested a rescue to Velander anyway. How does it feel to be free? Job security can be a problem, but— Ah, good, we turn here and cut across the field to the road that goes west, beside the river. Hold on, it's bumpy for a way."

"That, that, that, er, whatever it is—you mean *she* deliberately rescued *me*?" Senterri said, slowly catching up with what Laron had been saying.

"Yes. We're unwelcome sexual attentions about to be foisted upon you by the caravan master?"

"I— Ah, yes."

"Thought so. Velander is a little touchy about the rights of women in general, and violence against them in particular. I am, too, but I don't take it as personally as Velander, her being a girl—well, more or less, anyway. That is probably why she chose the caravan master to be first. He is Dinner Seventeen."

"She has killed seventeen people?" gasped Senterri.

"Oh no. If you count Breakfast Six and Lunch Two, it comes to twenty-five."

Senterri swallowed.

"Ah, and I nearly forgot about Midnight Snack Six and Afternoon Tea Two."

"Thirty-three deaths?"

"Her favorites are rapists, although she mostly makes do with ordinary bandits as a staple. She is also partial to bullies, wifebeaters, slavers, pimps, and burglars—oh, and corrupt administrators, she loves those. Then there are delicacies, like boring bards who sing out of tune, wine fanciers who will not shut up about the great cellars and vineyards they have visited, and religious fanatics who follow people about in the street reading tracts of scripture."

I have either gone raving mad or I am dreaming, thought Senterri. *Or maybe both. Perhaps the caravan master is ravishing me, and I have gone insane with shame and humiliation. I have vanished into my own head, where my spirit dreams it is free even though my body is—*

There was a muffled squeal followed by frantic scrabbling from the tray behind them.

"Velander!" shouted Laron, banging on the side of the cart. "Keep the noise down."

No dream, thought Senterri. *Far too ridiculous*. By Miral's light, Senterri saw long, gleaming fangs flash in Laron's mouth. So he was one, too! Senterri realized. One *what*? Whatever they were, they tore people's throats out and drank their blood. Perhaps she was being saved for later, as well . . . yet the treatment she was receiving was considerably better than that which her late masters had experienced.

She began to bind up her hair. This was something that did not require thought, and had not been permitted while she was a captive. In desert society, a respectable woman never showed her hair unbound in a public place. Her unbound hair was as much a symbol of her slavery as the padded shackle on her neck. They rode on in silence for a time, and presently the noises from within the cart's tray ceased.

"My lord, the caravan guards will soon be after us with dogs," Senterri warned, suddenly remembering the fate of other runaways.

"Dogs tend not to like tracking Velander," replied Laron. "Maybe it's because she likes dogs. It could be an acquired taste."

"She—she feeds on dogs, too?"

"Yes."

"How many more such, such—well, *demons* are there?"

"I told you, there is only Velander. She is quite enough, as you may have gathered."

"But what about you?"

"Me? Oh, you mean these!"

He removed his long fangs and dropped them into his purse. Senterri giggled before she could stop herself. *How long since I giggled about anything?* she wondered. *Back in Diomeda, months ago, at a belly-dancing lesson. So it is true, this is no dream. If I can laugh, then I truly am free.*

"Have to keep up appearances, you know," Laron explained. "I mean, when people see that Velander and I both have fangs, and then they see her tear heads off and get hit by arrows without showing any effects, well, they think I can do the same. Best way to win a fight is to frighten people into running away. Ah, this is a nice spot."

Laron reined in the horse and locked the wheels. Taking a body each, he and Velander carried them over to a ledge overhanging the river. Laron struggled under the caravan master's weight, but Velander had no trouble with the much-heavier bodyguard. Senterri watched as Velander carried two large rocks over to the bodies. Laron was waiting with a coil of rope.

"We always weight the bodies and sink them," Laron explained as he tied a rock to the bodyguard. "The fish clean off the flesh, the clothing rots, and tracker dogs are not at their best underwater. We seldom leave her, er, table scraps in open view. They would eventually become a trail that someone might follow."

Velander lifted the weighted body above her head, then flung it at least twenty feet into the deeper water. By now Laron was tying the second rock to the caravan master. When he was finished, Velander heaved the body into the water, then returned to the cart.

"You ruin this one!" she snapped at Laron as she lifted the decapitated body. "*Never* use strangle casting," she added for Senterri's benefit. "Big waste."

"As it stands, it seems as if the slaver and his bodyguard robbed and killed the caravan master, then escaped across the river to some hideaway," said Laron, following with the bodyguard's head. "Once the bodies are gone, we are just a boy and two women in a cart."

"But, my lord, I still wear the shackle of a slave."

Velander dropped the decapitated body, reached out with both hands, seized the shackle and twisted. The rivet broke. She tossed it aside. It traveled over halfway across the three-hundred-yard-wide river before hitting the water. Senterri rubbed her neck nervously as Velander continued to stare at her. Or at her neck, at any rate.

"Apologies," Velander suddenly muttered, looking away.

Laron weighted the body with a rock, then attached the head by its hair. Velander heaved it out into the water.

"Velander, wash your face," called Laron, as she turned back to the wagon.

"Am not finished," she said, vaulting into the tray and staring down at D'Alik.

Senterri saw that D'Alik's eyes were open and bulging wide with terror. He had apparently been awake for at least part of Velander's previous meal. He struggled against his ropes, but they had been tied with no less skill than a slaver would have used.

"You little pig!" exclaimed Laron. "Well, don't come running to me tomorrow night when you feel like a nice soft neck and there's nobody to hand."

For just a moment D'Alik caught Senterri's eye. Death was looming over him, licking her lips. A flicker of pity batted somewhere at the edges of Senterri's awareness. For so many months he had been her owner, her master, her monarch. Now he was Dinner Nineteen. Suddenly another thought crossed her mind. How many girls had D'Alik loomed over in the gloom of the bedchambers in Madame Voldean's establishment? With a dark, sharp stab of malicious pleasure, Senterri smiled at D'Alik.

"Do you think she wants some privacy?" asked Senterri, gesturing back to the tray as they set off down the road again.

"No, but if you value your sanity you should keep your eyes on the road ahead," Laron advised.

They reached the frontier before dawn. It was no more than a pair of stones flanking the road and the ruins of a watchtower annihilated during some border dispute of decades past. Laron hobbled the horse and left it grazing. Velander climbed out of the tray of the wagon, then looked to the river.

"For wash, is time," she said to Senterri, then strode away across the shingles to the water.

"She is right," said Laron, who was dragging sacks and bags out of the tray of the wagon. "That is good—not too much blood on the sacks and none on the bags and tent. She is not as messy as she used to be. Poor little thing, it must be hard for her, but she does try."

"She—she has not been like this for long?"

"Ah, no. Not at all, really. Only a matter of weeks. She saved my life once, you know. I tried to save her in turn, but I could not bring her back from the dead. Yet I did manage to bring her back, even though it's not quite the same. I have been trying to look after her ever since. Ah, would you please take these sacks to the water's edge and rinse out the blood?"

"I—I . . ."

Senterri stifled a sob. Laron took a pace back, looking concerned and still holding the sacks.

"I am sorry," he said hastily. "If blood upsets you I can do the washing. I would be grateful if you could tear up some grass for the horse's nosebag, though. We cannot stay here long, and he must be getting hungry. Story of my life, really, looking after hungry things that depend on me."

"No! Laron, no, you don't understand. Nobody has said 'please' to me for so very long. Yet again I realized that I was really, truly free, and it—it came as a such a shock. Give me the sacks."

"Are you sure?"

"Dammit, Laron, do you think I don't know how to wash clothes? I am an expensive and well-trained slave—well, until last night, anyway."

"Ah, damn, the slaver!" Laron exclaimed, as if remembering some minor and annoying detail.

Laron heaved D'Alik's body out of the tray and staggered unsteadily to the water's edge. Dropping the body, he went in search of a suitable rock to weight it with. *He will need rope,* thought Senterri. *Rope . . . and something to cut it with.* She approached the slaver's body with a coil of rope and an ax. Tossing the rope to the ground, she raised the ax and brought it down on the body's neck. At the fifth blow the head rolled free.

"What? Now I'll have to tie it by the hair!" exclaimed Laron as he returned with his rock. "Why did you do that?"

"A demon made me do it," Senterri sighed, the ax over her shoulders.

"A demon? Velander! Why in all hells did you tell her to cut off—"

"Not Velander!" protested Senterri. "A little joke—I couldn't help myself."

"Well, I like a girl with a sense of humor, but there's a time and place for everything."

"I *want* to keep the head," explained Senterri, and her tone made it clear that she was not open to negotiation.

"Amberwood hairpins, I collect," said Velander. "Laron, false fangs, you collect. Lady is liking heads, collect. Wasting other three. Sorry."

"You collect heads?" said Laron.

"Just this one," replied Senterri.

"But why? It has no particular virtues, and if searchers do find us, we are not just a boy and two women, we are a boy, two women, and a severed head. All that can be summed up by the word 'suspicious'."

Velander nudged D'Alik's head with her foot, then kicked it. The head arced through the air, and landed in the wagon's tray.

"Why are not you, ah, discarding fang collection?" she asked Laron. "Is suspicious, too."

"Well, point taken, but my fang collection is a lot smaller, and will not be reeking in a day or two."

"Miral down, myself am dead body," declared Velander. "Bigger than head, very suspicious. Yes?"

Laron opened his mouth, took a deep breath, then snorted and folded his arms. "Well, all right, keep your bloody head," he muttered to Senterri. "I suppose everyone needs a hobby."

Laron secured his stone to D'Alik's body, then Velander picked it up with one hand and heaved it out into the deeper water. Laron and Senterri applauded. Velander bowed. Laron began to tear up grass and stuff it into the feedbag, while Senterri attended the bloodstained sacks. The edge of the river flowed over stones, and was not at all muddy, so Senterri dumped the sacks into the water and trod them down. Not far away, Velander rose from the surface and began to strip off her black clothing. For a moment she stood naked in the green light of Miral, then tossed her tunic and trews to the riverbank. Ducking down again, she washed blood from her hair before striding from the water.

She noticed that Senterri was staring at her, the sacks beneath Senterri's feet forgotten.

"Something is matter?" asked Velander.

Senterri continued to stare, her mouth hanging open a little.

"Am not threaten you," said Velander. "Not afraid, being necessary. Ah, women of solidarity, I am believing in. Or is it solidarity of women, perhaps?"

"The finest Zel vase ever crafted is not as beautiful, delicate, and perfect as you," Senterri managed.

Velander blinked, her hands on her hips.

"Er, not understand."

"Compliment."

"Ah, *compliment*. Is peer, er . . . What is word? No hinting, please, trying to improve Diomedan . . . Approval! Peer approval. My thanks."

Velander gave a flourish with her arm, then bowed deeply. Laron came hurrying over with a bundle in either hand.

"Dry clothes. Velander, get into them with all haste. Senterri, get your slave gear off—don't worry, I shall not look—weight it with a stone, and throw it into the water. You can wear Velander's spare tunic and sandals—oh, and my cloak, if you are cold. Can I have the sacks, Senterri? And Velander, your wet clothes?"

Laron hurried back to the wagon.

"Is good soul in Laron," said Velander, wiping the water from her skin with her hand. "Him, if anyone hurts, I make sure is in pain of extremes, and takes long time to die."

✳ ✳ ✳

Dawn was glowing on the eastern horizon as they set off for the west again. Laron had erected the wagon's rain frame and tied tentcloth over it, after pointing to various colors in the sky and clouds, and insisting that it meant rain. Velander had the reins, ignoring Laron and Senterri as they breakfasted on dates and water.

"Do you not eat, my lady?" asked Senterri.

"Eat, that I do," replied Velander.

"She ate last night," Laron added.

"Ah, yes, I think I understand," said Senterri, shuddering. "Silly me."

Miral was touching the western horizon, jagged with the Lioren Mountains. Laron estimated they could reach the first of the inland cities by nightfall. Presently Velander stretched, in a strangely sinuous way, then climbed into the tray of the wagon.

"Soon to sleep," she announced, looking straight at Senterri. "Being nice to Laron, yes? Looking after me, big strain. Not say cross words to Laron. Else, myself unhappy. Myself unhappy, very dangerous."

With that she crawled beneath the bags and wet sacks. Laron

kept glancing at the western horizon until the last of Miral's rings had vanished.

"Velander will be asleep by now," he explained. "Actually, she is dead, but best not to say it like that—it hurts her feelings. She will become active again when Miral rises. You're stuck with my company for the next twelve or so hours."

Senterri was not sure what to think. Stuck with his company? Did Laron want her to pay for her rescue with the only currency she had to offer? At least it was the price of freedom, and he seemed nice enough, although a little scrawny. On the other hand, he seemed too . . . too well mannered and decent to demand that sort of thing.

"My lord Laron, what is your pleasure?" she asked softly.

Laron glanced from the road to her, then the tray, then west to the mountains.

"Now that you mention it, I could get great pleasure from about a half hour of sleep," he said as he handed the reins to her. "Just keep us pointed west, and on the road."

Senterri had never driven a wagon in her life, but she managed to more or less keep control while Laron tried to get comfortable on the narrow, bouncing driver's bench. Presently he began to doze, still sitting up. They proceeded west at a steady pace, and Senterri waved to the occasional peasant they passed. Light rain began to patter down, and slowly grew heavier. Laron teetered, Senterri put out a hand to steady him, then gently pulled him over until his head was resting on her thigh. He remained asleep. She stroked his wavy hair, then his beard. A tuft came off in her fingers. She choked down a giggle, then kissed the scrap of beard and gently pressed it back onto his cheek.

✳ ✳ ✳

Laron awoke with his head resting on Senterri's lap, her arm draped over his chest. He immediately tried to get up, but Senterri pressed him down again.

"Is the wooden seat more comfortable than my lap?" asked Senterri in a regal, confident voice.

"Ah, no," Laron admitted.

"Then stay where you are."

The girl is used to giving orders, thought Laron as he resigned himself to the warmth and softness of his unexpected cushion. She stroked his hair, then let her hand rest on his.

"You still look exhausted," observed Senterri. "When did you last sleep?"

"Ah, somewhere in the desert."

"I asked when, not where."

"Er, not sure."

"You do not look after yourself properly."

"I'm still alive," he pointed out. "That is not a bad test."

Laron finally noticed it was raining quite heavily, but the wagon's covering was doing a good job of keeping them dry.

"According to the milestones, we should be in Gladenfalle by sometime in the late afternoon," Senterri announced.

"Seems too quick," said Laron. "How long have I been asleep?"

"Perhaps eight hours, maybe ten."

"Eight hours!" exclaimed Laron, sitting up before Senterri could press him down again.

"Yes. My lap must have been very comfortable."

Laron blushed. Senterri giggled. Laron rubbed his hands together, hugged his knees, ran his fingers through his hair, stared at a rock they were passing in the hope that it was a milestone, then blew on his fingertips and rubbed his hands together again. They passed a real milestone.

"Well, goodness me, we must be quite close to Gladenfalle," he ventured.

Senterri reached across, put a hand behind Laron's head and kissed him very firmly on the lips. They avoided swerving off the road only because the horse was paying attention to where it was going.

"Velander said to be nice to you," whispered Senterri. "Was that nice?"

"Ah, yes," Laron admitted. "But I do not think she quite had that in mind."

"Oh. Would she be jealous?"

"No, but she does get sad about having cold blood and being dead. She cannot do things like, well, kissing. Too dangerous."

"I would not like her to be sad," said Senterri, turning back to the road.

"I feel that same way."

"Perhaps we should not talk about this to her."

"I agree. I am not sure I believe it, anyway."

"Why not?" asked Senterri, genuinely surprised.

"Well, you are lovely, and I am— Ah, well, I do not like talking about myself. It makes me depressed."

Senterri handed the reins back to Laron, then pressed against him and draped her arms around his neck.

"I'm cold," she said as she rested her head on his shoulder. "And don't you dare offer me the cloak in the tray."

Laron managed to take the cue, and he put his free arm around her. They passed another milestone. It was another hour to the city.

"What will you and Velander do now?" asked Senterri.

"Spread a little joy, do some charitable works in Gladenfalle, then move on. We like to think we do good, but we are never welcome."

"You mean killing evil and obnoxious people?"

" 'Kill' is a rather strong word. 'Selectively cull' is the expression I prefer."

"Are, er, Velander and you . . . That is, are you . . ."

"Are we what?"

"Intimate?"

"No!"

The vehemence of his reply suggested the idea was actually unthinkable, not just merely untrue.

"Yet you look after her."

"Yes."

"Why?"

"Because I am all that she has."

"But what do you get in return?"

"Nothing. It's mixed up with the idea of chivalry. Well, mostly. I get gratitude, I suppose. In her own way she has become such a sweet little thing since she died."

"You mean when she was alive she was *worse*?" asked the astonished Senterri.

"No—well, yes, but . . . it's complicated."

They rode in silence for another minute or so, but with the city so close Senterri felt emboldened.

"How did such a fate befall Velander?" she asked with genuine compassion.

Laron shook his head, as if wondering how much to tell her.

"She was a brilliant young priestess, with the rest of a great and wonderful life stretched before her, overflowing with promise. Then she did something very foolish, a magical experiment. She was killed. I—I found an echo of her spirit, after all others had accepted her death. I performed a casting. It was somewhat foolish, but then I am inclined to be somewhat foolish."

"But why? She was dead."

"Should your lover or your child die, would you not weep over the corpse? If bereaved, would you not save a loved one's portrait, ring, poetry, cloak, or lock of hair? People visit the graves of the dead, leaving flowers, candles, and even wine. All of this keeps the dead from fading entirely."

"Such acts are for the benefit of the living, not the dead," replied Senterri.

"Indeed? But is a fire truly dead when it has faded and cooled to a few lumps of charcoal and a spark?"

"No."

"Take that last spark away, use it to light a candle. Is the fire dead?"

"It is . . . no longer the same."

"Take that candle, use it to make those lumps of charcoal burn again. Did the fire ever die? The grate is the same, as are the coals. So is the flame. The fire is just a process, just like life. Velander's spark lingered in a calm, dark place for a very long time. By the time I found it, she was so weak that I could not bring her back to life . . . but I could bring her back."

"Yes, you used that expression before," Senterri said thoughtfully.

"I— Yes, so I did. You listened to what I said. That was very nice of you; most people don't take me very seriously."

Senterri tried to think it all through, but it was too hard. The metaphor Laron had used was not a good one, but it was hard to refute.

"So, she is, ah, not quite alive?"

"No, but there are countless people alive who do not deserve to be thus."

"She kills. That cannot be good or just."

"So does a soldier, or a king. The difference is that along with the bad, they often kill the good, the innocent, the generous, and the kind, because their wars are seldom about justice. Velander always kills the brutal, objectionable, cruel, greedy, and vaguely horrible—except for the occasional accident, anyway. She contributes more to the common good than most of us could. Had I alone confronted your late slaver master, his client, and their bodyguards with just a battle-ax, had I slain them in defense of your honor, would you have found it unseemly?"

Senterri was afraid of the only answer that she could have given. The thought of a handsome young hero standing astride the body of D'Alik with a bloody ax still seemed wonderful to her mind. The thought of the superhumanly strong Velander ripping out the slaver's throat filled her with horror, even though the vampyre had freed her.

"I . . . have not thanked Velander," Senterri admitted reluctantly, ashamed at her breach of good manners. "Do you think she will feel hurt?"

Laron shrugged. "Less than you or I would, but yes. The vampyre still remembers Velander's life, speaks with Velander's voice, and probably even thinks as Velander once did. When she is not hungry, at any rate. Velander tends to be rather focused when she is hungry."

"Is there hope for her?"

"Only one vampyre has been brought back to life in all of history, and the mechanism that was used to do it has been destroyed."

"And yet you remain Velander's companion, even though anyone else would shun her."

"Well, it seems the honorable thing to do. I try to follow the path of honor and chivalry, even though I seldom have company. She tries to care about me. Sometimes, when I am looking really doleful, Velander will sit beside me and hold my hand, and tell me I should find a nice girl."

"You should."

"And what girl would tolerate Velander, sleeping in a coffin, smelling of blood, and ripping out the throats of objectionable neighbors?"

"Well, yes, it could be valid grounds for divorce," Senterri conceded.

"What will you do now that you are free?" Laron asked cheerily, trying to lighten the mood of the conversation.

"Oh, go home, I suppose."

"Where is home?"

"Sargol."

"Really? Lovely place. I was there three years ago."

"But meantime I may stay in Gladenfalle for a while. I have a relative there, he will be glad to see me."

"Oh, splendid, perhaps I can help you find him. What is his name?"

"Prince Patrelias, he lives in the palace."

It took some moments for her words to sink in.

"But, but, he is the ruler of the city and surrounds," Laron quavered.

Senterri shrugged. "It's a living."

The cart rumbled on through the rain and the gathering gloom of evening as Laron tried to think of something to say. He failed. Senterri straightened her clothing and tightened her lacings. She and Velander had similar figures and were about the same height, so the fit was good.

"I want to look my best when we arrive," she explained, when it became clear that Laron was probably incapable of taking any sort of initiative, verbal or otherwise.

"Oh, but you always look your best, Your Majesty—or is it Your Highness? Which one is for a ruling monarch? I always get them confused."

"It's 'Highness,' actually," she said as she sat with her hands clasped between her knees. "Laron, what would you like as your reward? What is the worth of a princess?"

"Don't be silly, no reward required," he laughed halfheartedly. "I live cheaply, and Velander's food is free, although it does struggle a bit and sometimes has cross relatives. I mean, you washed the sacks, cleaned the ax-blade, and were nice to Velander. Not many people are nice to Velander, and I am sure she appreciated it. And you kissed me. How many boys can say they were kissed by a princess? Not that I *shall*, of course. Nobody would believe me, and if they did, I would probably be hung for, er, being lower class or something."

"Laron, it is you who is being silly. I could shower you with gold, make you a mighty noble . . ." She paused, thought carefully, then made a quick but important decision. "I might even sleep with you if you asked me nicely."

"I— Oh."

Laron managed to say no more. Senterri suddenly realized that a reply did not exist for the sort of offer she had just made—to a person like Laron, anyway.

"Don't hurt my feelings, Laron, what is your pleasure?" she continued now, trying to make it easier for him.

Laron frowned as he thought, then shook his head and laughed to himself.

"What is funny?" Senterri asked anxiously, feeling a little vulnerable about rejection after what she had just offered to him.

"Your High—"

"Just 'Senterri,' if you don't mind."

"Senterri, I *already* have my reward. I helped to rescue you, I defeated two guards while Velander . . . Well, she always goes for the plump ones, but— Oh, sorry. Look, I freed you, I made you happy, that is my reward. I've not made a woman happy since . . . Well, there were a couple of women in Diomeda that I would rather not think about, mostly, but—"

Suddenly Senterri burst out laughing, elbowed Laron in the ribs, then put her arms around his neck and kissed him greedily, and with considerable passion.

"Then *that* is for you to think about as much as you like," she explained.

"You are like house afire, getting along?" came Velander's voice from behind them.

✴ ✴ ✴

Gladenfalle was built on one side of a chasm, through which the Leir River flowed. The docks were cut into the rock of the chasm's west wall, and an array of immense cranes moved both cargoes and people from the city to the piers. Spanning the chasm at the city's level was a wide, arched bridge, and it was at the east side of this that Laron stopped the wagon.

"Velander and I shall walk behind with our packs," said Laron. "We have papers that name us as wandering scholars, in search of enlightenment. If you distract the guards with being a princess, we can sneak past during the fuss."

"My friends, this is really not the sort of parting you deserve," said Senterri.

"Maybe not, but it is what we need," Laron insisted.

"Remember plate," prompted Velander.

"Ah yes. Highness—that is, Senterri, may I request a small favor?" asked Laron.

"If I can do it, it shall be done," said Senterri at once.

Laron held out a his hand. From it Senterri took a small package, which was tied with string but not sealed.

"Please, have this delivered to the Metrologan Elder, in Scalticar, if you please," asked Laron.

"Is that all?"

"Yes. We dare not go there. The story is long, and this is not the time or place to be telling it. Now, let us enter Gladenfalle—you in triumph, we two as quietly as possible."

"No—I mean, Laron, or Velander, one question more. During the weeks and months past I have learned a lot. I was a princess, then a slave. I—I saw there is little separating the two. I can easily be both, yet neither of you could ever be slaves."

"Is true," said Velander.

"Please come to the point, Your Highness, it's seriously damp out here," said Laron.

"What difference is there between us?"

"Attitude," Velander replied at once.

"Attitude?" asked Senterri. "What do you mean?"

"Is answer. Attitude. Must learn for to understand yourself. If not, never understand."

"That is true," agreed Laron. "Velander died to learn that. Now, *please*, off you go, and try not to crash."

"Velander, Laron, once again, and with both of my hearts, thank you."

The guardpost beside the city gates grew slowly more distinct through the curtains of rain, and the great walls and towers of Gladenfalle loomed immense before Senterri.

"Halt and declare," called someone from under an awning.

Senterri drew back the reins and locked the brake-bar down.

"Senterri Millarien, to visit my uncle," Senterri called back through the rain.

Laughter greeted her words.

"Hey, that's a good one—now pull the other one, it yodels," cried the guard, walking out into the rain and holding up a lantern. "Now, who—?"

Suddenly the guard stared, then fished about for his Sargolan coin. Every guard and militiaman in the realm had been issued with a Sargolan coin bearing Senterri's likeness. He held the coin up to the light, then stared at Senterri's smiling face again.

"Sergeant!" howled the guard.

Moments later all six guardsmen of the post were kneeling in the rain beside the wagon.

"Your Highness, we had word that a slaver had ravished you," said the sergeant in charge of the shift.

"Untrue," said Senterri. "I escaped the slaver, with no more than my dignity harmed."

"Uh, well, where is he now, Your Highness? We need to avenge your dishonor."

"He is dead."

"Are you sure?"

"Well, reasonably so," Senterri replied softly. "I cut off his head. He seemed to find that rather hard to cope with."

With that, Senterri dropped D'Alik's head to the cobblestones before them. The guardsmen gazed at it in wonder, then admiration.

"Will you be long?" called Laron from behind the waggon.

"Shut up!" the sergeant called back.

"If you would take me to my uncle, please," said Senterri. "I have to stop my father and brothers from attacking the Toreans in Diomeda. They had nothing to do with my abduction."

"We're only poor students," called Laron.

"The palace awaits your arrival, Your Highness," declared the sergeant. "Your uncle will be overjoyed, and his city is yours to—"

"It's awfully wet back here," called Laron.

"Let them past," ordered Senterri with a little wave of her hand. "After what I have been through in the months past, I would wish misery on nobody else. Then please have someone guide me to the palace."

Laron and Velander were waved into Gladenfalle without inspection, a search, or even the demand for a bribe. They trudged past the cart and through the city gates, the rain streaming from their oilskin capes. Senterri turned back to the sergeant, who was reciting Gladenfalle's traditional welcome to foreign nobility, but when he had finished and she looked for her two rescuers again, they were gone. Only the horse and wagon remained as proof they ever existed.

Senterri enjoyed her uncle's hospitality for the next month, until a small flotilla of military racing shells came up the river and tied up at the docks cut into the face of the cliff, far below the city. Presently Prince Stavez and Dolvienne were carried up in one of the crane carriages, and a lavish feast was organized to celebrate their reunion with Senterri. The visitors stayed for a week, but when the time came to depart, Senterri had an unexpected announcement.

"You are not returning?" exclaimed her brother, unable to believe his own ears. "But—but the entire empire awaits you."

"Just thank them and say I am free, safe, and happy," said Senterri.

"We went to so much trouble and expense to get you back."

"And failed. I struck off my captor's head unaided, and got here for free. You have the head in a jar of vinegar, to present to Father with my compliments. Not much, as souvenirs go, but what can you do when traveling light?"

"Your face almost launched a thousand ships."

"Stavez, my brother, *nobody* is as pretty as that," Senterri laughed gently. "Back in Sargol, I would be no more than a princess. The idea does not appeal."

"*No more* than a princess?" he exclaimed, but Senterri held up her hand.

"It is true. Here, I am a symbol to all in the nearby regions where slaves are traded. I am a mere girl, yet I escaped. Others can, and others will. I have organized a refuge estate for slaves who seek sanctuary in this land. Uncle has provided the money, and work has begun already. Then there is other work. I plan to join a philanthropic religious order, and work to make the world a better place."

"But you can do all that in Sargol," began Stavez.

"Need I spell it out to you, brother of little wit? Were I to return to Sargol, I would be an embarrassment, a stupid little girl who got abducted while having secret dancing lessons. Rumors would flap about like fruit bats in the evening, rumors that I was ridden and ravished by every slaver from here to Diomeda."

"But that did not happen!"

"True, but who would believe it? A princess cannot afford to have that sort of rumor in her past. For a champion of the weak and powerless, however, some tragedy like that is almost mandatory."

Prince Stavez was unhappy, but he respected his sister's decision. It did solve a lot of problems—he had to admit it—and Senterri certainly was a changed woman. She was so radiantly happy, almost serene. Once he had taken his leave, to arrange the return voyage down the Leir, Senterri and Dolvienne were left alone to make their farewells. Senterri took out a small package and opened it. The wrapping itself was a note.

"Can you deliver this to the Elder of the Metrologan Order in North Scalticar?" Senterri asked.

"Anything," replied Dolvienne. "Back in the desert, I rode away in your service, but I failed to get you rescued. That shamed me. This time I am delighted to leave you in happier circumstances, and in this new mission I shall not fail. May I see the note?"

"Of course. It has no secrets."

Dolvienne frowned at the odd script, but could easily follow the Diomedan text. She read aloud.

" 'Most Excellent Highness Senterri, please have this conveyed to the Learned Terikel, the Elder of the Metrologans in the North Scalticarian city of Alberin. Give her my compliments, and say this is to remember all that we endured together. Ask her to convey good wishes also to my good friend Roval, and to my former mentor the Learned Wensomer, and to my surviving crewmates. Please explain that a matter of honor forced me to leave without a farewell, and please convey my regrets. Laron.' "

Dolvienne examined what was enclosed. It was a little brass rectangle with a hole at each corner. At one side was a medicar symbol; at the other, the crest of the Placidian Guild of Navigators, and across the center was, SHADOWMOON.

"This is all?" she asked.

"Look under the last fold," replied Senterri.

The writing was different, with a more exact and elegant script, but the Diomedan was not as good.

" 'Worthy Elder Terikel, forgiveness, please, am asking. Yourself, were right. If soulmate, again, yourself needing, if again yourself could liking me, sending word. To yourself, shall come. Loyal priestess of yourself, Velander.' "

"The words apparently carry far more meaning than we could guess at," Senterri assured her handmaid.

Dolvienne took a pace back and gazed approvingly at her princess.

"You have changed, and for the better," she declared.

"It is only a small shift in attitude, but it is the difference between being a slave and being a princess. Will you take the package to Elder Terikel, please?"

"I live to serve," declared Dolvienne with an elaborate flourish and a deep bow.

"I do, too," responded Senterri. "My thanks to you."

Epilogue

 The rain was pouring down on the darkened city as Laron fled through the alleyways with two town bullies in pursuit. In the light from a solitary public lantern he caught sight of a fruit vendor's handcart parked beside an awning that cascaded water into the street below. He ran for it.

A shadow dropped from the awning and knocked the second thief to the ground. Laron turned and engaged the other, cross-blocking his swagger-stick's blow, hooking a leg behind his, and pushing the swagger-stick against the man's throat. The thief toppled backward and struck the back of his head against the cobbles.

"Think this one's still alive, Velander," panted Laron.

He flung back the handcart's tarpaulin and heaved the unconscious thief up into the tray. It took him only moments to bind and gag his victim.

"Velander?" said Laron, dropping to his knees beside a pile of squirming shadows. "Not again! At least drag him into the cart before you start feeding. *Velander!* Listen to me: I can't lift you both."

A figure glided out of the shadows so silently that Laron did not notice until it was kneeling beside him.

"You take the body, I'll lift Velander," said a serene, reassuring, and very familiar voice.

"Senterri!" gasped Laron.

"Come on, lift! One, two, three!"

Velander lost her grip on the thief's neck, looked up, bared her fangs, and snarled savagely.

"Don't you growl at me, Velander Salvaras!" Senterri snapped, slapping Velander smartly across the face.

The vampyre's ferocity suddenly dimmed. Laron glanced from Velander to Senterri, then back again, astonished beyond words.

"Mine," Velander muttered sullenly.

Velander has actually backed down, he thought. *Velander has not backed down since, well, Velander has never backed down.*

"Help us get him into the handcart," ordered Senterri. "Then you can climb in and finish him."

Velander heaved the thief into the tray with one hand, then scrambled in after him. Laron hurriedly pulled the tarpaulin back over the handcart.

"I hope nobody wants to buy any fruit tonight," said Senterri as she and Laron stood leaning against the side, both limp with relief.

"What are you doing here?" Laron demanded without looking at her.

"I told my brother I was joining a philanthropic order dedicated to improving the world."

"But what are you doing— Oh no! You can't mean Velander and me!"

"Actually, I can and I do. Oh, and my handmaid has taken your package to deliver to Terikel. Dolvienne is very reliable."

"Senterri, go away. We are not nice company. Velander is more deadly than, than— Well, let's just say I've seen a pack of a dozen desert wolves flee from her with their tails between their legs. Except for the one that didn't run fast enough, that is."

"But she needs help, she's alone and vulnerable."

"And *I'm* helping her."

"I want to help, too."

"Go away, I saw her first."

"And *you* need someone to look to *your* welfare."

"Me? Absolutely not!"

"Did you know the beard is coming away from your left cheek?"

"Is it? My thanks— *Senterri!* I am *not* letting you into this traveling carnival of blood, death, horrible people, extreme danger, and occasional low comedy. I—"

Senterri suddenly wrapped her arms around him and jammed her lips against his. Moments later, two of the city's night watch strolled past.

"It's raining, have ye not noticed?" laughed one.

"Go home, do that in bed," said the other, tapping Senterri across the rump with his swagger-stick.

"Wouldn't happen to be in love, would ye?" the first called over his shoulder as they walked on.

Then they were gone. Senterri and Laron remained beside the cart, still embracing.

"You gave up everything for a dangerous and unstable fiend who once saved your life," said Senterri. "Why can I not give up everything for you, who gave me back my freedom and dignity?"

"Because, er . . ."

"Well? I have a right to be chivalrous, too. I listened to everything that Velander said about the rights of women."

There was a heavy thud behind her.

"Velander!" Laron cried suddenly.

Velander had crawled out of the cart and fallen flat on her face in the rain-drenched street.

"Requiring help, to walking," she announced as Senterri and Laron hauled her to her feet. "Am incapable."

"One of those idiots must have been drunk, and she does not hold her drink at all well," explained Laron. "Hold her up."

"So far tonight I have seen blood, death, horrible people, and extreme danger," said Senterri. "Is this the low comedy?"

Laron pushed against the cart, set it in motion, then steered it for the low brick wall at the end of the street. Moments later the two bodies had plunged nearly a thousand feet to the waters of the Leir River. Supporting Velander between them, Laron and Senterri set off through the rain and darkness.

"Wishing to apolop—er, apropol—Ah, sorry I snarl, at you," Velander managed in Diomedan, with considerable effort.

"Think nothing of it," replied Senterri.

"It's going to be an interesting night," said Laron.

"Are you saying it is not already interesting?" said Senterri. "Where are your rooms?"

"Fishbone Street, the Golden Crown, and it's only *one* room with only *one* double bunk," replied Laron.

"Bottom bunksh mine," slurred Velander.

"Laron and I will manage nicely with the top bunk," declared Senterri.

Laron's complaint that he would have to spend the night on the floor died on his lips. Rain pattered into his open mouth, driven by a light but gusty wind.

"Peeling off shilly beard, firsht, tell him," suggested Velander.

Laron's voice finally returned. "Look, Senterri, you're exquisite, you're enchanting, and I cannot say I don't fancy you, but *please*, think carefully," he pleaded. "There is still time to go back to your real life."

"Oh no, my chivalrous champion, within my hearts I ran away with you weeks ago, so now it is far too late."

And so Verral's smallest and strangest philanthropic order began. Laron and Senterri's first night in each other's arms was not really enhanced by Velander lying in the bunk below, breathing the reek of blood and alcohol into the air, belching etheric fireballs, muttering that her head hurt, and occasionally asking how they were getting along, but true love can cope with that sort of thing. The following morning they set off through the city gates and traveled deeper into the mountains with the horse and cart Senterri had kept in the palace stables ever since she had arrived. The sky was clear and a brilliant blue, while the air was intoxicatingly clean and fresh from the night's rain. Behind them, in Gladenfalle, quite a few people were missing whom nobody really missed, and the city was a slightly happier place as a result of the month Velander had spent there.

Under some blankets in the wagon's tray, Velander lay dead—at least until Miral rose again.

Look for

GLASS DRAGONS

by **Sean McMullen**

Available March 2004
by Tom Doherty Associates

Turn the page for a preview!

PROLOGUE

Even though the streets of Alberin were being lashed by a rainstorm and the wind was so strong that one could not walk through the gusts in a straight line, the two men who emerged from the mansion were relieved to be outside again. They never once looked back as they hurried to the outer gates of the grounds, and they ignored a guard who cheerily waved a bottle at them as they walked out into the street.

"I would like to point out that recruiting *her* to our cause was *your* idea, Talberan," said the taller of the pair.

"I had heard that she is eccentric, but this was too much," admitted his companion.

"Servingmen in rabbit fur g-strings, servingmaids in faun costumes, and as for what she and her guests were wearing! Had I not seen it, I would not have believed it."

"Are you sure that she is North Scalticar's most powerful sorceress, Lavolten?"

"There is no doubt of that. Lady Wensomer Callientor is also the only person in history ever to have refused a regrading to initiate thirteen. She said that *initate twelve* sounds elegant, and *initiate fourteen* has grandeur, but *initiate thirteen* has no style at all and she refused to have it after her name."

The storm had not dampened the night life of Alberin, it had merely moved it indoors. Music, pipe smoke and laughter poured out of warmly lit taverns as they hurried along, and the wind flung the scent of baking bread or roasting meat past them from time to time. A drunken apprentice came staggering along the street, a bottle in one hand and a tin flute in the other. Talberan and Lavolten separated to let him past.

"I wish I was in Alberin town,

When'er I'm down on me luck.
A lad's always welcome in Alberin town -"

They turned when the singing stopped abruptly, and noted that the youth had walked straight into a parked wagon and collapsed in a flooded gutter.

"He is already in Alberin, why does he sing about wishing he were here?" asked Lavolten.

"Degenerate nonsense, just like that sorceress. We offered her the chance to command the winds themselves!"

"She said she would rather command her guests to swap partners ever half hour."

"To rule the world."

"She said that she had been to lots of revels staged by rulers, and they were not nearly as good as her revels."

"To be immortal."

"She said that she knew plenty of immortals, and they were all boring."

"I mean, what does the woman want?" Lavolten demanded of the rainswept darkness, throwing up his hands in exasperation.

"She told us, Lavolten. She wants the secret of weight loss without exercise or dieting."

"Did she not understand that we were offering her the chance to become a god?"

"She said that gods all had beautiful bodies and narrow waists, and that being made a god sounded suspiciously like she would have to diet and exercise."

They turned off into an alley. Talons that glowed faintly blue burst from the toes of their boots and the fingers of their gloves, then they began to crawl straight up a sheer brick wall.

"Who should we try next?" asked Talberan as they climbed.

"Someone old, someone who has nothing more to hope for from life, yet someone with ideals."

"Astential?"

"Yes, the initiate fourteen. He is eighty one, and takes no interest in the delights of the flesh. He should quickly give in to temptation."

"Unlike that immoral glutton of a sorceress. Can you believe it? She flung our offer back at us because she said it was not at all interesting."

They climbed over the edge of the wall and onto the roof, and that was the last of their stay in Alberin. The next day a tiler checking a blocked downpipe found two cloaks washed into the roof's guttering. They were new, and had the stamp of a local tailor. Nearby were two purses, both containing twenty silver nobles. Being a practical and sensible man who was not inclined to bother the constables with trivia, he kept the silver, packed away the cloaks and purses to sell in the market, and charged the owner of the building for unblocking the pipe. By this time Talberan and Lavolten were on another continent, and having a very productive meeting with a wise, powerful, and temperate sorcerer who felt that he was admirably suited to wield the powers of a god.

✳ ✳ ✳

The ringstone site was not merely old, it was exceedingly ancient. It had last been used before the first cities had been built, but now it was no more than a circular mound, one hundred yards in diameter.

The three elderly riders who halted at the site were under the escort of a dozen mercenary cavalrymen, and had half a dozen labourers trailing after them. Unlike their guards, the old men carried no weapons and wore no armour. The mercenaries watched with no particular interest as they unpacked their saddle bags, then began to trace out the dimensions of the ancient mound with pegs and strings. One supervised the labourers, who were set digging three holes in the mound. They would not have called themselves the world's first archeologists, because the word had not yet been invented, yet that was what they were.

"This mound is mentioned in chronicles known to be thousands of years old," said the man with the longest beard, as he tapped a marker peg into the ground.

His companion took a scroll from a sling bag, unrolled it, and began reading.

"Devil mound . . . cursed place . . . place of death . . . said to increase virility if one lies on the summit during a solstice at dawn and -"

"All of that is folklore and hedgerow magic, Waldesar. We are concerned with its original purpose."

"Older than any kingdom or city," continued his companion.

"Ah! Very significant."

Before long the sorcerer-archeologists had the circular mound mapped and measured, and were making observations of the sun's elevation, position and movement. Two nearby goatherds also noted the sun's position, decided that it was noon, and sat down for lunch.

"They try to seem like nobles," said the shorter goatherd, inclining his head to the visitors.

"Aye," replied his companion, scratching beneath his false beard. "But nobles try to look noble, so they wear fine clothes and have a pack of hounds to chase game and bite peasants. Those three wear fine clothes, but have no weapons, hounds or crests."

"Sorcerers, then?"

"Aye, and they study an ancient site of power."

"Very significant."

Not far away, a woodcutter and carter were loading windfall branches onto a oxcart.

"The two with the strings and pegs are Most Learned Astential and Learned Waldesar," said the woodcutter.

"And the one having the holes dug?" asked the carter.

"Hard to say, can't get a clear look at his face. He spends too much time on his knees, looking into the holes, but he's younger than the other two."

"Learned Sergal is only seventy, and practices the cold sciences as well as magic."

"But Learned Sergal hates Learned Waldesar."

"Very true, but if Sergal and Waldesar are working together . . ."

"Very significant."

※ ※ ※

Upon the ancient ringstone mound itself, two lovers were lying in each other's arms in the grass.

"Astential, Waldesar and Sergal," whispered the girl as the boy kissed her ear.

"They keep mentioning Dragonwall," whispered the boy, who had exceptionally good hearing.

"Dragonwall was an ancient etheric engine used to turn men into gods, so that they could control the winds. Its secret was lost."

"Perhaps these folk have a mind to be gods too."

"Very significant."

※ ※ ※

On the summit of a nearby mountain, a pigeon trapper paused for a drink. Closer inspection would have revealed that the bottom of his bottle contained a lens, and that he had the neck to his eye.

"That's enough," said his companion. "You couldn't drink from a bottle for as long as that."

"They have the site mapped out," he reported as he lowered the farsight. They have placed seventeen pegs: sixteen in an outer ring, and one at the centre."

"Very significant."

※ ※ ※

Most learned Astential and Learned Waldesar sat down beside Learned Sergal's hole at the summit of the mound. Two of them had the curiously excited yet restrained manner of people who had achieved something stunningly important, yet did not want anyone else to know.

"The news is good," announced Sergal, holding up a slate.

"How can it be good?" asked Waldesar. "We are looking for a depression lined with melted sand a foot thick. This is a mound."

"My diggings show that this is indeed a depression one hundred paces in diameter. It was deliberately filled in five thousand years ago. Look down the hole. Fifteen feet down to a layer of melted sand, and the last five feet are below the level of the surrounding countryside. My outer trench is only two feet deep, and there is a lip of fused sand and stones one foot higher than this floodplain."

"Then it's definitely a Dragonwall ringstone!" exclaimed Astential. "It is lined with melted glass, one hundred paces across, five feet deep at the centre, and surrounded by a circular lip one foot high."

"Someone hid this site!" declared Waldesar, ever anxious to agree with his master while saying something intelligent. "No wonder it was lost for so long."

"Yes, yes, and now we have located them all," continued Astential. "We shall have to empty out the soil, of course, but that needs only horses, carts and labourers."

"Why would the builders have filled it in, most learned master?" Sergal asked Astential.

"The builders?" laughed Waldesar. "Why it might have been filled in by anyone at any time over the past five thousand years."

"I deal in proof and certainty," answered Sergal, "and I have proof of both this ringstone's age, and of when it was filled in."

"Proof?" laughed Waldesar. "You cannot prove anything's age, except by records."

"Oh no?" asked Sergal, pointing to the side of his trench with a quill. "Then what do these bands tell us?"

Sergal pointed to several alternating layers of dark and light soil. Waldesar stared at the layers for a moment, then turned to Astential.

"This is beyond me, most learned one," he admitted. "Can you deduce the message?"

Sergal was not yet aware that Waldesar had neatly sidestepped his attack, and was forcing him to make a fool of Astential.

"What spell must I cast to see the meaning behind them?" asked Astential.

"Oh, only common sense is needed," began Sergal, then his voice faltered.

Sergal was known for his scholarly brilliance, but diplomacy was not his strong point. It was now a little late, but even Sergal was suddenly aware that he had just told the world's only initiate of the fourteenth level to use common sense—and that Astential was getting nowhere by doing so. Astential began to allow the first signs of a frown onto his face.

"Well, actually, nothing magical is needed, nothing magical at all!" Sergal added hastily. "But, er, during my historical readings concerning this area I learned that there is a volcano twenty miles away. It erupts every six centuries, and is, ah, something of a curiosity, as volcanos go. Volcanos are somewhat irregular, you see."

"Please come to the point, Learned Sergal," said Astential, annoyed enough to address the lower initiate formally.

"Well there are nine layers of ash in the dirt above the river silt that someone used to fill in the depression. Nine times six centuries is five thousand four hundred years. That is roughly the age that the chronicles give for the Dragonwall machine."

Astential stroked his chin, which was always his reaction when very excited about something but trying hard not to show it. He took out a small book. Its covers had been recently fashioned from ivory and gold, but the pages were of exceedingly old parchment, and the writing was very faint.

". . . and four thousand years before Logiar was built, there was the ringstone of Dragonwall, which made wise men as gods, so that they commanded the very winds," Astential translated. "Logiar is known to be fifteen hundred years old, so that makes five thousand five hundred years. That is passably close as a match. Good work, Learned Sergal."

"Ah, perhaps the sorcerers who became gods filled it in," said Waldesar, hastily abandoning his indefensible position. "They must not have wanted others to use their ether machine."

"Then why were the others not filled in?" asked Sergal with theatrical impatience.

"Because all seventeen ringstones are needed for the ether machine to work. Hide one, and the rest are useless!"

"The sorcerer-gods removed the ringstones from every site, that was enough to disable them," retorted Sergal. "Why bury just one -"

"Gentlemen, please!" exclaimed Astential. "Some local chieftain might have had the site buried out of superstitious fear. We cannot know everything, but everything does not need to be known."

Astential seemed outwardly calm, yet he was fighting the urge to go running about in circles with his hands in the air, cheering. All the Dragonwall ringstone sites had now been located. Nothing stood between him and the reconstruction of Dragonwall, aside from the construction of two hundred and eighty nine megaliths, eight hundred and sixteen chairs with stone seats, and eleven hundred sorcerers.

"The soil covering this ringstone site must be removed," he said as he leaned over and peered into Sergal's excavation again.

"Oh I could organise for that to be done," said Waldesar at once.

"And guards will be needed."

"I know the local regent, Most Learned Sir, I could talk him around to it."

"An encampment will need to be built."

"I shall meet the cost with funds from my own estate."

It was no secret that Waldesar wanted to be regraded to initiate level thirteen, just as it was no secret that Sergal actually deserved to be regraded to that level. As the only living initiate of the fourteenth level, Astential could perform such regradings alone. The alternative was to wait for a meeting of the Board of Acreman Sorceric Examiners. That took place only once a decade, and the next meeting was eight years away. Astential needed the skills of both men. Waldesar was the better administrator, but Sergal commanded far more respect in sorceric circles. *Best to keep them both dangling.*

"Learned Sergal, there is still the matter of sorcerers to give life to Dragonwall," Astential said as he got to his feet. "Hundreds will be needed."

"Many will be reluctant," said Waldesar. "Why not just recruit those who show enthusiasm? I could have letters sent this very day."

"Because we must populate *all seventeen* ringstones, Learned Waldesar," replied Astential with a frown. Waldesar cowered. His actual movement was the merest fraction of an inch, but it was still a cower. "With four shifts of primary sorcerers and reserves, that will require nearly *every* sorcerer *anywhere*. Learned Sergal, all in the sorceric circles respect your scholarship. Could you persuade *every* sorcerer to participate in the Dragonwall?"

"I shall look upon it as a personal challenge, Most Learned Sir," replied Sergal.

"Splendid, splendid. Learned gentlemen, when Dragonwall has been rebuilt, it will be no surprise which of you will be preside as ringmaster at this ringstone."

Both initiates were aware that the first squad of ancients to be transformed into gods were said to have destroyed Dragonwall and barred the way to all others. Astential was confident that they would race each other in order to be included among the first sorcerers to use the Dragonwall, and that their work would be done all the sooner because of it.

The goatherds continued with their lunch as they watched the sorcerers pack, then go their separate ways.

"Interesting, they split up," observed the shorter man.

"I think they found what they wanted," said his bearded companion.

"Very significant."

"We should report this to the emperor."

"Those goatherds have just abandoned their goats," observed the timber cutter.

"Spies," replied the carter.

"Very significant."

"I'll report back to the councillium, you tell the Logiar regent."

"This double agenting will get us hung one day."

"But in the meantime it gets us paid double."

The pair of lovers was still a tangle of intertwined limbs in the
grass as they watched the timber cutter and carter hurrying on
their separate ways.

"Those timber cutters have abandoned their timber," said the
girl.

"Councillium spies, without a doubt," said the youth.

"Very significant. We must inform the castellon."

"Those lovers seem to have lost interest in each other rather
quickly," said a pigeon trapper to his companion as they sat
looking over the site from the central of the three crags.

"Alpennien spies, like I said," said his companion, peering
through the bottle-farsight.

"They also had horses hidden, ready for a hasty departure."

"Very significant. Time for us to make a hasty departure as
well."

An hour after the sun had set, an itinerant tinker lay under a
tree, settling down for the night. He was wrapped in his trail
cloak and using his pack as a pillow as he twisted the spigot of
his wineskin and swallowed several more mouthfuls.

"Ah, but it's for the cold," he told nobody in particular.

The immense, green disk of Miral shone down from nearly
overhead, its rings presented almost directly side-on. Suddenly
the summit of the nearby mountain moved. The tinker blinked.
Amid a shower of rubble and dust, a head appeared on a long,
serpentine neck. The summit now stood up and shook itself,
sending yet more cascades of dried mud and dust down the

mountain's slopes. The thing was glowing faintly as it spread a pair of wings whose span was greater than the length of most ships. Silently, it launched itself into the air, then swooped low over the ancient ringstone site and turned out to sea. The tinker scratched his head, then twisted the spigot of his wineskin again and allowed the remaining contents to pour out onto the grass.